# THE DEREK SMITH OMNIBUS

Library of Congress Cataloging-in-Publication Data
Smith, Derek Howe
Whistle Up the Devil
Come to Paddington Fair
Model for Murder

For information, contact: pugmire1@yahoo.com

# CONTENTS

# INTRODUCTION

John Dickson Carr is generally acknowledged to be the maestro of the locked room mystery, indeed of the whole sub genre of impossible crime. His first book, the intriguingly titled "It Walks by Night", appeared in 1930, and was followed over the next forty years or so by a catalogue of his further works, many of them among the finest, most cunning, most atmospheric mysteries ever penned.

He didn't have the field all to himself of course: there were many other excellent writers around including a few who, like Carr, specialised in the impossible crime sub genre. Authors such as Clayton Rawson, Hake Talbot, Joseph Commings and later Ed Hoch and Bill Pronzini contributed much that was also first rate.

But Carr's interest in the impossible crime didn't stop at his own books; he was also fascinated at the development of the form from the earliest examples by Poe and LeFanu, through Zangwill, Leroux and Futrelle right up to those books appearing at the time of his death in 1972. The variety of solutions dreamt up for this most mouth watering of problems was also something that very much occupied his mind. And being John Dickson Carr he didn't address the subject by publishing a dry analysis of it in the manner of a university dissertation; he put the words into the mouth of one of his two most famous detectives, Doctor Gideon Fell.

In "The Hollow Man" (American title "The Three Coffins") published in 1935, acknowledged to be one of Carr's masterpieces, the problems involving two murders in which "the murderer must not only have been invisible, but lighter than air" taxed his detective and his policeman colleague to such an extent that Fell decided to expound at length and explore all the possible ways in which:

An apparently hermetically sealed room could be breached (he listed seven in all), or doors and windows of the locked room could be gimmicked so that a criminal could escape from it (Fell listed five)

Carr was not the first author when tackling an impossible crime to suggest a variety of different solutions, with only one of them the real answer. As early as 1892, in "The Big Bow Mystery", in scenes set not only at the Coroner's Court, but also in the local press, author Israel Zangwill (whose brother Louis wrote an even more inventive impossible crime novel, "A Nineteenth Century Miracle" (1897)) advanced several different theories to explain how the locked room murder with which he faced his detectives had been perpetrated. This was a formula used by many later novelists right up to present day, including early detective fiction guru Carolyn Wells in her 1932 Fleming Stone mystery, "The Broken O", and never more delightfully limned than in Leo Bruce's "Case for Three Detectives" (1936) where a trio of thinly disguised big name detectives each offered a different explanation—and every one of them wrong! Carr himself, writing as Carter Dickson, had his other famous detective, Sir Henry Merrivale, expound on the subject in "The White Priory Murders" a year before Fell in 1934.

But very seldom did writers who followed Carr take the more analytical approach that Dr Fell had employed in "The Hollow Man". Foremost amongst them were Clayton Rawson (writing sometimes as Stuart Towne) and Anthony Boucher (writing sometimes as H.H. Holmes), both of whom were to become doyens of the impossible crime detective story and in Boucher's case one of the most knowledgeable and perceptive critics of many forms of genre fiction.

In Rawson's wonderful debut novel, "Death from a Top Hat" (1938), his detective the Great Merlini, like his creator a professional magician, and his cohorts in discussing a locked room problem with which they were faced, not only paid tribute to Fell's lecture but provided a detailed alternative of their own with overall more variations of method than those described by the good doctor, and as a bonus describing a further category which had not previously been covered.

Then in 1940 Boucher presented his detective, Sister Ursula, with a lovely meaty locked room murder in "Nine Times Nine" wherein, inter alia, her police confederate, Lieutenant Marshall, and reporter Matt Duncan, discussed Fell's lecture in some detail and reorganised the categories by reference to the timing of the various crimes, but otherwise added nothing new.

To this stellar list of detective novelists one final entry must now be made, someone whose work, though much less in quantity than those previously referred to, is not nearly as well known as it should be. In 1953 the publishing house of John Gifford (then the main publishing arm of the Foyle family's literary network) issued "Whistle up the Devil" a mystery novel in which a brace of sealed room murders occurred and a fascinating debate took place between detective Algy Lawrence and his friends on the subject of apparently impossible killings, and the earlier analyses to which they had been subjected by Carr and company. The book contained lots of locked room lore and was clearly written by a student of the form.   His name was Derek Smith.

The first piece I ever wrote about my own addiction to locked room murders appeared in Ethel Lindsay's idiosyncratic little fanzine, The Mystery Trader. Entitled "Lockedroomania" it pinned my colours firmly to the mast and generated a pleasing amount of interest and comment. However for me the most important knock on effect was that I received my first letter from Derek Smith himself. Starting with the more formal "Dear Mr Adey" but rapidly escalating to "Dear Bob" it began a correspondence which continued for more than two decades and was only interrupted for a couple of years in the early seventies when my wife Sue and I lived near Kingston upon Thames and Derek became a regular visitor, obviating the need for letters.

In his very first letter Derek provided details of more than twenty locked room mysteries which I had not included in the list I had made within my Mystery Trader article and I knew right away that I had come into contact with perhaps the most knowledgeable student of this form of detective fiction. When he visited it was invariably with books or copies of short stories to which my attention needed to be drawn, and after we moved out of the London area in 1972 the Royal Mail took over the job of seeing that I was kept up to date with Derek's latest information, often with accompanying tomes.

It wasn't quite all one way traffic. I was able to point Derek in the direction of a few items of which he was unaware and able to pick up for him when Sue and I visited America copies of books, particularly those by one of his favourite authors, Carolyn Wells, which he couldn't locate for love nor money in England. But the breadth of his knowledge on detective fiction in general and the locked room problem in particular was nothing short of phenomenal. Only when preparing this introduction and looking through my file of Derek's letters, the last of which was dated 7$^{th}$ August 1992, did I realise just how all embracing was the scope of his knowledge, seemingly overlooking virtually nothing. He had apparently inherited his love of books from his parents (he complained tongue in cheek in one letter about how his father had snaffled a recently acquired Gerald Verner from him before he had had time to read it himself!) and was a regular visitor to such institutions as The National Film Theatre, the British Library and Westminster's Central Reference Library; in fact anywhere he might investigate some new angle of mystery fiction.

Obscure stories from even obscurer magazines, volumes published by forgotten vanity press outfits, and loads of tips as to where the screen, large or small variety, might reveal more impossibilities, these were just some of the items and information that Derek passed on to me. Who else would have spotted miraculous crimes in such diverse films, both in date and style, as Conrad Veidt's 1929 "The Last Performance"; Peter Cheyney's "Alphaville"; "The Mackintosh Man"; "Death is a Woman"; the Czech made "Nick Carter in Prague" (now there's a title to conjure with); "Transatlantic"; "Blind Spot" (based on Barry Perowne's famous story); the humorous "The Fuller Brush Man" (Roy Huggins wrote the story on which it was based) and, undoubtedly the most unlikely source of all, at least from an impossible crime perspective, the 1956 German film, "Lianne, Jungle Goddess"?

On television he had noted episodes of MacMillan and Wife, and of McCloud (both of which I enjoyed myself), the whole Banacek series starring George Peppard, but outdid himself yet again by remembering a clever gimmick which he had seen in an episode, written by Jack Roffey, of the courtroom drama series, Boyd Q.C. (played by Michael Denison). While with radio, where Derek was very much a buff of many years standing, he drooled over the forgotten plays by Allingham and Christie, wrote at some length about his memories of Carr's wartime work and recalled with great fondness Philip Levene's locked room play, "Murder Beyond". Does a recording of that still exist somewhere I wonder?

He was also a devoted theatre goer and on one occasion sent me a playbill of the comedy thriller "Dead Easy" which he'd travelled out to the Wimbledon Theatre to see. On the back of it (typical Derek) he sketched out the lock trick the author had used but said not to read it if I thought that the play might come to one of our local theatres! Incidentally it never did. He even stumbled across a John Sladek impossible crime short story in a theatre programme for a Debbie Reynolds show for which he was actually queuing!

And he didn't confine his interest simply to texts in English, mentioning various French-language authors like Pierre Boileau and Jean Rey, the early German locked room mystery "Nena Sahib" (by Sir John Retcliffe (sic)) and even sending me a copy of "Qui a Tué Madame Skrof?", a French translation of a 1939 Finnish mystery by Mika Waltari, an author perhaps better known in England for the historical novel, "The Egyptian". He was very excited to read in the revised version of my locked room bibliography (1991) of the emergence of the young French locked room specialist Paul Halter and was positively salivating at the prospect of their translation into English.

He was also a long time collector of Old Boys' fiction and was able to identify for me miraculous crime examples from the very long running Sexton Blake Library, the Union Jack and the Magnet. He had large accumulations of magazines like The Thriller which contained stories by Verner, Gwyn Evans, Charteris and many other of his favourite authors. He even spotted a locked room problem in an ITV Pink Panther Special comic and bemoaned the fact that a Paul Temple strip from the Evening News containing a very neat sealed tower problem had never been reprinted.

Criminal cases from real life were another of his enthusiasms, not least where the method by which the crime was carried out defied logical explanation. He was especially taken with a murder which took place in France in 1830. The victim was Parisienne Rose Delacourt, whose locked room murder, possibly the earliest on record, had never been satisfactorily solved. Derek was eventually delighted to find a reasonably full description of the case in C.L. McCluer Stevens' "From Clue to Dock" (Stanley Paul 1927).

Derek's compass was so wide that in his letters he rarely found time to comment on his own personal favourites in mystery fiction. However he did say that two of the scenarios he most enjoyed were murder committed during a séance or where the crime took place on stage in full view of the audience. He also confessed that he found Harry Stephen Keeler difficult to read though admired his ingenuity; struggled, as I did myself, with Dillard's "The Book of Changes", but rated Melville Davisson Post, Jacques Futrelle and Thomas Hanshew very highly indeed. Perhaps surprisingly he liked the slightly comic Pat Rossiter (in his only outing, "Poison in Jest") even more than Carr's other detectives. Droodiana and Ripperology were not outside his purview either though he described himself here as a mere dabbler. Yet another minor passion of his was collecting jigsaw mysteries, all types and from all periods.

About his own writing he was extremely modest, almost to the point of self deprecation. When the publishers accepted "Whistle up the Devil" he was of course, like any author hoping to publish his first book, absolutely delighted though he commented ruefully that he wished that he had given it a thorough revision before it was published. He called his own locked room lecture in chapter 5 of that book "a semi parody of Carr's", a harsh judgement in my view. It's rather better than that.

The contract that John Gifford had drawn up with Derek was fairly typical of the treatment so often dished out to new authors. He wasn't paid all that much for the first edition and it had a relatively small print run (which explains why it is such an elusive book), and only nominal sums were paid for the second edition, which was issued under the Thriller Book Club banner, and for the foreign rights. Indeed although he eventually managed to get from Gifford a copy of an Italian translation, it was more than forty years before he received confirmation, and then from the noted French anthologist and impossible crime specialist Roland Lacourbe, that a French translation, "Appelez Le Diable!" had been published in the Le Masque series in 1953, and eventually obtained a copy for his own collection.

Derek had mentioned to me back in the early seventies that he had written two further impossible crime detective novels, one a second case for his detective Algy Lawrence, the other a Sexton Blake adventure. However they were both turned down, by Gifford and Amalgamated Press respectively, leaving Derek in many ways more disappointed about the failure of the Blake than the Lawrence, because as a devoted long time reader and fan of the Baker Street detective he felt that he knew exactly how to pen a tale for this series. For reasons he could never fathom AP did not agree.

The Sexton Blake novel has remained unpublished to this very day, but in 1997 Derek's Japanese friend Hidetoshi Mori and his partner S. Kobayashi published, in the original English, and with a very limited print run, Algy Lawrence's second investigation, "Come to Paddington Fair". But now when the matter of locating a copy of this very scarce paperback is mentioned, the term "hens' teeth" springs rapidly to mind. The book itself is longer and more complex in plot than "Whistle up the Devil" but Lawrence is on excellent form, and the impossible conundrum is a very good one with a really clever solution.

Sadly Derek is no longer with us, but I have no doubt whatsoever that, if he were, he would be drooling over the television series "Jonathan Creek" and "Monk", devouring the at last translated Paul Halter novels and chasing up other tales of the impossible with just as much enthusiasm as ever. He would have been delighted to see new authors emerging such as Christophe Fowler and his London based Peculiar Crimes Unit, Siobhan Dowd who set her mystery on the London Eye, and most recently of all Irishman Adrian McKinty with his top notch "In the Morning I'll Be Gone". He would have loved the suave Anthony Hopkins in "Fracture." And he would have been as proud as punch to see all three of his books finally appearing together in one sumptuous omnibus volume.

Bob Adey

# WHISTLE UP THE DEVIL
*A Detective Story*

## Derek Howe Smith

ROGER QUERRIN died alone in a locked and guarded room, beyond the reach of human hands. Algy Lawrence, with sleepy eyes and a lazy grin, refused to believe in ghosts. Yet with all his detailed knowledge of sealed room trickery, he could not explain the mystery of this "miracle" murder. And then, faced with a second crime which could not possibly have been committed, he began to wonder, at last, if somebody had conjured up an invisible demon who could blast out locks and walk through solid walls... *Whistle up the Devil* is an ingenious brain-teaser which plays completely fair with the reader.

"TELEPHONES," Algy told himself drowsily, "are the devil." He stretched out an arm from the blankets towards the black-enamelled receiver, stilled the persistent ringing, and yawned by way of greeting into the mouthpiece.

The tinny voice said briskly:

"Mr. Lawrence?"

"Mmmm." Algy settled himself more comfortably against the pillows.

"Chief Inspector Castle would like to speak to you."

"Steve!" Algy jerked into wakefulness, knuckling the sleep from drowsy blue eyes as he waited to talk to his old friend at Scotland Yard. "Hallo...Steve?"

"Hallo, Algy." The older man's baritone rang pleasantly over the line: cordial, yet with an odd trace of tension. "Where are you?"

Lawrence pushed the tousled blond hair away from his forehead and chuckled.

"In bed, of course. Where else, in the middle of the night?"

Castle laughed. "I thought so, you lazy young hound. Well, it's nine in the morning. And time you were up."

"Don't be tiresome, Steve." Algy yawned audibly. "Anyway," he added, remembering, "what are you doing in London? I thought you were on holiday in the country."

"I was: at Querrin House." Again that odd note of tension. "But you know the Yard, Algy. They recalled me suddenly. I've a job for you."

"I knew it" Lawrence groaned; but it was mainly pretence. Interest quickened his voice immediately. "Who's been murdered?"

"Nobody.... Yet. "

"Oh!" He hesitated. "Look, Steve. I don't think I'd be much good as a bodyguard."

"No, but——." The Inspector seemed to be finding it oddly hard to express himself. "Roger Querrin is a friend of mine. I wouldn't want to see him—that is, things are so indefinite—."

"They certainly are," said Algy kindly. "Look, Steve, you may know what you're talking about, but I don't. What do you want me to do?"

"Ah!" Castle drew in his breath with a vague sense of relief. "Well!

Querrin's brother is here with me. Will you speak to him?"

"If you like. Put him on."

"No," said the Inspector, with decision. "I'd rather send him along to you."

Algy sighed. "All right. But don't forget, you damned old slave driver, I'm only an unofficial detective, and if I don't feel like handling this blasted case of yours—."

"You won't. I know." The ghost of amusement in Castle's voice suggested he had heard something very much like this before. "Just listen to young Querrin, that's all I ask." Then, more seriously: "He's worried, Algy. And so am I."

The 'phone clicked and went dead. Lawrence slid the receiver back to its cradle, blinked at it thoughtfully, then pushed back the bed clothes and swung his long legs to the floor.

He was a tall, slim, athletically-built young man in his middle twenties, fair-haired, pleasant faced, and straight shouldered. He was invariably good humoured, and despite the amiable vacancy of his expression there was the unmistakably steady gleam of a high intelligence at the back of his lazy blue eyes. But just now he looked merely sleepy.

He kicked his feet into shabbily comfortable slippers and shrugged an old grey dressing-gown over sky-blue pyjamas. He went into the bathroom, twisted the taps for his morning bath, and shaved abstractedly in front of a steamy mirror. Then lounging in the water and soaping himself absently, he began to ponder over the Inspector's call.

Did it mean another case?

Lawrence shrugged his bare shoulders. It wouldn't be the first time he had taken a hand in such matters. Scotland Yard had a healthy respect for the young man's capabilities as a detective. "Unofficially, of course," as Castle would say, screwing up his eyes and rubbing his jowl; but the regard was real enough for all that.

A short spell of Intelligence work in post-war Europe had sharpened Lawrence's appetite for detection. On leaving the Forces he had discovered himself, like a good many other idealistic and adventurous young men, a hopeless misfit in a shabby world. He had drifted aimlessly.

Fortunately his parents, besides providing him with good health, a keen brain, and a romantic disposition, had left him an adequate private income.

And he had a good friend in Chief Inspector Stephen Castle. The burly man, shrewdly divining the young man's deep sense of frustration, had directed Algy's talents and interests into suitable channels.

Lawrence had quickly proved his worth.

He was an amateur but he was also a specialist. He could never hope to handle routine work with the quiet excellence which is the hallmark of the professional; but he could tackle the bizarre and the fantastic with expert skill.

So for two years he had drifted happily on the outskirts of crime, and if he had a deeper purpose than justifying his existence by assisting the police—.

As the Inspector said:

"The results of his work are good enough."

Lawrence had dressed and had breakfast before a sharp buzz announced the arrival of his would-be client. He grinned briefly at his own reflection in a mirror in the hallway and addressed himself gravely:

"An uncomfortable heat at the pit of your stomach? A nasty thumping at the top of your head? I call that the detective fever."

And with the words of Sergeant Cuff still lingering on his lips, he clattered down the stairs towards one of the weirdest adventures of his life.


Peter Querrin walked slowly along the quiet street in Kensington with a hard line of worry cut deep at the corner of his mouth. He stopped suddenly, fumbled in the pocket of his overcoat for a cigarette, and lit it with faintly trembling fingers. Drawing the soothing smoke deep into his lungs he paced on without enthusiasm.

The tension of the last few weeks had told on him badly, Castle's stay at Querrin House had given him a sense of security, though he knew well enough he would have no real rest till the whole fantastic business was over and done with; but now Castle was gone so unexpectedly... He stopped thinking.

On that chill grey morning, while his footfall rang hard on the pavement and the wind scurried leaves in the gutter, it came to him now that his last hope was an unknown man named Lawrence.

Castle had said as much an hour ago. "Peter, I'd like to help. But I can't now. This isn't a police matter," he hesitated, "yet." The tiny word had a nasty ring in the silent room, high over the Embankment. "But Lawrence is a good man and a friend of mine. If you can persuade him to go—."

"I must," Querrin had replied with finality. But now as he stood at the door of the young man's flat, he was no longer sure of anything. Except that his brother's life depended on Lawrence's answer.

He flicked away the half-smoked cigarette and stabbed a finger at the bell push. After the tiny buzz came the clatter of feet on stairs, and the door came open in the hand of a pleasant young man with a lazy smile.

"Mr. Lawrence? My name's Peter Querrin."

"Come in. Steve-—uh, Inspector Castle—said you were coming."

They went up the stairs together. Algy led the way into a room crammed with books. "A drink?"

"Please."

Under cover of some polite foolery with the decanter, Lawrence studied his visitor shrewdly. He saw a well-built young man of medium height, older than himself perhaps, but lacking any definite air of seniority. His face was pleasant without being handsome; definitely worried, and with a trace of weakness.

He took the tumbler from Algy's hand and drank quickly. The liquor flushed against his teeth and went fierily down his throat. It made him cough, briefly, but he felt better for the warmth of it.

Lawrence flicked an eyebrow. "Another?"

"N-no, thanks." Querrin handled his glass with unnecessary care as he perched on the edge of a chair. Algy sat down opposite, produced a silver cigarette-case, and opened it invitingly. Peter brushed the offer aside almost impatiently, though without rudeness, and said abruptly:

"I need your help." His voice wavered disturbingly. Fear that he might bungle his mission made him stammer slightly. "Did the Inspector tell y-you why?"

"No, he was rather vague. Probably thought anything he said might be taken down and used in evidence. Begin right at the beginning."

"Castle's been staying with us at Querrin House," said Peter hesitantly. "He's a friend of Roger's."

"Your-—."

"My elder brother." Querrin swallowed nervously, faltered, then:

"Mr. Lawrence, do you believe in ghosts?"

Algy's surprised grin pointed up the blunder. Peter banged down the empty glass, then shaded his eyes wearily. "I'm bungling this badly." He dropped his hand again and smiled without humour. "I suppose I'm too damned anxious to give the right impression."

Lawrence was soothing.

"Suppose you stop worrying about impressions and give me the facts."

Querrin nodded. "Yes. Well!" He steadied himself with an effort. "I'll have to tell you something about our family history, I'm afraid."

"Go ahead."

Peter said jerkily:

"The Querrins have lived for years in a little village called Bristley, not far outside London. That is, we've always kept up Querrin House, though we've been mostly too poor to live in it, properly speaking. Anyway, Roger re-opened it recently. He's a pretty shrewd business man and he's got the money to do it. My brother has more or less restored the family fortune, you might say. We've had some bad times in the past-—still, that's nothing to do with the story."

The words were coming to him more easily now. Lawrence lounged in his chair, discreetly silent.

"Like a good many old families, we have our own particular legend, tradition, or secret—whatever you like to call it. Ours is mild enough, I suppose, but the village gossips have given it a share of—of spurious glamour and mystery." He paused uncertainly, and realized with a vague uneasiness, it had been in just these words that the tale had been told a few weeks before, at the dawn of the terror. He drew in his breath and shook off the phantoms.

"They say the Querrins had a secret handed down from father to son for generations. And it really was a secret, too. Nobody ever knew except the head of the family and his heir."

Lawrence shifted suddenly and made as if to speak, but changed his mind and relaxed again instead.

Peter went on slowly:

"There was something of a ritual to all this, down the years. One month before the Querrin heir was to be married, his father would pass on the secret. Always alone," he hesitated, "always at midnight, and always in the same room. We call it the Room in the Passage.

"Well! This went on for years. Nothing much happened, except we were usually thought of as rather on the gloomy side, with a taste for the morbid and all that, until the story takes a nasty turn round about the middle of the nineteenth century.

"The head of the family then was a violent-tempered old martinet named Thomas Querrin. He had a son named Martin, who was equally wild and unprincipled. He was more than a match for the old man, by all accounts, though they stayed on fairly good terms till the young man decided to get married." Peter's eyes had shadowed. He seemed to be wandering in some misty country of the mind, only half aware of the other young man who was listening so patiently.

"They went through the usual ceremony, but this time something went wrong. Badly wrong.

"The servants were roused by the sounds of a violent quarrel in that old Room in the Passage. Knowing old Thomas as they did, they didn't interfere, until-—."

Querrin broke off and shrugged.

19

"Well, they heard a rather beastly scream, and then there was only silence. When they finally found the courage to go along to the room, they found young Martin lying on the floor with a knife between his shoulder blades, and his father sprawled in the corner in a fit."

There was a tiny silence. Lawrence broke it. "What happened then?"

Querrin started. It had been just that question which another had asked before.

He said softly:

"They never discovered what the quarrel was about. The old man died without recovering consciousness, and the secret died with him.

"The line carried on through a younger son, and with the famous old secret lost for ever, the Querrins were a humdrum crowd now.

"Except for one thing. A rather nasty old story began to grow up round that Room in the Passage. Village talk had the old man's spirit lingering there for all time, waiting for the Querrins to keep their traditional appointment. If they accepted the secret courageously and respectfully, everything was fine. If they didn't——."

He stopped.

"Yes?"

"They died like Martin."

And Peter Querrin, his tale completed, saw himself again with his brother, a girl, and the promise of death.

Audrey Craig, with a shiver, said:

"How horrible!"

Roger Querrin laughed. "You tell the story well, Peter. Almost as if you believed it."

Peter said queerly: "Don't you?"

His brother's eyes, lit with a smiling tenderness, slid back to the girl's. He replied obliquely:

"I have a weakness for these old traditions."

Audrey reached over and squeezed his hand gently, then turning back to Peter:

"But it is an old wives' tale, surely. I mean, there haven't really been any unexplained deaths here?"

The young man's gaze flickered uneasily round the room. A dim sense of evil, as yet undefined, seemed to be seeping into him like a presentiment. "Not to my knowledge, no. Though Bristley has it otherwise."

Roger stood up. "It's a good story, anyway." He added thoughtfully: "It might be—interesting to put it to the test."

Audrey's grey-green eyes rounded, and Roger smiled at her again. He was very like his brother, but sturdier in build, and with an air of strength and decision rather lacking in the younger man. He was very much in love.

"Well, darling, there it is. The curse of the Querrins. Still want to marry me?"

"More than ever." The curve of her lips was adorable. "Besides, it's not really a curse. And I don't believe a word of it."

"Well, now." Roger smacked his hand on the mantelpiece. "That's the story. This is the room. It could even be," and his gaze went upwards, "that that's the dagger."

Peter sounded angry. "Stop it, Roger!" He finished in half apology: "You're frightening Audrey."

She laughed. "No, he isn't. That is, not really." She looked up to where the knife hung over the mantel. "Though it looks evil enough."

Roger stretched up his hand and slipped the blade free from its sheath. He tested its edge on his finger. "It's sharp enough, too."

Peter said, not loudly:

"Put the damned thing back."

Roger stared at him.

"What's the matter?"

"I d-don't know. I've got the jitters this evening. Put it back, old chap."

The elder man reached up again, and the dagger slid home with a tiny "click!" against its casing.

Peter muttered: "Thanks,"

Audrey smiled at him. "You told that story too well," she murmured. "You nearly scared yourself."

The young man grinned back at her, though briefly. "Perhaps. I don't care for this room, anyway. This is the first time I've been near it since the house was re-opened."

Roger eyed him affectionately. "You're too imaginative." He added, with mock reproach: "And not very loyal. You ought to be proud of our family ghost."

Audrey commented:

"I don't see why. You couldn't call him a very likeable skeleton for the Querrin closet."

"Careful, darling. Do you want the old boy to take a dislike to you?" Roger stood with his back to the fire: a traditional stance, and one he loved.

"There's a thought," said Audrey lightly. "Do you think he'd approve of me?" Roger's eyes shuttered.

He said slowly:

"I've a damned good mind to ask him."

It took a long second for the exact implications of his casually appalling remark to reach the girl's consciousness.

Then she paled and began to whisper:

"Oh, no, dearest, I didn't mean ...."

But the sharper reaction was Peter's, for it was at this moment that the vague sense of evil oppressing him was obscure no longer: and it struck at him with sudden force.

He cried out violently:

"Damned is the word! Have you gone insane?"

It was a mistake, and he knew it immediately. There was a strong streak of obstinacy in his brother's make-up and opposition often hardened his determination.

Roger replied, with a dangerous politeness:

"I don't think so."

Audrey moved nearer, putting a hand on his shoulder. He smiled at her, bent his head and kissed her fingers.

She asked haltingly:

"But you didn't mean what you said. Seriously?"

His eyebrows went up. "Darling. We'll be married soon. I ought to keep my appointment with old Thomas if he intends to be here." He laughed. "Which I doubt."

Her voice had a hint of tears.

"But why must you do this?"

"The old yarn is something of a challenge. I feel I ought to accept it...." He laughed again, while the fire glowed ruddily behind him.

"Besides, it might be amusing— to whistle up the devil."

"Amusing," agreed Algy Lawrence, "but dangerous."

Querrin started. He had been so completely reliving the scene in memory that the quiet voiced comment jarred him oddly. He had, of course, been talking aloud and describing the episode exactly. Now he felt so played out emotionally, he knew he could put no clarity of expression into what came next, and the old deadly sense of failure swept over him again. But he struggled on with the appeal he had to make.

"We—we tried to dissuade him. But Roger's an obstinate man. He'd think it an admission of—of cowardice, or weakness, or something to back down now. ... He just laughs at us—says he can't see what's troubling us, as there's no real danger...."

"Well," said Lawrence mildly. "Is there?"

Peter stared at his polite unmoved face and replied wretchedly:

"I don't know. It's that I have such an oppressive sense of—of fear, and anger...." Even to himself, the words seemed lame and unconvincing. He tried to compensate with more feeling in his voice, then realized disgustedly he was verging on the theatrical.

Lawrence wasn't insensitive to the struggle going on in his would-be client's mind, but not being a psychologist, was finding it difficult to interpret. He was human enough to be slightly irritable about it, too: he didn't like mystery at both ends of his cases.

Querrin ploughed on.

"Inspector Castle is a friend of my brother's, and luckily he arrived for a visit a week or two ago. I had a talk with him right away and he promised to help. I've felt—more secure, since then." He realized with relief that the truth of this at least had managed to spill over into his voice. "But now he's had to leave us and—and...."

Lawrence said: "And you need a new guardian angel. Is that it?" Peter said defeatedly:

"More or less."

Algy nodded, not unsympathetically, but it was fairly obvious his mind was made up.

"Look, Peter, this is quite a story you've told me, but honestly, I don't see how I can help." He stood up and strolled over to the window, looking down into the quiet street.

"I'm only an amateur, you understand. I tell you frankly, I'd be no good as a bodyguard."

He turned round, resting his shoulder against the frame. He said slowly: "If one man's out to kill another—really determined, that is— the chances are he's going to do it. And nothing I could do would stop him." He smiled suddenly to take some of the grimness from his words. "That sounds brutal, but it's true.

"Now you want me to look after your brother. Peter, that's no job for an amateur. "I can recommend a dozen good private detective agencies who might take this work in the ordinary way.

"But this——." He shrugged helplessly. "You can't ask them to catch a ghost!"

"That's why," said Querrin helplessly, "I'm asking you."

Lawrence shook his head. He said gently:

"I'm sorry. You'll have to find someone else."

Querrin said hoarsely:

"There's no time to find anyone else. Roger's—appointment is to-night." There was a silence. Then Lawrence said again:

"I'm sorry."

It was a final refusal, and Querrin took it almost with detachment. He had salvaged a queer calm from this, the ultimate collapse of his hopes.

He said:

"My train leaves Victoria Station at noon. If you change your mind," his tongue tripped, "you could meet me there."

Lawrence began to make a tiny gesture of protest, then inclined his head in acknowledgment.

Twenty minutes later, Querrin had gone, but Lawrence was still slouched in the easy chair, staring opposite at where his visitor had been seated.

He said, aloud: "But how could-—?"

And: "Why should Steve-—?"

Then explosively: "Oh, hell!"

And he grabbed hat and raincoat and clattered impatiently down the stairs.

Algy Lawrence had completely regained his calm by the time he sauntered through the open gates and past the high stone pillars at the entrance of New Scotland Yard.

As he walked inside the building, the attendant policeman gave him something like a smile of welcome. The tall young man in the grey raincoat and crushed green hat was popular with the men of the C.I.D.

Algy murmured a question.

The reply came promptly. "Yes, Mr. Lawrence. The Chief Inspector's here, but I'm not sure if he's free. If you'll wait, I'll ring through and inquire."

Algy nodded his thanks and teetered on his heels while the constable spoke softly into the 'phone.

"He'll see you, sir. You know the way?"

Lawrence nodded again. As he wandered along endless bare corridors and up interminable stairs, he felt grateful that his friendship with Castle spared him the tyranny of form filling which is usually coupled to such requests for interviews.

Beating a cheerful tattoo on the drably familiar door, he pushed it open after the gruff but friendly response from within.

"Hi, Steve."

"Hallo, Algy." Castie swung round in the swivel chair —laboriously acquired, and in itself eloquent acknowledgment of his rank—and waved the young man to a seat.

The Inspector was a large man, urbane and shrewd of eye. He had an explosively good-humoured air that was disconcerting till you knew him, and beneath his frequent air of exasperation an inexhaustible fund of patience.

24

He was devoted to his wife and family and he was also a ruthlessly unsentimental man-hunter.

Just now, he seemed a trifle tense. Algy remembered the odd note he had caught earlier that morning.

Castle said, without preamble:

"So you turned young Querrin down."

"That's right." Lawrence tossed his hat at a coat-rack in the corner. It landed on the battered old raincoat which was almost the Inspector's badge of office.

Algy settled in a chair and eyed his old friend reproachfully.

"I turned him down," he repeated. "Did you expect me to do anything else?"

The Inspector countered this question with another.

"What's the matter—don't you believe in ghosts?"

"I live," said Lawrence carefully, "in the cold draught of a perpetually open mind. So maybe there are ghosts and maybe there aren't. But that's not the point, and you know it. I'm a detective, not a specialist in psychical research."

"Oh!" Castle began to thumb tobacco into the bowl of a villainous pipe. Then he said quietly:

"I'm asking you as a personal favour, to go down to Bristley this afternoon."

Lawrence looked at him sleepily.

He said:

"I'll go."

Then, as the Inspector bowed his head in an unspoken thank you, "Now tell me why."

Castle drew heavy brows together in a scowl.

"The devil of it is," he answered frankly, "I don't really know."

"Oh fine," said Lawrence sardonically. "Look, Steve, are you being troubled by the supernatural or indigestion?"

Steve chuckled deep in his throat. "Don't try so hard to be unsympathetic, Algy. You're overdoing it." He dropped the charred stump of a spent match into the ashtray, and began to draw comfortably on his pipe.

He went on soberly:

"We deal in facts here, not fantasies. And if the Commissioner could hear me now I'd probably be retired immediately. But I tell you now, and against all reason," and his voice rang loud in the silent room, "there's the smell of death in Querrin House."

Algy grinned lazily.

He said:

"Let's not play bogey-man, Steve. If you've smelt death and evil, you've reacted to a *human* intelligence."

Castle nodded slowly.

Lawrence went on: "If there's one thing that's certain in this business, it's that Peter Querrin is scared sick.

"You may be worried, but he's nearly off his head."

Castle said:

"It's his brother."

The amiable vagueness in his young friend's eyes had deepened to absolute vacancy.

Algy's brain was working hard. He murmured:

"Let's analyse this. Querrin believes his brother is in danger. Why? Does he really believe in this ghost he talks about so much?"

The question wasn't wholly rhetorical. Castle replied thoughtfully:

"I don't know the boy very well. It's hard for me to gauge his feelings exactly. I'm not even sure he knows them himself. I'd say,"—he scratched his jowl—"I'd say he's obsessed with the sense of a relentless evil."

"I'd say," supplied Lawrence with a flickering smile, "that you are obsessed with his premonitions." He stressed the pronouns heavily, and the Inspector nodded a rueful agreement.

Algy drawled:

"That doesn't help us much. If you've reacted so strongly to him"—he stifled a yawn—"it's because he has reacted to someone else."

Castle repeated gently: "Some *one*?"

"Of course." The corner of Lawrence's mouth twitched upwards, showing the teeth in his upper jaw. "Let's leave poor, dead old Thomas Querrin in peace. Doesn't Roger's—urn, appointment, mean a golden opportunity for a flesh and blood killer to strike and vanish—.'

He broke off, then finished flippantly: "With a flash of fire and the odour of burning sulphur."

He waved his hand and there was quiet in the room once more. Then the Chief Inspector smiled benignly.

"Of course," he said. "I saw that from the first."

The two men regarded each other with affectionate reproachfulness.

"You couldn't," remarked Lawrence with the hint of a rebuke, "have told me at the start? Instead of letting loose Peter with his brouhaha of family curses and homicidal ghosts?"

Castle put up a warning hand. "Don't let me mislead you, young Algy. If I begin thinking about murder, it's because I'm a soured old policeman and just naturally suspicious. I had nothing to go on. Otherwise I'd have called in the local police like a shot. Though in a sense," he added rather sheepishly, "I've done that already."

"The devil you have," said Algy (and reflected that mention of his Satanic majesty had crept far too often into the affair as it was): "I hope they have a broad-minded Chief Constable."

"My God," said Steve, profanely horrified, "I haven't done it officially. A nice fool I'd look. I've quite enough to put up with as it is. Hardinge has been giving me some very queer looks lately."

"Hardinge?"

"The local police sergeant. I had to take him into my confidence."

"Suppose you tell me exactly what you have done. I'm still groping round in a fog."

"Right." Castle began to puff vigorously at the pipe, and a blue haze eddied round his greying hair. "Well! When I got down to Bristley—and I went there for peace and quiet, the Lord pity me—what do I find but the house in a kind of polite but desperate turmoil; and all because my benighted friend Roger Querrin insists on spending the night in a haunted room."

"Turmoil my foot," said Lawrence disrespectfully. "You mean you were met at the door by young Peter with all his troubles instead of 'Welcome' on the mat."

His flippancy sounded a trifle forced.

Castle said:

"Not only Peter. Miss Craig, Roger's fiancée, is worried too. She's a nice girl, and deuced attractive." He squinted at Algy thoughtfully. "You'll like her."

Laurence felt his pulse skip unaccountably; and was annoyed.

"If she is so worried," he said with a shade of irritation," Why doesn't she persuade Roger to call the whole thing off? She ought to have the most influence, goodness knows. "

"It's not so easy," returned Castle with a frown. "Querrin's a friend of mine and a decent fellow, but he's bloody obstinate too. An iron will or a pig head, it's much the same in the end.

"Dammit, I asked him to drop the business myself and got laughed at for my pains."

"I don't think I like your Roger," said Lawrence dryly. "Maybe he thinks of himself as the one sane man in a world of craven half-wits."

Castle shook his head. "That's not very fair, Algy. He thinks Peter is making a fuss about nothing—as he may be, for all we know—that there's no danger and that it would be a sign of weakness to stop now." Steve twisted in his chair, which creaked in protest. "It's all in character, I can tell you that much. Roger has just enough sense of tradition to take an odd kind of pride in a family legend, just too little imagination to be afraid of the supernatural and just enough bravado to challenge it."

"Thank God I'm a coward," interposed Lawrence cheerfully. "Carry on."

"Well, Peter told me the story and asked me to help. Exactly what he expected me to do, I don't think either of us knew.

"Now whether he'd reacted unconsciously to the hidden menace of an atmosphere *or* a person, it was obvious he saw danger or death creeping round his brother like something physical... Blast it, he convinced *me*. Anyway, more to restore Peter's peace of mind than for any other reason, I took over."

"And did what?"

"Well," and the Inspector looked embarrassed, "there wasn't much I could do about the ghost. But I could at least see there wasn't any funny business otherwise."

"I suppose," murmured Algy, "you planned a guard for Roger on the night in question?"

"Which is to-night, incidentally. Yes, I did. Peter and I hammered out a scheme between us. Now," Castle tapped the desk top thoughtfully, "with us in the house were the girl and her uncle, who'd invited himself there on the strength of his niece's engagement. I couldn't use them, obviously. This was no work for a woman, and as for Russell Craig"— Steve gestured descriptively— "I wouldn't trust him to guard a hole in the road. Still, I needed assistance. This job called for a division of forces. Since Peter's too nervous to be left on his own, I decide I wanted a new recruit."

"And that," hazarded Lawrence, "is where you called on the local coppers."

"Yes. Fortunately," mused the Chief Inspector, "the local Sergeant is a decent chap. I gather Peter had already thought of him, too; though he would never have found the nerve to pitch him a tale like this. I hardly managed to do it myself. Still, Hardinge didn't tell me I was off my chump though he probably thought it. Here's what we agreed to do—."

Castle went into details. Lawrence nodded occasionally. And the villainous pipe smouldered and died unnoticed.

The Inspector leaned back at last and sighed.

"There it is." He slapped his hand heavily on the desk top. "Now it's up to you."

"All right, Steve." Lawrence stood up, strolled over to the coat-rack, retrieved his hat and squashed it on th back of his head. "I'll take over."

"Thanks, Algy." The Inspector hesitated. Then as the young man made to leave, Castle put words to a question which had puzzled him for two years.

He said abruptly:

"Just what do you get out of all this?"

Lawrence paused with his hand on the door-knob. He glanced over his shoulder, his face relaxed and impassive. He said politely:

"Maybe I just like to play detective."

Castle shook his head. "That's not the reason. At least, not wholly. You're not like that young scoundrel Vickers." —and the inspector smiled affectionately as he thought of another friend with a taste for detection—"It's all a game to him. But with you, it's different. If I wasn't afraid of being pompous," he hesitated, "I'd say you considered it your legitimate work for society."

"The trouble with you is," said Lawrence, "you're stuffy." Then he showed white teeth in an easy, pleasant smile.' "And I'm incurably— romantic. So long, Steve."

The door plopped shut behind him.

Peter Querrin, his face taut, stared along the platform. High overhead, the hands on the clockface pointed up the urgency of his vanishing hopes. There were only five more minutes to go. Meanwhile the noise and the tension rolled round the high vaulted roofs; the station seemed as impatient as he.

A newer clamour clawed up through the din: the crash-slam of doors along the drab length of the train. Peter shrugged helplessly. Lawrence wasn't coming. It was finished before it began. And Roger—Peter climbed back into his compartment.

He stared without vision out the windows, hardly noticing that his train had left the station.

The compartment door slid open and somebody stepped in from the corridor. Peter didn't look round. He was in no mood for company. A voice said mildly:

"I nearly missed you."

Querrin's head moved slowly, so slowly in fact, that Lawrence thought for a moment that Peter hadn't recognized his voice. Then their eyes met and he knew himself mistaken.

Querrin said inadequately:

"I'm glad you came."

"I thought you might be," grinned Algy. He swung a zippered grip on to the seat beside him, stretched out his long legs, sighed, and relaxed in a corner.

It seemed very likely he thought further comment unnecessary, but the varying shifts of relief and apprehension had driven Peter into an emotional confusion that fumbled for relief in talk.

He asked:

"What changed your mind?"

"Mmmm? Oh, Steve can be very persuasive."

Peter stammered:

"I ought to t—thank you—."

"Wait," said Algy dryly, "till I do something useful. I've never met a ghost before."

Querrin flushed.

"I know it sounds ridiculous. But I'm worried."

Lawrence eyed him shrewdly. Then he leaned forward and tapped him sympathetically on the knee. "I know you are. Believe me, I wouldn't have risked breaking my neck by scrambling on this blasted train at the last minute if you weren't. I'll do all I can to help."

He leaned back again and rested his arm on the bag beside him. Querrin glanced at it. He said politely:

"I hope you had time to pack all you need."

Algy grinned. "I shan't need much more than a tooth brush." He added mildly: "And this."

He had unzipped the bag and was groping inside it. Then something gleamed dully in his hand. Peter Querrin saw with a slight shock of surprise that it was an automatic pistol.

Lawrence slipped out the cartridge clip and examined it. Then he smacked home the magazine with the heel of his hand and looked up with a slight glint of amusement in his lazy blue eyes. He said:

"This wouldn't be awfully effective against a ghost."

The gun snout moved in a gentle arc. "But it does have its uses." Peter Querrin made a tiny sound deep in his throat.

Lawrence said quietly:

"Let's be frank. Are you sure you've told me everything?"

Querrin said:

"Put that thing away."

"Does it bother you?"

Peter said flatly:

"I don't like guns."

"Neither do I." Algy thumbed down the safety catch and slipped the pistol into his pocket. "But then I don't like murderers either. Which is the main reason why I carry it. "

"The point is," said Peter with a trace of humour, "the point is, do you use it?"

Algy chuckled. "Not often. Steve doesn't like me to shoot people." His eyelids drooped. "I asked you a question, Peter."

Querrin made a brief, oddly despairing motion with his hand. "I've told you all I know."

Lawrence shook his head. "No. Never mind the family ghost. I'm a detective, remember. I want to know if your brother has any *human* enemies."

Something stirred at the back of Querrin's eyes and his mouth slackened suddenly. He said: "Oh," very quietly.

Lawrence grinned again. He said:

"You see what I mean. Secrets are hard to keep in a small village. You have servants, I suppose? They might be talking." Algy stopped smiling.

He finished grimly:

"Anybody may hear of your brother's intentions. And Bristley wouldn't be particularly surprised to hear tomorrow that Roger had come to some harm. Old Tom has an evil reputation."

His voice dropped. "Roger will be alone to-night. He'll be an inviting target. It's my business to see nobody takes a shot at him."

Peter seemed upset. "The Inspector thought this, too?"

"Of course. Why else should he call in Sergeant Hardinge?"

Querrin nodded slowly.

Lawrence said:

"Well then. Let's look for a motive. Who would be interested in your brother's—death?"

It was the first time the word had passed between them, and it had an ugly sound. The train's whistle blasted shrilly, and Peter began to speak hurriedly.

"Turner," he said, as though the name hurt his mouth "Simon Turner. He's the  only one. The only man you could call Roger's enemy." He paused, then added: "As far as I know." He looked at Lawrence reproachfully, "I didn't want to tell you all this. It sounds so feeble."

"Never mind. Who is Simon Turner?"

"You remember I told you Querrin House had been closed for years. Well, old Simon was the caretaker who looked after it for us. He's a queer, skinnily built old fellow, crusty as the devil—and more than a little touched if you ask me. He'd lived in the house nearly all his life and looked on the place as his own."

Peter shrugged nervously. "I expect you can see what's coming. We re-opened the building and had trouble with him right from the start. Roger had the place entirely re-decorated and repaired, and Turner didn't like it. One way or the other, he made such a nuisance of himself we had to get rid of him. Roger offered him a fair pension, of course, but insisted Simon left the Querrin House at once."

"I can guess the rest," murmured Algy. "The old boy cut up rough?"

"Yes. I told you before he seems more than a trifle mad. He went stumping about raving that Roger had robbed him of his birthright, or some such nonsense. I believe his father was some sort of old family retainer, come to think of it. Not that it makes any difference."

"Except to a mental case," replied Lawrence. "Did he threaten your brother?"

"Yes," said Peter carefully, "and no."

"That's a good answer. What does it mean?"

Querrin smiled faintly. "Sorry. This is going to sound dam' silly." He hesitated. "Simon Turner threatened my brother with—the ghost."

"Did he now." Lawrence seemed to be falling asleep. "How, exactly?"

"He said Roger could do what he wished but he'd never escape the wrath of old Tom Querrin."

"That doesn't have to mean anything," returned Algy quietly. "Turner may believe what he says. But the wish can be father to the thought."

Peter said wearily:

"It's all very silly at second hand. You didn't see the cold malevolence on the old man's face."

Algy Lawrence studied him in silence. Then he laughed, leaned over, and clapped a friendly hand on Ouerrin's shoulder.

"Cheer up, Peter. We'll put such a guard on Roger to-night—no human hand will reach him."

Their train arrived at Bristley in the early afternoon. Lawrence had already decided upon his opening move. He needed a dependable ally, and the obvious man to approach was the local Sergeant.

Peter had been expecting this. He guided his guest towards the village police station.

It conformed to a pleasant tradition by looking exactly like the converted country cottage it was. Only the bars at the frosted windows marred its placid attraction.

The two men came to a halt outside.

Peter asked hesitantly:

"Would you rather see Hardinge alone?"

"Yes, I think so," agreed Lawrence.

A shade of relief appeared on Querrin's face at the young man's answer. Though he had been largely responsible for Castle's decision to call in the Sergeant, he hadn't been looking forward to another three-handed discussion of ways and means. Both Hardinge and Lawrence had much steadier nerves than he, and the coming interview—which might prove rather difficult—would be better left to them alone.

Algy was thinking much the same thing, though for a different reason. He was shrinking from the almost impossible task of convincing a hard headed policeman that a man might need to be protected from a ghost. "Still," he reflected cheerfully, "I can always put this blame on Steve."

Peter said:

"I'll take your bag and put it in your room." He paused. "Shall I wait here, or—."

Lawrence cut him short. "Don't bother, I'll find somebody to direct me to the house."

He grinned. "See you later."

Querrin nodded. He went down the street with a lighter step, swinging the zippered grip.

Lawrence turned his back on the post office across the way and went into the station.

He stepped into the porch, pushed open the inner door marked Inquiries, and found himself in the Charge Room.

The uniformed man behind the desk looked up politely. "Yes?"

"Sergeant Hardinge?"

"That's right."

"My name's Lawrence," Algy began, a trifle diffidently. A bright self confidence in his intellectual capabilities still hadn't yet endowed him with the traditional brashness of the amateur detective.

Hardinge smiled, stood up and came round the desk to shake hands. "Why yes, sir. Chief Inspector Castle 'phoned me you were coming."

Relieved to find that his friend had prepared the way, Algy regarded his new ally with amiable interest. Hardinge was a short thick-set man of around forty. Grizzled grey hair cropped close to his skull, a dapper moustache, and an upright bearing intensified his noticeably military air. He had keen blue eyes (paler than the young man's own) and a pleasantly strident voice: Lawrence respected him immediately.

Their handshake was friendly and vigorous. Hardinge led the way into his living quarters. Since they adjoined the station proper, he had only to leave open the communicating door to keep an eye on his official desk and the street entrance.

"Cosy," remarked Algy, "and compact."

Possibly suspecting a shade of patronage in his London visitor's comment, the Sergeant said dryly: "This isn't the Yard. But the cells are strong enough." Then relenting, he asked: "Would you like a cup of tea, sir?"

"Don't trouble, please."

"No trouble at all, sir," said Hardinge cheerfully. "The kettle's boiling."

A persistent whistle from the tiny kitchen emphasized the truth of this, and the Sergeant disappeared.

When he returned a little while later, he discovered Algy Lawrence at his ease in a comfortable chair. Putting down the tray, Hardinge said quietly:

"A council of war, sir?"

Lawrence said frankly:

"Yes. But I'll admit I'm at a disadvantage. You know these people, Sergeant, and I don't. Peter Querrin, now. What do you make of him?"

Hardinge shrugged. "Young Mr. Querrin? A likeable man. But impressionable and nervy. And when young gentlemen are nervy," pronouncing the word with a kind of good-humoured contempt, "they imagine things."

Lawrence laughed briefly, deep in his throat. Taking the teacup offered him, he said: "Then you don't believe in the Querrin ghost?"

"Scepticism," said the Sergeant politely, "is a policeman's stock in trade."

They sat in silence for a moment, drinking a tea brewed almost black.

Then Hardinge said abruptly:

"Chief Inspector Castle made certain arrangements for to-night, sir. Are you satisfied with them?"

Lawrence said slowly: "I think so. Steve's a good organizer. I haven't explored the ground yet, though."

"The layout's simple enough," supplied the Sergeant. "There are only two approaches to that room, as you'll see. You and young Querrin can take the one and I'll guard the other." He glanced out the window at a lowering rain-filled sky. "My post outside the house isn't going to be any too comfortable, I'll warrant."

"I'll take it, if you'd rather."

"No thanks." Hardinge shook his head. A slight smile played round his lips under the dapper moustache. "You keep an eye on young Mr. Peter. Else he'll see phantoms in every shadow."

Lawrence chuckled. "This business is going to look dam' funny when it goes into a report."

"No need for that, sir. To-night I'm off duty: on my own time. A private citizen, as you might say."

"That's very good of you."

"Not at all. I'm glad to help."

This polite interchange was followed by a slightly embarrassed pause. Then Lawrence said doubtfully: "You've realized—that is, I mean," he floundered, "a ghost isn't all we're worried about."

Then he looked into the Sergeant's shrewd blue eyes and stopped fumbling. Hardinge said softly:

"I understand, of course, sir."

Algy relaxed with a grin. "You don't miss much, do you?"

"We're trained to use our heads, sir." A twinkle of amusement showed in the Sergeant's voice. "And our eyes. That pistol, now—."

"Eh?"

"That pistol, Mr. Lawrence, which is ruining the hang of your coat. You do have a licence for it, I hope?"

Algy laughed. "You win, Sergeant. Yes, I do. And I'm sorry I tried to teach you your job." He sat up straight in his chair. "All right then. The question is, has Roger Querrin any human enemies?" He added slowly: "Peter suggested a man named Simon Turner."

"Old Simon Turner?" Hardinge seemed surprised.

"You sound doubtful, Sergeant."

"I am, rather. They've had words, I know. But Simon's a harmless old windbag. I doubt if he has either the brains or the courage—to stand in for a ghost."

Lawrence nodded thoughtfully. "Uh huh. I might speak to him

though."

"You might," agreed Hardinge, "but you won't. The old man's disappeared."

"What?" Lawrence was mildly startled.

"Sorry. I didn't mean to be melodramatic." The Sergeant stood up and began to load his tray again. Then he went back to the kitchen, saying as he went: "Turner has left the village. There's been no sign of him since yesterday."

Lawrence wondered what, if anything, the ex-caretaker's absence meant. He fished in his pocket for the silver cigarette-case, then let it slip out of his fingers again... Tobacco helped him to think but he liked his thinking to be constructive: and he needed more facts.

Hardinge came back. The young man asked a question.

The Sergeant said:

"No, I don't think it means anything—anything sinister, that is. Did I mention he left all his things at his lodgings? Well, he did." He sank back in his chair. "He's done this before, you know. He's probably gone on the booze somewhere."

Lawrence found his ally's calmness refreshing.

"That's all?"

"That's all. We don't have to worry. Believe me," said Hardinge firmly. "*Nothing* happens in Bristley."

Algy grinned. "You say that as if you were sorry."

"I am," said the Sergeant. For a fleeting moment the shadow of a deep rooted *malaise* peeped round the placidity in his eyes. "Believe me, sir, this is no place for an ambitious man."

He said no more, but Lawrence knew what was in his mind. No chance here for the bright piece of work that means quick promotion... Then Hardinge smiled. "Still," he admitted, "the quiet life has its advantages." He changed the subject. "I'll come over to Querrin House this evening, then. Just as soon as I come off duty and have a meal."

Algy nodded gratefully. "Thanks." He stood up. "With any luck," he added, half to himself; "I'll be home to-morrow." He turned to the door, then a sudden recollection made him swing round again. "Steve will want news before I get back to London, though. Can I 'phone him from Querrin House?"

"Oh, yes." Hardinge chuckled. "Only if you've any notions of privacy, be careful what you say."

Lawrence flicked an eyebrow.

Interpreting this as a question, the Sergeant went on equably: "Our village post mistress handles all the calls. Now Miss Watson is a nice old girl, one of the best, but she does have the habit—."

36

"Of forgetting to hang up?"

"Exactly."

"Maybe I'd better talk in shorthand."

"It won't make much difference," said the Sergeant blandly. "I'll wager all Bristley knows why you're here by nightfall."

Algy blinked.

"Miss Watson's post office," Hardinge reminded him gently, "is opposite the police station."

"Oh." The young man grinned. "And I came here with Peter."

"Did you? Then the secret is certainly out. She must have seen you. And there's only one reason why the Querrins should be entertaining strangers to-day."

"She knows about Roger's appointment?"

"The whole village knows about it."

"I gather," commented Lawrence, "that the lady can put two and two together?"

"And make forty-four."

Algy Lawrence strolled up the drive towards Querrin House, his grey raincoat open, and his hands plunged comfortably if inelegantly in the depths of his trouser pockets. The soft green hat, crushed as usual on the back of his blond haired head, had a certain air of jauntiness. Even his automatic pistol, thwacking as he walked, against his thigh with a troubled urgency, did little to disturb his new-found peace of mind.

Sergeant Hardinge's air of calm efficiency had impressed him greatly. He had, Algy told himself, at least one dependable ally. As for Peter... Lawrence thought rather smugly that the younger Querrin's fears were distinctly neurotic. A level headed Londoner would never have succumbed to them....

Algy continued cheerfully on his way.

He hadn't bearded the inappropriately named Miss Watson in her lair, but he had caught a glimpse of her as he left the police station. The flash of glasses behind a hurriedly adjusted curtain in the post office opposite had convinced him that the lady's official duties didn't prevent her from keeping the station under fairly constant observation.

He didn't mind. If the village knew he was there to guard Roger Querrin, idle mischief makers might be scared off. So much the better, thought Algy. I don't want trouble.

Following a bend in the path, Lawrence rounded a tall cluster of bushes, took his hands out of his pockets, and stopped in mild surprise.

A very attractive young lady appeared to be walking backwards down the drive towards him.

This, as he realized immediately, was just an illusion. The young lady was in fact staring back at the house.

Algy Lawrence had just enough time to note approvingly that her hair was a delectable shade of red-brown, sleek, and kissable, when she took another absent-minded step to the rear and stumbled into his arms.

"Oh!"

She twisted and nearly fell, but he held her securely. Then he looked into rounded, grey-green eyes; and felt his heart bump alarmingly.

He smiled down at her. "Hallo, there."

The alarm faded from her face as she smiled in return. "Hallo, yourself." The curve of her lips was intriguing. She added:

"You can let me up now."

"Oh, yes." She thought there was a distinct tinge of regret in the stranger's voice; and was flattered. He set her on her feet again and they smiled at each other once more.

Lawrence, who was an impressionable young man, decided she was lovely.

Her hair was long and curled mistily about her shoulders. Her grey-green eyes, piquant and mischievous, sloped slightly upwards; and thick lashes curved gaily at the corners. The moulding of her face wasn't classically beautiful, but it was clean and frank and free. Her hair swept softly behind her ears, leaving them bare.

She was engagingly Puckish; and wholly adorable.

Plunging slim hands in the pockets of her swagger coat, she inquired gravely:

"Mr. Lawrence, I believe?"

He returned with equal solemnity:

"Miss Craig, I presume."

Then they both laughed.

Audrey stepped forward, laid one hand on his arm, then pointed with the other towards the house.

"You're a detective," she said. "Make something of that."

Algy looked, but saw nothing unusual.

She stood no higher than his shoulder; he glanced down at her upturned face inquiringly.

"Those bushes," she said. "There by the house. They were moving."

There was no wind.

Algy Lawrence, who till that moment had felt nothing but pleasure at her touch, was conscious of a sudden chill.

Annoyed with himself, he said quietly:

"They're still, now."

His tone implied a question. She shook her head; and a wisp of hair strayed charmingly over her forehead.

"No, I didn't imagine it. Those bushes were moving. As if someone—
." She broke off.

Lawrence said:

"A poacher, perhaps."

"So close to the house?"

Algy had to admit it wasn't very likely. "Does it matter though? If it was a prowler, he's gone now."

She nodded, and colour touched her cheeks. "I'm edgy and nervous, I suppose."

"Of course. You're worried about Roger."

"Yes." She shivered. "He's determined to go through with this silly business." She tried to laugh. "Imagine! A tryst with a ghost. Ridiculous, isn't it? Yet I'd do anything—to make him change his mind."

Lawrence looked into her troubled eyes and decided Roger Querrin was a stubborn idiot who didn't appreciate his luck.

"Never mind," he said quietly. "We'll look after him for you."

She slipped her arm round his, and her face was sunny again.

"You're nice," she said. "I like you."

"Thanks," said Algy; and meant it.

"Come along," said Audrey. "I'll introduce you to the rest of the family."

"Weren't you going out?"

"I was only going down to the village. Don't worry about that."

They fell into step. Lawrence thought that she moved with a superb and cat-like grace, and he liked the engaging pressure of her arm against his.

He murmured: "You mentioned—the family," and inflected the words as a question.

She looked a trifle startled, then blushed. "Oh! I meant Roger, principally." She laughed. "Imagine. Already I'm making noises like a wife."

Algy said sincerely:

"Roger's a lucky man."

"Thank you." She looked into his pleasant, lazy face; and liked what she saw. She went on:

"Then there's Uncle Russ."

Algy recalled that Chief Inspector Castle's references to Russell Craig had been anything but complimentary. He detected too an odd trace of uncertainty in the girl's tone as she mentioned the name.

It was a mixture, almost, of affection and embarrassment. Then

Audrey said with amusement:

"I hope you won't disapprove of him."

"Should I?"

"Most people do, I'm afraid."

"Why?"

The twinkle of humour in her voice grew more pronounced. "He's an unhealthy influence."

Lawrence said he liked unhealthy influences.

By this time they had reached the house. Audrey drew free of Algy's arm and started up the steps, then turned back to the young man thoughtfully.

"We needn't," she murmured, "make a formal entrance."

"No?"

"No."

She hesitated. Lawrence said obligingly:

"I'm a furtive character. Sneak me in through the back."

She laughed. "I wasn't being rude. I thought you'd want to explore the ground."

Algy understood. He said:

"Hardinge mentioned there were two approaches to the Room."

(The capital letter was implicit and accepted in the minds of both: they had no need of definition.)

"That's right. From the passage; and from outside the house. That's the way"—she paused—"I'd like to show you now."

"Let's go then."

Lawrence stepped back, and the girl skipped gracefully down the steps to rejoin him.

She led the way along a flagged path that skirted the house and ran roughly parallel to its somewhat irregular contours. Between the path and the building proper lay wide, as yet unplanted, flower beds: the whole an expanse of soft brown earth broken only by a right-angled extension of the footway running up to a side door.

Audrey said:

"All this looks pretty barren now. But then, old Simon Turner was no gardener."

Algy glanced at her. She had spoken the name without any particular emphasis. He followed his thought out in words.

"Evidently you don't share Peter's suspicions."

She looked puzzled, then her face cleared again. Algy Lawrence decided approvingly that she was intelligent as well as beautiful.

"About Turner, you mean? Peter mentioned the talk he had with you." She paused. "No, I don't think old Simon's threats meant

40

anything."

She added: "He's rather stupid."

"You don't have to be intelligent," said Algy mildly, "to be evil."

A silence fell between them.

They turned another corner. The flagged path stretched on before them under the partial shelter of leafy trees. To their left it was bordered by thickly clustered bushes; but to their right, sloping up to the house, was the usual expanse of bare brown earth.

Audrey's face had altered subtly. A pulse pounded in her throat.

She said queerlv:

"That's—the room."

He let his gaze follow hers.

Large french windows, closed now, gave access to the house. Behind them a man moved dimly. Lawrence had the swift and disturbing impression of an animal in a trap.

He glanced at the girl, then stared in wonder: for her face had changed again and her eyes were bright with love.

She said softly:

"That's Roger."

Lawrence nodded and smiled, though an unreasoning envy had tugged briefly at his heart.

They stepped off the path and Algy felt his shoes sinking into the softness of the soil.

Audrey said, by way of apology:

"We've planned an extension of the path."

"Leading up to the house?"

"Yes. But these things take time."

She spoke absently. All her attention had slipped away to the sturdy man pushing open the french windows to greet them.

Algy Lawrence, with an inward sigh, allowed himself to be introduced to Miss Craig's fiancé.

Roger Querrin was a strongly built man some ten years Peter's senior. He had steady brown eyes in a pleasant unhandsome face. His jaw-line was etched with determination; strength and decision seemed apparent in the set of his shoulders.

Lawrence, regarding him with a prejudiced eye, reflected that Roger could also be a pig-headed ass.

The two men shook hands. Querrin's clasp was firm and friendly.

"Hallo, Lawrence. It's good of you to come. Though I don't mind telling you," Roger added with a smile, "you're wasting your time."

Algy grinned. He said:

"I hope so—for your sake."

Querrin stared. Then he put back his head and laughed.

"Good for you. Come in."

Lawrence walked through the open windows.

Then he stopped on the threshold, his mouth taut and unsmiling.

Perhaps it was the pinched look of fear on the girl's face as she went before him; perhaps it was the sight of Peter Querrin, standing uneasily in the shadows. Perhaps it was only the tyranny of his own imagination.

But he seemed to pass from the freedom and sanity of an outside world into the shade of a monstrous evil.

Lawrence saw with a slight start of surprise that Roger Querrin alone was quite unaffected by any premonition of danger. His laughter had sounded hollow enough, but it was entirely genuine.

His brother, however, seemed more nervous than ever. A nervous tic jumped intermittently at the corner of his mouth.

"Hallo. You found your way, then?"

"That's right," returned Algy gently. He could see that the other young man was trying to cover a deep anxiety with the tatters of banality.

Peter went on:

"I put your bag in your room." He paused. "You fixed things up—with Hardinge?"

"Thanks... Yes, I did. He'll arrive this evening."

"Eh, what's that?" Roger Querrin had caught their words, and turned away from his fiancée with a grin. "You're not dragging the good Sergeant up here too?"

Lawrence inclined his head. "That's the plan," he agreed.

"The devil take it, then," said Roger with a kind of bluff contempt. "Peter, you are a young ass. You've thrown everyone into a panic."

"Everyone," remarked Algy dryly, "except you."

Querrin might have had little imagination but he was not lacking in perception. He looked at Lawrence closely, then said quietly:

"You think I'm being unreasonable."

"Perhaps."

Audrey moved closer and put her hand on Roger's shoulder: he patted it absently, but kept his gaze on Lawrence.

"It hasn't occurred to you," he said without rancour, "that I've made no fuss about this—that I'm the only one in fact who seems to have kept his head?"

"I'd rather," said Lawrence coolly, "you kept your life."

Querrin felt the girl's fingers clutch hard on the cloth of his coat; and in the tiny silence, heard something rattle in Peter's throat.

Roger turned on his brother with something like relief.

"Peter." His voice was almost brutal. "You've gone white. Pull yourself together." He finished flatly: "You young fool."

Peter Querrin flushed, opened his lips as if to speak, then went in silence from the room.

Roger had the grace to feel slightly ashamed. When he turned back to Lawrence, the anger had died from his eyes.

"I'm sorry," he said. "But Peter's been getting on everybody's nerves, including mine."

"He's worried about you."

"I know it," said Querrin, with a good-humoured growl. "But, dammit, I didn't *ask* him to act like this." He eyed Algy shrewdly. "Be honest, Lawrence. If it wasn't for young Peter's hysteria, would you give this plan of mine a second's thought?"

Lawrence said honestly:

"Probably not. But the way things are, we'd all prefer you didn't keep this, um, appointment. What do you hope to gain by it?"

"Blast it, man," returned Querrin irritably, "I don't hope to *gain* anything. Where's your sense of tradition?"

Lawrence knew he had struck the hard vein of obstinacy in the older man's make-up, but made one final attempt to dissuade him.

"You won't change your mind?"

Roger felt the swift pressure of Audrey's fingers on his shoulder again, and he hesitated.

Then he said slowly:

"No."

The hope which had flared suddenly in the girl's eyes flickered and went out.

Lawrence said equably:

"All right, then. It's your funeral."

Querrin's mouth twisted wryly in humorous protest.

He said:

"You might have phrased that more tactfully. Come now," and he waved his hand vaguely round the room, "you don't really believe there's danger here?"

Lawrence, by this time, had thrown off the phantoms. He had surrendered his imagination to his intelligence; and now was concerned only with the threat of physical violence. Which, as he both admitted and hoped, might be entirely non-existent.

He glanced round the room with deceptive casualness. Avoiding Roger's question, he murmured:

"You haven't modernized this room much."

"No." Querrin shrugged away a slight discomfiture. "I had the whole house done over, yet somehow——."

He broke off and smiled at his fiancée. "Audrey doesn't approve. But I couldn't bear to tamper with this part of the building. That's why there's no electric light, either in here or the passage outside."

Lawrence eyed an old-fashioned oil lamp on the table and reflected on the price that is paid by lovers of the past.

Roger guessed what he was thinking.

"Don't you approve either?"

Algy said he liked his creature comforts.

"So," murmured Audrey gently, "do I."

Querrin smiled down at her. "You hate this room, don't you? You'd like to destroy it."

She nodded.

She said:

"It's so—oppressive."

It was all that, and more. Lawrence stared at the old grim-looking furniture, the long musty drapes by the french windows which were the room's only source of daylight, and the knife which hung over the mantel.

He crossed over to the fireplace and stretched up his hands to the dagger.

As the blade slipped out of its sheath, it glinted dully. He felt an indefinable sense of repulsion.

"A dangerous toy," he muttered softly.

Behind him, Audrey gave a little gasp.

Querrin said quietly:

"Put it back, Lawrence."

Algy slid the knife home again. The faint click of the blade against its casing seemed somehow very loud.

Audrey Craig said with muted urgency:

"Darling Roger. Won't you get rid of that horrible thing?"

Querrin soothed her.

"Perhaps, when our ghost is laid to-night. Till then," he finished with a smile, "I wouldn't feel justified in tampering with old Tom's property."

Lawrence asked:

"Is this really the knife that killed young Martin all those years ago?"

"It could be. Though," Roger admitted with a shrug, "we don't really know. The dagger is old enough anyway."

Audrey interrupted, with a shiver.

"Let's not talk about it."

44

Lawrence moved away from the fireplace. His face wore its usual expression of amiable laziness, but Audrey for one was not deceived. She knew he was inspecting the room with an eye to Roger's defence.

The fair-haired young man walked over to the french windows and examined them carefully. They could be secured top and bottom by two stout bolts. Not much danger there, he thought approvingly.

He peered through the glass panels at the double line of footprints he and the girl had left behind them. There was no way then of reaching the room from outside the house without leaving tell-tale traces... Better and better. He began to feel more cheerful.

There were no other windows, and the only remaining exit was the door in the opposite corner.

Lawrence crossed over to examine it.

The door had no bolt, but the lock was stout and new.

Algy straightened up, then looked a question.

"You see," said Roger Querrin by way of reply, "I haven't been entirely unco-operative. Steve Castle suggested a fresh lock, so I had a man down from London to-day. There's only one key. And this is it."

He pulled a key chain from his trousers pocket and showed Lawrence the bright new metal.

Algy murmured his approval. "Good. Hang on to that and we shan't have to worry about anybody making a duplicate."

Roger's eyebrows went up.

"There's no fear of that, surely?"

Lawrence was studiously banal. "You never know."

"No," said Querrin heavily. "I don't." His tone betrayed a certain impatience.

Algy said sleepily:

"Let's have a look at the passage."

He swung open the door and glanced outside.

A long corridor stretched before him between blank panelled walls towards closed double doors at the end of it. A solitary window, set half way along in the outside wall, did little to dispel the murky gloom.

Leaving Roger Querrin alone with his fiancée, Lawrence strolled out of the room and along the passage.

His footfalls were entirely muffled by a thick new carpet: the silence seemed brooding and oppressive.

Reaching the window, he examined it thoughtfully. Then he pushed up the frame and leaned out.

Immediately below, and stretching on either side, were the wide unplanted flower-beds. Straight ahead and parallel with the house, was the flagged path he had followed with Audrey Craig.

Once again, there was no method of reaching this part of the building without leaving clear traces in the soil.

He re-closed the window and pushed over the catch. All that remained now was to test its security from outside.

A voice broke in on his thoughts. He turned to find Peter Querrin at his elbow.

"C-can I help you?"

"If you like." Lawrence explained that he wanted to make sure that the window, once fastened, could not be opened from outside the house.

Peter nodded eagerly, then set off through the double doorway again.

A minute or two later, he appeared on the path outside. Walking rather gingerly over the bare brown earth, he picked up an old wooden box which was lying nearby and upturned it directly beneath the window. Using this as an improvised step, he brought himself up to a convenient level and began to rattle enthusiastically at the frame.

"All right," said Lawrence, through the glass.

Peter, however, was by no means finished. Clambering up on the wide sill, he redoubled his onslaught.

Algy, struggling with an impolite urge to laugh, waved him down. Young Querrin's unintentional comedy had at least convinced Lawrence that the window was secure against any attack short of actual destruction.

Peter climbed down. Algy made his way along the corridor to meet him as he re-entered the house.

Pulling open the double doors, Lawrence twitched aside the curtains that barred his way and found himself in the main hall.

A broad staircase swept up to the bedrooms above. To his right a short passage led up to the side door he had noticed on his walk with Audrey.

As he watched, the door pushed open and Querrin came in from the gardens.

Peter asked nervously:

"Are you satisfied?"

"Well enough," returned Algy.

"It wouldn't matter—about the window, I mean," continued Querrin jerkily, "only Roger won't let us stand guard in the passage itself. He says he has to be alone."

Algy grinned. "You weren't proposing to squat on the mat all night, were you?"

"There isn't," said Peter anxiously, "any mat."

"I was speaking," replied Lawrence patiently, "figuratively." He hoped Querrin's jitters wouldn't get the better of him. "We can stand guard here. Hardinge will watch from the garden. There's no need to worry."

Peter nodded, and fumbled a cigarette from a crumpled packet to gently quivering lips.

Lawrence pulled out his lighter and flicked up a flame. Querrin drew deeply and felt the soothing smoke seep down to his lungs. His nerves were still bad, yet the approach of zero hour was bringing its own queer calm, and he knew he could do what was required of him.

He said:

You can rely on me, Lawrence. I'll do whatever you say."

Algy clapped him encouragingly on the shoulder. "That's the spirit." Another cliché, he thought. Yet the bromides were soothing enough.

The curtains swayed behind them, and Roger and Audrey stepped in from the passage.

The girl saw that Lawrence had at last stripped off his raincoat and was twirling his crushed green hat absently round his hand. Steve Castle would have assumed he was looking for a suitable target at which to aim it... Lawrence had the unmistakable air of a man who delights in using the head-piece of a classical bust as a hat-rack.

Audrey said:

"I'll take you upstairs, Mr. Lawrence. You'll want to unpack."

"Eh?" Roger Querrin was recalled to his duties as host. "Oh, of course. Don't bother, Audrey. I'll show you to your room, Lawrence."

Algy followed him up the stairs.

The room to which he was shown was airy and comfortable. He prodded the bed approvingly. It was soft and well sprung. Not, as he reflected ruefully, that he would be spending much time in it.

Roger said:

"I expect you're rather hungry. Would you like some sandwiches?"

"Please."

"I'll have them sent up to you." Roger paused with his hand on the door. He hesitated. He said:

"I haven't been very gracious. I think you're wasting your time, and I've said so. Just the same," he finished awkwardly, "I'd like you to know I'm grateful."

Lawrence nodded pleasantly.

Querrin went out.

Algy dropped his hat and coat carelessly on a chair, transferred the gun to his jacket, then stretched out lazily on the bed.

It was all, he decided complacently, going to be very easy.

His eyes closed.

Somebody tapped on the door. Lawrence called out lazily. "Come in."

A tray chinked invitingly, and the appetizing aroma of coffee drifted past his nostrils.

Algy opened one eye, saw slim hands, and swung his feet hurriedly to the floor.

"Oh, it's you. Sorry," he ended vaguely.

Audrey Craig smiled at him delightfully.

"This is," she commented, "a very personal service. I hope," she added with a twinkle, "you're duly appreciative."

"I am," said Algy Lawrence, and regarded her with admiration.

She was indeed good to look upon. No longer hidden by the gay but unrevealing swagger coat, the moulding of her figure was exquisite. The gently-swelling breasts and the curves of her beautiful thighs and legs were innocent, frank, and completely seductive.

Lawrence said sincerely:

"You're very beautiful."

"Thank you." Audrey tried to be severe, but only succeeded in sounding pleased. "Shall I pour?"

"Mmm?"

"The coffee. Shall I pour?"

"Yes please."

Audrey balanced the tray on the bed and sat down cautiously beside it. She handed the young man a steaming cup, then leaned over and put the coffee pot, for safety, on the bedside table.

Pleasantly disturbed by her nearness, he noticed a rebellious tendril had once more shaken free from her sleek red-brown hair. He put out his hand and smoothed it gently away from her forehead.

The fleeting touch, brief as it was, startled them both.

Audrey, an unwilling surprise in her grey-green eyes, said faintly: "Don't spill your coffee."

"I won't." He put the cup carefully on the table beside him.

Then he dropped his hand over hers on the coverlet.

Oddly embarrassed, the girl said quickly:

"I wanted to thank you—for looking after Roger... "

"Don't thank me."

She struggled on inconsequentially:

"And wanted to ask you—why you became a detective...."

"Don't ask me," he murmured; then moved by an impulse he couldn't explain, leaned across and kissed her deliberately, full on the mouth.

Her lips were wholly unresponsive.

He broke away and stood up with sourness on his tongue.

The girl stayed where she was, her eyes rounded and a faint tinge of scarlet on her cheeks.

Lawrence said angrily:

"You ought to slap my face."

Audrey's voice was small.

"Wouldn't that be rather—Victorian?"

"I behaved like a cad." He smiled without humour. "That's Victorian, too."

The girl said shakily:

"It was only a kiss."

He replied obscurely:

"That's just the trouble."

Audrey stood up. "I'd better go."

The door closed behind her. Algy wandered over towards the window and stood staring out with an angry frown.

A blunder, he thought savagely. Of the worst kind.

At length the old placidity returned to his face and the lazy kindness to his eyes.

"At least," he murmured aloud, "I answered her question."

For Audrey Craig, no less than Stephen Castle, had wondered why Algy Lawrence should be content to spend his life exploring the labyrinthine ways of crime.

He followed a path that was sometimes dangerous, frequently weary, and always lonely. Yet he lived by a code and he lived for a quest.

For Lawrence was seeking his lady

All thoughts of romantic adventure, however, were far from Lawrence's mind as he descended the staircase in the early evening.

He knew that Audrey Craig was a good-humoured and well-adjusted young lady, unlikely to bother herself with a grudge. The incident in his bedroom could be politely ignored with profit to them both.

Nevertheless, the mild species of madness which had led him to the blunder had emphasized his distaste for the adventure as a whole. He reflected uncharitably on the imperfections of the Querrins: the neurotic fears of one brother, and the stubbornness of the other.

The devil take them both, he thought unkindly; then laughed at his own inconsistency. Their safety was, for the moment at least, his special charge.

He didn't believe there was any real danger, but just the same he intended his precautions to be detailed and his defences impregnable.

He had already examined the servants and dismissed them as negligible, either as a force for evil or for good.

There was, however, one member of the household whom he had not yet interviewed, and he intended now to remedy the omission.

Following his nose, he pushed open the door of the drawing-room and was immediately lucky.

An elderly gentleman with a large nose and silver-grey hair was sitting by the fire beneath the discreet glow of a standard lamp. He was smoking, with evident enjoyment, one of Roger's best cigars, and he was peering through enormous horn-rimmed spectacles at a book balanced on one elegantly crossed knee.

At the young man's approach, he looked up, nodded amiably, laid his book face downwards on the arm of his chair, and levered himself to his feet.

"Ah, Mr. Lawrence, isn't it? My name is Russell Craig."

They shook hands. Algy gazed at Audrey's uncle with considerable interest.

He was already aware that Mr. Craig had invited himself to Querrin House on the strength of the engagement, nominally as his niece's chaperon, but actually to indulge in the fleshpots.

Algy, despite Castle's implied disfavour and Audrey's half-serious misgivings, liked the old rogue's looks.

He was wearing, and in this manner showing an easy blend of comfort and formality, a soft shirt with his black tie and dinner jacket. In the matter of age, he seemed poised indeterminately between the middle fifties and the early sixties. There was a lusty glow of humour in his slate-grey eyes, and his manner was both courteous and distinguished. If he had a tendency to plumpness, it was largely obscured by the expert cut of his clothes. He had moreover the bland air of a man who forgot to pay his tailor.

"Well, my boy," said Russell Craig, "how would you like a drink before dinner, hey?"

Lawrence hesitated. He was the mildest of drinkers.

"You're not," said Craig, with sudden suspicion, "a teetotaller?"

Algy smiled.

"No. Not exactly."

"Good." Uncle Russ seemed relieved. "Horrid people, teetotallers. Addicted to all kinds of strange vices I believe."

He strolled across to a decanter on the sideboard.

Algy glanced at the book he had left balanced on the armchair. He saw with pleased surprise that it was a first edition of *The Man of the Forty Faces.*

Russell Craig turned back with a glass in each hand. Handing one tumbler to Algy Lawrence, he said:

"Fine stuff this, my boy. I don't mind admitting it's the prop of my declining years. When I was young"— he drew up his mouth in a horrible leer—"I had—other diversions. But now," and he sighed, "I find consolation in the pleasures of good whisky and bad detective stories."

Algy said with a grin:

"*Bad* detective stories?"

"Yes," said the old rogue earnestly. "And I mean that as a compliment. I have no patience with the modern conception of a detective as an ordinary young man with a polite manner and a weakness for quotations. I like my sleuths from the old school— wayward, arrogant, eccentric, and infallible."

Warming to his theme, Uncle Russ picked up his novel and waved it under Lawrence's nose.

"*You've* never heard of Hamilton Cleek," he thundered. "Or the Hanshews either. Tell me," he went on, with commendable fervour, but muddled logic, "that their writing was bad, their sentimentality embarrassing, and their drama wildly funny. Tell me all that and I'll agree with you. But, by God, they used ideas!

"A man walked into a room and vanished without a trace. Or died alone, from an explosion out of nowhere. Ingenuity, my boy! Not half-baked Freudian theory.

"Meet the Vanishing Cracksman and you might find also a nine-fingered skeleton, a monster footprint, an icicle shot from a crossbow, or a camera that takes the picture of a murderer from the retina of a dead man's eye.

"The Hanshews, Thomas and Mary," and he pronounced the names with affection, "knew the true detective story was only as good as its plot."

He paused for breath.

Algy Lawrence, a twinkle in his lazy blue eye, said thoughtfully:

"Mmmm... Of course, I'm no expert. But I see that's the first edition you have there, published by Cassell in 1910. Did you know it was reissued in 1913 as *Cleek, The Man of the Forty Faces*, with three of the original stories left out, and a new one included? In the U.S.A., oddly enough, the amended text was published five years *before* the original finally appeared as *Cleek, the Master Detective*."

"My boy," said Russell Craig with a new respect, "I see I've misjudged you. Have another drink."

"I haven't," replied Lawrence hastily, "finished this one yet."

"A trifling objection," said Russell Craig. He retrieved his cigar from the ash-tray and puffed at it sternly.

Algy Lawrence was about to answer when his eye was caught by a movement in the bushes outside. Uncle Russ, with commendable British fortitude, had left one half of the french windows standing slightly ajar, and in the dying light of the day Lawrence could see clearly a peculiarly localized disturbance of the foliage.

Exactly why this struck him as remarkable, the young man was unable to tell. Perhaps it was the memory of Audrey's earlier alarm.

Algy swallowed the remainder of his drink and strolled, as if casually, towards the windows.

Yes, there it was again: in the bushes beyond the path, an ominous rustling. Moved for the second time that day by an impulse he could hardly explain, Lawrence dropped the empty tumbler with a soft thud on the carpet, flung both the windows wide, and hurled himself out into the garden.

Moving without conscious thought, his long legs thudded over the ground. He reached the shrubbery with the blood singing in his ears and a soft curtain of rain striking mistily at his face.

The shaking of the bushes became violent and unconcealed. Algy charged into them without a second's hesitation, the wet leaves slapping at him in waspish protest.

53

There was a man there right enough, turned now in flight. Lawrence threw himself forward. His fingers scrabbled at the hem of the prowler's coat, and they went down together, rolling dizzily in the mud.

The fugitive came off best. Agile as a cat, he was already on one knee before Lawrence had time to do more than raise himself dazedly on his elbow.

Algy caught one glimpse of the prowler's face, scared and set with a desperate fury, before a skinny arm swept up, then down, and hurled him into blackness.

After a while the throbbing stabs of pain stopped driving through his head, and left only a villainous ache in his temples.

Lawrence opened his eyes and found Audrey's face very close to his.

He tried to speak, then closed his eyes again with a groan. The girl's fingers felt very cool against his brow.

She said anxiously:

"Mr. Lawrence! Are you all right?"

"I—I think so."

His voice seemed new and untried, and sounded strange even to himself.

He sat up wearily. A fresh wave of pain nearly swamped him once more, but he rode the storm doggedly.

"Ahhh…" He shook his head groggily. A thin trickle of blood stood out redly on his white face. Above him and around him, the bush leaves rustled wetly.

Audrey said again:

"Are you all right?"

"Yes," he returned weakly.

She put her hand on his shoulder. "What happened?"

"I caught a prowler. Then he hit me—with a stone, I think... Did you see him?"

She shook her head. "No. I came into the drawing-room just after you left. Uncle Russ and I followed you, and found you like this."

Somebody shifted awkwardly behind her. A lighted cigar glowed in the gathering darkness.

Russell Craig cleared his throat. "I don't wish to seem unsympathetic, my dear, but it's deuced uncomfortable here in the rain. If Mr. Lawrence can walk, I suggest we assist him back to the house."

The girl and her uncle helped him to his feet. He swayed unsteadily for a moment, then with an arm round Russell Craig's shoulders, made a halting journey back to the drawing-room.

The rain was falling more heavily now and he reached the lights and warmth with an excusable relief.

Audrey guided him to the sofa, then stood back with worry on her pretty face.

"You look terrible," she said frankly. "Shall I call a doctor?"

"I'd rather—you didn't."

"But—."

"My dear," interrupted her uncle, "there's nothing wrong with our young friend which a good stiff drink can't cure."

Audrey gestured helplessly, but he was already handling the decanter.

"Here, my boy. Take this."

"Uncle Russ!" The girl tut-tutted impatiently. "That's much too strong."

"Then," said Russell Craig with dignity, "I shall drink it myself."

And did so.

She scolded him briefly, then hurried through the door.

Lawrence closed his eyes. These cushions are very comfortable, he thought. If only my head didn't ache so much.....

Something cool sponged over his face. Audrey Craig was bathing his forehead.

"Keep still," she murmured.

Lawrence relaxed.

Audrey smoothed the tousled blond hair away from his brow and examined the wound with a frown.

The skin was torn and a bruise was already discolouring his temples, but now the clotted blood was washed away she could see that the damage wasn't as extensive as she had thought.

Algy opened one eye.

"How is it?"

She smiled. "You'll live. With a Grade A headache."

The door opened again. Roger Querrin hurried in, his face concerned.

"Lawrence, old fellow. What happened?"

Audrey explained briefly.

Her fiancé announced:

"I'll phone for the police at once."

"No." Algy roused himself to protest. "Hardinge will be here soon enough. I don't want to raise the alarm. I came here to look after you, don't forget. It won't help me to set the place in a turmoil."

"But we ought to get after the man who attacked you—."

"He's had time enough to get away. Leave it alone."

"Shouldn't we look for—for clues, or something?" Roger waved his hand uncertainly.

Lawrence grinned faintly. The first few words of his reply were drowned out by a long roll of thunder.

Querrin glanced round, startled. He seemed for once to be in danger of losing his air of bluff equanimity.

Lawrence said:

"There's your answer. That heavy rain will wash out every trace." Russell Craig turned away from the windows.

"That's true enough," he observed. "Look here, Roger, my boy." He pointed through the glass. "Our own footmarks are disappearing fast."

Querrin did not reply directly.

"Very well, then." He was looking towards Lawrence inquiringly. "What do you advise?"

"All I can suggest," said Algy, sitting upright, "is a policy—ouch!— of masterly inactivity." He put up his hand to his head. "In other words, there's damn all we can do. For the moment, at least."

"You," said Audrey Craig severely, "are going up to bed. At once."

He smiled at her. "That's not a bad idea. I need to be fit for to-night." Roger cleared his throat. He said gruffly:

"You're in no shape for a late night sitting. Couldn't you call off all this nonsense about a guard?"

"That's sound sense, my boy," said Uncle Russ from across the room. He added eagerly: "Let me take your place to-night."

Lawrence saw alarm spring into the girl's eyes, and grinned at her reassuringly.

Querrin said dryly, over his shoulder:

"I'd rather you didn't, thanks."

It was almost a snub. It seemed that Roger and Audrey both shared Steve Castle's opinion of Russell Craig's reliability.

"Nobody," said Lawrence firmly, "is taking my place to-night. I came here to look after you, Querrin, and by glory, I'm going to do it."

He stood up. "But now," he added ruefully, "I need a rest."

He went back to his room on Roger's arm, and was relieved they did not meet Peter on the way. He hadn't the smallest doubt that the younger Querrin would be thrown into a minor panic when he heard the news, and felt in no state to cope with him.

Oddly enough, his own spirits had lightened somewhat. That blow on the head had been painful but at least it proved his adversary was no ghost. The prowler had been both human and scared.

He should also prove easy to deal with....

That was before the nightmare closed round them all.


Algy Lawrence glanced at his wrist watch: thin black hands in a gold face right-angled at nine o'clock..

The young man sighed, swept long fingers over his smooth blond hair, and sat up gloomily.

A couple of aspirins and a brief sleep had done much to relieve the persistent throbbing in his temples, and his physical weakness had entirely disappeared; but mentally he was far from his best.

Not that it mattered. His arrangements were complete, and should work with precision. Besides, he had a least one reliable ally.

John Hardinge. Lawrence swung his feet to the floor. The Sergeant had probably arrived by now. He had better go downstairs and have a chat with him: there was still that wretched business in the garden to report.

That bump on the head had deprived Algy of his dinner, though sandwiches had once more been brought to his bedroom, this time by a pertly attractive young housemaid wearing her black dress stretched tight across shapely hips.

He had thanked her politely, and she had rewarded him with a bouncing exit which displayed her pretty legs to the best advantage.

Another twinge of pain stabbed through his temples: he groaned and stopped thinking about frivolous matters…He was conscious once more of a vague unrest.

Downstairs in the drawing-room, Sergeant Hardinge was also ill at ease. Audrey Craig had for the moment taken refuge with her uncle in the library, and left alone with the Querrins, the Sergeant was finding it hard to make conversation. Roger's air of faintly patronizing condescension did not help him at all.

They were practically strangers and in view of the peculiar circumstances of this, their first informal meeting, it was not surprising they were both reacting to the strain of the situation.

Roger, of course, considered Hardinge's presence, like the guard itself, completely unnecessary. He hardly bothered to hide his opinion.

Querrin, a forceful man, would have been surprised to learn that in the Sergeant's mind he figured only as a cipher. As human personalities, Hardinge was much more aware of Algy Lawrence and Peter Querrin: the one with an unmistakable intelligence behind a lazy facade, and the other with his air of patent unrest.

Peter was prowling uneasily round the room, contributing nothing to the small talk. Hardinge glanced at him and wondered. The young man seemed nervous in the extreme: would he lose his nerve?

(Lawrence in another part of the house was thinking much the same thing. And he reflected, if Peter goes to pieces, I shall have to cope with his hysteria. Oh, hell!)

Hardinge decided Peter's exact reactions would be unpredictable, and

57

hoped for the best while preparing fatalistically for the worst. It would mostly depend upon Lawrence, anyway... He began to think about that young man's scuffle in the shrubbery.

The Sergeant had so far heard only the vaguest details of the affair, and was entirely unable to account for it. It fitted nowhere in the pattern... Who was the man, and (this was more important) would he return?

Hardinge's jaw set grimly. He was a capable man and a determined one. No prowler could hope to get near the house while he stood guard outside.

He was rather relieved when Lawrence strolled into the drawing-room. He had taken a liking to this tall young amateur and had a healthy respect for his capabilities, which he knew well by reputation.

"Hallo, Sergeant."

They shook hands.

Hardinge glanced at the strip of plaster on Algy's forehead.

He said with a faint grin:

"I hear you've been having adventures."

Algy laughed. "None that I've enjoyed."

"Suppose you give me the details."

Lawrence did his best, but his description of the prowler was sketchy and confused.

Hardinge said, with a frown:

"It's all too vague. Of course, it might be—." He broke off "You'd know this man again?"

"I think so. Yes. If I see him again, I'll recognize him."

"Good." The Sergeant pondered.

Algy prompted him gently. "You said—it might be—.?"

Hardinge smiled and shook his head. "That description could fit a hundred men. I have only the vaguest of suspicions." He smiled again grimly. "I can promise! you this, sir. If it's the man I think, there's no more danger from him to-night."

Lawrence nodded. He shared the policeman's dislike of a hasty and possibly ill-founded accusation.

He said:

"All right. I think I can rely on you."

"You can, sir," agreed the Sergeant. He lowered his voice. "Can you rely upon Mr. Peter?"

Algy glanced across the room. The two brothers were; talking quietly. There was still a definite trace of impatience on the elder man's face: Lawrence wondered if Peter had again attempted to change Roger's mind.

Algy said softly:

"I think so. He won't crack."

"I hope not," responded Hardinge, grimly and sincerely. He added: "You've had enough, already."

Another long roll of thunder all but blotted out his words. Lawrence remarked:

"You'll get your feet wet."

The Sergeant replied indifferently:

"I've brought my rubbers."

The exchange was largely automatic. Neither man's thoughts were concerned with trivialities.

The door opened, and Audrey came in. The men rose: Algy prepared to be studiously formal.

The girl's pretty face was slightly worried. She said:

"I can't find Uncle Russ."

Roger smothered an exclamation. He said rather testily:

"I thought he was with you, in the library."

"No. He left me some time ago."

At that moment, a snatch of what was probably a highly improper song drifted to them through the panels. Then the door opened once more to disclose Russell Craig Wavering uncertainly on the threshold.

His gaze fell on Audrey. He inclined his head graciously.

"Hallo, m'dear." And he hiccoughed.

Lawrence realized, with an inward grin, that the old rogue was stewed to the gills.

Audrey said with horror:

"Uncle Russ! You've been drinking."

Craig blinked at her owlishly.

"My dear," he conceded, "you're right. I have," he admitted handsomely, "been drinking."

He turned to Roger and elaborated further. "I have been drinking," he said, "with your butler."

Querrin's face set hard. He said:

"With my butler?"

"With," agreed Craig, "your butler." He steadied himself, then added belligerently: "Whass wrong with that? A fine man, your butler... He buttles—hic!— most efficiently."

He dropped in an armchair and beamed round stupidly.

"Oh, Uncle," said Audrey despairingly.

Roger seemed angry. He said:

"You're too familiar with the servants. I've told you before."

Craig's only reply was a giggle.

Roger's face darkened. He strode forward and dropped his hands on the older man's shoulders.

His voice was sombre.

"You'd better go up to your room."

"Shan't," said Craig peevishly. Once more on his feet, he pulled free of Querrin's grasp and lurched over to Lawrence.

"My boy," he said courteously, "you look pale. Possibly the blow on your head has dis—dis—upset you. Have no fear. I shall myself"— Uncle Russ thumped his shirt front—"mount guard to-night."

Behind him, someone gasped.

Till then, Algy had felt only amusement. Now he began to worry about the effects of Craig's antics on Peter's already overstrung nerves.

The colour had wavered on the younger Querrin's cheeks. His voice seemed choked.

"You'll—what?"

Peter at that moment was incapable of logical thought. He was obsessed with the vision of Audrey's uncle crashing drunkenly through the careful construction of Roger's defence, which they had been at such pains to contrive.

Algy Lawrence, however, had no more intention than Peter of allowing Russell Craig to intrude that night.

He said soothingly:

"There's no need for that. I'd rather you went to bed."

Uncle Russ frowned.

"Is it possible," he inquired, with dignity, "that you are rejecting my offer of—of ..."

He tailed off muzzily.

"Yes," replied Lawrence simply.

"Then," said Russell Craig, "I shall withdraw. I shall withdraw," he continued, "immediately."

He hiccoughed gravely, and went out.

Audrey gestured helplessly with the same curious mixture of embarrassment and affection that Algy had noticed before.

"I'd better go after him," she said. An unwilling hint of laughter had struggled up behind her eyes.

Roger watched her exit with a frown, muttered something, then followed her out. Peter said softly:

"That damned old fool."

"Easy, there," said Algy. He clapped a hand on Peter's shoulder.

Querrin gave him a shamefaced smile.

"Sorry, Lawrence. I panicked unnecessarily. It's just," and his voice shook slightly, "I'm so concerned about Roger, and—and—."

60

"I understand."

Hardinge moved up to Peter suddenly. He said, quietly:

"Look, sir. You don't have to go through with this. You can go up to bed now, and leave it all to us."

The two men stared at each other.

Then Peter smiled. He said softly:

"Thank you, Sergeant. But it's all right now. I can do everything I have to."

"Of course you can," said Lawrence cheerfully.

His eyes and the Sergeant's met.

Peter had turned away; and Algy nodded quickly.

Hardinge was satisfied. He said:

"That's settled, then."

Roger Querrin hurried back to join them. He announced to nobody in particular:

"Craig's in his room at last. I've had more than enough... Oh, well." He broke off, then glanced at his watch. "Half-past nine," he murmured. "And my appointment is at twelve."

He gazed into three unsmiling faces. "We've plenty of time—to kill."

At eleven o'clock the four men stood up and made their way out of the drawing-room and along to the main hall of the house.

They did not talk among themselves.

Lawrence glanced up the broad staircase that led to the bedrooms and thought that the girl and her uncle would be asleep by now. Craig had been taken to his room an hour and a half before, and though Audrey had wished to remain with them, they had persuaded her gently she would be better off the scene.

The servants had also retired, on Roger Querrin's strict instructions. Testy already at the thought of his private affairs being common knowledge in the village, he intended no further details to reach the gossips.

In the hall, Hardinge picked up his cape and slung it round his shoulders. Outside in the gardens, the rain lashed down unceasingly.

Querrin lighted candles in a triple branched stand.

He asked quietly:

"Are we ready?"

They nodded soberly.

Roger turned to the doors that gave access to the passage. Peter stepped forward and held aside the curtains from the flame of the candlestick in his brother's hand.

The light flickered and danced in the gloom of the corridor.

61

Lawrence shifted uneasily. He was oppressed, once more, by the brooding silence.

Hardinge was the last to leave the brightly lit hall, and the curtains fell to behind him. The suddenly changing focus robbed his eyes momentarily of sight.

He murmured:

"Just a moment, sir. I've a better light than that."

He fumbled at his belt. A beam from his lamp cut through the darkness.

Roger nodded approvingly and made a motion to blow out the candles, before Lawrence dropped a restraining hand on his wrist.

He said quietly:

"I'll need those myself. I have no torch."

Querrin nodded again.

They set off down the corridor, passed its solitary window (shrouded now by musty curtains) and came to a stop outside the door of the old room.

A curious constraint had gripped them all. Lawrence fancied Querrin's hand was trembling as he twisted round the handle.

Inside the room, a dying fire glowed ruddily. Roger put down the candlestick carefully on the mantel above.

The tiny flames licked cautious light round the shape of the hanging dagger.

Querrin stepped across to the table, struck a match, and began to fumble with the old-fashioned oil lamp. As it flared into lambent life, the shadows retreated and lay in stealthy wait.

Roger said more cheerfully:

"That's better."

Then they were silent again. Hardinge put out his flashlight and stood by the door, relaxed yet attentive. Peter squeezed his hands, uneasily, into his pockets; and glanced towards Lawrence expectantly.

This is it, thought Algy. Here's where I take charge. And wondered at the hard knot of fear tied tight inside his stomach.

Roger said restively:

"I don't want to hurry you, but——."

"All right, Querrin." Lawrence scanned the room carefully. "This won't take along."

There was no place an intruder could hide. Assured of this, he beckoned the Sergeant forward.

Then, pulling back the drapes from the french windows, he glanced out at the darkness and murmured:

"You won't find it very pleasant."

"No matter, sir."

"That prowler might come back."

Hardinge said grimly:

"I can deal with him." He patted his truncheon meaningly.

Lawrence smiled. "Right, then. I leave it to you."

He tugged at the bolts securing the windows. They were stiff as well as sturdy. He had to exert his strength.

As the glass panelled doors pushed open, a thin spray of rain splashed over him. The moon was almost entirely obscured by thick clouds, and the night was forbidding enough. The Sergeant looked out without enthusiasm.

Lawrence murmured apologetically:

"Ready, Sergeant?"

Hardinge gave him a nod. Then he adjusted his cape; switched on his flashlight, and set off down the two steps that led from the room to the gardens.

Algy watched him as the uniformed man made his way across the unplanted flowerbeds towards the comparative shelter of the trees beyond the flagged path.

Hardinge turned and signalled.

Lawrence waved a hand in reply. Noticing absently that the heavy rain was already washing out the track of the Sergeant's footprints, he stepped back, closed the windows, and fastened them securely.

Roger said irritably:

"This is all very silly. He'll be soaked to the skin, by midnight."

Lawrence shrugged. "He'll make sure no intruder gets anywhere near the house."

His fingers strayed unconsciously up to the bruise on his forehead.

"Oh, very well." Roger poured himself a drink. He added dryly: "I don't anticipate a siege."

Lawrence drew the curtains across the windows.

He said quietly:

"You're safe here. You've only to cry out."

Peter put in, eagerly:

"We should hear you."

Roger looked at his brother with both exasperation and affection. However, he made no direct reply.

Lawrence let his gaze go round the room once more. Feeling slightly ridiculous, he stooped and peered under the table.

Ignoring Roger's scoffing laugh, he said amiably:

"You're entirely alone." Then, to Peter:

"We'll go now."

Peter's mouth trembled. He turned to his brother, as if to make a last appeal, then let his hand drop to his side helplessly.

Roger smiled at him.

He said jovially:

"Don't be an ass. Here, I'll give you a toast."

Snatching up his glass, he lifted it in salute.

"To the shade of old Tom Querrin! The devil take and keep him."

Peter drew in his breath sharply.

Lawrence spoke soberly. "Good luck to you."

He thought there was more than a tinge of fear beneath the other man's bravado.

Roger drained the glass and laughed again, though breathlessly.

Algy Lawrence asked:

"You still have the key?"

"Naturally." Roger pulled the chain from his pocket and showed them the bright new metal. Lawrence nodded.

"Good." He signed to Peter, who went quietly through the doorway.

Lawrence went across to the mantel and picked up the candlestick. His eyes rested for a moment on the dagger hanging above. Then he followed Peter out.

Roger closed the door behind them, and they heard the faint rattle of the key as it twisted in the lock.

Repressing his own uneasiness, the blond-haired young man smiled at his companion reassuringly.

"Come on, Peter," he said cheerily, and they set off down the passage.

They paused by the curtained window.

Handing the triple branched stand to Querrin, Lawrence held aside the drapes and inspected the catch. It was in position and the window was securely locked.

Algy let the curtains drop back, and the two men continued along the deserted corridor.

They regained the brightly-lit hall with something like relief.

Lawrence murmured:

"We may as well make ourselves comfortable."

Easy chairs had been provided for them, and Algy pushed one over near the entrance to the passage. Peter, however, seemed more concerned with his duty as a guard. He set open one of the double doors, and pulled aside the heavy curtain. Then shoving another chair by the dark oblong of the entrance, he seated himself at once.

Lawrence said with a chuckle:

"You won't see much from there. It's as black as a hat in the

64

corridor." Peter said tremulously:

"I can hear, at least—if anything goes wrong."

Lawrence said with a smile:

"Nothing will, I promise you."

And they settled down to wait.


At twenty minutes to twelve, the rain stopped, much to Sergeant Hardinge's satisfaction. As he said to Lawrence later: "It was no joke, waiting around in that downpour. Besides, when the clouds drifted away from the moon I had a much better view of the house."

Inside the building, Algy Lawrence glanced at his wrist-watch, shifted his cramped legs, and stifled a yawn.

Behind him lay the short passage that led from the main hall to the side door which, like every other entrance to the house, was securely locked from the inside. To his right was the broad staircase, to his left the entrance to the corridor, so near he could reach out his fingers and touch the half-drawn curtains.

And facing him was Peter Querrin, slumped in his chair, white-faced and uneasy.

Lawrence eyed him thoughtfully. He hoped that zero hour would bring no sudden attack of hysteria... It was a relief when Peter began to talk, nervously.

Recognizing the anxious chatter was a useful safety-valve, he listened sympathetically and interposed an odd word here and there.

As the hands of his watch crept round towards midnight, Peter's talk swelled up loudly, then suddenly stopped.

He said wretchedly:

"It's no good, Lawrence. I—I can't stand this any more."

Algy murmured a warning and peeped quickly at his wrist-watch. It was four minutes to twelve.

He said quietly:

"It will all be over soon."

Peter said, with a desperate calm:

"It's nearly midnight. We can't stay here... *I must be near to Roger.*"

Algy thought quickly. It would do no harm, at least... With sudden decision, he said:

"All right, then. Light the candles."

Querrin grabbed up the triple branched stand and touched flame to the wicks. Then he flicked away the spent and blackened matchstick, and looked expectantly towards Lawrence.

"Lead the way," said Algy.

He followed Peter into the gloom of the passage and blinked for a second. Then his eyes, like Querrin's, became more accustomed to the blackness, and they moved on cautiously.

The tiny flames licked aside the darkness, but did nothing to dispel the old deadly sense of oppression. Lawrence stared at the blank, panelled walls and shivered.

He glanced around, and upwards. The corridor was deserted.

"Come on," he murmured.

As they came abreast of the shrouded window, his footsteps slackened and stopped.

"We may as well check," he said quietly.

Peter, who was the nearer to the frame, nodded quickly, and placing the candlestick in Algy's grasp, turned his back and put his hands on the curtains. Stepping aside, he held the drapes back for Lawrence's inspection, and the fair haired young man could see that the catch was still in position and the window securely locked.

Algy noticed that the moon was once more riding free in the skies, then was diverted by the nearer vision of his own reflection staring grotesquely from the panes. He turned away hurriedly.

Peter let the curtains fall back into position, then followed Lawrence along the corridor.

Algy turned his head as his companion caught up with him. "What's the matter?" he asked.

"It's twelve o'clock," said Querrin; and his mouth trembled.

Lawrence looked at him thoughtfully. Perhaps it had been a tactless question, but he had wished to break the silence.

They were very near to the room now, and there was no more sound. A few seconds yet—.

Then they heard the scream.

It was high, and formless, and muffled.

There was something very wrong about that evil strangled sound. It came from the darkness like a ghost.

Its echoes rang in their ears.

Then Peter cried, in a high cracked voice:

"Roger...."

He hurled himself forward in a run, smacked wildly against the heavy panels of the door, and reeled back clasping his shoulder.

Lawrence brushed past and twisted hard on the door handle. The lock held firm.

Peter turned a whitely imploring face towards his companion.

"For God's sake, man," he whispered. "Do something... Quickly."

Lawrence jerked the candlestick towards him. As Peter's shaking fingers fumbled for a hold round the stand, the flames danced and flickered wildly.

"Don't let it go out," said Algy, between his teeth. He] pulled out his automatic and hammered with the gun butt on the wooden panels.

"Querrin!"

There was no reply.

"Querrin!" Lawrence cried again. "If you can hear me, man—stand away from the door!"

He thumbed over the safety catch, then levelled his' pistol at the door.

He fired once, twice, three times. As the sound rolled thunderously round the echoing passage, the bullets blasted through the lock and the cartridge cases spattered dully against the carpet.

Then Lawrence crashed his weight against the door and it flew open as he staggered into the room.

There was no light, save that from the dying fire.

Yet as Peter stepped up to the doorway and held the candles high, they saw the horror clearly.

Something was dragging itself, painfully, across the floor. Then it lurched upright, resting on its knees.

Peter gave a strangled cry of recognition.

"Roger...."

Roger Querrin's eyes blinked glassily, reflecting the tiny flame.

Then he choked, rolled over on his face, and lay still.

The haft of the dagger protruded like an evil growth from between his shoulders.


There was nobody else in the room. Lawrence saw that at once.

He said, with deadly quietness:

"Peter. Stay where you are." He added, half to himself: "We need more light."

He crossed to the table, still grasping his automatic, and keeping his eyes on the motionless form near his feet.

He scratched a match—the tiny sound seemed unnaturally loud in the silent room—and turned up the wick of the oil lamp.

As it flared once more into life, every detail of the strange scene stood out with pitiless clarity.

Lawrence glanced quickly under the table and behind the door.

Then he dropped on one knee beside the fallen man, touched his cheek gently, and felt without hope for the beating of his heart.

He stood up.

He said dully:

"I'm sorry, Peter. Your brother is dead."

Querrin's lips parted, and he cried out shrilly.

Lawrence stepped up to him and smacked heavily at his face.

Peter's head jerked wildly. Then his eyes cleared, and he nodded sanely. The marks of Algy's fingers stood out redly on his cheek.

"I'm all right now."

Lawrence nodded. His gaze travelled quickly round the room. Nothing had been disturbed, everything was in its place. "Except," he murmured softly, "the knife. Of course." The sheath over the mantel was empty.

He stepped across to the windows, and pulled aside the musty drapes.

The bolts were still shot, and the windows locked.

He stared at them hopelessly. The thin blade of fear stabbed through his heart and mind.

He mumbled:

"It's incredible...."

Struck by a sudden thought, he turned back to Roger's lifeless body. Kneeling beside him, he pulled gently at the chain that came out from under the dead man's coat and into his trouser pocket.

The door was locked, he thought. But if the key is missing—.

Bright new metal still glinted at the end of the chain.

Lawrence stared at the key with something like despair. He stood up once more and turned to Peter.

Querrin had not moved from the doorway. When he spoke, his voice shook badly.

"Shouldn't we—call a doctor?"

Lawrence said, as kindly as he could:

"Roger's beyond all help. But—yes someone should see him. You can telephone, if you wish."

Then he realized, with a shock, that the whole affair was now the business of the police.

Taking the oil lamp from the table, he strode across to the french windows and pulled back the drapes as far as they would go. Then, holding the light close to his face, he signalled urgently with his free hand.

From under the trees came the answering flare of; Hardinge's hand lamp. Then the Sergeant himself stepped out from the shadows and into the moonlight.

Lawrence pantomimed an instruction, then glanced towards Peter Querrin.

"Hardinge's going round to the side door."

Peter said tonelessly:

"It's locked and bolted. I'll go and let him in."

He hurried down the passage.

Lawrence was left alone.


John Hardinge stood under the trees, his keen gaze fixed upon the house. His breath soughed gustily, and his body was tense. The sound of the shots seemed to echo in his ears....

What was happening now, in that locked and guarded room?

He plunged one hand nervously into the pocket of his tunic. The other rested on the lamp at his belt.

He kept his eyes on the house, staring across the unmarked stretch of bare brown earth.

Suddenly the curtains, which had already been partially drawn, were swept fully aside and the figure of Algy Lawrence appeared behind the glass panes of the french windows.

He waved urgently and blindly. The Sergeant signalled an answer with his flashlight, then stepped out from the cover of the trees and on to the flagged path.

Lawrence pantomimed. His meaning was clear enough: the Sergeant was to follow the path to the side door.

Hardinge lifted his hand in salute, then strode briskly along, brushing heedlessly against the wet glistening leaves of the bushes that encroached across the way.

When he reached the side door, he found it standing open. This surprised him for a moment, then he heard Peter's voice from the hall and understood.

Querrin was hunched over the telephone, his voice strained and shaking. "D-doctor? Doctor Tyssen? Please come quickly...."

Doctor Tyssen also acted as police surgeon, so the call was grimly appropriate.

Somebody stumbled on the stairs.

Hardinge jerked his head upwards.

Audrey Craig, a dressing-gown over her pyjamas, gazed down with frightened eyes. She whispered:

"W-what's happened?"

John Hardinge was a man who prided himself on a calm efficiency and lack of emotion. Yet as he saw the distress on the girl's pretty face, he warmed to her with instinctive sympathy.

He said:

"I don't know, miss, exactly." He hesitated. "But I'm afraid—it's something nasty."

He looked towards Peter Querrin.

Audrey's lips trembled. Then her gaze followed his. They stood listening together.

Peter, unaware or heedless of his audience, went on spilling his urgency into the 'phone.

"My brother is dead...."

The four words seemed to swell and grow and distort like shadows across the brightness of the hall.

The girl's eyes darkened and the colour sponged suddenly out of her cheeks.

Hardinge thought, with alarm, she was going to faint.

Then she clutched hard on the balustrade, steadied herself, and ran lightly down the stairs.

She swept past him with desperate haste and vanished into the darkness of the passage.

"My God!" cried the Sergeant, genuinely shocked. "She mustn't see—."

He hurried after her into the corridor.

The darkness blinded him for a moment before he switched on his lamp and picked out the girl with its powerful beam.

"Miss Craig! Stop, please!"

He stumbled and the light jumped wildly.

Before Audrey could reach the room Lawrence appeared in the doorway and caught her in his arms.

She gasped and struggled. "Let me go... Roger! Roger!"

Her voice spiralled up dangerously. Lawrence was torn with an angry pity. He could feel her body shudder with panic.

He cried, brutally:

"*Audrey*... Be quiet!"

The harshness he had forced into the words quietened her like a slap in the face.

She whispered:

"Let me see him."

Algy shook his head. He said quietly:

"I'd rather—you didn't."

She searched his grave face fearfully. Then as he released her arms she stepped to one side and her gaze went past him through the open door.

He tried, too late, to blot out the sight with his body.

Then her eyes became strangely unfocussed and she swayed forward dizzily. Lawrence caught her once more and found she was crying, softly.

He patted her shoulders helplessly.

Somebody coughed. Hardinge was standing in front of him, formless behind the hard glare of the policeman's lamp.

Lawrence blinked. He said:

"Put that out, please."

The Sergeant obeyed. Lawrence and the girl became black silhouettes against the soft glow of light from the room at their backs.

Algy said gently:

"Audrey, my dear. There's nothing you can do. Please go up to your room."

She replied with a sob.

The Sergeant stirred restively. The girl deserved pity, but he couldn't forget he was a policeman. He had his duties, and must risk no accusation of slackness from his superior officers.

Lawrence was still soothing the crying girl when another form loomed up out of the blackness. It was Peter.

Algy turned to him with relief.

"Peter. Take Audrey away, there's a good chap."

Something that might have been assent rasped in Querrin's throat.

He said, tonelessly:

"The doctor's coming soon. I—I—."

He broke off, then led the girl down the corridor. Lawrence thought, with relief, that Peter at least had regained his self-control.

Hardinge said with a frown:

"That girl needs someone to help her. A relative, perhaps... Where's her uncle?"

"Still wrapped in his drunken slumbers," replied Lawrence with an uneasy flippancy, "I expect." He shrugged away Russell Craig's existence indifferently. He turned: back to the room.

Hardinge followed him through the doorway.

He looked at the body with blank, professional, policeman's eyes.

He said, with unintentional callousness:

"He's dead, of course?"

"I'm afraid so."

The Sergeant said:

"I heard a scream, and then shots—."

Lawrence pointed towards the door.

"The room was sealed. I had to force an entrance."

Hardinge peered at the shattered lock. The bullets had torn through the door obliquely and embedded themselves in the wall.

The Sergeant's eyes went from the lock to the key chain spilled on the carpet, then up to Lawrence, standing by; the drawn curtains of the french windows.

Hardinge said severely:

"You shouldn't have touched anything, sir. This is a police matter now."

Lawrence was conscious once more of his status as an amateur. He apologized.

"But," he added in defence, "I've hardly tampered with the evidence."

The Sergeant smiled. "No matter, sir. Anyway," he admitted, "you had to draw the curtains to signal me."

He crossed to the windows and inspected the bolts.

"No tampering here," he murmured. "That's evident... What happened, sir? How did the killer get past you?"

Algy laughed without humour.

He said dryly:

"He didn't."

The Sergeant stared.

"You mean—you have him?"

"I mean," said Lawrence quietly, "he seems not to have existed."

Hardinge said patiently:

"You know that's nonsense, don't you?"

"Oh, yes." The young man laughed again. "I know it. Yet there are only two exits to this room, and no man passed through either."

The Sergeant said:

"Nobody came through these windows, anyway. I had 'em under constant observation. Besides, there's not a mark on the ground outside."

"I believe you, Sergeant." Algy Lawrence grinned bitterly. "Will you believe me, when I tell you Peter and I stood unbroken guard inside, and no one came past us into the house?"

There was a silence, then Hardinge said flatly:

"That's impossible."

Lawrence said again:

"Oh, yes... It's impossible. But it happened."

The Sergeant said abruptly:

"I'll have to inform my Inspector."

"I'd say," returned Lawrence, "it was a matter for the Chief Constable."

"Perhaps. But it's not for me to say."

"Before you go," cried Algy suddenly. "May I borrow your lamp?"

"If you like." Hardinge detached the flashlight from his belt, then watched curiously as the young man took it from his hand and walked over to the fire, which had burned itself through to redly glowing embers.

Lawrence squatted on his heels. He said, over his shoulder: "A last chance," and directed the rays of the lamp upward, into the chimney.

Then he stood up, and said grimly:

"A cat couldn't climb up there."

Hardinge stared round the room. "There must be another way out." He added, protestingly: "There has to be."

"A secret panel, perhaps?" Lawrence shook his head. "No, Sergeant. It isn't going to be so easy."

"Then——." Hardinge racked his brains for a feasible suggestion. "A booby trap——."

"No." Lawrence was positive. "I've already looked. Though with your permission, I'll continue the search."

The Sergeant nodded. He left to 'phone.

Alone once more, Lawrence prowled restlessly round the room.

He touched nothing more. The fingerprint men would be here soon....

He was obsessed with a sense of angry inadequacy. Try as he might, he could detect no flaw in his defences. Unless——.

The fear closed round him.

Unless the crime was not a man's.

He straightened, then grabbed up his gun from the table, where he had dropped it while lighting the oil lamp. The hard butt gave no comfort to his hand.

He whispered aloud:

"I don't believe in you, Tom Querrin...."

The silence was its own reply.

Doctor Tyssen straightened up.

He said gruffly:

"That's that." He glanced towards Sergeant Hardinge. "D'ye want the technicalities?"

"Not now, Doctor. Thank you."

"No." The plump little man growled good-humouredly. "Doubt if ye'd understand 'em, anyway... Well, he's dead. Till I've done the post-mortem, there's not much else I can tell you... He's been dead for half an hour."

Lawrence said politely:

"We knew that, too. I was with him when he died."

"Were ye now?" Tyssen eyed him thoughtfully. "You didn't kill him, by any chance?"

Lawrence said: "No," soberly. He realized that, as an explanation, it would be hardly less fantastic than the truth. "Whatever," he told himself, "that might be." He closed his mind resolutely to the supernatural.

"Ah, well." Tyssen looked down, without compassion, at the thing that had once been a man. "There's a story about this room, isn't there? But," he finished disgustedly, "I don't believe in miracles. Even dark ones... Where can I wash my hands?"

Lawrence went to the doorway and called down the passage:

"Peter!"

Querrin came into the room.

Lawrence said apologetically:

"Would you show the doctor a bathroom?"

They went out. Peter, carefully, did not look at his brother.

Hardinge and Lawrence glanced at each other in silence. There seemed nothing to say.

The Sergeant cleared his throat.

He said:

"Inspector Hazlitt will be here soon. I'd like you to admit him, sir, if you would." He added an obvious comment. "I'd better stay here."

Lawrence nodded without resentment. The case was the Sergeant's till his superiors arrived.

"All right. I'll wait in the hall."

Hardly had he stepped out of the passage, however, before he heard the sound of tyres scrunching over the drive.

He went to the door, fumbled with its chain, then threw it open.

Three men climbed out of the police car, and made their way up the steps towards him. The leader was a uniformed Inspector, lean and caustic eyed.

Lawrence introduced himself. If the Inspector knew the fair-haired young man by reputation, he betrayed nothing in his manner.

"Hazlitt, County Police," he muttered sourly, by way of acknowledgment. He jerked a thumb towards his companions. "Sudlow, easy with that camera! Draycott, you'll look after the fingerprints." He turned back to Algy.

"Now, Mr. er—um—."

"Lawrence."

"Mr. Lawrence. Lead on, please."

Doctor Tyssen appeared on the landing above. He called down the stairs:

"Hi, Hazlitt! Get that body to the mortuary when you can, will you? I'm off now."

"Just a minute, Doctor. I shall want to ask you some questions."

"The devil you will." Tyssen towelled his hands vigorously. "Leave your blasted questions till morning... And don't tell me it's after midnight. I'm in no mood to split hairs."

He headed back to the bathroom.

The Inspector har-rumphed irritably and followed Lawrence into the passage.

Hardinge stiffened and saluted as his superior came into the room.

Hazlitt nodded a reply, then looked at the Sergeant without favour.

He said dryly:

"Why are you wearing your cape?"

Hardinge looked surprised.

"It was raining, sir. And I was on guard outside."

"Were you? Well, you're dry enough now, man. Go and take it off."

Hardinge went out, his face impassive.

Lawrence felt a thin flush of anger. He decided that he did not like the Inspector, and waited with perverse satisfaction... It wouldn't be long before Hazlitt found himself faced with the worst problem of his officious career.

The Inspector gave his men their orders, then drew Algy to one side while Sudlow and Draycott busied themselves round the body with chalk and camera. Plain clothes men, they worked with a smooth efficiency.

Hazlitt said importantly:

"Now, Mr. Lawrence. What can you tell me about this?"

Algy sketched a quick but thorough outline of the events leading up to the crime. He noticed with a faintly malicious glow of humour at the back of his lazy blue eyes, that the Inspector grew increasingly incredulous as the minutes slid by.

"So you see," finished Algy, "the way things are."

Hazlitt said, directly:

"Mr. Lawrence. Are you a fool?"

"No," replied the young man coolly. "Are you?"

The Inspector ignore d his question. He commented dryly:

"Then you must be a liar."

Lawrence grinned at him lazily. He said:

"Go ahead and arrest me. Though I ought to warn you. Everything I've told you will be confirmed by Peter Querrin. We were together every second since we left his brother in this room."

Hazlitt stared at him bleakly. Then he turned to his men.

"Sudlow, examine every inch of these walls for a secret, entrance. And don't forget the floor and the ceiling... We'll settle this damned nonsense once and for all."

Hardinge had returned and was standing quietly by the door. The Inspector said: "I'll question *you* in a minute."

A flash bulb glared as Sudlow manoeuvred his camera for a final shot of the victim. Hazlitt growled:

"Didn't I tell you... Oh, well. Finish your pictures first. And photograph the bolts on those french windows.'^ He looked at the shattered door. "And that." He asked Lawrence:

"Did you have to make such a mess of the lock?"

"I hadn't a picklock with me."

The Inspector's eyes were not friendly. He turned his head. "Draycott, go over this whole room for fingerprints. And examine that key chain, too. It looks as if it spilled out in a struggle."

Lawrence shook his head. "No, Inspector." He explained briefly.

Hazlitt was annoyed, but made no direct reply. Instead, he jerked towards Hardinge and said coldly:

"Nobody should meddle with evidence. You ought to have stopped him, Sergeant."

Algy broke in:

"The Sergeant was still outside in the gardens."

The Inspector ignored him.

He went on:

"You don't appear to advantage, Hardinge. You had no business here at all. And then"—he raised his voice slightly—"a man is killed and you let his murderer escape without lifting a hand to stop him."

Hardinge's eyes grew frosty, but he showed no other sign of resentment.

Lawrence admired his self control. He sprang to his ally's defence.

He said mildly:

"What does it matter? Since the evidence proves this killer can walk straight through solid walls of brick and plaster, where would you find a cell to hold him?"

Hazlitt reddened.

"Your story's fantastic—."

"Though it happens to be true. You know," continued Lawrence, who was beginning to enjoy himself, "I'm looking forward to the inquest. I can hear the jury now. They'll bring in a verdict of murder by a person or ghosts unknown."

With an angry exclamation, the Inspector turned aside.

He snapped over his shoulder:

"Spirits don't leave fingerprints. But I'll wager we'll find plenty here. Draycott!"

Draycott, who had already set to work with an insufflator, squatted back on his heels and listened patiently.

"Go over every surface in this room. Somehow or other, we're going to account for every print... There should be valuable traces—if Mr. Lawrence hasn't destroyed them all," added Hazlitt, with a faint sneer.

"I left you a few to play with," said the young man, equably.

The Inspector flew off at a tangent.

"Who reported this crime to the police?"

Hardinge replied. "Peter Querrin, sir." He added: "I thought I had better stay beside the body."

"Did you?" said Hazlitt. He managed to make the remark offensive. "I think I'd better interview that young man. We'll hear what he has to say."

"Handle him gently, Inspector," said Algy, cheerily. "He's my alibi." Hazlitt went on heedlessly:

'Sergeant, I shall want to interview everybody in the house. Round 'em all up together—yes, put 'em in the drawing-room, that will do—and I'll question them later." He looked towards Algy and smiled. "Oh, yes," He added softly, "and see that Mr. Lawrence has no chance to compare notes—with Mr. Peter Querrin."

Algy smiled, though wryly. It was a novelty to find himself considered as a suspect.

Hazlitt made as if to dismiss the Sergeant, then recalled him for questioning.

Lawrence listened incuriously to the Inspector's barking voice and Hardinge's low-toned replies. As he expected, the Sergeant's report was entirely negative: he had neither seen nor heard anything suspicious until the scream and the shots had sounded from the guarded;; room. Nobody had approached the house or left it.

Later, as the two men paced down the corridor, Algy murmured:

"You may have trouble with your Inspector. He acted as if he didn't believe your story either."

Hardinge chuckled grimly.

He replied:

"You can hardly blame him. This whole affair's incredible. Fortunately"—and he gave once more the ghost of a laugh—"my evidence is already confirmed. Or it will be, when the Inspector looks outside."

"How's that?"

The Sergeant responded with another question.

"Did you notice when the rain stopped to-night?"

"Some time before twelve."

"At twenty minutes to," said Hardinge. "Much to my relief. It was no joke, waiting around in that downpour. Besides, when the clouds drifted away from the moon I had a much better view of the house... However, that's not the point."

He began to speak more slowly, emphasizing the words. "The ground outside is like freshly dampened sand. You can't put a foot anywhere without leaving clear traces."

"Of course," said Lawrence. "And the only approach to the room is over bare, uncultivated soil."

"And," finished his ally triumphantly, "there isn't a mark of any kind in the earth outside the windows."

"Well, that's proof enough," agreed Algy thoughtfully. "Our murderer didn't leave that way. Though," he added with a wicked grin, "since we've already granted him the power of passing through brick walls, we might just as well believe him to be both invisible and lighter than air."

The Sergeant did not laugh.

He said gravely:

"There's trickery somewhere." He paused. "There has to be."

"Yes," said Lawrence. "But I'll lay you odds the Inspector, for one, can't find it."

They had paused in the lighted hall. Hardinge eyed his young friend shrewdly. He said:

"You'll stay on the case, of course."

It was not a question.

Lawrence responded with a nod. "Yes. Though I won't be welcome." He hesitated, then said slowly: "You know, Sergeant, I don't think I shall solve this case myself."

A query flickered in Hardinge's keen blue eyes.

He murmured:

"That's defeatist talk."

"No, not exactly," returned Algy. His face was relaxed and lazy. He said softly:

"I have a feeling the credit for clearing up this mystery is going to belong to one man only."

He grinned.

"To a certain Sergeant Hardinge."

John Hardinge was not a stupid man. He took Lawrence's meaning at once.

He murmured:

"Thank you, sir. But"—he hesitated—"I'm a member of the police. I couldn't step on the Inspector's corns."

"The Inspector's corns be damned!" exclaimed Algy, rudely. "I've no official standing. I have to pass on my theories to somebody. And I certainly don't intend to co-operate with Hazlitt. . . . Don't you see, man," he continued, coaxingly, "what a feather in your cap it would be—."

"If I explained the killing," finished Hardinge. "Of course." His eyes glimmered. "It would lead to promotion."

"It might," said Lawrence, "mean a transfer. To the Yard, perhaps."

"Pipe dreams," said the Sergeant wryly. "Oh, well. We'll see."

His face was impassive. Yet there was a keen pleasure behind the placidity in his eyes.

Audrey Craig's eyes were tired with too much weeping.

She said dully:

"There's nothing I can tell you, Inspector. Nothing at all."

Hazlitt, with difficulty, repressed his irritation.

He said:

"Come now, Miss Craig. You want to help us, surely?" He fiddled with the notes he had been making. "You went up to your room at half-past ten?"

"Yes. I wanted to stay, but Roger and—and the others, felt I'd be better out of the way—."

"Yes, yes. You didn't leave your room, then?"

"No. I went to bed, and tried to sleep." Her mouth trembled. "I dozed a little, I believe."

"And then?"

"I heard—sounds, like shots."

"My pistol, of course," said Algy from across the room.

"Mr. Lawrence!" The Inspector was testy. "Please don't interrupt... Now, Miss Craig."

Audrey's voice was only a whisper. "For a minute or; so I was too scared to move. Then I got up and put on my dressing-gown." She shivered, and not wholly with cold. "My bedroom is the farthest from the stairway. By the time I reached the hall, Peter was calling the doctor, and the Sergeant had come in from the gardens. Then—."

Hazlitt wasn't entirely without sympathy.

He said quietly:

"We know the rest." He sighed. "Very well, then. Is that all you can tell me?"

She nodded speechlessly.

Hazlitt said:

"It's not very much."

"I'm sorry."

The Inspector dropped his pencil. It made a tiny and irritable clatter on the shiny table.

They were sitting in the library. Hazlitt and his men, having completed their examination of the room and the grounds immediately surrounding, had begun the weary routine of taking statements from every person in the house. So far their questions had only served to deepen the mystery.

The Inspector said: "Very well," again. "Sergeant, take Miss Craig back to the drawing-room." He looked at the girl. "Or would you prefer to go up to your room?"

"Please."

Algy, who had been leaning against the book shelves, straightened up and stepped forward.

He said gently:

"You'll be all right?"

A smile touched her eyes, briefly.

"Yes."

He came over and squeezed her hand encouragingly.

She smiled once more, then he released her fingers.

The door closed behind her.

Hazlitt leaned back with a scowl.

"No help at all," he muttered. He rustled the papers on the table in front of him, and stared at his notes of Peter Querrin's evidence.

"Young Querrin, now," he said, disagreeably. "He did nothing but tell us of a lot of vague suspicions— though," he admitted, "some of them were justified. More's the pity. Hmmm… This part about Simon Turner, though." He turned his head. "Hardinge, you know the man, I believe. Think there's anything in it?"

"Frankly, sir," answered the Sergeant, "no. And I doubt if Mr. Peter really believes it himself."

"Agreed," said Lawrence. "He's just clutching at straws. He's trying to help us—but he's trying too hard."

"The Lord preserve me," said Hazlitt, "from over-enthusiastic witnesses." His eyes, resting on Algy's lazy face, added clearly: and from meddling amateurs.

Lawrence grinned. He turned back to the shelves and ran a hand over the backs of the closely packed volumes.

The Inspector looked at Sudlow, who had been taking down the statements in shorthand. He said:

"Let me have your transcripts of the evidence as soon as possible. I shall want to study them."

"Yes, Inspector." Sudlow resigned himself to a sleepless night.

Hazlitt scowled once more at his notes. Possibly he was annoyed because Querrin's story confirmed Lawrence's so completely.

He said:

"This crime's fantastic. It—it just couldn't have happened."

Lawrence took a book from the shelves, and glanced up with a smile.

"Easy," he warned. "You're playing the murderer's game. This killing was planned by a clever man. He's led us, as he intended, into a blind alley. So now we're facing the blank walls of an impossibility…   Just the same, there's an answer somewhere. And I'm going to find it."

It took the Inspector a long second to realize that this last remark was a challenge. Then he reddened, and snapped:

"You don't think I'll allow you to interfere and—and play detective again, do you?"

"Off hand," returned Algy gently, "I don't see how you're going to stop me."

The ghost of a smile flitted across the Sergeant's face. Possibly the Inspector saw it, for he immediately despatched his subordinate to the drawing-room to fetch Russell Craig for questioning.

Lawrence flipped over the pages of the book in his hand, concealing a grin. He fancied that Hazlitt had betrayed his knowledge of the young man's reputation.

The Inspector said, with an effort:

"There's no need for us to quarrel. Perhaps you can help me."

Lawrence never refused a friendly overture. He said:

"I have a fair grounding in locked room theory. Though frankly, I don't see how it will serve for the moment."

Hazlitt said disgustedly: "A sealed room murder!"

He made the four words sound like an obscenity.

"Say what you like," murmured Algy, "these crimes are fascinating problems." He turned the spine of the volume in his hands towards the Inspector. "And this is the book that began them all."

"What?"

It was an exclamation more than a question.

Lawrence grinned. "You can't arrest the author. He died in 1926." A pleasant fervour had crept into his voice. "This is *The Big Bow Mystery*, by Israel Zangwill. Published," he added, "in London, by Henry in 1892."

"Oh," said Hazlitt scornfully. "A detective story."

"Don't sneer," said Algy seriously. "A principle is a principle, whether in fiction or in fact. A sealed room may be fantastic, but it's a perfect protection. You can't possibly send the killer to trial without explaining how he escaped. "

"Well," said the Inspector restively, "does that book help us?"

"No," said Lawrence. Not, he told himself, unless you believe I'm the killer. Wisely he kept that to himself. "But it's a very rare item. Hallo, this is the 1895 edition. There ought to be a special Introduction... Yes, here it is."

He began to read.

" *'For long before the book was written, I said to myself one night that no mystery-monger had ever murdered a man in a room to which there was no possible access. The puzzle was scarcely propounded ere the solution flew up and the idea lay stored in my mind till, years later* (mm, ah, um...) *the editor of a popular London evening paper,'* " Lawrence mumbled again— " *'asked me to provide him with a more original piece of fiction.'* ."

"Well," said Hazlitt inadequately. "He ought to have been ashamed. Putting ideas into criminals' heads like that."

Lawrence slipped the book back into place, not without a trace of envy. He had been searching for a copy for years.

He looked up as the door opened and Russell Craig appeared.

Uncle Russ looked crumpled and irritated. He was apparently feeling the effects of his earlier carousal.

Lawrence doubted the usefulness of the old rogue's evidence. Hardinge and he had had the devil's own job to rouse him from his slumbers. He had locked his bedroom door, and they had been forced to hammer on the panels.

Craig was sober enough now, at all events.

The Sergeant crossed the threshold behind him and stood with his back to the door.

Hazlitt said:

"Sit down, Mr. Craig. You won't object if we take your fingerprints? Purely as a matter of routine."

"Purely as a matter of routine," said Uncle Russ, "why in hell's name should you?"

After a glance at the Inspector's face, Lawrence interposed hurriedly.

"You see, sir," he murmured, soothing the old boy's rumpled feathers, "we've found many fingerprints, and; we'd like to account for them all. If there are any we can't identify—well.... "

He trailed the sentence vaguely.

Craig squinted at him through horn rimmed spectacles. The old rogue's silver-grey hair was disordered and his velvet collared dressing-gown had obviously been  bundled on hastily, yet he still contrived an air of tremendous dignity.

He said:

"Very well, my boy. Though," he added shrewdly, "I'll wager you find none of mine in that particular room. I didn't venture into it any more often than I could help."

Hazlitt signed to Draycott, who took up Craig's hand with a muttered apology. Uncle Russ watched with interest as his fingers were smeared with ink.

The Inspector asked:

"You didn't believe that absurd ghost story, surely?"

"Not exactly. But I don't think it wise to take chances with—with the supernatural."

"Roger Querrin didn't agree with you there."

"Roger Querrin," said Uncle Russ incautiously, "was a pig-headed ass." The Inspector pounced.

"Weren't you on good terms with him, then?"

"Eh?" Craig blinked. "Oh, but I was. Of course. We were," he pursued unconvincingly, "like father and son." He looked anxious. "You haven't been listening to gossip have you?"

Draycott released his hands. Uncle Russ flexed his fingers nervously.

Hazlitt said softly:

"Whose gossip, Mr. Craig?"

"Eh? Oh, nobody's." Audrey's uncle did not look happy. "You know how things are in a small village. And the servants, too. They're never reliable."

"The servants," repeated Hazlitt. "Wait a minute. Didn't somebody tell me you were drinking with the butler yesterday evening?"

"That's right," said Craig unhappily. "I was."

Lawrence watched his discomfort with a sympathetic grin.

"And then," continued Hazlitt ruthlessly, "you were helped to your room."

"My offer to act as a guard," said Craig with dignity, "was rejected. So I withdrew."

The Inspector, whose handling of the subject had been reminiscent of a dog toying with a tasty bone, dropped it reluctantly.

His questions established little or nothing of value. Russell Craig said that, left alone in his room, he had gone straight to sleep and knew nothing more until repeated knocking on the door had roused him.

The Inspector, at last, dismissed him with a sigh.

He said, as the door closed:

"The devil take this case. All the witnesses have been the same." He tapped his thumbnail with the tip of his pencil. "Either they know nothing at all, or they swear to an impossibility." His expression was half angry, half humorous.

He sighed again.

"Ah, well. Let's see the butler."


Jexen was a slightly built man with a grave face.

He said:

"No, sir. I heard nothing. Neither, I am sure, did anyone else."

The Inspector's face said plainly: I knew it.

He said:

"Yes, yes. I know the servants' quarters are more or less sealed off from the rest of the house. But surely you heard *something*."

Jexen said:

"No, sir." He paused. "Mr. Querrin—Mr. *Roger* Querrin," he emphasized in parenthesis, "gave us; strict instructions to retire early. He mentioned particularly that no one was to pry"—he spoke the word with distaste—"into the room at the end of the passage."

Hazlitt muttered something. "All right, then. You were all in your beds. With your heads under the covers, probably."

Lawrence reflected that Roger's staff of servants had displayed even less initiative than old Tom Querrin's: unlike the Inspector however, he felt he could hardly blame them. Roger had been so anxious to keep them out of the way. Algy wondered if Hazlitt would pursue his inquiry into Russell Craig's peccadilloes.

Almost as if he had taken the thought from the young man's mind, the Inspector said:

"We've been told that you and Russell Craig were drinking together yesterday evening. Is that right?"

A faint smile flitted across the butler's lips.

"Yes, sir."

"Was that usual?"

"Hardly, sir. Though Mr. Craig and myself—." He hesitated. "Mr. Craig is a friendly gentleman, sir. The occasion was in the nature of a celebration."

"Oh? What kind of a celebration?"

Jexen looked slightly uncomfortable.

He said:

"This is rather difficult, sir. I suppose you could call it a farewell party."

"What?"

The Inspector leaned forward. Jexen moistened his lips. He seemed ill at ease.

Hazlitt said irritably:

"Come on, man. We've heard nothing of this before. A farewell party, you said. Who was leaving? Were you?"

"I? Oh no, sir. Mr. Craig intended to depart from Bristley very shortly."

"He told us nothing—." The Inspector broke off. "He's here with his niece. And Querrin and she weren't to be married for a month yet. Why was the old man going so soon?"

Jexen looked unhappy.

Hazlitt gave him no quarter. "Out with it, man. I asked you a question."

Jexen said slowly:

"Mr. Craig confided, sir, that—that Mr. Querrin had asked him to leave."

"Told him to get out, you mean?" This time the Inspector was really startled. "Why?"

"It's a delicate matter, sir."

"I've no doubt. Unfortunately I've no time for delicacy. Why was Craig told to go?"

Jexen was a loyal man, and he liked Audrey's uncle-but he had to answer.

He said, with an effort:

"Mr. Craig—assaulted one of the maids, sir."

"Assaulted one of the maids?" repeated Hazlitt, not without surprise.

"Why—and how?"

"Really, sir." The butler shifted uneasily. "I'd rather you learned the details from the young person herself."

"Oh, very well. Sergeant!"

Hardinge was sent in search of Susan York.

When she finally appeared and took the butler's place in the chair before the table, Lawrence recognized the shapely hipped young housemaid who had brought sandwiches to his bedroom. Her flimsy negligee displayed her pretty figure to pleasant advantage, and a wide blue ribbon lent a provocative touch to her loosened hair.

She turned wide brown eyes on the Inspector.

Hazlitt coughed. "You are Susan York?"

"That's right, sir." Her voice was soft and pleasing, with an overlay of movie-brand sophistication.

Algy looked at her with interest. The curve of her mouth was pertly attractive: he wondered if Uncle Russ had thought so, too.

Hazlitt continued:

"About Russell Craig... " He paused. "You know him, of course."

"Yes, yes, sir." Susan added impulsively: "He's an old dear. If you'll pardon my mentioning it."

She subsided guiltily.

The Inspector's eyebrows went up.

"We've been told he assaulted you."

Susan jumped to her feet.

"Nothing of the sort," she cried indignantly. "He's the perfect gentleman, I hope. Though he did—."

She broke off and giggled.

The Inspector did not look pleased. "Now, my girl. Be careful. We have definite information that Mr. Querrin had told him to go."

Susan looked remorseful.

"I know, sir. Mr. Roger was very strict. I didn't think the story would get to his ears, else I shouldn't have spoken. I didn't—don't want to get Mr. Craig into trouble. He's very nice, really."

"Yet he ill-treated you."

"No, sir. It was what any gentleman might do."

"What, then?" Hazlitt was getting impatient. "Did he kiss you?"

"Oh, no." Susan's reply was a trifle regretful.

"For heaven's sake." Exasperation sounded in the Inspector's voice. Answer me, girl. What did he do?"

A twinkle of amusement danced in Susan's eyes. She said demurely: "He smacked me. Hard. On the bottom."

And she rubbed her chubby buttocks reminiscently.

Russell Craig said defensively:

"It was only a playful slap."

He gestured descriptively, then dropped his hand hurriedly.

Lawrence strangled a laugh.

Uncle Russ passed a handkerchief over his forehead.

He said feebly:

"You know how these things happen. She was bending over, dusting, and—."

"Yes, yes," said the Inspector hastily. "You don't have to go into the details. We want Roger Querrin's reaction, that's all."

"Roger," replied Craig, glumly, "was most unpleasant."

"He told you to clear out?"

"You put it crudely, Inspector. But—yes, he did."

"May I ask why you kept this a secret?"

Craig protested. "Hardly a secret. I mentioned it to Jexen."

"In a moment," commented Hazlitt unkindly, "of alcoholic carelessness."

Craig blinked.

He said:

"Inspector, your interrogation is playing havoc with my nerves. I was indulging last night... And, frankly I'm in urgent need of a hair of the dog."

"You'll have to wait, Mr. Craig. There's no liquor here."

"Oh," returned the old reprobate courteously, "but there is." He turned to Lawrence. "My boy, if you would be so kind as to move those two volumes of Havelock Ellis—."

Algy grinned. Behind the psychologist's monumental and kindly work, he found the irreverent presence of a bottle and a glass.

"My refuge," murmured Uncle Russ, "in emergencies."

Lawrence poured out a drink. Craig seized the tumbler with relief.

Hazlitt tapped impatiently.

"Mr. Craig—."

"Hmmm? Oh, yes." The old rogue pulled himself together. "Well, Inspector, I told no one else of Roger's rather surly action because, frankly, I expected him to think better of it."

"You mean you expected to get round him somehow?"

"After all," replied Craig, with dignity, "he was engaged to my niece. And I confess that I considered a successful conclusion of tonight's— last night's venture might put him into a better humour."

The speech had a hollow ring.

Hazlitt threw down his pencil. "All right. You can go back to bed.

But remember," he warned, "this inquiry is only just beginning. Nobody leaves without my permission."

"I can assure you, Inspector," responded Russell Craig, "I shall be only too happy to extend my stay at Querrin House indefinitely."

"I bet he will," commented Hazlitt, when Uncle Russ had left. "This is a soft berth for that old rogue. Peter Querrin won't be rid of him in a hurry."

"You're forgetting the girl," said Lawrence. "She'll stay no longer than she's forced to."

The Inspector nodded. He seemed tired.

"I suppose not. Ah, well. Now we shall have to interview the rest of the servants."

"Forgive me," interrupted Lawrence, "if I don't stay to listen."

Hazlitt nodded again.

He said wearily:

"I don't imagine we shall learn anything useful."

Once outside the door, Lawrence leaned for a second with his back against the panels.

Fatigue and something like despair held him for the moment, then he straightened up and walked slowly towards the drawing-room.

Peter Querrin was still there, hunched in a chair and staring into the ashes of a burnt-out fire.

Lawrence went up to him slowly.

He said quietly:

"I'm sorry, Peter."

The travesty of a smile crossed Querrin's mouth.

"It had to happen, I suppose." He pinched the skin between his eyebrows. "That moment when we broke into the room... It was just such a horror as I've seen in dreams. Only now the nightmare is reality."

"Steady, old chap."

Querrin looked up suddenly.

"Lawrence, I have to know. How did my brother die?"

Algy dropped a hand on Peter's shoulder.

"He was killed by a man like ourselves. Not by a ghost."

Querrin clenched his fist, then rubbed it into the palm of his other hand. He said:

"We weren't able to save Roger. But at least we can avenge him."

"That's right," said Algy Lawrence.

His eyes were strangely dull.

John Hardinge walked wearily along the drive, away from Querrin

House. Hazlitt and his two assistants had already left. The Sergeant had stayed behind to hand over the care of the house and its occupants to a fresh-faced young constable from the village.

Now at last, Hardinge could return to the station. The dawn was already streaking light through the sky: he would have time for only a brief rest before returning to duty.

Every witness had been interviewed, and no new fact had been discovered. Hazlitt had gone to make his report at headquarters, and now—.

Hardinge shook his head. He wondered how the case would end.

He stopped suddenly.

A sound, beyond that of his own footfalls, had reached his ears.

He called sharply:

"Who's there?"

Something rustled among the bushes.

Hardinge ran forward, swept aside the foliage with one hand, and flashed on his lamp with the other.

The light picked out the figure of a hatless, crouching man. The Sergeant drew in his breath.

"Good Lord! It's—."

The prowler threw up a hand across his white face, shielding his eyes from the blinding glare.

"I want you," said Hardinge grimly. "I—."

He got no further. The shabby man, caught between fear and fury, hurled himself forward.

The move took Hardinge by surprise.

The prowler's shoulder crashed into his chest, driving him backwards. He staggered and fell.

He grabbed desperately as he went, and catching the cloth of the shabby man's coat, dragged him down.

Sprawling across the Sergeant's body, the prowler flailed down his fist in a desperate bid for escape.

Hardinge twisted aside. The blow caught him high on the temple.

Dazed but determined, the Sergeant brought up his knee in the other man's stomach.

His attacker gasped and rolled over.

Hardinge struggled up. He fumbled for his policeman's whistle.

Jamming it between his lips he sent blast after blast shrilling through the gloom.

Lawrence had not yet gone up to his room. Fie had stayed downstairs with Peter Querrin. Both men felt extremely tired, yet neither felt like sleep.

Querrin said, not for the first time: "It's all so completely—incredible."

They were standing in the hall and talking quietly. Hardinge had let himself out shortly before, and the young constable was sitting patiently beside the entrance to the long corridor.

Lawrence murmured:

"I know, Peter. There's nothing we can do for the moment. I—what's that?"

He broke off as the blasts of Hardinge's whistle sounded from the grounds outside. Police Constable Shaw jumped to his feet.

He cried:

"The Sergeant!"

With a sudden exclamation, Lawrence ran to the door and pulled it open.

Half falling down the steps, the three men raced along the drive.

Still in the lead, Lawrence rounded a bend, then skidded to a stop.

Hardinge was kneeling beside the prostrate figure of a man stretched out on the ground.

The Sergeant stood up shakily, brushing the dirt and gravel from his knees. He said:

"I'm glad you came."

Querrin pushed forward.

"What happened?"

Hardinge gestured. "I found this fellow prowling in the bushes that border the drive. The damn' fool attacked me when I challenged him. I fought free long enough to reach my whistle, then the struggle was on again. I'm afraid I had to stun him finally."

He rubbed his knuckles gently.

Lawrence said:

"I don't blame you." He added grimly:

"I wonder if I know the gentleman."

Hardinge glanced at the strip of plaster on the young man's forehead, and smiled.

"We'll soon settle that, sir. Constable!"

"Yes, Sergeant."

"Let me have your flashlight. Mine was damaged when we fell."

He took the lamp from Shaw's hand and stepped back to the fallen man.

As the beam drove the shadows from the unconscious face, Peter Querrin cried out in surprise.

"Good God! It's—."

The Sergeant interrupted. "Just a minute, sir. Now, Mr. Lawrence. Do you recognize this man?"

"I do," said Algy, with feeling. His fingers went up to the bruise on his temple.

"Ah! I thought so, from your description. Vague though it was." His suspicions confirmed, the Sergeant drew in a satisfied breath. "This is the man who attacked you?"

Lawrence agreed.

"We've certainly met before. His calling card was a stone."

"Yes." The Sergeant was grimly humorous. "Let's make that introduction formal."

He shut off the light.

"This man is Simon Turner."

Colonel Johnson was a ruddy-faced man with a hearty voice which was, for the moment, a trifle less friendly than usual.

He said:

"Frankly, Inspector, I don't appreciate your interest in this matter."

Stephen Castle stood—or rather, sat—his ground.

"In a sense, sir," he returned, "I am already implicated in the case. I was a personal friend of the victim's and I was also responsible for the presence in Querrin House of your chief witness."

The Colonel growled thoughtfully. The two men were seated in his study.

" 'Myes. This fellow Lawrence." He flipped through the papers on his desk. "Hazlitt seemed rather dubious of that young man's evidence."

The Chief Inspector replied firmly:

"Lawrence is completely reliable."

"Perhaps." The Colonel was not convinced. "Anyway, that's not the point." He slapped down his hand on the reports. "As Chief Constable of this county, I'm bound to support my men. Till they request assistance or I'm satisfied that they're not competent to deal with the matter, I see no reason to call in the Yard."

And when you do, thought the Chief Inspector, the trail will be cold.

But he could hardly put such a sentiment into words; and besides, he liked loyalty. So, repressing his feelings, Castle said respectfully:

"When I requested this interview, sir, it wasn't with any intention of over-riding your men's authority. I merely wanted to draw your attention to Mr. Lawrence's possible value."

"Possible value?" repeated Colonel Johnson. "Wait a minute. I *have* heard something of that young man' reputation. Wasn't he the fellow who—."

He mentioned details.

Castle nodded. "That's correct, sir. It occurred to me that he might be very useful to the County Police. He's no good with routine affairs. But he's an expert at resolving fantasies."

" 'Myes." The Colonel looked thoughtful. "Perhaps you're right. I'll speak to Hazlitt."

"Thank you, sir."

The Colonel said shrewdly:

"Now you've wangled the Yard its unofficial representative, maybe you'll tell me what else you want."

The Inspector chuckled.

"I was hoping, sir," he responded smoothly, "you would allow me to examine the reports of the case to date. Then before returning to London, I might have a brief discussion with Mr. Lawrence. A talk may clear up certain difficulties in the evidence."

"Very well. Though it seems to me," said the Colonel, "you are remarkably well acquainted with the affair already."

"Yes, sir," admitted the Chief Inspector. "Mr. Lawrence telephoned me in the early hours of the morning."

"Did he, by Jove?" The Colonel laughed. "So you fixed this up between you."

Castle made to protest, but the Chief Constable held up his hand. "Never mind. I wish your young friend luck."

He added sardonically:

"He'll need it."

Algy Lawrence strolled along the flagged path under the trees. He was thinking hard.

He believed, in the manner of the greatest of detectives, that the more bizarre a problem, the easier its solution. Yet he could not even begin to explain the mystery of Roger Querrin's death.

He grinned wryly. It was no consolation to reflect that Inspector Hazlitt was just as puzzled and even less confident of success.

He quoted aloud:

"The facility with which I shall arrive, or have arrived, at the solution of this mystery, is in the direct ratio of its apparent insolubility in the eyes of the police."

He took considerable pleasure from the sonorous roll of Dupin's words, and wondered if he dared apply them to himself.

Then he remembered Russell Craig's distaste for young men who liked quotations and grinned again.

His face sobered as he glanced towards the french windows of the room in which Querrin had died. Behind the glass panes, men were working busily.

Lawrence knew that Hazlitt, despite his own exhaustive search, still suspected the existence of a secret entrance. So now a team of experts had set to work examining every inch of the walls, the floor, and the ceiling.

So far they had found nothing. Lawrence had expected little else. Someone spoke his name.

He turned to see Audrey Craig. Touched by the distress on the girl's pretty face, he greeted her gently.

"Hallo, there."

Those were the words he had used at their first meeting. It seemed so long ago....

She said anxiously:

"I'd like to talk with you."

"Go ahead."

They fell into step.

"Algy." It was the first time she had used his Christian name. He felt a tiny shock of pleasure. "Algy, is it true that Simon Turner has been arrested?"

"Yes, it is."

She queried painfully:

"On what charge?"

"Assault, I imagine." He glanced down at her. "He attacked both Hardinge and myself, remember."

"Yes, I heard about that. But I thought, perhaps—."

She did not finish.

Lawrence took her arm.

He said:

"Audrey, my dear. I don't believe that Turner had anything to do with the—with what happened to Roger."

"But he must have been prowling round the house all the time. You remember, I saw somebody moving among the bushes yesterday afternoon—."

"Yes. But Audrey, you've forgotten one thing. The Sergeant was on guard last night. If Turner had ventured near Roger between eleven and twelve o'clock, Hardinge would have nabbed him like a shot."

"If the old man had approached him by way of the gardens, yes." Audrey was eager. "But supposing old Simon managed to smuggle his way into the house earlier in the evening?"

"After I was knocked out," Lawrence reminded her gently, "all the doors and windows were locked from the inside. On the ground floor, at least. And anyway," he finished, "I was on guard myself at the entrance to the passage."

"Just the same," returned Audrey mutinously, "somebody reached—and killed—him."

"That's right," said Algy Lawrence. His voice sounded tired and bitter.

Audrey glanced up quickly, then dropped her hand over his.

She said softly:

"I didn't mean to reproach you. You did your best."

"Yes, I did my best. But it wasn't—enough."

They went on a few paces in silence. Then Audrey made a brave attempt to change the subject.

"Uncle Russ has been disgracing himself again."

Algy grinned. He murmured:

"He merely responded to Susan's charms in his own inimitable style."

To his pleasure, Audrey laughed briefly.

"I suppose we can hardly blame him."

"No. She's a comely wench."

"She's a minx," returned Audrey with feminine ruthlessness. Then she smiled. "But I like her."

"So does Uncle Russ."

Affection and laughter struggled round the sorrow in her grey-green eyes. "He's an old rogue." Her voice faltered. "But he's all I have, now."

There it was again: the grief that stood between them.

The girl exclaimed suddenly:

"You didn't like Roger, did you?"

Lawrence replied awkwardly:

"I hardly knew him."

Audrey said quietly:

"That answer is only an evasion. No, you found him overbearing and obstinate. But, Algy, I have to say this, because somehow it seems important."

She paused, feeling for words that sounded to her only embarrassed and stilted.

"To me, Roger was all that is kind, and wonderful, and —and lovely in life. He was somehow the meaning of all existence...."

She finished with a hint of tears.

"You'll never understand."

Lawrence squeezed her arm tenderly.

He said:

"I understand, believe me." He added softly:

"We all need somebody to love us."

Something in his tone struck through the turmoil of her own emotions. She looked beyond the mask of his amiable laziness into the shyly romantic places of his soul.

She whispered quickly:

"I hope you find her soon...."


"Steve!"

Lawrence called the name with a mixture of surprise and pleasure.

Though he had telephoned his old friend early that morning, he had hardly expected the Chief Inspector to appear so promptly.

Castle stumped along the drive towards him, a bowler hat rammed down hard on his grizzled head, and one hand half in the pocket of his battered old raincoat.

After the girl had left him, Lawrence had continued his stroll in the grounds. He had just been thinking of his friend the Inspector when Steve had appeared at the open gates.

As the young man hailed him, Castle lifted his free hand and waved it in salute.

Lawrence hurried up and gave him a friendly clump on the shoulder.

"I'm glad to see you."

"So you should be," returned Castle gruffly. "I had the devil's own job to get here. And," he warned, "I can't stay for long. I fiddled leave of absence from the Yard— and lost about five good years of my life doing it—but I have to be back there this afternoon."

"Hardly," murmured Algy, "an extensive furlough."

"I put the time to good use, anyway. I had an interview with Colonel Johnson."

"Colonel—?"

"The Chief Constable." The two men walked on a few more paces in silence. Then the Inspector said, less belligerently:

"Well! You don't have to worry. I've wangled you semi-official status. Hazlitt won't bother you."

"Thanks."

Castle glanced at his young friend's impassive face and was not deceived.

He said quietly:

"Listen, Algy. Querrin's dead. So find his murderer. That's all that concerns you now... Don't blame yourself for anything that's happened."

"That's easy to say."

Steve pushed out a profanity with good humoured exasperation. Then he added, more calmly:

"I'll tell you this once, and then the matter's closed." He paused. He said slowly:

"No man's infallible. He can only do his best."

Lawrence shrugged.

"Cold comfort, Steve. I still let Querrin die."

Castle replied quietly:

"If you couldn't save him, no one could."

There was a pause. Then Lawrence said: "Thanks," again, as

impassively as before. But this time his tone had subtly lightened.

As they came nearer the house, the Chief Inspector asked:

"How's young Peter?"

"He's all right." Algy reviewed the moment of crisis when the raw edge of hysteria had shown in Querrin's cry. Yet after that ugly moment, Roger's brother had quietened rapidly.

Lawrence murmured:

"I misjudged him. He seems to have kept his head."

Castle nodded. He said abruptly:

"I don't want to see him."

He added:

"This isn't a formal call."

Lawrence said, not as a question:

"You came here to work."

Steve inclined his head. There was no need to elaborate. It wouldn't be the first time they had found a conference useful.

Inside the house, the Inspector removed his hat and peered round. "Where can we talk?"

"Let's go into the library."

Castle eyed his friend suspiciously. He said:

"I don't trust you among so many books."

Algy laughed. "I'll behave."

Once in the room, Steve glared round at the packed shelves and smacked down his hat on the table. He made no attempt to take off his battered raincoat. Lawrence often swore he had never been known to remove it while working.

Algy drew up a couple of easy chairs.

He said:

"We may as well make ourselves comfortable."

The Inspector cleared his throat. He growled:

"Before we start, young Algy, kindly remember this. Aside from the nervous strain involved in edging myself into this thing against official opposition, I've spent the last couple of hours studying nearly every report on the case to date. All this, mark you, since you dragged me down to the 'phone in the small hours of the morning. So for heaven's sake, don't lecture! I can't stand it."

Lawrence put on his usual lazy grin.

The Chief Inspector sighed. He fished out a notebook from one capacious pocket.

"I jotted down the main features of the affair. Though I don't see how it will help us, I admit."

Lawrence settled himself more comfortably.

He said:

"There's only one way to tackle this problem. You and I both know there are only a few basic methods of committing murders in sealed rooms. So if we examine every known principle—."

The Inspector groaned.

"We are bound," pursued Algy inexorably, "to arrive at the particular variation we need to explain the mystery."

Castle mumbled a not very hopeful protest. "At least," he murmured, "try to keep to the point."

Algy chuckled. He asked:

"Do you remember the case of the Dead Magicians?"

A spark of interest showed on the Inspector's rugged face. "You mean that odd affair in America, round about 1938? Yes, I remember. Homer Gavigan handled that for the New York Police Department. Though I believe most of the credit went to a man calling himself"—the Inspector's voice held a high pitch of unbelief—"the Great Merlini."

"That's it. Merlini solved the mystery, then wrote up the case as a novel, calling it *Death From a Top Hat*. He collaborated with Ross Harte—they used 'Clayton Rawson' as a pseudonym." Lawrence digressed slightly. "There have been four Rawson books to date, though only three have been published in England. More's the pity. Every one is first rate."

Castle stirred restively.

Lawrence said quickly:

"Here's the point. Merlini devoted the bulk of Chapter Thirteen to a lecture"—Castle groaned—"on the general mechanics of the sealed room murder. He indicated that every such crime falls within one of three classes, namely—."

The Chief Inspector held up his hand.

"I've read the book," he growled. "And before you go any further, I'm also well acquainted with Doctor Gideon Fell's famous Locked Room Lecture in *The Hollow Man*."

"Published in the U.S.A.," threw in Algy irrepressibly, "as The Three Coffins... I'm glad you know it. Fell and John Dickson Carr are experts."

Castle said:

"I have a feeling I'm not going to enjoy this discussion. I can't remember one of those crimes which was solved by an official representative of the police."

"Oh, come now," chided Lawrence. "You've forgotten Edward Beale and Joseph French. They were both Inspectors."

Slightly cheered, Steve Castle nipped through the leaves of his notebook. He said:

"This case is a topsy turvy affair, so let's start with Class Three."

"Which," supplied Lawrence dreamily, "includes those murders committed in a room which is genuinely sealed from the inside, and from which the killer does not escape, but stays there hidden until after the room is forced open from the outside. He leaves, of course, before the room is searched."

"Well," said the Inspector, "how about that?"

"Not a chance," returned Algy decisively, "I don't get caught with whiskery old gags like that. I was first in the room where Querrin died. There was nobody behind the door, under the table, or anywhere else, in or out of sight."

"That checks," admitted Castle, "with young Peter's evidence. He didn't move from the doorway till you sent him to let Hardinge into the house."

"Yes. Even if Peter hadn't been there, I'd still be certain. Once inside the room, I was much too alert to let any one escape."

"I like," commented the Inspector sardonically, "your modesty. But I believe you." He sucked at the stub of his pencil, then doodled absently in his notebook. "Let's slip back to Class One."

"Ah." Lawrence rasped a thumb along the angle of his jaw. "Death in a room which really is sealed because no murderer was actually inside."

"In other words," added Castle, "the killer contrives his victim's decease from outside the"—he finished with distaste—"hermetically sealed chamber."

"Mmmm. And this classification also includes accident or suicide which looks like murder, and the killing of the victim by the first person who enters the room—the dead man, of course, is lying on the floor apparently lifeless but in reality only drugged or unconscious."

"That's not much help," said Steve. "Unless you want me to arrest you."

Algy smiled. "Let's dispose of the other alternatives."

Castle scowled thoughtfully. "It certainly wasn't suicide, and a man doesn't take a knife out of its sheath and stab himself in the back by accident. I suppose you're sure he was unharmed when you left him?"

"If," replied Lawrence with restraint, "you're suggesting that Querrin was stabbed before he went into the room and locked it—." He broke off and laughed. "I think we would all have noticed a dagger between his shoulder blades. No, Steve. Roger was alive and unhurt when he secured the door behind us."

"Well," murmured Castle, "I'd be tempted to suggest another method—the one where the killer does his dirty work from outside, though it appears to have occurred inside—."

"Daggers fired from air guns, and bullets that melt in the wounds," interposed Lawrence helpfully.

"Yes. Except," finished the Inspector, "there was no opening at all in that room. No secret panels, whether the size of a man or a sixpence. And that knife certainly wasn't shot through the keyhole or a Judas window."

"And it didn't," grinned Algy, "fly down the chimney."

"You know," said Castle, "all this talk about daggers is nonsense. The knife was in its place on the wall when Roger sealed the room, so the murderer must have got in to take it down."

"You mean we should eliminate Class One entirely?"

"I don't know what I mean," confessed the Chief Inspector. "The whole point of every crime in Class One is that the doors and windows are locked by the victim himself. And we know that's what happened here. Roger sealed the room. So logically, the killer must have struck from outside."

"So logically," said Lawrence rudely, "nuts. That knife couldn't leave the sheath without somebody's hand on it. And I refuse to believe Querrin was so obliging as to co-operate with his murderer by helping him to rig a booby trap with it."

"Never mind who fixed it," said Castle eagerly. "Was there any sort of mechanical device in that room?"

Algy shook his head. "No. I searched it, remember. There was nothing capable of firing a spitball, let alone a dagger."

"Yes, that's true." The Inspector sounded depressed. "The County Police even examined the furniture."

"They're still at it," agreed Lawrence, with a grin.

"They're wasting their time," commented Steve, with a snort. "Hazlitt still thinks, against all reason, there's a secret passage somewhere. It's the sort of damn' fool notion he would get in his noggin."

"Anyway," smiled Algy, "it's probably the only way he can preserve his sanity."

"I sympathize there... What's left, then?"

"Not very much. We've exhausted nearly every possibility in Class One. Roger definitely wasn't the victim of any elaborate trickery such as Rupert Penny described in his brilliant *Sealed Room Murder*. And he wasn't driven to knife himself by poison, gas, or the sight of a horrible insect."

"So?"

"So," said Lawrence, "that's all, pal. We've eliminated Classes One and Three. Therefore the killer's method must be somewhere in

Category Two."

The Inspector nodded agreement, though he still looked worried.

"You mean that the room only seemed to be sealed, because the murderer tampered with the door or the windows."

"Yes. But," warned Algy, "be careful. There's a big headache in store. This room wasn't just locked. It was also guarded."

Castle swore.

He said:

"Don't confuse me, curse you. Our conclusion is this: the killer was in the room with Querrin. When he knifed Roger, he somehow contrived an escape."

"Mmmm. But how?"

"Don't ask me, for God's sake. But I'll tell you this. The medical evidence appears to confirm the theory. Roger's wound could not possibly have been self inflicted. Moreover, the doctor found a bruise on the back of his head under the hair. Suggesting he was stunned from behind, then stabbed while unconscious."

Lawrence was aware of the faintest of tremors. He had the sudden, appalling vision of a killer oozing like smoke through the solid walls.

He said abruptly:

"This is a devilish problem. How in blazes did the murderer break into the room in the first place?"

"He wasn't," inquired the Inspector, "hiding there when Roger locked the door?"

Lawrence emphasized the negative. "No. I made sure of that before we left him." He paused. "Wait a minute. I didn't look up the chimney. The fire was still burning."

Even as he spoke, he realized the quibble was ridiculous.

Castle said grimly:

"You can forget the chimney. It was examined thoroughly. It hasn't been swept for years. Nothing could pass up or down it without dislodging half a ton of soot."

"I judged it impassable," murmured Algy. "I'm glad you agree." Castle said unhappily:

"We're back to the door and the windows."

"Yes," agreed Lawrence unhelpfully. "Aren't we?"

"Oh, Lord," exploded Steve. "I'm foxed."

"Take some aspirin," advised Algy. "While I run through the known methods of hocussing locks and bolts. There aren't many, so it shouldn't take long."

Steve passed a hand across his forehead. Lawrence went on:

"The french windows were closed and bolted. Now, funny business with string, usually involving the keyhole of—or the gap under—a door, has often been employed to shoot bolts from outside. But in the first place, we're not considering a door, and in the second place, both bolts on the windows are so stiff they could never respond to any pressure from without."

Castle grunted irritably. He said:

"Granted. The only other way of fiddling the windows would be to remove a pane of glass, reach through and shoot the bolts, and then replace the glass from outside. And we know that didn't happen, because none of the putty was new."

"There is," mused Algy, "one other possibility. Somebody could have tampered with the hinges."

Castle dissented. "No. You can't do that without leaving traces. The screws hadn't been touched."

"Then," said Lawrence quietly, "I'll stake my life on this. Those french windows could only have been secured from inside the room."

The Chief Inspector scowled.

"You don't need to convince me, blast it. Let's consider the door."

Lawrence looked puzzled.

He said:

"This ought to be easy, on the face of it. Yet—." He broke off. "At least, since the key wasn't left in the lock, we don't have to concern ourselves with that hardy annual, the stem which was gripped and turned with pliers from outside."

"No," said Castle. He added incautiously:

"I wonder who thought of *that* first."

"Fitz-James O'Brien," said Lawrence promptly. "He wrote a yarn called The Diamond Lens, which appeared in 1858." He added: "It wasn't a detective story."

"Thank God for that, anyway," cried the Chief Inspector. "I should have known better than to ask."

Algy grinned. He asked:

"The lock on the door was new. Have you checked with the manufacturers?"

"Yes." Castle flicked through his notebook once more. "Though they sell a good many locks of that type, they never duplicate the wards. And they swear there was only one key made to fit, and that, we know, was kept by Querrin on a chain attached to his braces."

"Which rules out the possibility of anybody stealing it to take a wax impression." Lawrence rubbed his cheek. "Anyway, there would hardly have been time to cut a duplicate. The lock itself wasn't put in till yesterday morning." He grinned. "I'm beaten, Steve. I know how to lock a door from outside and then return the key to the mantelpiece by means of string and staples. But I've no idea how to get the key back to a dead man's pocket."

He snapped his fingers. "Did the killer use a picklock?" Castle shook his head.

"When you fired through the lock you made a mess of it. But there was enough of the inner mechanism left for the police to discount that particular possibility. They made a thorough examination... As you're aware, the exploring motions of a picklock or a skeleton key leave traces in the coating of grease inside a lock. The same applies to a paraffin-coated blank inserted and twisted till it touches the mechanism. The idea," he explained unnecessarily, "is to use the marks resulting as a guide to filing the key to fit. But that always leaves traces." He shook his head again. "No, Algy. There was no skele*ton, and no duplicate. The only key corresponding to the wards of* that lock was the one in Querrin's pocket."

Lawrence smiled again, entirely without humour.

"Then there was no way whatever of escaping from the room." Steve asked desperately:

"I suppose the door really was locked?"

Lawrence stared at him.

"If," he said politely, "you're implying that Peter and I were mugs enough to be fooled into believing a door could be secured when it wasn't, then all I can say is—."

"Yes, yes," roared Castle hurriedly.

Lawrence grinned. He said:

"I don't blame you for doubting my evidence. I'd be sceptical myself in your shoes. But the fact remains, there is simply no possibility of trickery of that sort— bolts being shot and keys replaced, etcetera, etcetera— after the door was forced, because I was the only person to enter and search the room until the police took over. Even Peter stayed in the doorway. He didn't venture across the threshold."

The Inspector gestured helplessly. He said:

"Perhaps we're mistaken in concentrating on the sealed chamber aspects of the thing. Let's consider the—the *accessibility* of the room."

Lawrence raised a quizzical eyebrow.

He said:

"That's a good principle. If you can't solve a problem, ignore it."

He pressed his finger tips together, and sank lower in his chair.

"Still, let's do things your way. First, the windows. By-passing the bogey of the bolts, and supposing our friend the Sergeant to be totally blind, we put our killer on the steps beyond the sill. All right, then.

How on earth does he manage to get to the path without leaving tracks in the soft wet soil of the flower-beds? The rain stopped twenty minutes before Roger died."

The Inspector scratched his nose. "It's impossible. It's much too far to jump, and a pole vault is out of the question."

Algy strangled a laugh. "And don't talk to me about ladders. Those beds are so wide, you'd need something like a thirty or forty foot ladder to get the right sort of incline against the house. And how could you possibly remove it without stepping off the path?"

Steve smacked his knee.

"All right, then. Nobody left through the windows. You proved that before."

"That leaves the door and the passage outside. I was guarding the corridor myself.

The only other exit from the passage was the window half-way along. That was locked—."

"Yes," interrupted his friend, "and we examined the catch. It couldn't conceivably have been secured from outside the house. And again, there were no footprints or marks of any kind on the earth between the house wall and the path."

"Besides," added Lawrence, "Hardinge tells me that from where he was stationed under the trees, he could see down that side of the house—Roger's room was on the corner, remember—and nobody came near it."

"Oh, Lord."

Algy continued:

"And the only other exit from the passage, the double doorway in the main hall, was under my own continuous guard."

"I wonder," said the Inspector, not very hopefully, "if anybody could have slipped past you as you went up the corridor."

"Stop wondering. I'm not blind. Neither is Peter. The candlelight wasn't strong, but it was adequate. That passage was entirely deserted. Besides, you're evading the most puzzling point of all."

"I know," said Steve, unhappily. "You heard Roger scream while you were standing in front of the door. I—. Wait a minute!" He thumped his leg with sudden excitement.

"What's the matter?"

Castle spaced his words carefully.

"Didn't I tell you just now that Querrin was stunned before he was stabbed? So how could he—."

"Scream when he was knifed?" Lawrence took the question away. "Hold your horses, Steve. You don't know Roger was unconscious. He might have been momentarily blacked out, and have come round as the dagger went in. Or he might only have been dazed and helpless. In either case he could have cried out."

"Oh." The Inspector slumped back. He said, with a brief show of spirit:

"Just the same, that scream might have been a fake."

Lawrence said slowly:

"I wondered if you'd suggest that." He shook his head thoughtfully. "I don't see it, Steve. You're forgetting I searched that room. There wasn't any sort of recording device there. No gramophone, no radio, no telephone, no dictaphone—not even a speaking tube. And even if it was a fake, you still haven't explained how the killer got out of the room and past the guards—either then or earlier."

"Oh, well. It was just an idea."

The Inspector was glum and rather angry.

He roared:

"God damn it, do you realize what we've done? We've eliminated every possibility, and—and proved this crime could never have been committed!"

Lawrence began to laugh. Then he stopped, suddenly.

Steve Castle asked curiously:

"What is it?"

"I was thinking," replied Lawrence in a small, queer voice. "We've made out a perfect case, and pinned the guilt square on the only possible culprit. But you'll never arrest him."

He laughed again.

He said softly:

"You can't put handcuffs—on a ghost."


Algy Lawrence stood at the top of the steps, watching Steve Castle as he stumped down the drive towards the gates.

He waved a lazy farewell, then re-entered the house. He stopped for a moment by the telephone and his hand strayed towards the receiver.

A voice from above called:

"Pssst!"

Lawrence glanced upwards. The large-nosed face of Russell Craig was peering down over the banisters.

"My boy," said that gentleman courteously, "I would like a word with you."

"Right."

Lawrence made his way up the broad staircase. He was rather surprised to find the landing deserted.

Then Craig's head appeared once more, disembodied and smiling, like Alice's Cheshire Cat. The old rogue was leaning out from behind the door of a room near the head of the stairs.

"This way, my boy."

Lawrence followed Uncle Russ through the open door and looked round with interest. This was apparently Craig's cubby hole, and it was very comfortably furnished.

Audrey's uncle indicated an easy chair, then seated himself on the bed.

"You called here last night," he murmured. "But I'm afraid I was too sleepy to invite you in."

"We had," agreed Algy, "the devil's own job to rouse you."

"Yes." Craig stroked the side of his nose. "I had slipped from the clutch of Bacchus to the softer arms of Morpheus."

Lawrence nodded. "This is a pleasant room. Do you spend much time here?"

"Not," confessed his companion, "usually. But just now the house seems crammed with detectives. And they all," he finished glumly, "disapprove of me."

Algy laughed.

"Never mind. I'll smuggle you a book from the library."

"I am," said Uncle Russ, "reasonably well supplied with reading matter."

He indicated a volume lying beside him on the bed.

"Krafft-Ebing," grinned Lawrence. "I hope you can understand Latin."

"My boy," returned Craig courteously, "I never fully appreciated the benefit of a classical education until I first saw a copy of *Psychopathia Sexualis*. However. Enough," he said expansively, "of frivolous matters. I have been employing my time more usefully of late."

"How, exactly?"

Uncle Russ said impressively:

"I have been evolving a solution to the mystery of Roger Querrin's death."

"Have you, now?" Lawrence eyed the old rogue quizzically. "I'd like to hear it."

"You will, my boy. But not just yet. In any event," Russell Craig admitted, "my analysis is not entirely completed." He hesitated. "There is one point, my dear fellow. I understand that in a measure you have, shall we say, the ear or confidence of the police? Yes. Well, then." He looked a trifle embarrassed. "Are they offering anything in the nature of a reward?"

107

Algy hid a smile. He replied: "I'm afraid not."

"Oh." Craig looked disappointed. "That's a pity."

Lawrence went on:

"Of course, Peter may——"

"Ah." Uncle Russ was cheered. "Peter. Yes, I may speak to Peter."

Lawrence stood up. "If that's all, then—."

He was interrupted by a knock on the door. As Craig called out: "Come in," Algy turned to see Susan York on the threshold.

She spoke to the young man demurely.

"Excuse me, sir. You're wanted on the telephone."

"Thanks." He nodded and smiled.

She went out with a sidelong glance at Russell Craig in which amusement and mischief showed clearly.

Uncle Russ turned slightly pink.

He said defensively:

"I hope the police aren't still brooding over that little affair involving Susan."

"Don't worry about it."

Craig fumbled an apologia. He said:

"I like to stroke a pair of pretty legs, or pat a sleek behind. There's nothing wrong in that, my boy. It's natural."

"This," murmured Algy, "was more than a pat."

"She has such a provokingly attractive *derrière*," said Craig. "A slap seemed the most appropriate salute."

A smile was still flickering at the corners of the young man's mouth as he picked up the receiver from the table in the hall below.

"Lawrence speaking."

"Hallo, sir. Hardinge here."

"Hallo, Sergeant. I'm glad you rang. I was thinking of calling you myself."

"Oh." Comprehension sounded in the Sergeant's voice. "About Turner, perhaps?"

"That's right."

"Good." Hardinge seemed pleased. He said:

"I'd like to speak to you about old Simon. I have an idea he might prove rather useful."

Interest quickened the young man's words.

"Of course. You're at the station, I suppose? Shall I come down to see you?"

"If you would, sir." The Sergeant said with decision:

"I'd prefer not to talk over the 'phone."

"I understand."

"One other thing, sir." Hesitation showed faintly in Hardinge's metallically distorted tones.

"Yes?"

"Mr. Peter, sir. He told us plainly enough last night he suspects Turner of complicity in his brother's murder——."

"Well?"

"Without offence, sir, Mr. Querrin is at the moment a trifle hysterical. Turner and he——."

"Had better not meet." Lawrence helped the Sergeant to finish. "I agree. Don't worry. I'll keep Peter out of the way."

Hardinge suggested:

"Miss Craig might be willing to help you."

"Mmmm," said Algy, thoughtfully. "That's an idea. She needs company. I'll mention the matter to her. Her uncle," he grinned briefly, "is otherwise engaged."

Hardinge said smoothly:

"I'll expect you, then."

"I'm leaving at once."

Lawrence dropped the receiver into its cradle. He stayed for a moment with his hand resting idly on the instrument. He was alone in the hall.

Somewhere above him, a door closed softly.

6

It was late afternoon before Algy Lawrence entered the police station again. The front door stood open. The fair haired young man walked over the step and found himself in the equivalent of a three-sided box.

Pushing open the inner door marked Inquiries, Lawrence went into the Charge Room.

John Hardinge was seated behind the desk, looking tired and a little worried. When he saw who had arrived, he stood up with a smile.

"Hallo, sir. I'm glad you're here."

"I came at once." Lawrence arched one eyebrow in a question. The Sergeant replied with brevity:

"It's Simon Turner."

Algy looked thoughtful. He fumbled for his silver cigarette-case, then let it slide out of his fingers once more.

He said:

"You're holding him, of course."

"Yes." Hardinge leaned against the desk. "We could hardly do anything else. He assaulted you, and he also attacked me." The lips beneath the dapper moustache curved in a brief grin. "That last offence is, I'm afraid, in the eyes of the police the more serious."

Lawrence laughed.

He said:

"Even that's trivial compared to the major crime last night."

Hardinge was serious. "I agree. That," he confessed, "is what's bothering me."

Lawrence was alert. "What is it?"

"I have the feeling," returned the Sergeant slowly, "that Turner knows something more than he's told us."

Lawrence said, not as a question:

"Hazlitt doesn't agree with you."

"No. Mind you, I don't blame him. I've no reason for thinking as I do. It's just a hunch."

Algy rasped the angle of his jaw.

"I'd like to see friend Turner."

"Ah," said the Sergeant, with relief. "That's what I thought. A talk may give you his measure. It's as well you came to-day," he added. "The Inspector is thinking of shifting old Simon away from the village.

Bristley is a peaceful place. I'm not used to guarding important prisoners in our cells."

Lawrence nodded. "Lead on, then."

Hardinge opened a door at the rear of the main room and the two men stood for a moment in the short corridor to which it gave access. The Sergeant indicated a cubby hole to their left.

"We use that as an office, when necessary. Down there," he pointed, "are the cells."

He jangled the keys in his hand.

Lawrence glanced at the solitary barred window and let a faint grimace of distaste flit across his face. He felt vaguely depressed.

Interpreting the look, Hardinge said lightly:

"Whoever converted this place into our police station had a fondness for iron grilles. Heaven help me, even the windows in my living quarters are barred. What I should do in case of fire, I shudder to think." He smiled. "Still, never mind that."

He stopped by the door of Turner's cell and twisted a key in the lock.

Old Simon looked up as the two men entered. He made no attempt to rise, but merely blinked at them suspiciously.

Lawrence, gazing at the old fellow's skinny frame, could hardly believe that this was the man who had attacked him so viciously the previous evening. Another glance showed him the crustiness in Turner's features and the malignity in his faded eyes.

Lawrence sat down on the bunk beside him.

Hardinge stood with his back to the door and remarked unnecessarily: "This is Simon Turner."

The young man said grimly:

"We've met."

He stroked the adhesive plaster on his temple.

Turner blinked again, apprehensively, but made no comment.

Algy said abruptly:

"How would you like to get out of here?"

A puzzling expression, almost of knowing amusement, peeped round the fear. Then Simon spoke, with a slur.

"Could y' fix it, then?"

"Well, now." Lawrence spoke slowly. "I might be persuaded to drop the charges against you."

Turner squinted at him.

"Y' wouldn't do that for nothing, would y' now?"

"No." Lawrence took the cigarette-case from his pocket. He asked politely:

"A smoke?"

Hardinge frowned but made no objection. Old Simon took a cigarette without noticeable gratitude. Lawrence shut the case and flicked up a flame from the lighter set in its spine.

He went on:

"You'd have to help me first."

"How?"

"Tell me anything you know about Roger Querrin's death."

Turner's response was a disgusted growl. He jerked a thumb towards the Sergeant. "Ask him. He already knows all I'm telling."

"Don't be impertinent." Hardinge's voice was a warning. "And answer Mr. Lawrence's questions."

The young man said patiently:

"I've no connection with the police. Naturally, you wouldn't want to incriminate yourself. But I promise you faithfully that if you can throw any light at all on the mystery, you certainly won't suffer by it."

Simon scowled. "What makes y' think I know anything?"

"You were prowling round Querrin House all day, weren't you?"

"Maybe I was. Maybe," said the old man bitterly. "I wanted to see that stiff necked bastard get what he deserved. I—."

"That's enough of that," interrupted Algy sharply. "We're not interested in your grudges. And unless you want us to believe you had a hand in Roger Querrin's death, you'd better not abuse him in our hearing."

Simon said obscurely:

 "I'm not worried."

"You should be. You've shown you don't shirk violence. Murder might be within your capacities."

Turner smacked his hands together. The cigarette jerked wildly between his lips.

"So I hit y'! That was your fault. Y' jumped on me, didn't y'? I had to get free."

"Why were you there in the first place?"

The faded eyes glowed with malice. Old Simon whispered:

"He robbed me of my home. Turned me out after a lifetime's service... I couldn't do anything about it." He laughed soundlessly. "I didn't have to. I just waited. I knew he wouldn't escape old Tom. Old Tom was my friend. Old Tom would avenge me...."

His voice dropped.

"I wanted to be there."

Hardinge broke the silence.

He said:

113

"I was on guard from eleven till midnight. You didn't come anywhere near the house."

Turner sneered. "You're clever, aren't y'?" His voice shifted tone. "I knew ye'd be there. So I wasn't outside Querrin's room. I was in the grounds, though. And I heard—the scream."

He finished on a note of obvious pleasure.

Lawrence felt momentarily sickened. "And then?"

A shutter seemed to drop behind the old man's eyes. He returned evasively:

"I wandered around. The police came. And I saw them take Querrin away."

Lawrence made a gesture. "Forget that. What else did you see, as you prowled about?"

"Nothing." Turner bit off the word sharply. "When the police left, so did I. At least I meant to, until—." Temper twisted his mouth. "Until the Sergeant caught me on the way out."

Simon drew hard on the cigarette, then dropped it on the floor and crushed the stub with his boot.

He looked up with a sneer.

He said deliberately:

"I didn't see or hear a thing."

Lawrence accepted defeat. He stood up. "Don't expect any help from me, then."

Again that puzzling expression, peeping round the weakness and the anger. Turner said slowly:

"The devil take y'."

Hardinge stood aside as the young man went past him out of the cell. Standing in the passage, Lawrence had one last glimpse of old Simon squatting disconsolately on his bunk, lips moving silently and faded eyes shifting, then the door swung shut and the Sergeant rattled the key in the lock.

The two men went back to the Charge Room.

Hardinge asked quietly: "What do you think, sir?"

He slipped the keys into his desk, and locked the drawer.

Lawrence said:

"I think you're right, Sergeant. That old rascal knows *something*."

"I'm glad you agree," Hardinge smiled wryly. "I was wrong about him once before—you remember, I told you there would be no more danger from *him* last night—so I was afraid I might be wrong again."

Lawrence perched on a hard backed chair. He mused:

"We needn't suspect him of any actual complicity in the murder. He obviously believes in his own ghost stories."

The Sergeant agreed. "He's not entirely normal. Some vague malice sent him prowling around Querrin House."

"Mmmm. But he may have seen or overheard something that could help us." Lawrence rubbed his cheek. "If we could only track his movements throughout the day."

"Quite impossible, I'm afraid, sir. The heavy rain obliterated every trace." Hardinge paused. "We did find some confused marks on the ground beyond the path skirting the building. They were probably made after midnight though, when we were all in the house. Turner saw Hazlitt arrive with his men, so he must have ventured as near to the room as he dared."

Lawrence nodded. "He'd be anxious to know exactly what had happened." He looked sleepy. "I wish we knew his precise position at the time of Roger's death."

Hardinge murmured:

"He says: in the grounds...."

"But was he?"

Interest sharpened the Sergeant's voice. "What do you mean, sir?"

"I'm wondering if Turner could possibly have made his way into the house."

"After you were knocked out," Hardinge pointed out, "all the doors and windows were locked from the inside."

Lawrence agreed wryly. It was a piece of evidence, and an objection, which he had already provided himself. "I know. Oh, Lord. I'm spinning round in circles."

Hardinge inclined his head sympathetically.

Lawrence stood up with a sigh.

He said:

"I might as well go back to Querrin House."

The Sergeant followed him to the door, his pleasantly strident voice ringing loud in Algy's ear and providing a not unwelcome distraction to the young man's troubled thoughts.

The two men stood for a moment in the porch, gazing down the village street. Then Lawrence caught a movement behind the curtained windows of the post office opposite, and smiled.

"Miss Watson," he murmured, "is still on guard."

Hardinge responded with a cynical yet tolerant laugh.

He said:

"That's only to be expected. Bristley has never known a more sensational affair than this."

"Neither," said Lawrence flatly, "have I."

The Sergeant snapped his fingers. "I nearly forgot. Your gun, sir. I

115

can return it to you now."

Since Lawrence's automatic had to some extent figured in the case, the police had confiscated the pistol to make their routine checks.

Hardinge re-opened the door marked Inquiries, and they re-entered the station.

The Sergeant indicated the communicating door on their left. "I left it in my quarters. I'll get it for you."

Lawrence rested one hip on the desk top and glanced after him lazily.

Hardinge came back with the pistol in his hands. "If you'll sign a reciept, sir—."

Algy scribbled his signature on an official scrap of paper and pocketed the automatic.

Hardinge sat down in the chair behind his desk.

He asked hesitantly:

"Had you any special reason for returning to Querrin House?"

Lawrence admitted:

"No. There's not a thing I can do there."

"Then," pursued the Sergeant, "I have copies of every report on the case. Would you like to study them? They might give you a lead."

Algy grinned ruefully. "I doubt it. Steve Castle and I—Wait a second. There was one report we didn't consider. The fingerprint analysis."

Hardinge slid open a drawer and produced a folder. He extracted some papers and passed them over.

Lawrence thanked him and sat down.

The Sergeant said politely:

"I'd suggest we went into my quarters, but I'd rather not leave the Charge Room as I've a prisoner to guard."

"Mmmm? Oh, never mind that. I'm comfortable enough." Lawrence flipped through the report. "You've studied this, of course."

"Yes." The Sergeant said slowly:

"It's not very helpful. We can account for all the identifiable prints. There was a confused medley of finger marks in the room, including the dead man's, your own, Mr. Peter's, Miss Craig's, the servants'—as you might expect, on the various surfaces. Mr. Roger's were the plainest, of course, overlying the others on the door, the key, the table, the mantel, the lamp, the bolts, the handles—."

Lawrence was paying no great attention. He interrupted:

"The dagger, now. There's a curious point here. The haft, I see, was *wiped clean.*"

Hardinge was puzzled.

"What of it? We didn't expect the killer to be so obliging as to leave his prints."

Lawrence gesticulated.

"You're missing the point. If the murderer had been wearing gloves, as I'd have expected, you would have found smudges on the knife."

"Yes. But in this case the haft of the dagger had been wiped clean—polished, almost. With a handkerchief perhaps." A query indented the Sergeant's forehead. "I still don't see any particular oddity there."

Lawrence said:

"It's the time element. Think of it. The killer was crouched over the body of his victim, and thinking only of escape. He must have needed all the time he could get to work his vanishing trick. Every second would be valuable. Why waste time rubbing the knife with a cloth when it's so much easier to slip on a glove before?"

Hardinge wrinkled his brow. He suggested:

"Perhaps the dagger was thrown. Then the killer would not have touched the haft. He'd hold the tip of the blade, which would wipe itself clean as it passed into Querrin's body."

Algy rubbed his cheek. "It wasn't a throwing knife. The weights and balances were all wrong."

Hardinge said reasonably:

"Such a minor point hardly matters when the whole case is a blazing impossibility."

Lawrence was rueful. "Maybe you're right… Were there any prints on the sheath above the mantel?"

"Yes," replied Hardinge, with a twinkle. "Yours."

"What?" The young man's mouth opened wide. Then he remembered handling the dagger the previous afternoon, and grinned. "Forget I asked." He pondered. "Roger's prints were on the oil lamp, you said. Did he turn it out, then?"

The Sergeant did not reply immediately.

He said slowly:

"I don't know. The prints were slightly smudged, so it's possible the murderer extinguished the light himself. With a handkerchief wrapped round his fingers, perhaps."

Lawrence felt a twinge in his temples.

He said:

"My head's aching. Let's change the subject."

Hardinge smiled:

"Shaw will relieve me at six o'clock. Till then we won't be disturbed. Let's just talk quietly. I'd be grateful for your company."

Lawrence nodded. He slumped back in his chair.

They chatted for a while, desultorily. Algy began to relax.

And somewhere in the recesses of his mind, a new idea was seeking the consciousness of thought.

A heavy footfall sounded on the porch outside, interrupting their talk. Lawrence turned his head and saw a formless blur behind the glass panels set in the upper part of the door marked Inquiries.

Then the door pushed open to disclose the figure of Russell Craig.

Uncle Russ said benignly:

"Ah, Lawrence, my boy. I thought I'd find you here."

"Your niece told you where I was?"

"Er, no." Craig said, with the appearance of great frankness:

"I happened to overhear your talk on the telephone to our friend the Sergeant."

Ignoring their quizzical glances, Uncle Russ removed his Homburg hat, placed it on a small filing cabinet, laid his gloves beside the hat, then crooked his walking stick through the metal handle.

He turned towards them, smoothing his silver-grey hair with delicate fingers.

He announced impressively:

"Gentlemen, I have solved the mystery of Roger Querrin's death."

Hardinge scratched his jaw. "The Inspector will be delighted to hear it."

Lawrence murmured unkindly:

"But he won't supply any reward."

Craig gazed at him reproachfully.

"My dear boy, I'm not a mercenary man. I shall be only too happy to fulfil my duty as a citizen, without the vulgar expectation of financial gain. I—."

"Yes, sir," returned the Sergeant. "But what have you to tell us?"

Craig was not to be hurried.

He seated himself, produced his spectacles from his breast pocket, polished them, and adjusted the horn rims over his large nose.

He said:

"I shall now begin."

"Please do," replied Lawrence politely.

Uncle Russ coughed.

"You must understand, my boy," he commenced blandly, "that the theories I am about to propound are largely tentative. I may need assistance with some minor facts of the case."

Lawrence concealed a grin and peeped towards the Sergeant. Despite the official gravity of his face, there was an answering twinkle in Hardinge's keen blue eyes.

Russell Craig cleared his throat.

He said:

"First, the scream that you heard at midnight. Has it occurred to you that cry may not have been genuine?"

Lawrence nodded. "It has. I don't see that it makes the problem any easier, though."

Craig squinted at him thoughtfully.

He said:

"You appreciate the fact it's very difficult to locate the source of sound, especially in the dark?"

"Yes."

Craig said slowly:

"There was another person with you. *Suppose he threw his voice?* It's not very difficult. You keep your lips still while talking, like this"—he demonstrated—"and produce a strangled muffled cry, deep in your throat."

He emitted a ghastly croak.

Algy laughed. He couldn't help it.

When he regained his breath, he said dazedly:

"Peter's no ruddy ventriloquist. And if you're suggesting that Roger was unharmed at the time, and Peter stabbed him as he entered the room—well, I can tell you now, Querrin never went near his brother's body."

"Oh." Uncle Russ was disappointed, but didn't seem nonplussed.

He said:

"I thought it advisable to test your reactions to the theory. However it doesn't affect my main hypothesis at all."

The Sergeant muttered something that sounded more like a profanity than a prayer.

Craig ignored him elaborately.

He continued:

"Let us suppose the killer to be concealed in the room when Roger entered: never mind where, for the moment."

Lawrence opened his mouth, then shut it again.

Uncle Russ went on:

"He emerges and strikes down Querrin from the rear. Then leaving Roger for dead, he turns out the lamp and unlocks the french windows."

About a dozen objections crowded into the Sergeant's mind at once. Catching his eye, Lawrence waved him hurriedly to silence.

Craig, however, did not continue immediately. He moistened his lips and said cautiously:

"I'm rather dry. I suppose there's no such thing as a —as a drink in the station?"

119

Hardinge stood up. "I'll make some tea."

He went through the communicating door. Uncle Russ stared after him without enthusiasm.

"That wasn't," he confessed, "exactly what I meant."

Lawrence knuckled his chin. "About this theory of yours. So far—."

"Please." Craig held up his hand. "Allow me to finish. I am no professional," he said smoothly, "but this could very well be an occasion when the looker-on sees most of the game. You, my boy are too close to this affair to view it clearly."

"How's that?"

"My dear fellow," said the old rogue expansively, "you believed your various precautions to be adequate. Since Roger's death proves them otherwise, you have retreated to the illogical acceptance of a patent impossibility. As a defence mechanism, you understand. I say this," added Uncle Russ hastily, "I hope, without offence."

Lawrence was gracious. "Quite. And I'm always ready to learn. Carry on."

"Thank you. I await the Sergeant's return." Craig folded his arms portentously.

Lawrence nodded.

Hardinge came back and announced cheerfully:

"I've put the kettle on."

Craig haa-humphed. "I will continue."

The Sergeant resumed his position behind the desk without betraying any great interest.

Uncle Russ went on:

"As I mentioned before, my analysis of the mystery depends upon the killer's exit through the windows. How then were the bolts secured behind him?"

"How indeed," echoed Algy, with a glint of mockery.

"You have forgotten," said Craig reprovingly, "one very important fact. *Roger was still alive*."

Lawrence stared.

"You're not suggesting that Querrin himself secured the windows after he was stabbed?"

Russell Craig was eager.

"Certainly. Put yourself in Roger's place. With his last reserves of strength, he drags himself upright. The windows are open, perhaps his murderer is still standing on the steps outside. What is the most urgent thought in Querrin's mind? To protect himself against a further assault. He slams shut the windows and shoots the bolts. Then utterly spent, he collapses."

Hardinge thought the theory preposterous. He was also angry at its implications. Unable to contain himself any longer, he burst out:

"Do you think I'm blind? And how do you imagine your hypothetical killer vanished from the steps?"

Craig was unmoved.

He said, not replying to the first question:

"It's simple. The murderer climbed *up*."

Lawrence grinned.

"Would you elaborate?"

"We know," continued Uncle Russ, "that he had no way of crossing the flower beds without leaving footprints. Obviously then, his only recourse was to climb the side of the house till he reached a window or the roof. He could have let down a rope from the guttering, ready for his escape."

"What," interrupted Algy, "about the scream?"

"That," returned Craig, "was the final touch. We will assume that the killer had reached the sanctuary of the roof. He drew up the rope. The time, I should add, was nearly midnight.

"One thing remained to be done. He had to provide himself with a small hand microphone—."

"What?"

"A small hand microphone with a long flex. He lowered this down the chimney—."

Hardinge groaned audibly, and even Lawrence was moved to protest. "Hold on. What about the fire?"

"My boy," Craig reproached him, "when you broke into the room the fire was nearly out. Only embers remained... The killer screamed into the microphone, and the sound was relayed through the speaker into the room. Then he wound in the flex and re-entered the house through the skylight."

The Sergeant asked with restraint:

"And the murderer's name?"

"That," admitted Craig, "is the one thing I don't know."

Hardinge was saved from further comment by the shrill blasting of steam. He said: "That's the kettle," and hurried out.

Uncle Russ said complacently:

"There, my boy. I'll leave you to work out the details."

Lawrence wondered how to spare the old rogue's feelings. He answered patiently:

"Let's take your theory step by step." He ticked off the points on his fingers. "First, you say the killer was hidden somewhere in the room. Yet I searched it before I left, and there was no one there. Roger was quite alone.

"Then you want us to believe Querrin re-locked the windows himself. Yet both the bolts are so stiff considerable exertion is needed to shift them. A dying man could never find the strength to shoot them."

Craig rallied. "What about the door, then?"

"The same objection applies. It isn't reasonable to assume that a mortally wounded man would drag out his key, lock the door, then carefully replace key and chain in his trousers pocket... Let's get back to your original theory.

"You say the killer escaped by climbing a rope to the roof—there aren't any windows immediately above the room where Roger died, by the way—but he couldn't do that without leaving slight traces. The police examined the roof, you see, and it's their opinion nobody's been up there for months. The inside of the skylight, also, was fringed with unbroken cobwebs.

"As for the chimney, it's so choked with soot that even the passage of a flex would inevitably have deluged the fireplace with dirt."

Craig appeared unconvinced. He said with spirit:

"At least, I've provided an explanation. Which is more than the police have done."

Lawrence grinned. "I have an idea their thoughts have already drifted in a similar direction. They searched the house and grounds, you see. There were no serviceable ropes or ladders at all."

Craig admitted defeat. "All right, then. Perhaps we should approach the problem from another angle." Uncle Russ laid a finger along one side of his large nose. "Look for the motive, my boy. Look for the motive."

"Which was?"

Craig said slowly and impressively:

"If Roger died intestate, his brother will inherit the Querrin fortune."

"Oh, Lord. Are you telling me Peter stabbed his brother before we left him alone in the room? That's crazy. I was the last to leave. Besides, what makes you think Querrin didn't make a will leaving the money away from his brother? It's possible."

"Surely we'd have heard if there were such a document in existence?" countered Craig. "You have only to contact Roger's solicitor."

"If Querrin killed his brother, why did he previously invite me down to guard him?"

"That's easy," said Uncle Russ promptly. "To divert suspicion."

Lawrence laughed.

He said:

"You've been reading too many detective stories."

Craig seemed slightly ruffled. "Very well, my boy. Very well. I shall submit my original theory to the proper authorities."

"Please do," returned Algy politely. "But I'd advise you to explain why Sergeant Hardinge saw nothing of all that funny business with ropes."

"Obviously," said Craig calmly, "the Sergeant saw everything. And is planning to blackmail the murderer."

John Hardinge pushed open the communicating door just as Craig made his last and least expected suggestion. For an instant, the shock and the surprise held the Sergeant motionless.

Uncle Russ had time enough to say cheerfully: "We shall probably discover Hardinge was Roger's illegitimate half-brother, or something of the sort," before Lawrence caught sight of the Sergeant's face and jumped up hurriedly.

Amusement, however, had already begun to seep round the anger in the policeman's eyes as he heard Craig's further contention.

Uncle Russ gazed at him uneasily.

Hardinge put down the tray he was carrying and handed the old rogue a steaming cup.

He said placidly:

"I'd prefer not to bring an action for slander, sir. So perhaps you'd better not mention that part of your theory to my Inspector... Sugar?"

Craig said with dignity:

"I had better retire." He picked up his hat, gloves, and stick. "Good day to you both."

The door closed behind him with a certain emphasis.

Hardinge smiled faintly, then replaced cup and saucer on the tray. He said:

"I suppose I should have expected something of the kind." He sounded rather tired.

Lawrence murmured a question.

"What?" The Sergeant fumbled for a reply. "You understand, sir. You're in much the same quandary yourself. Our evidence was substantially the same. We're both in the unhappy position of having to swear to an impossibility. No wonder we're not believed."

"Come on," said Algy cheerily. "Things aren't so bad as that."

"Aren't they?" The Sergeant seemed depressed. "I was on guard, and a man died. In Hazlitt's eyes, I'm guilty of criminal carelessness at the very least."

Lawrence reflected that Craig's wild talk had hurt the Sergeant more than he had thought.

He cried roundly:

"The Inspector's an ass."

"He's my superior officer," Hardinge reminded him wearily. "I may have to resign from the force."

"Not if I know it," roared Algy, shaken out of his habitual good humour.

He leaned across the desk. "Listen, Sergeant. I'm going to solve this problem... And when I do, the credit will be yours."

Hardinge shook his head. "You don't have to worry about me, sir."

It was a lame and inadequate reply, but as he realized the genuineness of the young man's intentions, he felt a warm flush of pleasure.

Algy picked up his cup and swallowed the tea rapidly.

He said:

"We've got to work."

He added:

"I have the feeling that every clue we need to explain the mystery is already in our hands.... "

They settled down to study the reports once more. The Sergeant's tea, standing unheeded near his elbow, grew cold and unpalatable in the cup.

At a quarter to six the Sergeant slapped the papers back into the folder and leaned back in his chair.

"It's no good, sir. We've made no progress at all."

Lawrence hunched one shoulder. He made no other reply.

Hardinge smiled suddenly.

"Don't think I'm ungrateful. But we're both very tired. I doubt if our brains are sufficiently alert."

"Maybe you're right." Glad enough to escape, Lawrence stood up in his turn. "Though I won't forget the problem completely."

"Sleep on it," advised the Sergeant. He added with a smile:

"Shaw will be here soon. I'd better see things are in order."

Lawrence exchanged farewells with Hardinge, then sauntered out of the station into the street.

He stood for a moment gazing at the post office, wondering if an interview with the vigilant Miss Watson would prove helpful.

Then he shrugged and moved on.

His head was still aching; and a sense of angry hopelessness was obscuring the clarity of thought... He frowned irritably.

He ought to know the answer.

Somewhere in the maze of questioning, analysis, and report, was the key to the crime's solution.

He shaded his eyes wearily. Faces and typescript sprang up on a mental screen, swirled together, blurred and faded. Voices sounded in a nightmare medley....

*He saw it!*

The question that was itself an answer, which pointed the way from the labyrinth.

He whispered: "How could—?"

He broke off, and the blood pounded in his throat.

He slumped against a wall, looking back without vision at the entrance to the station.

He fumbled the silver case from his pocket and jammed a cigarette between his lips.

He seemed relaxed and idle, but while the amiable vagueness in his lazy blue eyes deepened to absolute vacuity, the shutters in his mind flew open one by one....


Hardinge straightened up with shaking hands.

He backed out of the cell, then clattered heavily along the short corridor back to the Charge Room. His loud footfalls seemed to ring with a threatened panic.

"Mr. Lawrence!"

He began to call before he had even reached the door to the street.

"Mr. Lawrence!"

He wrenched at the handle, and stumbled through the porch. Standing outside, he cried out again.

Catching the urgency in the Sergeant's voice, Lawrence straightened up hurriedly. The cigarette dropped from his mouth unheeded.

"Mr. Lawrence! Come quickly!"

Algy shoved himself away from the wall and set off at a run. Coming up to the Sergeant, he grabbed his arm with unmeant force.

"What is it? What's happened?"

Hardinge said, with an effort; "In the cells, sir. Go quickly."

Lawrence stared into the other's strained face. Then without another word, he ran past him into the station.

In the passage behind the Charge Room, he stopped suddenly.

The door to Turner's cell was open. Lawrence went forward slowly.

Old Simon sprawled face downwards on the floor beside his bunk. Lawrence dropped to his knees beside him.

He lifted the old man's head gently, and looked into the sightless eyes. He shivered. The flesh was cold against his hands.

He stood up. His gaze went up to the small barred window above the bed, then round to the open door.

Hardinge stepped in from the corridor.

He said dully:
"I found him, like that." His tongue flicked briefly over his lips.
He whispered, incredulously:
"He's dead."

Hazlitt said coldly:

"This man was murdered."

His tone was an accusation.

Algy Lawrence made no reply. He was feeling slightly sick.

A barely controlled anger showed clearly in every cadence of the Inspector's voice. He came through the communicating door from the Charge Room and stood gazing at them sourly.

Lawrence and Hardinge had been waiting in the Sergeant's quarters. In the station proper, Hazlitt and his men were investigating Turner's death.

Hardinge stood up. His superior officer said grimly:

"You can sit down, Sergeant. You've no official status in this particular affair."

The words were ominous.

Lawrence asked, with an effort:

"How did old Simon die?"

The Inspector scowled. "Don't you know?"

"I'd say, at a guess, that the old man was strangled."

"It was," admitted Hazlitt, "a form of strangulation. Though not," he added, "the usual, rather clumsy, kind."

He walked towards them. He said:

"You can throttle a man in many ways. With your hands round his windpipe, with a cloth, with wire, even with the crook of a stick. But this—."

He broke off. "This was different. I'll demonstrate."

He stepped behind Hardinge's chair. The Sergeant sat upright, but kept his face impassive.

The Inspector said:

"I won't explain in detail. But roughly, this is the method. You approach your victim from behind, then dig your thumbs in the hollows of his neck just below the ears, like this"—he seized Hardinge's neck— "and press hard... I don't pretend to know all the medical details. It's something to do with the nerve centres, and the carotid arteries."

He dropped his hands.

"The pressure produces unconsciousness, then death. It's swift. And it's deadly."

Lawrence nodded. "So that's how Turner died. I suspected as much. You're right about the method, Inspector. It cuts off the supply of blood to the brain."

Hazlitt thanked him ironically. "There's no mystery there. My job is to discover who killed him."

"No easy task," said Lawrence thoughtfully. He was beginning to appreciate the complexities of this, the latest problem.

"That's right," agreed Hazlitt grimly.

He paced away from them, and turned his back.

He said, over his shoulder:

"Motive, means, and opportunity. Those are the three things we need to consider. We don't know why Turner was murdered, but we do know how he died." He twisted round to face them. "But *who* killed him?"

Lawrence swallowed. He said irritably:

"Get on with it, Inspector. We know what's in your mind."

Hazlitt said:

"First, let's establish the time of death." He looked towards Lawrence. "You, sir, arrived at the station shortly after four o'clock."

"Yes. Sorry I can't be more precise."

The Inspector went on:

"You interviewed the prisoner—I won't comment on that, for the moment—and left him in his cell about ten minutes later. At that time, he was alive and unhurt."

Algy nodded. "I'll swear to that."

"You may have to. Right, then. At seven minutes to six, you, Sergeant, made a routine check of the cells before your relief arrived."

Hardinge jerked his head. "Yes, Inspector. P.C.Shaw was to have taken over at six o'clock... The door of Turner's cell was open. I ran forward and found him on the floor. He was dead."

Hazlitt muttered:

"Then you called back Mr. Lawrence, and rang Tyssen and myself. Meanwhile Shaw reported for duty"—he mumbled—"we know the rest. Well, now."

He stared at them both. "We've established, then, that Turner died some time between fifteen or twenty-minutes past four and seven minutes to six. Those are wide enough limits. Fortunately we can narrow them down a little."

Lawrence interrupted. "I can help you there. I examined Turner's body. I'd say he'd been dead for at least an hour."

Hazlitt eyed him. He said stiffly:

"The Doctor agrees with you. The old man died some time before his body was discovered. But to be on the safe side, we'll say Turner was murdered somewhere between twenty past four and a quarter past five. Those are definitely the outside limits."

Lawrence's mouth tightened.

He mused softly:

"So he died while the Sergeant and I were sitting in the Charge Room."

"Exactly." There was an odd note in the Inspector's voice. "I suppose you're prepared to testify that nobody went through the door to the cells?"

"Yes." Lawrence and Hardinge spoke together.

"Thank you." Hazlitt was heavily courteous. He smacked his hands on the back of a chair, and pressed his fingers hard against the wood. He said slowly:

"Once more, your evidence proves the crime could not have been committed."

Lawrence protested, not very hopefully:

"Surely things aren't as bad as that."

"Judge for yourself." The Inspector twisted round the chair and straddled it. "Listen, both of you. Every window in this station is barred. You know that, Hardinge. You've complained of it often enough... There is no back door, no means of reaching the cells except by way of the door at the rear of the Charge Room, and no means of communication between that office and the Sergeant's living quarters except through this door here." He jerked his thumb behind him.

"In other words, there's only one entrance to the station. The front door."

"Oh, Lord," breathed Algy Lawrence. "We know that no one came through there except—."

"Except Russell Craig. Who went no further than the Charge Room, where you were talking."

"And left again soon after." Wisely, Lawrence made no mention of the old rogue's wild theories. "Wait a second. Could someone have been hiding in the station?" He answered his own question. "No, that's out. We searched everywhere, as soon as we discovered the body."

"Yes. It's hardly likely that any one could enter the station unseen. But in any case there was no way of leaving without detection." Hazlitt rasped knuckles against his chin. "Nobody tampered with the grilles, or walked through solid walls."

Lawrence shifted uncomfortably. Fear squirmed through his mind.

Hazlitt said:

"We have another witness."

He hesitated, then added half apologetically:

"Miss Watson, the post-mistress."

Algy remembered the lady with a shock. "Of course. She must have been watching us all the time."

"You're right. She was. Since we put old Simon in the cells, she's hardly taken her eyes off the station."

Hardinge chuckled faintly. "I can vouch for that."

The Inspector muttered:

"She's an infernal old busybody, but for once her prying has been useful." Hazlitt directed his next remark to Lawrence. "She saw you go into the station shortly after four. That roused her curiosity—she knows your reputation, apparently."

"Such," said Algy idly, "is fame."

The Inspector grunted. "Um. Anyway, that did it. She can't see into the station, thank God—the frosted windows cut off vision—but she kept her eyes on the entrance. She's willing to swear that nobody went into or out of this building between the time of your arrival this afternoon and mine this evening, except Russell Craig—."

"And the Sergeant and myself, when he called me back at five minutes to six. Oh yes, and the constable who arrived on the hour."

"We needn't consider Shaw," growled Hazlitt. "Or Tyssen."

"Right." Lawrence was thoughtful. "Well, that seems conclusive. Always provided that the old girl's reliable."

Hardinge coughed. He pointed out:

"We've agreed her testimony ourselves. You can't get into the station or the passage to the cells without passing through the Charge Room."

Hazlitt cut in:

"That's right. Besides Simon Turner, there were only three men in the building: the Sergeant, here; yourself, Mr. Lawrence; and Russell Craig."

His eyes slitted.

He repeated grimly:

"Only three."


Lawrence said flippantly:

"You pays your money, you takes your choice. Which of us killed him, Inspector?"

The Sergeant's face was strained. He protested:

"It's no joke."

Lawrence nodded. "I'm sorry."

Hazlitt stood up suddenly. "Let's get down to essentials. No one is above suspicion in a case like this, whether he's a Sergeant of Police"—

his gaze switched to the smiling young man with the smooth blond hair—"or a story-book amateur."

"Agreed," said Algy politely. "Fortunately, I have an alibi."

"We'll check it in due course," returned the Inspector coldly.

He pushed open the communicating door and called some instructions to his men. Turning back, he commented sourly:

"There was a case, a few years ago, where we found a trick exit in a police station wall. I'm making sure there's no such funny business here."

"You should rid yourself," remarked Lawrence brightly, "of this secret panel complex. It's hopelessly *vieux jeu*."

Hardinge glanced at his young friend sharply. He realized that Algy's flippancy was only a mask... Lawrence was obviously deeply troubled.

As if he had read the Sergeant's thoughts, Algy murmured:

"Don't mind me, gentlemen."

He grinned. "I haven't a clue."

The Inspector did not laugh. He said:

"Three men. We'll consider each of you in turn."

He paced the floor. "First, Russell Craig. He arrived about a quarter to five, and stayed fifteen or twenty minutes."

"Uh huh."

"During that time, he remained seated in the Charge Room. That's your evidence, Mr. Lawrence, and the Sergeant's. It seems conclusive."

He added in parenthesis:

"I've sent a man to interview him at the House. Though I don't imagine we'll learn anything we don't already know." Just the same, his tone implied, we'll put the old rogue through it.

Lawrence said sleepily: "So we eliminate Uncle Russ." He yawned. "One from three leaves two."

"Then," continued Hazlitt grimly, "there was Sergeant Hardinge."

Lawrence glanced at both the policemen curiously. He knew that neither was at his ease.

The Inspector said:

"We'll examine the Sergeant's movements in detail. The corroborative evidence is all yours, Mr. Lawrence. Check me if I go wrong."

Hardinge flushed painfully. He confided to Algy later: "It was the most awkward moment of my life."

Hazlitt, repressing his feelings and his professional pride, went on:

"The Sergeant escorted you to the cells, where you interviewed the prisoner. Turner was still alive when you left. Hardinge went with you along the corridor, through the Charge Room, and out on to the front porch. Then you re-entered the station. The Sergeant fetched your gun, then you both remained seated in the Charge Room until Craig arrived to interrupt your discussions. He stayed, as I said before, for about twenty minutes. During that time, the Sergeant left you twice—for brief periods— to make tea."

Hazlitt's tone suggested disapproval.

He continued:

"Craig left, and Hardinge and yourself remained in the Charge Room until just after a quarter to six. At that time, as we now know, Turner was already dead. And had been so, in fact, since (at least) one half hour before."

The Inspector relaxed and smiled.

"Well, Sergeant, that clears you. You had no opportunity to go into the cells. You were alone only briefly, while making tea in your quarters. Since every window is barred—and we've checked the grilles thoroughly— and there is no communicating door, you had no possible means of going from these rooms here"—he glanced round—"to the cells at the rear. The rest of the time, you were with Mr. Lawrence."

He looked towards Algy for confirmation. Lawrence inclined his blond head slowly.

He said quietly:

"Two from three leaves—one."

John Hardinge jumped up suddenly.

He said, with a faint trace of excitement: "Before you go any further, sir. I have an idea."

"I'm glad to hear it," returned the Inspector with ferocious humour.

The Sergeant pursued, undaunted:

"Perhaps we're approaching this problem from the wrong angle. All our evidence goes to prove that no one could have reached old Simon from the front—."

"The door in the Charge Room," interjected his superior testily, "is the only means of access."

"Yes, sir. But—." Hardinge followed a side trail momentarily. "I'd suggest that somebody was hiding in one of the empty cells, or in the office at the back, until the coast was clear; strangled Turner, then waited till Mr. Lawrence had left, and I hurried after him—."

"But—."

The Sergeant swept on breathlessly: "And slipped out of the station then. But we know that didn't happen, since Miss Watson was watching and swears that no one left. So we can disregard that particular theory."

Hazlitt thanked him ponderously. "I'm not a complete fool. That solution was the first I considered. So if that's all you can suggest—."

"It isn't, sir." The Sergeant sounded eager. "There is no back door. Nevertheless, the killer could still have struck from the rear."

"Through brick walls?" queried Hazlitt sarcastically.

"If I could demonstrate, sir—.?"

Hardinge trailed the question invitingly.

"All right," grunted the Inspector. "What do you want to do?"

The Sergeant explained quickly.

Hazlitt nodded again, then went to the door and called:

"Shaw! Go with the Sergeant, will you?"

Hardinge and the constable left the station. Lawrence and Hazlitt went through the main office and into the corridor behind.

Men were working in the passage, examining the walls.

The Inspector commented:

"Every inch of this building is going to be tested. If there is a trap, we'll spring it."

They went into the dead man's cell. The body had been removed, though chalk marks on the floor showed where it had fallen.

Hazlitt growled to himself. "What now? I—. Ah, there's Hardinge."

The Sergeant's voice floated down to them from the small window above their heads. There was the sound of a scramble, then Hardinge's face appeared behind the bars.

He said:

"I'm standing on the constable's back, sir, so we'd better not delay. Mr. Lawrence, will you act as Simon Turner?"

Algy agreed, not without a certain apprehension. He sat down on the bunk.

Hardinge called softly: "Simon!"

Lawrence glanced up.

"Here, quickly… Don't make a sound."

The young man clambered up on the narrow bed.

Hardinge whispered:

"I'll get you away."

The window was open. He pointed a hand through the bars. "What's that, behind you?"

Lawrence twisted. The Sergeant's hands shot round the bars, seized the back of his neck, and held him tight.

Algy struggled involuntarily, but did not succeed in breaking the other's grip.

Hardinge said calmly:

"Before Turner could escape, he would be unconscious. A strong

133

man wouldn't find it too difficult to support his weight. When old Simon was dead, his killer let him fall down to the floor."

He released his grasp. Lawrence co-operated handsomely, allowing himself to slide off the bunk and sprawl near the ominous chalk marks.

Hardinge said triumphantly:

"There you are, sir. I—. What's that? Oh, sorry, Constable. I'll get down."

He disappeared.

Lawrence stood up, brushing the dust from his clothes. He angled an eyebrow. "Well, Inspector. What do you think?"

Hazlitt shook his head.

"It's a pretty theory. But it won't hold water."

Lawrence squatted on the bed once more. "I can see one flaw, of course. But—."

The Inspector interrupted.

"I'll explain in a minute."

Footsteps sounded in the passage outside. Hazlitt went to the door and glanced out. "In here, Sergeant."

Hardinge appeared, followed by Shaw. The constable was rubbing his back ruefully.

Lawrence said, with a twinkle:

"Fine acting, Sergeant. You scared me silly."

Hardinge smiled. "I hope you weren't hurt."

"No," grinned Algy. "I fared better than the constable, here."

Hardinge said seriously:

"I didn't mean to suggest the killer had a confederate. He must have found some other support for his feet."

Lawrence grinned again. "I hate to picture even the most enterprising of murderers wandering through Bristley with a step ladder or an old soap box."

The Inspector frowned. "Please, Mr. Lawrence." He turned to Hardinge. "I don't like to disappoint you, Sergeant. Your explanation is fairly good. It fits most of the facts. Unfortunately, we know this crime was not committed in that way."

Lawrence sparked interest in his lazy blue eyes.

He said accusingly:

"You have something up your sleeve."

"Yes," returned Hazlitt, heavily.

He said:

"We have—another witness."

He finished wearily:

"Tell them, Shaw."

The young constable stepped forward. Pride and a certain embarrassment showed clearly on his face. It was his first experience of the spotlight.

He murmured:

"On the afternoon of—."

"You're not in the witness box now," interrupted the Inspector. "Just tell us informally."

"Yes, sir. Well—." Shaw moistened his lips. "I wasn't on duty this afternoon, as you know. When I left Querrin House this morning, I didn't have to report here till six o'clock this evening. But as I lodge in a house behind the station, and—and as I knew Turner had been arrested, I decided to keep watch."

"Like," interposed Hazlitt sardonically, "our Miss Watson. I think the constable suspected that the prisoner would attempt a movie-style break out."

Shaw flushed. "Anyway, there's a clear view of the back of the station from the window of my room. I kept an eye on Turner's cell."

"All the time?"

"From three o'clock till half-past five." He hesitated. "I had to get ready for duty. So—so my landlady took over then. She watched till six o'clock."

"Amateur detectives," growled Hazlitt. "Everywhere."

The comment was not unkindly meant.

Lawrence rubbed his cheek. "I know what's coming."

He paused invitingly.

Shaw said clearly:

"No one, at any time, approached the window of Turner's cell."

Lawrence slouched back on the bunk. He was not happy.

He said:

"That's that."

"Yes." The Inspector turned to Hardinge. "I'm afraid we've exploded your theory. In any case, there were other objections."

He pointed upwards. "That window was locked from the inside. We opened it ourselves after the investigation began. Then there was the door."

He stepped towards it. "You told us yourself it was open when you discovered the body."

Hardinge nodded slowly.

Hazlitt scowled abstractedly. "We've examined the interior of the lock. There were scratches inside—marks in the coating of grease—which suggest the use of a picklock, or a skeleton key."

135

"Held," supplied Lawrence, "in a phantom hand."

The Inspector made no reply.

He said:

"There's one other point. Turner may well have been stunned before he was killed. Doctor Tyssen found a bruise on the back of the dead man's head, under the hair."

Lawrence sat up. The words were oddly familiar. He snapped his fingers. "Roger Querrin. His head was bruised, too."

Hazlitt agreed. "That's not the only similarity between the crimes."

"Both murders," nodded Algy cheerfully, "being committed by an invisible man who walks through solid walls."

He added wickedly:

"According to the evidence."

The Inspector contradicted him with surprising mildness. "You may remember that the Sergeant interrupted my analysis of your testimony with his demonstration of a theory."

He stared down at the young man on the bunk.

"I was about to say that one person only had an opportunity to reach Turner's cell unseen. This man, for a brief but vital period, had no alibi whatever."

Algy's eyebrows went up.

"So you've found the guilty man. Who is he, Inspector?"

Hazlitt said gently:

"You are, Mr. Lawrence."


Lawrence asked equably:

"Am I under arrest?"

Hazlitt laughed, and broke the tension. Still enjoying the young man's discomfort, he said:

"No. But according to the evidence"—he accented the phrase maliciously—"you were the only man with sufficient opportunity. Logically, then, you killed Simon Turner."

"That kind of logic," murmured Lawrence, "doesn't meet with my approval."

Hardinge made a protest.

"Sir, I've already provided Mr. Lawrence with an alibi."

The Inspector shook his head. "No, Sergeant. Think. After you left the prisoner, you went with Lawrence to the front door. Then you both re-entered the station. Why?"

"I had to return his g—."

The word died on his lips.

Hazlitt was satisfied. "Exactly. You went into your living quarters to fetch and return this young man's gun." He broke off, and turned.

He said politely:

"You might let me have that pistol, by the way."

Algy grinned. He produced the automatic and levelled it at the Inspector. Then he laughed and reversed the gun, holding it by the barrel.

Hazlitt grasped the butt and thanked him politely.

He went on smoothly:

"At this point, Mr. Lawrence was alone in the Charge Room and had access to the passage leading to the cells."

Lawrence stretched his legs out lazily. "I'm willing to let myself be searched. You'll find I have no picklock with me."

"You didn't need one. The Sergeant had left the keys to the cells in his desk."

"The drawer," objected Algy, "was locked."

"It could still have been opened." Hazlitt went on hurriedly: "You could have reached the prisoner—."

Lawrence held up his hand.

"I dispute that, Inspector."

He stood up.

"I think," he said placidly, "we'll stage a reconstruction."

He led the way through the corridor and into the Charge Room. "Sergeant, would you please replace my gun in your quarters?"

Hardinge took the automatic from his superior's hand and went through the communicating door. He returned to find Lawrence sitting on the desk top.

The young man murmured:

"Let's say we've just re-entered the station. That's your cue, Sergeant."

Hardinge repeated mechanically:

"I left it in my quarters. I'll get it for you."

As soon as the Sergeant disappeared through the door, Lawrence straightened up and darted towards the entrance to the passage. He moved silently but with amazing swiftness.

Hazlitt followed him, holding open the door at the rear.

Hardinge came back with the pistol in his hands.

The Inspector called out: "Right, Mr. Lawrence. Stay where you are, please."

He turned back to Hardinge.

"Your timing was accurate?"

"Yes, sir. If anything, my movements were slower than formerly."

They went into the corridor. Lawrence stood just inside the cell. He grinned.

"Well, Inspector?"

Hazlitt shrugged his shoulders. "You win. You barely reached the cell before the Sergeant returned. Certainly you had no time to force an entrance, strangle Turner, and get back to the Charge Room... Your alibi stands up."

"Thank you." The amusement had gone from Lawrence's face. He murmured:

"Three from three leaves—what, Inspector?"

Hazlitt was too weary for anger.

He muttered:

"This crime is as crazy as the first."

Hardinge held up the gun in mute inquiry. The Inspector jerked his head impatiently. "You can give it back."

Lawrence took his pistol and stroked the butt gently.

Hazlitt smacked his hand, suddenly, against the wall.

"God damn it! How was Turner killed?"

Lawrence said honestly:

"I've no idea."

He stared down at his feet.

There was a silence, then he murmured:

"It's strange. You remember what Peter told us? Old Simon threatened his brother with the vengeance of a ghost." He looked up, and stared at the Inspector. "You talk about evidence and proof. We've proved these murders couldn't possibly have been committed. So what remains? Did Roger,"—he paused uneasily—"whistle up a devil? Or did Turner send him the shade of old Tom Querrin?"

There was no humour in his laugh. "But if Simon called up another spirit, to blast out locks and set him free—." He stopped, then mumbled: "This time, he lost control."

He finished slowly:

"This demon wrung his neck."

"Lawrence !"

Algy came to a sudden halt as he reached the gates of Querrin House. A figure loomed out of the darkness and repeated his name anxiously. Lawrence relaxed. "Hallo, Peter. I didn't recognize you."

Querrin seized his arm. He cried, without preamble:

"What's been happening at the station?"

The strain showed clearly on his face. He seemed almost haggard.

Lawrence gazed at him curiously. He had wondered how Peter would react to the news.

He said simply:

"Turner has been murdered."

Querrin's fingers slid away from the other man's sleeve.

He whispered:

"Old Simon—dead? But why… And how?"

The moonlight cast fitful shadows across his face.

Lawrence said gently:

"Let's go in."

They walked along the drive. Words began to spill worriedly from Peter's trembling mouth.

"The police came—from the village—to interview Russell Craig. We heard rumours, wild stories… I didn't know what to believe. Craig was no help. He keeps talking about invisible men, and goblins, and—and heavens knows what."

It looked as if Uncle Russ had been revelling in the dual roles of mystery man and key witness. Lawrence resolved to have a word with the old rogue. Meanwhile, he was more interested in the young man at his side.

Clearly, but with economy, he sketched out the main features of the puzzle of Turner's death.

Querrin listened with attention. Oddly enough, Algy's frank statement of the complexities of the case seemed to bring Peter a measure of relief.

Lawrence sensed the change, and Querrin tried to explain.

He said, remembering the shock the news had given him:

"When we heard—there had been another death— another murder which couldn't have been committed—."

Lawrence sighed. Peter hurried on jerkily:

"I was scared, horribly. It—it made the nightmare worse, somehow. There didn't seem to be any reason in the world, any sanity. Now I have the facts, and though you tell me that there's no conceivable explanation, yet I still feel easier in my mind. There's a solution somewhere, and I'm sure you'll find it."

Lawrence grimaced into the darkness.

Peter went on:

"I've never been able to put away the fear that my brother died because he tampered with the—with the supernatural... And I've always believed, as you know, that old Simon had something to do with his murder."

"You're wrong there," said his companion mildly. "Turner could not have harmed your brother."

Peter's speech, like his reasoning, became muddled.

"But we know, at least, that old Simon died at the hands of a man. Not a ghost."

Despite his own talk of demons, Lawrence was ready to agree. Yet he queried:

"What makes you say that?"

He was curious to hear Peter's comments.

Querrin replied:

"The cell door was forced open."

"The lock was picked, yes. Well? Oh, I see. You mean that was a man's trick, not a goblin's."

"Yes." Peter mused thoughtfully. "Why didn't Turner cry out when he heard someone tampering with the door?"

"Why should he? He thought somebody was helping him to escape." Lawrence shivered. He had a swift disturbing picture: of old Simon, eagerly and unsuspectingly awaiting the entry in his cell of a faceless man who wanted his life.

He murmured:

"A man who burst and vanished like a soap bubble."

"What?" Querrin was startled.

"Sorry, Peter. I was thinking out loud."

He asked:

"By the way, who told you the news?"

Querrin blinked. "One of the housemaids. Miss Craig and I went out for a walk—."

Lawrence remembered he had asked Audrey to keep an eye on Peter that afternoon, in case he should think of wandering near the station.

"—we've been together for most of the afternoon and evening, as it happens. Anyway, this girl Susan—."

"Susan York?"

"Yes, that's her name. She told us the police were here, interviewing Audrey's uncle, and gave us a garbled version of the affair. Whether she'd picked it up from one of the constables or by eavesdropping, I don't know—."

"It doesn't matter."

They walked on in silence, and reached the entrance to the house.

Lawrence made some excuses and strolled away, leaving Querrin on the steps.

He felt he had spent enough time wandering with Peter in the grounds. He wanted to think.

He sauntered along the flagged path round the building, and gazed thoughtfully at the room in which a man had died. Then he shrugged and retraced his steps.

He was not long alone.

A cigar glowed redly in the shadows, and a benign voice hailed him smoothly.

"Lawrence, my boy."

Algy groaned.

"It's Uncle Russ," he told himself gloomily. He was in no mood for any more of the old rogue's theories.

"My dear fellow," said Craig. "I'm glad I found you. I've had," he continued impressively, "another idea. What was that, my boy? Did you speak?"

"No."

"Another idea, as I say, about Roger's death."

Lawrence muttered something. He asked:

"Did you speak to Peter about offering a reward?"

"Er, yes." The old rogue seemed a trifle put out. "I did. I regret to say this, but Peter was rather offensive. He actually implied"—Russell Craig spoke more in sorrow than anger—"that my interest in the matter was completely mercenary. I disdained argument, of course."

"Of course. Well, what's your latest theory?"

"Hardly a theory. Merely a suggestion."

Craig removed the cigar from his mouth and gestured with the stub. "That is the outside wall of the passage between the hall and the room where Roger died."

"Uh huh."

"You observe the solitary window. Possibly the guilty man, after securing the door—."

Lawrence opened his mouth, but Uncle Russ gave him no opportunity to raise an objection. He hurried on:

"—made his escape from the house through that window."

Lawrence sighed. "It was locked."

"Never mind that," said Craig grandly. "To my mind, the only objection to my latest hypothesis is the absence of footprints on the flower beds."

"Well?"

"That can be explained." Craig pointed again. "You observe an upturned box beneath the window?"

"Yes."

"Doesn't its presence there strike you as rather odd?"

"No."

"No?"

"No." Lawrence explained briefly. "Querrin helped me test the window yesterday afternoon. He used the box as a step."

"Oh." Uncle Russ was disappointed. Then he rallied. "Even though its presence was fortuitous, the killer may still have used it to advantage."

"How?"

"He procured a plank—."

"A—what?"

"A plank, resting one end on the box, and the other on the path. Thus," finished Craig with pride, "he was able to cross over the soil without leaving a mark."

Lawrence stared. Then he roared with laughter.

"I'm sorry, sir. But, believe me, no one could leave that way. Those beds are much too wide. And the plank would dip in the middle under a person's weight. And the board itself would be too unwieldy to shift afterwards. And anyway, there was no such article in the grounds. And—."

"Never mind," interrupted Craig. "I withdraw the suggestion."

The young man choked back another chuckle. "If that's all, sir, I'll go in."

They went up to the side door, which Craig had left open. Inside the hall,

Lawrence said pointedly:

"I'm going up to my room."

Uncle Russ didn't take the hint. "Lead on, my boy."

Algy repressed his irritation. They climbed the stairs together.

In the young man's room, Craig settled himself comfortably in a chair. Lawrence eyed him with increasing impatience.

He said:

"If you'll pardon me, sir, I intend to spend the rest of the evening reviewing the evidence."

He decided with dismay that his speech was rather pompous.

Uncle Russ said cheerfully:

"By all means. I'll help you."

He began to lecture. He showed such a detailed knowledge of Turner's killing that Lawrence asked curiously:

"When the police came this evening, were they questioning you, or were you examining them?"

Craig looked amused. "The honours were approximately even." He drew heavily on his cigar, then stubbed it out. "I should be grateful, my boy, if you would apprise me of the latest developments."

Rather regretfully, Lawrence found himself once more discussing the mystery.

Craig listened attentively. He said:

"I have a shilling shocker mind. Are you sure that the inner and outer walls of the station are all they seem to be?"

"Yes. There's no chance of trickery of that sort. The building is everything it seems to be, no more and no less."

"The chimneys?"

"Impassable."

"Then," said Uncle Russ. "I can see only one possible solution."

Lawrence blinked. "Again?"

He went over to the dressing-table, and pulled out the gun from his pocket.

Craig said, to the young man's unresponsive back:

"Obviously Turner died the way Sergeant Hardinge described."

Algy stared into the mirror.

"That's impossible. Shaw was watching the window."

Uncle Russ smiled blandly.

"The constable was lying. He murdered old Simon himself."

"What?"

Lawrence swung round. The gun in his hand pointed like an accusing finger at the old rogue's head.

Craig shied away from the muzzle.

"My boy. Could you, er, direct that thing somewhere else?"

Algy grinned. "Sorry." He dropped the pistol in a drawer, which he locked.

He tapped the key on his thumb nail reflectively.

He said firmly:

"You'll have to be more discreet. You can't keep making these wild accusations. Really you can't. You'll be accusing the Chief Constable next."

"Was he," inquired Craig, "anywhere about?"

"Oh, dear." Stronger language deserted him.

Uncle Russ pressed home his case.

"You will have to admit, my dear fellow, that the hypothesis of Shaw's complicity is the only one that explains the facts as we know them."

"Oh no, it isn't," smiled Algy. "Maybe you and I were accomplices. Then you could have nipped into the cells while I kept up a one-sided conversation for the Sergeant's benefit."

Craig looked surprised. "But, my boy, we know that isn't true."

"We do," returned Lawrence. "But do the police?"

When Uncle Russ had gone, Lawrence settled down to work.

His methods were unique. First of all, he kicked off his shoes and stretched himself lazily on the bed. Then he clasped his hands behind his head, pressing them into the pillow, and closed his eyes.

He seemed to have gone to sleep.

Entirely lost to his surroundings, the young man was reviewing the case on a mental screen.

Roger Querrin had died in a locked and guarded room. Lawrence knew now, with a bitter and angry feeling of disgust, how Peter's brother had been murdered. And he knew who had killed him....

That wasn't the problem. Another man was dead. Another victim he might have saved.

Nausea gripped him. Was this the final crime, or was there to be more violence?

He shook away sick thoughts of failure. His thinking had to be clear....

How had Turner died? Like Roger?

No.

This room wasn't sealed, Lawrence told himself. It was merely inaccessible.

And this problem was worse than the first.

The crimes must have been linked. Could he believe the person who murdered Querrin had also killed old Simon?

Yes, surely.

And yet—.

Lawrence groaned impatiently.

The evidence was clear. He had to believe Miss Watson's story, and the constable's: they couldn't be lying, any more than he.

He grinned ruefully. His own testimony was the stumbling block....

The medical evidence? No, that couldn't possibly have been faked. Turner had died between twenty past four and a quarter past five. At a time when no man could have reached him.

Steady! There's trickery somewhere. There has to be.

Lawrence released his hands, then folded them over his chest.

He thought:

Hardinge's theory. Surely that can't be the truth. No, of course it wasn't. Shaw proved that.

Oh, hell!

He opened his eyes and gazed up at the ceiling.

The cell door. The lock and the handle had been wiped clean of fingerprints, both sides. What did that mean, if anything? Naturally, a person forcing the door wouldn't want to leave his prints... What about those scratches, anyway? Surely—.

Damnation! Lawrence pressed his fingers against his aching head.

Craig's wild ideas seemed to have driven away his powers of concentrated thought. He was glad now that he'd sent the old rogue away with something to worry about.

Lawrence sat up suddenly, and glared without vision through the window. Wipe away all preconceived ideas. Let X be the murderer.

Wait a minute!

The door to the cells had been under his own continuous guard during the vital times except for one brief period: while Hardinge and he stood on the porch outside.

Suppose X had slipped into the passage then?

He shook his head. Nobody had gone past them into the station. Unless—.

He caught his breath.

Suppose somebody had got into the Charge Room while they were questioning old Simon in his cell; suppose that somebody had hidden in the Sergeant's living quarters till they had gone out to the porch; suppose X then hurried into the passage behind—.

For a fleeting moment, Lawrence tasted triumph. And then he remembered.

Miss Watson.

No one could possibly have entered the station without her knowledge. And her evidence was clear.

Nobody had approached the entrance.

Lawrence himself had gone in just after four.

Russell Craig had arrived at a quarter to five, and had left at five past.

Lawrence had left just after a quarter to six; and at that time, Turner had been dead for—at least—half an hour.

Hardinge had hurried out to call Lawrence back at five to six, then they had both re-entered the station.

Shaw had arrived at six o'clock; then Doctor Tyssen, and Inspector Hazlitt, with his men.

These were the only people to pass into or out of the building—and nobody had the smallest opportunity to commit the crime.

Oh Lord, breathed Algy. It was almost a prayer.

He shaded his eyes, then squeezed his hands over closed lids. His head was splitting.

He decided, very suddenly, he wanted a talk with Audrey Craig.

She wasn't in bed.

He tapped on the wooden panels, and she came to the door with surprise on her lovely face.

"Algy!"

He asked without preamble:

"May I speak to you?"

She said doubtfully: "It's very late."

"Please."

His need was almost physical.

She smiled quickly. "Very well." She glanced round her room. "We'd better not stay here. Let's go down to the library."

They descended the stairs in silence.

In the book-lined room, she turned to face him. "What do you want to say?"

There was no impatience in her voice, only an instinctive sympathy.

"Sit down, Audrey." Lawrence balled one fist and smacked it reflectively into the palm of his other hand. He seemed uncertain how to begin.

He said:

"Roger died. He was murdered—and I think I know who killed him."

The girl said nothing, but her eyes grew wider.

Lawrence murmured softly:

"I'm confused, and I need your help. I don't know if what I'm doing is right... Old Simon is dead, too. I've no idea how he was murdered."

He was threatened with incoherence. Then he went on clearly:

"Audrey, I can drop the case now, with a fairly clear conscience... But if I go on, I go through to the end."

Her eyes were dark.

She whispered:

"What are you hinting?"

Lawrence sounded tired.

146

"Only that the truth might hurt you. That it might be better to continue believing that your fiancé died because he challenged the powers of another world."

There was a tiny silence.

Then Audrey spoke: distinctly, and with finality.

"I want you to find the truth."

Lawrence smiled at her. His face was once more lazy, placid, and carelessly good humoured.

"Right." He pulled out his silver case and offered it to her. "Cigarette?"

"No, thanks."

Algy nodded pleasantly. "You don't mind if I smoke myself?"

"No, of course not."

The young man lit up. The girl regarded him curiously.

Lawrence inhaled deeply, then took the cigarette away from his lips. He said:

"There's one small matter. You might be able to help me." He asked suddenly:

"Did Roger make a will?"

She seemed surprised. "Surely—his solicitors—."

Lawrence interposed quietly:

"We contacted them this evening. They say that Querrin intended to make a will, but they've drafted no document. As far as they know, he died intestate. Which means, of course, the property goes to his brother."

Audrey nodded slowly.

She murmured uncertainly:

"Roger told me—that when we married—he intended to leave most of his money to me. I had the idea—." Her voice caught. "I suspected he meant to give me the will on our wedding day." She was warm with affection. "That would have been the kind of gesture he loved."

Lawrence glanced at her sleepily. The dead man, for all his shrewd business dealings, had had a streak of the school-boy in his make-up. He might have by-passed his solicitors completely.

"Mmmm." He mused pensively.

Audrey said:

"Now it's my turn to ask a question. Algy, why did you ask me to look after Peter this afternoon?"

Lawrence started. "Eh? Oh, sorry, Audrey. I was day dreaming... Why? Well, frankly, I wanted Peter kept out of mischief. He believed Turner had something to do with Roger's death, you see. I didn't want him creating a scene while I interviewed old Simon in his cell."

He rubbed his cheek.

"Young Querrin is so nervy, you never know what he might do."

Audrey gave a tiny gasp.

"You don't mean—.

She stopped.

Lawrence eyed her curiously.

"Go on."

She said, with an effort:

"Turner was murdered. Did he die because Peter wanted his brother's death revenged?"

Lawrence smiled. "That's a query you can answer best yourself."

"I?"

"Yes. Where was Peter between the hours of four and six?"

The light died from the girl's eyes. She laughed ruefully.

"He was with me."

"Exactly. You're his alibi," Lawrence shook his head. "No, Audrey. Peter didn't kill old Simon."

She moved closer, and laid her hand on his sleeve. The touch was an unspoken question.

Lawrence replied:

"I don't know, Audrey. I can't explain the mystery."

Her voice was soft. "You'll find the answer."

"Perhaps. I'll try."

"Try now."

She went out. Lawrence stared after her with an odd smile on his lips.

The cigarette had smouldered down to his fingers. He threw it away, then took another from his case and tapped it absently on the silver.

He sighed. "Ah, well."

He settled himself in a comfortable chair, with a cushion behind his head and his feet on a padded stool.

His eyes closed.

There was silence in the room.


Susan York tapped on the door, then pushed it open. She gazed round the library with frank curiosity.

The only light came from a small reading lamp, obscured now by a blue-grey haze of smoke.

Algy Lawrence stirred himself as the girl entered, and eased his cramped legs to the floor. He blinked at the housemaid sleepily.

Susan excused herself demurely. "It's very late, sir. I looked in to see if you required anything more."

Lawrence croaked, then cleared his throat. He was feeling very tired. Susan said:

"My, sir. Look at all those cigarettes. You have been indulging."

"Tobacco helps me to think." Lawrence squeezed the skin stretched over the bridge of his nose. He stood up. "It's all right, Susan. I'm going up to bed."

He said obscurely:

"I've finished."

Susan York was an intelligent girl, and she knew why Lawrence had come to Querrin House.

She asked timidly:

"Are you still working on the case, sir?"

"Mmmm? Why, yes, I am. Is anything bothering you?"

Susan hesitated. She smoothed her hands over her shapely hips, then blurted out:

"It's about Mr. Craig. I didn't want to tell the police about—." She managed a creditable blush. "About that little affair between us. But they dragged it out of me, sir. And Mr. Craig is a very kind old gentleman, though a little impulsive. I shouldn't like to think of him getting into trouble, sir."

Lawrence concealed a twinkle. He said gravely:

"Don't worry, Susan. I'll see the police don't bother him unduly."

"Oh, thank you, sir." Susan fluttered her lashes. Her wide brown eyes were ingenuous. "You have such influence. And Mr. Craig would be so grateful. And I—I'd be grateful, too."

She stepped up to him quickly.

She whispered:

"I can be *very* grateful."

Lawrence blinked.

He said:

"Susan, you're a very attractive girl."

Her reply was a pleasant one. Her lips came up to his. The gentle pressure lightened, and went away.

She scurried away with a fleeting laugh.

Lawrence gazed after her with surprise. Then he grinned faintly and wiped his mouth with a handkerchief.

He murmured:

"That old rogue Craig! I wonder if he—."

He shrugged his shoulders. Then he turned out the light and closed the door behind him softly.

The humour had vanished from his face before he climbed the stairs. He felt physically exhausted.

For he knew, at last, the answer to every question.

The traps were sprung, and the ghosts were laid. The illusions were explained....

He smacked his fist against the balustrade.

This was the time he hated. He was now the hangman's ally.

He felt sick. A decision had to be made....

His mind rebelled.

He cried aloud:

"But not to-night!"

Then, ashamed, he went into his room. He undressed quickly and slipped between the sheets.

It wasn't any use. Sleep wouldn't come to him.

He sat up and clicked on the bedside light.

He lay back against the pillows. He needed something to ease the tumult in his brain. A book, perhaps. His old remedy.

He leaned out and dragged the zippered bag towards him. He never travelled without a selection from his library.

He thumbed over the much used volumes, then a smile of pure pleasure nickered across his lazy mouth.

He leaned back with a tattered, paper-backed novel in his hands. He studied the Savile Lumley illustration in red and blue on the cover, then flipped open the slim book.

It was a much-prized survival from his boyhood: *The Schoolboy 'Tec*, by Charles Hamilton.

For an hour and a half, he found his release in the adventures of Len Lex and Peter Porringe, of the Oakshott Fifth....

He closed the book with a sigh. He felt relaxed and happy.

For a while at least he had escaped from the grim problems he had still to face.

He turned back to the cover. The Schoolboys' Own Library, No. 353. Dated 3.11.38.

November, 1938. The smile faded from Lawrence's He had been a boy, then. Crime puzzles had been a game to him: comfortable affairs, between the covers of a book.

Even at that time, he had been gifted with a flair for analysis. He could solve any problem. It had all been fun.

But this time it wasn't amusing.

Now that the game was approaching its last and most deadly stage, it wasn't fun at all.

The tinny voice was urgent.

"You can't do it, Algy. It's too crazy for words."

Lawrence gripped hard on the receiver.

He said wearily:

"It's the only way. Haven't I convinced you?"

Steve Castle's pleasant baritone was distorted. It rang through the 'phone's diaphragm with the ugly force of fear.

"You've convinced me you've solved the mystery. You haven't convinced me this is the way to prove your theories."

Lawrence slumped against the wall of the booth.

He argued stubbornly:

"There's no evidence you can produce in court."

"That's our worry." Lawrence could hear his friend's heavy breathing. "Make your report to the Chief Constable. He'll know what to do."

"Colonel Johnson? That's an idea." Algy drew in his breath. "I'm practically on his doorstep."

"Aren't you in Bristley then?"

"Eh? Oh. No, I couldn't risk calling you from the village."

"You can't risk anything else, either. This crazy plan— it's dangerous."

"It needn't be." Lawrence was patient. "I've worked it out in detail. But I need co-operation."

"You won't get it." The Chief Inspector sounded positive. "Anyway, the Yard has no authority—we haven't been called in yet." He growled. "This isn't like you, Algy. Are you trying to earn yourself a medal?"

Lawrence said coldly:

"I don't want to be a hero. As for the credit, the local police are welcome to it. I've said that all along. Hardinge—."

"Never mind, never mind." Castle was gruffly apologetic. "You aren't a publicity hound, I know that... But why, why—."

Lawrence felt anger stir inside him. The placidity had vanished from his face.

He said:

"You know how Querrin was murdered. *Aren't you angry, too?*"

There was a pause.

Then the Inspector replied:

"Yes, burn it. I am. Roger was my friend."

The answer was in itself permission.

Lawrence sighed.

He said dully:

"All right, then. I'll speak to the Chief Constable."

He had won his point, yet he didn't seem happy.

Castle returned:

"Yes." He hesitated. "You can tell him—your plan has my approval."

"Thanks, Steve. Good-bye."

"Good-bye. And, Algy—."

"Yes?"

"Good luck."


Colonel Johnson's normally ruddy face was pale.

He said:

"It's incredible!"

Lawrence returned quietly:

"It's the truth."

The two men were sitting in the Chief Constable's study. The Colonel's hand opened, then closed again wearily.

He muttered:

"I believe you." He spread his fingers on the desk top. "What do you want me to do?"

Lawrence leaned forward.

He said gravely:

"I want you to co-operate—."

The Colonel barked:

"I won't authorize any such crazy scheme!"

"Suit yourself." Lawrence rubbed his cheek. "But the inquest is fixed for this afternoon. And your police won't show to advantage."

The Chief Constable reddened. He snapped:

"If you're looking for cheap notoriety—."

It was the young man's turn to interrupt.

He said, coldly:

"I don't hang murderers to flatter my ego. Whatever a killer's done, it makes me sick to trap him... I don't want to sound pompous, damn it, but I think I serve the cause of justice. And I believe, with all my heart, that the person who killed Roger Querrin deserves to be sent to trial."

Colonel Johnson gazed at him keenly.

Then he apologized. "I don't doubt your integrity. But this plan of yours—to force a confession—it might so easily go wrong."

"It won't. I promise you."

The Colonel hunched one shoulder. "My job is to guard the public, not to get men killed."

"It's a citizen's duty to help the police."

The Colonel clenched his fist.

"But the idea's so wild, so preposterous! How can I give it official approval?"

Lawrence said, dryly:

"Policemen aren't always so scrupulous. It's a shabby trick when a plain clothes man tempts somebody to serve him a drink after hours, or writes a letter asking for dirty postcards... This is a murder case, sir."

The Colonel inclined his head.

Still staring downwards, he said quietly:

"Very well, Mr. Lawrence. I agree."

He looked up sharply.

"You're certain," he asked, "*absolutely* certain that the killer is—?"

"Yes," said Algy Lawrence.


John Hardinge was startled.

Lawrence leaned towards him across the desk, his speech spilling urgently.

"Things are moving, Sergeant. To-day might see the finish." He relaxed, and grinned lazily. "I kept my promise. When you arrest—a certain person, you'll have the cuffs on a dangerous killer."

"But what—and who—."

"I haven't time to explain." Lawrence took his hands off the desk. "I've by-passed the Chief Constable, even. He puts his trust in Hazlitt... Stay by the 'phone, Sergeant. But when I call you, go out to Querrin House *as fast as you can*."

Hardinge jerked assent. His blue eyes glittered with suppressed emotion.

Lawrence smiled. He said sleepily:

"This could mean promotion."

He went out.


Lawrence went up the steps with dragging feet. He thought wretchedly :

"I don't want to go on. Yet I must."

He pushed open the door, and went into the hall.

The blood pounded in his throat.

This was the time....

His mind sketched the shape—of a hangman's rope.

He shivered. The house was quiet. It seemed to be waiting...

153

He walked past the entrance to the passage.

The curtains shrouding the double doors stirred suddenly, and a man stepped out from the corridor.

He said:

"My dear chap. I've been expecting you."

Lawrence turned his head. Fatigue, born of too little sleep and too much mental stress, dulled his eyes and slurred his tongue.

Yet a queer elation, sprung from a challenge and its acceptance, forced its way into his reply.

He said quietly:

"Come up to my room."


So many people were waiting.

While two men talked, there were others who stayed by their telephones.

In his room at the Yard, Stephen Castle worked steadily, but his mind was not completely occupied with the task in hand. His gaze strayed often to the black receiver on the desk before him.

His mind echoed:

"Good luck, Algy."

Colonel Johnson paced up and down his study floor. His ruddy face was anxious.

He exploded suddenly:

"These damned civilians!"

Then he smiled ruefully.

He told himself:

At least, young Lawrence is trying to save my face.

His eyes went back to the telephone.

Sergeant Hardinge fingered the twisted cord.

He thought:

One tug, and this instrument is out of commission. I'm tempted to do it, and save myself the tension. I could go out to the House at once—.

He laughed at himself. Keep calm.

Your thoughts are queer when you're puzzled. Lawrence will explain when he wants to. He's paid you a compliment....

He stayed in the station, waiting for his summons.

There were others: Hazlitt, and his men.

And a girl hugged cover in her bedroom, attentive for the alarm.

The minutes crawled by. Time seemed to be losing its meaning.

The duel was on.

Time passed....

Algy Lawrence reeled backwards. The blood showed, red and

154

angry, across his forehead. He crashed blindly over a chair, fell to the floor, and lay still.

Peter Querrin came out of his room and paused uncertainly in the passage. He stood listening. The sudden noise had jarred his nerves.

He heard a faint groan.

He mumbled foolishly:

"What—who—.?"

He went up to the door of Lawrence's bedroom and pushed it fully open. He stared in shocked surprise.

"Good Lord!"

He stumbled across the threshold, then half fell, half knelt beside the young man sprawled on the carpet.

"Lawrence!"

Peter gazed wildly round. The room was empty.

Lying on the floor, as if dropped from a hasty hand, was a stick with blood on its ferrule.

Querrin slipped his hand under Lawrence's collar and gently lifted the young man's head. Algy's eyelids stirred. He groaned again.

Peter spoke his name, urgently. "Are you all right?"

Lawrence mumbled:

"All ri'—."

His head fell back once more.

Querrin released his grip and straightened up. He looked round dizzily. Then he spilled water from a carafe on a clean handkerchief and began to bathe Lawrence's temples gingerly.

Algy's eyes flickered open. The intelligence seeped back to them rapidly.

Grabbing Peter's wrist with surprising strength, Lawrence croaked:

"Where is he?"

"Who?"

The blond young man did not reply. He levered himself up to a sitting position, muttering:

"He hit me with a stick—. Heavens! I remember."

He broke off abruptly.

His fingers pressed hard into Querrin's flesh. He mumbled incoherently:

"It all went wrong. I—I—you'll have to help me. The man who murdered your brother... Which way did he go?"

The shock held Peter silent. He shook his head numbly.

Lawrence cried:

"You must have seen him."

He struggled up, then sank back once more. He kept on talking.

"He was waiting for me when I came in… We talked. I meant to trap him, but I over-played my hand… God damn it! There's no time to lose. Where is he?"

Peter shook his head again.

He whispered:

"You don't understand. I was close at hand when you fell and cried out. I was coming out of my room, and the noise startled me. I was looking along the corridor. I didn't take my eyes from your door."

He paused, remembering.

He concluded fearfully:

"No one came out."


Lawrence's eyes blurred.

"So he's vanished again. It's a trick, Peter. A devilish trick."

He put out his arm. Querrin helped him to stand.

Lawrence gasped:

"I need a drink."

He lurched against the bedrail.

"Here." Peter pulled out a flask from his hip pocket, put it in the other man's hand. Lawrence let a few drops of the fiery liquid trickle down his throat.

"Thanks." He wiped his mouth. "I'm better now." New strength had surged into his speech.

He said bitterly:

"So much for my plans. Steve was right."

Peter cried:

"For heaven's sake! What happened?"

Lawrence muttered:

"You've a right to know. I should have told you before. Peter, we've discovered who killed your brother."

"Who, then?"

Querrin mouthed the words painfully.

Lawrence spoke a name.

Peter grew flushed and incredulous.

"What!"

The cry was mid way between a question and an exclamation.

He added sincerely:

"I can't believe it."

"Think, Peter. Think." Lawrence smacked his hand on the bedrail in emphasis. "Who was the man with no proper alibi—the man nobody saw for nearly an hour after Roger died? Who locked his bedroom door, and stayed in his room till the Sergeant and I roused him? Who said he heard nothing, though his room was near the head of the stairs?"

Querrin caught his breath.

"The scream—and the shots—."

"Yes." Algy was eager. "Audrey heard them, though her bedroom is farthest from the stairway."

Peter cried:

"I still can't believe it!"

Lawrence said grimly:

"This man was faced with the prospect of losing a comfortable home. He probably expected to stay here, once Audrey and Roger were married. But he made a mistake when he fooled around with the servants, and your brother told him to leave."

"That's no motive—."

Lawrence cut in ruthlessly. "We've been told that Roger died intestate. But did he? Maybe he made the will he intended."

"You mean—bequeathing the money to Audrey?"

"Yes. Perhaps there *is* such a document in existence. Perhaps our man has possession of it."

Lawrence finished tiredly:

"He gave himself away."

Querrin asked:

"How?"

Algy grinned briefly. "Those crazy theories. He did his best to confuse me. But he made one mistake."

He paused.

"He told me that when I broke into Roger's room, the fire in the grate was nearly out. Only embers remained."

Peter was puzzled.

"That was the truth, surely."

"Certainly. *But how did he know?*"

"But I—." Peter gulped. "I—I mean. That is—."

Lawrence helped him out.

"He must have been in the room himself, without our knowledge."

"Then how did he escape?"

Lawrence shook his head. "That's too long a story." He scuffed a foot against the stick on the carpet, winced, and put up his fingers to his forehead. Then his hand dropped suddenly.

He whispered:

"No...."

"Lawrence! What is it?"

Algy pointed. Querrin stared at the dressing-table. The fair haired young man said grittily:

"That drawer has been forced."

He sprang forward, and wrenched it open.

Then he twisted round with a desperate face.

He said, with a quiet hopelessness:

"He's taken the gun."

… Downstairs in the room where a man had died, the pistol was held in a podgy hand.

"Please don't move," said Russell Craig, politely. "I wouldn't like to have your death on my conscience."

Lawrence's mouth set hard.

He said:

"That old rogue is a murderer. He won't hesitate to kill again."

"For God's sake!"

All Peter's bewilderment exploded into the cry. He felt sick and confused.

Lawrence clutched hard on the bedrail. His knuckles showed white.

He muttered:

"I have to think. Now, as never before, I've got to think."

His eyes closed. . . .

Querrin was muddled. "Should we call the police?"

Algy's lids snapped open. "Yes. Ring Hardinge—. No, damn it, wait… There isn't time enough to reach him."

He jerked into action.

"Come with me, Peter. We have to settle this ourselves."

They hurried out on the landing. Peter gazed round helplessly. Lawrence called:

"This way."

They went down the stairs. Algy took three steps towards the double doors at the entrance to the passage, then stopped.

He murmured:

"No. We can't reach him that way. Follow me."

The side door came open at his touch. The two men ran silently along the path, skirting the outside wall of the corridor. As they neared the turn of the pathway, Lawrence laid a restraining hand on Querrin's arm.

"Easy. We have to be careful."

He moved forward cautiously and looked towards the french windows. Then he sighed with relief.

He breathed:

"The curtains are drawn. Come on, Peter."

They stepped off the path and walked noiselessly across the soft brown soil. Their footprints sprang up in silent commentary.

As they neared the room in which Roger had died, the sound of voices came like a ghost to their ears.

The french windows were unfastened. Lawrence eased one side partially open.

The voices grew clear and distinct. Through a gap in the curtains, he could see Russell Craig.

Two people were talking in that room.

One was an innocent person.

The other was a ruthless killer.


Uncle Russ said mildly:

"I've never murdered anybody. Though Lawrence thinks I was responsible for two deaths at least. But then, he's not very bright, is he? You fooled him easily."

The other said hoarsely:

"What do you want of me?"

Craig responded benignly:

"You'll learn in due course. In the meantime,"—here the old rogue shifted the pistol slightly—"don't make any sudden movements. I shan't hesitate to fire. That," he ended courteously, "is a warning."

There was a short, uneasy laugh. "I suppose there's a reason for your actions."

"There is," agreed Uncle Russ. He settled his back against the mantel. "But please sit down. Make yourself comfortable."

A chair creaked.

Craig continued:

"A word of explanation. I don't want you to misconstrue my motives. I know my duty as a citizen. If I choose to neglect it, it's not because I have a sentimental distaste for putting you on trial. I could watch you die with equanimity." His voice was hard. "No, I have another reason for letting you go free."

His companion was torn between relief and apprehension; but made no reply.

Craig went on smoothly:

"In this harsh world I have to look after myself. I'm not," he coughed, "financially secure. So I lack the little comforts due to me."

The light of understanding showed in the other's eyes.

"Go on."

"I need—you'll pardon the expression—a meal ticket. I'm an old man," said Uncle Russ, wrapped in self-pity, "and I want to see out my life in comfort. So naturally, I require money. You, my dear—."

159

The other interrupted.

"Blackmail!"

The word was sharp and ugly.

"Exactly." Craig's manner was benevolent and avuncular. "You are going to provide me with a substantial annuity. You may regard me, if you wish, as a remittance man." He chuckled. "Or a dependent relative. Though I don't advise you to show me as such on your Income Tax returns."

"I have no money."

"Oh, come now." Craig was reproachful. "Though it doesn't at the moment appear to do so; you know, and I know, that Roger's death has made you a wealthy person. You can spare a little for me. In fact," he laughed, "you will have to spare a good deal."

The other's voice was soft.

"You're playing a dangerous game."

"I agree. But don't think you can scare me." Craig indicated the pistol in his hand.

"You won't always have a gun."

The old rascal eyed his companion thoughtfully.

He said:

"You're not wise to threaten me."

There was a silence.

Then Craig murmured: "It makes no difference. I shall strengthen my defences."

The reply was almost a sneer.

"How?"

"Ah." Craig placed one finger along his nose. "You'll see."

The other stirred.

"I've listened to you patiently. And you're talking nonsense. You can't keep me here for ever. When I leave, I shall go straight to the police station, and—."

"I don't think so." Craig was unruffled. "I've nothing to fear. I shall give my evidence at the inquest this afternoon."

"Your evidence?"

Unwilling fear showed in the question.

"Yes." Craig smiled. He looked like a cat playing with a mouse. "You see, I wasn't asleep—the night friend Roger died. I heard the scream, and then the shots—."

There was the sound of an indrawn breath.

"I got up hastily. My room is near the head of the stairs. I looked down over the banisters—."

He paused.

Something rasped in the other's throat.

"Well?"

Craig said gently:

"I saw you come out from the passage, through the double doors and into the hall."

"Querrin and Lawrence both swore—."

"That nobody passed them in the corridor. I know. Please don't quibble. I also know why they didn't see you." Craig was brisk. "Let's continue. I watched you leave. Then," he smiled broadly, "I went back to my room, locked the door, and climbed into bed. I needed time to think."

"That's your evidence?"

"Yes."

"And for a price, you'll suppress it?"

"Yes."

"All right. I agree."

The reply had over-tones of relief.

Uncle Russ seemed amused.

He said unexpectedly:

"You think you've beaten me, don't you?"

"What?" The other was caught off balance.

Craig continued:

"I'm not a fool. I've made false statements to the police, but not under oath. So far I haven't committed myself. But if I perjure myself this afternoon, I weaken my position. To-day, I can give you away. Next year, I can't. You're counting on that. Aren't you?"

"I—I don't understand."

"Come now." Craig grinned unsympathetically. "I can't make myself an accessory after the fact. I don't want my neck in a noose."

"So?"

The word held menace.

"You'll have to help me."

Craig slipped his free hand into the inside pocket of his coat and extracted a thin sheaf of folded papers.

He said:

"Read this."

He tossed the papers into the other's lap.

The pages rustled gently.

Craig watched his companion warily.

The reaction came swiftly. "This is a confession!"

"Yes," returned Uncle Russ, politely. "In your name. Read it, please. I had to use my imagination in places. But I think you'll find it

161

essentially accurate."

There was a laugh.

"I'm to put my name to this? You must think I'm a fool."

"No," replied Craig equably. "But you will do as I wish."

There was another silence while the other read swiftly.

Then:

"So you know that, too?"

"Oh, yes," said Craig. "I've omitted nothing."

The papers rustled angrily.

"I can't sign this."

"You will sign," returned Craig gently, "every page."

There was menace in the room. It seeped round the shadows, and flared up with the lighted lamp. Lawrence, peering through the crack between the drawn curtains, watched the old rogue curiously. He noted, without surprise, that in spite of the tension betrayed by the beading of sweat at his hair-line, Uncle Russ was enjoying himself immensely.

Craig held the gun with unwavering steadiness.

He said:

"I need your confession, for obvious reasons. I don't intend to be your third victim. And I shan't allow my part in this affair to be known by the police. If at any time you fail to provide my—ah—allowance, those papers will be despatched—anonymously—to New Scotland Yard."

"I could still name you an accessory."

"How," inquired Craig politely, "could you prove it? "

There was no reply.

Uncle Russ said smoothly:

"With those papers in my possession, I shall have nothing to fear. From you, or the Director of Public Prosecutions."

The other said flatly:

"I won't sign."

"The choice is yours." The old rogue shrugged delicately. "Either you put your name to that confession or I tell the Coroner everything." Craig chuckled. "The true story of this crime should make a bigger sensation than any fantasy I've advanced myself."

He added:

"I shall make an excellent witness."

"You—."

The other's arm jerked upwards.

Craig thrust the pistol forward. He snapped:

"No abuse, please." He relaxed. "And no violence." He finished benignly: "Though I could handle you well enough."

His voice hardened once more.

"Have you made your decision?"

There was a moment of terrible calm. Then a pen scratched furiously over the surface of the papers.

Craig chuckled wordlessly.

Outside in the garden, Lawrence looked at Peter. Querrin had heard every word. His face had gone white, and bloodless.

Lawrence swung back to the curtains. His body tensed.

Uncle Russ inquired:

"Have you finished?"

"Yes." The response was quiet and resigned, yet with strange undertones. "Here."

Somebody moved in the dusky room. Lawrence saw Craig's eyes flicker briefly as his companion stood up with the signed confession. The other said gently:

"Take it."

As Craig grasped the papers, his gaze shifted down involuntarily. In that brief moment, the killer was on him like a wildcat.

Two desperate hands clutched at the gun in his fist, seizing the pistol by muzzle and butt. Craig felt the automatic turn out, around, and in, trapping his finger in the trigger guard.

He shrieked with pain.

The pressure eased, then a blow crashed into his already contorted face. He lurched to the floor, only half conscious.

"Now!"

The other's eyes were steely. The gun swung up, reversed in a merciless hand.

It clubbed down viciously.


For a long second, Lawrence felt paralysed with fear and shock. Then as Uncle Russ went down, the young man wrenched aside the curtains and hurled himself at the old man's attacker.

He grabbed the killer's wrist, and wrenched with all his strength. The gun butt missed Craig's temple by a hair's-breadth.

The force of the onslaught carried Lawrence on to the other's back. They rolled over together, struggling wildly.

The pistol, jarred from the killer's hand, slid over the floor; and struck against Querrin's shoe as he came through the windows from the garden.

Lawrence's head crashed against the table leg. The lighted lamp rocked crazily.

His senses reeling, the young man pulled himself up.

His adversary, standing also, met him with a dead face.

Lawrence couldn't afford to be squeamish. He lifted his leg, stepping inside the other's crotch. The killer was thrown to the ground with Lawrence on top.

Algy tucked his opponent's toe under his own left arm, then turned the other over with his body, sitting in and locking the fallen one's leg over his own. He lay back and applied pressure.

He gasped: "For your own sake, keep still!"

The command was not obeyed. The killer struggled in a frenzied bid for escape. Lawrence gritted his teeth. He heard a choked cry of agony, then the other lay still.

Lawrence wiped the sweat from his forehead. He didn't feel happy: he hated violence.

He looked round for the gun.

It was in Peter's hand.

Querrin came forward slowly. One curtain had been swept fully aside, and the daylight streamed in behind him.

Lawrence said queery: "Give me the pistol."

Peter Querrin shook his head. An odd smile drifted over his mouth. He said:

"No."

His voice sharpened. "I'm warning you. Don't move."

Russell Craig stirred suddenly.

Querrin snapped:

"Get up. Stand over there, behind Lawrence."

The old rogue hesitated.

Algy called sharply: "Do as he says."

Craig levered himself up painfully. A thin smear of blood showed on his cheek, and the trigger finger of his right hand was red and swollen.

He tried, with pitiful ineffectiveness, to straighten his disordered silver-grey hair. He walked slowly across the room.

"That's right," breathed Peter Querrin.

Lawrence shifted position.

Peter jerked the gun.

"I said—don't move!"

Algy felt the body beneath him squirm. A voice squeezed, painfully:

"Make him—let me go… "

Querrin's mouth trembled.

He muttered:

"No. I don't trust you." His voice altered pitch. "You gave me away."

Lawrence stared at him, coolly. Then, with calm and lazy movements, he stood up and released his prisoner.

Peter's features contorted angrily.

"You swine! Do you want me to shoot?"

Algy Lawrence said mildly:

"You won't kill me, Peter. You haven't the guts."

The speech had the flick of contempt.

Querrin flushed. His crooked finger trembled against the trigger.

Lawrence leaned one hip against the table.

He said, conversationally:

"You'll always need another"—his glance went sideways and down— "to do your dirty work. And this time, Peter, you have no hired assassin."

He relaxed, and closed his eyes.

"Tell me, Peter. When did you decide"—he paused— "that your brother had to die?"

Something rasped in Querrin's throat.

He said:

"Give me that confession."

The papers were still clutched in Craig's hand. He had retrieved them when picking himself up from the floor.

Lawrence leaned over and wrenched them from his grasp.

Querrin's eyes went blank and deadly.

He whispered:

"Give me those papers."

Lawrence shook his head.

He said:

"You'll have to kill for them, Peter. There's no easy way."

"Shoot!"

The hoarse voice startled them both.

Querrin's accomplice struggled up, then sank back with a cry of pain, rubbing an injured leg.

Lawrence grinned without humour.

"That's good advice. Take it."

"I don't want to kill you—."

"But you'll have to kill me, Peter. You'll have to kill us all."

Querrin seemed on the verge of angry tears.

"Damn you!"

Lawrence shrugged.

"You're no gambler, Peter. And the stakes are a little too high. You should have stopped and considered before you plotted Roger's death."

Querrin's face had crumpled.

He whispered:

"I didn't want him to die." His tone was thin with hysteria. "It was this room—this room, I tell you. There's evil here... I hate you, old Tom Querrin! You made me do it all."

Lawrence said brutally:

"You're crazy."

Querrin's nostrils pinched.

He breathed:

"That night—when I told them the story—Audrey and Roger, here together, I felt evil seep into me... I saw— how easy it would be—."

"To murder your brother, and inherit his fortune."

Peter jerked back like a man from a whip lash.

He cried:

"It was his own fault! Audrey and I—we pleaded with him...    He wouldn't change his mind. He insisted on keeping—his appointment... He wouldn't remove —the temptation."

Lawrence said:

"You hadn't the nerve to kill him yourself. So you called on—."

He gestured wordlessly.

Querrin's mouth hardened.

"You know, then?"

"Oh, yes." Lawrence was casual. "I knew within eighteen hours of Roger's death." He laughed. "You didn't believe that fairy story I spun upstairs?"

He grinned at Russell Craig. "Sorry, sir. I've been blackening your character dreadfully."

"Shut up, damn you." Querrin's face was white. "I've nothing to lose. I shall hang anyway, whether I kill you or not."

"You fool." His accomplice was bitter and scornful. "Get that confession, and don't waste time. It's enough to hang us both."

Querrin snarled.

"You signed it, blast your eyes."

"I hadn't any choice."

Lawrence smiled gently.

He said:

"You may as well give yourselves up."

Peter's mouth thinned.

"Give me those papers."

"Take them, you fool." His confederate cried out with rage and pain. "If I could only get up—aaah! My leg...."

"I'm sorry," said Lawrence, with an odd but genuine concern. "But you shouldn't have struggled. You crippled yourself."

Querrin shouted:

"Be quiet!"

166

The pistol shook wildly in his hand.

He backed towards the window.

His accomplice gasped madly:

"You poor fool! Don't give up now. Keep your head. Shoot him—get the papers—come back!"

Querrin seemed to shrink.

Lawrence said:

"It's no use. Querrin can't kill in cold blood."

He thought, with gratitude:

"I've won. Thank God."

Peter whispered:

"I have—to get away."

Lawrence said nothing, and Craig kept silent, but there was another and vicious reply.

"They'll hang you, Querrin."

"What?"

"You can't get away like this, leaving all the evidence. . . . They'll find you and they'll hang you. They'll come into your cell one morning, and bind your arms, and stand you on the trap—."

"You—."

Peter's voice was a shriek. He ran forward blindly, and lashed his tormentor's cheek with the muzzle of the gun.

"Stop that!"

Lawrence sprang towards him and grabbed his arm.

Querrin, with desperate strength, hurled him back.

He crouched like an animal.

Lawrence, sprawled back across the table, saw death in Peter's eyes.

His finger tightened on the trigger....

A new voice ordered:

"Drop that pistol."

Querrin's eyes lost focus.

Then he turned his head slowly, and stared at the uniformed man who had stepped in through the windows.

The policeman was holding a revolver.

Lawrence said quietly:

"I'm glad you arrived, Inspector."

Nobody moved.

A tear ran down Peter's cheek.

Then he twisted the gun in his hand, and they heard the sound as the muzzle smashed against his teeth.

Then his finger jerked hard on the trigger, and the shot blasted cruelly through the silence.

For one horrible second, Peter Querrin stood upright, his face a distortion in pulp and blood.

Then he crashed on the floor like a broken doll.

Lawrence straightened slowly.

He looked down with compassion.

He said:

"It's over now."

"Not quite," returned Hazlitt grimly. He stepped back to the heavy, shrouding curtain, and pushed it aside. Daylight flooded the room once more, driving out the shadows.

The Inspector called:

"Sergeant, call Doctor Tyssen. Then"—his gaze flicked back over his shoulder—"make arrangements. We have a prisoner."

He walked back, skirting the dead man with distaste.

He said:

"I have a warrant—."

Peter's accomplice said wearily:

"Let's skip the formalities. I want a word with Mr. Lawrence."

Hazlitt hesitated.

Lawrence nodded. "There's no more danger."

"Very well." The Inspector thrust the revolver in the young man's hands. "Take this."

He went out. Craig followed, a handkerchief over his mouth.

Lawrence asked:

"Does the leg still pain you?"

"No." The other said abruptly:

"Give me a smoke."

"Surely." Lawrence opened his case, and eased a cigarette between the other's lips. The revolver he slipped, carelessly enough, into the pocket of his coat.

His companion inquired:

"You aren't afraid I'll try to grab the gun?"

"No. You can't escape with the police outside. And you're not thinking of suicide."

"That's right." The conflict resolved, the two had dropped back to their old relationship. "I'm not such a fool as Querrin."

There was a moment of silence, then—.

"You haven't beaten me yet."

Lawrence shrugged. "I have your confession."

"Forced," said the other triumphantly. "I shall deny everything. I won't go down without a struggle."

Lawrence lifted one shoulder.

"Let's not wrangle. You'll have a fair trial. The rest is up to the jury."

"And the hangman." The other laughed bitterly. "What's the use. I'm too honest to fool myself. And Peter's left me to face things alone."

Lawrence asked, suddenly:

"Why did you do it?"

"Who can say? I was bored, and frustrated... I've never shirked—a calculated risk. And you said yourself, the stakes were high. It was a gamble, that's all. It might have paid me well."

Lawrence said softly:

"I'm sorry."

He looked curiously at the man for whom he still had a genuine liking.

"You needn't be," replied the other. "I challenged you, in effect, when I murdered Querrin and Turner. You were too clever for me. I've no grudge against you."

He grinned, briefly.

"Though I admit it's humiliating—."

He paused, then—.

"To be beaten by a damned amateur," finished Sergeant Hardinge.

"Peter Querrin," said Lawrence slowly, "wasn't a very efficient criminal. And he wasn't a good actor. You and I,"—he stared at the burly man opposite—"both knew he was nervous, tense, and scared."

"Yes." Stephen Castle scowled. "His emotions were genuine. We misinterpreted them, that's all."

His voice was bitter.

Lawrence felt, once more, the stirring of an old anger. After a moment's hesitation, he remarked sanely:

"We can't blame ourselves now. We were fooled, yes. But we couldn't know that by guarding Roger we were exposing him to danger."

The Chief Inspector seemed tired.

He said:

"You'd better explain from the beginning."

Lawrence nodded. The two men were sitting in the library. The young man swept his hands over his smooth blond hair and began.

"Peter was weak, and entirely dependent on his brother. He must have resented Roger's wealth and authority for a long time."

Steve commented:

"Roger was my friend, but he could be arrogant and overbearing. He wasn't an easy man to understand."

Lawrence went on:

"When his brother decided to marry, Peter saw a fortune going out of his reach. He might even have lost his home, since newly weds usually," Algy chuckled, "prefer to be alone.

"However, he didn't think of murder till Roger advanced his crazy plan of keeping the Querrins' traditional appointment. To do Peter justice, I'll admit he tried to dissuade his brother—he was scared of his own capacity for evil.

"Roger was obstinate, and Peter couldn't resist the temptation. He made up his mind that his brother had to die.

"He knew Roger had made no will, so the wealth would pass to him. That money was Hardinge's bait."

Algy was careful to avoid his old friend's eyes.

He continued:

We shall never know their exact relationship. It's safe to say Hardinge and Peter were fairly intimate. They must have known each other's characters."

Castle shrugged. "We can investigate. Not that it matters now."

Lawrence mused:

"The Sergeant knew Roger hardly at all. Their first informal meeting was on the night Hardinge came to kill."

Castle swore. His professional pride was hurt.

Lawrence said mildly: "Policemen are human beings, with human faults and vices. The Sergeant was bored and frustrated, with a dead end job in a tiny village. He had few hopes of promotion and no way of making money.

"When Peter suggested his crazy scheme—timidly enough, I imagine—John Hardinge seized his opportunity. From that moment, the Sergeant took charge. Young Querrin was only the pawn. There was no fear of a double cross. Hardinge was the stronger man. He knew that once Roger was dead, he could force from Peter as big a share of the Querrin fortune as he wished.

"He began to make plans. The first essential was to provide Peter with an unbreakable alibi.

"That's where you came in, Steve. You arrived here for a holiday, and they tagged you the perfect witness.

"Peter, plagued with doubts and indecision, yet determined to see things through to the bitter end, told you his colourful ghost story. You agreed to help, and what's more"—Algy grinned slightly—"Querrin managed to persuade you it was your own idea to call in Sergeant Hardinge."

Castle looked glum.

Lawrence smiled at him gently, and went on:

"They jockeyed you into position. In all good faith, you agreed to stand guard with Peter—at the end of the passage—while the Sergeant waited outside in the gardens.

"That was a necessity. The whole illusion was to depend on it.

"Right! Everything was settled, and then suddenly you were recalled to the Yard.

"That nearly wrecked their plans. The whole scheme required an irreproachable witness to swear to Peter's alibi. Querrin was, after all, the obvious suspect. They had to establish his innocence.

"You dropped out. They looked round for a substitute. In all innocence, you told Peter to call on me."

Algy's eyes had lost their kindness.

"I was his last hope. Truly, his brother's life depended on my answer.

"If I refused to go with Peter, he would have to abandon his plans. ...

172

I had only to stay in London."

He smacked his hands together angrily.

"But for me, Roger would still be alive."

Castle's mouth twisted.

He said:

"I made you go. I'm sorry."

Lawrence lifted one shoulder.

"I fell into the trap, as you did. Querrin couldn't hide his feelings. He was near collapse, through fright and worry... But it wasn't concern for his brother. It was fear of the hangman."

Even as he spoke, Algy realized that Peter had also been scared he would lose his only opportunity to bring about his brother's death.

He shivered, with sick reproach.

He said abruptly:

"I don't like to think of the dark conflicts in Querrin's mind. Let's say he fooled us, and leave it at that.

"I went with him to Bristley.

"As you had done before me, I smelled both security and danger. So, with relief, he handed me over to his accomplice.

"Hardinge was a very different man. He was cool and efficient. He was also, though I didn't know it then, completely ruthless."

Lawrence grinned. "Oddly enough, I liked him on sight. I still do, come to think of it."

He rubbed his cheek. "The Sergeant was a man without passion. The elder Querrin was to him no more than a cipher—an obstacle to be removed."

He went on quickly:

"Hardinge eased me gently into position. I had no suspicion—."

"Don't blame yourself for that," grunted the Chief Inspector. "He fooled me too. He had already persuaded me to stand guard inside the house. You simply took my place."

"Even so, I could still have wrecked their schemes, merely by altering the existing arrangements. But"— his face was grim—"I didn't. And Peter tricked me again.

"I let him help me test the window in the passage. He grabbed the opportunity of upturning an old wooden box directly beneath the sill."

Steve looked puzzled. Lawrence said:

"I'll explain later. That box had to be in position. Unwittingly, I gave him the chance of averting all suspicion."

"It was unlikely," supplied Steve, "that the police would ask questions about it anyway."

"So they believed." Lawrence closed his eyes. "Let's digress for a moment.

"I don't suppose they intended to direct my attention towards old Simon. But I rattled Peter in the train, and he decided the story of Turner's dismissal would serve as a useful red herring.

"Old Simon had, in fact, been prowling round Querrin House all day. He was the only man who believed in the ghost story—and he wanted to see Roger come to grief.

"Hardinge was puzzled when he heard I had been attacked, but judged the prowler would be too scared to return. That was a bad miscalculation.

"However, he had other things on his mind. He was wondering if Peter would lose his nerve. That could mean disaster for them both. Querrin's part in the murder was small enough, but it was vital—as you'll see.

"Peter nearly cracked up when Uncle Russ got drunk and tried to join the guard. That might have spoilt everything. Still, that crisis passed, and—."

Lawrence broke off and chuckled grimly.

"And Hardinge actually told Peter, in my presence, that he didn't have to go through with the killing if he wanted to cry off."

"What!"

"In guarded language. But that's what he meant. Querrin replied: 'I can do everything I have to,' and the die was cast.

"Well, now. Roger obviously would have no suspicion of the men who'd been set to guard him.

"It was raining heavily. Soon after the elder Querrin had been left alone Hardinge left his post on the path and crossed over the flower beds, back to the house. The rain washed out his footprints once more.

"Standing on the steps, he tapped lightly on the glass panes. Roger was surprised, but he had no reason to be suspicious. He pulled back the curtains, saw who it was, and opened the french windows.

"The Sergeant, I imagine, had taken off his cape and left it under the trees. He had removed his goloshes after crossing the wet soil, so he brought no mud into the room from the gardens.

"He made some excuse to Querrin, and put the rubbers by the fire to dry.

"It wasn't long after eleven, so Roger raised no objection. It wasn't till later, when the time for his appointment drew nearer, that Querrin told the Sergeant to go.

"Hardinge stepped behind him, and stunned him with his truncheon—."

Castle pushed out a muffled curse.

"—catching him as he fell, so there would be no loud noise. He let him slip to the floor. Then he slid out the dagger from its sheath, and waited."

Lawrence settled himself more comfortably. "Much to the Sergeant's satisfaction, the rain stopped at twenty minutes to twelve. That was a stroke of luck. Previously he had intended his alibi to depend solely upon the windows which Roger had re-locked from the inside. Now he had the unmarked soil of the flower beds to back up his story.

"At ten minutes to twelve, he replaced the goloshes over his shoes—if there was any dried dirt on the soles he shook it into the embers of the fire—picked up the knife, and slid the blade into Roger's back.

"He polished the handle quickly. He didn't want to leave smudges of any kind on the hilt.

"He may have been wearing gloves—of rubber, or thin cotton—or he may have wrapped a handkerchief round his fingers. He turned out the lamp, so no light would escape into the corridor—."

Castle leaned forward attentively.

Lawrence said slowly:

"Using equal care not to obliterate Querrin's prints on the handle, he opened the door—."

"Now wait just a moment!" Steve was exasperated. "We know darn well that's impossible—."

Algy grinned sadly. He said:

"The trick's so simple I'm almost ashamed to explain it. Peter knew there was to be a new lock on that door, so when he came up to London with you, he went along to the manufacturers and bought a new key to the same type of lock—."

Castle swore.

"This key he gave to Hardinge when he arrived at the house that evening, and the Sergeant substituted it for the true key on Roger's chain after he'd knocked him senseless.

"Hardinge unlocked the door, slipped into the passage, then re-locked the door from outside.

"He went noiselessly along the corridor till he reached its solitary window. He climbed through, pulled down the sash once more, and squatted on the upturned box beneath the wide sill.

"Meanwhile, Peter and I had been waiting at the entrance to the passage. Peter had managed to manoeuvre himself into the commanding position, but even if I had looked into the corridor at the wrong moment, it's unlikely I would have seen anything in the blackness.

"Moreover, Querrin was there to divert my attention. The two conspirators were working to schedule, of course. At ten minutes to twelve, Peter began talking loudly, to cover any slight noise of movement.

"At four minutes to twelve, when he was sure his accomplice was out of the way—probably he'd caught the brief flicker of moonlight as Hardinge moved the window curtains—Peter made me go with him into the passage.

"I suggested we check the window. They had expected that.

"Peter pushed the candlestick he was carrying into my hand, turned his back, and put his own hands on the drapes. Pretending to draw them aside, he slipped the catch into position—a tiny movement which I didn't notice; his body shielded his fingers—then showed me the window securely fastened.

"Hardinge was crouched under the sill out of sight. And the candle turned the glass into a mirror, obscuring my vision still more. Besides, my attention was fixed on the catch... I hope that doesn't sound as if I'm making excuses."

"Go on," said the Chief Inspector gruffly.

Lawrence shrugged. "Then Querrin worked the same trick in reverse. I turned away. Under cover of replacing the curtains, Peter released the catch.

"We reached the door to Roger's room. It was twelve o'clock.

"The Sergeant straightened up, rested his hands on the sill, and pressed his face against the window. He screamed—."

"Oh, no!"

"Oh, yes. Russell Craig, amidst all his nonsense, said a true thing. It's very difficult to locate the course of sound, especially in the dark ... I thought at the time there was something very wrong about that evil, strangled sound. As, of course, there was. It came from behind, not in front of us.

"But Peter gave me no time for reflection. He cried out his brother's name, and the misdirection was complete.

"We smashed open the door.

"Once more, they had the devil's own luck. Roger had regained consciousness. With his last reserves of strength, he was dragging himself towards the door. The effort was too much for him. He died without speaking.

"Peter's hysteria was genuine. The narrow escape, combined with the scene of slaughter, was almost too much for him."

Lawrence paused, remembering.

"Hardinge had been waiting patiently outside. He didn't expect me to shoot open the door, but he didn't lose his head. As soon as I forced my way in, he slid open the window and dropped into the corridor. Peter had stayed in the doorway to block my view of the passage.

"Hardinge locked the window, carefully leaving no prints on the catch. Then he ran quickly along the corridor—the carpet was thick, and muffled his footfalls— through the double doors into the main hall, and then up the short passage to the side door.

"He unbolted the door and hurried through. He ran along the path skirting the house, back to his original position under the trees. He had time to put on his cape, then—."

Lawrence paused.

"I can picture him standing there under the trees, his breath soughing gustily, tensely watching the house. One hand in his pocket, perhaps, nervously fingering the key he had to replace.

"His greatest fear was that I should detect the substitution. I did, in fact, examine the chain in Roger's pocket, but"—he shrugged—"one new key is much like another, and I didn't have time to try it in the lock."

Algy smiled ruefully. "I stepped over to the windows, and signalled the Sergeant. Peter at once offered to let him in. That was to make sure that nobody else examined the side door, which was, of course, no longer locked and bolted.

"Hardinge marched along the path. He was dry when he should have been wet but his cape had been left in the rain, and he brushed against the damp leaves as well."

Lawrence grinned again. He said, with self-reproach:

"Hazlitt noticed the Sergeant was dry enough. I didn't....

"Hardinge had a nasty moment when he saw Roger's key chain spilled on the carpet. He knew I must have examined it, and promptly snapped at me for tampering with the evidence.

"That was a mistake, though I didn't spot it immediately."

"Eh?" Castle pondered. "Oh, I see. If Hardinge was the innocent man he pretended—."

"He couldn't have known I had pulled out the chain. It might have fallen from Querrin's pocket in a struggle. The Sergeant knew that wasn't the case, jumped to the correct conclusion I'd been examining the key, and gave himself away. He was quick witted, though. He saw his error and turned his remark at once. He implied he'd been referring to the curtains by the french windows.

"He had still to replace the key before we discovered that the one on the chain didn't fit. So he told me to wait in the hall, and switched keys before the Inspector arrived. The false one he slipped into his pocket to dispose of later. Any questions?"

"Yes. Where did old Simon fit into this?"

"Ah, Turner was unlucky. He couldn't keep away. Hardinge knew well enough no prowler would venture near the house while he stood guard, but once he was in the room with Roger—."

He shrugged. "Turner came closer, making those confused marks in the ground beyond the path. He heard the scream, and a little while later, saw the Sergeant hurrying back to the trees.

"Old Simon faded away discreetly. He didn't want more trouble. Unfortunately for him, he lingered too long and bumped into Hardinge as they were both leaving in the morning.

"There was a struggle, with no time for comment or explanations. Hardinge would never have arrested him if he had known what old Simon had seen. But Turner was knocked unconscious, and then we arrived, so he had no choice. He put him in a cell.

"They talked. The Sergeant couldn't afford to let the old man's story go any further. Once anybody suspected that Hardinge wasn't the impartial witness he appeared to be—."

Lawrence stopped. "Old Simon had to die."

Castle said nothing.

His friend continued:

"Hardinge found himself on dangerous ground. When Turner was killed in the police station, the Sergeant would inevitably be considered as a suspect. So he had to prove himself innocent."

"He did, too." Castle scowled. "God damn it! Argue how you like— Hardinge couldn't possibly have reached him."

"Impossibilities," replied Algy, "were the Sergeant's speciality. Once more, I was to be the dupe. He called me down to the station—."

"Wait a second. You interviewed old Simon at Hardinge's invitation. How could he risk that?"

"Don't confuse me, Steve. I'll explain in a minute. Before I analyse the second illusion, I'd better explain how I solved the first."

Castle nodded. "You weren't very explicit over the 'phone."

Lawrence linked his hands.

He said dully:

"Hardinge himself gave me the clue. It took me an hour and a half to realize its significance. In that time, another life was lost."

Castle studied his young friend sympathetically.

He said again:

"Don't blame yourself."

Lawrence looked up with a lopsided grin.

"I can only do my best... Oh, well." His tone altered. "Hardinge showed me the fingerprint analysis. Roger's prints had been found, overlying any others, on a number of objects in the room where he died—*including the bolts securing the windows.*"

He paused expectantly. Castle looked puzzled, then caught his breath.

Lawrence nodded. "Yes. I locked those windows myself. The prints you found ought to have been mine.

"Obviously then, Roger had first drawn, then re-shot the bolts after we had left him.

"Why? Clearly, to let somebody into the room from the gardens.

"That could not have been done without Hardinge's knowledge. Therefore his evidence was false.

"Now, Roger wasn't a fool. He knew we were guarding him. He would let nobody into the room, without raising the alarm, whom he didn't know and trust. Only three men besides himself had any business in that place, at that time.

"Peter and I were in the hall. That left only Hardinge. So it was reasonable to suppose the Sergeant was Querrin's visitor."

Castle nodded agreement. He murmured: "Hardinge probably made some excuse about the weather."

"Uh huh. Asked for shelter till the rain stopped. Something of the sort... To continue:

"Once inside, Hardinge could easily dispose of his victim." Lawrence was deliberately banal. He was trying to reduce the blood and the pain to the comfortable anonymity of a newspaper report. "But how could he escape? Through the windows? No. He couldn't hocus the bolts, and he couldn't get back to the path without leaving footprints.

"So—." Lawrence shrugged. "He must have gone through the door. There was only one key, so he must have removed it from Roger's body. Yet I had found it myself, still in the dead man's pocket.

"I saw my mistake. I had found a key. I had only assumed it was genuine... A fake, then. Yet the police must have tested it in the lock. Therefore the real key must have been replaced before they arrived.

"Only the Sergeant had a chance to do that. I had stayed in the room myself, till I left to meet Hazlitt. Nobody could have switched keys while I was watching.

"Next question: How had Hardinge vanished from the corridor? He didn't go through the double doors. He wasn't hiding in the passage. Therefore he must have gone out of the window.

"How could he, without leaving footprints? There was only one answer. He had stood on the box outside.

"That brought me up against another impossibility. The window had been locked... I had examined it myself.

"I reviewed the exact circumstances, and saw how Peter could have—must have—fooled me.

"It all fitted in. Once I was sure of the two men's guilt, every mystery was explained."

Lawrence rubbed his cheek. "There was another point. Put yourself in the Sergeant's place."

Steve looked surprised.

Lawrence went on:

"I set you to guard Roger Querrin. You're waiting in the gardens. You hear a scream, then three shots. The man in your charge is in danger. Quick, now! What do you do?"

"I run forward to the windows, to see what's—."

Castle's voice died slowly. His mouth stayed open. Lawrence said with satisfaction:

"Exactly. You're there to save Roger from harm, not to preserve evidence....

"Naturally, Hardinge wouldn't step on to the flower beds. He didn't want to spoil the illusion. But no innocent person would have had the superhuman control— or the callousness—to ignore an obvious cry for help.

"Only a guilty man could have any reason to stay where he was."

Castle mused: "The curtains were drawn, and he could see nothing. Or he might have been afraid—."

He stopped. "No, those objections are too flimsy. You're right, Algy. Any man's immediate reaction would have been to run forward."

Lawrence inclined his head. "I had just about reached this point in my reflections when I was faced with the news of Turner's death. Frankly, I was stymied.

"It seemed only reasonable to assume that Hardinge had killed him. Yet my own evidence proved it impossible.

"I span round in circles. And then I saw the truth.

"Between the hours of four and six there were only four men in the station: myself, Hardinge, Craig and Turner.

"We had accounted for the movements of three.

"*We knew nothing of the fourth.*"

Castle smacked his knee, suddenly.

"Burn it! Old Simon himself—."

"Right. I knew he'd been in his cell at a quarter past four. I had also found him there at six o'clock. He had been a prisoner, so we automatically assumed he had stayed where he was. Yet who had locked him in? Sergeant Hardinge...."

Lawrence closed his eyes.

"The Sergeant told us he found Turner in his cell at seven minutes to six. There was nothing to prove it."

Castle muttered something.

Algy went on:

"Since two vital pieces of Hardinge's evidence were not confirmed, it was possible to suppose that old Simon had walked out of his cell.

"Now, the door from the passage opens into the Charge Room. Turner's only opportunity to slip through it was during the brief period when I stood on the porch outside the station."

The Chief Inspector groaned. "You don't have to go on. Obviously, old Simon hid himself in the Sergeant's living quarters."

Lawrence said:

"Let's go back to the beginning.

"Turner believed Roger died because he meddled with the supernatural. He didn't realize Hardinge was a murderer. He thought the Sergeant guilty only of neglecting his duty.

"So when he found himself under arrest, he told Hardinge he needed help. He threatened he'd tell the Inspector how the Sergeant had left his post—."

Castle interrupted. "Turner didn't see Hardinge go into the room, surely?"

"No. But he knew nobody was guarding the french windows at midnight. When he saw the Sergeant hurrying back a little while later, he probably assumed that he'd wandered off carelessly."

Lawrence cleared his throat. "Turner knew he'd almost certainly be convicted of assault, even if he persuaded Hardinge to drop one of the charges. So he decided to escape.

"He demanded the Sergeant's help. Hardinge pretended to agree.

"He said: Look here. I don't want my superiors to know I neglected my duty. But I shall get into worse trouble if it's known I let you escape. You'll have to protect me.

"So he told the prisoner his plan. Turner swallowed the bait.

"Hardinge 'phoned me, coolly suggesting I provide Peter with an alibi."

The Inspector balled his fist. He growled angrily.

Lawrence said:

"Querrin had to be protected. He was the Sergeant's meal ticket. And I don't imagine he knew then what new danger was threatening.

"I went down to the station. I talked to old Simon.

"Hardinge had warned him to be careful. Even so, he had to cue him twice during the interview.

"We left the old man in his cell. Hardinge pretended to lock the door, but did nothing more than rattle the key in the lock.

"We went back to the Charge Room. As soon as we left the corridor, Turner slipped out of his cell and waited behind the door, listening to our talk.

"As soon as he heard us go out on the porch—Hardinge was speaking rather loudly, as a signal—he hurried through the Charge Room and hid himself in the Sergeant's quarters.

"Then Hardinge 'remembered' my gun, and led me back into the station."

"Wait a minute." Castle was scowling horribly. "Suppose you'd made no move to leave?"

"Then the Sergeant would have taken me into his rooms while Turner slipped out from the corridor and hid himself behind the communicating door. Then the Sergeant would have accompanied me back to the Charge Room, talking still—to divert my attention—and while our backs were turned, old Simon would have slid round the open door into Hardinge's living quarters."

Castle thought for a moment, then nodded. "A dangerous plan. But it might have worked."

"Hardinge wasn't afraid of a calculated risk. And he coached his victim well."

Steve asked:

"How did he fool old Simon?"

"I imagine he told him something like this. Turner was to stay hidden in his rooms till after dark. Then the Sergeant would divert the constable's attention while old Simon slipped out of the station. Thus the prisoner would appear to have escaped while Shaw was on duty, absolving Hardinge from blame."

Castle nodded. "The old man, I'm told, was rather stupid. It wouldn't be hard to fool him with a plausible story."

"Uh huh. Hardinge filled out the yarn with circumstantial detail. Turner suspected nothing.

"He hid himself in the Sergeant's bedroom. Russell Craig arrived unexpectedly. Hardinge, a born opportunist, suggested making tea.

"He put a kettle on the stove. He also stepped into the bedroom and stunned Turner with his truncheon."

Lawrence interrupted himself. "Don't let me mislead you. The Sergeant did nothing he hadn't already planned. But Craig's presence was a help. It strengthened his alibi, and distracted my attention.

"Leaving old Simon stretched out on the floor, Hardinge came back to the Charge Room. When he left again a few minutes later, he went back to the bedroom, crouched over Turner, and choked him."

There was a tiny silence.

Lawrence mused:

"He'd already prepared some tea in a thermos flask. He poured it into three cups, washed the flask quickly, poured away the boiling water from the kettle, then rejoined Craig and me."

Algy grinned. "Uncle Russ was propounding his theories, and gave Hardinge a momentary scare. He thought we'd guessed the truth. Even then, he didn't lose his head. When, like a sap, I sympathized, he didn't lose the chance. His 'unhappy position' was to be his eventual excuse for resigning from the police force."

Castle growled again.

Lawrence continued:

"At a quarter to six, he got rid of me. As soon as I left, he carried the old man's body back to the cell. He turned to the door and wiped over the lock and handle quickly, to remove Turner's fingerprints."

"What about the scratches inside the lock?"

"I imagine he'd made those previously—and not necessarily with a picklock. An old piece of wire could have made those marks."

Castle frowned. "Why did he bother with the fake at all?"

"Because he was in charge of the keys. He preferred us to think the door was forced… He didn't want to puzzle us with a second sealed room. He didn't even want to confront us with another impossible crime. He simply wanted to provide himself with an alibi."

Lawrence shrugged. "He 'explained' the murder later. That was a mistake, since he had already told us he had found the cell door open. But he hadn't foreseen Shaw's evidence, and anyway—."

"He wanted to confuse you," supplied the Chief Inspector. "So he spun you his yarn about hands at the window. He didn't care whether you accepted the theory or not."

Lawrence nodded. "The point's not important… As things worked out, the killing was proved 'impossible'. But since Hazlitt was convinced of Hardinge's innocence, the Sergeant didn't mind much."

Algy sighed. "There's not a great deal more. Hardinge arranged old Simon's body in much the same position in which it had been lying on the bedroom floor. He didn't want his evidence contradicted by the condition we call 'post mortem lividity'."

The young man finished quickly:

"The stage was set. He straightened up with shaking hands—by this time the strain was telling—and rushed after me into the street.

"Since his alibi depended on the time of Turner's death, he wanted the old man's body examined immediately."

Lawrence gestured. "You know the rest."

Castle blew out his cheeks.

He commented inadequately:

"A complicated affair."

"Not really." Lawrence thumbed the angle of his jaw. "Hardinge had an eye for detail. For example, when he returned the key to Roger's chain, he remembered to press Querrin's fingers over the surface."

"Don't tell me how clever he was, burn it!" The Chief Inspector was irascible. "Tell me how you trapped him."

Lawrence looked unhappy.

He said, slowly:

"Unlike most hunters, I have no taste for the kill. In most cases, I tell you my theories, and leave the police to prove them."

His face set grimly.

"I'm not proud of myself. But this time, I was angry." He shaded his eyes.

"Two men had died. I should have saved them. Perhaps—." He laughed dryly. "Perhaps my pride was hurt. And it's so easy to confuse revenge with justice. For the first time, I wanted the killers to die."

Castle said sharply:

"You did no more than your duty." Lawrence lifted one shoulder.

He said abruptly:

"I took Russell Craig into my confidence. He agreed to help."

There was much that was left unsaid. Uncle Russ, dragged from his bed in the early hours of the morning, had been hard to convince.

Yet Craig soon realized he owed the conspirators a grudge. They had robbed him of a comfortable home, since he had hoped to stay with his niece when she married.

Besides, the old rogue was pleased at the thought of appearing as chief witness in a sensational murder trial. There were, he reflected, commercial possibilities in the situation....

Lawrence preferred not to analyse Craig's motives.

He went on:

"I talked to Colonel Johnson. I needed his co-operation. And, anyway, I wanted to save his face. Hardinge was a member of the County Police. It was only right that they should take the credit for his capture.

"Then I interviewed the Sergeant himself and told him to stay by the telephone.

"I went back to Querrin House. Uncle Russ was waiting. We went up to my room to talk over the final arrangements.

"Craig had already warned Audrey to keep out of the way. Peter, luckily for us, was also in his room.

"Craig 'phoned Hardinge—using my name—and asked him to come out to the house. He met him on the drive, and took him into the room where Roger died.

"I'd been watching from my window. I staged a little comedy for Querrin's benefit."

Lawrence smiled ruefully. "I coaxed open the wound on my forehead, then smeared some more blood over my temple from a cut finger."

Castle interjected: "You also smeared the ferrule of Craig's stick."

"Yes. When I saw Uncle Russ take charge of Sergeant Hardinge, I attracted Peter's attention by crashing backwards over a chair." He winced. "I was too damned enthusiastic... Oh, well.

"I told Querrin that Craig had killed his brother."

Seeing the question in the Chief Inspector's eye, the young man explained:

"My whole object was to confuse Peter and make him lose his head. He was the weaker partner. I thought he'd crack more readily.

"I gave him no time to think. He didn't realize my talk of wills and motives was absolute nonsense." Algy laughed, shortly. "He nearly called my bluff.

"I said that Craig could only have known the fire in the grate had been reduced to embers"—he drew breath— "by being in the room himself.

"That was silly. As Peter nearly admitted, he had told Craig that himself, while waiting to be interviewed by the police. Fortunately for me, Querrin thought he might as well leave me labouring under a delusion."

"Half a mo'," growled Castle. "Why did Peter go out of his way to tell Craig a minor point like that?"

"He didn't." Lawrence was patient. "But Hazlitt herded all his suspects together in the drawing-room. Naturally, they talked. Peter, besides myself, was the only eye-witness. I daresay Uncle Russ indulged in his incorrigible curiosity, and questioned Querrin thoroughly. That's how he found out about the fire."

"Skip it," Castle yawned. "It's a trivial matter."

"Uh huh. I showed Peter the drawer—which I'd forced myself—and told him my gun was missing. Then I rushed him down the stairs.

"Meanwhile, Craig was playing the part of a blackmailer with gusto."

"Was there any truth in the story he told Hardinge?"

"Not a scrap. I primed him with every detail. . . . The shots I fired might very well have roused Craig in time to catch sight of the Sergeant running out from the passage. Actually," Algy grinned, "Uncle Russ remained wrapped in his drunken slumbers."

He rubbed his cheek. "The story seemed convincing. Hardinge believed it. He signed the confession I'd typed myself."

Algy's voice died.

Castle was gentle. "Well?"

Lawrence sighed. "By this time, Peter was nearly off his head. I planned to confront him with his accomplice. Before I could move, Hardinge made a desperate attack on Uncle Russ. Craig was taken off guard. The pistol I'd given him was no protection.

"You know the rest. I defeated the Sergeant, but lost the gun to Querrin.

"Fortunately, Hazlitt and his men were waiting in the grounds. As I'd arranged with the Chief Constable: as soon as I went into the room with Peter, the police moved up to the windows.

"They heard Querrin's confession. And the Inspector saved my life."

He finished dully:

"He didn't save Peter's."

Castle grunted.

Lawrence stood up. He said, more cheerfully:

"That's all, Steve. You can send your man to trial. But," he warned, "Hardinge is tough. He'll fight you, Steve. He'll fight you like the devil."

The Chief Inspector scowled. "He's finished."

"No. He'll put all the blame on Querrin. He'll claim his own confession invalid, since he signed it at gunpoint."

Lawrence repeated:

"He'll fight you like the devil."

Castle's face was stern.

He said, grimly:

"He'll hang."


"Lawrence, my boy!"

Russell Craig hailed the young man as Algy strolled out of the library. Lawrence looked about him and saw the old rogue standing in the passage with one hand clasped round his niece's slim waist.

Lawrence smiled at them both.

"Hallo, Audrey. Hallo, sir. You're none the worse for your experiences this morning, I hope?"

"Indeed, no. I enjoyed them all," lied the old rascal unblushingly. "Though I confess I was relieved to see the Inspector's timely arrival with a revolver."

"You'd never believe," grinned Algy, "the trouble I had persuading the Chief Constable to arm his police."

The girl moved suddenly. She brushed aside their talk impatiently, and said with soft appeal:

"Algy. I'd like to talk to you."

"Of course." He took her arm, and they walked into the drawing-room. She sat down.

Lawrence straddled a chair and gazed at her with polite inquiry.

She said painfully:

"I suppose—I should thank you—for trapping the men who killed my—."

Lawrence shook his head. He said gently:

"No, Audrey. You can't thank me for sending two men to their deaths. We're not made that way, you and I."

He paused. "The man you loved was murdered. But you must think of the future. You can't let your life be corroded with bitterness and hate."

The girl's lips trembled. Then she hid her face in her hands and sobbed.

Lawrence watched her with distress in his lazy blue eyes.

Then he stood up, and gazed down at her shaking shoulders.

He dropped a hand on her sleek red-brown hair and stroked it gently. She looked up with tears streaking her cheeks.

She said:

"Roger died because I loved him."

She cut short his protest with bitter self-reproach.

"No, no. Don't lie to me. You warned me it might be better to continue believing my fiancé died because he challenged the powers of another world. I didn't know what you meant then. But I know now.

"Roger was killed because he wanted to marry me. It's as simple as that. I loved him. And I sent him to his death."

Lawrence replied quietly:

"You're wrong to blame yourself. Roger wouldn't wish it."

He hesitated.

He said, with sudden decision:

"I told you the truth might hurt you. It might also console you."

There was a question in her lovely grey-green eyes.

Algy went on quietly:

"I have something to tell you. It won't help you now, because the pain's too strong. But listen to me. Listen carefully.

"Hasn't it occurred to you, Audrey, that it's a queer brand of evil"—he paused uncertainly—"which makes a man so twisted he plots his brother's death?"

The girl's lips parted.

Lawrence said dully:

"Perhaps that was the curse of the Querrins. Perhaps that was why young Martin turned on old Tom with fury, all those years ago.

"Perhaps the old man told his son that their blood was tainted with madness. Perhaps that was the secret. A scarlet thread of insanity in the weave of a Querrin's soul.

"So one Querrin stabs his son, and another kills his brother.

"But remember. Killers or victims—the taint was in them all."

There was a long silence.

Then the girl said queerly:

"You're right. What you have told me—it doesn't help me now."

Her voice dropped to a whisper.

"But I think—one day—it might help me, very much...."

Lawrence left her.

Craig was waiting outside. He caught the young man's arm, and asked eagerly: "Is she all right?"

Lawrence responded mildly:

"I think so."

Uncle Russ attempted to pass him. Algy laid a warning hand on the old rogue's sleeve.

He murmured:

"Don't speak to her now. She would rather be alone."

"Very well, my boy."

The two men walked away together.

Craig said suddenly:

"Audrey is very precious to me."

He spoke sincerely, then his instinct for self-dramatization came to the fore again. He said tragically:

"I'm an old man. There is no one else—to care for me. "

Lawrence laughed out loud.

He said rudely:

"Don't you believe it."

"Hey?" The old rogue was thrown off balance.

Algy pursued:

"You're a marked man, Uncle Russ. You may as well give up."

"My boy. I don't follow—"

Lawrence said, with amusement:

"Girls are often attracted to—older men. And one young lady has already demonstrated her affection for you."

Craig looked nonplussed.

"You don't mean—."

"Uhhuh. Susan York." Algy chuckled. "She tried to vamp me last night. And why? Because she wanted me to keep you out of trouble with the police."

He clapped a hand on the old rogue's shoulder.

Uncle Russ turned pink.

Lawrence grinned.

"Too bad," he sympathized. "It seems you're caught at last."

Craig squared his shoulders.

"My boy," he returned expansively, "I am a gentleman. I shall accept my destiny." And he strolled off, jauntily.

The blond-haired young man gazed out the window of his bedroom and let his thoughts wander idly. Then he sighed, and returned to his packing. He thought:

It's less than three days since the Querrins came into my life. And now they're both dead.

He tugged on the zipper viciously.

His mouth was dry with defeat. Hazlitt had told him that the police had discovered traces of Simon Turner's fingerprints in Hardinge's bedroom. Another nail in the Sergeant's coffin....

Lawrence shrugged into his raincoat, then jammed on his hat.

He didn't feel proud. He had brought a murderer to justice, yet blamed himself for failing to prevent his crimes.

He laughed wryly. He thought:

Audrey and I. We're a pair. Is it some sort of conceit which makes our consciences so tender?

He went on thinking about the girl.

Somewhere below him, a horn blasted shrilly. Lawrence picked up his bag and hurried out.

... He stood for a moment on the steps, looking down at the car parked in the drive.

Castle cranked down the window and stared out.

He called:

"Come on, Algy. I want to get back to London before nightfall. Burn it, I only hired this car for a day."

Lawrence nodded. He pulled open the rear door and pitched his bag on the seat.

He gazed back at Querrin House. The figure of a girl appeared at the open door.

The young man's jaw tightened. A thin flush crept up behind his cheeks.

It was as if he had seen her for the first time. He breathed:

"Audrey...."

Then he slammed the car door shut and ran towards her, up the steps.

He seized her gently by the elbows.

He was very conscious of her loveliness.

"Audrey, my dear. I can't leave you like this. You're alone—and I'm lonely too."

He was clumsy and gauche, but he didn't care. He stumbled on: incoherent, but painfully sincere.

The girl said nothing in return, but emotion welled up round the grief in her grey-green eyes. She drew a deep breath; and there was exquisite beauty in the moulding of her firm young breasts.

"Algy—I—."

He pressed his mouth to hers.

Their heartbeats met and mingled. Lawrence's hands slid over the graceful contours of her hips. The warmth of their bodies was the languor and the sweetness of an innocent intimacy.

He felt her lips open under his. Their tongues met in a long French kiss. Then she pushed him away and cried out desperately:

"It's no use, Algy. It's no use!" She blinked back the tears.

She said, gently:

"Let's not be foolish. You don't love me, and I don't love you."

"Audrey—."

"No, my dear. I belong to Roger still, and you—." She hesitated. "You belong to the lady you've been seeking."

Algy smiled at her tenderly.

He put up his hand and smoothed back a soft tendril of hair which had wisped over her ear. Then he kissed her again, without passion.

He said, softly:

"Good-bye."

She watched him go.

Then, as she had done before, she whispered quickly:

"I hope you find her soon...."

The words were a sad farewell.


THE END

# APPENDIX

# Letter from Derek Smith to Doug Greene

In 1980, Douglas Greene wrote to Derek Smith, whom he had known for some years, regarding what he considered to be a weakness in the story

The author's entire reply is reproduced below, minus a list of British Carr books he had found for Doug (page numbers refer to the Thriller Book Club edition):

"14 Crescent Lane
Clapham Park
London SW49PU                                                    1st. June 1980

Dear Doug,
          Thanks for your letter, which came as a welcome distraction at a very worrying time. I'm glad you enjoyed WHISTLE UP THE DEVIL, which was intended as a light-hearted "homage" to both John Dickson Carr and Clayton Rawson, though in the event I was too diffident to send it to either of them.

You have put your finger on the one big mistake in the novel, which has given me inward qualms since I first saw the book in proof—and you are, incidentally, the first person to point it out! I am not quite so bad as Raymond Chandler who, when asked who killed the chauffeur in THE BIG SLEEP, is reputed to have replied, "Damned if I know!"

I have an explanation for the point about the unmarked ground and the rain, which is implied in chapter 10, quote one: "Previously he had intended his alibi to depend solely upon the windows which Roger had re-locked from the inside. Now he had the unmarked snow of the flower beds to back up his story." (Page 202)*. Quote two: "But no innocent person would have had the superhuman control—or the callousness—to ignore an obvious cry for help... Any man's immediate reaction would have been to run forward." (Page 209)*.

Since I foolishly neglected to spell the explanation out, I'm glad of the opportunity to write it down now -- I think I'll pop a copy of this letter into my file copy for future reference. Here goes:

The rain provided an unplanned chance to pile on an extra impossibility.

Had the weather been dry, Hardinge would have (literally) covered his tracks in this fashion: He would have made his way across the unplanted flowerbeds as described on page 65*, leaving a single line of footprints. When Lawrence had left the haunted room, leaving Roger Querrin alone, Harding would have crossed and re-crossed the flowerbeds a few times in the same line, messing up his own footprints—his excuse being that he was periodically getting to close quarters, watching and listening outside the French windows and making sure that Roger had come to no harm. Then he would have persuaded his victim to let him into the room, as described on page 201*, and proceeded to kill as planned. After the crime (midnight) he would have made his way back to his official position under the trees and waited for Lawrence to break into the room. When he heard the noise of this happening, he would once again have crossed the flowerbeds and would have been waiting immediately outside the french windows for Lawrence to look. He would of course have claimed to have heard the scream, to say nothing of the noise of Lawrence's forced entry, and so he had naturally come up to the windows again to find out what was happening. There would be one less line of footprints than there would have been, but since he had effectively trampled the soil going backwards and forwards a few times, it's very unlikely that would be noticed. The locked french windows would have seemed to prove his story and his alibi.

Like the Sergeant, I was a bit too tricky here for my own good. Were I plotting the novel now, I would cut most of the "footprints in the flowerbed" stuff out and have a flagged pathway outside the french windows, which would be much more natural anyway, leading over to the trees.

I think that clears it up. I don't mind leaving psychological loose ends, but hate matters of fact to go unexplained.

About Algy Lawrence himself you are, also, absolutely correct. He is a somewhat shadowy and unconvincing figure, I was in danger of ending up with exactly the sort of detective I don't like—what Nicholas Blake defined as: "as undistinguished as a piece of blotting-paper, absorbing the reaction of his subjects; a shallow mirror... a pure camera-eye." What I had intended was a developing portrait of a young idealist, highly intelligent, yet rather naive and slightly sentimental—a romantic who would eventually be caught in the trap of his own sensibilities.

Somewhere in my papers is a terrible handwritten piece of juvenilia (I was about seventeen at the time) which covers the end of what I had hoped would be a mini-series of three or four books (only the second got written). Since my own taste in detectives is much the same as Uncle Russ's—wayward, arrogant, eccentric and infallible—to which I would add "slightly comic," I think now my work would have been more of a commercial proposition if I'd abandoned my original intention and made Uncle Russ himself the detective in subsequent tales... though the line between blundering and genuine detection is very difficult to tread. Something between Darlington's Mr. Cronk and Webb's Mr. Pendlebury would be best I suppose.

I'm quite a fan of Judge Dee, so I'd certainly be interested in your van Gulik material. Back in the early days of ITV there was a dramatisation of the "murderess who died and believes herself in hell" episode from DEE GOON AN (with Donald Wolfit as the Judge) but a later series with another actor was not nearly so successful.

I'm keeping my fingers crossed about your John Dickson Carr volume [The Door to Doom] to say nothing of the projected radio play collection [The Dead Sleep Lightly]. I'd like to comment at length, but am afraid I'll have to leave that for a later letter.

To get back to my personal affairs, I'm having a bad time at the moment as my poor old mother is ill in hospital and I'm spending most of my free time at her bedside to encourage her. So I haven't been able to make my usual pilgrimages through the London bookshops.

Meanwhile, cheerio and very best wishes, Derek"

---

## Letter from Derek Smith to Tony Medawar (extract)

Another friend of Derek's, Tony Medawar, was asked to make changes to his copy as follows, both to page 209*.

Replace the following text:

Castle mused: "The curtains were drawn and he could see nothing. Or he might have been afraid—." He stopped. "No, those explanations are too flimsy. You're right, Algy. Any man's immediate reaction would have been to run forward." Lawrence inclined his head.

by

Castle asked: "What would he have done if there had been no rain to wash out his footprints?"

Lawrence shrugged. "My guess is this: Hardinge would have walked to and from the french windows three or four times, ostensibly to peer in through a crack in the curtains to check on Roger's safety, but really to churn up the ground in one straight line, preparing for his final dash across when the alarm was given. Of course, there would have been one less line of footprints returning than there should have been, but it's unlikely that would be noticed."

These changes have not been included in this current edition.

*Editor's note: Pages 65, 201, 202 and 209 in the Thriller Book Club edition correspond to pp 63, 174, 175 and 180 respectively in the LRI edition.

# COME TO PADDINGTON FAIR

*A Detective Story*

## *Derek Howe Smith*

*Dedicated to the memory of*
John Dickson Carr
Lord of the Sorcerers

# CONTENTS

# PART ONE
# THE CURTAIN RISES

# CHAPTER ONE

Richard Mervan went through the wide portals of the bank into the street outside. He was a soberly dressed man in his thirties with a thin, intelligent face and vaguely anxious eyes.

A taxi was waiting. Mervan turned towards it, taking a firmer grip on the leather case in his hand. He never enjoyed these trips to Head Office. Leaving the branch might have its advantages when the work was more than usually boring, but returning with the money invariably disturbed his peace of mind.

"It's only a few hundred pounds," the Accountant had told him airily. "You won't need an escort."

Mervan had disagreed— silently. He had gone into Head Office with a hollow sense of apprehension. It was becoming a premonition of disaster. Mervan swallowed nervously. He started towards the waiting taxi. The driver was watching him. Mervan saw alarm wash the ruddiness from the man's face and swivelled round instinctively. Through fear-blurred eyes, he glimpsed a distorted face. Something metallic gleamed in an upraised hand.

The cosh swept down viciously.

Mervan's mouth contorted in a ghastly grin. He dropped the case and brought up his arm to ward off the blow. His forearm crashed against the other's raised arm. The ugly weapon clenched in the threatening fist was arrested in mid-air. Pivoting quickly, Mervan swung his body under the stranger's armpit immediately after grabbing his arm with both hands. With one hand on the man's wrist and the other above his elbow, Mervan held on firmly. He heard a sobbing gasp of alarm and laughed hysterically. He leaned forward. Helpless in the young clerk's grip, the would-be robber felt the world spin round him dizzily. His own weight brought him over the young man's shoulder. He crashed on the pavement with a cry of pain.

Almost bewildered by the success of the manoeuvre, Richard Mervan made his first mistake. He should have pressed with his leg and pulled the other's wrist. It was a ruthless hold which could have broken the man's arm. Perhaps Mervan was too squeamish. Perhaps he was too concerned about the safety of the money in his charge. He loosed his grip and stepped back, looking for the leather case.

Racked with pain, the bandit made a desperate bid for freedom.

Spitting like a cat, he hurled the cosh at the bank clerk's head. Mervan dodged instinctively. He heard somebody shout, then realised with surprise that the noise came from his own throat. Something crashed against his neck and he went down, huddling over the case he had just retrieved. The world was a breathless muddle. He was dimly aware of shouts and the thud of feet against the pavement. He closed his eyes wearily....

Somebody was supporting his shoulders. "Are you all right, guv'nor?"

Mervan opened his eyes again. A ruddy face was very close to his own. "Eh? Oh. Yes, I'm all right." He winced. "My neck..."

"It's bleeding, guv." The taxi-man sounded anxious. "I'd better get you to a doctor."

Mervan shook his head. Pain flared through his neck and he gasped. He felt the torn skin cautiously, then stared at his fingers. They were sticky and red. He looked up. "That man... Where is he?"

"He got away, guv. Down that side turning."

Mervan glanced into the expectant, slightly foolish faces of the passers-by who had formed a half-circle round him on the pavement. "Didn't anyone follow him?"

The driver shrugged. "Things happened too fast, guv'nor. And I was more worried about you than 'im."

Somebody shouldered his way roughly through the crowd. It was a bank messenger, uniformed and important. Mervan stilled the question on the messenger's lips with a slightly sardonic grin. "It's all right. The money's safe."

The taxi-man said again:

"I'd better get you to a doctor."

Mervan refused obstinately. He added dully:

"Take me back to the branch."

The driver and the messenger spoke together in protest.

"The police—."

"They'll want a statement—."

Mervan said stubbornly:

"They can follow me to the branch. I must deliver this." He clutched the leather case.

The messenger nodded. "I'll explain, then." He picked up the cosh and examined it with interest.

The taxi-man said: "Fingerprints—" and Mervan said: "He was wearing gloves," at the same time.

Then they both lost interest in the sawn-off piping in the messenger's hand and the driver helped the young clerk up from the pavement.

Giddy and breathless, Mervan bundled himself into the taxi and leaned back against the cushions. As the cab moved off, he mopped his neck with a handkerchief. His fingers were trembling and his heart was thudding painfully. With sudden revulsion, he pushed the case away from him along the seat.

The journey to the branch office seemed all too short. Struggling for composure, Mervan carried the leather case into the bank and handed the money to the head cashier. His arrival created something of a sensation.

The Accountant came forward to meet him. He said with mild distaste:

"Mervan, you look a wreck."

The clerk struggled with an insane desire to laugh. He replied weakly:

"I suppose I do." He shaded his eyes wearily. "I feel rather tired. Do you mind if I sit down?"

His chief unbent. "Come this way." He led the young man into his own cubby-hole behind the counter. The junior hurried forward with a chair. The Accountant perched himself on a seat behind the desk. He was a short, ill favoured man with wiry hair. His brusque manner made him unpopular with the staff, but he was hard working and efficient. Speaking with unusual affability, he jerked:

"Well, Mervan. It seems you're quite a hero."

The clerk smiled weakly. He could feel the blood oozing down his neck, soaking his collar.

The Accountant continued:

"Head Office 'phoned—told us to expect you. Understand you refused to wait for the police." He frowned. "Don't know I approve— they'll follow you here. Still, never mind that. No harm done. The money's safe. That's the main thing."

Mervan said:

"Yes, Mr. Spurling. That's the main thing."

Spurling coughed. After an awkward pause, he went on:

"I hope you're not hurt. Your behaviour was commendable. Most commendable. You were courageous and quick-witted. The Manager"—he spoke in capital letters—"wishes to thank you personally."

Mervan nodded. There was a sour taste in his mouth.

Spurling regarded him with closer attention. Mervan looked very bedraggled. Unable to keep a tinge of disapproval from his voice, the Accountant said rather severely:

"You'd better not see him like that. You can clean yourself first."

He broke off, then said abruptly:

"That wound on your neck is a messy affair."

Mervan replied:

"It isn't so bad as it looks." He felt strangely indifferent. He wondered if he would be given the rest of the day off.

Spurling said gruffly:

"Well, well. We've sent for a doctor. Meanwhile, bathe your neck downstairs."

Mervan nodded again. He stood up wearily. He made his way to the stairs leading down to the basement, walking uncertainly.

The clatter of typewriters stopped abruptly as he went past the girls' corner. The younger of the two typists looked up with a sudden, friendly smile. Mervan's gait slackened. He returned her smile immediately. She dropped her head in pretty confusion. Mervan moved on with a springy step.

When she left the bank that evening, Richard Mervan was waiting for her. He had been loitering by the shops opposite for half an hour, waiting for her to appear. When he saw her at last descending the steps, he strolled across with a casual air. He raised his hat. "Good evening, Miss Barre."

Her blue eyes widened with surprise. "Mr. Mervan!   I thought you'd gone home."

"The Manager gave me the rest of the day off," he admitted. "But it was hardly a holiday. I had to make a statement to the police. And then I had to look through the pictures in the rogues' gallery at the Yard."

"At Scotland Yard?"   The girl's eyebrows arched.

"Yes. They hoped I could identify the man who attacked me." Mervan was speaking mechanically. He was regarding the girl with admiration. She was very lovely.

"Oh." Keenly aware of his gaze, she dimpled becomingly. "And did you?"

Studying the delicate planes of her face, he almost missed the question. Then he responded hastily:

"No. No, I couldn't find him in the gallery. I'm not sure I could recognize him anyway." He added doubtfully: "He had a stubbly chin and greying hair... That's all I can remember." He looked rather glum.

The girl laughed sympathetically. "You were too busy defending yourself to notice his face."

Mervan said: "Yes," rather lamely; there was an awkward pause.

The girl adjusted the long strap which looped her handbag over her shoulder. "Well, I must be getting along."

Mervan said desperately:

"Don't go. I— ." He broke off. He felt ridiculously shy. It was the first time he had struck up a conversation with her.

"Yes?" Miss Barre waited with an expression of demure enquiry.

Mervan took his courage in both hands. "Will you have tea with me?"

There was a faint flicker of mischief at the back of the girl's blue eyes. She asked directly:

"Why?"

Mervan swallowed. Then he said baldly:

"I like you."

Her lips quivered, then curved in a roguish smile. She said sweetly:

"I like you too. Let's have some tea."

Almost dizzy with elation, Richard Mervan made a confession. "I was too nervous to speak to you before."

They were sitting at a table in a crowded tea-shop. The girl's cheeks indented. "Were you?"

"Yes. I'm rather shy."

The girl said seriously:

"I know." She added sympathetically: "It's an unusual quality. But it does you credit."

Mervan's face lightened. "Thank you, Miss Barre."

"Lesley," she corrected gravely.

"Lesley," he repeated with pleasure. "It's a lovely name."

"I think so," agreed the girl with an odd kind of pride. She laughed. "That sounds conceited. But I am rather fond of my name." She gestured prettily. "Well, sir. What's *your* Christian name?"

"Richard."

Lesley said with decision:

"I shall call you Dick."

Mervan looked at her happily. He said suddenly:

"You're very beautiful."

Lesley was a girl who never blushed. She thanked him demurely. "Now *that's* established," she continued with a hint of laughter, "what happens next?"

The clerk replied eagerly:

"I'm going to take you to the pictures."

She smiled. "You make that sound like a declaration of eternal fidelity."

Mervan said quietly:

"Don't laugh at me, please."

Briefly she dropped her hand on his. "I won't, Dick. I promise."

He felt absurdly pleased. He asked: "Where shall we go?"

"You choose."

"There's *You Only Live Once* at the London Pavilion— ."

"The Fritz Lang movie? Yes, I'd enjoy that."

Mervan smiled. He had suggested the film rather doubtfully, wondering if its finer points might be lost to Lesley. But her reference to the director had pleased and reassured him.

Lesley waited by the entrance while he paid the bill. When he rejoined her, she linked her arm through his.

As they walked through the city streets, she began:

"Dick, you didn't tell me——." She hesitated.

He prompted her. "Yes?"

Lesley began again. "We've been working together at the bank since you were demobbed——."

Mervan nodded. He had been released from the Army at the beginning of 1946 and had at once returned to his old employers.

Lesley's voice was soft, almost tremulous. "That was months ago. But you've never approached me as a friend before. What made you speak to me today?"

Mervan replied:

"What gave me the courage, you mean?" He mocked himself with a dry laugh. "The answer's simple, Lesley. You gave me a friendly smile."

The reply seemed to please her. She stared for a moment at the wide bandage around his neck. Then she murmured:

"You were quite a hero. I thought you deserved— a smile...."

They strolled through the dark streets holding hands like children.

They were silent. It was as if they felt that this new intimacy which they shared was a precious, brittle thing that might be broken by speaking.

The girl sighed. She said at last.:

"It's getting late."

"Yes."

Their steps rang on the pavement. Lesley murmured:

"It's been a lovely evening."

He didn't reply. Instead, he turned his head and brushed his lips against her soft hair.

She laughed a protest. They walked on in silence. When they reached her home, she turned to face him. She was a tall girl— five feet seven— and their eyes were level. Mervan felt a pulse throbbing hard in his throat. She was very near to him.

Lesley whispered. "Goodnight, Dick."

Her mouth found his in a fleeting caress. Then she was gone.

It began with a kiss. It ended with murder.

# CHAPTER TWO

Two men came through the well-guarded doorway into the great hall of the prison. Their footsteps rang on the metal stairway as they climbed up to the first gallery which stretched along the side of the hall. They spoke in low tones.

The Chief Officer said:

"Oh, yes. He's a good prisoner. He doesn't complain, he's obedient, and he doesn't make trouble. And yet—— ." He paused.

His companion finished shrewdly:

"And yet he worries you."

"Yes." The Chief Officer nodded. "It's nothing he does and nothing he says. It's rather what he doesn't do, what he doesn't say...." He broke off. He snapped:

"I don't like first offenders! Give me the old lags. You know where you are with them."

Detective Inspector Castle chuckled. He was a large man, urbane and shrewd of eye. He was wearing a battered old raincoat and a bowler hat. He said:

"That's prejudice."

The Chief Officer grunted. "Maybe. Maybe not. Laugh if you like, but I'll tell you this. Young Mervan scares me."

Castle made a noise which was politely incredulous.

The Chief Officer said grimly:

"He's a man with an obsession. He's polite and reserved. And he's ruthless."

Castle stared. "You're describing a different man."

His escort returned dryly:

"He's been here for several months."

Castle said mildly:

"I see what you mean."

They continued on their way.

The Chief Officer nodded curtly to the landing warder and came to a halt outside one of the cells. He twisted a key in the lock and thrust open the door. The room beyond was as wide as it was high and four strides deep. The discoloured walls were slightly damp, and uncertain light filtered through the tiny panes of opaque glass set in the heavily barred window. The air in the cell was cold and stale and permeated with the animal smells of prison. Castle shivered involuntarily.

The man who rose from the truckle bed in the corner was dressed in grey. His face was almost the same colour as his ill-fitting uniform. He did not speak.

Castle tapped his escort on the shoulder and murmured in his ear. The Chief Officer hesitated, then turned and went out on the landing. He closed the heavy door carefully.

Castle grunted:

"Sit down, Mervan. I want a word with you alone."

Richard Mervan spoke with an odd suggestion of mockery beneath the servile flatness of his voice. "You're forgetting the regulations. A police officer when interviewing a prisoner——."

"Should do so under the supervision of a member of the prison staff. I know." Castle looked tired. He took off his bowler hat and thumped it absently. He said:

"This isn't an official visit."

A flicker of curiosity showed on the thin, intelligent face. The ex-clerk sat down on the truckle bed, spreading his hands on the coarse blankets covering the hard mattress. "You should have seen me in the Visiting Room. This 'peter' isn't very comfortable." He gazed sombrely round the cell.

The Inspector regarded him with a gleam of sympathy. He commented obliquely:

"You're picking up prison slang."

"By degrees." Mervan added bitterly:

"I have plenty of time to learn."

"Ah, yes. The sentence was——."

"For long enough." Mervan's mouth was hard.   "I must wait for my freedom for many years."

"You can't complain. You robbed the bank."

Mervan bit his lip. "I've never denied it."

"No," said Castle. "You haven't. But you've told us nothing of value. And we've yet to recover the money you took from the strong-room."

Mervan shrugged. He made no reply.

Castle rubbed his jowl. He mused:

"You were caught and convicted. But you worry me still."

Mervan's fingers crooked. "Forget me."

"I can't." Castle shoved aside an enamel bowl and jug and perched himself on the edge of a table which had been built into the wall. He began to speak in level, confiding tones. "The case intrigued me from the first. As you probably know, I handled most of the preliminary investigations."

He paused, as though inviting comment. Mervan nodded, but said nothing.

Castle continued:

"The first report was a simple one. You were found in the street one Saturday in the late afternoon. You seemed to have been the victim of an attack. You were taken to hospital and were found to be suffering from concussion. There was a bad wound in your scalp." He smiled grimly as Mervan winced and fondled the back of his head reminiscently. "Obviously, you had been coshed." He pronounced the word with distaste. "That was clear enough. But the motive for the attack was obscure. You didn't appear to have been robbed."

Mervan grinned wryly.

Castle squinted at him thoughtfully. "You were carrying your identity card, so we knew who you were, and we soon discovered where you worked. You were also carrying a bunch of keys which apparently belonged to the bank. You were still unconscious, so we couldn't question you. But we contacted your employers. They weren't particularly alarmed, even when we mentioned the keys. They explained their system.

"The strong-room was always secured under two sets of keys. The Accountant or another senior official held the first bunch, while one of the clerks held the other. The duty went by rota. That week-end, it was your turn to hold the keys. But your set was useless without the other. Nevertheless—." Castle gestured vaguely. "We persuaded your employers to check the safes in the vaults. We had to wait for the Accountant— a fellow named— ." Castle snapped his fingers.

"Spurling," said Mervan tonelessly.

"That's right. Spurling. We needed his keys, besides yours, to open the strong-room. And when we did— ."

"All hell broke loose."

"Yes. The safes had been raided. Bank notes, treasury notes, negotiable securities—you had taken the lot. The examiners put the loss in thousands of pounds."

Mervan asked curiously:

"Did you ever doubt my complicity?"

Castle blew out the negative with a short laugh. "Not once. It was obviously an inside job. Nothing had been forced except some tin boxes on the cashiers' trolley. Everything else had been opened with keys. You were obviously responsible for the robbery. We found your fingerprints everywhere. You had even left us the hammer and chisel you had used to break open the boxes. Yours was the work of a rank amateur."

Mervan bit his lip hard. "So I made your task an easy one."

Castle frowned. "'It wasn't that easy. There were several questions I couldn't answer. You had never had access to the Accountant's keys— yet you must have used them to effect the robbery. At first I thought Spurling might have been your accomplice— .'"

Mervan laughed involuntarily.

Castle continued equably:

"But he had an air-tight alibi, so I soon dismissed him from my mind. The keys in his possession had not been used that afternoon—so you must have had duplicates."

Mervan's silence was an admission.

Castle shot out a question. "Where did you get 'em? And how?"

Mervan's face was a mask. "I have nothing to say."

Castle drummed stubby fingers on the brim of his bowler hat. "You have nothing to say." He mimicked the prisoner's voice without derision. "That's what you said when we arrested you."

"You gave me the usual warning."

"Yes. Sometimes," sighed Castle, "I wish I could ignore Judges' Rules. If I could have had a confidential talk with you... Ah, well." He rubbed his jowls. He continued briskly:

"My theory was this. You must have had an accomplice—and this person was the probable source of the duplicate keys. With these—and those officially in your charge—you were able to return to the deserted bank in the afternoon to open the strong-room and raid the safes. It was Saturday, the bank had closed at twelve o'clock, you had a clear field. You filled a suitcase with money and left. It was as simple as that."

Castle scowled. "What happened then? I can only guess... You rejoined your accomplice. You thought you were leaving together— fleeing the country, perhaps. But—." He gestured vaguely. He said grimly:

"You were double-crossed. You were knocked on the head and abandoned. Your accomplice escaped with the loot. And you were left with nothing."

Mervan grinned savagely. His fingers crooked.

Castle said:

"It's not an uncommon story. But your reactions were unusual. You knew you couldn't escape conviction; but you might have got off with a lighter sentence. You could have co-operated with the police. I expected you to name your accomplice and make a full confession. But you didn't make a statement of any kind. You pleaded guilty— and left the rest to us."

The muscles of Mervan's face had frozen around his last savage smile. He rubbed his hand across his mouth.

Castle grunted: "And now you've nothing more to lose. You might as well tell me everything."

Mervan repeated dully. "I have nothing to say."

"No?" Castle paused imperceptibly. Then he said gruffly:

"You could tell me about— Lesley."

The name mushroomed across the chamber like an exploding shell. Then there was a deadening silence in which the Inspector became gradually aware of the sound of the watch ticking against his wrist.

Mervan's cheeks had hollowed. His eyes were fever-bright.

Castle sighed. "I can see I shall have to soliloquize. Ah. well!" He scratched his chin. "Let's go back to the beginning. You were unconscious for some time. You were also delirious. You talked."

Mervan's eyes were fixed in painful concentration.

Castle went on:

"You kept mumbling a name. The name of the person who had double-crossed you—."

Mervan made a sudden, involuntary movement.

Castle smiled grimly. "Don't worry. You weren't very explicit. We had placed a detective in the hospital to watch you. He reported little more than the name 'Leslie'—which we took to be a man's. You seemed to think this person had betrayed you."

When Mervan spoke, his voice was low. "Is that all?"

"That's all," agreed the Inspector. "It was a slender clue. You had been speaking in a delirium—it might have meant nothing. But I checked, of course."

Mervan muttered. "Well?"

"Well!" Castle blew out his cheeks.   "I found that a girl named Lesley Barre had been employed for a while in the bank as a typist."

The prisoner said tonelessly:

"I knew her slightly. She left some time before the robbery."

"A few months before," agreed the Inspector. He paused, then said mildly:

"I discovered the location of her flat." He regarded Mervan owlishly. "Oddly enough,"—an ironic note crept into his voice—"it wasn't far from the street where you were found suffering from concussion."

Mervan's jaw muscles tightened.

Castle said dryly:

"I had a look around that flat. It was deserted. Miss Barre, it seems, had left without supplying a forwarding address. I wasn't able to make contact with her."

217

"So?" The word wasn't much more than a breath.

The Inspector grunted. "That's all, I'm afraid. Miss Barre had disappeared. It can happen, you know, even in these days of national registration."

"You didn't,"—Mervan had difficulty in phrasing the question—"you didn't succeed in tracing her?"

"No. I could hardly ask my superiors to institute a nation wide search. After all, I was only following a hunch. We had no real reason to look for Miss Barre. Had we?" The question was a challenge.

Mervan reacted violently. He snapped:

"I think you'd better go."

Castle grunted. "Not so fast, young man. Hear me out."

"You're just wasting your time."

The Inspector growled. "Maybe. But I don't like unfinished business. When I handle a case, I like to tie up all the loose ends neatly."

He banged his hat against his knee. "That's why I'm here. Officially, the case is closed—unless you give me an excuse to open it again. Understand? I need new evidence."

"I have nothing to tell you."

Castle said without heat:

"I think you're a fool. Yet I'm sorry for you. And, believe me, I rarely feel sympathy for criminals."

Mervan shrugged. He seemed indifferent.

Castle said softly:

"I'd like to know what changed you from the decent young man who fought a robber in the street to the reckless crook who raided his employers' strong-room. The change is too violent, too sudden, too strange..."

Mervan muttered: "A man in love—." He broke off.

Castle pounced. "Then it was a woman. Lesley— ."

Mervan said stubbornly:

"I've told you nothing."

Castle regarded him with puzzled eyes. "I can't understand you, Mervan. You gain nothing by protecting this girl. You can't want her to go unpunished. Unless— ."

He caught his breath. He stared at the man in prison grey. In the uncertain light which filtered through the heavy glass behind him, Mervan's face seemed scarred with hate.

Castle murmured:

"You were safe and secure and respectable. But that's all finished now. You'll never return to the life you knew... You're a broken man. Thank Lesley for that."

Anger lit the prisoner's eyes. He choked:

"You can taunt me now. But one day——."

"You'll be free." The Inspector tensed. "And then?"

Mervan's pupils contracted. Sanity came back to his eyes. "You needn't worry. I have nothing against you."

"No," rumbled Castle. "But you frighten me... Men go sour in prison. Maybe they go mad—I don't know. But I do know this..." He hesitated, then said bluntly:

"You're a man with an obsession. And you're dangerous."

Mervan forced a laugh. "You're mistaken."

Castle shook his head. "No. I understand you now. You won't betray this girl— "

"There's nothing to betray."

"Don't lie." Castle was brusque. "You won't implicate this girl. Why? Because you don't trust us. You mean to take your own revenge..." The Inspector paused. He had played his hand. He could do no more until Mervan responded.

A tiny smile drifted over the prisoner's lips. "Good-bye, Inspector."

Castle scowled. He clapped his hat on his head and smacked the crown angrily. He turned and hammered on the heavy door with the flat of his hand.

Then, as footsteps sounded along the gallery outside the cell, the burly man made his last appeal.

"Forget revenge. Leave the girl to us."

The flicker in Mervan's eyes was an unspoken question.

Castle answered it quietly. "You're a decent young man. I don't want you to destroy yourself." For a moment, Castle thought he had succeeded.

Mervan's face had changed: he looked like a hurt child. Then he took refuge in his bitter pride. He said again:

"Good-bye."

Castle lifted his hand and dropped it in a gesture of defeat. The door opened. He went out of the cell.

Richard Mervan stood listening as the sound of footsteps died away in the distance. Then he spoke aloud.

He said, as though making a vow:

"Lesley, my love, we'll meet again. I'll look for you and find you." He finished in a whisper:

"And then I shall kill you...."

# PART TWO
# THE STAGE IS SET

# CHAPTER THREE

Algy Lawrence said bitterly:

"God damn and blast all telephones!"

He was just settling himself in his morning bath when the persistent ringing began in the bedroom. He cursed again wearily, then raised his slimly built, athletic young body from the warmly inviting water and scrambled out of the bath. Kicking wet feet into shabbily comfortable slippers, he draped a towel round his dripping thighs and tramped unhappily through the adjoining doorway to his bedroom.

He grabbed the telephone with a damp hand and snarled rather than spoke into the receiver. "Hallo!"

"Hallo, Algy."

"Steve!" Most of the young man's irritation disappeared. "You old son of a gun. How's crime?"

"It doesn't pay. Or so they tell me." Chief Inspector Castle cleared his throat. "I'm not offering you a case, Algy. This is a social call."

"Uh huh."

Castle said, rather too casually:

"Let's go to a theatre this afternoon."

"Well, now." Lawrence rocked gently on his heels. "What's the show? If it's Revudeville at the Windmill, then I'm your man. There's a lovely young lady named Carole Logan—."

"No, no, no." Castle was irritable. "I have tickets for the ☐atinee at the Janus."

"The Janus? Oh, yes. It's a mystery play there, isn't it? Well, I don't know, Steve...."

Castle said quietly:

"I'd like your company."

An odd note in the older man's pleasant baritone caught Lawrence's attention. He made up his mind at once. "Right, then. I accept your invitation."

"Good." The Inspector seemed pleased. "Shall we meet for lunch?"

"Yes, of course . How about—?" He named a pub in Kensington.

Castle growled approval. "Fine. Now, let me see." Lawrence heard the faint rustle of papers as his old friend thumbed through them quickly. "I have a fair amount of routine work, but— Oh well, the Yard can do without me for once."

"Yes."

"Dammit," chuckled Steve, "you needn't agree so readily...I can be at that pub by one o'clock. Will that suit you?"

"Certainly. I'll order you a good meal."

"That'll make a change. I usually have to make do with sandwiches on the desk. But you wouldn't know about things like that, you lucky young idler."

They exchanged a few pleasantries, then broke the connection. Lawrence let his hand linger for a moment on the telephone and murmured sleepily:

"Steve, you old fraud, there's something on your mind. I wonder what?"

He went back to the bathroom with a questioning gleam at the back of his lazy blue eyes.

Chief Inspector Castle—six years after the final interview with Richard Mervan, but still wearing the same battered raincoat and bowler hat— threaded his way through the cluster of tables.

Algy Lawrence rose to greet him. "Hi, Steve! Over here."

Castle grunted. His young friend had secured a table for two in the corner. A glint of approval showed in the policeman's shrewd grey eyes. "Hallo, Algy." They shook hands.

"I've already ordered," smiled Lawrence. He signalled to the waitress. "Roast beef and baked potatoes. Right?"

The burly man was conservative in his tastes. He growled contentedly.

Lawrence sat down again and stretched his long legs under the table. He eyed the Inspector quizzically.

Castle wrenched his hat from his grizzled head and banged it on a clothes-rack in the corner. Almost as an after-thought, he stripped off his raincoat and suspended it from the peg beneath his bowler.

Algy grinned. He knew the Inspector's affection for the disreputable old coat was a standing joke at Scotland Yard. He said:

"I bet you're glad we're going to a ☐atinee. You might have had to wear evening dress in the orchestra stalls at the eight o'clock performance."

"Evening dress be damned," grunted Castle. "I—Wait a minute! How did you know I have tickets for seats in the front stalls?"

"I didn't," confessed Algy. "But I thought this little outing might be in the nature of a reward for the occasional—uh—assistance I render Scotland Yard from time to time. And knowing your kind heart and generous——."

"All right," said Castle gruffly. "Don't labour the point... I'm disappointed in you, young Algy. I thought for a moment you'd done something clever."

"Intuition," returned Lawrence comfortably, "is better than deduction. It's easier, too. Ask Mr. Fortune."

"Anyway," said Steve, "you're right. We'll be sitting in the front row. The most expensive seats in the house. And," he finished abruptly, "they didn't cost me a penny."

Lawrence angled an eyebrow. "Complimentary tickets?"

"Yes," said the Inspector carefully. "And no."

Algy grinned lazily. He said:

"Let's not play games, Steve. Tear off the false whiskers. Tell me the real reason for our trip to the Janus."

Castle dragged out a chair and sat down heavily. "What makes you think I have an ulterior motive?"

"A □atinee à deux," smiled Algy, "is a purely feminine habit. It's not your idea of the ideal way of passing a Saturday afternoon. Besides,"— laughter wrinkles deepened at the corners of his sleepy blue eyes— "you've been drooping hints with all the delicacy of a man hurling bricks through a plate glass window."

The two friends grinned at each other.

Then Castle flung up his hands in a comic gesture of surrender. "All right, then. Take a look at this."

He took an envelope from his pocket and tossed it across the table.

Lawrence glanced at the typewritten address. "New Scotland Yard, London, S.W.1 Hallo! You've been demoted, Detective Inspector Stephen Castle."

"My correspondent," growled Steve, "is a few years behind the times. I was made a Chief Inspector in 1948. While you," he added irrelevantly, "were fooling around Europe in Intelligence."

Lawrence rubbed his cheek. "The letter was delivered this morning?"

"Yes. It seems to have caught the last collection yesterday evening... Look at the post-mark again."

"London, S.E. 1."

"Does that suggest anything to you?"

Lawrence's finger traced idle patterns on the table-cloth. "It's a large area, Steve. It contains two hospitals, two main line stations, a cathedral, the Imperial War Museum, and County Hall... But only one theatre. The Old Vic."

"Exactly. The Janus is on the other side of the river in the heart of theatre-land."

"Uh huh." Lawrence opened the envelope and took out a folded piece of paper. The young man examined it carefully. It had been printed for a famous ticket agency, and was a form of admission for two persons to that afternoon's □atinee at the Janus. The relevant details had been scrawled across the face of the ticket in indelible pencil.

Lawrence murmured: "That settles it. These seats aren't a gift from the management."

"No. Free tickets sent from a theatre are always issued at the box office and stamped COMPLIMENTARY."

Lawrence replaced the slip in its envelope. He said brightly:

"The conclusion is obvious. You have a benefactor who prefers to remain unknown."

Castle scowled.

He said unexpectedly:

"*Timeo Danaos et dona ferentes.*"

"Don't quote Virgil, Steve," grinned Algy. "It confuses me... So you fear the Greeks and the gifts they bring." His fingers strayed towards the envelope. "What makes you think this is a Trojan Horse?"

"I'm damned if I know," admitted Castle frankly. "Maybe I'm just a soured old policeman. But in my experience,"—he hesitated—"you rarely get something for nothing. Besides... there was something else."

"In the envelope?"

"Yes." Castle took a thin strip of pasteboard from his wallet and passed it across the table.

Lawrence picked it up, holding it delicately by the edges.

"You needn't worry about obscuring fingerprints," said Castle dryly. "There aren't any."

The implied admission made his young friend smile. "So you had it tested. You're a thorough man, Steve."

"When my curiosity is aroused."

"Mmmm. This is rather intriguing." Algy seemed puzzled. "What the devil does it mean?"

He dropped the card face upwards on the table-cloth. Four words had been rubber-stamped in gummy black ink across the pasteboard.

The message read simply:

COME TO PADDINGTON FAIR

Sydney Short, stage door-keeper of the Janus Theatre, leaned out of his glass-enclosed cubby hole and called shrilly:

"Miss Christopher!"

Lesley Christopher turned her lovely blue eyes towards him enquiringly.

"Yes, Sydney?"

"A letter for you, Miss. Just a second." The door-keeper hopped off his stool like an ungainly old bird flopping down from its perch.

Lesley waited patiently by the stage door through which she had just entered while its custodian scrabbled clumsily through the litter at the back of his shabby sanctum.

"Here it is, Miss. Came by the mid-day delivery." Short hesitated. Then garrulity overcame discretion. "It's marked Personal and Urgent."

An inquisitive note sounded clearly in his voice. Lesley detected it and strove to repress her instinctive irritation.

"Thank you, Sydney." She took the envelope from his bony hand and resisted the temptation to snub him. There was no point in falling out with the old fool now. She never slighted a man unless she was sure she could find no use for him.

"That's all right, Miss." Short eyed the letter rather wistfully.

Lesley slipped it into her handbag and turned away. Then she hesitated briefly and turned back, her long silky hair swinging like a curtain against the collar of her coat.

"Oh, Sydney!"

"Yes, Miss?" The door-keeper leaned out of his cubby hole once more.

"Has Mr. Trent arrived yet?"

"No, Miss." He scanned the face of the clock above the door. "He may be late."

"He usually is." Behind the professional warmth of Lesley's smile, a keen observer might have detected a chill of anxiety. "Please ask him to go to my dressing-room when he arrives."

She walked away along the passage with superb grace and poise.

Short gazed at her retreating figure with admiration, .then withdrew to the cover of his cubby hole again. He shook his balding head, sighed sentimentally, and said at random:

"She's a proper lady."

A voice answered in the crude idiom of the streets.

"She's a—."

The third word was partially smothered by an indignant cry of protest from the door-keeper. "What the 'ell do you mean by that, Albert Wix?"

"I mean what I say," returned his companion inside the glass box. Wix, the property master, was a tired-looking man in his middle fifties. He had a seamed and anxious face and a morose gleam at the back of his faded eyes.

"Look 'ere—." Short glared at the other man's unresponsive back.

227

Wix was crouched over an evil-smelling oil lamp, coaxing a kettle of water to the boiling point.

Wix said over his shoulder:

"Don't get excited, Syd. You've got one opinion about our precious leading lady. Well, I've got another."

"I can't understand why— ."

Wix interrupted. "You've never felt the rough edge of her tongue. I have."

Short muttered rebelliously.

Wix said:

"We won't quarrel about her. She isn't worth it."

Short seemed ready to continue the argument, but bit back the retort which sprang to his lips. Instead he snapped testily:

"Ain't that ruddy tea brewed yet?"

"Don't get impatient. There's plenty o' time."

The remark set Short's thoughts flying off at a tangent. He stared at the clock and muttered.

"Not for Michael Trent, there isn't. He's been late for every performance this week. If he wasn't playing the lead—." He broke off and shook his head. "What's the matter with him, anyway?"

The property master's lined face crinkled with one of its rare smiles. He gestured eloquently with his elbow.

"Drink, you mean?" said the door-keeper doubtfully. "Maybe, maybe. He carries it well, then. Does it affect his performance?"

Wix shrugged. "He looks all right from the wings." He busied himself with an old teapot and a couple of mugs. "But star or no, his nibs will give him hell if he's late again this afternoon."

His nibs was the stage manager.

Short said:

"He'll give you hell too if you don't take him those blank cartridges soon."

Wix scowled. "He's an old woman sometimes. Doesn't trust anyone with that revolver but himself. I bring him the blanks every day, don't I? So why doesn't he leave me to load the blasted gun?"

Short looked bored. "It's fired in the big scene, they tell me. I s'pose he likes to make sure that nothing goes wrong."

When Wix had a grievance, he liked to talk about it. He continued to grumble as he finished making the tea. "Fuss, fuss, fuss. That's Mr. Jack Ruddy Austin. Like 'the barber's cat, full o' wind and—."

Short hissed a hurried warning. Then he said in an unnaturally clear voice:

"Hallo, Mr. Austin. Anything I can do for you?"

The property master swallowed an inaudible curse as a long shadow fell into the glass box. He put down the teapot and turned with an insincere smile. "Just coming, Mr. Austin. I have the blanks here."

He rattled a box in his pocket by way of illustration.

Jack Austin nodded curtly. The stage manager was a stockily built man about thirty five years old. He was wearing a loose fitting jacket over a turtle necked sweater, plus grey flannel trousers and tennis shoes.

"Never mind that, Props." The familiar diminutive sounded odd and unfriendly in Austin's clipped, precise speech. "I've other things to attend to."

He turned towards the stage door-keeper. "Have you seen Mr. Trent this afternoon?"

Short replied rather diffidently:

"No, Mr. Austin. Not yet."

Austin's face darkened angrily. "You mean he isn't in the theatre?"

Short glanced apprehensively at the clock but made no response.

"What's troubling you, Jack?"

Austin turned his head. His face cleared slightly. "Hallo, Victor...It's Michael Trent. He promised me yesterday he'd be here early for the ☐atinee, but it looks as if he's going to be late again."

He glared at his wrist-watch, then corrected himself angrily. "He is late again."

Victor Friern, general manager of the Janus Theatre, was a distinguished figure in evening dress. He was tall, erect, and square-shouldered. He had greying hair and aristocratic features. He said smoothly:

"Don't worry, Jack. Give him a little licence. He hasn't let us down yet."

Austin responded gloomily. "There's always a first time."

Friern shrugged. "Speak to Denzil. Warn him to be ready. He'll be pleased to play Michael's part."

Douglas Denzil was the Juvenile. He was also Trent's deputy.

Austin asked:

"What about Denzil's own understudy? He's barely competent."

Friern smiled. "It's not an important role. As Douglas would be the first to tell you. But...." He shrugged again. "There's no need to worry. Trent will be here soon."

The stage manager cracked his knuckles. "I wish I could be certain of that."

Friern took his arm in a friendly fashion and led him gently away. Austin left the general manager at the entrance to the dressing-room passage. Friern strolled along the corridor. Pausing before the door marked with a golden star, he raised his hand and tapped lightly on the panels.

A muffled reply came from within the room. Taking the call as an invitation, Friern pushed open the door and looked inside.

Lesley Christopher was sitting on a chair in front of the dressing-table, staring at her reflection in the lamp-shaded mirror.  She turned hurriedly. "Michael, I— ." She broke off. "Oh! It's you, Victor." She forced a smile. "Come in, do."

Friern studied her curiously. Behind her make-up, the colour of her cheeks was wavering. He closed the door and said mildly:

"You've dropped something."

Her sudden turn had sent a card and an envelope sliding to the floor.

Friern bent down to retrieve them. His gaze fell on the card which was resting face upwards on the carpet.

He read the rubber-stamped message in an instant.

It ran:

WE MEET AT PADDINGTON FAIR.

# CHAPTER FOUR

Friern said lightly: "A curious message." His voice inflected in a question.

Lesley smiled nervously. "From a crank, of course. It came by the mid-day delivery."

Friern studied the torn envelope. "Anonymous letters are common enough. But this one hardly follows the usual form. For instance— what's Personal and Urgent about it?"

"Oh, really, Victor! I can't explain it. I told you—it must be from a crank."

She seemed tired and. Irritable. Friern eyed her quizzically, then murmured:

"Forgive me, my dear. I didn't mean to upset you."

Lesley turned back to the mirror. "You haven't upset me, Victor. But—Oh, well. Throw the wretched thing away."

Friern dropped card and envelope into a basket by the dressing table. He said:

"This kind of thing is annoying because it's pointless. But it shouldn't worry you, unless..." He hesitated. "Forgive me again, my dear. But are you in trouble of any kind?"

Lesley was still peering into the mirror, painting her lips a deeper red. She froze for a second, then countered his question with another. "What makes you ask that?"

Friern said gently: "I know you well enough. For the past few weeks you've been nervous, tense, troubled in your mind. Would you like to tell me why?"

"Victor, I—."

Friern interrupted without discourtesy. "Face me, my dear. Please."

Lesley sighed prettily, then obeyed. Despite the heavy mask of make-up pancaked over her face and the white cloth pinned over her hair to protect it, she was a very attractive young woman.

Friern gazed at her with a fleeting hunger in his deep-set eyes. He continued:

"Troubles can be shared. Won't you let me help you?"

Lesley squeezed her slender hands together. She said:

"I'm in no kind of distress. Truly, Victor, you're exaggerating... I admit I'm not myself. But then the part I play—." She hesitated. "It's exacting. It takes a lot out of me." She forced a laugh. "It isn't easy to 'die' at every performance."

"It isn't easy for Michael to commit murder eight times a week," commented Friern lightly. "The 'shot' he took at you last night was most unconvincing." He added more seriously:

"But I agree—your role is emotionally exhausting. Perhaps you need a holiday."

Lesley's mouth hardened. "I have a run of the play contract."

Friern gestured grandly. "A leave of absence can be arranged. Two weeks or three...."

"No, thank you, Victor." Lesley emphasized the negative with a frown. "I'm not going to lose this part."

"You're relying on your nerves."

"That's how I give of my best." Lesley turned back to the mirror. "This is my first big success, Victor. I'm not going to throw it away."

"The decision is yours, my dear. But be careful."

"Don't worry." There was little humour in her laughter. It was hard and brittle. "I'm not going to break down. I shan't miss a single performance." She concluded venomously:

"Tell that to Penny Valentine."

Friern smiled. "You misjudge her, my dear. She doesn't want to take 'Marilyn' away from you."

"You men!" returned Lesley scornfully. "I'm surprised at you, Victor. Can't you see she'd give anything—anything—for a chance to play 'Marilyn'?"

"She has a good part already."

"But she is also my understudy! Why do you think she was so anxious to take the job?"

Friern was tactful. "She plays one role and understudies another. That's not an uncommon arrangement in any company. Denzil is in the same position."

Lesley said bitterly: "You'll never understand."

Friern, on the contrary, understood her completely. But as an old hand in the profession he was used to meeting extremes of generosity and pettiness. He said gently:

"'Marilyn' is yours, my dear. For as long as you wish."

Lesley softened. She murmured. "Victor, dear. You're rather sweet."

Friern put his hands on her shoulders and twisted her gently till she faced him once more. He said:

"I can't make pretty speeches. But remember this, I beg you. You're a special person, Lesley. And there's nothing I would not do for you." He took her hand in his and then, bending his greying head, kissed her lightly on the inside of her wrist.

Lesley's lips quivered. Mingled amusement and triumph showed briefly in her eyes. She whispered:

"Thank you, Victor," and let the tips of her fingers flutter across his cheek.

Friern straightened up. Smiling wryly, he said:

"I mustn't forget I have a rival." He looked pointedly at a framed photograph hanging on the wall.

Lesley followed his gaze. She said, rather too quickly:

"Michael's an old friend. Nothing more."

"As an old friend," replied Friern smoothly, "you should give him a word of warning."

"Of warning?" Alarm sounded in her voice.

"Yes. Trent has been late for every performance this week. The S.M. does not approve—and if Austin advocates extreme measures, then as the general manager I shall have to back him up."

Lesley relaxed. "Oh. Is that all?" She stressed the pronoun lightly.

"All?" repeated Friern. "Isn't it enough?"

"Of course, Victor. I spoke carelessly." She frowned imperceptibly. "You mean Michael is late again this afternoon?"

"He wasn't in at the half." Friern glanced at his watch. His jaw tightened. "He may miss the quarter call as well."

Lesley said anxiously: "But you'll hold the curtain?"

"If necessary. Trent hasn't let us down yet. But this kind of thing can't go on."

They were interrupted by the arrival of Lesley's dresser, a plump and muscular woman with bright, beady eyes. She put a packet on the dressing-table. "Your cigarettes, miss."

"Thanks, Maggie. Now help me into my dress, will you?"

Friern made his exit as Lesley was preparing to throw off her dressing-gown. Outside in the corridor, he found a wizened little man with a gloomy face who was obviously worried.

The cause of his agitation was clear to Victor Friern. "Hello, Ben. Are you looking for Mr. Trent?"

Ben Cotall, Michael Trent's dresser, ducked his head nervously. "Yessir. Is he—is he ill?"

"No," replied Friern rather grimly. "But he's certainly in trouble."

Ben began to gesticulate, suddenly became very conscious of his hands, and plunged them into the pockets of his shabby black jacket.

Friern led the way towards the stage door. Ben trailed after him disconsolately. Sydney Short had left his cubby-hole and was peering through the door into the gloomy alley-way outside. Hearing their

233

footsteps, he signalled the two men eagerly.

"Here he comes now, sir!" he called, addressing the manager.

"Trent? Thank the Lord for that," muttered Friern.

Cotall's gloomy face brightened. He ran forward to meet his employer as he came into the theatre.

Michael Trent was a tall and handsome man with well defined features and glossy black hair. The boyish charm of his smile was off-set by an attractive suggestion of wickedness in his intelligent grey eyes. He swayed slightly as he greeted them. "Lo, all. Am I late?"

Friern said coldly:

"You're drunk."

"That," returned Michael with dignity, "is a canard. A calumny. I go further. A foul slander. I'm not drunk." He seemed to be searching for the right word. "I'm happy." His diction was only slightly slurred. Friern decided with relief that Trent was in a fit state to go on.

Michael himself had no doubts. "Come on, Ben, you old scoundrel. Help me to my dressing-room. No, God damn you," he swore good-humouredly. "Don't try to carry me. I can walk by myself. I've been doing it for years." Cotall led him away.

Friern shrugged. The expression on his face was enigmatic.

A voice in his ear startled him momentarily. "Trent's here at last, then?"

"Oh, it's you, Jack... Yes, he's here. Ben is looking after him."

The stage manager said grimly:

"I'll have a word with Mr. Trent."

Friern patted his shoulder. "Leave it till after the performance. Michael isn't drunk, but he isn't sober either. He might get argumentative. You know what children actors are." Remembering that Austin had once trodden the boards himself, he smiled to rob the words of offence.

The S.M. nodded glumly. "Perhaps you're right. I shall round on him after the show. Meanwhile...."

"Meanwhile," said Friern smoothly, "you might have a word about another matter. His business with the revolver in the last act—."

"Hell, yes!" Austin cracked his knuckles. "Even now, that needs more rehearsal. The way he handles that gun—." He broke off. "Which reminds me—." He interrupted himself again, half-turned, then shook his head and muttered: "First things, first. I'll speak to Trent now."

"Be tactful,'" smiled Friern. "You can reprimand him later."

Austin nodded. He hurried along to Trent's dressing-room.

The call-boy was just knocking smartly on the door, chanting:

234

"Quarter of an hour, please." Catching the stage manager's eye, the lad added rather guiltily: "One minute late."

Austin grinned briefly, tapped perfunctorily on the wooden panels, and pushed open the door. Michael Trent glanced over his shoulder. He was standing by the wash-basin, twisting the taps. "Hallo, Jack. Have you come to lecture me?"

Austin said:

"No," without a smile.

"That's good," murmured Trent. But for a scarcely perceptible inability to focus his eyes, he looked reasonably sober. He bent over the wash-basin and splashed his face liberally. He straightened up with a sigh. "Ben! Towel, please... Thanks." Cotall watched anxiously while his employer rubbed himself dry. Austin leaned against the wall, stony-faced.

"That's better." Trent slipped into the dressing-gown his dresser held out for him and turned towards the mirror by the basin. "I look human again."

Austin said:

"Trent, I—. "

"Please, Jack." Michael spoke in mock reproach. "Don't keep me from my paints and powder. The show must go on." He added an elaborately whispered aside. "What a damn' silly line."

Austin snapped: "Stop fooling, Michael. I'm not sure I should let you go on."

"Remember," murmured Trent, "my public." He began to put on his make-up. The S.M. glared at the back of the actor's head. Catching his eye in the mirror, Michael winked impertinently.

Austin mustered what patience he could. "Listen, Michael. This is important. You must take more care with your business with the revolver in the last act."

Trent lifted an eyebrow. "In what way?"

Satisfied that he had caught the other's attention at last, Austin replied heavily: "Aim the gun before you fire it. You're supposed to shoot 'Marilyn' through the heart."

"Well?"

"Last night you didn't sight the gun at all. If there had been a live cartridge in the chamber the bullet would have gone into the O.P. box."

Trent laughed. "Don't worry, Jack. I'll be careful. I'll level the gun at Lesley's heart." He added:

"This afternoon, I promise you, the audience will see a convincing murder."

Jack Austin hesitated outside the door of the adjoining dressing-room. Would it be wise, he wondered, to go in? Making up his mind at last, he rapped on the panels beneath the golden star.

"Come in!" Lesley Christopher, fully made-up and ready for her entrance, was sitting in the chair in front of her dressing-table. Seeing Austin, she gave him a tiny frown. She turned to her dresser. "I don't need you for the moment, Maggie. See if Miss Valentine needs any help." Maggie left, a gleam of curiosity in her bright, beady eyes, promising:

"I'll be back for your first call, miss."

Austin remarked:

"That was a generous thought."

Lesley shrugged. "You know I don't like Penny. It was just an excuse to get rid of Maggie."

"So that we might be alone?"

"So that you," replied Lesley dryly, "might be saved from making a fool of yourself in public."

"Lesley, I—."

She cut off his words with her own. "Has Michael arrived yet?"

"Yes."

"I thought I heard his voice." Lesley frowned again. "Damn! I left him a message, but he hasn't been in to see me."

Austin .said impatiently: "He has no more time to waste. And he's not in the best of condition."

"You mean he's been drinking again?"

"Yes. But he's fit to go on. Ben Cotall's looking after him now."

Lesley shook her head slowly. She said softly:

"Poor Michael..."

"Never mind him now." Austin's voice was rough. "What about – us?"

There was a long silence. Then Lesley said coolly:

"Give me a smoke." There was a packet on the dressing-table. Austin picked it up, took out a cigarette and placed it between the girl's lips. Lesley said:

"Now light it."

Austin struck a match with trembling fingers. Lesley held the cigarette to the tiny flame, inhaled deeply, then blew out a streaming cloud of smoke.

Austin threw the burnt out match into the basket on the floor. "Lesley—." She said insolently: "I hope you're not going to be tiresome, Jack."

Tiny muscles tightened angrily along the line of the S.M.'s jaw. "I asked you a question, Lesley."

"Yes, you did." She smiled unpleasantly. "And here's your answer. There's nothing between us, Jack. There never was and there never will be."

Austin felt his throat constrict. He spoke with an effort. "That's not good enough, Lesley. You led me to believe—."

Lesley didn't allow him to finish. She said:

"You should never mistake a smile for a promise."

Hating himself for his weakness, Austin began to plead. "But, Lesley, I love you."

She answered coldly:

"But I .don't love you." His foolish face annoyed her. Anxiety and fear had set her mind in a turmoil. Powerless to ignore or suppress the dangers which threatened her security, she turned on the only man she could hurt without wounding herself. She savoured the words as they came to her lips. "I don't even like you."

"Lesley!"

She smiled with a poisonous sweetness. She said:

"You revolt me..."

Austin flushed deeply. Then his nostrils pinched and his face went muddy-white. He lurched forward and grabbed her wrist, bruising her delicate skin. "You little vixen, I—."

Lesley laughed. Poising the smouldering cigarette between her fingers, she mashed the glowing end against the back of Austin's hand. He jerked it away with a curse. The sudden pain brought water to his eyes. The contempt in her voice hurt him more. "Go away. You silly, greedy boy."

Speech strangled in his throat. Before he could move, a knock sounded at the door. A young voice called:

"Five minutes, please!"

"Thank you, Billy."

Lesley peeped at herself in the mirror. The door, which had opened a few inches, closed again. The call-boy's voice died away down the corridor. The interruption had been enough to recall the S.T. to his duties. In a few minutes he would be ringing up the curtain. Without another glance at the girl he loved and hated, Austin wrenched open the door and hurried out of the room.

Immediately, the cruel smile faded from Lesley's lips. Staring at the framed photograph on the wall, she said aloud:

"Help me, Michael. Help me." She whispered:

"I'm afraid.... "

A man was walking slowly across Westminster Bridge. A cold wind from the river plucked at his shabby clothes and stung momentary colour into his pallid cheeks. His shuffling frame was thin and strangely lifeless. His gaze seemed fixed on the ground in front of him, dull as the pavement itself. As he passed in the shadow of Big Ben, the great clock began to chime the half-hour.

The man looked up and smiled. He said:

"I'm coming for you, Lesley." He had cheap cotton gloves on his hands, a self-loading pistol in his pocket, and murder in his heart.

# CHAPTER FIVE

The first act of THE FINAL TROPHY closed with a complete black-out. An enthusiastic burst of applause drowned the swish of the invisible, falling curtain. Then the house lights went up suddenly, disclosing an audience whose individual members began to fidget and flutter self-consciously, as if ashamed to be discovered enjoying themselves.

Seated in the front row of the stalls, Chief Inspector Castle scowled at the curtain. He said abruptly:

"Let's go to the bar."

Algy Lawrence glanced at his wrist-watch. "If this were a nasty, uncivilised foreign land," he remarked, "we could buy a drink any time we wanted it. But Britons never, never shall be slaves—except to their censors and bureaucrats. Do I have to remind you about our licensing laws?"

Castle cursed them unprofessionally. "Come along, anyway. I'll buy you a lemonade."

"You devil, you." Lawrence followed his friend to the nearest exit, pursued by the rattle of tea-trays. In the almost deserted bar, they bought two soft drinks and carried them to a table in the corner.

Glowering at his lemonade, Castle asked suddenly:

"Well, what do you make of it?"

"Of the play? Not much. I still wish we'd gone to the Windmill."

Castle was impatient. "Don't blather, Algy. I mean who sent us those tickets? And why?"

Lawrence tapped his glass thoughtfully. "I don't know, Steve. The house isn't papered. The play seems to be doing good business."

"We've already agreed," growled the Chief Inspector, "we're not guests of the management. But why should anyone else want to see us here this afternoon?"

"I've no idea. Neither," admitted Algy wryly, "can I tell you where to find Paddington Fair."

"That's not surprising. The place doesn't exist."

Lawrence slumped in his chair. "It did once. The name's vaguely familiar. I wish I could remember...." His voice trailed away aimlessly.

Castle snorted. "It's gibberish." He drank his lemonade noisily.

Slamming down the glass, he muttered testily:

"Something's out of true."

His young friend nodded. "Uh huh. There's an odd kind of tension in the air. I can't locate the cause. Though of course,"— he hesitated— "the leading man isn't entirely sober."

"Eh?" The Inspector's eyes widened. "How can you tell?"

"Little signs." Algy opened his hand and shut it again. "I can't go into details. But I'm sure he's been drinking."

"I envy him," commented Castle gruffly. He fished a programme out of his pocket and turned to the cast list. "What's his name, now? Trent. Michael Trent. Know anything about him?"

"No." Lawrence looked sleepy. "But he has a talent for improvisation."

"Huh?" Castle looked blank.

"Didn't you notice? The girl playing 'Marilyn'—."

"Lesley Christopher."

"Yes. As I was saying, she missed her cue. Dried up completely."

"Did she? I didn't notice."

"Thanks to Michael Trent. He ad-libbed masterfully. Drunk or sober, he keeps his wits about him."

"I missed all this. How did you manage to spot it?"

"I have that kind of mind," confessed Algy ruefully. "To coin a cliché, I take my pleasures seriously."

"Maybe you do. But you seem to be particularly alert today."

"Somebody wanted you to see this performance and I want to know why." Lawrence felt for his cigarette case, then let it drop back in his pocket again.

He said softly: "I wonder why she missed her cue."

Castle shrugged. "Actresses do."

Lawrence nodded. "I'm probably making a mystery out of nothing. But it was an odd coincidence."

"What was?"

"A man came into the box on our right at that very point. He was late, and he came in quietly. It seemed to me—." He paused.

Castle was impatient. "Well?"

"I think Lesley Christopher saw him too. She dried up at once. I got the impression she was—." He broke off again.

"Yes?"

Lawrence said quietly:

"Scared."

A bell above the bar rang sharply. It was a warning. They went back to their seats in silence.

Jack Austin had left the prompt box and was standing on stage with his back to the curtain, his gaze roving round the set. Somewhere out of sight the call-boy was chanting:

"Second act beginners, please!"

Penny Valentine was already on stage. She said amiably. "Don't look so fierce, Jack. Nobody's walked off with the props."

The S.M. spared her a brief, amused glance before returning to the prompt box. He was to remember the interruption later. Unimportant though the remark was, it had helped to drive another matter from his mind.

Unperturbed by the clatter around her, Penny Valentine moved Up Centre and stood regarding the closed double doors at the back of the set. The doors opened to disclose a solid-seeming lobby which resolved itself on closer inspection into a few skilfully painted "flats". Penny concentrated her attention on the man who had opened the doors. "Hallo, Douglas."

Denzil returned the greeting rather too warmly. He was slim, good-looking man with a young-old face. Across the footlights he exuded youthful charm, mixing shyness with boyish impertinence. He was a competent Juvenile, and had been for several years. Off stage, his manner was not so attractive. Denzil asked:

Did you want me, sweet?"

Penny returned his gaze with a faint glimmer of amusement at the back of her cerulean eyes. She replied:

"In a way. But don't build your hopes too high! It was only to ask you to be careful with your cues. You gave me one the wrong way round and I nearly fluffed my lines."

"Sorry, sweet." Denzil caricatured a bow of apology. "My mind was wandering." He added:

"I'm no Stanislavsky."

Penny laughed. "No, my pet. You're not."

Denzil said stiffly:

"My role wouldn't be worthy of such effort.    But don't think I'm not capable of the necessary concentration. With the right part, now...."
He paused in invitation.

Penny covered a smile. "Michael's?"

Denzil eyed her suspiciously. "Well, yes. After all, I am his understudy."

"And I'm Lesley Christopher's."

"Well?"

"Both our principals are in the best of health. Don't fool yourself, Douglas. You have about as much chance of playing 'Regan' as I have of playing 'Marilyn'. Which means no chance at all."

Denzil pouted. He said maliciously:

"Dear Michael may soon be resting again. He can't have his own way for ever."

A betraying glint of anger showed in the girl's eyes. She said evenly: "Drunk or sober, he can act you off the stage."

"Oh, pardon me," said Denzil with a hint of viciousness. "I forgot you and Michael were—uh—friendly."

"Darling Douglas. You're quite a stinker, aren't you?"

"I have that distinction," agreed Denzil graciously. One of his more maddening characteristics was a determined refusal to take offence until it suited him to do so. He said:

"I'm also a damn' good actor."

Penny had quickly recovered her equanimity. She smiled:

"I know you are, my pet. But be careful you're not early with your final curtain."

Denzil's painted face creased in a surprised smile. "There's little fear of that, sweet."

"After all," said Penny pointedly, "the means are to hand."

She indicated the revolver hung by pegs on the painted "wall" of the lobby behind him. It was a Webley & Scott with a long jagged scratch on the barrel and the initials "H. W." engraved above the butt.

Denzil stared at the gun with casual interest. He remarked: "I may not be popular. But even in the hand of an enemy, a gun loaded with blanks couldn't do me much harm."

Austin's voice barked suddenly:

"Clear, please!"

Denzil winked and retired to the "lobby" once more. Left alone on the stage, Penny took up her position Down Left.

"Stand by!" The S.M.'s fingers depressed a switch on the board in the prompt corner. A light glowed green in warning. High in the flies, the signal was accepted by the waiting stage-hands. The light went out. Austin drew a deep breath, then switched on the red for "Go".

The curtain went up.

"There's your call, miss." Maggie Boyd stared at her employer curiously. She didn't like Lesley—few women did—but the intimacy of their work together had awoken in the older woman's heart an odd concern for the girl she dressed. She said again:

"There's your call, dear."

"What? Oh... Oh, yes." Lesley seemed to be suffering from some kind of shock. Beneath the flat monotone of her reply was a subtle note of fear.

Maggie said:

"I'll come with you down to the stage." She spoke gently, as though to a child. Lesley stood up.

As she went through the door, she mumbled:

"I saw him. And I dried stone dead."

Maggie followed her from the dressing-room with a hand-mirror and a powder-puff. "What did you say, dear?"

Lesley mumbled:

"In the box...." She spoke no more till they reached the stage.

Michael Trent was waiting in the wings on the prompt side. Ben Cotall was standing behind him, flicking his master's shoulders with a small brush. "That's enough, Ben," murmured Trent as the women approached. "Don't fuss." He smiled at Lesley. "Hallo, angel."

"Michael, I—." Her voice was unnaturally loud.

A hurried "Ssh!" came from the prompt corner.

Lesley continued in a lower key. "Michael, I have to talk to you." She sounded hysterical. Trent's face sobered. The two dressers exchanged enquiring glances.

"*Pas devant les enfants*," said Michael in schoolboy French.

Ben kept his face impassive but Maggie pursed her lips in disapproval.

Heedless of them both, Lesley blurted:

"Michael, you don't understand! He's out there, watching." She finished fearfully:

"Waiting...."


Chief Inspector Castle sat slumped in his seat scowling at the stage. He was not enjoying himself. He grunted, then looked sideways at his companion. Lawrence's blond head had drooped slightly forward, and his sleepy blue eyes were half-closed. Castle was not deceived by his young friend's indolent posture. Lawrence always kept his wits about him. Remembering their conversation in the interval, the Inspector looked past his friend towards the box on their right. He clicked his tongue with annoyance. The man in the box was sitting well to the rear, eluding the glare reflected from the stage. To the Inspector's eyes, he was only a formless blur.

Castle turned his attention back to the play. He was coming to Paddington Fair.

The second act curtain fell on another black-out. Lesley Christopher and Penny Valentine, who had shared the final scene, stayed motionless and invisible till the lights came on again. Then Lesley hurried away through the prompt entrance, like an animal escaping from its cage. Penny followed slowly, a thoughtful look in her eyes.

Wix, the property master, was standing in the wings. He nodded. "Hallo, Miss Valentine."

"Hallo, Props." Penny sounded amused, but a trifle irritated. She knew that the property master tended to regard her as an ally in his feud with Lesley Christopher.

Wix jerked his thumb over his shoulder. He said darkly:

"Her ladyship's not herself today."

Penny smiled briefly. "She can't be. She just forgot to kill my big laugh."

"Ah." Wix shook his head wisely. "Something's upset her, I reckon. Proper scared, she seemed." His lined, anxious face was unusually cheerful. He rattled something in his pocket with an air of gloomy gaiety.

Penny chuckled. Side-stepping the property master neatly, she headed for the dressing-room passage. She hesitated for a moment outside one of the doors, then tapped the panels lightly. The door opened. Ben Cotall peeped out.

Penny asked:

"How's Mr. Trent?"

Before Cotall could reply, a voice from within cried gaily:

"Penny, darling! Come on in." Michael Trent was lounging in a wicker chair by the further wall. He was wearing a dressing-gown, and his face glistened thinly with sweat. He smiled at Penny wickedly. Without taking his gaze from the girl, he said softly:

"Leave us, Ben. For a minute. But," he warned, "don't go far away."

When they were alone, Michael grinned at the girl engagingly. "Penny, my love .Give me a kiss."

"There's no time for that," she replied practically. Taking some tissues from the dressing-table, she began to blot the perspiration from his face. Michael submitted with a fairly good grace. Penny stood back and studied him with a tiny frown. "You need more powder. Otherwise you'll pass muster."

"Yes, ma'am." He stood up.

Penny rested her hands on his chest. Michael stroked her fingers gently. Her mouth trembled. She asked abruptly:

"Have you spoken to Lesley?"

Trent seemed embarrassed. He said:

"Damn it, Penny. These things take time. I can't just blurt out suddenly—."

"That you love me, and you don't love her?"

"I love you," whispered Michael. "That's true, indeed." His hand moved in a long caress over the curve of her spine. Penny's lips moved silently. Michael covered them with a kiss. The door behind them opened.

Lesley Christopher came into the room. "Michael, I—." She stopped suddenly.

There was a long pause.

Then Lesley spoke in a choking voice. "You'll be sorry for this. I promise you." She went out.

Penny was trembling. Michael tried to soothe her but she pushed his hands away and slipped from his embrace. Running to the door, she called unevenly:

"Ben! Ben, come here, please." She stumbled out.

Michael bit his lip. He turned back to the mirror. Almost unconsciously, he began to tidy his make-up. His intelligent eyes were anxious. Abruptly, his fingers stilled: he began to swear fluently and tonelessly. Cotall had shuffled back at Penny's call. Like a second mirror, old Ben's face reflected the anxiety in his master's.

The thin man with the pallid cheeks sat well to the rear of the box, shielded by the curtains from the front stalls. His programme lay unopened on the ledge. A pulse was throbbing in the thin man's temple, blue-veined beneath the skin. His gloved hands were trembling. As the lights went down, he leaned forward.

Taking the self-loading pistol from one shabby pocket, he examined it carefully. Then he placed it on the empty seat beside him, ready to hand. His head went forward. He paid no attention to the drama on the stage. He would pay none till Lesley reappeared. His head drooped.

He seemed to be praying.

# CHAPTER SIX

As the curtain went up for the third act Algy Lawrence slumped in his seat and stretched out his legs in front of him.

His lazy blue eyes were moody. They roved absently over the set resting for a moment on the stuffed bear which stood to the rear of the stage on the audience's left. The huge animal was sitting upright on its hams, and from its circular dais seemed to be glowering at the occupants of the boxes on the right. Its paws were spread realistically and its mouth was open in a menacing snarl.

Lawrence shifted uneasily. Though the play appeared to be shaping for a climax, it was beginning to bore him. He was too uncomfortably aware of a larger tension beyond the artificial contrivances of dialogue and plot. When Lesley Christopher made her next entrance, he watched her attentively. He fancied he saw an odd flicker—as of fear—in her eyes as she glanced, perhaps involuntarily, towards the box on his right. Lawrence tensed. The invisible "fourth wall" which separated the audience from the stage seemed to have been shattered by that fleeting glance. Then the moment passed .and he wondered if it had existed only in his imagination.

He turned his head slightly and stared hard. It was quite useless. He couldn't see past the curtains which shrouded the side of the box. He directed his attention back to the stage. After a while, he gave up listening to the dialogue. "Paddington Fair" loomed larger in his mind. I should know what it means, he told himself irritably. I've heard the name before. Suddenly, he tensed. An isolated phrase from the dialogue forced its way into his mind and stayed there obstinately.

The shadow of Tyburn Tree... The Tree... and Paddington Fair. Was there a connection? Lawrence closed his eyes, scanning a mental screen. A memory formed, then faded like breath from a mirror. Damnation! Lawrence opened his eyes and glared vacantly at the stage. Penny Valentine made her exit on the O.P. side, leaving Michael Trent alone on the stage. Taking advantage of a spatter of applause that followed the girl through the painted door, Lawrence leaned over and whispered in his friend's ear:

"Steve, I—."

An indignant "Ssssh!" came from the row behind. Lawrence subsided, ignoring Castle's grunt of enquiry. The double doors at the rear of the set opened suddenly. Lesley Christopher appeared on the threshold, clutching something in her hand. Lawrence leaned forward instinctively. He could see it was a Webley & Scott revolver—the gun which had been fixed by pegs to the "wall" of the lobby behind her.

Michael and Lesley went into their big scene. It was a tense duologue which commanded even Lawrence's flagging attention. "Marilyn" threatened "Regan" with the gun. He shrugged, turned away, then wheeled and grabbed her wrist. Silently, the audience watched the struggle. They saw "Regan" wrench the revolver from "Marilyn's" hand, then back slowly away, covering her with the gun. "Now it's my turn, baby."

She whimpered. She backed away from the menacing weapon. The stuffed bear behind her seemed to be spreading its paws invitingly. Lawrence's eyes were on Michael Trent. Sweat glistened behind the actor's heavy make-up. Lawrence chilled. He watched with fascinated revulsion as Trent thumbed down the hammer of the revolver and steadied the gun carefully.

Lesley's heels tapped against the dais, and she seemed to freeze with her body almost within the animal's clumsy grasp. The gun in Trent's hand tilted gently, its muzzle pointing like an accusing finger towards the girl's heart. She whispered:

"No...."

Trent was standing Down Left very near to the setting line with his back to the boxes on the audience's right. Lesley's frightened gaze was fixed on the gun in his hand— Or on something or someone in the box behind him? As the startling question formed in Lawrence's brain, a memory unsealed. And he knew, with a chill of fear, the meaning of Paddington Fair.

He tried to shout a warning, but the sound died in his throat.

Trent was smiling tightly. His crooked finger squeezed against the trigger and the revolver blasted in his hand. Lesley's body jerked. A sick, puzzled look appeared in her eyes and she swayed back against the animal behind her. Something bubbled thickly in her throat. A red, spreading stain showed briefly on her breast before she fell face downward upon the floor.

Castle stared in bewilderment. Lawrence's voice sounded in his ear.

"There were two shots—two spurts of flame—." Castle jerked his head. He had a second's glimpse of his friend's white face before the lights faded in a complete black-out. Dazed and bewildered, he waited helplessly in the darkness. He could see nothing.

And then he heard the laughter. It was a crazy sound. And it was evil.

Lawrence leaped to his feet. He blundered through the darkness wildly. Nothing relieved the blackness except the lights above the EXIT doors. And they did no more than shape the letters of the signs. They threw no light into the auditorium. Fighting a rising panic, Lawrence battled his way towards the box on his right. He kept his body against the low partition which divided the orchestra well from the front stalls and groped along, ignoring the startled cries of enquiry that followed him. Then the footlights glowed, illuminating the fallen curtain.

Lawrence gasped with relief. He swung his legs over the partition and lurched towards the box. He had no time to feel afraid. He put his hands on the ledge and vaulted into the gloom. He stumbled against a chair and recovered his balance quickly. A man was scrabbling at the door in the rear of the box. He jerked round as Lawrence reached out for him and swung a clumsy blow at the young man's face. It caught him on the side of his jaw and he stumbled back, momentarily dazed.

He shook his head. His vision cleared. His assailant was a thin man with pallid cheeks. He wore shabby clothes and cheap cotton gloves. He was holding a pistol in his right hand. Lawrence said grimly:

"I knew I saw a gun flash."

"Shut up!" The man's voice was hysterical. He muttered:

"Get back against the wall. Hurry up, damn you! I've used this gun once. I can use it again."

Lawrence obeyed. He said quietly:

"Don't be a fool. You can't escape."

"I said, shut up! And put up your hands."

Lawrence raised his hands above his head. He said again:

"You can't escape."

"Damn you!" The shabby man was trembling. "Why did you have to interfere?" He moved nearer, holding the pistol close to Lawrence's chest. There was a strange gleam in his eyes, frightened yet ruthless. He had the look of a man who had killed once and who would not hesitate to kill again...The muzzle shook.

Lawrence thought: He's mad... He's going to shoot! Lawrence moved quickly. He dropped his left hand and knocked the thin man's pistol hand to one side. At the same time he turned his right shoulder forward. The gun blazed but the shot passed harmlessly under his left armpit and the bullet thudded into the wall behind him. Lawrence grabbed the shabby man's right wrist with his left hand and slid his right foot behind the other's right heel. Then he jabbed his right hand forward. The tips of his fingers thudded into the tenderest part of the other man's throat.

The shabby man collapsed with a sickly choke. Lawrence pulled the gun from his hand and stepped back wearily. He felt ill. He had always hated violence. The house lights went up suddenly. Lawrence leaned over the ledge, ignoring the startled faces that were turned towards him. "Steve! Come quickly."

Castle was already on his feet. "Are you all right?"

"Yes." Lawrence rubbed the sweat from his face. "But hurry." The Chief Inspector turned to face the crowd behind him. He raised his arms and shouted: "Quiet, please!" His authoritative manner subdued the noisy, startled crowd. He said clearly:

"I am a police officer. You will kindly keep your seats." Beckoning to a uniformed attendant, he muttered some hasty instructions. Then he stumped towards the box.

Lawrence shoved the chairs to one side and bent over the fallen man, who was only semi-conscious. Algy stared at the thin, pallid face and felt pity stir. Then he remembered the girl and his lazy eyes hardened. The door behind him opened and Castle appeared, ushered into the box by a frightened programme seller. The Chief Inspector growled:

"Just what in blazes is happening here?"

Lawrence straightened up.

He said:

"You saw that stain over Miss Christopher's heart. It wasn't stage blood. It was real."

Castle nodded slowly. "I feared as much. And so?"

"Two guns were fired, though we heard only one report. I saw a second flame spurt from this box."

"A gun flash?"

Lawrence held out the pistol in a wordless reply. Castle scowled. "So that's it. When the blank was fired on stage our friend here—."

"Fired a live cartridge at the same target," finished Algy grimly. "Using the noise of one explosion to cover the other."

"A bold plan," grunted the Chief Inspector. "But a clever one. He might have escaped if you hadn't kept your wits about you."

Lawrence shrugged. "He gave himself away when he laughed so crazily."

Castle shivered. "He must be mad."

"Perhaps." Lawrence stared at the pistol in his hand. It was small but deadly—a Colt .25. "But not in the legal sense."

"No," agreed Castle. "This crime was premeditated. And if that girl dies, then this man will hang."

Lawrence muttered unhappily. "Don't let it bother you," advised the Chief Inspector. "Ah, well! Let's get to work."

The shabby man groaned.

"He's coming round," said Lawrence. He smiled uneasily. "I thought for a moment I'd killed him."

"You merely bruised his neck," returned Castle grimly. "The rope will break it."

Michael Trent groped about in the blackness, fighting a rising panic. The echo of the shabby man's macabre laughter rang in his ears, and he remembered with a shudder the ugly stain which had appeared on Lesley's breast in the appalling seconds before the lights went out. He steadied himself with an effort. Clutching hard on the butt of the Webley & Scott, he called:

"Austin! For God's sake, put on those lights!" When the bulbs flared up, they blinded him. He shut his eyes, then opened them.

"Lesley!" He ran across the stage to the crumpled figure lying at the base of the dais, ignoring the confused babel of sound from the other side of the fallen curtain.

"What's wrong?" The stage manager had appeared from the wings. Standing by the prompt entrance, he asked again:

"What's happened?"

Michael turned a blind face towards him. He whispered:

"Lesley – she's been hurt."

Austin said blankly:

"I don't understand."

Trent lifted the girl's shoulders and stared at the wound in her breast. He choked. He said hoarsely:

"She's been shot."

"B-but—." Austin's mouth worked stupidly. Before he could say more, a gun blasted on the other side of the curtain. Trent let the girl's body slide to the ground once more and moved his hands in an odd gesture of protest. The stage manager cried:

"Good God! What's that?"

Trent shook his head helplessly. Austin cracked his knuckles. He muttered nervously:

"Something's happening out front. They'll need the house lights. I'd better give the signal." Still mumbling, he returned to the prompt corner.

Trent stroked the dead girl's hair gently. He said aloud:

"Good-bye, Lesley." Somebody moved behind him.

A scared voice whispered. "Is she dead?"

Trent stood up. He looked at the questioner dully. He said. "Yes, June. She's dead."

June Merritt was the assistant stage manager. Her plain, rather podgy

251

face was set in a bad caricature of astonishment. "What happened?" The stage manager returned in time to hear the question. He echoed it.

Trent passed his free hand across his forehead, smearing his make-up. "I---I don't know exactly." He looked down at the revolver in his right hand with a kind of dull horror. Then he shook his head, as if rejecting an impossible suspicion. He said:

"Somebody… somebody fired a gun from the box behind me. I—." He swallowed. "I felt the wind of a bullet as it passed my body. Lesley collapsed with blood on her breast. The lights went out."

He finished tonelessly:

"And then there was—the laughter."

Austin and his assistant stared incredulously. Then June Merritt burst out wildly:

"But things like this don't happen in England."

Austin laughed harshly. "Don't be so insular, June. This isn't our first public assassination."

"For God's sake!" Trent's voice shook. "You sound so callous. Aren't you going to send for a doctor?"

"What for?" asked Austin coldly. "You said yourself—she's dead."

Michael stared at him. The S.M. seemed to have recovered his composure rapidly. Had there been a trace of savage satisfaction in his reply? Surely not. And yet… Trent put the thought aside. He cried:

"Don't you understand? Something must be done!"

"Calm yourself," said Austin curtly. He added dryly:

"And put down that gun."

Trent brought up his hand and stared at the revolver once more. He cried with sudden loathing:

"Take it then!" He thrust the gun into the stage manager's hands.

Austin looked vaguely surprised. Then he slipped the revolver into one capacious pocket and shrugged indifferently. "As you please." The rough material of his jacket chafed against his hand. Withdrawing it from his pocket, he fingered the burnt flesh gently....

Victor Friern pushed his way past the startled attendants and went into the box with a haggard face. His erect carriage was gone, but he spoke with his usual formality. "Good afternoon, gentlemen. I am the general manager."

Castle nodded briefly. "I'm Chief Inspector Castle of the C.I.D. I'm glad you're here, sir. You know what's been happening?"

Friern nodded his greying head painfully. "I heard—." He broke off.

Castle grunted. "I've made an arrest. But there are certain formalities which must be observed." He indicated the audience. "These people will have to be questioned. Some may be required to give evidence. And, for the moment, no one will be allowed to leave this theatre. Will you make the necessary arrangements?"

"I'll do anything I can."

"Good. Perhaps you'll take Mr. Lawrence here to a telephone. Algy!"

"Yes?"

"You know what to do. Call the Yard and make a full report. Say I've taken charge. They'll send the right people."

Lawrence nodded. "Right, Steve." He followed Friern away.

The shabby man was still on the floor. He sat up, rubbing his throat ruefully. Castle stood over him, his shrewd grey eyes alert. He scanned the other's pallid face. He asked abruptly:

"What's your name?"

The thin man said sullenly:

"You should know."

"What's that?" Castle scowled with surprise. "Wait, now. Your face does seem familiar, but...."

"We met a long time ago."

"I don't remember you."

"I'm not surprised." The shabby man sneered. "Prison life has changed me for the worse."

"You don't talk like a convict," said Castle bluntly. "Or a madman. Who are you?"

The thin man said bitterly: "I'm a decent young man who destroyed himself."

Castle recognized the words as a paraphrase—or a parody—of his own. He caught his breath. "Hell's blazes! You're—."

"I'm a murderer," said the prisoner savagely. "I made a vow and I kept it."

"And the girl?"

"Her name was Lesley Barre. Mine is Richard Mervan."

# CHAPTER SEVEN

Algy Lawrence replaced the receiver, then turned from the telephone with a sober face. "That's that. The police will be here soon."

Victor Friern clenched his fist. He said painfully:

"It's incredible!"

Lawrence replied:

"It happened."

"But Lesley...." Friern choked on the name.

Lawrence glanced at him sleepily. "Did you see the shooting, sir?"

Friern shook his greying head. "No. I was here—in my office. An attendant came for me after—after—." His voice shook.

Lawrence made his own tone brisk. "Let's take a look back-stage, sir. There may be something we can do."

Friern asked. "Are you an officer too?"

Lawrence grinned crookedly. "I'm not a policeman. But I'm well known at the Yard. My—uh—interference won't be resented."

Friern took a key from his desk, then led the way out of his office and climbed a flight of stairs on the left. Lawrence followed him through a door giving access to the Dress Circle. The manager murmured:

"This way, please."

They went down the wide stairs flanked by the left-hand wall, ignoring the frightened, angry people squirming restlessly in the plush-lined seats. Friern muttered anxiously:

"We can't keep the audience here much longer."

Lawrence shrugged. "Don't worry. Steve knows what he's doing."

Friern said doubtfully:

"I hope so."

By this time, they had reached the front of the Dress Circle. Friern pushed aside a curtain to disclose a short, narrow passage. He said:

"This gives access to the box on this level."

He knocked politely on the door and led the way in. The occupants of the box—a man and a woman—looked round nervously. The manager murmured a few courteous words, then unlocked the pass-door in the wall nearest the stage. Murmuring a caution, he led the way down a narrow stairway.

Lawrence looked about him with interest flickering in his lazy blue eyes. It was the first time he had been behind the scenes in a theatre. His first impressions were rather confused. He seemed to be lost in a world of bewildering activity, of hoarse voices and hazy lights. And it was something of a shock to discover that the solid-looking "room" he had seen from the stalls was mainly composed of rectangular wooden frames covered with canvas.

The manager said:

"This way."

Lawrence followed Friern through what he later discovered to be the O.P. entrance and found himself on the stage set. He felt vaguely uncomfortable and out of place.

"Victor! Thank the Lord you're here." A man in a loose fitting jacket and flannel trousers broke away from a group of people on the other side of the stage and hastened towards them.

Friern made a hurried introduction. "Mr. Lawrence, Mr. Austin." He took the stage manager's arm. "How is she, Jack?" Austin shrugged. "I'm afraid there's no hope. But—. " He pointed to the rear of the stage. "I called for a doctor. He's examining her now."

Friern dropped his hand. He said:

"She mustn't die."

Austin's jaw hardened. He turned away without replying.

An efficient little man with deft hands was bending over Lesley's prostrate form. He straightened up as Lawrence and Friern approached him. The manager said:

"Doctor?" on a note of enquiry. Recognizing the unspoken question, the little man shook his head sadly. "I'm afraid there's nothing I can do. The young lady is dead."

Friern swayed. Then he steadied himself with an effort. He asked:

"Did she—did she suffer?"

"I don't think so. Death was probably instantaneous. The bullet appears to have penetrated her heart." He added kindly:

"No, she didn't suffer."

"Thank God for that." Friern's voice was firmer. "And thank you, Doctor, for your help."

"It was little enough, I'm afraid." The small man hesitated. Then he asked:

"Shall I return to the auditorium?"

Lawrence interposed. "Not yet, Doctor. The police surgeon will be here soon. I expect he'll want to talk to you."

"Ah, yes. Of course."

Lawrence stared down at Lesley's body with pity in his eyes. He said abruptly:

"I hate waste."

Victor Friern said:

"She was rather"—he hesitated—"a special person." His eyes were blind with pain.

Lawrence nodded slowly. Someone tapped him on the shoulder.

"Have you got the devil who did this?" Michael Trent was standing behind him. The actor's glossy black hair had lost its sleekness, and his handsome features were blurred with emotion. He asked again:

"Have you found the man who murdered Lesley?"

Lawrence said:

"A man has been detained."

Trent asked hoarsely:

"He—he admitted his guilt?"

Lawrence said dryly:

"He could scarcely deny it. I took the gun away from him myself."

Friern interrupted. "Michael, you look all in."

"Never mind that," snapped Trent impatiently. His eyes were feverish. "This man—who is he?"

"I don't know." Lawrence was gentle. "He's under arrest. It won't take long to identify him."

"Under arrest!" repeated Trent stupidly. "I don't understand this at all. How did the police arrive so quickly?"

Lawrence explained patiently. The shock seemed to have scattered the actor's wits. Algy said:

"Chief Inspector Castle was a member of the audience. So was I." He added:

"I'm Algy Lawrence."

Trent stared. "You were in the audience too?"

Lawrence repeated softly:

"Too? What made you say that?"

Trent's eyes flickered. He swallowed. "I—I—." He finished with decision. "I'm going to be sick." He stumbled towards the prompt entrance. A wizened little man in a shabby black jacket tried to assist him, his bony hands plucking ineffectually at the actor's coat. Trent. Pushed him away with a curse. "Damn you, Ben! Leave me alone." He lurched into the wings, leaving Cotall blinking unhappily.

Friern murmured.:

"Poor old Ben! He's Trent's dresser, you see, and devoted to him. But his fussiness drives Michael crazy."

Lawrence nodded. "Trent seems to be near collapse. I wonder why?"

Friern hesitated before replying. Then he said with restraint:

"Michael and Lesley were very good friends."

"I see." The two men fell silent, looking at the girl's dead body.

Friern sobbed suddenly. The sound was so harsh and unexpected that Lawrence started involuntarily, then looked away awkwardly. Friern said:

"Forgive me, please. I'm not becoming hysterical. It was a—a stab of memory."

"Yes?"

The manager was himself again. He explained:

"I was talking to Lesley in her dressing-room before the show. She said—." He broke off. Lawrence prompted him gently.

Friern finished grimly:

"She said it wasn't easy to die at every performance."

Lawrence said uncomfortably:

"A macabre comment."

Friern spread his hands. "She was nervous, tense, and troubled in her mind."

Lawrence showed interest. "Why?" ·

"I don't know. I've been wondering if that queer message had upset her more than she admitted."

"What message?" asked Lawrence sleepily.

"It was on a card in a letter which was delivered to the theatre this afternoon. It was an odd message. It was something about a fair."

The amiable vagueness in Lawrence's eyes was approaching absolute vacancy. "Where is the card now?"

"In her dressing-room, I suppose. I threw card and envelope into the basket. At Lesley's request."

Lawrence nodded. He said with apparent irrelevance:

"Chief Inspector Castle was given two free seats in the stalls. That wasn't a gift from the theatre, was it?"

"Heavens, no." Friern looked surprised. "At least, well, I'll have to check with my business manager before giving a definite answer. But to the best of my knowledge the free list has been entirely suspended. We're doing good business, you know. We're not playing to the Wood Family."

Algy blinked. "What was that again?"

Friern's smile was fleeting. "Sorry. That was theatrical jargon. I was referring to unoccupied seats; empty benches; the Wood Family, in fact. And as I say, business is good. We don't find it necessary to paper the house."

"Now that," said Algy, "is a term I understand. You don't give away free tickets." He spoke absently. Then he asked abruptly:

"Where are the dressing-rooms?"

Friern's reply was interrupted by the arrival of a number of men in uniform and in plain clothes. Lawrence recognized the man in charge as Detective Inspector Wemyss, a capable investigator who frequently worked with Stephen Castle. Leaving Friern to greet the party, Lawrence slipped through the double doors at the rear of the seat. He noticed in passing that the Webley & Scott revolver had not been replaced on the pegs on the lobby "wall." The inner "room" or lobby terminated abruptly beyond the audience's line of sight. In contrast to the standing set, the rest of the stage was dimly lit. The odour of size solution was very strong.

Both disillusioned and fascinated by his glimpse behind the scenes, Lawrence looked around for the entrance to the dressing-room passage. It was close at hand. Lawrence strolled into the corridor and eyed the walls gloomily. The green distemper was shabbily depressing. Then he smiled with simple pleasure. A girl was standing outside the door to one of the dressing-rooms and Algy, who was an impressionable young man, viewed her with frank approval.

She was slapping the panels with her open hand. "Michael! Michael! Please let me in."

Lawrence coughed discreetly.

The girl's eyes met his, and she said:

"Oh," very softly. She stepped away from the door. She was very attractive. Her hair was styled in a page boy bob; it was dusty blonde and streaked with gold. She smiled, and tiny lines of laughter deepened at the corners of her cerulean eyes. Her mouth was warm and kissable. Algy smiled in return.

"Hallo. Let me introduce myself. My name is—."

"Algy Lawrence," said the girl unexpectedly. "I know."

He angled an eyebrow. "You recognized me?"

"From your photographs. The papers all carried your picture when you solved the Querrin House mystery."

"I see." Lawrence was sombre. The case was one he didn't like to remember. He shrugged away the phantoms. He said lightly:

"And you're Penny Valentine."

"That's right."

Lawrence said:

"I'm glad I crossed the barrier of the footlights. Though I wish we had met under pleasanter circumstances." His voice was admiring.

A responsive twinkle of mischievous amusement showed in the girl's clear eyes. Then she remembered. She said gravely:

"I can't pretend I liked Lesley. But I'm sorry she was killed."

Lawrence drew a bow at a venture. "And sorry," he murmured, "that

Michael had to watch her die?"

"Poor darling." Penny's eyes were troubled. "He's locked himself in his dressing-room." Her lips trembled. "And he won't let me in."

"There are times," said Algy mildly, "when a man prefers to be alone. Trent is probably being sicker than a dog."

"Oh!" Amusement, sympathy, and confusion showed in her face. She retreated along the corridor.

Lawrence gazed after her, admiring the supple motion of her body, the graceful sway of her hips. Then he opened the door marked with the golden star and walked into the dressing-room. It was empty. Lawrence located the basket by the dressing-table and examined the interior eagerly. "Ah!" He picked up the card with the enigmatic message, holding it delicately by the edges. He placed it carefully on the table top. WE MEET AT PADDINGTON FAIR.

Lawrence read the words aloud. He murmured. "I wonder... "

A heavy tread sounded in the passage outside. Algy turned to discover Castle in the doorway. Castle gave a good-humoured growl. "Look here, young Algy. Are you tampering with the evidence again?"

Lawrence grinned an apology. "Sorry, Steve. My curiosity outran my discretion." He indicated the card. "I found that in the basket."

Castle pursed his heavy lips. He lumbered across the room. Then he swore violently. "Paddington Fair!"

"Yes. Friern tells me the message came by the mid-day delivery.   It was addressed to Lesley Christopher"—Lawrence stooped over the basket again—"and was enclosed in this envelope." He added:

"The postmark is London, S.E.1."

Castle confessed his bewilderment with another blood-curdling oath.

Lawrence said wearily:

"I know what it means, Steve. So should you"

"Eh?"

There was a bitter taste in the young man's mouth. "A line from the play gave me the clue. I saw the truth—too late."

Castle scowled. "You'd better explain."

Lawrence sighed. "You recall the reference to Tyburn Tree?"

"What about it?"

"The Tree was the gallows. And Tyburn is in the parish of—."

"Paddington." Castle flushed with excitement. "Hell's blazes! You mean...."

"When our forefathers went to Paddington Fair," said Lawrence dully, "they went to witness a public execution."

He closed his eyes wearily. "We accepted a killer's invitation. We came to the Fair today."

# CHAPTER EIGHT

Castle sighed noisily. "So that was it! A prosy message of defiance. 'See me commit murder. And catch me if you can.'"

Lawrence shivered. "A challenge like that," he muttered, "is crazy."

"It's the product of a mind unhinged," agreed the Chief Inspector. "Mervan lusted for revenge."

"Mervan?"

"We've identified the man. He's an old... acquaintance of mine." He laughed uneasily. "Funny—I nearly said friend."

Lawrence regarded him, thoughtfully. "You have a story to tell."

"Later," said Castle flatly. He sounded tired. "There's work to be done." Lawrence followed him out of the dressing-room. As they made their way back to the stage, Castle grunted an aside. "I found two spent shells on the floor of Mervan's box—the cartridge cases ejected from his pistol. Calibre .25." Lawrence nodded absently. This was routine work. Matched with the bullets from the wall and Lesley's body, the empty cases would prove the prisoner's guilt.

"You're going to give him a fair trial," said Algy suddenly, "and then you're going to hang him."

Castle said patiently:

"This isn't a frame-up. There'll be no miscarriage of justice."

Lawrence grinned a rueful apology. "I know, Steve. I'm sorry. But I don't like capital punishment."

Castle replied grimly:

"I don't like murder."

They went through the prompt entrance in silence. Lawrence discovered that much had been done during his comparatively short absence. Lesley's body had been removed and was now on its way to the mortuary. Algy glanced at the chalk outline and the red stain which marked the place where the girl had fallen, then looked away with clouded eyes. The stuffed bear seemed to be snarling in triumph.

Detective Inspector Wemyss approached his chief and spoke in low tones. "The police surgeon has just left, sir. He has promised to perform the post-mortem at once. He will let you have the bullet as soon as he recovers it from the dead woman's body."

"Good." Castle grunted approval. "I shall want an immediate report from ballistics."

"Right, sir. The .25 pistol and the two ejected cartridge cases are on their way to the laboratory. And I'm about to recover the second bullet from the wall of that box."

"I'm glad," said Castle ferociously, "that we haven't got to dig it out of Mr. Lawrence's chest." He glowered at his friend affectionately. "You took an awful chance, young Algy."

Lawrence shrugged. "Someone had to tackle Mervan."

Castle asked Wemyss:

"Have you begun to question the audience?"

The Detective Inspector nodded. "Each person will be interrogated before leaving the theatre."

Lawrence looked surprised. "Are you taking statements from everybody?"

"No. Just names and addresses."

Castle broke in:

"Every man, woman, and child in the auditorium witnessed a murder this afternoon. We must know where to find them."

"I suppose so."

Wemyss lowered his voice. "What shall we do with these people, sir?" He indicated the men and women huddled together in a corner of the set.

Castle grunted. "I'll speak to 'em now." He stepped forward and cleared his throat noisily. "Ladies and gentlemen! Your attention, please." Silence fell like a blanket. The Chief Inspector said:

"We shall be taking statements from you later. Meanwhile, those of you in costume"—Castle's gaze fell on Denzil and his companion, an attractive young girl in a fringe—"may go to your dressing-rooms and change. I must ask you, however, not to wander about the theatre. And nobody should leave the building without permission."

There was an uncertain pause. Castle coughed. "Thank you. That's all for the moment." Rather to his surprise, no one moved.

Then Victor Friern detached himself from the group and advanced with the air of a spokesman. Castle eyed the manager's sunken cheeks. The tragedy had evidently affected Friern deeply. "Chief Inspector—." It was a false start. The manager's voice pitched oddly, then faltered and died away.

Castle growled, not unsympathetically:

"Yes, Mr. Friern. What is it?"

"Your—your work will be finished soon?"

"I imagine so." Castle squinted inquisitively. "Why do you ask?"

Friern said baldly:

"We have another performance scheduled for this evening."

Castle stared. "You're surely not asking me for permission to give a show tonight? After all that's happened?"

"I am."

"But good God, man! No one will expect you to open tonight."

"We like to keep faith with the public."

Lawrence and Castle exchanged glances. Then Algy murmured:

"If somebody says 'The show must go on', I shall probably cry aloud."

Friern said with dignity:

"The phrase may be hackneyed. But I can assure you it represents a very real tradition of the theatre."

Castle thought:

he speaks sincerely. But... He shrugged. "Suppose I agree? You've lost your leading lady."

"She has—had a competent understudy."

Castle scowled thoughtfully. "Well, now. We shall probably have completed our routine work here before eight o'clock."

Friern said, not eagerly:

"That gives us time enough." He gestured. "This is a standing—that is, a permanent—set."

Castle spread his hands. "Very well, then. You can give the performance. But remember," he warned, "our work takes precedence. I shall expect you all to hold yourselves at our disposal."

Friern nodded. His face was slightly flushed.

Castle beckoned to Wemyss. "I'm leaving you in charge. You know what to do."

Lawrence asked: "Where are we going, Steve?"

"We?" echoed the Chief Inspector. "This is no case for you, young Algy. No sealed rooms. No black magic. No hocus pocus. Just a straightforward killing." He finished sarcastically:

"Mere routine."

Lawrence said:

"I wonder."

Castle started. "What the devil do you mean by that?"

Lawrence grinned lazily. "Nothing, probably. But I'd like to see the case through to the end."

Castle grunted. "All right, then. Come with me. I'm going to question Richard Mervan."

The two friends left.

Douglas Denzil waited till they had disappeared from view, then crossed the stage and clapped Victor Friern on the back. "Good work, sir. You handled the Dogberry well." He was grinning hugely.

Friern regarded him with distaste. The manager said coldly:

"It's hardly a matter for congratulations. I don't think of it as a victory. I simply want to keep faith with the public."

"Of course," said Denzil on a subtle note of mockery.

The manager frowned. He said with a spurt of irritation:

"Stop smiling!"

Denzil's expression sobered. But his eyes remained lit with malicious amusement behind the mask of gravity. He murmured. "I'm sorry." He coughed. "May I break the good—the news to Penny?"

"I suppose so." Friern looked tired. "Someone must tell her to be ready. It might as well be you."

"Right." Denzil capered away. Arriving in the dressing-room passage, he paused for a moment outside the door marked with the golden star. Setting his face in a grotesque caricature of melancholy, he bowed to the emblem. Then he knocked on the adjoining door and glanced into Trent's dressing-room.

Michael was huddled in a chair, looking rather the worse for wear. Ben Cotall, having at last reclaimed his charge, was fussing round him anxiously.

Denzil said:

"Hallo, Michael."

Trent spoke without any particular emotion. "I wish I'd kept that damn' door locked."

"Naughty man," said Denzil calmly. "You can't offend me, Michael."

"I can try."

Ben Cotall began anxiously:

"Gentlemen, please—."

"Shut up, Ben," said Denzil pleasantly. "I have news for you, Michael. The show goes on tonight."

"What! But I can't—I mean—oh, hell!" Michael bit his lip.

Denzil grinned maliciously. "It's too late for objections now. Friend Victor has made up his mind. And the Dogberry is amenable."

Trent ran a monogrammed comb through his thickly-growing hair. Then he swore softly and dropped the comb carelessly.

Denzil's eyes narrowed. "Squeamish, Michael?" His smile was feline. "You don't have to go on tonight. I'd be happy to deputize."

Trent's response was terse.

Denzil retreated gracefully. "Don't worry, Michael. I'm not trying to step into your shoes. Or tread on your toes. The part is yours."

Outside the door he added softly:

"For the moment...."


Penny Valentine looked up with a start when the door of her dressing room opened. "Who's there? Oh, it's you, Douglas." Her voice flattened. "Don't you bother to knock?"

Denzil ignored the question. "Hallo, sweet. I bring good news."

"That's nice," said Penny equably. She smeared grease over her face.

Denzil pointed his toes like a dancer. He cried:

"Marilyn the first is dead. Long live Marilyn the second."

Penny was removing her make-up. Her fingers faltered for a moment, then busied themselves again.

She said wearily:

"That may be a joke, Douglas. But I don't feel like laughing."

Denzil pouted. "I'm not fooling, Penny. THE FINAL TROPHY goes on tonight with you in the lead."

The girl stared at her reflection in the mirror. "But the police—. "

"Have given us permission."

Penny said:

"It's hard to believe."

Denzil put his hands on her shoulders. "This is your big chance. Make the most of it."

Penny whispered:

"But to get it like this, because Lesley was killed...." Her eyes shadowed.

"I feel as if I were robbing a grave."

# CHAPTER NINE

Chief Inspector Castle said gravely:

"I'm speaking unofficially. But I think I ought to tell you"—he coughed behind his hand—that you might be wiser to keep silent."

Richard Mervan slumped in the hard-backed chair. "What's the use? I'm done for anyway."

"Very well." Castle scowled at the table between them. He said impersonally:

"Richard Mervan, it is my duty to warn you that anything you say will be taken down and may be used in evidence."

The prisoner's mouth twitched.

He said abruptly:

"For God's sake, give me a cigarette."

Castle nodded a signal. Lawrence stepped forward and held out his silver case. When the cigarette was between the prisoner's lips, Lawrence reversed the case and flicked up a flame from the lighter in its spine.

Mervan inhaled deeply. "Thanks."

He blew out a streamer of smoke.

Castle waited patiently. Lawrence retired to a seat in the corner. The station shorthand writer flipped open his notebook.

Mervan took the cigarette away from his mouth.

He spoke with uneasy bravado. "Well, Inspector. Where shall we begin?"

"Anywhere you please." Castle's voice was gentle, almost sympathetic. "I'll help you compose a formal statement later."

Mervan asked abruptly:

"You know why I killed her, of course?"

Castle nodded. "She was Lesley, the girl who betrayed you."

"Yes." Mervan's cheeks hollowed. He forced a laugh. The sound was harsh and ugly.

Castle prompted him gently. "Tell me about her."

Mervan said desperately:

"I loved her... "

He went on:

"It all began on the day a thug tried to rob me outside Head Office. I downed him with a simple piece of Judo—it was one of the tricks that the Army taught me. I take no particular credit for it.

"But I did save the bank's money. And I hoped for some small reward."

"Did you get it?" asked Castle.

Mervan laughed shortly. "I received," he said bitterly, "a personal letter of commendation from the Directors. Which had no cash value." He dragged smoke from the cigarette. "That was the start of it all. My discontent. And my friendship with Lesley."

He paused, remembering. He said angrily:

"I can see now how she played upon my resentment. I could have forgotten the disappointment in time. But she kept reminding me about it. She acted as if the Directors had cheated me—she spoke as if they owed me something...."

"I thought she was genuinely indignant and speaking out of sympathy and friendship. But I can see now that she was preparing me for what I had to do."

He choked. He said:

"I thought she loved me. I knew I loved her. She seemed so good, so kind, so beautiful—."

He broke off with a stifled sob.

Castle waited patiently.

Mervan bit his lip hard. His voice was unsteady. "I asked her to marry me. She refused. I said I wanted to make a home for her. She said you needed money to make a home."

He hunched his shoulders. "She was right, of course. An over-worked, under-paid bank clerk couldn't hope to provide for her. She wouldn't be content with love in a cottage. She wanted a place in the sun.

"Money became an obsession with me. With it, I could buy happiness... I could have Lesley."

A hungry look came into his eyes. "I watched the money pass to and fro across the counter, watched it packed each night in the vaults. I kept thinking about the strong-room. All that money, the property of rich, idle, worthless people... They had so much, while I had so little.

"I talked to Lesley. I felt as though I were in a trap. She asked me if— if I had the courage to break free. I was afraid, but I had to listen. She put into words all the secret longings and convictions which crowded my mind.... "

Mervan choked.

He went on:

"She showed me it was only fear that restrained me. I had taken nothing. But here—inside—I was no longer an honest man.

268

"I had no more illusions. I was ready to do whatever she wished. And then she gave me the keys."

Mervan stared at his hands. "I could hardly believe my eyes. There were the keys—duplicates of those held only by the senior officials. Lesley said that they had been struck from wax impressions taken from the originals.

"I pressed her for an explanation. She said only that the impressions had been taken of the keys while they were in Spurling's charge, without his knowledge, and in circumstances that made complaints impossible... You understand?

"I was mad with jealousy. But she swore that there was no longer anything between them. And I wanted her too much to let my anger take command.

"She bewitched me. I was ready to do anything for her."

Mervan looked up. "Once the decision had been made, the rest seemed easy. We had only to wait for a favourable opportunity.

"Lesley resigned from the bank and we kept our association a secret. It seemed the safest course." Mervan laughed bitterly. "And it was—for her."

He brooded. "I waited patiently. At last, the moment came. My name went up on the duty list to hold the keys one Saturday. That meant they would be in my charge for the week-end—and the strong-room wouldn't be examined until Monday morning.

"It was Spurling's turn to hold the other set of keys, as it happened. That was the irony of fate—nothing more.

"We locked up the safes, the Accountant and I, and then we left the bank. But I returned in the middle of the afternoon and let myself into the building.

"I had my keys and Lesley's duplicates. I opened the strong-room and filled up a suit-case with money. It was as easy as that."

Sweat glistened thinly on Mervan's forehead. He continued in a low voice:

"I went to join Lesley. We were going to smuggle the loot abroad and build a new life in another country... Lesley was waiting in her flat. I 'phoned her first to let her know everything was all right, then went to her with the money."

Mervan finished in queerly hurried tones, as though forcing himself to speak. "She called me into the bedroom. I went through the door... Something crashed on my head. My brain seemed to swell and burst with pain."

His eyes were tortured. He whispered:

"Somebody had been waiting behind the door. But I saw no one but

Lesley. She was looking at me. And laughing."

There was a long silence. Then—

"I came to in an alley-way behind the flat. I struggled into the street, then collapsed again... You know what happened next."

The cigarette had smouldered down to Mervan's fingers. He dropped the charred stump into an ash-tray and continued wearily:

"All those years in prison... Only one thing kept me alive. The hatred in my heart."

Castle sighed noisily. He spoke with genuine feeling. "You should have listened to me. I told you to forget revenge, to choose justice."

Mervan laughed bitterly. "I could have told you the whole story. You might have believed me. You might have found Lesley. Would you have been able to convict her?"

"Perhaps."

"And perhaps not. I wanted a real revenge. I wanted—her life."

Castle sighed again. "Go on."

Mervan slumped in his chair. "I came out of prison with only one thought in my mind. To find Lesley."

"And exact retribution."

"Of course. I had one clue—her name."

Castle looked puzzled. "Her name?"

"Yes. 'Barre'—that meant nothing to her. But 'Lesley' was a lovely name, and she was proud of it. I knew she would never change it."

"I see," said Castle heavily. A small vanity, he thought. And yet it had helped to bring a girl to her death.

The muttering voice went on. "One of the Aid Societies helped me find a job. In my free time, I carried on the search."

"And then?"

"I found her."

Castle grunted. "Did it surprise you to discover she was an actress?"

Mervan said:

"I might have guessed." His voice trembled. "She made me believe her when— when she told me she loved me."

Castle said nothing.

Mervan continued:

"I saw her picture in a magazine." He paused, remembering the thrill of discovery. The face in the photograph had altered with the years, but it was still Lesley's. And it was still lovely.

"I went to the theatre. I sat in the gallery, watching performance after performance."

He pressed his palms against the table top, staring down at the backs of his hands. "I wanted to watch her without being seen. So I went into the gods." His waxy face grew animated. "I felt like a god myself. A god with the power to snuff out a human life."

He looked up. He said more calmly:

"I bided my time. I could afford to wait. I knew that she couldn't escape me now.

"I think she glimpsed me from time to time, in the theatre or on the streets. It didn't matter. Nothing could rob me of my revenge... I made my plans.

"The gun itself wasn't hard to find. No, Inspector"—he smiled wryly—"I shan't tell you where I got it. I used to be in prison, remember. I made some useful contacts."

Castle knew all about the underworld's illegal trafficking in firearms. He growled:

"Go on."

"I booked that box for this afternoon. It gave me the best position for a shot at the stage. Besides, there was an exit nearby.

"I came late—deliberately. I had my .25 automatic. I waited for the close of the first scene of the third act. For the moment when Lesley— died."

His voice faded.

He remembered the pleasure-pain of the moments spent waiting for the covering blast of the blank cartridge on stage. He recalled the feel of the gun against his gloved hand, the flame-spitting roar as the bullet sped towards its target. There was a hot, salty taste as of blood in his mouth.

He said:

"I turned the make-believe into reality. And as the bullet crashed into her body, I think she knew that I was the man who killed her."

His eyes blazed suddenly, accentuating the prison-pallor of his cheeks.

"That was the instant—when we were one at last."

There was silence in the room. Lawrence shivered and licked dry lips.

Castle shifted his bulky frame. He said brusquely:

"You've left something out."

Mervan shook his head. "I don't think so... I was giddy with triumph. I laughed, I remember. I was a god."

The glow faded from his eyes. "I thought I could manage to escape before you discovered the girl was dead. But your friend vaulted into the box. You know the rest."

Castle scowled. "I was talking about the cards. The messages sent to Miss Barre and to me. About Paddington Fair."

Mervan looked puzzled.

He said wearily:

"I sent no cards. I know nothing of Paddington Fair."

Chief Inspector Castle looked tired.

He said tonelessly:

"Well, there it is. Mervan's full statement, signed and witnessed."

Lawrence commented unhappily:

"His death warrant."

Castle squinted at him. He said:

"We can't afford to be squeamish. Mervan is a murderer. He will have to pay the penalty."

"I know." Lawrence scuffed his foot against the carpet. Mervan had been taken back to his cell; the two friends were alone.

A tiny frown marred the serenity of Algy's pleasant face. He said abruptly:

"I can't understand why Mervan persists in denying he sent those cards."

"Neither can I. But it doesn't matter."

"Doesn't it? I wonder. He might be telling the truth. If so...." He shrugged helplessly.

Castle stared. He said doggedly:

"Mervan must have sent those cards. Everything points to it."

Lawrence nodded slowly. "A crazy message of defiance to you. A melodramatic warning to his victim. Well, perhaps. But—."

Castle said:

"The proof is self-evident. Take the message to me. It was addressed to Detective Inspector Stephen Castle. That was my rank at the time Mervan was convicted. He didn't know I'd been promoted.

"Besides that, the post-marks on both envelopes were the same. London, S.E.1. Now look at Mervan's address. It's in the same area."

He concluded:

"Everything fits neatly."

Lawrence said softly:

"Too neatly."

Castle's head jerked up. "Hey?"

Lawrence grinned lazily. He said:

"Steve, old friend. This looks like a frame-up."

Castle roared like a wounded bull. "What the devil do you mean by that? Hell's blazes! I never saw a clearer case in my life."

He stopped to draw breath. He grumbled:

"We've established the motive, opportunity, and means. We made an on-the-spot arrest and we've obtained a full confession. What more can you possibly want?"

Lawrence didn't reply directly. Instead, he said dreamily:

"Consider the situation. A man commits—or appears to commit—murder. In the presence of hundreds. All of them, mark you, potential witnesses for the prosecution. What's more, the man himself is convinced of his guilt and makes a full confession. And yet—."

He paused. Then he finished lightly:

"He's innocent."

Castle stared at his friend for a long time.

Then he said heavily:

"And a brilliant young amateur sets himself the impossible task of proving the man's innocence. Is that what you mean?"

Algy laughed. "Don't worry, Steve I was only day-dreaming. But you must admit it would have been a wonderful situation."

He was saved from Castle's wrath by the timely arrival of the station sergeant. "Telephone for you, sir."

The Chief Inspector grunted: "It's probably Wemyss. He knows I'm here."

He stumped out of the room. Lawrence stared out of the window moodily.

He had an uneasy feeling that the case was far from finished. And yet....

When Castle came back, he had an odd look on his rugged face.

He spoke in an uncharacteristically subdued voice.

"We'd better go back to the theatre, young Algy. Something has happened."

# CHAPTER TEN

Trudy Ann was a very pretty girl. She was also extremely determined. She said:

"You really must help me, Douglas."

Denzil gave her a feline smile. "You fret too much, child. You know your lines. And I don't feel like rehearsing now."

Trudy Ann pouted. "It's all very well for you. But it isn't easy for me. Penny is playing 'Marilyn' tonight. That means I take the second lead. It's my big chance. I don't want to spoil it."

They were standing at the back of the stage, well beyond the set. Ignoring the notice stencilled on the bare brick wall behind him, Douglas Denzil lit a cigarette.

He sighed out smoke. "You've persuaded me, wench. I'll help you run through your lines. Though to hear them now—."

He affected a shudder. 'It's a wretched play."

"It is not," said the girl firmly. "Mr. Windsor has written a very good play. With a fat part for you."

Denzil rejected the contention. "For Trent you mean. Now if I had his part—." His eyes gleamed. "Ah, well. Where shall we go for this impromptu rehearsal?"

"To the greenroom," suggested Trudy Ann. "Or are the police there?" she concluded doubtfully.

Denzil shrugged. "They're everywhere, my dear. They're positively crawling out of the walls... But we can try—."

"Denzil!"

The stage manager was hurrying towards them. He frowned at the cigarette between the actor's fingers, then gestured towards the notice. "You know better than that, Douglas. Smoking is forbidden here."

Denzil looked bored. "You're stuffy, Jack. But"—he twitched his shoulders—"I won't argue. Come along, child." He took the girl's hand. "Let's be off."

He tossed the cigarette away. It bounced off the side of a fire bucket and rolled along the floor, its tip glowing red.

Denzil left with the girl. Austin stared after him angrily.

Detective Inspector Wemyss came out of the dressing-room passage. Catching sight of the stage manager, he walked towards him.

Austin was stooping to recover the discarded cigarette. He pinched it out, then dropped it tidily into the fire bucket. Something caught his attention. He smoothed away the sand and picked something out of the bucket. "That's odd," he muttered.

Wemyss coughed.

Austin glanced up with a wondering gleam in his eyes. He said quietly. "Look at that."

Wemyss stared at the object resting on the stage manager's open palm.

It was a blank cartridge.

"There are five more buried in the sand here," said the Detective Inspector. He was squatting on his heels beside the fire bucket. "Five plus one makes—."

"Six," muttered Austin. "Six cartridges. That's a full load—."

"For the average revolver. Yes." Wemyss looked at the stage manager thoughtfully. He stood up.

He said on a note of enquiry:

"Such a gun is fired in the course of the play?"

"Yes. It's a Webley & Scott."

"I haven't seen it."

"No." Austin clutched his pocket. "As a matter of fact, I had forgotten all about it. I've been carrying it about with me. Trent gave it to me immediately after the curtain fell—."

"Quite," said Wemyss shortly. "May I see the gun now?"

"Yes. Of course." Austin pulled the revolver out of his pocket. Wemyss took it from his hand and studied it carefully.

The stage manager mumbled. "Please don't take it away. We shall need it for the evening performance. I was about to reload it."

"With blanks, of course."

"Yes. As I do at every performance."

Wemyss broke open the revolver and examined the magazine. His face changed oddly.

He asked:

"Did Michael Trent fire this gun on stage?"

Austin stared. "Yes."

"At Miss Christopher?"

"Yes. I—."

"You took it from him immediately afterwards?"

"You know I did," snapped the S.M. impatiently. "Why do you ask these pointless questions?"

"Because," said the Detective Inspector woodenly, "there are five

276

live cartridges in the cylinder of this revolver. And an exploded case in the chamber under the hammer."

The revolver had been tied to a piece of thin wood, through which holes had been bored for the fastenings. Chief Inspector Castle was scowling at it pensively.

Detective Inspector Wemyss was saying:

"It was an odd discovery, sir. I thought it best to notify you at once."

Castle nodded. 'I'm glad you did.' He raised his voice. "Mr. Friern! Will you come here, please?"

They were sitting in the general manager's office. Victor Friern came forward with laggard steps.

Castle showed him the revolver. "I'd like a formal identification. Is this the gun used in your play?"

Friern bowed his head. "Yes. It's a Webley & Scott, calibre .32."

"Thank you." Castle scratched his chin. "Well, sir. You heard what the Inspector said. This revolver was found to be loaded with live ammunition. And a bullet has been fired from it recently."

"I can't explain," said Victor Friern. His voice was harsh and troubled. "We use blanks – "

"Like the ones concealed beneath the sand in the fire bucket?"

"Yes." Friern's hands were trembling. "Loading the gun—that's Austin's responsibility. Wix, the property master, brings him the blank cartridges half an hour before each show. Austin sees the revolver is fully loaded—."

Castle interposed a question. "You mean there are always six blanks in the magazine? Wouldn't one be enough?"

Friern replied. "Austin is a cautious man. He checks and double checks. As stage manager, it's his job to see that nothing goes wrong. With only one blank in the gun, he felt there would always be the danger—however slight—of a misfire. And if the hammer fell on an empty chamber the whole effect of the first scene of the third act would be ruined."

"I see." Castle rubbed his heavy jowl.

He asked Wemyss:

"Have you questioned Austin?"

"Not in detail."

Castle sighed. "All right. Let's go back-stage."

Austin spoke defensively. "I can swear to this, Inspector. The gun is in precisely the same condition now as it was when I took it from Michael Trent."

Castle studied him shrewdly. The stage manager seemed sincere. The Chief Inspector felt sure he was telling the truth. And yet....

Castle grimaced. Austin looked about him nervously. The two men were standing on stage, like actors waiting for the curtain to rise.

The Chief Inspector said wearily:

"Let's go back to the beginning. Is this the revolver fired on stage?"

"Yes, of course. It's the only gun in the theatre."

"Describe it, please."

"But why—Oh, very well." Austin spoke rapidly, impatiently. "It's a Webley & Scott revolver, calibre .32. I can't tell you the number, because it has been filed off. But it's easily identifiable. The gun has a long, jagged scratch on the barrel and some initials—'H.W.' — engraved above the butt."

Castle nodded. "That's correct. Well, now." He thumbed his chin. "You saw that the gun was loaded with blanks for the □atinee?"

"Yes."

Castle considered. "Hmmm... Friern tells me that you follow a definite routine. The property master brings you a box of blank cartridges half an hour before each performance. You load the revolver in his presence, making sure there are six blanks in the magazine. You then place the gun on the pegs in the lobby 'wall' and return the box to Wix. Right?"

"Yes, that's my normal routine. I ---.'

A noisy argument broke out in the wings. Austin swallowed the rest of the sentence and swung round nervously. "What the devil's that?"

He hurried through the prompt entrance and added his voice to the clamour.

Castle followed to discover Algy Lawrence conducting a long distance conversation with a stage-hand who was half-way up a long iron ladder stretching up to the grid above.

The Chief Inspector made expressive noises. "Algy! What the blazes ---."

Lawrence grinned. "We're having a slight difference of opinion, Steve. I want the curtain raised. Our friend aloft considers it should remain where it is."

The stage-hand appealed to his chief. "Mr. Austin! Your orders was to keep it dahn."

The S.M. said tiredly:

"I'm not giving the orders any more. Ask the Chief Inspector."

Castle growled an aside to Lawrence. "What the hell are you playing at? If this is one of your damn' fool jokes—."

Algy's pleasant face sobered. "It's no joke, Steve. I give you my word."

Castle squinted thoughtfully. Turning to the stage manager, he said mildly:

"Raise the curtain, please."

Austin shrugged. Craning backwards, he called out a brief instruction. The stage-hand clattered up the ladder into the flies.

Castle hunched his shoulders. "What happens now?"

"Now," said Lawrence lightly, "we reconstruct the crime."

As they returned through the prompt entrance, the curtain began to rise. Castle stared into the empty auditorium and felt vaguely disturbed.

Lawrence said cheerfully:

"Ghostly, isn't it?"

Austin re-entered. Algy hailed him. "I'm going to ask you for more help."

Austin shrugged assent.

Castle was restive. "For Heaven's sake, Algy."

"Patience, Steve." Lawrence's eyes were unusually serious. "Mr. Austin, I'm asking you to deputize for Michael Trent. Steve, you'll stand in for Richard Mervan."

"Eh?"

"Into the box, old friend." Lawrence spoke with gentle firmness. "Mervan's gun has gone to the laboratory, so we'll have to improvise. Use your pipe, Steve. I'd call it a deadly weapon. Its effects are well-nigh lethal."

Castle allowed himself to be shepherded across the footlights. Still clutching the board to which the revolver had been tied, he stepped from the corner of the stage to the ledge of the box, then manoeuvred his bulk down into the box itself.

"Right." Lawrence pulled his ear thoughtfully. "Mr. Austin, will you come here, please."

The S.M. obeyed. Lawrence said quietly:

"Let's speak plainly. The revolver has been in your possession since the curtain fell this afternoon. You could therefore—since then—have tampered with the ammunition in the cylinder. The Chief Inspector must have considered that possibility."

Austin looked unhappy. "I swear—."

Lawrence interrupted without discourtesy. "If you have any such suspicions, Steve, discard them." He paused, then said slowly:

"I'm convinced of this. If Austin had broken open the gun immediately after taking it from Trent's hand, he would have found it in exactly the same condition as it is now."

Castle's chin jerked upward. "But—."

279

He broke off.

He said grimly:

"Go on."

Lawrence continued:

"First, we'll set the scene." He glanced at Austin. "This is the prompt side, I believe?"

"That's so." Austin cleared his throat. "In case you didn't know, the actors' left is the audience's right. In other words, though a man in the stalls would say we are now standing on the right-hand side of the stage, we are actually positioned Down Left."

Castle glowered.

Lawrence said amiably:

"And the other side, on the player's right?"

"Opposite prompt—the O.P. side."

"Uh huh. Now, as I remember it, Michael Trent was standing close to the footlights when he pulled the trigger."

"Yes. His heels were almost touching the setting line. That's the boundary of the acting area, or the point on both sides from which the building of the scene commences. Or to put it another way, it's an imaginary line running between the edges of the proscenium returns."

"Let's not get too technical," smiled Algy. "In layman's language, Michael Trent was standing about eighteen inches up-stage from the front curtain. On the extreme edge of the set, with his back to this box."

Castle grunted:

"With a murderer behind him."

Austin seemed to hesitate.

Then he said abruptly:

"He told us he felt the wind of the bullet as it passed his body."

Lawrence nodded. "Take his position, please."

Austin obeyed.

Lawrence said softly:

"Hold it, now," and backed across the stage till his heels tapped against the dais.

He said:

"My position now is—uh—Up Right, I suppose. Anyway, I'm standing diagonally opposite to you both."

They watched him silently. He said:

"Aim, please." Holding a fountain pen at waist level, Austin pointed it towards Lawrence's heart. Looking equally sheepish, Castle held up a large and virulent pipe in the manner of a gun.

Lawrence didn't smile. A rare spark of excitement illumined his sleepy eyes. He said:

"It's as I thought. The angle of each weapon—and the range of both shots—they were virtually the same."

He walked away from the dais. Austin held his pose as if frozen. With the dummy "gun" tilted in his hand, his sleeve had fallen away from his wrist.

Lawrence murmured:

"You can relax now. Hallo! You've burned your hand."

Austin bit his lip. "It's nothing. Nothing at all."

Behind him in the box, Castle roared impatiently. "What's all this about?"

Lawrence grinned lazily. "I think you know, Steve. But to put it into words...."

He spread his hands.

He said mildly:

"There were no blanks in the Webley & Scott revolver. Michael Trent fired a live cartridge at Lesley Christopher this afternoon."

Austin's face was as livid as the scar on the back of his hand. "But that's impossible!"

Lawrence shook his head. "No. Somebody took the blanks out of the revolver before Lesley carried it on stage in the third act."

"But I—."

Austin's voice faltered and died.

Lawrence said sympathetically:

"It's the only explanation. You must accept it."

The S.M. nodded dumbly.

Then he said hoarsely:

"But there weren't two wounds in Lesley's body."

"No. Two shots were fired. But one of the bullets missed her."

Castle asked softly:

"Which one?"

Lawrence gave him a fleeting smile. "That's a question which can only be answered by an expert in ballistics."

The Chief Inspector grunted. "To hell with ballistics. I can use my common sense."

Lawrence looked a question.

Castle growled:

"I remember the careful way Trent steadied his revolver. The muzzle was pointing towards the girl's heart."

Austin asked hoarsely:

"Do you mean—he couldn't have missed?"

Castle's silence was an eloquent reply.

Lawrence said suddenly:

'"Somebody's laughing at us, Steve. That somebody is the person who really murdered Lesley Christopher. And yet he's safe, because another man has already confessed to the crime—."

He broke off, then said with wonder:

"Richard Mervan is innocent and doesn't know it himself!"

# CHAPTER ELEVEN

"In other words," growled Stephen Castle, "Mervan is only a murderer by intention. But not in fact. Well, it fits the pattern. He's made a mess of everything else in his life. It isn't surprising he bungled this."

Lawrence said softly:

"I'm glad he did."

Castle shook himself like a huge dog. "So am I. But-this means our job has only begun. So let's set to work... There's something you haven't explained."

"What's that?"

Castle drummed his fingers on the ledge of the box. "You say both Mervan and Trent fired at Lesley Christopher. One bullet lodged in the girl's heart. The other missed. Very well, then. Where is it?"

"Ah," said Lawrence. "That's the question. But I think I can answer it."

Motioning his friend to stand clear, the young man jumped lightly into the box. He said:

"Mr. Austin, will you take up your position again, please."

In an undertone, he continued:

"Look, Steve. By moving to the rear of the box, Mervan could sight his pistol past Trent's body at the girl's. Now where was she standing?"

"Diagonally opposite," replied Castle. "In front of that stuffed bear."

"Exactly," said Lawrence with a satisfied smile.

"You mean—?"

"Watch," grinned Algy. He climbed out of the box on to the stage.

Tapping Austin on the shoulder he asked:

"Is that animal ever moved?"

The S.M. shook his head. "No. This is a standing set. We don't strike the flats or shift the props."

"Good."

The bear seemed to glower at Lawrence's approach. Algy stopped at the base of the circular dais and stared into the brute 's face.

"He's no beauty, is he?"

Castle clambered out of the box. "Algy—" he began. "Patience, Steve." Lawrence's eyes slitted. He had taken a miniature torch from his pocket and was playing the light on the animal's muzzle. 'I think I see—Ah!'"

"What is it?" asked Castle.

Lawrence side-stepped. "Look there, Steve. Into the bear's mouth."

He angled the rays of the torch. The Chief Inspector caught his breath. "By God, yes! There's a hole inside—."

He grabbed the light from his young friend's hand.

Lawrence circled the dais, then raised his fist and tapped the bear lightly on the head.

He said sleepily:

"Bruin has a hard skull. It's succeeded in stopping a .25 calibre bullet."

Stephen Castle replaced the telephone receiver and stared blankly at the wall opposite. "That settles it," he mumbled.

Victor Friern's anxious voice forced itself through the detective's barrier of preoccupation. "Chief Inspector—."

"Huh?" Castle roused himself. He had been called to the telephone immediately after the discovery of the missing bullet, and had left Wemyss in charge on stage. "Yes, Mr. Friern. What is it?"

"Am I—am I to understand that L-Lesley was not murdered by the madman you arrested?"

"I'm afraid so. Unpleasant though it sounds, the brutal truth is this: Miss Christopher was murdered by a member of your own company."

"But—." Friern put out a hand to steady himself. "We know that this man Mervan shot at her from his box."

Castle explained patiently:

"Mervan fired a .25 self-loading pistol—a so-called 'automatic'. He meant to kill the girl—make no mistake about that. But he missed. Continuing on its upward flight, the bullet passed over Lesley's head and lodged instead in the skull of the stuffed bear behind her."

"But why wasn't the bullet discovered at once?"

"Because it went into the brute's open mouth," continued Castle. "The hole of entry was hidden to all but a searching look... We haven't yet established the exact composition of the stuffing in the bear's head. It was tow, I expect. Anyway, it was sufficient to trap the bullet and prevent its exit."

Friern said unhappily:

"Then Lesley—. "

"Died," said the Chief Inspector. "But not by Mervan's hand. By

284

Michael Trent's."

"I still can't believe it! Damn it all," said the manager helplessly. "You were certain that Mervan had killed her. Why didn't you discover the mistake at once? You had the evidence. The range of the shot—the angle of the bullet—."

Castle sighed. He spoke with the same mechanical patience. "Our error was an honest one. Excusable too, I think... Mervan was only a few feet—two or three yards at the most— to the rear of Michael Trent. In other words, the range of each shot was virtually the same. Ballistics can tell us a lot. But it's impossible to say whether a shot has been fired from five yards or from twenty.

"As for the bullet's passage into the girl's breast"—Castle spoke with deliberate flatness, ignoring the pain in the manager's eyes—"well, a surgeon can't work miracles. He can indicate the general direction of the bullet, but no more. He can't be precise to a degree—not when he's dealing with a human target."

"I suppose not," said Friern dully.

Castle fingered his jowl. "In one respect at least," he growled, "ballistics is an exact science. We can match a bullet with the gun that fired it... Lesley Christopher died with a .32 bullet in her heart. And it was fired from a Webley & Scott revolver."

"Is that—certain?"

"Yes." Castle pointed a stubby finger at the telephone. "That call was from the police surgeon.  He'd just finished the post mortem. The bullet extracted from the girl's body was a .32. And the Webley type of rifling—."

Friern looked blank as the Chief Inspector went into technicalities.

"—was distinctly engraved on the bullet. Seven broad grooves, a right handed twist and narrow lands—that's the rifling used in all Webley revolvers."

Friern shrugged helplessly.

Castle muttered:

"All that remains now is to match up the bullet with this revolver." He indicated the gun which had been tied to a piece of thin wood to preserve all possible clues. "I'll have it sent to the laboratory at once."

"I suppose," said Friern, "that's hardly more than a formality."

"A very necessary one," jerked Castle. "But, as you say, a formality. There's no further doubt. This is the murder weapon."

"But I can't believe —-that Michael Trent—."

Friern's protest died away unfinished. Castle eyed him quizzically. "I said that Miss Christopher died by his hand. Not that he murdered her."

"You mean—."

"I mean," replied Castle, "that if"—he stressed the word briefly— "if Trent didn't know he was firing live ammunition, then he wasn't guilty of murder."

Friern murmured his relief.

"Remember I said 'if,'" warned the Chief Inspector. "All we can be certain of is this. Somebody put six bullets in this revolver. Who? We don't know. It could have been Michael Trent. For that matter," added Castle benignly, "it could have been you."

"I?"

Castle was bland. "Everyone back-stage had access to the weapon."

"Including the manager," said Friern with a touch of bitterness. "Well, sir, I had a high regard for Miss Christopher. I wouldn't have harmed her for the world. Will you take my word for that?"

"Certainly," returned Castle politely. "But it would help if you could also prove an alibi,"

"I believe I can." Victor Friern frowned thoughtfully. "Let me see, now. I must prove I was given no opportunity to extract the blanks from the gun and refill the magazine with bullets."

"Yes."

Friern's face cleared. "I was talking with Austin half an hour before the performance. At that time he hadn't yet loaded the revolver with. Blank cartridges.

"We parted at the entrance to the dressing-room passage. I went into Lesley's room—."

"Why?" asked the Chief Inspector.

Friern hesitated, then outlined his conversation with the girl. Castle made no comment.

The manager continued:

"I left when Maggie Boyd arrived."

"Maggie Boyd?"

"Miss Christopher's dresser. Lesley had sent her out for some cigarettes... When I left, I found Ben Cotall outside in the corridor. He was looking for Michael Trent.

"We went back to the stage door. When Trent arrived, Cotall helped him to his dressing-room. Michael was—hm!—indisposed."

"Drunk?" asked Castle mildly.

"Tipsy," said the manager with a frown. "No more. As I say, his dresser took charge of him... Austin joined me at the stage door. We talked again.

"After Austin left, I exchanged a few words with Short, the door-keeper. Then I left, too."

"By the stage door?"

"Yes. As you know, there's a pass-door in the proscenium arch; but it's always kept locked when the theatre is open to the public."

"Go on."

"I walked round the building to the front entrance and went through the foyer into my office. I didn't go back-stage again. You can check with the stage door-keeper. He never leaves his post during a performance."

Castle nodded slowly. "I shall question the people you've mentioned. If they corroborate your story—as I've no reason to doubt they will—I think I can accept your alibi."

"Thank you, Chief Inspector." Victor Friern looked relieved. He hesitated, then said with difficulty. "Lesley—Lesley was very dear to me. If there's anything I can do to help you, I—I—."

He choked.

Castle eyed him sympathetically.

He said:

"We'll find the man who murdered her. He won't escape."


Friern and Castle came through the O.P. entrance on to the standing set. The men from the Yard were hard at work.

Detective Inspector Wemyss caught his chief's eye and threaded his way towards him. Castle growled a greeting, then repeated the surgeon's report to his colleague.

Wemyss received the news unemotionally. "It looks like our work is just beginning."

"There's a lot to be done," agreed the Chief Inspector. "We shall have to take statements from everybody back-stage. Mr. Friern!"

"Yes?"

"I need hardly say that there will be no performance tonight. I'm closing the theatre until further notice... Meanwhile I want to interview every member of your staff who went back-stage this afternoon."

Friern suggested:

"You could examine them in the greenroom. And I could tell them all to wait for you in the wardrobe room."

Castle nodded. "That will leave the stage clear for your men, Wemyss."

Sweeping his hands under the tail of his battered raincoat, he stumped to the rear of the set. Regarding the open double doors up-stage and centre, Castle said:

"As I remember it, the revolver was resting on pegs in the 'wall' of the lobby there."

Friern agreed. "Yes. The 'wall', of course, consists of a number of painted flats. The pegs are fixed to a horizontal rail nailed across the frame to the stiles—that is, the uprights—behind the canvas."

"Is the gun always left on the pegs?"

"Yes. Except when Austin hands it to Props to be cleaned and oiled."

"Props?"

"Wix, the property master."

"Ah, yes. I've yet to speak to him."

Friern hesitated.

Then he spoke with a trace of discomfort. "I don't know what the man will tell you. But I advise you to treat his statements with a certain amount of reserve."

"Huh?" Castle's eyes snapped. "What d'you mean by that?"

Friern replied with distaste:

"It's all rather silly. But Wix seemed to imagine he had a grudge against Lesley after she'd spoken to him rather sharply once or twice. He was somewhat resentful."

Castle said softly:

"Speak plainly, sir. Are you suggesting that Wix may have put real bullets instead of blanks into the revolver?"

"Heavens, no!" The manager seemed shocked. "I meant only to warn you that the man's evidence might be distorted—no, that's not the right word—might be coloured by his dislike for Miss Christopher... As for loading the gun, he leaves that to Austin."

Castle nodded absently. He walked through the open doors.

The tail of his eye caught a flicker of movement. A vague figure was disappearing round the last flat of the lobby "wall" into the obscurity of the deserted stage behind.

"What the—."

Castle took a stride forward, then stopped with a shrug. The eavesdropper, whoever he was, was gone.

The Chief Inspector turned back to the pegs in the "wall." On those flimsy supports, the gun had rested. A gun that had been harmless until an unknown hand had filled it with six shiny messengers of death. An unknown hand, an unknown man.

Castle's face was grim. He spoke his thoughts aloud.

He said:

"You have a name, my friend. And I'll know it soon, I promise you."

# CHAPTER TWELVE

Algy Lawrence looked up with a smile as the door of the greenroom opened.

"Hi, Steve. Make yourself at home."

Castle gave a good-humoured groan. His young friend was sprawled in a saddlebag chair with his blond head on a cushion and his feet on a magazine rack. A large, heavy volume lay open on his lap.

"Algy! What on earth are you doing now?"

"Merely examining the theatre library." Lawrence indicated the packed shelves at his side. "I've found some interesting volumes. For instance,"—a glint of bibliomania showed in his lazy blue eyes—"take this one here...."

Castle held up his hand.

"I refuse to hold up another case while you talk about your blasted books."

Lawrence grinned.

He said disrespectfully:

"I know policemen only read books when they are trying to find an excuse to ban and burn 'em. But honestly, Steve, this one should interest you. It's a bound volume of the Gentleman's Magazine for 1783—."

"Not," said Castle firmly, "another word."

He stared around.

An electric fire glowed in one corner. The room had been furnished with a number of easy-chairs and was well supplied with books and periodicals. Some theatrical posters and portraits hung on walls which had been painted a cheerful green. It was, Steve decided, a cosy place.

He said with approval:

"This will do."

"For what—the inquisition?"

"For the interviews," returned Castle heavily.

"That which we call a rose," quoted Algy, "by any word would smell as sweet."

He replaced a marker between the leaves of the volume on his lap, then slipped the book into its place on the shelves.

"Algy—."

"What's in a name?" mused Lawrence. "What indeed?"

He said with maddening persistence:

"Really, Steve, you ought to read the Gentleman's Magazine for 1783.... "

Austin cracked his knuckles nervously. His glance flickered towards the expressionless man with the open note-book, then returned to meet the level gaze of the Chief Inspector.

Castle said:

"You will appreciate the importance of your evidence. I don't have to tell you that it's vital. Well, now! Let's start from the beginning. Your name and occupation, please."

Austin swallowed. "Uh... Jack Austin. Stage manager."

Lawrence interposed a question. "Jack—that's for John, I suppose?"

"Yes."

Stephen Castle glared at his young friend.

Algy murmured: "I thought so," and seemed absurdly pleased with himself.

The Chief Inspector said: "If you've finished, we'll proceed... Mr. Austin! I want you to describe in detail how you loaded the revolver this afternoon."

The S.M. licked his lips. "I followed my usual routine. The property master brought me the blank cartridges half an hour before the performance—."

"Just a minute." Castle squared off his notes with his thumbs. "Victor Friern told me he was talking with you at that time. You hadn't then loaded the revolver."

"No. I'm afraid my mind was on other things." Austin hesitated. "I was waiting for Michael Trent. Actors are always supposed to be in at the half, but Trent had been late throughout the week. He—he drinks." The S.M. licked his lips. "I discussed the matter with Victor Friern. He told me not to worry."

Castle consulted his notes. "You left him at the entrance to the dressing-room passage?"

"Yes. I saw him go into Miss Christopher's room."

"And then?"

"I returned to my post back-stage. Props brought me the blank cartridges and we went to load the revolver."

"Ah!" Castle blew out his cheeks. "At what time?"

"About—about five minutes past two."

"Right. Now describe your actions in detail."

Austin shifted uncomfortably. "I removed the Webley & Scott from its pegs on the flat—."

"Is the gun always left on the lobby 'wall'?"

"Nearly always. We regard it as part of the standing set."

"Go on."

"I broke open the gun—it's a break-down, not a solid frame model – and pulled the extractor."

"Emptying the magazine?"

"Yes. I had followed my usual routine the night before: I had replaced the gun on its pegs after taking it from Michael Trent after the Third Act curtain... There were five unfired blanks and one exploded blank left in the cylinder."

"So?"

"I removed the exploded cartridge, examined the five remaining blanks, added another from the box Wix handed to me, then—after testing the action of the gun—I refilled the magazine. Then I replaced the revolver on its pegs."

"And returned the box of cartridges to Wix?"

"Yes."

"Hmmm." Castle thumbed his chin. "Are you absolutely certain that the six cartridges in the gun were blanks?"

Austin was definite. "I couldn't mistake a live cartridge for a blank. It's quite different in appearance." The S.M. paused, then said abruptly. "Wix will confirm my statement. The gun was loaded with harmless blanks when I replaced it upon the peg."

"M'yes." The Chief Inspector relaxed in his chair. "Now, then. You and Wix were standing in the lobby. That part of the set is separated from the main scene by double doors. Were those doors open?"

"No. They were closed in readiness for Act One."

"So," said Castle softly, "you and the property master were alone at the vital time when the gun was loaded?"

Austin blustered. "I don't like your insinuation!"

"I've made none." The Chief Inspector was dangerously calm. "But I'd like to remind you, Mr. Austin, that a murder has been committed. And your own carelessness made the killer's task an easy one."

Austin flushed, then paled. "I—I don't understand."

Castle said. "Before a stage revolver can be fired, a licence must be obtained from the police."

"We have a licence," cut in the S.M.

"But not, I imagine," said Castle gently, "for this particular gun. Since the registration number has been filed off, it might fairly be described as an illegal weapon."

Austin looked unhappy. "Props supplied the gun."

Castle screwed up his face. "There's another thing. The barrel should have been stopped up. Even if you had done nothing more than plug it with a wad of paper, it would have made the murderer's task more difficult."

Austin fingered the burn on the back of his hand. "You're right, I suppose. But none of us dreamed—."

He broke off, then said flatly:

"We used a property gun at rehearsals. But the author complained that it looked like a toy. The producer agreed: he has a passion for realism. He decided to use a real gun with an unplugged barrel. He wanted nothing to interfere with the full effect of the explosion."

Castle made an ironic interjection. "He wanted the audience to see a convincing murder."

Austin caught his breath, then expelled it with a hiss. "Good Lord!"

Castle asked: "What's the matter?"

The S.M. said slowly, unwillingly:

"The words you used—they startled me. Michael Trent used them in his dressing-room before the show."

"Oh?" Castle scribbled a note. "Repeat them, please."

Austin mumbled reluctantly. "Michael told me: 'This afternoon, I promise you, the audience will see a convincing murder.'"

"As it did." Castle dropped his pencil on the table top. The noise of its fall seemed very loud.

The S.M. said, rather too eagerly. "A coincidence."

"But a strange one," commented the Chief Inspector. "Perhaps you had better explain."

Austin sketched out what he could remember of his conversation with Michael Trent. Castle listened in silence. When the S.M. had finished, the Chief Inspector said dryly:

"That's interesting. But you haven't answered my original question."

Austin's mouth hardened.

He said sullenly:

"Props and I were alone."

Lawrence coughed politely. "The double doors were closed. But the lobby isn't masked on the prompt side, is it?"

"No." Austin frowned thoughtfully. "It's visible from the wings. Anybody passing might have seen us. But I don't think anyone did."

"It can't be helped," said Castle mildly. "We'll have to take your word."

Austin spoke with sudden violence. "Why should I want to harm Lesley?   Damn you, I loved her!"

Castle's eyebrows quivered.

Austin looked away, feeling angry and foolish.

Castle asked:

"Did she love you?"

"No." Austin laughed harshly. "She knew how to use men. But she cared for no one but herself—and Michael Trent."

Castle remembered the photograph on the wall of the dead woman's dressing-room. "Trent, eh? I—."

The door of the greenroom flew open with a bang. Austin started nervously, Castle bit his tongue, and the shorthand writer scored a jagged line over the surface of his open notebook.

Only Lawrence was undismayed. He gazed with evident admiration at the graceful figure of the girl who was standing on the threshold.

"Where," she enquired, "is Chief Inspector Castle?"

Steve was annoyed. He snapped:

"Young lady, I—."

He wasn't allowed to finish. The girl's teeth met with a tiny click of anger. "Ah! So you—."

She approached Castle like a particularly beautiful tigress advancing upon its prey.

Lawrence studied her with interest. She had hazel eyes, slanting eyebrows, wide cheekbones, and a tiny but determined chin. She wore her hair in a kiss curl fringe. And her figure was exquisite.

She paused with her hands on her shapely hips.

She said to Castle:

"You are a very nasty man."

Lawrence chuckled. "Steve, I disown you now."

Castle spluttered.

The girl transferred her attentions to Lawrence, who met her glare with a winning smile. He said promptly:

"Forgive us, please, for whatever we've done to offend you. And may I congratulate you on your performance this afternoon? You were delightful."

She had a charming smile, as Castle noted with some relief. He scowled horribly to re-establish command of the situation.

"Now, young lady," he began.

She waved a disdainful hand. "I shall talk to your friend," she announced. "He is a gentleman."

Steve turned purple. Lawrence disguised a laugh with a cough. He said:

"You mustn't be too hard on the Chief Inspector. Uh—what has he done?"

The girl answered tragically:

"He has closed the show."

293

Castle shut his eyes, then opened them again. He had already recognized the girl as the actress who had played a small part in the first and second acts: he had last seen her with Douglas Denzil when he had given them permission to go to their dressing-rooms and change. He explained patiently:

"Young lady, I had no alternative. This case is no longer the simple affair it once seemed."

Lawrence interposed tactfully:

"Closing the theatre—that's only a temporary measure. It will soon be re-opened. Of course," he added brightly, "to finish their work, the police will need the help of everyone in the theatre."

The girl paused, her lovely face puckered in thought.

Then she said sweetly:

"I shall co-operate."

"Good." The Chief Inspector breathed heavily. "Please sit down."

The girl nodded graciously. She seated herself in the chair Austin had vacated, crossing pretty legs and smoothing her skirt over nyloned knees.

Castle said hastily: "Ha-hmmm... Your name, please."

"Trudy Ann."

"Trudy Ann what?"

"Nothing."

Castle growled inaudibly. Then he continued:

"Young lady, I want your full name."

The girl widened her lovely eyes.

She replied with an air of kindly patience:

"You have it. My name is Trudy Ann. You know—like Vera-Ellen. But without the hyphen."

"Oh." Castle digested this information in silence. Something about it disturbed him. "Very well, Miss Ann—."

"No, no," she cried. "Don't split my name. I can't bear it."

"I understand," said Lawrence gravely. "These things are important to an artiste."

She favoured him with a dazzling smile.

Castle regarded his young friend with some bitterness. Then he returned to the girl. "What shall I call you, then?"

She said simply. "Call me Trudy Ann."

Castle surrendered. "Very well, miss. Ha-hmmm! I imagine you all know now how Miss Christopher was killed?"

"Yes, indeed." She sighed. "Poor Michael."

"Huh! Be that as it may," huffed the Chief Inspector. "The problem facing us now is to plot everyone's movements back-stage from the half hour call till the gun was actually fired. So, miss, let's start with you."

Trudy Ann pouted prettily.

Before she could speak, Jack Austin asked:

"May I go now?"

Castle shook his head. "No, Mr. Austin, not yet. You can wait here; this won't take us long."

He turned back to the girl. "Now, miss! Describe your movements, if you please."

Trudy Ann folded her hands with an air of schoolgirl primness. She said:

"I reached the theatre about three quarters of an hour before the matinee. I went to my dressing-room to make up. I stayed there, reading, until the five minutes call. Then I went on stage."

Castle asked:

"And then?"

"I played my part. It isn't," added the girl reproachfully, "much more than a walk-on. But I do my best with it"

Lawrence guessed that such unusual frankness meant that Trudy Ann had her eyes on something better. He made a mental note.

The Chief Inspector continued:

"And what did you do when you weren't on stage?"

"I waited in my dressing-room for my calls. Billy makes the rounds."

Castle frowned. "You were alone, then?"

"Yes. I like privacy. And I can't stand back-stage talk—it's all theatre shop." She fluttered her lashes ingenuously. "And these back-stage feuds are such a bore."

She darted a mischievous glance at the Chief Inspector, as if daring him to rise to the bait.

Castle looked down his nose. He said:

"You didn't appear in the first scene of the last act."

"No. I don't appear in Act Three at all. I was in my dressing-room when I heard about Lesley's death. Then I joined the crowd on stage."

"I remember." Castle said keenly:

"You had made your final exit in Act Two. Yet you were still in costume."

"Of course." The girl spoke with pitying tolerance. "I was waiting to take the curtain calls."

Lawrence interrupted again. He said cheerily:

"I'll take the opportunity of applauding you now."

He was rewarded with another warm smile. Castle growled. "Shut up, Algy, for Heaven's sake. Or for mine at least... Now, young lady, I

295

understood you to say that you divided your time between appearing on stage and waiting in your dressing-room."

"Yes."

"Didn't you leave your dressing-room at all?"

"Only," said Trudy Ann demurely, "for the natural emergencies."

Castle continued hastily:

"You mentioned back-stage feuds. Was Miss Christopher concerned in them?"

"She was indeed."

"Ah!" Castle paused invitingly.

Trudy Ann said nothing.

Castle prompted her. "Had she any enemies?"

The girl answered naively:

"I don't think anybody liked her, once they knew her really well. Not even Michael Trent. Though he sometimes went to bed with her."

Castle broke the point of his pencil and swore inaudibly. He said:

"I asked you if she had any enemies."

Trudy Ann considered "I wouldn't call them enemies. But many had cause to dislike her. Especially—."

She stopped abruptly, her lips framed silently about a name.

Castle leaned forward. "Yes?"

Trudy Ann smiled piquantly. "I don't think I'll tell you now."

Castle breathed hard. He said coldly:

"You promised to co-operate."

"Perhaps I did. But," said the girl accusingly, "I can see that you have a nasty, suspicious mind. And I don't want to help you make trouble."

Lawrence interposed hastily. "Trudy Ann, the Chief Inspector is only doing his duty. And Lesley Christopher has been murdered. Don't you want the guilty person to be punished?"

"No," she replied, "I don't think I do."

"Why?" roared Stephen Castle.

She answered gently:

"I didn't like Lesley Christopher."

"But—." Castle fought for breath.

Lawrence asked mildly:

"Why didn't you like her?"

"She was a bitch," said Trudy Ann with disarming frankness.

# CHAPTER THIRTEEN

Lawrence smothered a laugh.

He said gravely:

"Not even a bitch deserves to be murdered."

"N—no," said Trudy Ann doubtfully. "But—."

Lawrence coaxed her. "Unless we learn the truth, the wrong people may suffer. You wouldn't want that to happen, would you? Be a good girl, Trudy Ann. Tell us all you know."

"W—well—." She hesitated. Then she said with a mutinous pout:

"Lesley really was a bitch, though. Ask Penny Valentine; she suffered the most. She could act La Christopher off the stage. But she was only the second lead. And she didn't know all the dirty tricks, while Lesley did. She trod on Penny's lines and killed her laughs—."

Castle was sharpening his pencil with vicious slashes. Snapping shut his penknife, he said grittily:

"This is interesting, but not strictly relevant. Unless Miss Valentine is the special person you had in mind."

"Penny? Why, no. It was J—."

She broke off. Lawrence saw the stage manager start.

Castle commanded:

"Go on."

Trudy Ann said, very softly:

"It was Jack Austin whom I saw leaving Lesley's dressing-room."

Algy Lawrence spoke lightly. "That's not necessarily cause for suspicion. Is it, Mr. Austin?"

Trudy Ann was regretful. "I'm sorry Jack. I didn't mean—."

"Whatever you meant," said Austin bitterly, "you'll have to explain it now."

Trudy Ann gazed at the Chief Inspector with an air of innocent enquiry. "Must I?"

Castle replied heavily:

"You're not compelled to tell us anything."

He managed to surround the speech with an aura of menace.

Trudy Ann took the hint. She said without conviction:

"It was nothing, really. But I couldn't help seeing—. "

She stopped. After a tantalizing pause, she continued:

"I left my dressing-room after the five minutes call. As I was walking along the corridor, I saw Mr. Austin. He came bursting out of Lesley's dressing-room with a face of thunder."

Castle was prosaic. "You mean he seemed angry?"

"He was furious," said Trudy Ann. "He went on to the stage like a bat out of hell. I was almost afraid to follow."

"You've made your point," interrupted Austin thinly. "Don't over-act."

The girl's lashes brushed her cheeks "I'm sorry, Jack. I didn't want to tell them. Truly I didn't."

"You haven't told us anything yet," said the Chief Inspector caustically. "Continue, please."

"W—well," hesitated Trudy Ann. "I couldn't help wondering what had upset Mr. Austin. So a little while later I asked young Billy, the call-boy. And he said—.'

"Really, Inspector," said the stage manager restively. "Is this sort of thing evidence?"

"Not in a court of law, perhaps," replied Castle. "But it's permissible during the course of an investigation... Please don't interrupt. Go on, young lady."

Trudy Ann continued: "When Billy calls the times he knocks on the door and opens it an inch or two. Sometimes"—she smiled demurely—"he opens it more than he should. And he told me—in confidence, of course—that before he made the five minutes call, he overheard the sounds of a quarrel and then a cry of pain in Lesley's dressing-room. So when he knocked, he pushed open the door and peeped in."

"And?"

"He saw Mr. Austin. Jack was nursing his hand.'

Algy Lawrence angled an eyebrow. "Was that when you burned it, Mr. Austin?"

The S.M. compressed his lips. He made no reply.

The Chief Inspector shuffled his notes and spoke to the girl. "We needn't keep you now. I shall. Probably ask you to sign a statement later."

He stood up with an air of dismissal.

Algy Lawrence escorted the girl to the door. She said in a low voice: "I hope I haven't made things too unpleasant for Jack."

Lawrence grinned at her lazily. "You haven't told us enough to hang him. So don't worry. But—."

She peeped through thick lashes. "Yes?"

"Uh—you haven't explained why you were so cross with Steve for closing the theatre tonight."

Her hazel eyes were innocent. She said obliquely:

"Though there are five characters in the play, we have only two understudies on the pay-roll—one for me and one for Douglas Denzil. You see, Douglas deputizes for Michael, and Penny for Lesley."

"So Penny Valentine"—Algy spoke thoughtfully—"will now play 'Marilyn'."

"It's her big chance," agreed Trudy Ann.

Lawrence murmured. "I'm sure Miss Valentine has everyone's good wishes. But if she has been promoted, who now plays the second lead?"

Trudy Ann's lips parted in a slow sensuous smile.

She lifted her hand and stroked cool fingers against his cheek.

"Silly boy," she cooed. "This is my big chance, too."

Algy Lawrence closed the door behind her and turned to discover the S.M. in the hands of the Inquisition.

Austin was perspiring freely. He said miserably:

"All right, then. I admit it. We were quarrelling. I lost my head and grabbed Lesley's wrist. So she—she stubbed out her cigarette on the back of my hand." His fingers moved nervously over the burnt flesh. "I stormed away. I –I was blind with anger."

Castle spread stubby fingers over his jowl. "So your feelings for the dead girl could hardly be described as friendly."

Austin's head jerked up. "I was angry with her, yes. But that doesn't mean I murdered her!"

"Perhaps not. But why did you tell us you loved her?"

"Because it was true! But she didn't love me. That's what the quarrel was about. I was a fool—I pressed her too hard." Austin's voice wavered. "She was capricious and cruel. But I loved her."

His chin sank. Castle's gaze met Lawrence's over the stage manager's bowed head. Algy nodded slowly.

Castle continued mildly:

"Now I'd like to put your movements into sequence—from the time you loaded the gun with blanks till the moment of the tragedy."

Austin paused for a moment to collect his thoughts. "After Props and I had seen to the revolver, I busied myself back-stage. As stage manager, I have a lot to do.

"I went to the stage door to see if there was any sign of Michael Trent. I arrived in time to see his dresser take charge of him... I exchanged a few words with Victor Friern"—he described the conversation briefly—"then went to see Trent. I've told you about that. I left Michael's dressing-room and went into Lesley's." He flushed. "You know what happened then."

Castle nodded. "You took up your duties back-stage. You gave the signal to ring up the curtain. What did you do then?"

Austin smiled faintly. "I hope you don't imagine my work was finished. I was in the prompt corner—that's my post back-stage. I spent most of the afternoon on the book—."

"The book?"

"The prompt script. I always hold it. You never know when an actor is going to dry—forget his lines."

"As Lesley did," commented Lawrence, "in the first act."

The S.M. nodded. "Yes. She dried stone dead. I gave her the word—prompted her—but she didn't seem to hear me. Trent managed to cover up for her."

Castle gestured impatiently. "That's by the way... Continue, please."

Austin dabbed his forehead. "As I say, I spent the afternoon on the book, giving signals from the prompt corner switchboard."

"You didn't leave the prompt corner?"

"I—I left it for a brief period after the curtain had gone up on the third act."

"Oh? Why?"

"For no sinister reason, I assure you." Austin gave an uneasy laugh. "I wanted to check on a special effect that was due to be given in the final scene. You didn't see it, so I needn't bother you with details." He continued rapidly. "I put my A.S.M. on the book and left her in the prompt corner. I wasn't away for more than a couple of minutes, and was back in my corner with June before—before—."

"Before Miss Christopher died." Castle tapped his thumbnail with the pencil. "Thank you, Mr. Austin. I shall ask you to sign a statement later. Now I would like to interview the property master."

Austin stared. "You mean I can go?"

Castle spoke in a neutral tone. "We may recall you later."

The stage manager made his escape.

"Exit Antigonus, pursued by a bear," commented Lawrence idly. "Tell me, Steve. Is friend Austin's harassed air the sign of a guilty conscience, or is it the natural result of your third degree tactics?"

"There's been no third degree."

"You were rather rough with him, though."

"I'm not sure he was telling the truth."

Lawrence nodded.

He said:

"I wonder."

Castle glared at the property master accusingly. Wix fidgeted and drummed his bony fingers on the table between them.

The Chief Inspector snapped. "Sit still, man! Please."

The morose gleam in the other's faded eyes deepened perceptibly. His tired mouth quivered.

Castle said, more mildly:

"I want you to answer my questions as clearly and concisely as you can. You are the property master, and your evidence will be very important."

Wix eyed him suspiciously. "You've already seen Mr. Austin—ain't he told you all you want to know?"

"We'd like to confirm his evidence, if we can."

Wix nodded energetically. "Ev'rything he told you was the truth."

"You don't know what he told us—yet," said Castle softly.

The seamed face reddened. "R'you tryin' to trick me?"

"It's more than likely," returned Castle dryly, "that you're trying to trick yourself. Come off it, man. We know why you're on the defensive. We've heard about your feud with Lesley Christopher—."

"Feud!" Alarm sharpened the lines etched in the surface of the property master's face. "What the 'ell 'r'you saying? Are you tryin' to make out I put bullets instead o' blanks into that ruddy revolver? I—."

"Control yourself, man!"

Algy Lawrence dropped a casual remark into the silence that followed. "Nobody has suggested that you put cartridges of any sort into the gun. We know that the stage manager himself—."

"Yes." Wix licked dry lips. "Yes, that's right. Mr. Austin loaded the gun. I watched him do it."

He forced a smile of apology. "Sorry, gents. I didn't mean to get excited."

He confirmed Austin's story in every detail. He had brought the S.M. a box of cartridges. He had watched Austin emptying the revolver, testing the action and reloading with six blanks. He was positive that no error had been made. "Believe me, gents, his nibs don't make mistakes."

"Hmmm." Castle scratched his nose. "Can you account for your movements after five minutes past two?"

"If you mean can I prove an alibi," said Wix sulkily, "the answer's no. I don't move about under escort. When I wasn't in the wings, I was in the prop room—alone. But"—his faded eyes gleamed—"I didn't go near that blasted gun again and you won't find anyone to tell you different!"

Castle asked:

"Where were you when the girl was shot?"

"I wasn't watching her, if that's what you mean," sneered Wix. "I was having a break—drinking tea with Syd Short."

"The stage door-keeper?"

"Yes. He likes to brew up in his box."

Castle produced the six blank cartridges which had been found in the fire bucket. "Can you identify these?"

"What d'you mean, identify 'em?"

"Are they the blanks you gave Austin to put into the revolver?"

"'Ow the 'ell should I know? You can't tell one bloody blank from another!" Wix clawed a half-empty box from his pocket and slapped it on the table. "Look for yourself. That's the box I took the fresh cartridge from this afternoon."

Castle examined the blanks in the box. They matched those hidden in the sand.

The Chief Inspector grunted. He said abruptly:

"Let's talk about the revolver. The Webley & Scott with the engraved initials. Are they yours, Wix?"

The sudden question startled the property master. But he replied quickly. "Course not. My name's Albert. You don't spell that with an H."

"But you did supply the gun?"

Wix was sulky. "What if I did? That's no crime, is it?"

Castle was benign. "It could be. It was an unlicensed weapon and the number has been filed off. Would you mind explaining how such a gun came to be in your possession?"

"I—I—." The faded eyes flickered. "I gave 'em a prop gun for the rehearsals. They didn't like it. Said it looked like a toy. The producer— the author—."

He stopped suddenly. His eyes shifted focus. Then Wix said rapidly:

"The author—he was the man. He asked me if I had a real gun. When I said no, he produced one himself. The Webley & Scott .32. 'H.W.' Those were his initials above the butt."

"Well, well." Algy Lawrence teetered gently on his heels. Then he turned and tipped a mock salute to the poster on the wall behind him.

"THE FINAL TROPHY," he read. "By Herbert Windsor. The man who set the stage—for murder."

# CHAPTER FOURTEEN

After Wix had gone, Lawrence stood staring at the closed door with dreamily vacant eyes. As Castle knew, this was invariably a sign that his young friend's brain was working hard.

Before the Chief Inspector could phrase a question, the door opened again. Castle grunted a greeting to the man on the threshold. "Hallo, Wemyss. Have you anything to report?"

The Detective Inspector was as emotionless as ever. "We've extracted the bullet from the bear's head. As we expected, it's a .25. I've sent it to the laboratory for examination." He paused, then added: "We have also plotted the trajectory of the bullet. It was delicate work, but we think it's accurate."

Lawrence pricked up his ears. "You mean you've managed to demonstrate the actual path of the bullet?"

Wemyss nodded. "Yes."

Lawrence turned to his friend. "I'd like to see this, Steve."

"Do what you like," returned Castle tiredly. "We don't need you here."

"So I feared," said Lawrence cheerfully.

He went out.

As he headed for the stage, he passed Michael Trent. The actor was on his way to the greenroom in the company of a policeman.

Trent's easy air of self-possession had deserted him completely. Lawrence looked at his haggard face and wondered... That air of grief seemed genuine. Yet it could have been assumed.

Trent was, after all, an excellent actor.

Arriving on stage, Lawrence studied the figure of the bear with interest. A long piece of twine stretched from the animal's mouth across the stage to the interior of the box which Mervan had occupied.

"Looks as if he's having a tooth pulled, doesn't it?" came a cheery voice in the young man's ear.

Lawrence nodded to the speaker, a detective sergeant who usually worked with Wemyss. "Hallo, Bob. This is your work, I suppose?"

Robert Penrhyn was an amiable and obliging young man who had only recently been promoted. He liked to talk about his work. "It is. Shall I explain?"

"If you promise not to blind me with science."

Penrhyn grinned and crooked a finger. "Come here, then. Br'er Bear calls for closer study."

Lawrence obeyed.

Penrhyn said:

"To some extent, this animal is a museum piece, a survival from the past. Taxidermists today have abandoned the old idea of stuffing a skin with tow and fixing the posture with wire. Nowadays they model the body first and place the skin around it... Bruin shows the influence of both methods. In particular, he has a hard skull. Beneath the hide we found an outer layer of some hard substance and beneath that, tightly packed tow rags."

"Which could stop a .25 bullet."

"Yes. When you come to think of it, a stuffed head is not so very different from the boxes of cotton waste that our ballistics men use to catch bullets in the lab."

"Go on," said Lawrence keenly.

"As you know, the bullet entered the interior of the animal's open mouth. It penetrated the roof of his mouth somewhere below the snout, continuing on its angled, upward course not far beneath the surface. Ploughing through inches of tow, it finally lodged in the hard outer layer which prevented its exit through the back of Bruin's head."

"And was, of course, invisible beneath the furry skin."

"Right," agreed Penrhyn. "The bullet had virtually disappeared. There was nothing to betray its presence. If you hadn't thought of examining the bear's mouth—."

Lawrence shrugged speculation aside. "You examined the bullet, of course."

"Yes. Even if it had been set up and deformed we could have told by the weight that it was calibre .25. But it was quite undamaged—it had passed through the tow cleanly and showed clearly defined markings. We shall be able to match it with the pistol that fired it."

"I'm with you," mused Lawrence, "so far." He pointed to the length of twine. "Now explain that."

Penrhyn spoke with boyish enthusiasm. "It marks the path of the bullet. We were able to calculate the exact angle of penetration—and project it to its origin."

Lawrence raised a mild objection. "That's only possible if you can be sure that the target itself has not been moved."

Penrhyn scoffed. "Sure? Bruin weighs a ton. And he's securely fixed to the dais. The whole contraption would need half a dozen stage hands to move it."

Lawrence remembered the producer's reported passion for realism and his insistence upon using the genuine article. For once, he felt grateful for it.

He said:

"Then the impact of the bullet—."

"Was absorbed immediately," finished Penrhyn. "I doubt if Bruin swayed a fraction of an inch."

Lawrence nodded. He asked:

"How did you project the bullet's angle of penetration?"

"We sighted along the line of entry—in reverse, of course—using one of our special gadgets. It sends out a pencil-thin beam of light."

"Marking the path of the bullet?"

"Yes. The spot from the flashlight hit the rear wall of the box which Mervan had occupied. We marked the spot on the wall, then ran the twine from there to the hole inside the bear's head. As a final check, we matched the line against the angle of penetration and found it to be identical."

Lawrence said:

"From the academic point of view this is all very interesting. But," he added pessimistically, "you've only proved what we already knew. It hardly helps us now."

Penrhyn was undismayed. "I'll chalk it up to experience."

Lawrence was not so volatile. He nodded a gloomy farewell to the sergeant and walked through the open doors at the rear of the set.

When he reached the entrance to the dressing-room passage he turned and scanned the stage thoughtfully. From this position he could see the reverse sides of the painted flats which formed the back "walls" of the scene but was unable to see into the lobby itself. But by taking a few steps into the wings in the direction of the prompt entrance he obtained a clear view of the lobby "wall" on which the revolver had been placed.

Frowning slightly, he returned to the dressing-room passage.

The corridor was deserted but the sound of voices pressed against his ears. The voices weren't loud but were hard and persistent. They belonged to Douglas Denzil and Penny Valentine. The two seemed to be quarrelling.

The door with the golden star stood open. Lawrence edged towards it. He was prepared to eavesdrop shamelessly.

Denzil's malicious tones shaped into words as the listener approached.

"... make the most of it, sweet. Dear Michael won't be playing 'Regan' to your 'Marilyn' for long."

Penny's reply was incoherent but angry.

Denzil continued, unruffled:

"Or Romeo to your Juliet. Tell me, sweet—is he good in bed?"

There was a clear note of sexual jealousy in his voice. Without giving the girl any chance to reply, he continued impertinently:

"You'd find me better."

Her answer was as cold and clear as a piece of ice. "You flatter yourself, Douglas. But if you are as good as you seem to think—are you sure I'm worthy of your favours?"

Denzil said coolly:

"You'll suit me very well."

As Penny told Lawrence later:

"He looked at me as insolently as if I were a prize sow in a market."

"Are you sure?" Penny spoke with ruthlessly controlled fury. "You don't want to cheat yourself. You should consider the vital statistics. Now my figure's good, but hardly voluptuous. Bust 34, waist 22, hips 34. Height, five feet three. Weight—."

"Stop it, Penny. Verbal strip-tease doesn't suit you."

Penny replied with a hard little laugh. "I have my faults. You'll have to take me as I am."

Denzil said arrogantly:

"I can take Michael's place—on stage and off. And tame you as well."

"You flatter yourself," said Penny again. "Or perhaps—."

She broke off. She went on.

"Maybe you're trying to prove something to yourself. But I think you're bluffing, Douglas. I don't think you really want me. I don't think you want any woman."

There was a brief silence.

Then Denzil hissed:

"You little—."

There was the sound of a scuffle, a gasp of pain, and the crack of a hand across Denzil's face.

Then the door wrenched wide in Penny's grasp and the girl hurried out into the corridor. She paused for a moment as she sighted Lawrence. Her lovely face flushed. Then she ran past him without a word.

Lawrence looked into the dressing-room and discovered Denzil nursing his cheek. Though the angry marks of Penny's fingers stood out redly against the whitened flesh, Douglas did not seem unduly abashed.

He smiled a casual greeting. "Hallo, friend. You're the Dogberry's assistant, aren't you?"

"In a way." Lawrence eyed Denzil curiously. The actor looked cool and composed: it was as if he had already forgotten the flare of temper which had betrayed him into an undignified scuffle with the girl.

"I suppose you're going to tell me I should be waiting in the wardrobe room." Douglas grinned boyishly. "I slipped away while the bobby was escorting dear Michael to the Torquemada's chamber. Well—I apologize."

"You needn't. You're not a prisoner. But—."

"Yes?"

"I would like," said Lawrence carefully, "to know what you're doing in Lesley Christopher's dressing-room."

Denzil spoke in portentous parody. "I was looking for clues to this dastardly crime."

Lawrence angled an eyebrow. "Shouldn't you leave that to the police?"

Denzil grinned impudently. "Perhaps. But you've no right to reproach me. I've placed you now. You're not a professional sleuth. You're an amateur, just like me. Why do you spend your time hunting murderers?"

Lawrence stuck his tongue in his cheek. He said firmly:

"It's my legitimate work for society."

Denzil used a rude word pleasantly.

He continued:

"Amateur detectives are like morality leagues and censorship boards. They ascribe to themselves the worthiest motives and claim to be working in the best interests of society. But they're really meddlesome busybodies who love to poke their noses into other people's business."

Lawrence grinned wryly. "Perhaps you're right. But my status as a sleuth is at least quasi-official. Yours isn't."

Denzil gestured gracefully, if theatrically. "I won't argue. If you insist, I shall withdraw gracefully. But don't think I'm idly curious. I am concerned in this— ah—odd affair."

"As a suspect, perhaps," said Lawrence gently.

Denzil laughed. "I asked for that. But dig into my past—you'll find no grounds for suspicion. I'm one of the few people in this theatre who had no reason to want Lesley dead."

He spoke with confidence.

Lawrence shrugged. "That's for the police to decide."

Denzil said softly:

"Aren't we splitting hairs? Several people had motives—but only one person killed her. He's the man you will have to arrest."

Lawrence stared. "You mean—."

"Michael Trent."

"But—."

Denzil waved his hand. "He shot her through the heart. That's all you need to prove. You must arrest him."

Eyes glinted maliciously in the young-old face.

Lawrence said:

"Wait now. It's not as simple as that. Trent killed her, yes. But unless we can prove he knew he was firing a live cartridge, no jury will call him a murderer."

"But—."

It was Lawrence's turn to interrupt. "He will have to appear at the inquest, of course. And the Coroner or his jury may commit him for trial on a technical charge. But it won't be more than a formality. And I can't see the police opposing bail. Trent's in no danger yet."

"I see." A shutter seemed to drop behind Denzil's eyes. He rasped his thumb over the point of his jaw. It made an impatient, irritable sound in the silent room.

He said. "In the meantime—."

"It's up to you all to assist the police," finished Lawrence politely. "Shall we return to the wardrobe room?"

Denzil nodded reluctantly. "I gather my short career as a detective is already at an end. Dear me. It's really too sick-making. However—."

He broke off and moved towards the door. Lawrence stood aside to let him pass.

Algy said:

"You wouldn't have found any clues here. The police have already searched this dressing-room."

Denzil stopped. "No?" His lips curved in mockery. "The police aren't infallible, though. And sometimes a clue is too obvious to be seen by clever fellows like you."

His gaze flicked briefly towards the photograph on the dressing-room wall.


"Mr. Lawrence!"

There was a tremor in Penny Valentine's voice and troubled shadows in the depths of her cerulean eyes.

Lawrence gave her a friendly smile. "Yes?"

Penny spoke with an effort. "I want to talk to you—about Michael Trent."

"Of course. Uh—is this private enough?"

They were standing in the corridor outside the wardrobe room. Lawrence had just returned Denzil to the friendly custody of the

308

constable he had eluded.

The girl answered:

"Yes," to Algy's question, then paused. She murmured:

"It's rather difficult to put into words."

Lawrence guessed she was wondering how much he had overheard outside Lesley's dressing-room door. He said sympathetically:

"If it's anything to do with Denzil, you needn't worry. I don't take anything he says very seriously."

A smile touched her lips briefly. "You know that we quarrelled.    It was all very childish and silly. I—hit him."

Lawrence was tactfully silent.

Penny continued:

"I had asked the constable for permission to go to my dressing-room to fetch a handkerchief. On my way back, I saw Douglas in Lesley's room. He seemed annoyed when I challenged him. He wouldn't tell me what he was doing. Instead he began to taunt me. He told me Michael was in serious trouble—."

"Now look," said Lawrence firmly. "If Denzil believes Trent is going to jail then either he knows very little about law or he's indulging in wishful thinking."

He repeated to the girl what he had already told Denzil. Penny listened attentively.

She asked like a child seeking reassurance.

"Then Michael is—safe?"

"Unless we discover new evidence."

Penny's hands had clenched into two small fists. She opened them slowly.

She said softly:

"I don't think you will."

Lawrence smiled rather sadly. "Now it's my turn to ask a question."

"Yes?"

"Why are you so worried about Michael Trent?"

Her smile was a shaft of sunshine through the clouds. "Because I love him."

She walked away. Lawrence strolled back to the greenroom with a slightly rueful expression on his pleasant, lazy face. He had forgotten the mystery he was trying to solve.

He was thinking instead of the luminosity of Penny's blue eyes, and the streaks of gold in her dusty blonde hair.

# CHAPTER FIFTEEN

Trent's romantic successes might have made him a man to be envied, but Lawrence felt glad he was not in the actor's shoes when he returned to the greenroom. Slipping unobtrusively into his seat, he studied the other's handsome face.

Michael Trent seemed near collapse. His cheeks were grey and he drew raggedly on a cigarette. His mouth trembled: smoke spilled out with words. "For God's sake! I've told you all I know."

Castle regarded him thoughtfully. "You haven't been very explicit about your relations with the dead woman."

Trent shaded his eyes wearily. "I had no—relations with her."

"No?" The Chief Inspector was mild, almost gentle. "One witness at least has suggested that Miss Christopher was your mistress."

Trent dropped his hand and looked up. An oddly distorted smile drifted over his lips. He said in a brittle voice:

"She certainly wasn't my—mistress."

"You were just good friends," supplied Castle sardonically. "Tell me, Mr. Trent: how long had you known her?"

"For ten years," replied Trent with mechanical quickness. Then his jaw slackened and the skin stretched taut over his cheekbones.

Castle's eyes glinted. He said:

"Thank you, Mr. Trent. That will be all. For the time being."

Trent stumbled to his feet. His hands lifted, then dropped. He went out.

Castle looked at Wemyss. "Well—what do you think?"

"I think," answered the Detective Inspector cautiously, "that Mr. Trent knows rather more than he has told us."

"Just what," asked Lawrence, "has he told you?"

Castle grunted. "Precisely what you'd expect—no more and no less. He didn't know there were live bullets in the gun and he's shocked half out of his wits to discover he was used to kill the girl." The Chief Inspector waved towards the shorthand writer. "When the report has been transcribed, you can read Trent's statement for yourself. But I've given you the essence."

Lawrence asked gently:

"How much of the statement is true?"

Castle replied with brutal frankness. "Not very much, in my opinion. What do you say, Wemyss?"

The Detective Inspector answered unemotionally. "Trent is, of course, the most obvious suspect. He pulled the trigger and he was the only person who could have been certain that the bullet would go through the girl's heart."

The quiet words sent a chill through Algy Lawrence. He thought: Poor Penny, and wondered if he was wholly sincere.

He said:

"You surprise me. I thought Trent was safe from arrest."

"He is," growled Castle. "Make no mistake about that. We've no real evidence to prove his guilt. We can't even suggest his motive."

Algy's sense of fairness made him speak. "I can help you there. Friern told me that Michael and Lesley were good friends. Trudy Ann's account was blunter. Let's accept her version for the moment."

"Well?"

Lawrence said, not very happily:

"Penny Valentine is also involved with Michael Trent. I think they're lovers."

"Do you now?" Castle's eyebrows went up. "Then the two girls were rivals— off stage as well as on?"

"Yes. And if Trent preferred Penny to Lesley—."

"Miss Christopher might not have accepted her dismissal." Castle looked grim. "Trent wouldn't have been the first man to discover he had to murder his mistress to discard her."

Lawrence said coolly:

"That sounds a little too melodramatic to be convincing."

Castle glared. "Dammit, Algy. You yourself—."

Wemyss interposed smoothly:

"I think we should keep an open mind. We haven't heard all the evidence yet."

Castle turned down the corners of his mouth. "You don't mean evidence. You mean back-stage gossip."

"If it's gossip you're after," commented Lawrence, "I know a promising witness."

Castle snorted. "So do I. And I may be prejudiced, but he's not a man I like." He sighed noisily. "Oh, well. Let's have him in."

Douglas Denzil displayed an engaging smile. "I'll be frank with you, gentlemen. I didn't have any special feelings about Lesley Christopher one way or the other. So"—he drew in his breath with a little hiss—"I can't say her death distresses me. But that doesn't mean I would care to protect her murderer"—his smile became feline—"even if he turns out to be one of my colleagues."

Castle's tone was neutral. "Just tell us what you know. Your responsibility ends there."

"I'm ready. Ask your questions."

The Chief Inspector began by charting the actor's movements from the moment he had arrived at the theatre. Denzil was not evasive, but neither was he specially helpful. "You see, I'm a wanderer. Actors have a habit of straying from their dressing-rooms and getting into the most peculiar places. I'm no exception."

Castle persevered. "You say that you spent most of the time between the half hour call and your first entrance in your dressing-room."

"Yes. For once, I was on my best behaviour. You see, I'm Trent's understudy—and dear Michael's movements have been uncertain of late. He wasn't in at the half, so the S.M. warned me—."

"Austin warned you? When?"

Denzil said vaguely:

"Before the quarter... He told me Trent was missing, but would probably turn up. He asked me to wait there in my dressing-room, to be ready to make a quick change if I had to play the lead. He said he'd send word by the A.S.M. if Michael didn't arrive in time. But, of course"—Denzil grinned rather savagely—"Trent did."

"So you played your usual part." Castle considered. "Now, sir. Will you detail your movements during the first and second acts?"

"Oh, really, Inspector!" Denzil chuckled ingenuously. "You're asking too much. As I told you before, I'm a wanderer."

Castle sighed. Close questioning, plus an examination of the prompt script and the time sheet, enabled him to pin-point Denzil's appearances on stage; but the actor was not particularly helpful about his movements behind the scenes.

At the time when Lesley had died, he had been in the dressing-room passage talking to Penny Valentine. After hearing the news, they had hurried on stage. Trudy Ann had joined them later. And by that time a crowd had collected.

Castle blew out his cheeks. "This tells me nothing I didn't know before. Nothing valuable, that is. Nothing that has any bearing on the crime."

Denzil said cautiously:

"I don't want to speak out of turn. But I might be able to help you."

"I'm listening."

"I don't want to tell tales out of school." The gleam in Denzil's eyes betrayed him. "But I suggest you ask Michael Trent to tell you what happened in his dressing-room during the second act wait."

Castle fiddled with his notes. "The second act wait—that's the interval between the second and third acts?"

"Yes. I don't want you to think I was eavesdropping—. "

"No," said Castle dryly.

Another man might have flushed. Denzil merely grinned. "I was strolling along the passage. I saw Lesley go into Michael's room. She left the door open. She said in a loud, choking voice: 'You'll be sorry for this. I promise you.' Then she came out."

The Chief Inspector frowned. "Well?"

"I think she interrupted something. Penny Valentine followed her out, called for Ben Cotall—Michael's dresser: he was nearby—then scampered into her own dressing-room. None of them seemed happy."

"And then?"

"I walked away."

"Is that all you have to tell me?"

Denzil countered the question with another. "Isn't it enough?"

Castle was deliberately obtuse. "No. You'll have to be explicit."

"All right." Denzil's reply was tinged with anger. And the mask had slipped badly: his face was nakedly spiteful. "I'll tell you this. Trent's too damned attractive for his own good. When he wants a woman, he takes her. Drops her, too, when he's had enough. But Lesley wouldn't stand for that—she was too possessive. She—."

He stopped suddenly.

He relaxed. He smiled boyishly. He said:

"No. I shan't tell you any more. You can draw your own conclusions."

After Denzil had left, Wemyss said quietly:

"The dead woman may have discovered a liaison between Mr. Trent and Miss Valentine. But does that provide Trent with a motive for murdering her?"

"I think so." Castle rubbed his jowl. "Lesley Christopher may have been in a position to make things bad for him."

The Detective Inspector hesitated. He repeated softly:

"'You'll be sorry for this. I promise you.' Was that a strong enough threat to bring murder in reply?"

"It could have been," said Castle stubbornly. "If Trent had a guilty conscience—if he knew that Lesley knew some secret in his past—."

Lawrence protested. "You're guessing wildly."

"Am I?" grunted Castle. "You heard Trent tell us he had known the woman for ten years. He spoke without thinking. Then he looked like a man who had made a guilty admission."

"You mean—."

"I mean," said Castle quietly, "we know what happened seven years ago. Richard Mervan robbed a bank. He was betrayed by Lesley Barre, alias Lesley Christopher. She took the loot and escaped. With an accomplice. With... Michael Trent?"

Ben Cotall muttered rebelliously. "You can't make me tell tales about Mr. Trent. He's the best employer a man ever had—yes, an' friend, too."

"You've been with him a long time?"

"Five years or more." Pride showed clearly in the dresser's wizened face. "He gave me a job when no one else would look at me. He was unknown then. Now he's a star."

Castle said:

"Tell me about Miss Christopher."

Cotall scowled weakly. "She was no good for him. But he couldn't give her up."

"Or get rid of her?"

Ben's mouth snapped shut. He made no reply.

Castle shifted ground. "Let's consider your own movements from the time you arrived at the theatre this afternoon."

Cotall was frank but uninformative. He had gone back-stage about an hour before the performance was due to begin. He had gone to Trent's dressing-room to prepare it for his master. He had uncovered the dressing-table, laying out the articles of make-up, and had taken Trent's costume for the first act out of the wardrobe. After he had conscientiously attended to every little job he could think of, there had been nothing to do but await his employer's arrival.

"Mr. Trent was late?"

"Yes. He was— unwell."

"You mean he had been drinking."

"What if he had?" Ben stuck out his jaw pugnaciously. "There's plenty that do worse."

He had taken charge of his employer as soon as Trent had passed through the stage door. And from that moment he had followed him like a shadow. Or—.

"Like a faithful dog," mused the Chief Inspector, as the door closed behind old Ben. "They say no man is a hero to his valet. Evidently that doesn't apply to his dresser."

"In Cotall's case, no," smiled Wemyss. "But I think we shall find that Miss Christopher's dresser took a more objective view of her employer."

Maggie Boyd said bluntly:

"No, I didn't like Miss Christopher. Few women did "

"What about"— Castle hesitated— "the men?"

Maggie's bright beady eyes glinted cynically. "They were attracted to her. So she used them."

"And?"

"They meant nothing to her. She loved nobody but herself."

"And Michael Trent?"

Maggie jerked beefy shoulders. "Perhaps. There was some kind of a bond between them—I never knew what, exactly. But she always turned to him when something was troubling her. As she did this afternoon."

Castle said:

"Tell us about this afternoon."

Maggie folded plump hands. "I'm not one to gossip. But it won't help Miss Christopher to keep her secrets now... Something happened during the first act. Miss Lesley came back to the dressing-room as pale as a ghost—and trembling. She didn't tell me what had upset her. But she mumbled something about seeing a man in one of the boxes."

Castle shuffled his notes morosely. He already knew that the sight of Richard Mervan had given Lesley a shock. This was old news now.

Maggie prattled on. "I went into the wings with Miss Lesley. Mr. Trent was there with his dresser, waiting to make his entrance."

"In the second act?"

"Yes. Miss Valentine and Mr. Denzil were already on stage."

"I remember," grunted Castle. "Go on."

"As I say, the four of us were waiting in the wings. Miss Lesley appealed to Mr. Trent—said she had to talk to him. It was like a cry for help."

"Oh?" The Chief Inspector was interested. "How did Trent react?"

Maggie pursed disapproving lips. "He tried to put her off—made excuses because Ben and I were there. He said something silly in French. Not in front of the children—something like that. But he couldn't keep Miss Lesley quiet. She blurted: 'Michael, you don't understand. He's out there, watching. Waiting...'"

Lesley's voice echoed faintly from Maggie's throat.

Somebody moved sharply.

Then Castle asked mildly:

"And Mr. Trent—did he understand?"

Maggie Boyd frowned. "He didn't answer. But I think he knew what

Miss Lesley meant."

Castle gave a satisfied rumble. "There you are, gentlemen. Was I guessing so wildly?"

Maggie Boyd had left. The investigators were alone.

Wemyss spoke dubiously. "I'm not sure—."

Castle interrupted. "Lesley Christopher was obviously referring to Richard Mervan. So Trent must have known all about him—and the robbery, too. I think Trent was very probably the man who helped the girl to double-cross Mervan by knocking him out in her flat."

"That's guess-work," objected Wemyss half-heartedly. "But if you're right"—he spread his hands—"then Trent had a motive for murder."

Castle nodded. "Crazed with fear and jealousy, Lesley could have given him away. She might have come to us in a moment of malice or panic. Trent had to stop her mouth."

Wemyss coughed. "This is only a theory," he reminded his chief. "We can't prove it. Of course," he added shrewdly, "we've yet to question Miss Valentine. She may be able to help us."

Stephen Castle was moody. "She could. But I don't suppose she will. If she loves Michael Trent, she won't be eager to put a rope round his neck."

As the Chief Inspector had feared, the interview was unrewarding, though Penny Valentine answered all his questions about her movements with an air of perfect frankness. She agreed that she might have had one or two opportunities to tamper with the ammunition in the gun but—with no display of resentment, anger or fear—quietly denied having done so.

Castle tried to question her about Michael Trent, but had no success at all. When he began to make clumsy hints about her relationship with the actor, the girl's eyes glimmered mischievously but she made no direct reply.

Castle started to perspire. He said bitterly:

"Young lady, you're not helping me at all."

Penny replied calmly:

"I don't have to answer your questions. You know that as well as I do." .

"If you don't answer," huffed Castle, "you can't blame us for being suspicious."

"Be anything you wish." Penny was tranquil. "I love Michael Trent. I won't deny that. As for the rest"—she dimpled suddenly—"you'll have to use your imagination."

"Very well," said Castle, making up his mind, "you may go back to the wardrobe room. I shall ask you to sign a statement later. And I may question you again soon."

Penny left, with a quick smile for Lawrence.

The young man said quietly:

"Leave Penny to me, Steve. I think I've won her confidence."

Castle looked down his nose. "And I'm just a blundering policeman. Is that what you mean?"

Lawrence grinned. "No. But I can move amongst these people freely, unhindered by rules and regulations. I can gain their friendship, win their trust. You can't."

Castle scratched his nose. He admitted: "The Valentine girl may talk to you. If she does"—he gestured—"ask her what happened in Trent's dressing-room during the second act wait."

Lawrence nodded.

Wemyss cleared his throat. "Trent may be our Number One suspect. But we mustn't lose sight of the others."

"You're right," growled Castle. "Every person back-stage had a chance to load the gun with bullets. We'll have to chart everybody's movements from the half-hour call—."

He bit back his words and swallowed them.

He sighed. "Oh, well. Let's begin."


Afterwards, Stephen Castle recalled the interrogations as a nightmare procession of faces, for the most part blurred and indistinguishable. A few sharpened into focus: June Merritt's, plain and podgy with a lingering expression of shocked astonishment; the call-boy Billy's, youthful and scared, yet pleasurably horrified; and others. But mostly they were just faces: fleshy frames for mouths shaping meaningless words.

Heavy-eyed, the Chief Inspector yawned over a mounting pile of statements. They had all been laboriously compiled from shorthand notes, read back to their originators, and then signed and witnessed.

At last, Lawrence stretched and yawned. "I shall take advantage of my amateur status. I'm going home to bed."

Castle consulted his watch. "It's getting late. I'm tempted to follow your example. What d'you think, Wemyss? Is there anything more we can do here tonight?"

The Detective Inspector shook his head. "I think not, sir."

"Then—."

Somebody knocked on the greenroom door.

Castle called:

"Come in... Oh, it's you, Mr. Friern. You look worried. There's nothing wrong, I hope?"

The manager said jerkily: "Yes... No... I'm sorry, gentlemen, if I sound confused. I've been having rather a difficult time. Your decision to close the theatre—that meant we had to turn away the ticket-holders this evening. And then there were the reporters—."

"Dear me, yes," commented Castle with unusual mildness. "I had forgotten them. They gave you no trouble, I hope."

"I—I gave them the statement you authorized. I'm afraid it didn't satisfy them."

"Devil take 'em," growled the Chief Inspector. He laughed harshly. "Cheer up, sir. You'll be re-opening soon. And this publicity won't do you any harm."

Victor Friern replied simply:

"Increased business is no compensation for the loss of a very dear friend."

Castle said gruffly:

"You're right, of course."

He added in half-apology: "Perhaps my job makes me callous. Ha-humph! Have you a night watchman?"

"Yes. He has already arrived."

"He'll have a companion tonight. I'm leaving someone to keep an eye on things. Wemyss! Have you told off a man for duty?"

"Yes, sir. Bailey is staying."

Friern asked:

"Have you finished your work?"

"We're doing no more tonight. Everyone can go."

Wemyss and Friern went out.

Castle lumbered to his feet and banged both fists on the pile of statements. "Hell's bloody blazes! What a case."

Lawrence chuckled. Castle eyed the young man suspiciously. Algy had strolled back to the bookshelves. Steve glared at the back of his friend's blond head. "Come away from those ruddy books! You're wasting time."

"No, I'm not," said Lawrence mildly. "No case is complete without one red herring." He turned with a heavy volume in his hands. "And here it is."

Removing a marker, he opened the book and put it on the table facing the Chief Inspector. Castle regarded the pages with lack-lustre eyes. "What's this?"

"A bound volume of the Gentleman's Magazine."

"That's the blasted book you were babbling about hours ago."

Lawrence said quietly:

"Read it, Steve."

Castle obeyed with a grumble. His glance fell at random on the old print.

... From Newgate to Tyburn he behaved with great composure. While the halter was tying, his whole frame appeared to be violently convulsed. The Ordinary having retired, he addressed himself to the populace: "Good people, I request your prayers for the salvation of my departing soul; let my example teach you to shun the bad ways I have followed; keep good company, and mind the word of God."

Castle looked puzzled. "What's so interesting about this?"

"Look at the date. The 7th of November, 1783."

"Well?"

"That was the date," said Lawrence, "and this is the description – of the last public execution at Tyburn."

Castle narrowed his eyes. "I believe you're right."

"Uh huh. I've already checked up. I 'phoned a librarian I know."

Castle said:

"This is interesting. But we don't want to get Paddington Fair on the brain."

Lawrence's eyes glimmered. "Did you notice the name of the man who was hanged?"

"Huh? Why it was—."

Castle found the name.

Then he looked up with startled eyes.

"It's—."

"Yes," said Algy Lawrence.

# CHAPTER SIXTEEN

It was one o'clock in the morning. Outside in the streets, a fine, light rain was falling. It misted the nimbus of light about each lamp-post and transformed the pavements into black mirrors.

Fitful moonlight played over the two faces of Janus, guardian spirit of the doorway. Below the pagan emblem, the unilluminated tubes of a neon sign ghost-spelled the legend of THE FINAL TROPHY, a play by Herbert Windsor. And beneath the fade, a darker shadow moved against the wall of the theatre, then was gone.

"... And that makes thirty-one."

Bailey watched his companion gloomily as the night watchman bent over the cards, counted the hands, and pegged the scores on the cribbage board.

The policeman said abruptly:

"I'm tired of this—d'you mind if we drop the game?"

Tom Purrett shifted the pipe to one corner of his mouth. "No, I don't mind. Anyway,"—he glanced at the clock—"it's time I made my rounds."

The two men were sitting in the night watchman's cubby-hole, a small room at the back of the theatre. A kettle was spluttering wisps of steam on a gas-ring in the corner.

Purrett glanced at it and asked:

"Would you like a cup of tea?"

"I'd prefer something stronger," answered Bailey without much hope.

Purrett lowered a leathery eye-lid. "Mebbe I can oblige."

He stood up, scratched his thigh, then lumbered across the room. Opening a cupboard under the sink, he groped inside and extracted a beer bottle. It was empty. Purrett studied it with regret, mumbled: "Must've finished it last night," and returned it to the cupboard.

He straightened his back with a grunt. "Mebbe it's for the best. Beer makes you sleepy—an' on my job you're s'posed to keep awake." He glanced at his companion. "No reason I can see why we should both stay up, though. Why don't you take a nap while I'm doing my rounds?"

Bailey replied regretfully:

"I have orders to stay awake."

Tom Purrett sniffed. "Please yourself." He sorted out a heavy electric torch and, gripping it tightly in a horny fist, stamped out of the room.

Bailey sighed. He gathered the greasy playing cards together, then cursed briefly and slammed the deck down on the table.

He felt bored and unhappy. Routine work like this would never bring him an appointment to the C.I.D. If only there was some way to prove his worth—.

He brooded. Somewhere in the theatre, there might be a valuable piece of evidence waiting to be found....

He hesitated. It might not pay to interfere. His job was to see that nothing was touched until the Chief Inspector and his men returned to complete their investigations. But—.

The temptation was too great. With no real plan in mind, but day-dreaming wistfully of a spectacular piece of detective work which would win him instant promotion, Bailey made his way out of the room and along the dark corridors in the direction of the dressing-room passage.

The beam from his flashlight drove back the shadows. At the entrance to the passage, Bailey paused and listened. Behind and above him, something moved and creaked high in the grid. An old back-cloth perhaps, stirred by the fugitive wind sighing its way in through the top of the theatre.

It was an innocent sound. It meant nothing, except that the theatre was somehow alive—and waiting.

Something moved in the passage.

Bailey's heart leaped. He swung his flashlight wildly. The beam slashed into the black corridor like a knife-blade. The passage was empty. But one of the doors was partly open. It was the door with the golden star.

"Who's there?"

Bailey's voice cracked. He cleared his throat and called again. "Who is it?"

Silence. Bailey felt glad he was still in uniform. He drew his truncheon and moved forward cautiously. There was no further sound, beyond that of his own soft footfalls.

Bailey began to relax. Perhaps it was a false alarm.

He reached the Number One dressing-room. Standing against the wall, he reached out with his truncheon and thrust against the panel. The door with the star swung open to its fullest extent.

Nothing happened.

Bailey directed the rays of his flashlight into the inner blackness. The room was empty.

Bailey laughed shakily. He made to turn.

Then a savage, crashing blow on the back of his head hurled him through a tunnel of pain into oblivion.

Tom Purrett had returned to his cubby-hole. He was frowning round the empty room.

The kettle still spluttered on the gas-ring. The night watchman looked at it absently. Then he padded across and twisted the tap, extinguishing the tiny flames.

He paused for a long moment, exhibiting a curious air of indecision. Then he seemed to make up his mind to act.

He picked up the heavy electric torch and lumbered out of the little room, slamming the door behind him. He began to call in a curious monotone. "Mr. Bailey! Mr. Bailey!"

His voice echoed eerily along the dark corridors. Ghost calls returned in sardonic parody.

Purrett came to a halt on the night-shrouded stage. He swung his torch uneasily. He seemed unwilling to proceed.

"Mr. Bailey! Where are you?"

Somebody groaned.

The night watchman caught his breath, then expelled it in a long and toneless "aah". He stumbled towards the entrance to the dressing-room passage.

The torch eye jumped, then steadied. Its rays focused on the body of a man on the floor.

"Gawd!" Bailey was lying on his face with his head and shoulders over the threshold of the Number One dressing-room. Purrett lumbered towards him. He half-fell, half-knelt beside the prostrate figure.

Old Tom put out a cautious hand. The back of the policeman's head felt soft and warm and sticky. Purrett stared at his fingers in the torch-light. They were streaked with blood.

Bailey groaned again. Purrett put the heavy torch down carefully. He put both hands on the policeman's shoulders and rolled him over.

Bailey's eyelids stirred. His mouth quivered helplessly. "Aaahh... "

Purrett's voice cracked. "Are you all right?"

Bailey's eyes opened in a sightless stare. Then he groaned again and his head rolled limply.

Purrett scanned the waxy face with fear-filled eyes.

He whispered:

"For God's sake, man! I don't want you to die.... "

The police surgeon's face was tired and irritable, but his hands were deft and kindly.

Stephen Castle was watching anxiously. "Well, doctor?" he asked at last.

The police surgeon stood up. He said:

"Bailey is suffering from severe concussion, but I' don't think there'll be any permanent damage. He was lucky. That blow might have fractured his skull."

The Chief Inspector nodded grimly. He commented:

"I'm glad you could give him prompt attention. Fortunately the night watchman had sense enough to 'phone us immediately. And he didn't attempt to move him."

He looked down at the unconscious man. He asked abruptly: "How was the blow delivered?"

The doctor shrugged. "With the traditional blunt instrument, I suppose. I couldn't tell much from the wound. The scalp was torn and bloody. So the weapon was probably heavy and metallic. Take your choice between the butt of a gun and a section of lead piping—your guess is as good as mine."

The two men were not alone in the dressing-room passage. Purrett was standing some distance away, watching uneasily. And the Chief Inspector had brought a small band of assistants with him.

Castle said:

"We've sent for an ambulance. I – Good! It must be here."

The theatre was by now ablaze with light. Two uniformed men had arrived with a stretcher. They lifted the injured man on to it gently.

Castle watched in gloomy silence.

Suddenly, he tensed. "Hallo! What's that?"

He was gazing at a small object on the floor which had, until then, been concealed under Bailey's body.

The police surgeon said irritably:

"Bailey must be taken to the hospital as soon as possible—."

"Huh?" Castle started. "Oh, get him away by all means. I don't want to delay you. But what do you make of that?"

The doctor signed to the attendants who continued on their way back to the ambulance with the unconscious man. Then the police surgeon's gaze followed Castle's pointing finger.

He answered:

"It's an ordinary comb."

Castle grunted. "In an extraordinary place—under an injured man's body. And whose is it? Not Bailey's. Not Purrett's."

"How do you know that?"

"It's monogrammed. Look at those initials."

Leaving the police surgeon staring, Castle stepped forward and put his head round the dressing-room door. "Penrhyn! Come here, will you?"

The detective-sergeant obeyed. His chief indicated the comb. "See that? I want it tested for prints."

"Right, sir." Robert Penrhyn called two men out of the dressing-room and gave them precise instructions. Then he turned back to Castle. "Sir, there's something in here you should see—."

"Oh, very well." The Chief Inspector was gruffly good-humoured. He stumped over the threshold. "What is it, what is it? I—Hallo!"

His eyes narrowed. His lips pursed.

The photograph of Michael Trent was no longer in its place on the wall. The shattered frame was lying on the dressing-table and the photo itself had been ripped out and flung to the floor.

"Well, well." Castle scowled thoughtfully.

Penrhyn answered the unspoken question. "We've tested the fragments. There are no identifiable prints—only smudges. I expect our man was wearing gloves."

"He'd need them to protect his hands." Castle studied the splintered glass and the shattered frame. "But what the devil was he doing?"

Penrhyn said:

"I think he was looking for something which had been hidden behind the picture."

Castle nodded slowly. "Lesley Christopher may have concealed some important paper inside the frame under the photograph. Her murderer may have wanted it. But he couldn't get at it while we were here—."

"So he came back tonight." Penrhyn spoke eagerly. "He meant to break into the theatre, take what he wanted, and slip away unseen. But Bailey must have heard him—.'

"And got knocked on the head." Finished Castle grimly, "before he could make an identification. Our unknown friend is a dangerous man."

"Or woman."

"Huh?" Castle jerked his head in surprise. "I suppose it's possible Bailey's assailant was a woman. But it's damned unlikely."

Penrhyn smiled. "I was trying to keep an open mind."

Castle grunted. "That's the right attitude. But at the risk of setting you a bad example, I'm going to say now that the man who murdered Lesley Christopher was also the man who cracked Bailey's head open. And, God damn it, I'm as certain of his name as I am of my own."

Penrhyn asked softly:

"Michael Trent?"

Before his chief could reply, a roar of wrath sounded behind them. "That's the daftest notion I ever heard!"

Tom Purrett lumbered through the doorway. His face was red with anger. '"Michael Trent is no murderer. He's one of the kindest, gentlest, most generous men there is. Oh, I know"—he held up a horny hand – "he's not a saint! He's a devil with the women and he drinks too much. But he ain't a ruddy killer!"

The Chief Inspector bit his lip. Silently, he cursed the unguarded words the night watchman had overheard.

He said abruptly:

"I've accused no one. You needn't spring to Trent's defence."

Purrett scowled. "I know what I 'eard. An' if you coppers are gettin' funny ideas about Mr. Trent you're going to make bloody fools of yourselves—an' that's the truth."

"That's enough!"

Mumbling ominously, the night watchman turned to go.

"Wait!" snapped Castle. "As you're here, you may as well answer a few questions."

Purrett said impatiently:

"I've told you all I know. I made my rounds, everythink was in order, I didn't hear nothin' suspicious. Mr. Bailey was gone when I got back to my room. I went to look for him—."

"Yes," agreed Castle. "I've heard all that before. Now! You found Bailey with his head and shoulders across the threshold here."

"Yes."

"Did you move him at all?"

Purrett replied sulkily:

"I rolled him over on his back. The poor bleeder was lying on his face."

"Ah!" Castle drew a satisfied breath. "Did you notice anything on the floor by his side?"

Purrett scratched himself thoughtfully. "There was his truncheon. It looked as if it 'ud fallen out of his hand."

"Not that. A—a smaller object."

Old Tom shook his head. "I don't remember nothing else. Course, I was worried 'bout Mr. Bailey."

"Of course." If Castle was disappointed, he didn't betray his feelings. "But if there had been such an object by his side, can you explain why we found it under his body?"

"I told you," snapped Purrett. "I turned the poor basket on his back. Mebbe I rolled him on top of this object of yours—whatever the ----ing thing was."

"Good," said the Chief Inspector. "That was the answer I wanted."

Purrett looked at him suspiciously. "Can I go now?"

"You may."

The night watchman lumbered out.

Castle said expansively:

"Here's my theory, for what it's worth. Bailey was prowling round the theatre; playing detective, I'll bet. He heard a sound from this passage. He thought it came from this room. Well, he was wrong. The man he wanted had slipped into the room next door. That's—."

"Michael Trent's."

"Ah hah!" Castle's eyes gleamed. He continued:

"Our man waited until Bailey poked his head into this room, then stepped out from his real hiding-place and attacked him from behind. How's that?"

"It seems likely enough," agreed Penrhyn cautiously. "Do you think the picture was smashed after the attack – or before??

"It's hard to tell." Castle frowned pensively. "The frame seems to have been broken apart by a man in a hurry."

"That's true, sir. As a matter of fact"—Penrhyn paused dramatically— "he left part of his booty behind."

"What!"

"Yes, sir. I should have mentioned it before—."

"You should have indeed." Castle spoke with unusual restraint.

"Sorry." Penrhyn produced a cellophane envelope and handed it to his chief. "You mentioned a hidden document. This seems to prove your theory. As you see, sir, it's a scrap of paper—."

"I'm not blind." Castle's growl was amiable. He studied the contents of the transparent envelope. The paper looked vaguely official and seemed to have been torn off the corner of a certificate of some kind. "You found this—?"

"Caught in the splintered frame," replied Penrhyn. "Our man must have missed it in his haste."

Castle said savagely:

"That wasn't the only mistake he made." He went to the door once more. "You, there! Have you found any dabs on that comb?"

"Yes, sir." The reply came promptly. "There are several prints. They're badly smudged. But they're identifiable."

"Good." Castle chuckled grimly. "Photograph 'em." He turned back to Penrhyn, rubbing his hands. "We've taken fingerprints from everyone in the theatre. It won't take long to identify those on the comb."

Penrhyn coughed. "This comb, sir. Was it the—um—object you

found under Bailey's body?"

"It was," answered Castle. "You heard me question Purrett. He confirmed my theory. The comb must have fallen out of our murderous friend's breast pocket. He was probably bending over Bailey's unconscious body—perhaps to see if he was still alive."

"And the comb fell out unnoticed." Penrhyn whistled. "Jove, sir! A mistake like that could hang a man."

"I hope it will," returned Castle grimly.

He reclaimed the comb from the fingerprint men. "Look at this, Penrhyn. Can you identify its owner?"

The detective-sergeant studied the monogram.

Then he replied:

"I know of only one suspect with the initials 'M.T'"

"Indeed you do," said Castle softly.

# CHAPTER SEVENTEEN

Michael Trent cried desperately:

"All right! All right! The comb is mine. I admit it. But that's all, damn you!"

His voice died away in a frightened whimper.

Chief Inspector Castle studied the actor curiously. Michael Trent was no longer the suave, self-possessed and handsome man who nightly projected the wicked charm of a strong personality across the footlights. Perhaps, as Castle told himself cynically, Trent needed a sympathetic audience. Now, as he struggled to convince three stony-faced policemen of his innocence, he seemed to be subtly disintegrating. Even his normally well-defined features appeared to be blurred; and fear had driven the intelligence from his frank grey eyes.

Trent said hoarsely:

"For God's sake, give me a cigarette."

Castle looked at Wemyss and nodded. While the Detective Inspector ministered to the actor's needs, Castle stood up and stretched. He went to the windows and sighed imperceptibly. The blinds were down: daylight framed the corners.

Castle turned back. He said baldly:

"That's a nice suit, Mr. Trent. Do you always keep a folded handkerchief in the breast pocket?"

Trent dribbled smoke from the corner of his mouth. He answered shortly. "Yes."

"A comb, too?"

"Sometimes." Michael's face gleamed waxily in the harsh, artificial light. His eyelids stirred warily. "Why do you ask?"

Castle was gentle. "Smudged fingerprints were found on the comb by Bailey's body. The prints are yours. And the comb could have fallen out of somebody's breast pocket as he crouched over his victim."

There was a brief silence.

Then Trent choked out:

"The comb is mine—I haven't denied it. But I didn't take it with me when I left the theatre yesterday evening."

He looked at the blank, unresponsive policemen's faces and said bitterly: "That's the truth. But what does it matter to you? You've found a scapegoat. That's all you care about."

Castle said:

"If you're an innocent man you have nothing to fear. Tell us about the comb."

"I've told you before... Oh, very well." Trent dragged soothing smoke into his lungs, then expelled it jerkily. "I left the monogrammed comb in my dressing-room. I don't remember where." He pressed his aching head. "I don't recall the last moment I saw it. I had—other worries.  You hadn't been giving me an easy time."

Castle thumbed his chin. "If you didn't remove the comb from your dressing-room, then somebody else did. Who knew you had such a comb?"

"Everybody back-stage."

Castle yawned hugely. "Perhaps, perhaps." His voice changed abruptly. "Where were you at one o'clock this morning?"

"I—I can't tell you."

Castle smiled without humour. "You weren't at home. I sent a man round to your flat. He had to wait until two o'clock before you arrived."

Trent tore the cigarette out of his mouth and flung it across the room. "I can't tell you where I was because I just don't know! Don't you understand? By the time you let us leave the theatre last night I was so sick and confused I didn't know what I was doing. I didn't want the company of my friends and I found I couldn't stand solitude either. I left my flat and went drinking. There are places, if you know them. By one o'clock I had tired of that, too. I found myself wandering aimlessly through the streets. By two o'clock I felt exhausted. I thought I could sleep at last. I went home."

He finished dully:

"I found a detective waiting for me. He was very polite. He brought me here. And that's all I know."

Castle waited until the last echoes of the speech had died away, then paced across the room and slowly ground the still-glowing cigarette between his heel and the floor.

He said:

"We're all rather tired. We need a break."

He went to the windows and raised the blinds. Daylight streamed into the room. A shaft of watery sunlight struck Trent's eyes and made him blink. He huddled in his chair.

Castle nodded to Wemyss and the shorthand writer, then clicked off the electric lights and went out of the room. He rubbed his eyes wearily, then shook himself like a huge dog and stumped across the passage and went into his own office.

Algy Lawrence was waiting. He had been standing by the window, looking down on the Embankment with an enigmatic gleam in his lazy blue eyes.

He turned with a grin. "Hi, Steve."

Castle growled a reply. Lowering himself into the swivel chair behind his desk, he asked abruptly:

"How much do you know about last night?"

"Not a lot. I came to the Yard to discuss the case. I arrived to find you were holding Trent for questioning."

Castle nodded. He thumbed tobacco into his large and virulent pipe. Lighting up, he began to describe the events of that strangely peaceless Sunday morning. As he talked, a blue haze eddied about his greying head.

When his friend had finished, Lawrence said quietly:

"I think you're making a mistake, Steve. There seems to be a lot of evidence against Michael Trent. But it's only circumstantial."

Castle laughed grimly. "Most murderers are hanged by circumstantial evidence."

Lawrence said dryly:

"That's a good argument against capital punishment."

Castle gestured impatiently. Lawrence continued:

"Circumstantial evidence is like a signpost pointing in opposite directions. Or to put it another way"—he hesitated briefly—"like Janus, it has two faces."

Castle shrugged. "Be specific"

Lawrence accepted the challenge. "You believe that the comb fell out of Trent's breast pocket. You say that its position against the folded handkerchief in the same pocket was responsible for smudging his fingerprints."

"That's right. I do."

Lawrence grinned crookedly. "But suppose I say that the prints were blurred because another person had wrapped that comb in a handkerchief to preserve them—however imperfectly?"

Castle shifted uncomfortably. "You mean the comb was a plant—it was deliberately dropped by Bailey's side to incriminate Michael Trent?"

Lawrence smiled. "It's as good an explanation as yours."

"But dammit, Algy!" Castle was irritable but uneasy. "I'm sure Trent's guilty. Look! Bailey was assaulted soon after one o'clock. The night watchman gave the alarm almost at once. I found the comb by Bailey's body. I sent a man round to Trent's flat. Trent wasn't at home

331

and he didn't turn up until two. He told us this preposterous yarn about wandering through the streets—."

Lawrence chuckled. "I like that story. It's thin enough and unlikely enough to be literally true."

Castle made impatient noises.

Lawrence said sleepily:

"Let's tackle the problem from another angle. Admit that there's no direct proof as to the identity of the person who attacked Bailey... Now how did this unknown man get into the theatre?"

"We don't know," admitted the Chief Inspector. "There were no signs of a forced entry."

"Then let's suppose the intruder was carrying a duplicate or skeleton key. He was also carrying a bludgeon. And he left the theatre with some kind of stolen document. Did you find any of those three articles in Trent's possession?"

"No," confessed Castle. "But that doesn't mean much. He could have cached them—or chucked 'em into the river."

"I suppose so."

Castle scowled at his fists. "Trent covers his tracks well... I 'm sure he was mixed up in that bank robbery seven years ago. But I can't prove it."

"It hardly matters now."

"Perhaps not. But why should he escape, while that poor devil Mervan—." Castle broke off and shook his head gloomily. "Mervan doesn't know, even now, that Trent was the man who double-crossed him."

"Then don't tell him," advised Lawrence. "We don't want another murder on our hands."

"There's no fear of that." Castle was forbidding. "Mervan has lost his liberty now. He will have to answer two charges: shooting with intent to cause grievous bodily harm; and unlawful possession of a firearm.   That will be enough to send him back to jail for a long time."

"Poor devil."

Castle said, almost defiantly:

"I can't afford to worry about him."

Lawrence's eyes were vacant. He said:

"Mervan may be able to help us."

"How?"

"There are two questions I'd like you to ask him. Wait—I'll write them down." Lawrence grabbed pen and paper from Castle's desk and scrawled quickly. "There, Steve."

Castle squinted at the questions. "I don't see why—."

Lawrence grinned.   He drawled:

"A doll is innocent in itself. But if you follow the strings attached to its limbs you find the puppet-master."

Before Castle could demand an explanation, a knock sounded on the office door.

"Come in!"

Chief Inspector stood up as Victor Friern entered.

The manager seemed to have aged considerably since Lesley Christopher's death. His erect carriage was gone and his face was lined with grief. But his voice was still calm and his manner authoritative.

He said sombrely:

"I have just been informed of the night's events. And I understand"—he seemed suddenly angry—"I understand you are holding a member of my company a prisoner in this building."

The Chief Inspector sighed noisily. Then he said firmly:

"Michael Trent is not a prisoner."

"You haven't arrested him?"

"No. But"—Castle paused momentarily—"I would be less than fair if I didn't admit that he is under the gravest possible suspicion."

The flare of anger had burnt itself out. Friern passed a hand over his twitching mouth. "I can't believe—."

Castle interrupted. "Perhaps I'd better explain."

He summed up the situation with meticulous fairness. He concluded:

"You see? Mr. Trent has much to explain."

Victor Friern nodded reluctantly.

Then he said rebelliously:

"I'm not given to melodrama. But I tell you this in all sincerity. I would stake my life on Trent's innocence."

Big Ben was chiming eleven as Algy Lawrence left New Scotland Yard.

He scanned the Embankment with thoughtful blue eyes. Then he looked both surprised and pleased, and walked briskly towards one of the public seats.

"Penny! Uh—Miss Valentine."

She was simply and unobtrusively dressed, and there was very little make-up on her lovely face. She was wearing a beret and a belted raincoat and her fingers were pressed hard on a plain grey handbag. Her cerulean eyes seemed almost blind.

She looked up with a tiny smile as the tall young man approached. But the smile died quickly as she returned his greeting.

Lawrence spoke with deliberate flippancy. "For an actress, you're almost in disguise."

The smile came back. "I don't feel very flamboyant this morning."

Then her mouth was sad again.

Lawrence seated himself beside her. He said softly:

"You mustn't worry."

She answered without reproach. "That's easy to say. But—."

She broke off, then asked painfully:

"They've arrested him, haven't they?"

Lawrence said:

"No. They just believe Michael can help them with their enquiries."

Penny parodied a smile. "I've seen that phrase often enough in the newspapers to know what it means."

Lawrence produced his silver cigarette case and offered it to the girl. She accepted a cigarette and put it between her lips. Algy touched flame to the tip from the lighter in the case's spine.

He said quietly:

"I can reassure you. As matters stand now, Michael cannot possibly be arrested for murder."

Penny seemed not to have heard. She said dully:

"Something happened at the theatre last night."

"Yes. But how did you know?"

"I was—told." Penny's voice dropped.

Lawrence regarded her thoughtfully, studying the soft curve of her cheek. She was very lovely.

He said gently:

"I think you need a friend to confide in."

She nodded. Lawrence waited patiently.

Penny turned her face away. She spoke in a muffled voice:

"There's something—."

"Yes?"

"Something I have to do." She choked. "God knows I don't want to! I've been sitting here watching—waiting—trying to make up my mind—."

She turned back to face him. He saw with distress she was crying.

"Penny, my dear—."

She cried desperately:

"Don't stop me now. Here, take it quickly."

She snapped open her handbag and snatched out a crumpled paper. She thrust it into Lawrence's hand with trembling fingers, then watched dumbly as he unfolded the paper and examined it. It was dated some five years before. It was the certificate of a marriage between Michael Trent and Lesley Barre.

# CHAPTER EIGHTEEN

Lawrence said gently:

"You mustn't over-rate the importance of this thing. The Chief Inspector will be interested in the marriage certificate. But he won't swear out a warrant for Michael's arrest on the strength of it."

Penny smiled wanly.

"Now"—Lawrence gave her an encouraging grin—"explain from the beginning."

The girl nodded. She cradled her hands round a cup of steaming coffee.

The two young people were sitting in a Westminster tea-shop. Lawrence had insisted on removing Penny from the public seat on the Embankment, and they had found a secluded corner in the restaurant where they could talk in private.

Penny said:

"This won't be easy. But I'd rather tell you than a policeman. I—."

She faltered.

Lawrence smiled at her. "Take your time."

Penny started again. "Michael—Michael didn't tell me that Lesley was his wife. I knew that she had some kind of hold over him, but at first it didn't seem to matter. She made demands on him but—but he was tactful. He knew how to handle her. And I think she had her reasons for not claiming him publicly as her own."

Lawrence nodded slowly.

Penny flushed very slightly. "Michael and I—we became lovers several months ago. We used to meet secretly. He explained that Lesley must know nothing. He didn't say why and I was too much in love to ask him to explain."

"Was?"

"And am." Penny's flush deepened. "Michael is the only man in the world for me. If I should lose him—."

Lawrence said:

"You're not going to lose him."

She thanked him with a warm smile. She continued:

"We tried to keep our secret. But it wasn't easy. We were living in a small, well-integrated group with our lives revolving around the play. That's one of the penalties of a long run: you get to know your fellow players too well.

"Douglas Denzil soon discovered our secret. I think Trudy Ann knew, too. She doesn't miss much, bless her designing little heart." Penny was indulgent; there was no sting in her words.

"Fortunately, Lesley herself was the last to know. It wasn't until yesterday afternoon in Michael's dressing-room—."

Penny faltered again.

Then she said more firmly:

"She had been suspicious, of course. She had never liked me. It was professional jealousy, I suppose. But it was becoming something worse towards the end...

"Michael suffered, too. She became increasingly possessive. She began to make"—Penny hesitated—"physical demands upon him again. Michael hated it, poor darling."

Lawrence waited in sympathetic silence.

The girl continued:

"Things were getting steadily worse. We had to give up our meetings. Lesley was making Michael's life a hell. And he was drinking too much, poor sweet." A spark of anger showed in her beautiful eyes. "She was destroying his life. And I had to watch."

Lawrence asked:

"And you—what was she doing to you?"

Penny shrugged gently. "She had her knife into me. She was out to kill my performance at every show. Not that that mattered, so long as I could be sure of Michael's love for me."

Her lips trembled. "But I was afraid of losing him. I thought Lesley was succeeding in driving us apart. Then at last I couldn't stand it any more. I went to Michael and told him—."

"Yes?"

"That he must break with Lesley. Or with me."

Lawrence asked:

"Was that wise?"

Penny blinked back a tear. "Don't you see? An ultimatum—that was my only chance. I had to make him act before it was too late. Before Lesley—."

She choked. She said dully:

"She was killing him. And killing his love for me."

She drank some coffee. It seemed to refresh her. She continued:

"When I told him that, it shocked him. And then I knew he still loved me. He—he said he'd rather die than live without me. He swore that he would break with Lesley. With her consent or without it."

Lawrence said nothing. But his face was grave.

Penny said:

"I know what you're thinking. But it isn't true. He didn't resort to murder."

"I hope not." Lawrence added mentally: for your sake.

Penny said desperately:

"Michael isn't a murderer. You must believe that."

Lawrence replied:

"I'll try to. I can't say more than that. Go on with your story."

Penny looked away. "I didn't know that Michael was Lesley's husband. He didn't tell me, even then. But he vowed he would break the hold she had over him. He meant to tell her he loved—only me."

She smiled faintly. "I believed him. But he must have lost his courage again. He began to drink more heavily than ever. It affected his work.

"He had been late for every performance last week. He was tipsy again yesterday afternoon. And he still hadn't managed to tell Lesley the truth.

"Then chance took the matter out of his hands. Lesley must have suspected us, but she had never actually known. Until—."

She hesitated, then said flatly:

"Until yesterday afternoon. She came into Michael's dressing-room during the second act wait. She found me in his arms."

Lawrence murmured:

"And said: 'You'll be sorry for this. I promise you.'"

"How did you know that?"

"It doesn't matter, Penny. Go on."

The girl answered in a low voice:

"Lesley's face was evil. And—and scared, too, in some strange way. As if her last hope had failed her, making her despairing and vengeful at the same time."

Her hands clenched. "She frightened me."

Then Lawrence said cheerfully:

"All right, then. You've cleared up several obscurities. But this is only half the story. Now you must tell me about the marriage certificate."

Penny nodded. Her face changed.

She said uncertainly:

"It's an odd story. Something happened this morning which made me feel wretched. Yet now it seems rather silly... I hardly know whether to laugh or cry."

Her mouth quirked.

She remarked with apparent inconsequence:

"I'm afraid Douglas is a rather incompetent blackmailer."

"Denzil?"

"Yes. He gave me the certificate."

"Did he, now?" Lawrence's eyes were sleepy.

Penny nodded again. She said:

"I couldn't tell this story to anybody else but you. Certainly not to a policeman."

"Don't you trust the police?"

"I suppose so. But I don't like them."

Lawrence grinned. "Nobody does. Not since they became the custodians of morals and motoring... Tell me about Denzil."

Penny pushed aside her cup and saucer. She drew a deep breath and obeyed.

"He came to see me this morning...."

Penny Valentine regarded her visitor with unfriendly eyes. "You do have a thick skin, don't you? I thought I'd made my feelings plain."

Denzil smiled unpleasantly. "You did, my sweet. But I don't take offence until it suits me to do so. And as for the slap"—he rubbed his cheek lightly—"I've already forgiven you."

Penny thanked him dryly.

She was wearing a black night-gown, a filmy black ☐atinee☐, and fluffy black slippers. Denzil stared at her with cool insolence. She stirred restively under his gaze. "I can't imagine why you came here."

"Let me in and I'll tell you."

Penny shrugged and stood aside. Douglas strolled into the living room while the girl closed the front door of her flat.

She followed him. "Now, Douglas—."

He mimicked her. "Now, Penny." He moved towards her. He said:

"You know you're very beautiful. And you smell deliciously of flowers."

It was almost a deliberate caricature of his manner on stage. Amusement shimmered briefly in Penny's lovely eyes. Then she yawned slightly and turned away.

"Ah—pardon me, Douglas. But it is rather early. And I usually sleep till noon."

Denzil said:

"I have something to show you. I think it's of interest."

He spoke maliciously.

It was his usual tone; but an alien cadence caught Penny's ear. She felt suddenly afraid.

She sat down on the sofa. "Well?"

338

Denzil seated himself beside her. Unhurriedly he withdrew a folded paper from an inside pocket and put it into her hands.

Penny examined it with puzzled eyes. "It's——."

"A marriage certificate," said Denzil pleasantly.

Penny read the names. She said nothing. A clock ticked loudly in the room.

Denzil relaxed against the cushions. "Penny, my sweet. Haven't you anything to say?"

Penny folded the paper carefully.

She said:

"No. Except that this isn't your property. And I didn't think you were a thief."

Denzil's eyes glinted briefly. He answered smoothly:

"I'm not. As a matter of fact, my conduct has been beyond reproach." The mockery in his voice became more pronounced. "As a public-spirited citizen, I have an obvious duty. To hand this paper to the police."

Penny caught her breath.

Denzil had been watching her closely. He smiled a cat-like smile. He said softly:

"That wouldn't help Michael. You know what policemen are. They might think he had a motive for—ah—removing his wife."

Penny said clearly:

"I don't think you need worry about Michael. It might be better to consider your own position. The police may ask you some inconvenient questions."

"I can answer them all," returned Douglas lightly. "If necessary." He stressed the word "if." He continued: "You see, sweet, I didn't steal that certificate. I found it."

The girl asked:

"Where?"

The word was only a breath.

Denzil replied:

"In my letter box."

Penny shook her head. "I don't understand."

"Neither do I, sweet. But there it is. And was." Denzil's eyes slitted. "You know I have a flat in a mews not far from the theatre. When I got up this morning, I found this certificate in the letter cage inside my door. Some unknown hand had delivered it during the night."

His young-old face seemed puzzled. "There was no note, no explanation of any sort. I was curious, of course. I decided to telephone Michael."

He grinned slightly. "There was no reply. He wasn't at home."

"But—."

"Patience, sweet. Next, I rang the theatre. I found myself talking to a policeman. A charming fellow, you understand, but uncommunicative. The police are so discreet... I told him Michael was missing—."

Penny said:

"You're so thoughtful of others."

Denzil grinned. "True, my sweet. But to continue: my policeman hemmed and hawed for a while but eventually unbent. He told me there had been trouble of some sort at the Janus in the night and he believed that Mr. Trent was assisting the police in their enquiries—I believe that's the phrase?"

Penny's hands clenched. "Michael—."

"Oh, don't worry, darling. The beloved is in perfect health."

The girl relaxed.

Denzil went on:

"I 'phoned the Yard. Yes, Mr. Trent was there. No, I couldn't speak to him. He was still—h'm—assisting the police."

Penny stood up. "I must go to him."

"Not so fast, my sweet." Denzil's voice flattened oddly. "We have things to discuss."

"What things?"

Denzil said softly:

"I don't believe the police have arrested Michael. But they obviously suspect him. What do you suppose they'll think when they discover that he and Lesley were secretly married?"

Penny said dully:

"I don't know."

"Then I'll tell you. The police know about you and Michael. And they know that Lesley was a jealous, possessive woman. They'll say that Michael had to kill her to get rid of her."

"No!"

"Yes." Denzil was persuasive. "You have to face it, sweet. This certificate makes all the difference. The police already know that Michael had the means and opportunity. Now they can prove he had a motive for the crime as well."

Penny tried to speak, but no words came.

Douglas gave her a side-long glance. The corners of his mouth lifted.

He said gently:

"Of course, the police don't have to know about the marriage. Do they?"

"Aren't—aren't you going to tell them?"

"Well. That depends."

"On what?"

"On you, my sweet." Denzil stretched like a cat. He said, very quietly:

"You might be able to persuade me to forget about that certificate."

Penny's breasts rose and fell beneath the gentle, caressing confinement of black chiffon. She asked:

"Persuade you—how?"

Denzil told her.

The girl paused, remembering. Then she laughed rather shakily. She told Lawrence:

"Douglas made a certain suggestion. It wasn't exactly a surprise, though something of a shock. Douglas can be rather crude at times. You probably heard what he said to me in Lesley's dressing-room yesterday. And he looked at me as insolently as if I were a prize sow in a market."

Lawrence rubbed his cheek. "I gather you didn't accept his offer."

"Proposition," said Penny, "might be the better word." There was a fleeting gleam of amusement in her eyes. Then she said more soberly: "No, I didn't accept. I love Michael too much to cheat him."

Lawrence nodded. "You couldn't have kept the secret, anyway. Even if Denzil had been willing to keep silent about the marriage, another might have spoken."

"Another?"

"The man who sent the certificate." Lawrence frowned thoughtfully. "Why the devil did he give it to Denzil?"

Penny suggested. "To do Michael a bad turn."

"Perhaps. But—." Lawrence hesitated briefly. "Finish your story, Penny. How did Denzil act – "

"When I refused him?" The girl smiled. "He didn't appear unduly perturbed. I suspect he was rather relieved... He didn't try to reclaim the certificate. He said he would leave it with me while I made up my mind what to do."

"So you brought it to me."

Penny said:

"Meeting you was a lucky chance. I couldn't make any real decision. I came here because I had to be near Michael. Yet I dared not go into the Yard. I could only wait on the Embankment, wondering what to do." Her mouth trembled. "I was so afraid—for Michael."

Lawrence remarked with a question in his tone:

"But you gave the certificate to me."

Penny put out her hand impulsively. "I had to give it to somebody. And I felt I could trust you as a friend."

Lawrence felt a warm flush of pleasure. He squeezed her fingers gently. "Thank you."

He released her hand and said briskly:

"I shall have to surrender the certificate to the Chief Inspector. You knew that, of course."

Penny agreed reluctantly. "He'll have to know about the marriage."

Lawrence explained:

"It's the certificate itself which is so important. I believe it was stolen from Lesley's dressing-room last night."

He told Penny about the attack upon Bailey at the Janus. When he had finished, the girl cried excitedly:

"But surely—this proves Michael's innocence! He might have taken the certificate to destroy it. But he wouldn't have put it into another man's hands."

"Least of all, Denzil's," agreed Lawrence. "That's true. But Castle may not agree." He paused, then said quietly:

"I think I see a way for Michael to prove his innocence. But it won't be easy. And he'll have to trust me completely."

Penny said softly:

"I can persuade him to do that."

Lawrence smiled, but spoke sombrely. "Penny—."

"Yes?"

"I must warn you. In my modest way, I stand for the truth... I don't think Michael is a murderer. But I've been wrong about such things before and I may be wrong again. And if I am—."

He halted.

Penny finished the sentence. "You won't protect Michael. Even for me."

She smiled. "I knew, you see? You didn't have to tell me."

# CHAPTER NINETEEN

Chief Inspector Castle spoke with grimly controlled relish. "This is it, Algy. The genuine article."

He thumped a stubby finger on the marriage certificate. "See that? One corner has been torn off. Do you know where that scrap of paper is now? It's already in our possession. We found it caught in the splintered frame of the portrait of Trent in the dead woman's dressing-room."

Lawrence rubbed his cheek. "So Lesley kept her marriage lines hidden behind the photograph of her husband. Somebody wanted that certificate urgently enough to break into the Janus and assault a policeman. Why?"

"Ask Michael Trent."

Lawrence studied his friend's expressive face. "Do you really believe he did it?"

Castle said. "Yes," a little too firmly.

Lawrence chuckled. "Then explain why he shoved the certificate into Denzil's letter box."

Castle looked unhappy. "How should I know what was in the fellow's mind? Perhaps he was playing an intricate game of double bluff."

"You don't really believe that, Steve."

"Maybe not. But I'm not going to abandon my theory until you provide me with a better one."

"All right, Steve. That's a bargain." Lawrence smiled seraphically. "But I shall expect you to co-operate. You'll have to release Michael Trent. You can't keep him here indefinitely. And you can't arrest him—you don't have enough evidence."

Castle relieved his feelings with a heart-felt curse. Then he asked unwillingly:

"What do you suggest?"

Lawrence explained....

Castle fingered his jaw. He mumbled:

"I can't say I like it. But if you can produce the right results—."

He stopped short. Penny Valentine had returned.

The girl said dully:

"I've made a statement and signed it. Now may I go?"

"Of course." The Chief Inspector was polite.

"And Michael—may he leave, too?"

Castle hesitated. His eyes met Lawrence's. Then he shrugged and said:

"Wait just a moment. If you please."

He left his office and opened the door across the corridor. The police officers pushed back their chairs. Trent didn't move. He sat slumped in his seat, looking pale and ill. A half empty teacup stood on the table at his elbow. The charred stump of a cigarette had been mashed soggily into the saucer.

Castle rested his fists on the table.

He said pleasantly:

"Well, sir. Have you completed your statement?"

Trent's lips moved stiffly. "Ask your friends."

Wemyss coughed discreetly. "Here it is."

Castle took the paper-clipped pages from the Detective Inspector's hand and leafed through them quickly. "Hmmm... Isn't there anything you would care to add about your relationship with Miss Christopher?"

Trent's words were pebbles dropped into a muddy pool of silence.

"I've told you everything."

Castle's eyebrows came together in a frown. Then he shrugged. "I don't think we need detain you any longer. Thank you for helping us."

He turned away.

Trent said:

"You mean—I can go?"

Castle spoke over his shoulder. "Of course. You're not under arrest." He went out of the room.

Trent followed slowly. When he saw Penny in the corridor, a faint flush crept over his cheek-bones.

He forced a smile. "Hallo, darling."

"Michael!"

The girl put her hand on his forearm. He patted it gently. "It's all right, Penny. I'm leaving with you."

"And with Mr. Lawrence." The Chief Inspector spoke from the doorway of his office. "He wants a talk with you."

Trent's mouth hardened. "Haven't you finished with me yet?"

Lawrence said amiably:

"I have nothing to do with the police. I might even be able to help you."

Penny said softly:

"That's true, Michael. I think he's our friend."

Trent smiled at her eager, up-turned face. "If you say so, darling."

He nodded to Lawrence. "Shall we go?"

"Just a moment." Stephen Castle spoke with deceptive mildness. "Before you leave—."

"Well?"

"You might like to look at this."

He held out the marriage certificate. Michael Trent took a swift step forward, then stood rigid. As he read the names, his hands clenched hard.

His gaze shifted to the Chief Inspector's face. He seemed to be asking a wordless question.

Castle answered:

"That's all for now. Goodbye, Mr. Trent. We may call you later."

Michael Trent said thoughtfully:

"So that's how Castle got hold of the certificate."

"Yes." Penny's eyes were anxious. "You do understand, my darling, that I—that I—."

"Couldn't keep the secret? Of course." Michael squeezed her hand. "But as for Denzil—." His face set grimly. "By God, I'll make him suffer."

Algy Lawrence grinned lazily:

"You can kick Denzil's spine through the top of his head, but"—his eyelids drooped sleepily—"it won't solve any of your problems."

Michael and Penny drew closer together.

They were in the actor's flat. Lawrence was reclining in an easy chair, apparently on the point of falling asleep. He continued drowsily:

"Castle will arrest you if he can. He is still convinced that you murdered your wife."

Trent murmured a shocked protest.

Lawrence shrugged. "You can't blame him. You might have known the police would find out about your marriage. You should have confessed it at once."

"It wouldn't have helped them."

Lawrence said gently:

"That wasn't for you to decide."

Penny had been watching the fair-haired young man closely. She asked quietly:

"Why do the police think Michael is a murderer?"

Lawrence answered:

"There's one damning factor." He spoke directly to Michael Trent. "You've asked us to believe that the real murderer put live bullets into the gun to make you his catspaw. But this man couldn't have been sure

Lesley would die. You might not have dealt her a mortal wound. There was only one man who could have been certain that the bullet would go crashing through her heart. And that was the man who aimed the gun and pulled the trigger."

There was a brief, appalled silence.

Then Trent said in a tortured voice:

"It's a nightmare. I can argue. But I can't escape."

Penny cried a pain-filled protest.

Lawrence avoided her eyes. "You might as well know the worst. There's a case against Michael—I'll state it point by point."

Trent nodded mutely. Lawrence said:

"I'll begin at the beginning. You weren't exactly sober when you arrived at the theatre yesterday afternoon. Right?"

Michael stared. "I'd been drinking, certainly. Isn't that a point in my favour? I would have needed a clear head to carry out a premeditated murder."

"You might have needed Dutch courage, too."

Penny cried:

"That's monstrously unfair!"

Lawrence grinned wryly. "I'm not trying to be fair. I'm putting the case for the prosecution… Next! You told the stage manager: '

"'This afternoon, I promise you, the audience will see a convincing murder.' As indeed it did."

Trent put his hand to his throat. "Good God, man!   Do you think I'd have been mad enough to use those words if I had really been planning to kill her?"

"No, I don't. You'd have been a fool to invite needless suspicion. But a jury would take your words at their face value."

"But what I said—." Michael paused helplessly. "It was quite innocent. We always talked of murder when we discussed that scene. We simply meant the business on stage." He licked his lips. "You can make any statement sound like a guilty admission when you quote it out of context."

Lawrence shrugged. "You made another unfortunate remark."

Trent had a hunted air. "When?"

Lawrence didn't reply directly. He mused:

"Somebody sent the Chief Inspector two tickets for the show. Castle's presence in the audience was therefore to be expected; but no one could have known he would invite me to accompany him. So my arrival back-stage must have surprised the man who sent the tickets."

"Well?" muttered Trent.

"When I told you my name," said Lawrence gently, "your first words were: 'You were in the audience too?'"

Michael bit his lip hard. "I meant nothing important. I knew your name and your reputation. You had already told me about the Chief Inspector. Then you disclosed your own identity. The remark I made— it was natural enough."

Lawrence nodded. "I can accept that explanation. But there's still—."

"The damning factor." Trent's hands moved in an involuntary gesture of protest.

"Yes." Lawrence rubbed his cheek. "You levelled the gun at Lesley's heart. That's something—it can be argued—an innocent man would not have done. You thought the revolver was loaded with blanks. But even a blank cartridge isn't the harmless article it seems. It contains a heavy charge of powder which can burn and tear anyone in the line of fire. It also contains wadding in lieu of a bullet—and even that can be painful if it scores a hit. You must have known the golden rule: never point the gun at the human body. Even if you hadn't learned the lesson by previous experience, your producer must have warned you of the danger."

Strangely, Penny laughed.

Trent smiled too. He spoke with a return to his old, light-hearted manner:

"You've been giving the matter some thought. But there's one point you've overlooked. Our producer is a whale on realism. That's why we use a real gun with an unplugged barrel. And that's why he made me level the gun at Lesley's heart."

He paused, then continued:

"At the first rehearsals, I behaved like every professional. I pointed the gun away from Lesley's body. But the producer and the author didn't approve. They wanted the scene to be as realistic as possible. So I was told to sight the gun carefully."

"Didn't you object?"

"Of course. I said Lesley might get hurt. But we experimented and proved she was perfectly safe. You remember that I stood some way from Lesley when—when—."

"You fired the revolver. Yes. Go on."

Michael pulled himself together. "The powder grains from the blank never reached her. And the wadding always fell short of her body. At that distance, I could fire the blank safely, even though the gun was levelled at her heart."

"As it was yesterday. But it wasn't always so exactly aimed. Was it?"

"Wh—what do you mean?"

"I mean," said Lawrence softly, "you were notoriously careless with that gun. You rarely bothered to sight it precisely. On Friday evening you aimed it so wildly that"—Lawrence seemed to be quoting—"if there had been a live cartridge in the chamber the bullet would have gone into the O.P. box. In other words, anywhere but Lesley's body. But on Saturday afternoon, on the only occasion when there was a real bullet under the hammer, you aimed so carefully that the shot went through her heart."

There was a terrible silence.

Then Trent said thickly:

"Oh, my God."

He collected himself with an effort. "Look here, man. I admit I'd grown careless with the gun. That was partly due to my drinking and partly due to an instinctive return to the golden rule you mentioned. And it's true I sighted the revolver with particular care yesterday afternoon. But that doesn't make me a murderer! I was only obeying a stage manager's order."

Lawrence said coolly:

"I know that Austin told you to aim the gun before you fired it. He repeated the conversation in your dressing-room to us."

"Then that puts me in the clear."

"Not necessarily. You might have been deliberately careless with the gun at previous performances knowing that the S.M. must eventually tell you to follow the producer's orders. Then you could have slipped live ammunition into the revolver. You had been told to aim carefully—who could blame you if Lesley died?"

"God Almighty!" Trent looked at Lawrence with horror in his eyes.

Penny's voice shook. "You can't believe Michael capable of such – such—."

"Devilish subtlety?" Lawrence grinned crookedly.

He said:

"Let's be frank. I haven't made up my mind about Michael one way or the other. But if he is innocent—."

"Yes?"

"There's only one way to prove it."

"Well?" Trent's hand clenched. "Out with it, man, before you drive me crazy."

"Michael." Penny spoke in gentle warning.

She regarded Lawrence gravely. "Go on. Please."

Lawrence addressed Trent. "The only thing that can save you now is complete and utter frankness. You've tried to conceal the truth about your relationship with Lesley Barre and you've failed miserably. Now, let's wipe the slate clean and start again. I want to know everything about her."

"But I've already told you—."

"You've told us nothing. But don't think we don't know about you and Lesley and Richard Mervan."

Trent caught his breath. "I don't understand."

Lawrence smiled. "I think you do."

Michael looked at the girl, then turned back to Lawrence in mute appeal. Algy understood. He said amiably:

"Penny, my dear. You said you trusted me."

She nodded.   "I do."

"Then do what I say. Leave us now. And don't ask questions."

The girl's eyes widened. She stood up without a word.

Trent put out a restraining hand. "Penny! Don't go."

She bent over and kissed him lightly. "I must."

"But—."

"Call me when you've finished. I'll be waiting by the 'phone."

She left.

Lawrence remarked:

"She's a wonderful girl."

Trent was angry. "Why did you send her away?"

"To save your face. She knows nothing of your criminal past."

"Criminal!"

"You robbed a bank," said Lawrence blandly. "That's a crime, I believe."

Trent tried to laugh. "You're raving."

Lawrence continued inexorably: "You took the loot and escaped with Lesley. Mervan was left to pay the price."

Trent's breathing had quickened.

Lawrence eyed him quizzically. "I hope you're not going to bluster. It would only waste time."

Trent regained his composure. He answered lightly:

"I'm not going to deny anything. I don't have to. You can't prove your accusations."

Algy agreed equably. "I can't. What's more, I don't want to. That's why we're going to work together."

Trent was wary. "You'd better explain."

Lawrence settled himself more comfortably in his chair. "I'm not trying to convict you of a seven year old robbery. I want to solve yesterday's murder."

"Then why—?"

349

"Am I pulling skeletons out of the closet? Well, now. Perhaps it's because the essential clue to the mystery may lie somewhere in Lesley's past. Or perhaps it's because"—Algy grinned widely—"I'm humanly inquisitive. I don't like unexplained mysteries. Don't forget: Mervan could tell me only half the story of the robbery. I want to hear the rest from you."

"You want to trap me." Trent was bitter. "You'd like me to convict myself."

"Don't be an ass," said Lawrence roundly. "I've sent Penny away. There are no witnesses. We're alone."

"You mean—."

"I mean," said Lawrence deliberately, "you can admit any crime without fear of punishment. You couldn't possibly be put on trial. It would only be my word against yours. You could even sue me for slander."

Trent eyed him suspiciously. He said cautiously:

"That sounds reasonable. But—."

"There aren't any buts," said Algy Lawrence. "I give you my word I mean no trickery. Of course, you don't have to believe me. You can search the flat for hidden microphones. But you'll find nothing."

Trent studied the young man's lazy face.

He said abruptly:

"I believe you."

"Thanks." Lawrence rubbed his cheek. "Are you going to tell me the whole story?"

Trent hesitated. He asked bluntly:

"Where's the catch?"

Lawrence answered frankly. "I shall report our talk to the Chief Inspector. That is, I shall repeat as much of it as I consider is necessary for him to hear."

Trent's voice was hard and angry. "Do you expect me to agree to that?"

"Oh, yes." Lawrence was mild. "I think so. We know most of the story already. Telling us the details won't make it easier to prove. Besides, Castle doesn't want to arrest you for robbery. He wants you for murder."

Trent swallowed. He lit a cigarette with a shaking hand. "You're very frank."

"I'll be franker still. Castle knows my plan. That's why he released you."

"What?"

Lawrence laughed. "Don't misunderstand me.   Castle is convinced you're a murderer; I'm not. Castle knows that. But he also knows I shall play fair with him. I won't conceal a material fact."

"So?" The word trembled out in a cloud of smoke.

"Castle thinks you'll be eager to argue away his suspicions. So he thinks you will talk—too much."

"I see." Trent took the cigarette out of his mouth. "He thinks I shall out-smart myself."

"Yes. And you probably will—if you're guilty of murder. You won't find it easy to walk along the dividing line between truth and falsehood."

"It comes to this." The actor's voice was brittle. "I'm caught in a web of circumstantial evidence. The only thing that can save me is complete frankness. But if I'm guilty—."

"You will almost certainly give yourself away." Lawrence grinned crookedly. "So you'd be a fool to talk at all. Wouldn't you?"

Trent met the challenge in the other man's eyes.

He flung away the cigarette.

He said tightly:

"I'll tell you everything you want to know."

.

# CHAPTER TWENTY

"I'm not going to make excuses." Trent's voice was low. He sat with linked hands, staring into his palms. "But you must understand the situation... Mine is one of the toughest professions in the world. It's also the most over-crowded. There are about ten thousand actors and actresses in this country at the present time. Less than half of us can expect to earn our living on the stage; and we spend about five months in the year out of work."

Lawrence nodded without speaking.

Trent drew a deep breath. "Well! That's the situation now. It was worse seven years ago.

"I hadn't been long out of the Navy. I thought I was going to take the Theatre by storm. But I couldn't land a shop anywhere."

"Land a—?"

"Theatrical engagement. I couldn't even get a walk-on... Lesley was having the same trouble. We weren't amateurs. We'd both had previous experience. But no management wanted us.

"Well! We had to eat. So Lesley took a temporary job in this bank. They were short of staff; and Lesley was a qualified typist. She had been trained for a business career by her guardian: he hadn't approved of her theatrical ambitions. But the stage was Lesley's life: she had to act or die... She meant to return to the theatre as soon as she could, but in the meantime—."

He gestured.

"She didn't talk about her real profession, of course; and nobody at the bank knew of her relationship with me."

Lawrence asked:

"Was it something to be ashamed of?"

Trent grinned suddenly. "Respectable bankers would have considered it unconventional. We weren't married then: that came later... Besides, Lesley was naturally secretive."

"So?"

"We met when we could. We made love when we met... That's all."

Lawrence said:

"You made love. Were you in love?"

Trent frowned. He confessed. "I—don't know."

He groped for words. "Ours was a queer relationship. It's hard to describe... Take Lesley, now. She was a cold fish, for all her seeming warmth and charm. Men found her attractive, but they meant nothing to her. She used them; she never liked them. And yet—."

"Yes?"

"If she loved anybody at all she loved me. She could be passionate enough. And I was hers—with a great big 'L' branded on my back."

Trent laughed rather savagely. Lawrence said dryly:

"We've been told she was a possessive woman."

"She was," returned Trent in a sombre tone. "I fooled around with other girls. But when Lesley whistled—I came running."

Lawrence angled an eyebrow. "You didn't protest?"

Trent shrugged. "She suited me well enough. I was younger then. And easy-going. I always took the line of least resistance. And there was a quality of—of steely determination in her which I found irresistible. She had the drive and force I lacked. So, in a dozen different ways, she made herself essential. I thought I prized my independence. But I couldn't do without her."

Lawrence nodded slowly. "I think I understand. But you haven't explained why you turned to crime."

Trent looked ashamed. He said unhappily:

"I was a damned fool. And I was having a hard time. I couldn't land a shop. I began to drink and gamble... That made things worse. I got myself in the hell of a hole; so I went to Lesley for help." He muttered:

"By God, if I'd known what was in her mind—."

Lawrence grinned sardonically.

Trent flushed. He said sombrely:

"I know what you're thinking. I'm not just a crook, I'm a coward as well. Lesley's dead; she can't defend herself. I can hide behind her grave... But—God help me—I'm telling you the truth. Hers was the brain behind the crime."

Lawrence said:

"I'm inclined to believe you. She was the puppet-master. You were the doll."

"Yes. Richard Mervan was another. Poor devil!"

"Poor indeed."

Trent bit his lip. "I'll never forgive myself for what we did to him. And yet—then—I hardly thought of him at all. He wasn't a man. He was just a puppet."

He relapsed into moody silence.

Then he continued:

"Lesley struck up a friendship with Mervan. A. thug had attempted to rob him in the street: she told Mervan he deserved a reward for saving the bank's money. When he didn't get it, she played on his natural feelings of resentment. And, of course, she made him fall in love with her."

Lawrence said mildly:

"We know how she trapped him. Let's hear your side of the story."

Trent muttered:

"I didn't take any great part in the business. Lesley must have been planning it for months. An accountant named Spurling had given her the idea—unintentionally, of course. He had been pestering her. So she made use of him.

"She took him to her flat one night when he was holding the keys to the safes. She drugged a drink she gave him. When he passed out she struck an impression of the keys."

"Impressions are useless in themselves," said Lawrence. "Who cut the duplicate keys?"

"I did," confessed Trent. "It wasn't a hard job. And I had some amateur skill as a locksmith." He added uncomfortably. "I wasn't happy about it. But I always did what Lesley asked."

Lawrence made no comment. He asked:

"Was there any trouble with Spurling?"

"No. He didn't realise the keys had been copied. He didn't even know he'd been drugged. And Lesley dropped him at once. He dared not protest."

"No," mused Lawrence. "Bankers pride themselves on their respectability. The directors would have sacked him if they had heard about his amorous adventures."

"Right. Lesley was a fellow employee—she could have made things awkward for him." Michael smiled reminiscently. "She could lead a man up the garden path. Then she would side-step neatly—and pitch him into a bed of thorns."

Lawrence ignored the metaphor. "Lesley had one set of keys. Then she went to work on Mervan for the other."

Trent nodded.

He said unhappily:

"He believed everything she told him. And she—she set him up like a clay pigeon. While I—."

He halted painfully. "God, I'm so ashamed!"

He swallowed, then continued:

"I went to Lesley's flat on the morning of the robbery. We waited till Mervan 'phoned. Then—."

He bit his lip. "Lesley was ready to leave. Mervan thought she was going with him. But when he arrived with the loot, she called him into the bedroom—."

"And you were waiting behind the door with a bludgeon," finished Lawrence coldly.

"Yes," said Michael dully. "I struck him down from behind. We took the money and left."

"Leaving Mervan to the police."

Trent retorted:

"He could have saved himself! Nobody knew about that duplicate set of keys. The police couldn't have proved that Mervan had ever had them. Lesley had taken them from his pocket before we left...."

"The robbery would have remained an unsolved mystery if Mervan had kept his head. He could have gone back to the bank and bluffed it out. Instead, he gave himself away."

Trent seemed to be arguing against his own conscience. Lawrence thought that the actor was too intelligent to deceive himself with sophistry. He said dryly:

"So Mervan had only himself to blame?"

Trent flushed. He said bitterly:

"I can't pretend to be anything but a damnable scoundrel, can I? Maybe I should hang—for what I did to Mervan."

Lawrence said amicably:

"That wasn't technically murder. If you really want to salvage something from the wreck of Mervan's life, you'll have an opportunity to help him later. Meanwhile let's concentrate on Lesley."

Trent continued slowly:

"I'm just realising how little I really knew about her. She was always an enigma."

"Let's stick to the facts as you know them."

"There's not much more to tell." Michael's voice was low. "We took the money and left London at once. Lesley had to disappear for a while. We didn't know what Mervan would tell the police: he might have put them on her track. But we weren't seriously worried. Mervan couldn't possibly trace us himself and we thought he would be too busy trying to save himself to implicate us."

"You thought he would bluff it out?"

"Yes. I told myself—that is, I hoped—he would. But, as we saw from the newspapers, he threw in his hand at once."

Lawrence said levelly:

"His whole world had collapsed."

"Yes, I realised that." Trent bit his lip. "I was—I am— very sorry."

Lawrence made no spoken comment. He shrugged, then said quietly:

"Tell me about your marriage."

Trent answered frankly. "It wasn't much more than a legal formality. Our relationship didn't change at all. It wasn't that Lesley wanted to be my wife instead of my mistress. She was completely amoral. But—."

"She was a possessive woman. And now you were partners in crime. Perhaps that gave her a feeling of insecurity," suggested Lawrence. "She would want to make binding the tie between you. Marriage would give her a legal claim upon you."

"I suppose that was it," agreed Michael slowly.

"But why did you keep the marriage a secret?"

"Lesley," answered Trent, "wanted to have her cake and eat it too. She was determined not to lose me, but"—he grinned cynically— "considered she would get further in the theatrical rat-race if she was thought to be unmarried. Of course," admitted Michael, "the situation gave me certain advantages too." He smiled reminiscently.

He responded to Lawrence's questions with engaging frankness. They had cached the loot and gone into semi-retirement. Trent had found a temporary job and had stuck to it. They had followed the reports of Mervan's trial attentively. His silence had puzzled but relieved them. When they were satisfied that the hue and cry had died down, they had returned to their chosen profession.

"We used the money as our stake in the great gamble. And this time we were lucky."

A brave but short-lived venture in a 'little theatre' in the provinces had ended in financial failure, but their work had won critical esteem. This, plus a successful season in repertory, had served as a springboard to various engagements in London.

"We were still a long way from the top, you understand. But we were climbing the ladder."

Lawrence interposed a question. "You were in the public eye again. Weren't you worried about Richard Mervan?"

Trent nodded. "I was," he confessed. "Though Lesley hardly ever considered him. He had grown shadowy and unreal. It was as if the prison sentence had ended his life for her. She simply put him out of her mind."

Lawrence rubbed his chin. "You were safe, of course. Mervan would have no reason to connect Michael Trent the actor with the unknown man who had struck him down from behind. But Lesley—."

He shook his head. "Didn't she take any precautions?"

Trent shrugged helplessly. "Her ego blinded her to the danger. She had gone so far as to adopt 'Christopher' as her surname and to alter the style of her hair. But beyond that—nothing."

He hesitated, then added:

"Somehow, she believed that when she reached the top, nothing could pull her down."

"I think I understand." Lawrence's eyes were sleepy. "She might have argued that Mervan had lost his chance to harm her when he refused to expose her after being arrested."

"Yes. But she didn't guess that he meant to take the law into his own hands." Trent gave a short, uneasy laugh. "That was a fear that came later."

"It came, then?"

"Yes—a few weeks ago." Trent paused uneasily. "Hell!---I'm not proud of myself. I've failed everybody, even Lesley. She came to me for help. And all I could do was to reach for the bottle."

Lawrence was patient: "She knew Mervan had found her again?"

"Yes. She caught sight of him in the theatre. And again in the street. She told me about it. He just looked at her–and smiled."

"What did you do?"

"Nothing. What could we do? Mervan didn't approach Lesley. He just let his presence play on her nerves. That was a move which couldn't be countered."

"Did you try?"

"I," said Trent with bitter self-reproach, "took refuge in alcohol. The strain was telling upon me, too. Don't forget—I had other troubles as well."

"You were in love with Penny."

"Yes. I wanted to marry her. Yet I couldn't get rid of Lesley. She would never have given me a divorce—I dared not ask her. I suppose I was afraid of her. Yet I was also frightened for her."

"You thought Mervan would harm her."

"I suppose so. But I never dreamed—The crazy fool! Yesterday afternoon—everything seemed to happen at once. You've heard that Lesley left a message with the stage door-keeper—."

"That she wanted to see you? Yes."

Trent frowned. "I never found out why she wanted to talk to me. Perhaps she wanted reassurance—all the moral support I could give her. For days she had had a premonition of danger. Yet she was determined not to run away. The play was our first big success, you see, and she couldn't bring herself to abandon it..."

"You had advised her to stick it out?"

"Yes. I expect she wanted me to reassure her. But I wasn't exactly sober, and I was late, and there wasn't time to see her. We exchanged a few words in the wings, but—.'

He grimaced.

Lawrence asked:

"Did you know Mervan was out front?"

"No. Not till the beginning of the second act. I knew that something had given Lesley a shock, of course, because she had dried in Act One—I had to ad-lib to cover her. She had spotted Mervan in the box, though I didn't know that then. She told me later, in the wings. But we weren't alone and I had to shut her up."

"We've been told about that," murmured Lawrence.

"Not by Cotall," said Trent with decision. "Old Ben is devoted to me. And he's discretion itself."

"Maggie Boyd," drawled Lawrence, "was more communicative."

Trent nodded.   He continued:

"We couldn't talk in front of the dressers. That's why Lesley came to my dressing-room in the second act wait. But then—."

"She found you with Penny."

"Yes."

Lawrence nodded. He quoted softly:

"'You'll be sorry for this. I promise you.'"

Michael's face was pale. "That's what she said. It— it scared me."

"You were afraid of what she might do?"

"Yes. To me. Or to herself, perhaps. I had loved her once, you see."

There was a pause.

Then Lawrence asked mildly:

"Did you murder her?"

Trent met his gaze squarely.

He answered firmly:

"On my honour—no."

Lawrence grinned sleepily. "I'm inclined to believe you."

Trent relaxed. He said with relief:

"Then it's all been worth while."

"Our talk," returned Lawrence cautiously, "hasn't been an unqualified success. I haven't found the essential clue I was hoping for, though," he admitted cheerfully, "I may have been too blind to see it. However!   At least you've cleared up several minor mysteries. I hate loose ends; so that's a relief."

"But—."

"What about you?"

"Yes. Have I proved my innocence?"

Lawrence grinned. He said frankly:

"No. But you've passed the test, so far as I'm concerned. I don't think you put the bullets in that gun. And I'm going to do my best to prove it.'"

Michael Trent nodded his thanks.

Then, as Lawrence rose to leave, the actor asked hesitantly:

"And—Mervan?"

For an instant, Lawrence's lazy face was uncharacteristically stern. Then he said abruptly:

"Richard Mervan is going back to prison. He'll stay there for a long time."

Trent stared at the floor. "I'd like to help him."

"You can."

Trent looked up. "How?"

Algy mused sleepily. "Well, now. You're doing well in your profession. You must be quite a wealthy man. Or will be soon."

Trent's face lightened. "So?"

"You owe that bank a lot of money. But they're wealthy enough – and they've long since written off that debt as a dead loss. So—."

"Mervan needs the money more," finished Trent eagerly.

"Yes," agreed Lawrence. He added engagingly:

"It's a most immoral suggestion. But it holds an element of poetic justice. And I never cared much for the letter of the law."

Michael laughed. Then his face clouded. "I couldn't give Mervan the money without arousing his suspicions."

Lawrence shrugged. "I'll take care of the details."

"You'll see the money gets to Mervan?"

"Yes. I'll be the go-between. You can let me have your cheque—but not," Algy warned, "until the case is closed. I don't want Steve on my tail."

Trent laughed again. "I'll pay the first instalment on the day the murderer goes on trial," he promised.

He added uneasily:

"If I'm not in the dock myself."

Lawrence said amiably:

"I don't think you will be."

Trent said awkwardly: "I was—I am—in a nasty hole. I can't find the words to thank you."

Lawrence replied:

"You don't have to thank me."

He was thinking of the tears in a girl's lovely eyes.

He said, almost roughly:

"I'm not doing this for you."

# CHAPTER TWENTY ONE

It was a gloomy Monday morning.

Algy Lawrence was emerging from his flat. He eyed the rain-misted street without enthusiasm, then flipped up the collar of his raincoat and pulled his hat forward over his brow.

Behind and above him, a bell began to ring.

"Blast that telephone!"

Lawrence banged shut the door and clattered up the stairs towards his bedroom. The 'phone's shrill summons ceased as he picked up the receiver. "Hallo!"

"Hallo... Mr. Lawrence?"

"Penny!" Pleasure tinctured his voice.

"Hallo, Algy." The girl paused briefly. "I didn't disturb you?"

"I was on my way to the Yard."

"Oh." Her breathing quickened. "To see the Chief Inspector—about Michael?"

"Y---yes." Lawrence hesitated. He had reported to Castle immediately after leaving Trent the previous afternoon. He said cautiously:

"I've put Michael's case to the Chief Inspector. Steve won't commit himself—but I know he'll play fair. If Michael's innocence can be proved, then Castle will prove it."

Penny said:

"I know Michael isn't a murderer. But if there's a doubt in your mind—I may be able to dispel it."

"I'm listening."

"I've been thinking about"—her voice flattened oddly—"the damning factor... You said that Michael was the only man who could have been certain that Lesley would die."

"Yes."

"That may be true. But you've overlooked something." Penny's voice pressed triumphantly against Algy's ear.

"What?"

"The man who put the bullets into the gun was a murderer morally and legally. But he may not have cared whether Lesley lived or died!"

Lawrence said slowly:

"I don't understand."

Penny's laugh was tinged with sadness. "You will—when you know us better."

She rang off.

Lawrence went down the stairs and into the street with strange new thoughts working through his mind.

The young man found Castle in his office. The Chief Inspector appeared to have given himself up to gloom. He sat hunched at his desk, regarding a pile of papers with lack-lustre eyes.

Lawrence lowered his slim frame into a chair which had lately been occupied by Michael Trent's dresser. "I saw Ben Cotall in the corridor. Have you been grilling him?"

"We've been questioning him," returned Castle heavily, "yes." He buried his face in a huge handkerchief and blew his nose lustily. He looked up with a scowl. "Michael Trent is a scoundrel. Why is everyone so anxious to protect him?"

Lawrence chuckled. "Stop making noises like a policeman. You can't catch him now for a seven year old robbery. So forget about it."

"And the attack upon Bailey—shall I forget about that, too?"

"You don't really believe Trent knocked out Bailey."

Castle was belligerent. "Somebody did. And he didn't break into the theatre like an ordinary burglar. He must have used a key—a skeleton or a duplicate."

"So?"

"Trent told you himself he was an amateur locksmith."

"Steve—you're catching at straws."

"Perhaps." Castle picked up a pen and began to doodle on his blotter. He said:

"I've been thinking about the confession Trent made to you... I'm not saying that I wasn't impressed by the man's show of frankness. But though he told you a lot about his past life, he said very little about his movements on Saturday afternoon."

"Oh, come now. You already have that information. You've made him account for nearly every minute of his time."

Castle scowled. "Yes, dammit. And I've spent most of the week-end checking his story."

"Searching for a flaw that wasn't there?"

"Yes, I suppose so." Castle stabbed the pen into the pad with a tiny show of violence. "Blast it! I was sure Trent was guilty of murder.  He had both the motive and the means, but"— he stressed the word heavily—"he didn't have the opportunity."

A glimmer appeared in Lawrence's eyes. "You've established his alibi."

"Yes," growled the Chief Inspector. "While you were persuading him to talk, I was checking on his movements. I wanted to discover exactly when he could have put those bullets into the revolver."

Lawrence searched his memory. "Your starting point was—um—at five minutes past two on Saturday afternoon."

"Right. That was when Austin and Wix went to load the gun with blanks. At that time, Trent wasn't in the theatre. He was in a taxi."

"Have you traced the driver?"

"Yes. He put Trent down at the entrance to the alley-way, then watched him go down to the stage door. When he saw the door-keeper take charge of Trent, he drove away. This was as ten minutes past two.

"Victor Friern confirms this. He met Trent at the stage door, then handed him over to Ben Cotall, the dresser, who helped his employer to his dressing-room. Trent stayed there until it was time for him to make his entrance in the first act."

Lawrence commented:

"So he couldn't have tampered with the gun before the play began."

"No. I thought Trent must have had several opportunities to switch the cartridges during the actual performance. The double doors were closed on the 'lobby' a good deal of the time, you remember. But—."

"Yes?"

"I was wrong." Castle sounded angry with himself. "Trent wasn't at any time in or near the lobby without a companion."

"That's definite?"

"Yes, curse it. Old Ben was Trent's second shadow. He went with him to the stage and watched him from the wings. And nearly everybody else back-stage had their eyes on Trent as well. They all knew he was tipsy."

"Didn't he make any exits or entrances through the double doors masking the lobby?"

"Not unaccompanied."

"Where was he during the black-outs at the end of each act?"

"On stage with Douglas Denzil during the first. The doors were closed then. There wasn't time for either man—with or without the other's knowledge—to reach the lobby and find the gun before the lights went on again. And one of the stage hands was actually standing at the mouth of the lobby at the time. He swears nobody went into it," concluded the Chief Inspector mournfully.

"What about the second black-out?"

"At the fall of the curtain on Act Two? Trent was already in his dressing-room with Ben Cotall." Castle paused, then finished gloomily: "So far as I can establish, Trent didn't get his hands on that gun until he took it from Lesley Christopher in Act Three. And he couldn't have filled it with bullets in full view of the audience."

"So Trent," mused Lawrence, "has been cleared."

"I'm afraid so," snorted Castle. "I'd like to believe that Cotall is lying about his master's movements; but there's too much corroboration from other sources... I've tried to find a loop-hole, mind! As I've already explained, Trent couldn't have reached the gun while he was on stage or in the wings; but it's barely possible he might have slipped back to the set while he was officially off stage and in his dressing-room with Cotall."

"That's hardly likely."

"No," admitted Castle. "It isn't. Too many people were popping in and out Trent's room to see how he was. He couldn't have slipped out without being seen... Besides, I've been questioning Cotall closely – grilling him, if you like—and I don't think he's lying. He was genuinely worried about his employer and he was sticking to him like glue."

"Then Michael Trent owes him a debt of gratitude."

"Which is more than I do," said Castle sourly. "His evidence wrecks my original theory. Hell's bells! The inquest has been set for Wednesday. I have to present some kind of case to the Coroner—and I know damn all about the murder."

"You've covered the ground."

"And turned up nothing." Castle scowled in disgust. "I've been proving a series of negatives. Trent couldn't have done it. And neither could Victor Friern."

"You've established his alibi, too?"

"Yes. I've questioned Austin, Maggie Boyd, Ben Cotall, and Short, the stage door-keeper. They agree that Friern had no chance to handle the gun during the period he spent back-stage.

"He went back to his office at the front of the theatre before the play began. He didn't go back-stage again until after the shooting—Short confirms that."

Lawrence said:

"There's a pass-door in the proscenium arch."

"Yes. But it's always kept locked while the auditorium is open to the public. And to reach it you have to go through a box on the upper level—."

"On the O.P. side."

"Yes. And the couple in that box say that nobody went through the pass-door until Friern opened it for you after the killing."

"That clears Friern, then."

"Yes. But it hardly helps me. I need a new line to follow."

"I might be able to suggest one when we've tidied some of the complications out of the way. But—."

Algy paused to consider.

Castle eyed his friend hopefully. He picked up a stack of papers and showed it across the desk. "Would you like to study these reports?"

Lawrence selected a paper at random. It proved to be the autopsy report, with a detailed description of the dead woman's physical characteristics and the nature of the wound which had killed her. It told him nothing he did not already know.

The next report was the fingerprint analysis. It was equally unrewarding.

Castle said:

"The revolver had been handled by too many people to retain tell-tale prints. Austin's and Trent's were the clearest, as you'd expect; and we developed some underlying impressions of Lesley Christopher's. But the rest were too badly smudged to be distinguishable."

Neither the bullets nor the blanks had retained any identifiable prints. Lawrence dropped the report. "I presume there were none on the card sent to Lesley?"

"'We meet at Paddington Fair'? The dead woman's and Victor Friern's. That was what we expected." Castle sighed noisily. "We can't deduce much from those messages, Algy. Both the Paddington Fair cards were cut from a thin strip of pasteboard which can't be traced. And the messages themselves were rubber-stamped. They had been built up letter by letter on a child's printing block. You know the sort of thing I mean—you can buy it at any toy-shop."

Lawrence nodded. "And the tickets—."

"Which were sent with our invitation? We can't trace the buyer. They were bought from one of the busiest agencies in the West End – the staff sell hundreds every day. Nobody can remember the man or woman who bought those particular tickets."

Lawrence turned to the ballistics report. It merely confirmed what they already knew. The bullet in Lesley's heart had been fired from the Webley & Scott .32; the bullet in the bear's head and the bullet in the wall of the box had been fired from the Colt .25: both .25 bullets matched the ejected cartridge cases found on the floor of the box which Mervan had occupied.

Lawrence pushed the reports aside. "These tell me nothing."

Castle drew a malevolent caricature on the blotter. "I'm going to follow a new line. It's not strictly relevant, but I can't ignore it."

Lawrence looked a question.

Castle mumbled a name. "Albert Wix. The property man. He told us he got that damned Webley & Scott from the author of the play, a fellow named Herbert Windsor. I've got the chap's address. I think we should pay a call on Mr. Windsor. That blasted revolver was an unlicensed weapon. He has some explaining to do."

Lawrence nodded indifferently.

He asked suddenly:

"Have you interviewed Richard Mervan?"

"I have." Castle spread his fingers over his jowl. "He knows now that he failed in his bid for revenge. The news crushed him... He has thrown his liberty away for nothing. Poor devil!"

Lawrence's eyes were sleepy.

He murmured:

"I gave you two questions."

Castle grunted. "I put them both to Mervan." He looked puzzled. "The answer to the first disturbed me. But I don't see the point of the second"

Lawrence smiled. "Where," he quoted, "did you book for the box you occupied on Saturday afternoon?"

"Answer," growled Castle, "'I reserved the box and paid for it at the box office in the foyer of the Janus Theatre.'"

"When?"

"A few days before the ☐atinee."

"Hmmm." The amiable vagueness in Lawrence's eyes deepened. "Now tell me the answer to my first question. How did Mervan identify Lesley Barre as Miss Christopher?"

Castle said immediately:

"He saw her photograph in a theatrical magazine."

He paused, then finished gruffly:

"The magazine was sent by post. It was delivered in a large envelope to Mervan's lodgings in London. The magazine had a front cover picture of Lesley Christopher. Mervan recognized her at once."

Lawrence leaned forward.

Castle answered the question before he asked it.

"I don't know who posted the magazine. It certainly wasn't sent by the publishers—though Mervan thought it was. But they don't send out complimentary copies in that way."

"Then—."

"Yes," said the Chief Inspector. "It looks that way, doesn't it? Someone meant to put Mervan on Christopher's track."

Lawrence's face was grave .

He said abruptly:

"Somebody has been playing God, Steve. And I don't like it."

He whispered:

"I don't like it at all."


Trudy Ann said drowsily:

"Darling... Your beard. It tickles."

Herbert Windsor replied indistinctly. "I'll shave it off tomorrow." He continued to nuzzle her neck.

Trudy Ann fondled his hair.

Windsor raised his head.

He said pleasedly:

"*Tu as les beaux tétons.*"

His fingers strayed. Trudy Ann smacked them gently.

She murmured:

"You may admire. But you mustn't touch."

"Dammit," protested Windsor. "You're not the Elgin Marbles."

Laughter bubbled through her lips into his.

Then the door-bell rang.

"Oh, blast!" said Herbert Windsor.

He stood up. The divan gave a twang of relief.

Windsor stalked into the hall and wrenched open the door. "Well?" he roared.

Chief Inspector Castle teetered on the front step. Lawrence stood behind him. Both men stared at Herbert Windsor.

He was wearing an untidy beard which matched his tangled hair. His canary yellow shirt had lost most of its buttons and disclosed a broad chest.  He wore corduroy trousers and open-toed sandals. The general effect was somewhat startling.

Castle fell back. Lawrence gave him an encouraging push from the rear.

The Chief Inspector cleared his throat.  "Mr. Windsor... Mr. Herbert Windsor?"

That gentleman eyed him narrowly. "I am."

"You are the author of a play—."

"Never mind about me. Who the blazes are you?"

Castle produced his warrant card.

The result was alarming. Windsor's roar rattled the windows.  "My God, a policeman!"

"Mr. Windsor—."

"A ruddy copper," continued the playwright, driving the point home.

Castle continued doggedly:

"You are the author of a play entitled. THE FINAL TROPHY—."

"You can't put me in jail for that. It's been licensed by the Lord Chamberlain. Go and bully someone else."

Castle realised he was suffering for the sins of his colleagues. He protested:

"You've made a mistake. I have nothing to do with prosecutions for obscene libel—."

"So I should hope," said Windsor sternly. "Bloody lot of witch-hunters..." He added some pithy remarks about the Home Office.

Castle was perspiring gently. He said:

"I am conducting an enquiry into the death of Miss Lesley Christopher..."

"Oh." Windsor's face changed. He said: "Come in."

He led the way into his study.

Trudy Ann was still seated upon the divan. She looked sleek and well-satisfied like a cat after swallowing cream.

Lawrence greeted her with a smile. She returned it demurely.

Castle squinted. "I didn't expect to meet you here."

Herbert Windsor said briefly:

"Trudy Ann is a friend of mine."

"A very close friend," agreed the girl. Her eyes glimmered with mischief.

Castle regarded her suspiciously. "You didn't tell me this before."

The girl rested a slim finger against her pretty chin. "You didn't," she said gravely, "ask me."

Castle snorted.

Windsor spoke impatiently. "I've known Trudy Ann, for quite a while. We're very good friends. And—if you're still curious—I wrote my play with the girl in mind."

Trudy Ann pouted. "The part you gave me was hardly a plum."

Windsor grinned at her affectionately. "Light of my life—your talents are obvious. But they are not necessarily those of a Bernhardt."

The pout became a smile. "At least," the girl murmured, "I have both my legs." She lifted her skirt to display them. "And they are rather nice. Aren't they?"

Windsor and Lawrence expressed unqualified agreement.

Castle breathed heavily.

He said in a grinding voice:

"Mr. Windsor! You appear to have helped in casting your play. Were you by any chance responsible for engaging Miss Christopher?"

The playwright stared. "Lord, no! I pulled a few strings for Trudy

Ann; but the rest of the casting was out of my hands. You'd better speak to Victor Friern. He's the general manager."

"Hmmm." Castle thumbed his jowl. He said abruptly:

"You didn't like the prop gun which was used at the first rehearsals."

Windsor was not disconcerted. "It was ludicrous—an obvious toy. I told What's-his-name—Wix—."

"The property master."

"Yes. I told him that no ruddy pop-gun was going to spoil my third act. I asked him to produce a real revolver. He hemmed and hawed a bit, but in the end—."

"You provided one yourself."

"Huh?" Windsor's beard bristled. "Where did you get that idea?"

"Wix told me so."

"Then Brother Albert," said the playwright, "is a flaming liar."

Castle stared. "You didn't give him the Webley .32?"

"Of course not."

"But your initials are on the butt—."

"Oh, no, they're not. Windsor is only my pen name. I was christened Herbert Higgins. But," he added ferociously, "breathe that to another living soul and I'll have your guts for garters."

Castle's brow was furrowed. "But Wix said—."

He broke off.

Windsor smiled.

His eyes were shrewd. He said softly:

"I believe that Props has a son named Harold."

Castle swore.

His voice was hard. "Can I use your telephone?"

"It's in the hall."

Castle stamped out.

Lawrence followed. He caught his friend by the shoulder. "Don't be hasty, Steve. Wix is on the hook. Now play out the line and land him gently."

The Chief Inspector grunted. "What d'you mean?"

Lawrence smiled. "His lie about the revolver is comparatively unimportant. But we may be able to use it to break the case."

Castle regarded him suspiciously. "You know something you haven't told me."

"No. But Wix does."

Castle grabbed the 'phone. "You can explain later. I'm going to contact Wemyss. He's working at the Janus. Wix should be there with the rest of the theatre staff. If he is—."

He broke off.

He snapped into the receiver. "Hallo! This is Chief Inspector Castle. I want to speak to Detective Inspector Wemyss...."

Lawrence turned away.

He went back to the study.

Windsor greeted him with a roar. "Great Godfrey! Isn't it time you left me alone with Trudy Ann?"

Lawrence kept a straight face.

He said gravely:

"I'm not sure that I should. Your intentions may not be honourable."

The girl smiled demurely.

Herbert Windsor replied with dignity. "They aren't... I have a reputation to live down to."

The Chief Inspector returned.

He said grimly: "I'm going to the Janus. Are you coming with me?"

Lawrence nodded. "Lead the way."

"I'll see you out," said Trudy Ann.

Windsor sprawled on the sofa in mock disgust.

In the hall, Lawrence squeezed the girl's hand. He murmured:

"It's none of my business. But—."

He hesitated.

She smiled with complete understanding.

She said softly:

"Don't take Herbert too seriously." Her mouth curved gaily. "He's a lycanthropist."

"A—what?"

Trudy Ann explained:

"He only thinks he's a wolf."

# CHAPTER TWENTY TWO

The Chief Inspector Stephen Castle stumped into the Janus theatre with a horrible scowl on his face. Glaring at the fresh-faced young constable who had been chatting desultorily with the stage door-keeper, he barked an enquiry.

As the constable stammered a reply, Algy Lawrence sauntered past and disappeared back-stage.

The young policeman was saying: "Y—yes, sir. Nearly all the staff are back-stage. The Inspector has been questioning them—."

"I know all about that." Castle was impatient. "Tell Albert Wix I want to see him. Quickly."

"Yes, sir." The uniformed man saluted and hurried away.

Castle glowered at Sydney Short. The door-keeper blinked uneasily. Perched on a stool in his cubby hole, he looked more than ever like an ugly old bird in its cage.

The Chief Inspector snapped:

"You know Mr. Lawrence—."

Short nodded quickly. "Yes, guv. He just went past."

"That's right. If he comes back this way, tell him I'm in the greenroom with the property master."

He strode away.

Short shook his head dolefully. To judge from that copper's manner, old Bert was in for it now.

He said aloud:

"I wonder what he's done."

An ugly suspicion formed in his mind. He tried to dispel it with a mumbled "No," then looked up guiltily as a long shadow fell into the glass box.

Castle glared round as the door of the greenroom opened behind him. "Oh, it's you," he growled.

"It is, indeed." Algy Lawrence seemed rather pleased with himself.

Castle eyed him suspiciously. "You've been up to something."

Lawrence grinned. "I've been talking to June Merritt."

"June—?"

"The A.S.M."

"Oh, yes. What about her?"

"I asked her a question. And the answer was: 'No, none that I know of.'"

"Well"—Castle was irritable—"what was the question?"

"Guess."

Castle breathed hard. "Now, look here—."

Lawrence stopped smiling. He said seriously:

"You ought to know, Steve. You've read the prompt script, too."

Interest sparked in Castle's shrewd grey eyes. "You've spotted something I missed?"

Lawrence said carefully:

"I had a suspicion which may soon be verified. You came here to grill Albert Wix. But be alert. You may discover more than you expect."

Castle wore a puzzled frown. "He lied about the gun. But—."

Lawrence interrupted without discourtesy. "It was the small, silly lie of a frightened man. Your questions had rattled him. And you had told him it was a crime to be in possession of an unlicensed gun. So he blurted out the first silly story which came into his mind."

"But he must have prepared the lie," objected Castle. "It came so quickly. We hadn't even mentioned the author's name."

"No mention was needed," smiled Lawrence. He pointed a long finger. "There's his name—in big print—on that poster."

Castle stared at the playbill on the wall. He muttered disgustedly.

Algy sprawled in the saddlebag chair. "I remember how Wix's eyes shifted focus when you were questioning him. He must have caught sight of that poster. The coincidence of the initials 'H.W.' struck him suddenly—so he told you Windsor had given him the gun."

"That's plausible," said Castle grimly. "But now—."

"He'll tell the truth."

"He will indeed," growled the Chief Inspector.

Lawrence said casually:

"I may ask a question. You won't object?"

Castle regarded him with sudden suspicion. "What—?"

The question died on his lips as the door opened after a perfunctory knock.

Albert Wix hesitated on the threshold. His faded eyes flickered uneasily. "You wanted to see me?"

"I did," said Castle quietly. "Come in and sit down."

Wix obeyed, his lined face set in a sullen mask.

Castle swept his hands under his coat-tails. Standing over the property master, he glowered down. "I'm not going to waste time, Wix. You've been lying to me. Now you're going to tell me the truth."

Apprehension muddied the other's eyes. "I dunno what—."

Castle's head went forward. "You told me the Webley & Scott came from Herbert Windsor. That was a lie. Wasn't it?"

"I—I—."

Lawrence had been watching the scene through half-closed eyes. Now he said gently:

"It's no use denying it, old chap. We know you supplied the revolver yourself. Why bother to lie about it?"

The tired mouth quivered.

Then Wix cried:

"What the 'ell did you expect? I'm the property master. I 'ave to get the producer what he asks for. I didn't think I'd be called a criminal— just 'cause I brought him a gun!"

Lawrence said smoothly:

"You needn't be afraid. Technically, it's a crime to be in possession of an unlicensed gun. But you probably have a reasonable explanation—."

"Yes, I have." Wix was pathetically eager.

"Well, then. Let's hear it." Algy gave his friend a meaning stare. "The Chief Inspector won't be vindictive. I'm sure he doesn't want to make trouble for you."

Castle's grunt was non-committal. "I'm waiting for an explanation."

Wix interlaced his bony fingers. "I told you before. The producer and the author—they both wanted a real gun for the play. So I brought 'em one from home."

"You kept the revolver in your home?" asked Castle sternly.

"It—it wasn't mine," Wix answered sullenly. "It was my son's. It was part of a collection he once had."

"Your son's?"

"Yes. Collecting guns—that was an 'obby of his. He was in the Army." Pride gleamed momentarily in the sullen eyes. "He was a good lad. Saw service in some rough places, I can tell you."

"Was?" interposed Algy gently.

"Yes. He—he died in Korea." Wix faltered, then continued:

"He'd got rid of most of his collection 'fore he went there, you understand. But he liked that Webley & Scott; he'd had his initials engraved on it. 'H.W.'—Harold Wix."

"I see."

Wix nodded miserably. "Yes. He'd left the gun with me 'mongst his other things. Then, when I heard he'd been killed, I kept it as a kind o' keepsake."

"I understand." The Chief Inspector was not unkind. "But"—he stressed the word heavily—"that's no excuse. You should have surrendered the revolver at once. Even if your son had had a right to it—which he hadn't—you weren't entitled to retain it after his death. Illegal possession of a firearm—."

Lawrence shot his friend a warning glance.

He said smoothly:

"That's not important now, Steve. You don't want to bring charges—."

"Bring charges!" Alarm sparked the faded eyes. "Gawd!" Then Wix whined:

"Now you know why I made up that story about Herbert Windsor. I didn't want trouble—and he was to blame anyway. Nagging me about that blasted gun—."

"All right, man." Castle was brusque. "Don't whine! I'm not going to hound you."

Wix looked relieved.

Then Lawrence said gently:

"You see? I told you the Chief Inspector wouldn't be vindictive."

Castle jerked his head sideways, impatiently. Interpreting this as a gesture of dismissal, Wix rose hopefully. Then Lawrence's amiable smile brought him to a sudden halt.

Algy asked mildly:

"But aren't you going to explain the other lie?"

Something rasped in the property master's throat. He repeated painfully:

"The other lie?"

"Yes."

"I—I don't know what you mean."

Lawrence said casually:

"I think you do." His eyelids drooped lazily. "You told us the stage manager loaded the revolver with blanks—."

"That's right! I watched him do it!"

"Oh, no." Lawrence shook his head. "You filled the cylinder yourself... With blank cartridges—or bullets?"

The property master's body jerked uncontrollably.

He cried:

"With blanks, I sw—."

The word died in his throat. In the silence that followed, he could hear the thumping of his heart.

He sank into the chair, his thin lips quivering. For a moment, he seemed on the verge of tears.

The Chief Inspector was startled. He turned a questioning gaze on his young friend, but Lawrence was concentrating on the forlorn figure of the property master.

Algy said sympathetically:

"You see? You've given yourself away."

Wix tugged at his collar, fingering his neck as though it were bruised. He whispered with stubborn weakness:

"You're twisting me up—confusin' me... "

Lawrence smiled:

"You're confusing yourself. I knew you were lying from the first."

He rubbed his cheek reflectively. "We questioned you on Saturday. You were a little too anxious to confirm the stage manager's evidence – before you knew what it was. And then you asked the Chief Inspector if he was trying to make out you put bullets instead of blanks into the gun... Remember? And I pointed out—."

"That nobody had suggested that Wix had put cartridges of any sort into the revolver," finished Stephen Castle. He glared at the property master. "That was Austin's job, not yours. But the inference was—."

Wix strangled a cry. "I never done nothing!" He drew a sobbing breath. "Maybe I said—what you say I said. But it was just a slip o' the tongue."

Lawrence grinned a negative. "No. We gave you the benefit of the doubt then. But you made a similar mistake a short while later. We were questioning you about the box of blanks. You produced it and said: 'That's the box I took the fresh cartridge from this afternoon.' But you had previously confirmed Austin's version of the story. Which was that you had merely handed him the box—leaving the extraction of the fresh blank to the S.M. himself."

"I— I—."

Wix floundered helplessly.

Castle's heavy face set grimly.

He said:

"Albert Wix, I—."

"Hold on, Steve." Lawrence was deliberately informal. "We know Props loaded the gun himself. We know that with Austin's help he concocted a lying story to cover up. But we don't know why. Do we?"

Castle grunted. "The conclusion's obvious."

"And probably wrong." Lawrence was gentle. "I don't believe Mr. Wix is a murderer. Do you?"

Wix flailed the air with a bony hand. "I swear—."

"Calm yourself, man!" Castle clapped a heavy hand on the property master's shoulder. "I'll give you one last chance. Tell the truth now, or—."

"I will, I will!" Wix was frantic.

The Chief Inspector released him. "All right. Begin."

Wix dabbed his face with a grubby handkerchief. "I didn't mean any harm. It was just my filthy luck—the only time I ever loaded the gun—an' then the woman got shot—."

Castle studied the frightened face. "Are you telling me that you made a mistake? That you put live bullets into the gun?"

"No, no!" Wix sobbed hysterically. "They were blanks—same as always. Only I can't prove it 'cause I was alone—. "

"You were alone?   Then where was Austin?"

"I don't know." Wix struggled for calm. "I'd already told him I 'ad the blanks for him. That was our routine, you see. I always brought him the box half an hour 'fore the show began—."

"Yes. We know."

Wix continued sulkily:

"Mr. Austin's a ruddy old woman 'bout those cartridges. He'd never trust me to load the blasted gun myself. But just this once he wasn't there, see? I'd already reminded him, but he'd told me never mind now—that was at two o'clock." Wix squeezed his palms. "So I went to the set and waited. Come quarter past two, Mr. Austin still hadn't turned up. I couldn't see the A.S.M. about either—not that Miss Merritt ever had anything to do with the gun, you understand."

Castle nodded impatiently. "Go on."

"Well, you see how it was." Wix pouted. "I had the blanks in my pocket and there was the gun on the pegs. I couldn't see no sense in waiting, so I loaded it myself."

He had lifted the Webley & Scott from the "wall" and had broken open the cylinder. He had emptied the chambers, removed the exploded blank, taken another from the box in his pocket, then had refilled the cylinder with the six cartridges.

Castle asked:

"You're sure they were blanks and not bullets?"

"Of course." Wix was indignant. "I'm not stupid. I did just what Mr. Austin always did—even tested the action first."

"Did you tell the stage manager what .you'd done?"

Wix responded with a sulky negative. "No. I went back to the prop room."

"Hmmm." Castle scratched his jowl. "That's a reasonable story, but"—he pointed an accusing finger—"why the devil did you lie about it?"

The slack mouth quivered. "'Ow d'you think I felt when I heard Lesley Christopher hadn't been shot by the crazy bloke in the box. It was the gun I had loaded which had been used to kill her! And I'd been alone. I couldn't prove I'd filled the cylinder with harmless blanks."

"So you persuaded Austin to lie for you."

"It wasn't my idea," said the property master weakly. "S'welp me, it wasn't... Mr. Austin had a word with me after that there demonstration o' yours—."

Lawrence nodded.

"—an' he said he was afraid you might suspect me 'cause I'd been alone with the gun. He said it was a pity I hadn't stuck to the usual routine 'cause then he'd have been with me and I would have had an alibi. And then he said he wouldn't mind stretching a point to help me out... "

Castle snorted. "So you faked your evidence."

"I didn't want to, I tell you! I told Mr. Austin I didn't wish to lie to the police."

"But you did."

Wix responded sullenly. "That was Mr. Friern's fault."

"Friern's?" Castle's eyebrows went up.

"Yes. I heard what he told you 'bout me and Lesley Christopher – how I was supposed to be holding a grudge against her."

"Wait a minute." Castle's voice was sharp. "How and when did you hear this?"

"It was just before you herded us all into the wardrobe room." Wix stared at the floor. "You were on stage with Mr. Friern, talking about the revolver. I was out of sight behind the set, so I stopped to listen."

Castle clicked his fingers. He remembered the vague figure he had glimpsed as it disappeared back-stage. "You were standing in the 'lobby'?"

"Yes," Wix admitted. "I scarpered when you came through the double doors. But I'd heard what Mr. Friern had told you. And I was afraid you'd think I had a motive for murdering the girl, 'specially when you found out about me and the gun."

The man's eyes, like his speech, became muddled.

"So I told Mr. Austin I'd made up my mind."

"To lie to the police?" Castle was stern.

Wix avoided his eyes. "I had to."

A knock sounded on the door. Detective Inspector Wemyss came in. He said quietly:

"I hope you weren't discussing confidential matters."

"What's that?" Castle spoke in mild surprise. "Why not?"

"Someone was listening at the door." '

Castle muttered a curse. "Who?"

"Douglas Denzil, sir. He walked away when he spotted me. But I'm sure he was eavesdropping."

Algy Lawrence laughed. "He must be playing the amateur detective again."

Castle said a rude word. Then he snapped:

"I've stood enough nonsense. Now I'm going to put my foot down."

Taking Wemyss by the arm, he gave him a rapid but precise summary of the discoveries they had made. Then he turned back to Albert Wix. He said grimly:

"I'm handing you over to the Detective Inspector. You're going to make another statement. And this one is to be true in every particular. If it isn't—."

He left the threat unuttered "Take him away, Wemyss."

Wix retreated with a chalky face. Castle glared at the door as it closed behind him. "Curse him!"

Lawrence chuckled. "Don't be so savage, Steve. You can't complain. You're unravelling the skein."

Castle scowled. "You're not much help. You knew Wix and Austin were lying—."

"I suspected it."

"Then why the devil didn't you say so?"

"Be reasonable, Steve. You wouldn't have listened to me before. When we left the theatre on Saturday night, you were already convinced that Michael Trent was the guilty party. Subsequent events merely confirmed your first impression. I had to demonstrate Trent's innocence before we could proceed."

"Don't lecture me, confound you!"

"I'm sorry," grinned Algy. "But I had to tackle things in their order. We've tidied several complications out of the way. Now we know what we're doing."

"Do we?" Castle seemed doubtful.

"I think so. Wix has helped us considerably. Once we've settled Austin's part in the affair, then—"

"We'll reach the solution?"

"Perhaps not. But at least we'll know the problem."

# CHAPTER TWENTY THREE

"Greetings, gentlemen."

Douglas Denzil strolled across the threshold without visible qualms. He rested one buttock on the table top and grinned at Castle insolently. "Friend Wemyss says you want to see me. It seems I've been a naughty boy."

"Sit down!" barked the Chief Inspector. "And don't play the fool."

Denzil shrugged, then lowered himself into a chair, striking an exaggerated pose of humility.

Castle said accusingly:

"You were listening at the door."

"I suppose I was."

"Why?"

"My dear chap! The answer's obvious. I was humanly inquisitive." Denzil made a pyramid of his fingers. "I came into the theatre at your heels. I heard you storming at the stage door-keeper and I questioned him discreetly. Then Lawrence and Wix joined you in the greenroom. Things seemed to be happening; so I succumbed to my baser instincts and took up my post at the door."

"You heard—."

"Everything." Denzil smiled maliciously.

Lawrence said: "You mustn't be cross with him, Steve. He fancies himself as an amateur sleuth."

Douglas murmured:

"I hope you're not reproaching me."

"On the contrary." Lawrence was gracious. "I remember our conversation in Lesley's dressing-room. You were quite right. Sometimes a clue is too obvious to be seen"—his voice flattened—"by clever fellows like us."

Denzil's eyes hooded. "I wonder what you mean by that."

Lawrence grinned. "You seemed to be referring to the photograph of Michael Trent. We know now that an important document lay hidden behind that picture. And somebody smashed the frame—and Bailey's head—to get it."

"Ah, yes. Friend Bailey. I hope he's well?"

"He's recovering. But let's talk about that document. It was a marriage certificate. It was taken from its hiding-place. And it next appeared"—Lawrence smiled politely—"in your possession."

Denzil was not put out of countenance. "An odd coincidence."

"Yes. If it was—a coincidence."

Denzil said coolly:

"I didn't attack Bailey, if that's what you mean. And I didn't steal the certificate."

"But you did know it was hidden in the portrait?"

"As a matter of fact—I didn't. But to save you the trouble of making any more clumsy suggestions"—Denzil's tongue was sharp—"I'll make an admission. I did have my suspicions about that picture. And if I hadn't been disturbed in Lesley's dressing-room, I would have had it off the wall to examine it."

Castle asked: "What made you curious about the picture?"

"Lesley seemed to have an exaggerated regard for it. I wondered why."

"Hmmm." Castle eyed Denzil suspiciously. "Can you explain why the certificate was delivered to you?"

Denzil said blandly:

"No."

Lawrence laughed. "You don't question a gift from the gods."

"I'm sure," said Douglas virtuously, "I don't know what you mean."

Algy was quizzical. "You may not have known where the certificate came from. But you were ready to make use of it."

Denzil bared his teeth in a savage grin. "You've been talking to Penny."

"And you," hazarded Lawrence, "have been talking to Michael Trent. Uh—that is a bruise beneath your eye?"

Denzil fingered the faint discolouration ruefully. Then, surprisingly, he laughed.

"Michael did," he admitted, "become distressingly physical. I couldn't restrain him. Penny—sweet girl—had been telling him stories."

He paused, then added pointedly:

"Fairy stories."

"You mean the—uh—bargain you proposed—."

"Existed only in Penny's imagination," finished Denzil sardonically.

"I don't believe," said Lawrence politely, "that you're telling the truth."

"Perhaps I'm not," returned Denzil carelessly. "But you can't prove it."

Lawrence grinned. "Tell us your version of the interview."

"I showed the certificate to Penny without comment. Michael wasn't available, you remember. Penny said she'd surrender the certificate to the police. So I left it with her."

"That's not a convincing story."

"It doesn't have to be," sneered Douglas.

The Chief Inspector rumbled:

"You claim—."

"I claim nothing," interrupted Denzil. "I found the document in my letter cage on Sunday morning. I know no more than that. I've had two of your detectives on my door mat looking for clues—let them explain the mystery. If they can."

"You can't help us?"

"I can only suggest," said Denzil spitefully, "that you check up on Michael Trent."

"We've done that," said Algy Lawrence, "as you probably know. We can't prove he didn't steal the certificate. But we can prove he's not a murderer. Right, Steve?"

Castle looked down his nose. But he grunted an affirmative.

Denzil bit his lip.

Then he shrugged philosophically. "Oh, well. I—."

He was interrupted.

The fresh-faced young constable, after knocking cautiously, came into the greenroom. He saluted. "The stage manager's outside, sir. Do you want him now?"

Castle nodded testily. "Wait five minutes. Then send him in."

The constable withdrew.

The Chief Inspector returned to Denzil. "Now then—."

Douglas said swiftly:

"Don't dismiss me. I have a fancy to remain."

"Eh?" Castle was monetarily disconcerted.

Lawrence had been watching Denzil with a lively interest. He was wondering if the actor knew more than he had admitted. If so....

Algy said smoothly:

"Let him stay Steve. He can't do any harm."

"Thank you," said Denzil waspishly.

"I think—yes?" murmured Lawrence. He indicated a screen in the corner.

Denzil nodded. He settled himself in a chair behind the screen.

Lawrence turned back to Castle. The Chief Inspector had been following his young friend's activities with growing exasperation. "Look here, Algy."

"Hush, Steve." Lawrence's lips framed the words: his voice was

381

barely audible. "I'm playing a hunch."

Castle blew out his cheeks. Then he smacked his hands together and stumped to the door.

Dragging it open, he roared into the corridor. "All right! Send him in."

He glanced at Lawrence, adding sotto voce:

"And Heaven help you both."

Jack Austin was obviously ill at ease. His voice wavered perceptibly. "You—you wanted to see me?"

"I did." Castle was dangerously calm. "Sit down, Mr. Austin."

The stage manager obeyed, licking his dry lips nervously. The Chief Inspector regarded him with a level stare. Then he put out a big hand and drew his brief-case towards him. Withdrawing some stapled sheets of paper, he looked from the typescript to the stage manager.

"Do you know what this is?"

"N-no."

"It's a copy of your statement. Listen."

Unhurriedly, the Chief Inspector began to read aloud. Austin shifted uneasily as Castle, in a dry and emotionless tone, recited the S.M.'s testimony from beginning to end.

Silence fell.

Castle looked up.

"This is your statement?"

Austin nodded without speaking.

Castle smiled savagely. He tore the papers across and dropped the torn leaves into Austin's lap.

"And that," he growled, "is what it's worth."

Austin flushed, then paled.

He cracked his knuckles nervously. "I—."

Castle slapped his open palm against the brief-case. "Don't bother to lie. We've been talking to Albert Wix. He has told us the truth at last."

Pitilessly, he outlined the substance of the property master's story. He concluded ominously:

"Wix is rather stupid. He doesn't appear to have wondered why you were so ready to suppress the truth. No, don't tell me it was mistaken altruism. You wanted to mislead us for reasons of your own. And I want to know what they were—and are."

Austin opened his mouth. But no words came.

Castle said:.

"I'm waiting."

The stage manager croaked:

"Chief Inspector—I—."

The mumble died away.

Lawrence asked unexpectedly:

"Mr. Austin, do you read the Gentleman's Magazine?"

Castle shot his friend an angry glance. But the very incongruity of the question loosened Austin's tongue.

The stage manager said faintly:

"I don't quite understand."

"More exactly," continued Lawrence, "do you know this particular volume?"

He lifted a book from the shelves and brought it across to the stage manager. Austin shook his head. "I don't believe I do."

"I always look into books," mused Lawrence. "And I found this volume here, amongst others, on Saturday."

Austin looked puzzled. "It's part of the library. There's nothing important about it, surely."

"It's old," said Algy mildly. "Which is interesting in itself. But that's not what I meant. I was only browsing. I doubt if I would have given it a second glance if I hadn't noticed one intriguing item."

He put down the bound volume and allowed it to fall open, then looked up with a smile. "A marker had been slipped between the leaves. I wondered why."

"Get to the point," said Castle gruffly.

Lawrence shrugged. "That's how I found this particular item. Somebody had evidently been studying it."

"What is it?" asked Austin.

Lawrence answered:

"It's an account of the last public execution at Tyburn in November, 1783. The final month of Paddington Fair. But that wasn't what caught my attention.  It was the coincidence of the name."

"The name?"

"Look for yourself," said Algy Lawrence. "The man who was hanged was called—."

"Yes?"

"John Austin."

There was a moment's silence. Then the stage manager gave a puzzled laugh. "That's interesting. But it doesn't really mean anything. Does it?"

"No," agreed Algy. "But it suggests—."

"What?" Austin seemed more at ease.

Lawrence continued slowly:

"I'm trying to get into the murderer's mind. He brought Paddington Fair to the stage of this theatre. And I think he hoped we would find this article. Which might mean—."

"Yes?"

"He's trying to direct our attention towards you."

"I don't see that," commented Austin in genuine surprise. "You can hardly suspect me of murder just because a namesake of mine was executed a hundred and seventy years ago."

"No?" Lawrence's eyes glimmered. "Well, perhaps not. But if this is just a red herring—as I think it is—then you don't want to play the killer's game. In other words, don't complicate the case by lying." His voice hardened. "You were lying, weren't you?"

Austin passed his hand over his mouth.

He said wearily:

"Yes. I didn't tell you the truth about the gun."

Castle broke in with an accusation. "You meat to mislead us from the very beginning."

"No!" The denial came promptly.

Austin continued with a rueful smile:

"Friern misled you originally. Not intentionally, though."

"Friern?"

"Yes. Before you questioned me, he had already described my usual routine."

"That's right. He had," muttered the Chief Inspector. "But—."

"You repeated it to me for confirmation." Austin chose his words carefully.

"And you said: 'Yes, that's my normal routine.'"

"Which sounded like confirmation. But I was about to add: 'I didn't follow it this afternoon, though' when—."

"We were interrupted," groaned Castle. He swung round on his friend. "Algy! That was your doing!"

"I'm afraid so, Steve," admitted Lawrence. "I was having my friendly argument with that stage-hand about raising the curtain."

"And then," recalled Castle, "we set about reconstructing the crime. You found the bullet in the bear's head and—."

He halted, then finished softly:

"And you, Mr. Austin, decided to lie. I want to know why."

Lawrence saw the furtiveness creep into the S.M.'s face. He said quietly:

"First things first, Steve. Let's hear why Mr. Austin didn't load the gun himself."

Castle lifted his shoulder.

"Well?" he grunted.

Austin said wretchedly:

"I always attend to that job myself. But on that afternoon, I forgot about it. Wix reminded me, but my attention was on other things. Michael Trent hadn't turned up, and I was worried about that. I had to warn Denzil to be prepared to take the part over—and I had to get into contact with Douglas's own understudy by 'phone."

Lawrence hazarded:

"You were also worrying about Lesley Christopher."

"Yes." Austin bit his lip. "I—I was anxious to talk to her. You know about that."

Castle said impatiently: "Let's hear about the gun."

"Yes. Well." The stage manager hesitated. "I had a talk with Victor Friern—."

"At what time?"

"About five minutes past two. As I told you. I left him at the entrance to the dressing-room passage."

"But you didn't go back-stage to load the revolver."

"No. I was worrying about Michael Trent. I wasn't so certain as Friern that he would turn up. So—as Victor had suggested—I went to see Denzil. Friern didn't see me go into his dressing-room—he had already gone into Lesley's. After I had warned Douglas he might have to deputize for Trent, I went to 'phone Denzil's own understudy. I couldn't contact him—that didn't restore my peace of mind. Fortunately, Trent himself arrived on the quarter call. Friern informed me of his arrival—and something Victor said reminded me about the revolver. But I went to see Michael first, and then I had that row with Lesley" he flushed and fingered his wrist—"and that drove everything from my mind."

He paused to collect himself.

He continued.

"I was on the prompt book and I forced myself' to concentrate on that. I might have remembered about the gun in the first interval—I went on stage to check the set before raising the curtain on the second act. But Penny made some casual remark and distracted my attention once more."

He smiled humourlessly and added:

"I still wasn't myself, you understand."

Castle had been following him closely. "Go on."

Austin's eyes seemed to lose focus. "There—there isn't any more to be said. I forgot about the gun completely. Until—until—."

"Until after the tragedy?" supplied Lawrence.

"Y-yes." Austin drew in a sobbing breath.

Castle put in a question. "Then you cooked up a story with Wix after you'd witnessed the discovery of the .25 bullet in the bear's head?"

"Yes " Austin's tongue flicked over his lips. "Props had told me about the revolver after the show—how he'd loaded it himself. It didn't seem important then. But after Mr. Lawrence had shown us how it must have been used to kill Lesley...."

He fell silent.

Lawrence said sleepily:

"You saw that he had no alibi. So you manufactured one."

"Yes." Austin spoke with difficulty. "I didn't want him to be accused of the murder."

Lawrence angled an eyebrow. "But how did you know that he hadn't put real bullets into the gun?"

Austin's voice grew fainter. "He couldn't have."

Lawrence was gently insistent. "But how could you know?"

"I—I—."

Lawrence rubbed his cheek thoughtfully. "Did you touch the gun at all before Trent handed it to you after the tragedy?"

"No—no—."

"You didn't go into the 'lobby'," suggested Algy, "after the curtain went up on the third act?"

"No. I was on the prompt book—."

"But you left it for a while," smiled Lawrence. You told us so. You put your A.S.M. on the book."

"Yes, that's right." Austin was breathing quickly. "I wanted to check on a special effect that was due to be given in the last scene—the one you didn't see—."

"Ah, yes. That special effect. You know, I was curious about that. I checked the prompt script for it. And oddly enough, I couldn't find it."

Austin's face was pallid. "I—I—."

"What's more," continued Lawrence benignly, "I made an enquiry. I asked June Merritt if there was any special effect in the final scene. And her answer was—."

"'No, none that I know of!'" The Chief Inspector broke in with a roar.

Austin's stocky frame seemed to shrink.

"She's mistaken—."

Castle's face was thunderous. "You're lying! You went into the 'lobby' to get the gun—."

"No, no, I swear I didn't!"

Castle bit back another reckless accusation. But he clenched his fists menacingly. "Out with it, man!"

Austin was weak but stubborn. "I didn't touch the gun—I didn't...."

There was a long moment of silence.

Then somebody chuckled reprovingly.

Denzil's voice sounded from behind the screen.

"It won't do, Jack,'" he said with malice and mockery. "Really, it won't."

# CHAPTER TWENTY FOUR

Douglas Denzil reappeared with an insolent gleam in his eyes. Pushing aside the screen, he gave Austin an unpleasant smile.

"You could say," the actor remarked, "'Lady Teazle, by all that's damnable!' But I suppose it wouldn't really be appropriate."

"No," said the stage manager coldly. "I see you more properly as Sir Benjamin Backbite. Or Mr. Snake."

Denzil's smile broadened into a grin without humour. "Touché," he murmured.

The Chief Inspector had been following the exchanges with growing impatience, but Lawrence kept him silent with a tiny gesture of warning. Behind the mask of indolence, the young man was keenly alert.

Austin and Denzil faced each other like duellists. Then the actor turned away with slight shrug. "I'm sorry, Jack," he said without noticeable regret. "But I can't let you tell such naughty fibs."

"You yourself," said Austin thinly, "have such a high regard for the truth."

"Oddly enough," agreed Denzil, "I've told no lies to the police. Though I haven't been entirely frank."

Castle could stand no more.

He roared:

"If you've something to say, for God's sake say it!"

Denzil winced. "My dear Chief Inspector! You're putting me off."

Lawrence interposed:

"I think we should let Mr. Denzil tell his story in his own way."

"Thank you," said Douglas ironically. "I propose to do so."

Lawrence grinned. He extended his silver case in mute invitation. Denzil selected a cigarette and lit it. The centre of attention, he moved with deliberate and irritating slowness.

He blew out a cloud of smoke.

He said softly:

"You questioned me after the killing. My statement was true. But it wasn't complete."

He leaned against the wall. "I didn't have much to do in the first scene of the third act. It was Michael's and Lesley's, of course. But you may remember that Penny appeared with him, too, in quite an effective passage."

The detectives nodded. The S.M.'s face was devoid of expression.

Denzil continued:

"That's not important in itself. But it explains my presence in the wings at the time. I was waiting for Penny to make her exit. I wanted a word with her—."

"About what?" Castle interrupted gruffly.

Denzil replied coolly:

"Personal matters. Oh, well"—he grinned wryly—"I needn't make a mystery of it. I wanted to question her about that little contretemps in Michael's dressing-room. Discreetly of course," he added sardonically.

"And did you?"

"No. At least, not then." Denzil paused, as if to marshal his thoughts. He gave Austin a sidelong glance. He said* "Something distracted my attention."

"What?" Castle was impatient.

Denzil was not to be hurried. "I came out of the dressing-room passage. I saw somebody going into the 'lobby' at the rear of the set—.""

"What's that?"

Douglas lifted a finger. "Patience, my friend. Well, now! I'm naturally inquisitive. I sauntered into the wings and glanced idly along the 'lobby'. And I saw this particular somebody take the revolver from the 'wall' and break it open."

Something rattled in Austin's throat. Denzil threw him a mocking glance and continued:

"I watched this somebody empty the cylinder and refill it. I won't say that made me suspicious; but it made me thoughtful. I decided not to wait for Penny in the wings. I went back to the dressing-room passage."

"And Penny joined you there," remarked Algy Lawrence.

"She did," agreed Denzil. "I turned on the charm and detained her. She wasn't very communicative, though. I was still trying to pump her when we heard that Lesley had been shot."

"And who," rumbled the Chief Inspector, "was this...somebody?"

Denzil threw away the line.

"You tell them Jack," he suggested.

Austin said hopelessly:

"I didn't know you'd seen me."

Then anger animated his dead face. "Why didn't you speak before?

Do you like to play cat and mouse?"

"Now that," mused Lawrence, "is a good question." He looked at Denzil. "What's the answer?"

"Guess," invited Douglas.

Lawrence smiled. "I think I know."

Denzil was feline. "I think you do, too."

He added in a whisper:

"But you can't prove it. And it wouldn't help if you could."

Algy's eyelids drooped. "There it is, Steve. Mr. Denzil has misled us. But he hasn't lied to us and he hasn't made a false statement on oath. So perhaps he's telling the truth now."

Castle grunted. "Mr. Austin hasn't denied it."

The stage manager shook his head. His voice was weary. "I was a fool to lie about the gun. But I was frightened."

Castle began: "You admit—."

Then he checked himself and said in a flat voice:

"Give us your own explanation."

Austin moistened his lips. He spoke with difficulty. "I told you I had forgotten about loading the revolver. That was true. But when we reached the scene in which it was to be used—after the curtain had gone up on the third act—I suddenly remembered."

He rubbed his palms nervously. "I was on the book. I handed it over to my A.S.M. June's a good girl—she doesn't ask tiresome questions...

"I didn't have time to find Props and get the box of blank cartridges from him. But at least I could examine the gun and see it was in order. The double 'doors' were closed, you see; I could move about the 'lobby' quite freely. I took down the gun and broke it open—."

Castle frowned. "But why? You had no fresh cartridges."

"No. But even if the gun hadn't been touched since the previous performance, there would still have been five unexploded blanks in the cylinder. I intended to rotate it if necessary and make sure that the hammer would fall on an unfired cartridge. It would be a simple precaution—enough to put my mind at ease."

Castle nodded. "I see. Go on."

Austin cracked his knuckles. "I examined the gun and found I had been worrying needlessly. Wix had obviously seen to it himself. It was in perfect working order and held a full load of six blank cartridges. I replaced it on the pegs and went back to the prompt corner. I didn't know anyone had seen me." He regarded Denzil with dislike.

"Everything was in order?" Castle seemed dubious.

"Yes." Austin nodded emphatically. "I didn't think about the revolver any more until the live bullets were discovered inside it. And then—after Mr. Lawrence's demonstration—."

"Yes?" Castle's voice was steely. "What then?"

Austin swallowed. "I realised what a horrible position I was in. You would be looking for the person who had taken the blanks out of the revolver before Lesley carried it on stage in the third act. And I had handled it myself."—he choked—"a few minutes before. You were bound to suspect me."

Algy Lawrence said sleepily:

"You had quarrelled with Lesley before the show."

Austin nodded jerkily. "I felt I was in a trap. I had to escape."

"So you went to Wix," said Castle grimly.

"He was my only chance," the S.M. whispered. "I told him how Lesley had been killed. He got scared too. I played on his fears.... "

"You implied he would be suspected of tampering with the cartridges."

"Yes. He—he didn't know I had handled the gun myself."

"So you persuaded him to lie." Castle's jaw jutted accusingly. "He thought he was protecting himself. But he was really shielding you."

"I didn't want to fool him." Austin spoke with painful intensity. "But I —-had to."

"You fabricated," rumbled Castle ominously, "an ingenious and effective alibi. Was that the action of an innocent man?"

"I swear—."

Austin choked on the protest.

Algy Lawrence asked mildly:

"Didn't your conscience bother you?"

"No." Austin emphasised the negative with a blow from his fist on his knees. "Props had loaded the gun with blanks. I had examined them and replaced them in the gun. Neither of us knew anything about the bullets—but now could we prove it? If only we'd been together...."

"As you usually were."

"Yes. If we could only make you believe that we'd followed our usual routine, then you would have no reason to be suspicious of either of us."

"And you were prepared to wreck the entire structure of the case to divert attention from yourselves." Castle was dangerously calm. "We've been proceeding on the assumption that the substitution of bullets for blanks could have taken place at any time between five minutes past two and the moment the gun was carried on stage: Now we must confine the investigation to narrower limits."

The Chief Inspector's voice sharpened. "You say that .the gun was still loaded with harmless blanks when you replaced it on the pegs."

"Yes, yes!"

"Very well," glowered Castle. "But it was—by your own story—only a few minutes before Miss Christopher herself carried the gun on stage. In that brief interval"—the Chief Inspector's words were hammer blows—"could any one have tampered with the ammunition?"

Austin cried:

"The murderer must have got to the gun somehow! Before—before Lesley went into the 'lobby' – "

There was a brief, incredulous silence.

Then Douglas Denzil said flatly:

"I'm sorry, Jack. That just won't do."

He turned to the Chief Inspector.

He continued:

"I have something more to tell you. I had decided not to wait in the wings—."

"So you returned to the dressing-room passage." Castle nodded impatiently. "I remember."

Denzil said:

"Yes. I was still thinking about that little scene in the 'lobby'. At the entrance to the passage, I looked back. Austin was just leaving the set on his way back to the prompt corner. At that same moment—."

He paused with calculated effect.

Then he finished softly:

"Lesley passed me on her way to the stage. I made some casual remark; she mumbled a reply and went into the 'lobby' to wait for her cue."

"Wait a minute!" Castle was excited. "That means—."

"It means," said Denzil dramatically, that Lesley went into the 'lobby' almost on Austin's heels. And nobody could have reached the gun after he had left it!"

Castle scanned the stage manager's frightened face. "Well, Mr. Austin?" he grunted.

The stocky man gasped. "I—I—."

The Chief Inspector was pitiless. "Miss Christopher was waiting in the 'lobby' for her final cue. When she made her last entrance, she went through the double 'doors' and took the revolver with her. It was loaded with live ammunition—yet you say you left it filled with blanks. How was the substitution made?"

"I don't know!" Austin searched desperately for an explanation. "Perhaps somebody joined her in the 'lobby'—."

"And switched the cartridges before her very eyes?" asked Castle with portentous scorn.

The stage manager seemed on the point of collapse. "My God. I— Wait!"

Hope lit his eyes. He stood up and grabbed Denzil's arm. "Tell them, Douglas. You were watching. You must have seen!"

The actor seemed amused. "Don't gabble, Jack," he murmured.

Austin clutched harder. "You saw me empty the gun. You saw me examine the blank cartridges and replace them in the cylinder. You saw me, Douglas. Tell them!"

Denzil disengaged his sleeve and smoothed it delicately.

He said lightly:

"I saw you empty the gun and palm the cartridges. But then you turned your back and your body obscured the movements of your hands. You may have replaced the blanks. But you could also have refilled the cylinder with bullets."

Nobody moved.

Then Castle said gently:

"I think we should go the Yard. Then you two gentlemen can make your statements in the proper manner."

His hand fell like a father's on Austin's shoulder.

# CHAPTER TWENTY FIVE

Lawrence had just finished breakfast on the following morning when a sharp buzz announced the arrival of an early visitor. Pausing by a mirror in the hallway, he eyed his reflection quizzically and murmured: "I wonder?"

Then he clattered down the stairs and opened the front door of his flat. He smiled delightedly. "Penny!"

The girl said gravely:

"Hallo , Algy. May I come in?"

"Of course." He stood aside, glancing quickly along the quiet street outside.

Penny smiled. "I wasn't followed. Perhaps the reporters were looking for me. But—what you called my disguise—it fooled them."

She was wearing the same simple costume he had admired on Sunday. He thought again: She's beautiful.

They went up the stairs together. Algy took the girl into a room crammed with books. She turned and faced him gravely. "I want to talk to you. It's rather important."

Lawrence nodded. "Please make yourself comfortable."

Penny stripped off her beret and shook out her tresses. A fugitive gleam of sunlight from the window behind her touched golden highlights in the dusty blonde of her hair; she was very lovely.

Lawrence caught his breath. He helped her out of the raincoat; her nearness made his fingers tremble.

When he came back from the hallway, he found her gazing round the room with a tiny smile on her red lips. He looked a question.

She answered:

"I was thinking: this room—it's you."

"It certainly lacks a woman's touch."

She studied him curiously. She said softly:

"You're lonely, aren't you?"

"Well..." Lawrence temporized. "Let's say—."

"Yes?"

"I'm still looking for my lady."

Penny's eyes softened. "You'll find her soon," she murmured sympathetically.

Lawrence looked at the girl with a pang of regret. "How's Michael?"

he asked abruptly.

Her face grow bright with love. "He's himself again," she replied. "Thanks to you. But—."

Her eyes clouded.

Lawrence dropped into a chair opposite hers. "But what?"

"I didn't come here to talk about Michael." The girl hesitated, then asked suddenly:

"Is it true about Jack—has he really been arrested?"

Lawrence rasped his thumb against the angle of his jaw. He answered carefully:

"Austin has not been arrested. But…."

He shrugged eloquently.

Penny breathed quickly. "He can't have had anything to do with Lesley's death."

Lawrence hunched his shoulders. "I'll tell you what we've discovered.   You can judge for yourself "

He began to describe the events of the previous day. Penny listened attentively.

"So you see," he finished at length, "if what Denzil says is true, we seem to have proved that nobody could have reached the gun after Austin had left it. Which means…."

He left the conclusion unspoken.

Penny frowned. "But—."

She bit her lip.

She repeated slowly:

"If what Denzil says is true... But why shouldn't Douglas be lying? You know how unscrupulous he can be."

"Austin doesn't deny handling the gun," replied Lawrence.

"But you've only Douglas's word to prove that Lesley went into the 'lobby' as Jack left it."

"True," said Algy. "But we've talked to the A.S.M. and we've examined the time sheet and the prompt script. We know when Austin returned to the book; we know when Lesley made her last entrance. The times very nearly coincide."

The girl was mutinous. "I don't care. You can't trust Douglas—."

She broke off.

She seemed to be making an appeal. "If his story is true, then why didn't he speak before?"

"Ah." Lawrence grinned sleepily. "That's a question I've asked myself. Denzil won't explain. But I think I know the answer."

"Yes?"

Lawrence put the tips of his fingers together. "He told us once that he didn't have any special feelings about Lesley Christopher. Her death didn't distress him. He wouldn't protect her murderer. But—." He gestured. He continued:

"Denzil has a devious mind. And he's an unscrupulous opportunist. Do you agree?"

Penny nodded.

Lawrence said slowly:

"He had two ambitions. One was to take over the starring role in THE FINAL TROPHY from Michael Trent. The other—ahem—."

Penny's eyes twinkled.

She said solemnly:

"I know what you mean."

Lawrence laughed. "Good. Now here's my theory. Denzil didn't care who had murdered Lesley Christopher. But he meant to use her death to further his own plans."

Penny frowned. "He hoped that Michael might drink himself out of the part. And then, after Lesley died—."

"He told you that Michael would be arrested. That was wishful thinking."

"I made it clear to him that Michael was in no danger. But Denzil was determined to push Trent out of the play, even if he had to get him charged with murder.

"So he said nothing about the stage manager. But he told the police about that little scene in Michael's dressing-room—."

"When Lesley interrupted us."

"Yes. Denzil was doing his best to make us suspicious. He didn't want Trent to be hanged—."

Penny caught her breath.

"—but he did want to see him taken into custody. He longed for that starring role. Denzil was going to be an overnight sensation," finished Lawrence sardonically.

"Go on," breathed Penny.

"You know what happened next. Someone broke into the theatre and stole Lesley's marriage certificate. Michael was taken to the Yard.

"Douglas found himself with the certificate. He used it in an attempt to further his other ambition. He went to see you." Lawrence paused delicately.

Penny remarked, with a glimmer of humour:

"You don't have to elaborate. We know what was in his mind."

"We do," agreed Algy. "Well, now! You turned him down. But he probably consoled himself with the reflection that the revelation of Lesley's secret marriage would clinch the case against Michael Trent."

"And so it would," said Penny warmly, "if it hadn't been for you."

"Perhaps." Lawrence shrugged his shoulders. "Anyway, Castle could find no flaw in Michael's alibi. Denzil's scheme had come unstuck. He realised this—."

"Michael hammered home the lesson," interrupted the girl, "with more force than charity."

Lawrence nodded. "I saw Denzil's eye," he murmured.

He continued:

"Douglas had been unable to oust Michael from his leading role. He had also been frustrated—uh—in his designs upon your person. He had sense enough to admit defeat. So there was no longer any advantage to be gained by keeping Austin's secret... And though his ruthless ambition may have blinded him to the dangers, he knew he was concealing important evidence. He didn't want to become an accessory after the fact; so when he found we were on the S.M's track—."

"How did he discover that?"

Lawrence grinned. "Douglas fancies himself as an amateur sleuth. I encouraged him. His sense of the dramatic did the rest." Algy rubbed his cheek. "He may also have developed a conscience. But—whatever his motives—you may be certain of this. He has told the truth at last."

Penny bit her lip. "Even so," she faltered, "I can't believe that Jack is a murderer."

Lawrence said flatly:

"The evidence is damning."

Then he grinned ruefully. "But I think he's innocent."

Penny sighed with relief.

"Why?" she demanded hopefully.

Lawrence hesitated. He said slowly:

"Well, now. I remember a remark Austin made after I had shown him how Lesley had died. I said that somebody had taken the blanks out of the revolver before Lesley had carried it on stage. Austin began: 'But I—,' then stopped. I think he was going to say: 'But I examined it myself a few minutes before she took it.' That's the remark of an innocent man."

Penny looked disappointed. "But that's only guess-work."

"True. But there is something else... Austin didn't know Denzil had seen him going into the lobby. That's a point in his favour. As an innocent man, a stage manager concentrating upon his professional duties, he would have been thinking only about the job in hand—the inspection of the gun. He would have no reason to conceal himself or cover up his actions. But a guilty man plotting a murder—."

"Would have been on the watch!" cried Penny.

Algy nodded. "Austin would have been looking round to see if his movements were being observed. He wouldn't have dared to tamper with the gun if he had known there was a witness about; and he would have spotted Denzil if he had been on the alert."

Penny began: "That proves—."

"It proves nothing," said Lawrence quietly. The Chief Inspector won't listen to arguments like that. He wants facts."

"Facts!" The girl was scornful.

Lawrence hunched his shoulders. The stage manager was the last person to handle the gun before Lesley carried it on stage. Austin says it was loaded with harmless blanks. If that were true...."

He gestured eloquently.

Penny said stubbornly: "It is true."

She added in a small voice:

"If Jack says so."

Lawrence shrugged. "Then how did the bullets get into the gun—by black magic?"

Penny's hands clenched. She voiced a challenge. "You're not afraid of impossible crimes. You've met them before."

"I can't ask Castle to think of this as a 'miracle' murder. He has his explanation."

"But...."

Lawrence said flatly:

"You have to state a problem before you can solve it."

"I see." Penny's eyes were downcast.

She asked:

"Then what will happen now?"

Lawrence pulled his ear thoughtfully. "The inquest has been fixed for tomorrow. Castle will present his evidence to the Coroner; and the jury will bring in a verdict. It may be murder by person or persons unknown. Or—."

"Jack Austin may be accused." Penny's voice trembled.

"Yes," said Lawrence without evasion.

Penny looked up.

She spoke with decision. "It isn't too late. We may still be able to save him."

"How?"

Penny didn't reply directly. Instead, she murmured:

"I trusted you once. And you asked me to do what you said, without asking questions."

"Yes."

"I'm asking the same favour from you."

Lawrence sighed imperceptibly. "Very well."

"You have influence with the police." The girl's voice was steady and clear. "They won't interfere. I want you to call the company together."

"The—?"

"Yes." Penny's gaze was sombre. "I know every line, every move of Lesley's role. I shall play 'Marilyn'. And tonight at the Janus we will stage the third act of' THE FINAL TROPHY."

"But—."

"You promised not to ask questions," the girl said gently.

"Yes, but—."

"I can't explain now." The girl spoke urgently. "But this I can promise you. If you do as I say, I may be able to clear Jack's name and—and state your problem."

She met his gaze squarely.

Lawrence felt his pulse skip. Then he laughed and reached for the telephone. "You win, Penny. I'll call Steve now."

She smiled warmly.

Lawrence paused with the receiver in his hand. He grinned at her wryly.

An answering glimmer of mischief showed in her cerulean eyes. "What are you thinking?"

"That I'd like to kiss you," he replied.

"You can if you like," the girl said equably. "But it wouldn't mean anything. Would it?"

He laughed rather sadly. "To you? No. Ah, well."

He turned back to the telephone with a sigh.

# CHAPTER TWENTY SIX

The Chief Inspector and his young friend were making their way through the gathering dusk towards the Janus Theatre.

Castle was grumbling mechanically. "I can't see what you hope to prove by this reconstruction."

Lawrence said mildly:

"It's Penny's idea, not mine."

Castle leered incredulously. "Come off it," he growled. "You have plans of your own, I wager."

"No." returned Algy. "I'm waiting to hear from Penny. But I'm glad she wants us to re-enact the crime. It may give me a lead."

Castle continued an old argument. "You're creating a bogey-man. You can't accept the simple explanation. You'd rather go chasing a faceless phantom—a black magician who can change blanks into bullets without handling the gun."

He snorted contemptuously.

Lawrence replied unhappily:

"I can't accept your simple explanation because I don't believe Austin is guilty."

"He must be." Castle was belligerent. "This was no 'miracle' murder. It was the impulsive crime of a jealous and frustrated man."

"No, Steve. It wasn't." Lawrence objected quietly. "This was a coldly planned, premeditated crime. The Paddington Fair cards prove that."

Castle growled like a disappointed dog.

Lawrence continued:

"I don't know who murdered Lesley Christopher. But"—he tapped his head—"a picture is growing in my mind. It's shadowy and indistinct. But one day soon"—his voice dropped—"I shall recognize the features in the portrait."

Castle grunted. "Meanwhile...."

Algy's tone lightened. "Meanwhile," he said more cheerfully. "I can sketch the outlines."

Castle's gaze sharpened. "I'm listening."

"The person we want is a special kind of murderer—a man with a devious mind. He stays behind the scenes and lets others do the dirty work."

Castle agreed cautiously. "So?"

"He was also well acquainted with the circumstances of his victim's past. He knew all about Lesley's part in the robbery and her relations with Michael Trent—if the theft of the certificate is anything to go by. He knew about Richard Mervan—."

"Huh?"

"Someone sent her photograph to Mervan. He might never have found her otherwise."

"You think—." Castle's eyes gleamed. "By God!" he muttered. "There's only one man who meets those qualifications. And that's Michael Trent."

Lawrence tut-tutted reproachfully. "Don't go off half-cocked, Steve. You've forgotten—."

"Yes?"

"Lesley herself "

"Eh?" Castle's mouth opened in an O of astonishment.

Lawrence grinned. "This is only speculation. But it's a working hypothesis.

"Let's suppose that Lesley had some secret confidant—a man with whom she was having an affaire, perhaps. In an unguarded moment, she let slip something about her past.

"The man remembered. For some reason, he later decided that she had to die. But he didn't want to kill her himself—oh, dear me, no. He wanted a catspaw.

"He thought of Mervan and went to work. He had patience and cunning and a clever brain. He checked up on the robbery. He went through the files of old newspapers—."

"And found my name!" Castle spoke with unwilling interest.

"And your former rank of Detective Inspector," agreed Lawrence. "He traced Mervan after his release from prison. That wouldn't have been hard to do—he could have engaged a private detective.

"He was, of course, gambling on Mervan's having a lust for revenge. He took great care not to approach him in person—that would have given the game away—but he sent the photo to put Mervan on Lesley's track. When the man began to haunt her, our unknown friend must have hugged himself with glee.

"But Mervan was too slow. He seemed to have no homicidal intentions. Our devious friend was disappointed.

"So he looked around for another catspaw. Michael Trent was made to order; and when Lesley died by his hand, he would almost certainly be suspected of murder."

Castle looked uncomfortable.

Lawrence continued blandly:

"Our man had also discovered that Mervan had booked a box for Saturday's ☐atinee. So he fixed on that date for the murder."

"As another red herring?"

"Yes. Lesley would die and Mervan would be discovered in the audience. Any detective might be pardoned for assuming cause and effect."

Castle grunted. "If Mervan was identified."

"The Paddington Fair cards took care of that. One was despatched to Lesley to bolster up the revenge theory; another was sent to you—apparently from Richard Mervan."

"It wasn't signed," objected Castle.

"That would have been too obvious. Our unknown moves subtly. He sent it to Detective Inspector Castle and posted it near Mervan's lodgings."

"In the S.E.1 district. Jove, yes!" The Chief Inspector breathed hard.

Lawrence nodded. "He probably reckoned you would spot Mervan in the box. Then, after the shooting, you would be too busy investigating either Mervan or Trent or both to bother about anyone else back stage."

Castle mumbled disgustedly.

Lawrence paused, then continued:

"The strength of this plan lay in the safety it gave to the real culprit who was in the happy position of a puppet master, alone and unseen, who was manipulating the strings of his dolls. And even the dolls didn't know they were being used."

"Never mind the metaphor," jerked Castle.

Lawrence continued imperturbably:

"Mervan's belated attempt on Lesley's life complicated the situation without materially affecting it. Like us, our mystery man may not have known at first by whose hand the girl had actually died. But dead she was, and by his manipulations. So he cut the strings—."

"And left his dolls to our tender mercies." The Chief Inspector was sarcastic. "You argue persuasively. But I'm not convinced."

The two friends had reached the Janus Theatre. A constable stood guard outside. Returning the uniformed man's salute, Castle stumped past him into the foyer. Lawrence followed.

Castle said:

"You've made no attempt to explain Austin's part in the affair."

"That may yet explain itself."

"Perhaps." The Chief Inspector grunted disconsolately.

Lawrence smiled mysteriously.

Castle returned to the attack. "There's another flaw in your theory."

Lawrence paused by the box office. "Yes?"

"You say that the murderer knew Mervan was coming to the ☐atinee performance."

"Yes." Lawrence leaned against the ticket window. "Mervan hadn't advertised his plans. How could our man have discovered them?"

Lawrence smiled. "I put two questions to Mervan. Have you forgotten his reply to the second?"

Stephen Castle considered. "No. It was—."

"Chief Inspector!"

Castle turned to find Victor Friern behind him. The manager had just emerged from his office. His appearance was something of a shock: he seemed to be aging rapidly.

Castle eyed him sympathetically. "Hallo, sir. Is everything ready?"

"It is." Friern spoke with an effort. "The company has been assembled. But —-."

He swallowed.

Castle's brows became circumflex accents. "But what?"

The manager bowed his greying head. "This reconstruction—can it serve any real purpose? It seems so—so grisly."

Castle pursed his lips.

Lawrence interposed gently:

"We believe it will help us to find Lesley's murderer."

Friern's mouth tightened. "That's all that matters, of course." He squared his shoulders. "Very well, gentlemen. I shall do all I can to help you."

"Thank you." Castle's bluffly determined face betrayed none of his inward uneasiness "And now—."

Lawrence said smoothly:

"Steve, you were going to superintend operations back-stage. Mr. Friern and I"—he smiled at the manager politely—"will go into the auditorium."

The Chief Inspector grunted. "Right."

He waved a meaty hand. "I know where the pass-door is." He left them in the foyer and stamped up the stairs to the Dress Circle. Lawrence and Friern continued on their way through the entrance to the stalls.

The auditorium presented a somewhat ghostly and forlorn appearance. Dust sheets covered the seats like so many shrouds about corpses.

Lawrence shrugged away the macabre thought. He led the way down the centre aisle towards the stage.

The curtain was up. The set itself was illuminated by a single

404

working light—the pilot. Two people were already on stage. With the light behind them they looked shadowy and unreal from the auditorium. Then they moved back from the setting line and assumed character and substance.

Trudy Ann was saying in her clear, candid voice:

"But Douglas, I can't see what it's for."

Denzil put on a mocking smile. "Angel child, you should use your pretty head. The Dogberry and his assistant have gone back to the Bard for precedent."

The girl looked a question, charmingly. "?"

Denzil explained:

"Hamlet. Act Two, Scene Two." He quoted:

"I have heard, that guilty creatures sitting at a. play,

Have by the very cunning of the scene,

Been struck so to the soul, that presently

They have proclaimed their malefactions.

For murder, though it have no tongue—."

"Will speak," concluded Algy Lawrence, "with most miraculous organ." He added mildly: "I never quite knew what that meant."

Denzil turned. "It's Shakespeare," he said sarcastically. "It doesn't have to mean anything."

Lawrence and Friern had by this time reached the orchestra well. The manager frowned. "Don't be flippant, Denzil. This is serious business."

"I'm sorry," said Douglas without noticeable regret. "I was merely explaining to Trudy Ann the most probable reason for our presence here today."

Lawrence grinned. "I agree," he murmured, "that the play's the thing. But you shouldn't assume we're here to catch the conscience of a king."

Denzil smiled with cynical disbelief.

"I," said Trudy Ann ☐atinee☐ously, "I don't know what anybody is talking about."

Denzil blew her a kiss.

Victor Friern said abruptly:

"We're ready to begin. You have only to say the word."

Lawrence nodded. "Thank you. The Chief Inspector should be with us soon."

They waited in silence. Lawrence noted with inward amusement that Denzil's air of detachment was less convincing; he seemed to be finding it difficult to maintain his pose of the sardonic, amused observer. And even Trudy Ann appeared more subdued and less volatile than usual.

Presently the Chief Inspector emerged from the wings. Michael and Penny followed. Like Douglas and Trudy Ann, they were wearing full make-up and costume.

Algy paid Penny no special attention. The role she had played behind the scenes was to remain a secret until after the reconstruction.

Castle lumbered towards the footlights. "I've posted my men," he grunted. "Now"—he swept his hands under the tail of his raincoat—"it's up to you."

Lawrence nodded. "Right-ho, Steve." He raised his voice. "Mr. Austin! Miss Merritt! Will you come on stage, please?"

The stage manager and his assistant, pale-faced and ill at ease, entered from the prompt side. Clasped in Austin's hand was the Webley & Scott .32.

Trudy Ann drew in her breath with a little hiss. Her perfect teeth made momentarily bloodless indentations in her pouting lower lip.

Lawrence said quietly:

"The Chief Inspector has released the gun for this experiment. But there's no need to worry. All the tests have been completed. And now it's loaded with harmless blanks."

Austin agreed huskily. "That's so."

June Merritt did not speak. Her pudgy face was anxious.

Lawrence said: "Good! Now you probably know what's been happening back-stage. The company and staff have been assembled. Everyone is at his post: the door-keeper, the property master, the dressers—."

He gestured. "Everybody."

Castle nodded agreement. "They all have their instructions."

"Yes." Lawrence explained: "While you are re-enacting the third act of the play, your colleagues back-stage will be retracing their steps behind the scenes. We are putting the clock back to last Saturday afternoon."

Denzil laughed. "Everyone will co-operate—."

"We hope so."

"Save the murderer," finished Douglas wickedly.

Lawrence gave him a tranquil smile. "The Chief Inspector has stationed his men at strategic points back-stage. They will be watching. And waiting."

Friern moved sharply. Algy continued:

"Here, on stage, the situation is rather different. Mr. Trent and Mr. Denzil are playing their original roles. As for the ladies—."

He spread his hands. "Lesley Christopher is dead. Her part will be played by Miss Valentine, and Miss Valentine's"—he bowed slightly—"by Trudy Ann. Fortunately the role originally played by Trudy Ann isn't featured in this particular scene—."

"I think," said that young lady engagingly, "Mr. Windsor made a bad mistake there."

"Hush, child," grinned Denzil. He took her hand and patted it.

"So," finished Lawrence, "no problem arises. Well, now! We're ready to begin. Mr. Austin, you can place the gun on the 'lobby' wall—."

Footsteps sounded in the aisle behind them. Lawrence saw Trudy Ann's smile widen and turned to discover its cause.

Herbert Windsor was striding briskly towards them. The playwright was wearing suede shoes, corduroy trousers, and an enveloping duffle coat. A homburg hat was crushed over his cheerfully tousled hair.

He waved a salute. "Greetings, souls!"

"Hallo, pet." Called Trudy Ann in a proprietary tone.

Windsor regarded her with undisguised admiration. "Light of my life," he announced, "you are bewitching. In that get-up you could seduce an anchorite."

Trudy Ann was demure. "As that," she murmured, "you hardly qualify."

Douglas Denzil intervened. He said unpleasantly:

"These exchanges may be interesting. But they hardly concern the evening's business."

"True," admitted Windsor, with a maddening air of condescension. "But I don't yet know what the—ah—business is."   He appealed to the Chief Inspector. "I obeyed your summons. May I now know why you called me to the theatre?"

Castle jerked an open hand. "It's your show, Algy," he growled. "You explain."

Lawrence said smoothly:

"We are re-staging Act Three of THE FINAL TROPHY. It's just an experiment. But we hope it may help us solve the mystery of Lesley Christopher's death. So we've invited all interested parties. You, as the author—."

"I see." Windsor removed his hat and crushed it thoughtfully. "But…."

"Yes?"

"I've been following the case. And I thought you knew the identity of the man"—Windsor did not look at Austin—"who put the bullets into the gun."

The stage manager paled.

Lawrence replied:

"That's the crux of the problem. But perhaps we've been too preoccupied with the question of opportunity. What's that without motive?"

Windsor's gaze sharpened. "Go on."

Lawrence said dreamily:

"The man with the best opportunity had the weakest motive." He didn't miss the expression of relief which appeared on .Austin's face. He continued: "There were others who had a more direct interest in removing Lesley from the stage."

"You mean—."

"I mean," said Lawrence, "that we may have made a serious mistake in assuming that the murderer wanted Lesley to die!"

"What?" roared Castle.

Lawrence grinned apologetically. "It's a new conclusion, Steve. And one I might never have reached." He gave Penny a fleeting smile, acknowledging her help.

He explained:

"The murderer used Michael Trent as his catspaw. That gave him personal security. But it also made the crime itself a chancy business. The bullet Trent so unwittingly fired might not have hit a vital organ and Lesley might not have died."

Windsor said eagerly:

"But she was almost certain to be wounded."

"Yes. And even a minor wound would have secured her withdrawal from the cast."

Trent said angrily:

"Oh, my god."

He put his hand on Penny's arm and squeezed it protectively. She responded with a sad little secret smile.

Lawrence continued:

"That might have suited the unknown's book. He—or she—might not have cared whether Lesley lived or died so long as she was unable to play 'Marilyn'."

Douglas Denzil said quietly:

"Penny, my sweet. Your protector is turning against you."

Lawrence continued imperturbably:

"It's true that Miss Valentine was Lesley's understudy. And she would certainly be the next to play the leading role. But Penny's own part was a good one—and Lesley's removal would also effect a promotion for Miss Valentine's own deputy."

Denzil chuckled. "He means you, Trudy Ann."

"Why, Douglas. You pig," said Trudy Ann with more amusement than irritation. She turned her disarming gaze on Algy Lawrence. "It's true I wanted the second lead. But I wouldn't have killed either Lesley or Penny to get it."

"Why, thank you, dear," said Penny with the ghost of a laugh."

"I mean it," announced Trudy Ann.

"I'm sure you do." Lawrence smiled at her. "And you're not the only suspect. Lesley's death set off a kind of chain reaction which nearly resulted in the arrest of Michael Trent."

"Which," supplied Herbert Windsor with satanic relish, "would have secured his withdrawal from my play. H'm! You are Michael's understudy, aren't you, Douglas?'"

Denzil flushed angrily. "Look here—."

He broke off and steadied himself with a laugh. He said more coolly: "This is rather ridiculous. Follow the argument to its logical conclusion and you suspect my understudy—and he doesn't figure in the case at all."

Lawrence said amiably:

"I was merely suggesting a line of enquiry. But now we can abandon theory for experiment. Let's get to work."

His suggestion was adopted with a general air of relief. Castle disappeared into the wings. Victor Friern seated himself in the front row of the stalls. Windsor made to accompany him, but Lawrence caught his arm."

Algy said amicably:

"I have a role for you to play."

"Eh? I'm no actor."

"It doesn't matter. Come with me."

Lawrence lead Windsor out of the stalls into the corridor giving access to the stage box on the prompt side. "This is the box Richard Mervan occupied."

"Mervan? That's the fellow who took the boss shot at poor Lesley."

"Yes." Lawrence opened the door. "He missed her and hit the bear. You can see where."

Windsor went into the box and stared at the stage. "I can see something like an outsize toothpick sticking out of the animal's mouth."

Lawrence smiled. "We calculated the bullet's angle of flight and marked it with twine. But we had to remove it this evening to allow the actors free passage about the stage. So we fixed that rod instead, to remind us of the shot. That stick represents the exact path of the bullet as it entered the bear's head."

409

"Oh." Windsor was dubious. "What am I supposed to do about it?"

"Nothing." Lawrence was casual. "Mervan is in jail. You're his stand-in."

"Eh? D'you want me to take a pot-shot at Penny?"

"That won't be necessary." Algy's voice was dry. "Just sit there. And watch."

He closed the door behind him gently, leaving Windsor alone. He glanced along the corridor.

A policeman was standing with his back to the exit doors. Lawrence signalled silently. The uniformed man gave a nod of understanding and moved quietly towards him. Lawrence left him at a new post—facing the door of the box.

When Algy returned to the auditorium, he found the Chief Inspector in the seat which he had occupied at the fatal ☐atinee. Lawrence settled himself beside his friend. He murmured tritely:

"Here we are again."

Castle grunted. "I wish I knew what you had in mind."

"So do I."

Castle covered an exasperated squawk. He raised his voice. "Mr. Austin! We're ready."

The stage manager cracked his knuckles nervously. But he slid without difficulty into his customary role. Standing with his back to the footlights—the curtain had not been lowered—he looked round the set, making a final check. Then he went to his post in the prompt corner.

His voice boomed hollowly:

"Clear, please!"

Then—.

"Stand by!"

And finally—.

"Curtain up!"

The last performance began.

# CHAPTER TWENTY SEVEN

Lawrence stared moodily at the stage. He felt vaguely unhappy and a little scared. It was as if he had set into motion forces he would be unable to control—and yet.

Resolutely, he focused his attention on the play.

"We are putting the clock back to last Saturday afternoon." His own words recurred with frightening force: he could almost believe they were literally true.

Wearing an exact duplicate of the dead girl's costume, Penny Valentine had brought both 'Marilyn' and Lesley back to life. Every word, every gesture was Lesley's. Lawrence knew this was not unusual: an understudy is always expected to follow his or her principal. Nevertheless, the illusion was scarifying.

He glanced quickly to his right. Victor Friern was leaning forward in his seat. The manager's face was white, and the hand on his knee was clenched in a tight fist. His breathing was harsh and irregular.

The play progressed...

Trudy Ann made her exit on the O.P. side leaving Michael Trent alone on the stage.

Lawrence tensed. This was the climax.

The double doors opened. Penny came out of the "lobby" with the revolver in her hand.

Lawrence felt a constriction in his throat. He watched the players, hardly daring to breathe.

Michael and Penny made the most of their final duologue. Their acting was faultless.

"Marilyn" threatened "Regan" with the revolver. Then he grabbed her wrist and the struggle for the gun began. "Regan" wrenched it from her hand, then backed slowly away, covering her with the revolver.

"Now it's my turn, baby."

Penny whimpered.

She backed away. The huge stuffed bear seemed ready to seize her.

Once again, Lawrence watched with fascinated revulsion as Trent thumbed down the hammer of the Webley & Scott. The gun in his hand steadied.

Penny's heels were touching the dais and her body was nearly within the animal's grasp. She was watching the gun in Michael's hand.

411

She whispered. "No.... "

Lawrence followed her gaze. Trent was smiling tightly. His finger was about to squeeze the trigger...

Somebody moved in the stage box behind him. Herbert Windsor rested his clasped hands on the ledge. His eyes reflected greenly, like a cat's.

Lawrence's glance went back to the girl. The rod in the bear's mouth was brushing lightly over the top of Penny's head and pointing like an accusing finger at the figure of the playwright....

The clasped hands parted. Something metallic glinted bluely against Windsor's palm....

Lawrence half-rose in his seat. His mouth shaped a call but the sound was lost in the sudden, shocking blast from Trent's revolver.

Penny's body jerked. She swayed back then forward. She fell to the floor.

Slowly, the curtain descended...

"Algy!"

The Chief Inspector's voice was alarmed.

There had been no black-out, and in the glow from the foot-lights he saw that his young friend had left his seat and was running towards the box on the prompt side.

Lawrence was moving blindly, without conscious thought. Fear had gripped him.

He lurched past Victor Friern and scrambled over the low partition into the orchestra well. A long stride brought him to the box. He put his hands on the ledge and pulled himself over. He crashed against a chair and half- fell to the floor.

Windsor had bounded up in alarm. "What the—."

In the face of Lawrence's head-long arrival, he pressed himself back against the wall. The metallic object dropped from his hand on to the carpet.

Lawrence grabbed for the fallen prize. It was shaped like a miniature gun....

Algy stood erect, his chest heaving painfully.

A voice sounded behind him. "Mr. Lawrence! What—."

Algy answered tiredly:

"All right, Mr. Friern. It's over now."

The manager stared into the box. His gaze was on Lawrence's fist. "Wh—what's that in your hand?"

Algy replied:

"It looks like a gun."

Windsor had recovered his composure. Amused understanding appeared in his eyes. He drawled:

"It's shaped like a pistol. But its contents are hardly lethal. Ah—allow me."

He took the gun out of Lawrence's hand and squeezed the butt... A cigarette popped out of the muzzle.

Algy stared at it stupidly.

Windsor smiled. "I have a fondness for gadgets."

Lawrence found his voice. "And for melodrama."

The playwright grinned. "It was merely playing my part as Mervan's deputy. This cigarette case was a useful prop." The mockery deepened. "However, I didn't expect you to enter into the spirit of your own role quite so thoroughly. Er—you were acting? You didn't really believe...."

He looked at the "gun" and laughed.

Lawrence flushed.

He said abruptly:

"It's finished."

A cool voice called his name. He turned.

The curtain had been raised again. Penny Valentine, alive and unhurt, was smiling contentedly. She had taken the Webley & Scott from Trent's hand; crossing the setting line, she proffered the gun. "Here, Algy. You'll want this."

Then in an undertone, she added swiftly:

"Come to my dressing-room. Bring the Chief Inspector."

Lawrence looked into her luminous eyes and realised that the experiment had been a success.

When they reached the dressing-room they found the girl in her dressing-gown. She had removed most of her make-up.

Her skin was almost translucent. She was glowing with an inner excitement; and she was very beautiful.

Lawrence regarded her gravely. She smiled happily in return. "Come in, please."

Maggie Boyd was attending her. Chief Inspector Castle indicated the dresser with a sidewise glance.

Penny took a small towel from the plump woman's hand and said politely:

"Thank you, Maggie. Be a dear and leave us now."

Maggie eyed the two men suspiciously and sniffed. "Very well, m' dear. Call me if you want me."

She left the room with a twitch of her beefy shoulders. As the door

413

closed, Lawrence spoke with unusual formality. "Your portrayal of 'Marilyn' was superb."

"Thank you," smiled Penny. "But you didn't come here to discuss my acting ability."

"You have something to tell us?" grunted Castle hopefully.

"I think so." Penny dropped the towel on the dressing-table and studied herself in the mirror. "But first you must answer some questions. I—."

Someone tapped on the door. It opened to disclose Michael Trent.

Penny turned and smiled. "Come in, Michael. This concerns you, too."

Lawrence and Castle exchanged glances. The Chief Inspector's hand opened in a tiny gesture of assent.

Trent crossed the room and squeezed Penny's shoulders. "Darling, you were wonderful."

She patted his fingers and laughed. "Sit down, my love. This is serious business." She sobered. "It may mean Jack's salvation."

The three men studied her with keener interest. Lawrence was the spokesman. "Go on."

Penny said slowly:

"You saw the scene as Michael and Lesley played it. And you saw how we played it today. Was the interpretation identical?"

Lawrence nodded agreement. "Every move, every action was the same."

"Good." Penny seemed pleased. "Now think of the business with the gun. I had taken it from the lobby 'wall'—."

Lawrence said quietly:

"You threatened Michael. He grabbed your wrist and wrenched the revolver from your hand. He backed away, thumbed down the hammer, and fired."

"Just as he did last Saturday?"

"Exactly."

Penny drew a deep breath. Her voice shifted tone. "Think carefully now. Think of the day Lesley died. Would you swear—."

She faltered.

Lawrence pressed her. "Yes?"

She finished quickly:

"That the gun he fired was the one he took from Lesley's hand?"

"What!"

"In plain terms," said the girl, "could he have pocketed the gun he took from Lesley and fired instead another loaded with live ammunition?"

414

"Penny!" Michael's voice was shocked and reproachful.

"Trust me, Michael. Please... Well, Algy? What's your answer?"

Lawrence grinned broadly. He passed the question to Castle. "You tell her, Steve."

The Chief Inspector considered the suggestion wistfully. Then he shook his head and grumped.

"I wish I could say yes! But I can't."

"I agree," said. Lawrence quietly. "Like the rest of the audience, I was watching the struggle closely. And now—I have a clear mental picture of it. Michael took the gun from Lesley's hand and held it in full view of the audience till the moment he fired it. He couldn't have tampered with the gun in any way. Nor could he have switched revolvers."

Castle nodded. "Anyway," he growled, "such a theory would make nonsense of the ballistics report."

Penny closed her eyes. She said gratefully:

"I knew it. But I had to hear you say so."

Lawrence leaned forward. "And now?"

"And now," said Penny tranquilly, "I have something to tell you."

She turned to the Chief Inspector. "Last Saturday I was playing the second lead. Just before Lesley died. I made an exit."

Castle inclined his head. "I remember. You went off, leaving Trent alone on the stage. Miss Christopher made her entrance from the 'lobby' and they played the final scene."

"That's right." Penny was speaking coolly and confidently. "I made my exit on the O.P. side. That meant that to get back to my dressing-room I had to cross the stage behind the set to reach the entrance to the passage."

"Yes?"

"As I passed the flats which make up the lobby 'wall' I heard an odd sound. I don't want to be melodramatic, but"—Penny hesitated briefly—"it seemed to be a sob of fear."

The girl paused.

She continued softly:

"I knew that Lesley would be there, waiting for her cue. I was curious. I looked round the flats into the lobby.

"Lesley was standing by the double doors. She was holding the Webley & Scott in her hand. She seemed over-wrought."

"As I watched, she broke open the revolver and extracted the blanks. She examined them quickly, then—."

Castle snapped:

"And then?"

415

"She replaced them in the gun."

"But—."

Penny was firm. "She seemed strangely relieved. I wondered what was in her mind. I might have spoken to her, but before I could do so, she opened the doors and made her last entrance—with the gun she had just examined."

Silence. Then—.

"Good God!" roared the Chief Inspector. "Do you realise what that means?"

Lawrence gave a short, harsh laugh.

"Of course she does," he answered wryly. "It means we must solve the mystery of yet another crime which couldn't possibly have been committed."

# CHAPTER TWENTY EIGHT

"This case," said the Chief Inspector gloomily, "will probably drive me insane."

Lawrence chuckled.

The two men were alone in the greenroom. They were waiting for Penny to finish changing.

Castle felt spiritually battered. He had been unable to find any flaws in the girl's story and, impossible though it seemed, he had had to accept her evidence as the truth.

Lawrence said:

"You may not like it, Steve. But Penny's story rings true."

Castle nodded glumly.

His friend continued:

"Emotionally, Lesley Christopher was near collapse. She had been living on her nerves for weeks. Her role was emotionally exhausting; she was jealous of Penny's talents; she had quarrelled with Austin; and her past was threatening her once more.

"Mervan's presence in the audience had given her a nasty shock; and the discovery of Michael's infidelity had come as the final blow. She felt wretched and alone, plagued by jealousy and fear. She was waiting in the 'lobby' for her cue with the revolver in her hand. And then—."

"And then," said the Chief Inspector, "she remembered what Denzil had told her."

"Douglas?"

"Yes." Castle thumbed his jowl. He quoted slowly: "'Lesley passed me on her way to the stage. I made some casual remark; she mumbled a reply and went into the "lobby" to wait for her cue.'" He squinted thoughtfully. "That casual remark was rather important."

"Uh huh?"

"Yes. I've questioned Denzil. He can't recall his exact words but he admits it was a—a jocular warning about the gun."

"Of course!" Lawrence ran his hands over his smooth blond hair. "He had just seen Austin handling the gun. A furtive suspicion was in his mind. It wasn't his way to take direct action. But he soothed his conscience—."

"If he has one," snarled Castle.

"By dropping a hint to Lesley," finished Algy with a smile. "It fits, Steve! Lesley had quarrelled with Austin—and now her attention had been drawn to the gun he had loaded. She broke open the revolver and examined the cartridges.    She discovered to her relief that they were harmless blanks and put them back into the cylinder. And then—."

"She died," said Castle grimly. "By black magic."

"It's a dark miracle," agreed Lawrence. His voice was hard. "Lesley knew the gun was harmless. She brought it on stage herself. And from that moment it was never out of the audience's sight. Yet when Trent wrenched it out of her hand and fired it—."

"The blanks had been replaced by bullets," mumbled Castle. "And the harmless load was suddenly lethal."

He finished in an awed whisper:

"It's impossible."

"But," said Lawrence, "it happened."


"I'm ready now." Penny Valentine was standing by the open door.

Michael Trent was with her. He clasped the girl's arm protectively, then frowned at the Chief Inspector. "Where are you taking her?"

"To the Yard," replied Castle forbiddingly. "I have to present this blasted case to the Coroner tomorrow and there's a lot of paper work to be done. We must put Miss Valentine's statement into proper form."

"But—. "

"Don't fuss, darling." Penny smiled affectionately. "Go home now. I'll 'phone you later."

"I'll be waiting." Michael's voice was soft.

They kissed.

Lawrence looked away.

Castle grunted. He prepared to leave. "Coming, Algy?"

Lawrence shook his head. "The problem has been stated.    Now I must find the solution.    That requires thought—and tobacco." He grinned faintly. "I might as well stay here."

"Call me," growled his friend, "if you have any useful ideas."

There wasn't much hope in Castle's command.    He stumped out of the greenroom, ushering Trent away.

Lawrence called Penny's name. She turned back with a smile. "Yes, Algy?"

"I want to ask you a question."

"Yes." She closed the door.

Lawrence asked:

"Why did you tell us about Lesley and the gun?"

418

"To save Jack." Penny was tranquil.

"You've cleared Austin," agreed Lawrence. "His story has been proved to be true. But why didn't you speak before?"

Penny's eyes glimmered. "Don't you know?"

"Tell me, please." Lawrence regarded her with peculiar intentness.

She sighed. "I had seen Lesley examining the gun. I knew it must have been loaded with blanks. And Michael was the only other person to handle the revolver before it was fired."

Lawrence nodded gently. The implication was clear.

Penny clenched her hands. "I didn't doubt Michael myself. You understand? I knew he was innocent.   But I knew the police would be bound to suspect him. They might suggest he had palmed a bullet which he slipped into the breech after taking the gun from Lesley—."

Lawrence laughed. "That's quite impossible. The audience was watching his every move. Even a skilled illusionist couldn't have pulled off a trick like that."

Penny smiled faintly. "I thought that too. But I could guess what the police would think next."

"They would say that Michael had switched revolvers."

"Yes. But he would have to have done it on stage. And I knew the scene well—he would have had no opportunity. But the police—would they be satisfied? Or would they perhaps…."

She bit her lip.

Lawrence said without reproach:

"You didn't trust them. You thought they might force an arrest."

Penny nodded. "I suppose there was some such fear in my mind. I thought it best to keep silent. But then—."

"Austin fell under suspicion."

"Yes. And only my evidence could clear him. But what would happen to Michael? When the Chief Inspector heard my story, he would be bound to suspect him again."

Her mouth trembled. "I could see only one way out. I would have to force the police to admit that Michael could not have tampered with the gun. Then—and only then—would I tell them what I knew."

Lawrence drew a long breath. "I see... You left them no escape. This was, as you claimed, an impossible crime. And you made them admit it."

She nodded. "I set the stage. I recreated the past—."

"And stated the problem." Lawrence grinned ruefully. "But you didn't provide the solution."

She laughed gently. "I leave that to you."

She turned to go.

Lawrence straightened. There was a query in his lazy eyes.

"Penny—."

"Yes?"

"One thing puzzles me." He ran his hands over his smooth blond hair. "You knew Austin was innocent—."

"I did."

"But you wouldn't speak until Michael was in the clear. Now supposing—just supposing—your plan hadn't worked... Suppose Castle had answered: 'Yes, Trent could have tampered with that revolver.'"

Penny's eyes clouded.

Lawrence asked softly:

"Would you have told us about Lesley then?"

"No."

Lawrence pressed her hard. "But Austin was an innocent man. Only your evidence could save him from arrest."

Penny hesitated. Then she said clearly:

"You could have taken him to the scaffold. I would still have been silent."

Lawrence looked blank. "You would have done even that for love of Michael?"

She recognized the question as a protest.

She answered defiantly:

"All that. And more."

"Oh."

Lawrence seemed bewildered.

Penny was suddenly a stranger.

Then she smiled. Her cool fingers brushed over his cheek in a fleeting caress.

She whispered:

"Poor Algy! You're awfully clever. But you don't know much about women, do you?"

With a laugh, she was gone.

The reader is respectfully requested to
PAUSE FOR REFLECTION---
and play the great game of
WHODUNIT? and HOW?

# PART THREE
# THE CURTAIN FALLS

# CHAPTER TWENTY NINE

The theatre was almost deserted.

Alone in the auditorium, a man was sprawling limply in a gangway seat in the stalls. He seemed to be sleeping; but his eyes were open. They were vacant and lifeless, serving only as mirrors reflecting the light from the stage.

At last, the man stirred. He fumbled with a silver case and slipped a cigarette between tired lips. Flame spurted; he inhaled deeply. Blue smoke drifted sluggishly in the cloud above his head.

Then, with a sigh, he crushed the cigarette into the ash-tray fixed to the back of the seat before him. The tray was already full: stubs had fallen to the floor.

Lawrence licked parched lips.

He asked aloud:

"What shall I do?"

He felt sick and lonely.

And afraid...

He knew the truth at last.

"Hallo, Algy."

He turned his head slowly.

"You," he said hoarsely.

Penny Valentine nodded. "Yes."

The soft carpet had muffled the girl's footfalls; he had had no warning of her approach.

He asked:

"How did you get in?"

She shrugged the question aside. "It doesn't matter." Her face was taut; her eyes were fever-bright.

She gazed around. Interpreting her thoughts, Lawrence said gently:

"We're quite alone."

"I'm glad."

She seated herself in the row behind him.

She said flatly:

"You've solved the problem."

He stared moodily at the stage. "I think so."

Her mouth slackened. Her fingers pressed hard on the handbag in her lap.

Then, as he turned, she composed her face and spoke calmly:

"I've solved it, too."

Something stirred behind his eyes. "You have?"

"Yes."

Lawrence twisted in his seat. "Tell me."

Penny said painfully:

"There's only one way to explain the crime—."

"This 'miracle' murder." Algy's voice was hard.

Penny seemed to gather her strength.

She said coldly:

"It wasn't murder."

Lawrence said nothing, but his gaze was watchful.

Penny continued:

"You didn't know Lesley. I did. She may have thought she loved Michael. But it wasn't really love—it was a selfish passion which could turn in an instant to hate."

"Perhaps."

Penny said urgently:

"Lesley had been driven to the point of collapse—by herself and by others. This crazy man Mervan was a constant threat to her peace of mind. And she was jealous of me as a woman and as an actress. And then—."

She faltered.

Lawrence said gently:

"She found out about you and Michael."

Penny nodded. "It must have been the final blow. She knew she had lost everything. She had nothing to live for."

"You mean—?"

"She decided to die." Penny was breathing quickly. "Don't you see? It's the only explanation. She put the bullets into the gun herself."

Lawrence admitted:

"She may have had a motive for suicide. But why should she choose such a crazy method?"

"She was jealous and vindictive." Penny's colour was high and her voice was excited. "She wasn't satisfied with suicide alone. She meant to take Michael with her."

"Michael?"

"Of course! It would be the perfect revenge. She meant to die by his hand, to brand him a murderer. I was to lose him too. She could hit at us both from beyond the grave." She paused triumphantly.

426

Lawrence considered. "The mystery of Lesley's death isn't the only problem we have to solve. You haven't explained the attack upon Bailey."

Penny clenched her fists. "That had nothing to do with the shooting. It was Douglas—."

"You're accusing Denzil?" Lawrence sounded surprised.

"Yes! Nobody else wanted the marriage certificate. Only Douglas could use it."

"To blackmail you... Hmmm." Lawrence mused. "That's reasonable. But there are flaws in the suicide theory."

Penny's knuckles were white. "No."

Lawrence contradicted her gently:

"Yes. Remember your statement. You watched Lesley break open the gun, extract the blanks, examine and replace them in the cylinder."

The girl responded to the challenge. "I made a mistake. I described what I thought I saw. But now I realise it must have been bullets she was putting into the gun."

Lawrence asked mildly:

"She made her entrance immediately afterwards. How did she dispose of the blanks? You were watching her. How could she hide them in the fire bucket?"

Penny bit her lip. "There must have been a way. I—."

"No, Penny." Lawrence gave her no quarter. "The theory's a fantasy. The suicide could not have been premeditated—yet the means were magically at hand. Where could Lesley find live ammunition? Did she conjure the bullets out of thin air?"

"I—I—."

The girl faltered miserably.

Lawrence watched her gravely. His eyes were sombre.

Penny's lips were trembling.

She spoke in a whisper. "Very well. The theory is a fantasy—a last desperate attempt to explain the impossible. Why can't you accept it? It will satisfy the police. Isn't that enough?"

"No."

"What, then?" The question was a cry of pain. "If you reject this--- what remains?"

Lawrence said sadly:

"The truth."


Silence settled like dust.

Penny spoke at last. She said hopelessly:

"You know it all."

"Yes."

The word was a knife-thrust. Penny closed her eyes in a spasm of pain. Open again, they were misted with tears.

She whispered:

"It isn't too late. Forget it all."

"I can't."

She was beautiful in her distress. His heart swelled with pain.

She said desperately:

"For pity's sake don't tell them. If you have any regard for me at all—."

"Oh, my God." He could no longer bear to watch her. He turned abruptly, gazing once more at the stage. "Can't you see this is as difficult for me as it is for you? Do you think I want to hurt you?"

"Then why—."

"Listen, Penny." His voice was muffled. "I warned you once. I can't be stopped; I go on to the end. I stand for the truth—because truth can't be denied."

"Algy—."

"It's no use, Penny. It's too late to protest. I wish I'd never solved this case. And I pity you." His shoulders slumped. "Believe me. But I won't cover up a murder. For you—for anybody."

A solitary tear streaked Penny's cheek.

Her lips moved silently.

Then her hands seemed to move of their own accord. She opened her bag and groped within...

Her voice was a breath. "You leave me no choice."

The muzzle of the gun touched Lawrence's neck.

The girl said dully:

"I have to kill you now... "

There was sourness in his mouth. It might have been the taste of fear. But his voice was steady.

"Shoot if you must. You will silence me. But destroy yourself."

He heard her sob. "The secret must be kept."

He said quietly:

"Castle will know why I died."

Her voice was tremulous. "You've told him nothing yet."

"That's true." His head was aching.

He continued tonelessly:

"But he won't need me now. You've already given him the key to the problem. He has only to turn it. As I did."

Penny spoke with dreadful decision. "I may not escape. That's the chance I have to take... Good-bye, Algy."

She whispered:

"Forgive me... "

Lawrence closed his eyes.

This is it, he thought. This is how it ends. The cold kiss of metal; a blasting roar; a moment's unimaginable pain. And then—.

"Penny! Stop!"

"Michael—keep away!" Her cry spiralled into a scream.

Lawrence could no longer feel the touch of the muzzle against his neck. He threw himself sideways out of the seat.

No shot came.

There were the sounds of a scuffle, abruptly terminated. The crack of a fist against bone...

The gun thudded to the floor.

Lawrence picked himself up, retrieving the revolver. "A .32," he murmured. "Of course."

His gaze focused upon the initials...

Then, for the first time, he looked at the man who had intervened.

Michael Trent was gazing with haggard eyes at the girl he loved. Penny lay slumped in the seat. Despair lingered on her unconscious face.

A bruise was forming on her jaw.

Trent said dully:

"I had to hit her."

Lawrence passed a weary hand over his mouth. "You saved my life," he muttered.

Trent laughed harshly.

"And what," he demanded, "will be my reward?"

Lawrence shivered.

"The hangman's rope," he answered sadly.

# CHAPTER THIRTY

It ended, as it began, in Richard Mervan's cell.

Algy Lawrence said sombrely:

"You, if anyone, have the right to know the whole truth of the matter."

Mervan nodded slowly.

The flesh of his face seemed to have shrivelled away, leaving only the skin stretched over his skull; but his eyes were alive and strangely hungry.

He muttered:

"Tell me."

Lawrence stared at the floor. "You don't have to speak. I want you to listen. That's all."

Mervan nodded again. "I understand."

There was a pause.

Then Lawrence spoke in a muted voice:

"Michael Trent was a man of violence. Bailey was one of his victims. You were another."

Mervan clenched his hands.

Lawrence said:

"Trent was the thug who first tried to rob you in the street."

Mervan's voice was husky. "Trent was the man who attacked me?"

"Yes. It was a foolish and clumsy crime which failed as it deserved. But Lesley turned it to her advantage. You expected a reward for saving the bank's money. When you didn't get it, she played upon your feeling of resentment---. "

Mervan said painfully:

"I don't want to talk about that."

"Very well." Lawrence squeezed his palms together. "You know how Lesley trapped you. Trent's plan had ended in failure. But Lesley's schemes were subtler—and they succeeded. Trent was content to follow her orders."

Mervan's knuckles were white. "I'm thinking about that fight in the street. I saw the robber's face. Why didn't I recognize Trent when I saw him again?"

Lawrence's voice was toneless. "Trent was an actor. He could have been wearing a disguise."

"Yes." Mervan relaxed. "He could have powdered grey into his hair, grown stubble on his chin—."

He broke off. He said:

"This may be true. But how do you know what happened?"

Lawrence replied:

"Trent told me many things."

He paused, recalling that last sombre talk in the darkened theatre. Trent had thrown away his last chance of escape. He had saved Penny from becoming a murderess. It would cost him his life.

Lawrence said:

"He no longer had any reason to remain silent."

Mervan's eyes were glassy. "But you already knew—Trent had murdered his wife?"

"I knew how the crime had been committed. Trent didn't have to tell me anything about the murder."

Lawrence stared at the floor.

His voice was low. "I had already realised my mistake. I had been looking at the case through a distorting lens. Trent appeared to be the killer's catspaw: an innocent man who had been tricked into slaying his wife. But Penny knocked away the lens—and then the picture was very different."

He looked up.

He said:

"Michael Trent was the murderer's accomplice. And he will hang. But he didn't kill Lesley Christopher."

Something rattled in Mervan's throat.

Lawrence studied him curiously.

He said distinctly:

"You shot her, Mervan... "

The walls of the cell enclosed the silence.    It was thick, oppressive and suffocating...

Mervan spoke at last.

He said tightly:

"That's ridiculous."

Lawrence shook his head. "I wish it were." His face was shadowed. "Castle tried to save you years ago. But you wouldn't let him. And now you've destroyed yourself."

Mervan's jaw-line hardened. "Go on."

Lawrence looked away. "You loved Lesley once. But she cheated and betrayed you. Then there was no longer love—only hate. You wanted your revenge."

Mervan said thickly:

"I needed it as other men need air to breathe."

Lawrence sighed. "You served your sentence, treasuring your hatred. Lesley was going to die by your hand. But you meant to cheat the hangman—that was the essence of your plans... You waited. You were released. You began the search for Lesley. And you found her at the Janus."

Mervan began:

"Someone sent me a magazine containing her photograph—."

Lawrence shook his head. "That isn't true. You lied to set us on a false trail... No one helped you to find Lesley. You traced her yourself. And with her you found—another."

Lawrence paused, then continued:

"You recognized Michael Trent. You identified him as the man who had attacked you in the street. You knew him, too, as Lesley's accomplice. You must have caught a glimpse of him before he knocked you out in her flat...

"You knew him. But you didn't hate him as you hated the girl. You probably thought of him as a dupe of Lesley's like yourself. So you decided not to kill him. But you meant to make use of him."

Lawrence smiled sadly. "You contacted Trent secretly. You told him what you knew about his part in the bank robbery. You threatened to inform the police, unless—."

"Unless?" repeated Mervan.

"Unless," finished Lawrence, "he agreed to help you murder his wife."

Lawrence went on: .

"Trent agreed. He was by no means an unwilling accessory. He loved Penny and he wanted to marry her. But he dared not break with Lesley. In a jealous rage, she might have lost all sense of caution. She could have gone to the police and ruined them both.

"Trent had become a success. He was prepared to do anything to safeguard his position in the theatre and to escape from the past. He wanted Penny and a new, clean life. You showed him the way."

Lawrence hunched his shoulders. "The basic plan was yours; Trent contributed his inside knowledge of the theatre and its staff. You plotted the crime together. It wasn't meant to be a 'miracle' murder—you just wanted unbreakable alibis. But—."

He gestured.

He continued:

"We now know that Trent had access to the Janus at any time. He had made a friend of Purrett, the night watchman; and he had struck a duplicate key to an outside door. He could enter the theatre whenever he wished, with or without Purrett's knowledge.

"Meanwhile, you were using the underworld contacts you had made in prison. You had already obtained a .25 self loading pistol. Then you located a .32 Webley & Scott revolver.

"Trent showed you the revolver which was used in the play. You examined it carefully, then set about turning your own .32 into an exact duplicate.

"You filed off the registration number, you had the initial 'H.W.' engraved above the butt, and you copied from the original that long jagged scratch on the barrel. At last you were satisfied. The forgery would pass muster. Only the rifling inside the barrel could betray the duplicate."

Lawrence rubbed his cheek. "The day of the murder came at last. Lesley was to die in the afternoon. But much work had to be done first, in the early hours of the morning.

"Trent had approached Purrett the previous evening. He had handed him a bottle of beer—a casual gift which old Tom accepted unsuspiciously. He counted himself a friend, he was used to such small favours.

"Saturday morning. The night watchman made his rounds at one o'clock. Then, as always, he retired to his cubby-hole for a drink. The beer had been drugged—and he fell asleep."

Mervan's eyes were wary.

Lawrence continued:

"You went with Trent to the theatre. Michael crept into Purrett's room and found him dead to the world. If there was any of the drugged beer left, Trent must have emptied it away. He wouldn't want it to be discovered later. But there was no real danger. Old Tom might realise that the beer had made him unusually sleepy; but he wouldn't realise that he had been doped...

"Trent reported that all was well. The coast was clear, you set to work.

"You were probably wearing rubber gloves. The .32 revolver was in its usual place on the lobby 'wall'. Taking care not to obscure any existing fingerprints, you emptied the cylinder and transferred the load—five unused and one exploded blank cartridge—to the duplicate revolver you had prepared. It was time to make the substitution. You placed the second Webley & Scott on the pegs fixed to the flat. The original gun was not going to be used in the play that afternoon—you needed it for deadlier work."

Lawrence paused, then said quietly:

"You had your .25 Colt. You went into the box you had booked for the ☐atinee. You levelled the .25 at the stuffed bear and put a bullet into the animal's mouth."

In the silence that followed, Lawrence lowered his head. He said wearily:

"You didn't need a silencer. The building was deserted. And the night watchman was insensible. You were safe enough.

"But it was tricky work. You needed all your skill as a marksman. You had to place the shot exactly. Its presence must not be detected until after the murder. The bullet hole had to be invisible: safe from passing eyes."

"An error now would force you to abandon the plan. But—." Lawrence opened his hand, then closed it. "You made no error. Lesley's fate had been decided. You could say she died then—many hours before you murdered her."

He paused, then continued:

"The night's work was quickly finished... You removed all traces of your presence.

"The .25 was a self-loading pistol—a so-called automatic. You had fired one shot and a cartridge case had been ejected. You picked up the empty shell and pocketed it. You had a final conference with Trent, then you left the theatre. You took the two guns with you—your .25 and the original .32.

"The substitute Webley had been left in its place on stage. Wix, Austin, Lesley herself—they all handled the duplicate without suspicion. It seemed to be the same revolver they had used every day since the play began.

"But, of course, the original gun was now in your possession. And when you brought it back to the theatre, there were six live bullets in the cylinder."

Lawrence shaded his eyes.

He said bitterly:

"You needed a stooge. You picked on Stephen Castle. Trent had already obtained two tickets from an agency: you sent them to Scotland Yard. You baited the hook with an enigmatic message.

"Who thought of Paddington Fair? Trent, I fancy. He had been browsing through an old volume in the greenroom and he had chanced upon a description of the execution of the stage manager's namesake. It was a pleasing coincidence which might serve as a red herring.

"And the messages themselves were apt enough. Lesley was to he executed in public... You had posted the cards on Friday night. One was addressed to Castle. The other went to Lesley."

Lawrence sighed. "The stage was set. Trent prepared his alibi. He stayed clear of the theatre, then made a belated arrival on Saturday afternoon. He was feigning drunkenness. He meant to attract attention and keep it focused upon his movements.

"The plan worked well. Ben Cotall, his dresser, became a second shadow. And everyone else was watching Trent closely. He would be able to account for every second of the time he spent in the theatre. And the police would have to admit that he could not possibly have tampered with the revolver."

Mervan smiled emptily.

Lawrence's face hardened. "You were ready for the kill. You arrived at the theatre with your two guns and the empty cartridge case."

"You dropped the spent shell on the floor of the box. You took the .25 pistol out of your pocket and placed it on the chair beside you.

"The curtain rose on Act Three. You withdrew the .32 revolver from another pocket. You thumbed down the hammer. And waited."

Mervan's eyes gleamed savagely. His fingers crooked into talons.

Lawrence looked away. He said:

"Trent fired his Webley & Scott—the duplicate gun which you had so carefully prepared. It contained harmless blanks. But at the same moment, you fired the original revolver—and sent a .32 bullet crashing through Lesley's heart."

A sick cry squirmed in Mervan's throat.

Then he said hoarsely:

"Go on. Damn you! Go on."

Lawrence was sombre. "The scene ended with a black-out. As the curtain fell, you tossed the revolver on to the stage. The cylinder had not rotated; the gun wasn't cocked. There was only an exploded cartridge case in the chamber under the hammer, so there was no danger of an accidental shot.

"As you threw the gun, you laughed crazily. You meant to cover the sound of the revolver's fall. And you wanted to attract attention to yourself: you meant to be caught. You hoped the Chief Inspector would arrest you.

"You snatched up the .25 pistol and turned to the door of the box. You weren't trying to escape. You were waiting for Castle or for some other foolhardy member of the audience to make a bid to capture you." Lawrence grinned wryly. "I came for you myself. You fired your .25. You weren't trying to injure me: you intended the shot to go wide."

436

Mervan muttered:

"Then why did I fire?"

Lawrence smiled tightly. "The weapon was cold. A routine test would have shown that it had not been used that afternoon. But you shot again—and then there was nothing to prove that the first bullet had in fact been fired into the bear's head in the early hours of the morning."

Mervan bit his lip.

Lawrence continued greyly:

"Meanwhile, Trent was playing his part well. He had fired a blank cartridge from the substitute revolver. That gun had to be hidden at once. As soon as the lights went out, he jammed the Webley into his pocket. You tossed the murder weapon on to the stage at his feet. He bent to retrieve it.

"That must have been a nasty moment. It was completely dark: he could see nothing. I can imagine him groping about in the blackness, fighting a rising panic. Then he put his hand on the revolver and clutched it by the butt, calling for the lights... "

Lawrence added reflectively:

"The S.M. might have put up the lights before Trent found the gun. But Michael could have claimed to have dropped it in a moment of fright...

"His frantic scramble across the stage towards Lesley's body was probably a cover-up for another task. A tell-tale piece of wadding had been blown out of the blank he had fired—it had to be found and hidden. It went into his pocket with the duplicate gun.

"The original Webley remained in his hand. You had handled the gun with care. It still retained some of Lesley's prints. You had been wearing gloves which left only unidentifiable smudges. Trent covered those with his own prints, then passed the gun to Austin. There was nothing to show that it had ever been in your possession.

"Sooner or later, the revolver would be identified as the murder weapon. Meanwhile, Trent could use the delay to advantage.

"He had to dispose of the duplicate .32. No one must know what was in his pocket. That's why he drove his dresser away with a curse. And that's why he locked himself in his dressing-room and pretended to be sick.

"He found a temporary hiding-place for the gun in his dressing-room. It was safe enough. But he had to prevent an exhaustive search.

"That's why six blank cartridges were planted in the fire bucket. Trent was perhaps over-cautious, but he reasoned like this: the police will think that the blanks were removed from the Webley to make room for the bullets. Therefore they will search for the blanks in the hope of finding them in the murderer's possession.

"And a search, if prolonged, might uncover the hidden gun. So the missing blanks had to be easy to find.

"He planted six in the fire bucket. He need not have taken them out of the revolver. He could have taken them from the property room long before planting them that morning.

"But he still had to dispose of the gun. He dared not smuggle it out under the noses of the police. He decided to return to the theatre during the following night.

"It seemed the safest course. But he had bad luck. He recovered the gun from his dressing-room, but he was interrupted by the man we had left on guard. He clubbed Bailey with the revolver to save himself from identification. But he knew that danger still threatened.

"The police would assume that the murderer had returned to the theatre. They would probe for a motive. Trent had to keep our suspicions from turning in the right direction.

"He improvised brilliantly. He knew that his wife had hidden their marriage certificate behind his photograph in her dressing-room. He smashed the frame and deliberately left a scrap of the document behind. The rest of the certificate was to reach us by a roundabout route.

"You see, he didn't have to keep the marriage a secret from the police. So long as we knew nothing of his partnership with you, it didn't matter what other suspicions we entertained. Trent had an unbreakable alibi to protect him.

"He went to Denzil's flat and pushed the certificate through the letter box. That was a clever move."

Lawrence rubbed his cheek. "The next problem was to dispose of the gun and the key to the theatre. Trent didn't know he had dropped his comb by Bailey's body but he did know that he had to be ready for an instant investigation. He dared not hide such incriminating evidence in his flat. So he had to go elsewhere"

The young man sighed. "He had another—and secret—apartment. He was Penny's lover; he had taken this other flat for her. But they were no longer using it: they had had to give up their secret meetings... It was quite deserted. Trent went there to hide the gun and the key. Then at last, he returned to his home. A policeman was waiting to take him to the Yard.

"Trent had only to play the part of an innocent man caught in a trap. His dupes—Penny, Denzil, and myself—went hurrying to his rescue."

Lawrence laughed grimly. "Douglas thought he was working against Michael. Unwittingly, he was playing Trent's game...

"Denzil delayed matters with a clumsy attempt to blackmail Penny, but the marriage certificate reached us eventually—as Trent had expected. The burglary had been 'explained'—and Denzil had brought suspicion upon himself.

"Trent was well content. His alibi would soon be proved and meanwhile he could win my confidence with a pose of frankness." Lawrence's mouth was hard. "He could afford to be completely frank about his part in the old bank robbery. There was no longer any evidence against him. And no witnesses: Lesley was dead—and you were silent."

He scanned Mervan's face. It was set like a mask.

Lawrence muttered:

"Together, you had plotted a murder. It was almost the perfect crime. You had invited suspicion in order to dispel it. The detectives themselves had established your alibis."

He laughed harshly.

He continued:

"Trent would escape scot-free. As for you...."

Mervan stirred. He croaked:

"As for me?"

Lawrence shrugged. He said abruptly:

"You had had your revenge. And you were escaping the gallows. You didn't care how long you had to spend in prison now. It was the safest hiding-place in the world."

He paused, then went on: "And, of course, one day you would be free again. But—."

"But?" The word was a whisper.

"Chance was to betray you. Chance—and a girl's generous heart." Lawrence paused. He continued more briskly:

"You hadn't intended to frame Jack Austin. But he had fallen under suspicion. And only Penny Valentine could clear him.

"But Penny wouldn't speak until she was sure of Michael's safety. She believed him innocent—and she meant to prove it. That's why she persuaded me to stage a reconstruction of the crime. And once the police had been forced to admit that Michael couldn't be guilty, she was ready to save Austin too.

"But she had made a tragic mistake. Unwittingly, she had betrayed her lover."

Lawrence bit his lip. He said sombrely:

"Once the problem had been fairly stated, I was bound to find the solution. And Penny herself gave me the essential clue."

Lawrence shook his head. He said with regret:

"I should have seen the answer before. I ought to have wondered why you were still at the door of the box. You could have escaped minutes before—under cover of the black-out—through a nearby exit to the street. And a man who knew something about Judo should have been able to counter my attack. I should have realised that you wanted to be captured."

Mervan smiled faintly.

Lawrence went on:

"And nothing could really explain the monstrous coincidence of two independent attempts on Lesley's life. Oh, I tried to rationalise it—as you meant me to. I created a phantom—a master-mind—a puppet-master." He grinned wryly. I spoke of such a man to Castle on our way to the theatre last night. And I was thinking of Victor Friern: he could have seen you at the ticket window from his office when you were looking your box for the ☐atinee. Ah, well!" He sighed ruefully.    He continued:

"That theory was soon forgotten. Penny herself showed me the truth.

"She took Lesley's place in the reconstruction. I watched her back away from the gun in Trent's hand. Like Lesley, she stood with her back to the stuffed bear, her body almost within the animal's grasp. The rod which marked the passage of the .25 bullet into the bear's mouth was brushing lightly over the top of Penny's head...

"And that was the essential clue! Penny is five feet three inches tall. The dead woman was five feet seven.

"Lesley could not have been standing in front of the bear when you fired the .25 automatic. Those extra inches would have brought her into the path of the bullet. Instead of passing harmlessly over her head, the bullet would have crashed into her skull."

Defeat showed greyly in Mervan's face. He closed his eyes.

Lawrence said sadly:

"Once I realised that, the whole crime was within grasp. Sitting in the deserted theatre, watching an empty stage, I peopled it with phantoms. You and Trent and Lesley: you all played your parts."

Incredibly, Mervan smiled. "A command performance."

He brooded, then asked:

"The Valentine girl—what made her return?"

Lawrence replied:

"She had learned the truth, too."

"In God's name—how?"

Lawrence sighed. "Michael had taken another flat—I told you about that. Penny still had a key, of course. She left the theatre and went to their apartment. She 'phoned for Michael. She was deliriously happy.

She wanted her lover. And then—."

"Yes?"

Lawrence said dully:

"She found the key to the theatre. Some ammunition. And the .32 Webley & Scott."

He shuddered. "I don't like to think of that moment. It was the end of the world for Penny. She saw the truth at last. Michael was a murderer. And she had put the rope around his neck.

"I was the man she feared. She knew I must inevitably discover the truth. But she meant to save Michael if she could."

"She crammed some bullets into the revolver and hurried back to the theatre. She made a desperate attempt to persuade me that Lesley had committed suicide—the only other possible solution to the crime. She failed. When she realised I knew the truth, she made her final bid to save her lover. She tried to kill me."

Lawrence shaded his eyes. "I can't blame her for that. She loved him, you see."

He looked up. His voice grew stronger. "But Michael loved her too. And he wouldn't let her risk death—or damnation... "

"Trent had reached the flat to find her gone. The gun was missing. So was the key to the theatre. He guessed she had gone to the Janus. He followed.

"I can find it in my heart to admire him. Penny was about to send a bullet crashing through my neck. Michael must have guessed why she wanted to kill me. But he wouldn't let her destroy herself for his sake. He knocked the revolver out of her hand."

Lawrence lifted his shoulders. "Finis."

The travesty of a smile distorted Mervan's lips. He said tonelessly:

"You have yet to prove your theory."

Lawrence shrugged again. "I leave that to the police. They have the duplicate revolver. And Trent will probably confess to protect Penny. Nothing will be said about her attempt on my life. I shall see to that."

Mervan's voice was emotionless. "And Trent will implicate me."

Lawrence smiled humourlessly. "And we have your own confession. It omits important details. But it's true enough for all that."

Mervan showed his teeth in a death's-head grin. "It will be an interesting trial."

Lawrence opened his hand.

He said dully:

"That's all, then. I may as well go."

But he made no move.

Richard Mervan said slowly:

"I suppose I ought to hate you. But I feel only a sensation of mild curiosity."

He gazed at Lawrence squarely. "This is an unofficial visit—one that breaks all the rules. You didn't come here to trap me into a confession."

"No."

"Why, then?"

Lawrence licked his lips. "There's something—I want to know... "

His voice faded.

He stumbled on. "I thought perhaps—you could tell me...."

"Yes?"

Lawrence finished in a whisper:

"What makes a killer kill?"

Mervan's face was a mask.

He muttered:

"The spirit of murder sleeps in everyone's heart. Once awakened—."

He gestured emptily.

He said, more strongly:

"I can tell you this. I destroyed myself before I killed."

Darkness gathered in the cell. Mervan's voice was a flickering flame. "I had to have my revenge. But then I was left with—nothing.

"I was no longer a man. I was just an empty shell."

He said hollowly:

"Revenge isn't sweet. It's only futile."

He added strangely:

"Remember that."

Lawrence inclined his head. He stood up slowly, easing cramped limbs. He went to the door and called for a warder.

He left the cell without looking back.

# APPENDIX

Hidetoshi Mori on Derek Smith
Tony Medawar on Derek Smith
Nigel Moss on Derek Smith

## Hidetoshi Mori on Derek Smith

I met Derek Smith for the first time in June 1994 at the antiquarian book fair held in the Hotel Russell in London. I had been talking to a book dealer specialising in mystery fiction, who told me about Derek, who lived in London and would be attending the fair later. He introduced us, and Derek and I discussed our favourite topic—locked room mysteries—over coffee. When I told him that I had quite enjoyed his locked room novel (*Whistle up the Devil*, 1953), he informed me that there was another Algy Lawrence novel which had not been published, entitled *Come to Paddington Fair*.

It became customary for me to visit that same book fair every year, up to and including 1997. After that year, my workload in Japan became heavy; I've never been abroad since and I doubt that I ever shall (I must read and review more than 200 books every year for various magazines.) It was in 1996, I think, that Derek gave me a Xerox copy of *Come to Paddington Fair* and also a copy of a Sexton Blake novel *Model Murder*\*, which had never been published either. At the time, he expressed his hope that *Come to Paddington Fair* would be published some day. After I returned to Japan, I read the manuscript and thought it a masterpiece—even better than his first book. I wrote to Derek to say that I would like to publish it in Japan if he could not find a publisher in England or USA. Thus the book was published in the spring of 1997 by Susumu Kobayashi, who edited and created the layout of the book, and myself. The production was limited to 80 copies because publication costs were very expensive here in Tokyo: 45 copies were sent to Derek (which went to his friends and fellow collectors) and 35 copies remained in Japan (which went to fellow locked room fans here.)

Towards the end of May of that year, he sent me a letter saying: "You and your friend S. Kobayashi deserve the highest praise for the way you have produced my book. It's almost exactly the way I visualized in my daydreams of a private publication these last forty years—'Thirties style but with modern improvements: slightly larger than usual paperbacks, but easy and comfortable to hold. The paper is excellent, the binding sturdy, and the print size fine for smoothly easy reading. The pagination (270 plus) is just right, the stiff paper binding fine and intriguingly decorated and your paper jacket nicely designed with a appropriately drawn "Curtain" motif. Altogether a splendid piece of work. I can only hope readers find the story as intriguing." I myself designed the paper jacket he mentioned and was happy to hear that he liked it.

After the book was published, Derek remembered that I had suggested a Queen-style Challenge to the Reader, and regretted that he hadn't inserted one at the end of Part Two of the book. He suggested it be worded: "The reader is respectfully requested to PAUSE FOR REFLECTION—and play the great game of Whodunit? and How?"

Readers may wonder why we did not publish *Model Murder\** at the same time as *Come to Paddington Fair*. It was simply because the novel was based on a character not created by Derek Smith! Although it would have been quite easy to get permission to publish from Derek, we weren't sure whether we had the right to publish a novel based on a character not created by the author (You may imagine the situation of Sherlock Holmes or Hercules Poirot parodies and pastiches these days.)


Hidetoshi Mori

Tokyo, June 2014


*\*Editor's note:*

There is some question over the precise title, see page 616

# Tony Medawar on Derek Smith

I met Derek Howe Smith at Bouchercon XXI, at London in 1990, where our mutual friend, Bob Adey, was the Fan Guest of Honor. Derek was an absorbing companion, full of anecdotes about the many famous detective story writers with whom he had corresponded or met and gifted with the ability to recall in precise detail the many, many books in the genre he had read, however well-known or obscure. Though some 40 years apart in age, we quickly established a shared enthusiasm for John Dickson Carr, the American writer so aptly described as the "King of Misdirection" by none other than Agatha Christie, and Derek revealed that he had had the good fortune to see the original production of one of Carr's wartime stage plays, "Inspector Silence Takes the Air." I had recently discovered the script of this and three other plays by Carr in an obscure archive at the British Library so I was able to give Derek a copy of the script of the play which he told me he had thought about "for nearly fifty years". It was Derek's idea that the scripts should be collected together and published, as they eventually were by Douglas Greene's company Crippen and Landru. Sadly Derek did not live to see what he had rightly envisaged would be received by Carr's many enthusiasts as "a magnificent treat".

Derek was absolutely delighted to have the opportunity to read once more the script of "Inspector Silence Takes the Air" and, in return, he generously gave me a copy of the first edition of his own novel "Whistle up the Devil," an ingenious locked room mystery that was Derek's homage to our favourite writer. Ever the perfectionist, when he gave me the novel, Derek pointed out a corrigendum he had tipped in clarifying one aspect of the solution, which he had realised was ambiguous only on reading the published text. He did the same thing some years later when giving me a copy of the 1st edition of his novel *Come to Paddington Fair*, in which he had marked a number of minor typesetting errors and included a Challenge to the Reader of the kind made popular by Ellery Queen. Derek's interest in the construction of plots made him an ideal person to discuss ideas with and in the mid 1990s he advised me how to handle a key element of the plot of a locked room mystery I was then writing, indeed still am writing. Like many fans of detective fiction, I carry numerous plots in my head—truly ingenious problems with even more ingenious solutions. But, like many fans of detective fiction, I have not yet committed any of these self-judged masterpieces to paper. We can therefore be grateful that Derek was able to do what so many of us find difficult and not only thought up delightful problems, steeped in the Golden Age, but found the time to turn those thoughts into words with the result that today, many years after his death, Derek Smith is still able to challenge us to play "the great game of Whodunit? and How?".

Tony Medawar

London, June 2014

*Editor's note*: The dedication to Tony Medawar's copy of *Come to Paddingon Fair* reads:

"To Tony Medawar—incomparable finder of lost treasures—this surviving trifle from the vanished world of the early Nineteen Fifties—from a fellow devotee of the Master

(signed) Derek Smith"

## Nigel Moss on Derek Smith

I was first introduced to Derek at a book fair in London in the late 1990's by Mori-san, a prominent Japanese collector. It was around the time that Mori had published *Come to Paddington Fair* in the Japanese private press first edition. Below is a letter to me from him, dated September 1998:

"Dear Nigel Moss,

I hope you will forgive my long delay in replying to your letters. I have no real excuse – it's just that my winter blues seem to have lasted through the summer, and I have neglected everything.

However, here at last are the bits and pieces for you to add to your copy of COME TO PADDINGTON FAIR. There are only thirty to forty copies of the book in the Western half of the world—who knows, they may become collector's items! I shall be eternally grateful to Mr. Mori and his friend S. Kobayashi for recuing the novel from obscurity.

I personalized all the copies that went through my hands – all signed, and most with individual inscriptions. The enclosed should do the same for your copy.

(one) the title page, to be inserted before the dedication to John Dickson Carr

(two) the inscription page, to go opposite the CONTENTS leaf, with a specially composed piece of doggerel which I hope will amuse you, and

(three) a polite "challenge to the reader" which goes before Part Three, page 252.

In addition, I sealed up that portion of the book, following JDC's own practice with his earliest novels.

With some hesitation, I enclose a further fragment from my youth: circa 1948, on my first typewriter, when I was happily hammering out any story that popped into my head for the fun of it. Needless to say, none were published, and most have vanished, though fragments sometimes appear in my old personal papers, mostly of yarns I thought might be revised or expanded. Paradoxically, this one has survived in near pristine condition because I thought it too feeble to send anywhere! I thought it might amuse you now as a curiosity—the carbon has long since disintegrated, so the item may be awful, but at least it's unique.

With very best wishes,

(signed) Derek Smith

P.S. I'm keeping an eye open for the books on your wants list, but so far without success. I'll keep looking.   D.S."

Nigel Moss

London, January 2014

*Editor's note*: The "fragment" alluded to in the letter is a short story entitled "The Imperfect Crime," which appears on page 617. The dedication to Nigel's copy of *Come to Paddingon Fair* reads:

"To Nigel Moss—with many thanks for his kind interest in my stories.

(signed) Derek Smith

Miracle murders, well designed
May drive a sleuth out of his mind!
So turn the key in puzzle's lock—
The truth may tease, surprise or shock:
When night's black agents shroud the way
Then Reason pure will light the day"

# MODEL FOR MURDER

## (Sexton Blake's Sealed Room)

### *Derek Howe Smith*

# PROLOGUE

Behind the soundproof doors, a blow was struck, viciously.

Leo Garvary reeled back and collapsed into a chair. He stayed for a moment with his head against his hands. Then he looked up and wiped away the thin trickle of blood which showed redly at the corner of his mouth.

He said quietly:

"I'll forgive that burst of bad temper. But—."

The burly man stood over him with menace in his clenched fists. "You—." Garvary cut in sharply: "Touch me again and you'll regret it. I promise you."

Cold fury touched the other's eyes. Then his hands opened and he turned away with a half-spoken curse.

There was a silence in the studio. Garvary adjusted the gold rimmed spectacles and ran nervous fingers over his moustache and neatly pointed beard before he spoke again.

He murmured:

"We don't have to quarrel. I —."

"I want that book!"

The violence in his companion's voice made Garvary quail momentarily, and fear pinched up his face. Yet he went on doggedly. Incredibly, the frightened man in the hard backed chair was master of the situation.

He returned: "You can't have it."

The burly man cried angrily:

"You broke into my room and stole it."

A glint of humour showed in Garvary's eyes.

"Why don't you complain to the police?" he asked smoothly.

"If I thought you meant to shop me, I'd kill you."

The words seemed to spread like shadows across the room. Then Garvary said crisply:

"Don't worry. I need you,"—he hesitated—"and you need me—now. That's why I took such desperate measures. It was your own fault. You cut off my supplies."

"The stuff's there, if you want it. And can pay for it."

"I might say the same," replied Garvary slowly, "about your little black book."

453

A dark flush of anger crept over the other's cheeks. He controlled himself with an effort. "Look here, man. I need that book for my business."

The formal word had an odd ring. Garvary smiled. "I thought of that. Here."

He took a thin strip of film from the pocket of his long white artist's smock. The burly man took it suspiciously. "What's this?"

"Microfilm. I photographed every relevant page. You'll find all the information that's necessary to carry on your business."

There was a terrible silence. Then the burly man strode stiff-legged across the room, twisted hard on the lock, and pulled open the door.

He called over his shoulder:

"This isn't the end, believe me. I'll—."

He broke off suddenly. Footsteps had sounded on the stairs outside. He closed the door and stood with his back against it. He said:

"It's that fool from upstairs."

"Tenison?"

"Yes. I don't want to meet him."

The door bell shrilled. Garvary said equably:

"I shan't answer. That young man calls much too often."

His companion grunted. He asked without interest:

"Why?"

The artist replied:

"I suspect he's in love with my model." A dry rasp of exasperation was audible in his voice.

The bell sounded again. Neither man regarded it.

Garvary said abruptly:

"You'll have to admit you're beaten."

The reply was flat and dangerous. "You think so."

"I know it. If that book was sent to Scotland Yard,"—the artist stepped back involuntarily as the fury flamed once more in the other's face—"you'd be finished."

He was answered with a vicious obscenity. "If I thought the book was in this studio, I'd wreck the place to find it."

Garvary smiled mirthlessly. "I'd be a fool to hide it here. But don't worry. It's safe enough. It won't fall into the wrong hands, unless—."

"Unless?"

"Something should happen to me," finished Garvary, with a shocking death's-head grin. "So...."

The two men eyed each other warily.

The burly fellow laughed. "I under estimated your resourcefulness. All right. I can't threaten you, so perhaps I can buy you." A hard line of anger cut down from one nostril to the corner of his mouth. "How much?"

Garvary seemed strangely contented. He breathed:

"I don't want money."

"What, then?"

The artist smiled crookedly. He whispered:

"You know *exactly* what I want."

# CHAPTER ONE

Linda Martin hurried along Baker Street, her fleece-lined boots clacking with troubled urgency against the pavement.

She was a very beautiful girl. She was also very scared.

Presently she reached the old houses near the north end of the street and scanned the numbers eagerly. She knew there would be no name plate to guide her. The man she was seeking neither wanted nor needed publicity.

She identified the house, hesitated, then ran lightly up the steps and pressed the bell-push hurriedly.

Standing on the front porch, nervously fingering her handbag, she glanced downward through the old fashioned area at the windows of a comfortable looking sitting room.

Behind the curtains, somebody moved, dimly. Then a little while later footsteps sounded and the door came open in the hand of a buxom and maternal-looking old lady with kindly eyes.

Linda said faintly, almost as if she were seeking reassurance:

"You're Mrs. Bardell."

"That's right, dear," replied that lady comfortably. "What can I do for you?"

"I—I'd like to speak to Mr. Blake."

Mrs. Bardell shook her head regretfully. "You're out o' luck, my dear. Mr. Blake's away. I don't properly know when to expect him, neither."

The girl burst out:

"But I must see him! Please. Isn't there anything you can do?"

The elderly lady eyed her shrewdly. With a sudden air of decision, she nodded and smiled. "Come in, miss."

Linda found herself standing in the dim, old fashioned hallway. Mrs. Bardell nodded once more in the manner of a friendly conspirator, and whispered:

"Mr. Tinker is home. I'll tell him you're here."

Leaving the girl staring rather fearfully at the marks of bullets in the wall, the old housekeeper climbed painfully up the staircase to the first floor. When she reached the landing she paused for a moment to regain her breath, then banged heavily on the consulting room door.

A cheery voice sang out: "Come in, old dear!"

Mrs. Bardell pushed open the door and gazed affectionately at the

457

young man by the windows overlooking the street.

Sexton Blake's youthful assistant was sprawled easily, if inelegantly, in the chair behind his desk. His feet rested on the blotting pad by the telephone, and he was reading a gaily jacketed novel.

He looked up with a grin as the old lady entered. "Hallo, beautiful. What's troubling you?"

"Mr. Tinker," said Mrs. Bardell, with great dignity, "I believes as 'ow you're a well known detective—."

"Bless you for those kind words," interrupted the young man irrepressibly. "So?"

"So there's a client downstairs who wants to consult you—poor girl."

"I can't see anybody now," said Tinker firmly. "I'm much too busy."

Mrs. Bardell stared grimly—and significantly—at the book he had just laid on the desk. Tinker said hurriedly:

"Mr. Blake told me to take no more clients."

"He also told you," returned the old lady, "to read that book with the jaw-breaking name."

"The *Handbuch fur Untersuchungsrichter*," supplied Tinker modestly.

Mrs. Bardell blinked, but rallied gamely. "Anyway,"she said, "it wasn't *Jack of All Trades*."

Tinker said defensively:

"Frank Richards is considerably more entertaining than Hans Gross any day. Besides," he added peevishly, "you know these learned old German johnnies. Their idea of a little handbook was a series of umpteen enormous volumes—."

"Be that as it may,"commented the housekeeper patiently, "what shall I do about the young lady downstairs?"

Tinker hesitated. "You know what the guv'nor said," he muttered dubiously.

Mrs. Bardell had evidently taken a liking to Linda Martin. She said persuasively:

"It wouldn't do no harm to see her, at least."

Tinker grinned suddenly. "All right, old dear. Show her up."

While Mrs. Bardell made her way down to the hall once more, Tinker swung his feet off the desk, ran his hands quickly over his dark, untidy hair, straightened his tie, and began to examine some completely unimportant papers with portentous solemnity.

The plump and motherly lady who reigned supreme in the Sexton Blake household re-entered and announced:

"Miss Linda Martin."

Tinker looked up politely as the girl crossed the threshold. Then he stared, frankly. She was easy to look at.

She was small and slender, and carried with her a curious air of delightful intimacy. She had a delicate, heart-shaped face, smooth, rippling, raven black hair, and large, slanting blue grey eyes. Tinker, who was an impressionable young man, felt his heart bump alarmingly.

Linda walked with an intimate, swaying grace. And her figure was exquisite.

Tinker stood up slowly, and took her hand. It was satin smooth, and it made his fingers tingle. He gulped:

"Miss Martin."

She smiled. He noticed that her lipstick had slipped a little wide of the mouth. "Mr. Tinker. It's good of you to see me."

"Uh — not at all. It's a pleasure," returned the young man sincerely. "Won't you sit down?"

"Thank you." Her voice was as delightful as her face.

Tinker offered the girl a cigarette and studied her quickly under the cover of some polite foolery with a lighter. He felt a little tremor of excitement crawl over the nerves at the back of his neck.

For Miss Martin was poised, polite, charming — and afraid.

Tinker's spirits rose. He was a romantic young man who would do anything for a lady in distress.

He smiled. "Now how can I help you?"

Linda said abruptly:

"I'm a model. An artist's model."

"Of course," replied Tinker, greatly daring. "With your face and figure, you couldn't be anything else."

"Thank you." She seemed faintly surprised by the compliment. She went on rapidly: "I work for a sculptor. You may have heard of him. His name is Garvary. Leo Garvary."

Tinker shook his head. 'No. I'm sorry.'

"He's rather famous." She sounded a little reproving. "I've been working for him for some time now. He's a fine artist. Though a trifle eccentric, perhaps."

"Yes." Tinker doodled idly on the blotter in front of him. "What's the trouble?"

Linda stubbed out her cigarette nervously. "It's Mr. Garvary. There's something bothering him. He's been worried, and—and edgy, for weeks." She smiled faintly. "He made me jittery, too. I asked him what was the matter. At first he didn't want to talk about it. Then he said it was the letters."

"What letters?"

"Anonymous letters. Threatening letters. They were coming all the time."

"Did you ever see them?"

"No. That is——."

"Yes?"

"Not till this morning. When I arrived, he looked haggard, almost desperate. Excited, too. He said he couldn't work, not then. There had been another letter."

"This letter had upset him?"

"Yes."

"More than usual?"

"Yes. It wasn't only that. He said he'd finally guessed who sent them, and why."

"Oh." Tinker dropped his pencil with a tiny clatter on the desk top. "Did he explain?"

"No. He only said that he had to have help at once." Linda's mouth trembled. "He looked terrible. His face was nearly grey. It threw a scare into me, just to look at him. I haven't got over the shock even yet."

Tinker nodded sympathetically. "What happened then?"

"I suggested he went to the police. He said there were several reasons why he couldn't do that."

Tinker pulled a wry face. "So he sent you to us."

"Yes." Linda hesitated. She murmured: "He said: 'There's only one man who can help me now.'"

"And his name is Sexton Blake," finished the young man cheerfully. "Unfortunately, the guv'nor's away."

The girl said quickly:

"I'm sure that you, yourself——."

Tinker looked into her magnificent eyes and was lost. "I'll do all I can to help. But why couldn't Garvary come here himself?"

Linda flushed. "I told you. He's eccentric. And he looked so ill. He's helpless somehow. I felt sorry for him. So I left for Baker Street at once."

"Did he give you the letter?"

"Yes." She took it out of her handbag and passed it over the desk. Tinker murmured a thank-you, then examined the letter carefully. It was a large square sheet of grey paper, creased into quarters. The message was unsigned, and typewritten throughout. It was brief, malicious, and vaguely threatening. 'You'd better be careful, damn you. I won't wait much longer.'

Tinker said cheerily:

"This may mean something to Garvary, but it doesn't mean a thing to me."

He folded the letter up again. Except for a slight crumpling at the corners, it wasn't creased any more. Garvary had evidently treated it carefully. But then he hadn't had it very long.

Tinker broke in on his own thoughts to say: "This came this morning?"

"Yes. So he told me."

"Do you have the envelope?"

She nodded quickly, and groped in the handbag again.

The envelope was oblong, white, made of cheap paper, and postmarked: London, W.C. The address was typewritten, like the letter itself, but different machines had obviously been used on each.

Linda looked puzzled when the young detective told her this. "Is that important?"

"I don't know," replied Tinker frankly. "All we know now is that the writer had access to two machines. That might help us trace him. Or," he grinned ruefully, "it might not." He fumbled absently, folded the note across, fitted it into the envelope, and passed it back to the girl. "The other letters you mentioned. Do you have them with you?"

"No. Mr. Garvary destroyed them."

"Why?"

"I don't know why." Linda was nonplussed. "Perhaps he thought they weren't really important, just irritating. At first, that is. Oh, I don't know." She sounded rather helpless. "I told you, he's—.'

"I know. Eccentric. I expect he glows in the dark." She bubbled briefly with laughter.

Tinker leaned back in his chair and scowled thoughtfully.

"I doubt if the guv'nor will handle a case like this," he murmured, half to himself.

"Oh, but—."

The telephone rang shrilly and cut short the girl's protest. With a faint smile of apology, Tinker picked up the receiver and angled it against his ear.

"Hallo. Why, hallo, guv'nor!"

"Hallo, old son." Sexton Blake's deep and pleasant voice crackled through the diaphragm. "All's well, I hope?"

"Uh.Why, yes." Tinker darted a glance towards Linda Martin. She looked tactfully away. "I'm glad you called guv'nor. Are you coming home?"

"Not till tomorrow. Is there anything to report?"

"We have another client."

"Turn him down," said Blake decisively. "I can't handle any more cases till this business is cleared out of the way."

"'Taint a him," said Tinker, "it's a her. And she really needs help."

"A lady. Hmmm." The ghost of a chuckle echoed in the famous detective's voice. "Not, by any chance, a young and attractive lady?"

"Er—yes."

"I thought so. Look here, old son, not for the most charming girl in Christendom could I abandon the case I'm on at the moment."

"What are you doing, guv'nor?" asked Tinker, with pardonable curiosity.

Sexton Blake was evasive. "Let's call it work of national importance."

Tinker grinned. He said flippantly: "I suppose you're helping the Home Secretary to recover his collection of French postcards."

"Cheeky beggar!" laughed Blake. "You need discipline, young man. And something to occupy your mind. Is the 'Index' up to date?"

His assistant looked over one shoulder at the row of red-bound volumes which made up the famous 'Baker Street Index.'

"Yes, guv'nor."

"And don't forget the *Handbuch*."

Tinker coughed and changed the subject hurriedly. "What about Miss Martin, guv'nor?"

"Miss Martin? That's your would-be client, I assume. Well, what about her, old son? Would you like to handle the case yourself?"

"Would I?" Tinker's eyes danced. "Certainly I would."

"All right, then. I leave her to you."

"Dick Hamilton," said Tinker dreamily, naming his friendly rival, "will be green with envy. I hope."

Blake laughed. "Goodbye, young 'un. I'll see you tomorrow."

"Goodbye, guv'nor."

Tinker replaced the receiver and grinned at the girl triumphantly.

She smiled back shyly. Against the sombre background, her beauty stood out like a flame.

"Mr. Blake is busy," said Tinker. "You'll have to put up with me."

Worry touched her eyes once more. "Mr. Garvary is waiting."

"We're on our way," the young man reassured her. He stood up and walked across to a coat rack in the corner. He shrugged a mackintosh over his tweeds and jammed a tweed camp over his dark, curly hair.

Linda followed him to the door. They went down the stairs together.

# CHAPTER TWO

Leo Garvary lived and worked in one of the quietest corners of old London, in an aged and somewhat queerly shaped mansion which had been converted into flats.

As he accompanied Linda Martin through the doorway of the building, Tinker rubbed his hands with relief. It was a cold winter's day, and the snow had only just ceased falling. The young detective's raincoat barely protected him against the chill.

He said, not very profoundly: "Brrrr!" Linda smiled, but made no comment.

Tinker glanced round. A sleepy looking man was seated at a telephone switchboard behind the reception desk. He looked up and nodded a greeting to the girl.

Linda murmured: "This way." She hesitated. She asked timidly:
"What is your name?"

The young man grinned. "Just call me Tinker," he said. "Everybody does."

They went up some stairs at the rear of the hall. Linda explained, rather nervously:

"Mr. Garvary's apartment is on the first floor, in a corner of the building. It's very peaceful. Isolated, almost. Mr. Garvary likes solitude and silence."

"In this day and age," commented Tinker, "he's lucky to get it."

They reached the landing and found themselves at the end of a long corridor. Linda indicated a door at the further end.

"There. That's his studio."

"Right," said Tinker, and led the way. The soft carpet cushioned their feet like cotton wool. Before they had gone more than a few steps, the studio door burst open with the suddenness of farcical comedy. Tinker caught a brief glimpse of a tall man wearing a long white smock, a tam-o'-shanter, a dark moustache, a neatly pointed beard, and a pair of gold rimmed spectacles. The apparition gesticulated wildly, made an agitated skip, and the disappeared into the studio once more behind a slamming door.

Tinker blinked. "What on earth—?"

"That," said Linda, "is Mr. Garvary."

"Who is," returned the young man carefully, "eccentric. I can well believe it."

"I think he's pleased to see us."

"He has an extraordinary way of showing it."

Linda smiled nervously. "I told you he was on edge."

Tinker said flippantly:

"He seems to have slipped over it."

They continued along the corridor, keeping their eyes on the entrance to the studio. When they reached the door, Tinker raised a lightly clenched fist to knock.

Linda put her hand on his arm.

"He won't hear you," she murmured. "The studio is soundproof."

"Soundproof?"

"Yes. Mr. Garvary can't stand noise while he's working, so he had the walls processed and a special door fitted. There isn't even a key hole."

"I can see that." The young detective pointed. "It's a Yale lock. You say he can't hear us?"

"That's right."

"Then how do we get in?"

"He knows we're here, surely. But anyway, you can ring the bell."

Tinker put his finger on the buzzer. He muttered:

"I hope this thing is working. What's the matter with the chap?"

He jabbed the bell again. Linda shifted uneasily. He could feel her nervousness growing steadily. He wasn't happy himself. Garvary's conduct seemed inexplicable.

He stood back with puzzled eyes, while the minutes slithered by.

"This is crazy." He scratched his chin. "Suffering cats! Anything might be happening in there, without us hearing a thing. Is there a way we can get in?"

"This is the only door."

"Granted. But can we get hold of a key?"

"Well—." The girl sounded uncertain.

A door scraped open somewhere above them, then feet clattered down a little back stairway to their right.

Following the sounds instinctively, Tinker turned his head and witnessed the arrival of a pleasant faced young man in a battered blue suit. He was clean shaven, vague and amiable of eye, and tall enough to top Tinker by two or three inches. He hailed Linda Martin immediately. His voice was rather colourless, and his breathing heavy.

"Linda! I heard you talking. Is anything wrong?"

"No, Bob. Not really. It's just that—." She broke off abruptly. "Bob, this is Sexton Blake's assistant. Tinker, this is Mr. Tenison. He lives upstairs. He's an artist, too. A painter."

"Not a very good one, though," grinned Tenison. "I can't even claim the distinction of rejection by the Royal Academy." The two men shook hands. Bob queried:

"What's the trouble?"

Linda shrugged helplessly. "Mr. Garvary is being difficult. He sent me to fetch Mr. Blake. I came back with Tinker. And now Leo won't open the door."

"I hope," said the young detective, "that isn't cause and effect." He rubbed his cheek thoughtfully. "If Garvary won't come out, I think we should go in. Is there a way we can manage it?"

Tenison suggested:

"Borrow a key from the desk clerk."

Linda said doubtfully: "Do you think we should?"

Tinker cut in: "I don't see why not. We ought to do something."

Tenison said agreeably:

"I'll go down and speak to the clerk." He set off along the corridor.

Tinker watched him go, and commented:

"Nice chap."

Linda.said impulsively: "He's a dear."

The young detective angled one eyebrow. "Is he your boy friend?"

She smiled, and shook her head. "No. I just like him, that's all."

Tenison came back after a while and slipped a key into Linda's hand. He said, with a wry grin:

"I had to bribe the desk clerk. And he made me promise to see Garvary made no trouble."

"I'll see to that," replied Tinker. "Even if I make him swallow his chisel."

Tenison laughed, nodded pleasantly, then ran lightly up the stairs again. Linda slipped the key into the lock, turned it, and pushed open the door. She hesitated.

"Tinker, I—."

"Right ho." The young man took the lead. He walked into the studio. Linda followed. They stood on the threshold of a comfortable, spacious room. Wide windows in the facing wall gave excellent light. A door in the corner was locked and bolted. The left and right hand walls were lined with cupboards.

An unfinished, life size statue of a half-nude girl dominated the room. Tinker's voice echoed queerly. "Where," he asked, "is Garvary?"

Linda whispered:

"I don't know."

Tinker glanced behind the open door, then walked across the room slowly. He stopped by the statue, and saw that it was Linda. The sculptor had caught her beauty to perfection. Except for a brief cloth, held to her with a wonderful impression of modesty, she was unclothed.

Tinker asked softly:

"This is you?"

"Yes." A thin flush of blood showed behind the delicate skin of her cheeks. Tinker said soberly:

"You're very beautiful."

"Thank you."

He passed on to the windows. They were in three sections. The middle, and largest, consisted of two big glass panes which could be opened outwards like French windows, and which were securely fastened from the inside by a handle and latch at the centre. Flanking this section were two more windows, each in two halves. The bottom half of each was an immovable sheet of glass set in the wall. Above, the top half was hinged like a transom, and was secured by a triple notched bar that holed over a small iron upright set in the ledge at the base.

Tinker stepped on a long box seat under the windows, and raised the slender bar of the left hand section. The window pushed outwards and upwards. As the hinge opened, he stretched up his hand and ran his fingers idly over the disclosed upper metal edge. It was clean, he noted absently. He was looking down at a little courtyard which was covered with an unmarked carpet of snow. Opposite, there was only the blank wall of a warehouse.

He shut the window again: it fitted snugly in its frame. Linda watched him silently. Tinker shrugged. "Well, he didn't go this way." The young detective glanced towards the inner door.

Linda followed his glance. "That leads to Mr. Garvary's living quarters. But he can't be there, can he?"

"No. The bolts are shot on this side." Tinker rubbed his ear, tilting his tweed cap to a crazy angle. Feeling rather silly, he opened the box seat and glanced inside. It was empty.

He clicked his fingers irritably. "The man must be here somewhere. He couldn't have left the room, obviously. Let's look into those cupboards."

Linda giggled, then stopped, a chill in her eyes. "I'm sorry. But I thought—why should he be hiding? The idea seems so silly."

"Miss Martin," said Tinker grimly, "it's insane." All the humour had gone from his face, and the line of his jaw had tightened.

There were three cupboards each side, let into the walls. Tinker pointed. "Look there, please." He went himself to the opposite wall.

He wrenched open the first two closets, and found only a miscellaneous collection of artist's materials. Across the room, and more slowly, Linda opened the first, and then the third.

Tinker looked into his last cupboard and blinked at a surrealistic cast in soft clay.

The young man shook his head ruefully and turned around just as Linda pulled open the middle door.

He saw her stiffen suddenly. Then she turned with dreadful slowness and he saw that her mouth had gone slack like a doll's.

She said hoarsely:

"I've—found him."

# CHAPTER THREE

Linda Martin was fighting for control. Tinker walked over to her slowly, and gave her a half grin of encouragement.

She choked suddenly. "Oh, Tinker—."

She stumbled towards him. He put his arm round her shoulders and whispered gently. "Easy there. Take it easy."

He liked the crisp, clean smell of her raven black hair.

After a while she stopped shaking, and stepped back. Then he put his fingers under her chin, tilted her face upwards, and smiled.

"All right, now?"

She murmured: "Yes," very quietly. Tinker went to the cupboard and looked inside.

The closet was wide and roomy. Garvary lay on his back, among the rubbish on the floor, with his head and shoulders against the wall.

Dark untidy hair straggled stupidly under the tam-o'-shanter. The gold rimmed glasses were hooked precariously over one ear and one lens rested crazily on the man's chin. His eyes were glazed and wide open, and his mouth was slack and silly.

He was freshly dead.

The long white coat was holed and stained. It had fallen open at the front, showing an unbuttoned tweed jacket and a pale blue pullover.

One of the bullets had smashed his shoulder and another had pierced his side. Tinker knelt down and touched the dead man's jacket gingerly. It was stiff with blood.

There was a third bullet in Garvary's leg. The fourth was through his heart.

Blood welled slowly from the powder marked hole in the pale blue pullover: pale blue turning slowly red.

Tinker straightened up. He could see a pistol lying near the body, close to the dead man's hand.

Tinker didn't touch it.

Linda whispered: "Is he dead?"

"Yes."

The tiny word seemed very loud in the still and silent room. The girl's mouth trembled. Tinker took her hands gently.

"Look, Linda." It was the first time he had used her Christian name. "This chap Tenison— he's a friend of yours, isn't he? Can you trust him?"

"Bob? Of course."

"Right. Tell him everything that's happened. Tell him to telephone New Scotland Yard and ask for Detective Inspector Stevens."

She repeated the name mechanically. Tinker nodded quickly. "If Tenison gets the Inspector, he can tell him Sexton Blake's assistant discovered the killing." He released her hands with a final squeeze. "The both of you wait upstairs until some one comes to fetch you."

He snapped his fingers. "One thing more. Contact whoever's in charge here and tell him no one's to leave the building until the police arrive." He smiled boyishly. "Can you manage all that?"

Linda nodded. She asked: "And you?"

"I shall stay here."

He turned away and began to prowl restlessly round the studio. He seemed worried and almost afraid. Then the old cheery grin flickered over his face again.

He said: "What a case! Look here, Linda." He pointed a long finger. "We were watching that outer door from the moment Garvary re-entered this room." He paused.

She whispered, as if in reply to a question:

"No one came out."

"Right. And the door in the corner is bolted on this side." He pointed again. "The windows were locked. There's no chimney. There isn't even a keyhole. *There's no way out.*"

She looked at him with frightened eyes.

Tinker said softly:

"When Garvary came back into this studio, somebody picked up a gun and shot him. And—."

He paused. The girl's mouth picked up the word and framed it in silent query. Tinker finished simply:

"And vanished."


Detective Inspector Steven Stevens was large, urbane, and shrewd. He was loyal to his friends and devoted to his family. He was also a ruthlessly unsentimental man-hunter.

He stumped into the studio and eyed Tinker quizzically. He grumbled a greeting, then growled:

"Well! What have you let me in for this time?"

Tinker grinned. "Nothing much," he replied affectionately. "Only a murder that couldn't possibly have been committed."

Stevens eyed him with distaste. "What is it," he glared, "that makes me avoid you so eagerly?" Then he laughed. "All right, young fellow.

Tell me the worst."

Tinker pointed wordlessly towards the open closet. The Inspector grunted, then nodded to the men with him. They set to work in a maze of cameras and flashlights. An occasional muttered curse drifted out of the haze of activity.

Stevens drew his young friend to one side. "Where do you fit into this affair, my lad?"

Tinker plunged his hands into his pockets. "I'm looking after my client's interests."

"Who's your client?" Stevens accented the adjective sardonically.

"Miss Linda Martin."

"And who's Miss Linda Martin?"

"A model. You'll meet her."

The Inspector swept his hands under the tail of his battered raincoat. "Where is she?"

"Upstairs." Tinker gestured persuasively. "Look, Steve. Don't you want to hear my story?" The inspector sighed. "Go ahead. And don't call me Steve!"

Tinker told his story swiftly and economically. When he had finished, the Inspector stared at him and swore briefly.

"Hell's blazes! A sealed room murder."

"You can call it that." Tinker breathed reverently. "What a case!"

"Don't sound so pleased about it, curse you! A man was killed while you,"—Stevens spluttered—"were ringing the doorbell."

"Be reasonable, Steve. The room is soundproof. I couldn't possibly know what was happening."

"All right, all right." Stevens was irritable. He put up a hand and slapped the crown of his bowler testily. "Wait a minute. You mentioned a letter. Let me see it."

The girl had given up the note to Tinker. He passed it to the Inspector. Stevens pursed his lips thoughtfully. "I'll have this tested for fingerprints."

"Certainly," said Tinker helpfully. "You'll find mine, Miss Martin's, Garvary's, and your own. That should please the Assistant Commissioner."

Stevens eyed him malevolently. "You're a great help."

He walked across to his assistant, Detective Sergeant Wyatt and conferred with him briefly. Then he turned back to Tinker with a jerk of his head. "Let's see Miss Martin."

They went out into the corridor and up the little back stairway to the floor above. Standing outside Tenison's flat, the Inspector pounded on the door with his fist. The artist answered the call immediately. He

471

looked vaguely worried. He asked:

"Are you from the police?"

Stevens identified himself curtly. Tinker followed him into Tenison's flat.

The studio was almost exactly similar to Garvary's, and directly above it. It was cluttered with all the usual paraphernalia of an artist's and also with—surprisingly enough—odd pieces of gymnastic equipment. Bob removed an Indian club from the seat of a chair and murmured by way of apology:

"I like to keep in condition."

Stevens sat down and removed his hat, disclosing iron grey hair cropped close to his skull. He said:

"Mr. Tenison. You 'phoned my office at the Yard—."

"Yes," the artist agreed. "Miss Martin—."

"Ah, yes," the Inspector interrupted ruthlessly. "Miss Martin. I want to see that young lady." Tenison nodded. He went to a door in the corner and tapped on it softly. He pushed it open. Linda had been warming herself by the fire in the inner room. She looked up quickly. Bob stood in the doorway and gave her an encouraging smile:

"Linda. The Inspector wants to speak to you."

Stevens looked at the girl curiously as he rose to greet her. She was pale, but steady. She walked over and seated herself in the chair Tinker pushed forward.

Stevens sat down again and studied the girl without being too obvious about it. He said abruptly:

"I understand Leo Garvary was your employer and that you discovered the body. Would you please tell me your story from the beginning?"

Tinker had strolled behind the Inspector. He gave the girl a friendly grin over the big man's shoulder, then moved across to a heavy raised couch under the windows. He sat down and began to ponder. His eyelids drooped.

He opened an eye to see the Inspector thumbing his chin absently. It was something of a danger signal.

Stevens asked benignly:

"Are you absolutely certain nobody came out through the studio door after Mr. Garvary went in?"

"Absolutely."

"I see." The Inspector's voice was an ominous rumble. "You do realise, Miss Martin, that your story makes nonsense of the murder?"

Linda wanted to cry. "I can't help it! Ask Tinker—he was there, too."

"That's right," said the young man irrepressibly. "Our evidence

472

proves that Garvary couldn't possibly have been killed. So laugh that over with the body."

Stevens glared at him. "Don't be funny. I'm investigating a murder. I intend to get at the truth,"—his gaze swung back to the girl—"whoever obstructs me...."

Tenison caught the glance and the innuendo. He said hotly:

"Dammit, Inspector, you've no right to—."

"Young man, I'll tell you again. I'm investigating a murder. Allow me to do it my own way."

Tinker stood up and grasped Tenison's arm. He steered him away. "Don't mind the Inspector. His bark's a lot worse than his bite."

"But Linda—."

"Linda will be all right." Tinker regarded the painter curiously. Bob Tenison had no personality, yet when he spoke of the girl his face came live and warm. Tinker murmured:

"You like her, don't you?"

Bob said simply:

"I love her."

Then, as if ashamed of the admission, he said hurriedly:

"You'll see she's not bullied, won't you?"

"Of course." Tinker answered sincerely, but absently. He was puzzling over the crime, trying to evolve a theory. He asked:

"Are there any rooms above these?"

"No. This is the top floor."

"Hmmm." The young detective mused. "Is there any way on to the roof?"

"None that I know of." Tenison looked puzzled. "It's pretty steep, and the tiles aren't too secure."

Tinker smiled. "Next question. Are there any other tenants in this part of the building?"

"There's somebody on the ground floor, below Garvary. He's not a very sociable fellow. I hardly ever see him."

Tinker nodded. "I think I'll pay him a visit."

Stevens was still questioning the girl. The young man from Baker Street slipped through the door and descended the stairs.

Outside Garvary's studio stood a thin man with a small bag. He seemed to be nursing a grievance. Tinker recognized Whitfield, the police surgeon.

The doctor snapped:

"I've been calling my head off. Where's the Inspector?"

"He's upstairs," returned Tinker politely.

Whitfield clattered up to the next floor to make his report. Tinker

473

grinned, then ran lightly down the narrow stairway to the bottom.

There was a sign outside the apartment door. It read:

Please Do Not Disturb.

The young man glanced at the name above the bell push. Alan Raven. Tinker put his finger on the buzzer and kept it there.

# CHAPTER FOUR

After a while he heard the slam of a door inside and the slow drag of footsteps across the floor. Then the outer door opened to show a burly man with tangled hair and sleepy eyes. He was wearing ash-grey silk pyjamas, a thick blue bath robe, and battered carpet slippers.

Tinker greeted him pleasantly. "Good morning, Mr. Raven."

"The sign," murmured Raven, "says don't disturb."

Tinker grinned. "It's more polite," he returned smoothly. "It says please."

He strolled past the burly man into the flat. There was a comfortable chair in one corner. He sat in it.

Raven said without rancour: "You've got a nerve." He shut the door and fumbled in his pocket. "Want a smoke?"

Tinker shook his head. "No, thanks."

Raven shrugged, thumbed out a cigarette from the packet and jammed it between his lips. He scraped a match into flame.

Tinker, watching him, said abruptly:

"Garvary has been murdered."

Raven's eyes were squinted against the smoke, and Tinker could read no expression in their depths. But the match flame crept down and scorched the burly man's fingers.

Raven dropped the charred stick and said softly:

"So?"

"Aren't you surprised?"

"Naturally." The burly man had recovered his balance. "But what has it got to do with me? Are you from the police?"

Tinker identified himself.

"Sexton Blake's assistant, eh?" Raven's voice was soft and pleasant, in contrast to his face. He had the malformed nose of a prize-fighter. "Come into my bedroom. There's a fire there."

He ushered Tinker through the inner door, then sat down on the bed amid tumbled sheets and blankets.

Tinker murmured:

"You sleep late."

"I work at night," returned Raven absently. "I came home at four o'clock this morning." A trace of wariness crept into his deep set eyes.

"Then you probably can't help us." Tinker walked across to the window, which was barred. He glanced through the glass. Everything outside was covered with an unmarked carpet of snow.

Raven replied. "I've been sleeping since I returned."

Tinker asked:

"Were you a friend of Garvary's?"

"I hardly ever saw him." Raven pinched out his cigarette and flicked the stub away carelessly. "How did he die?"

"Somebody shot him." Tinker explained the circumstances briefly. Raven listened attentively. The young detective finished:

"The police will probably ask you for a statement."

Raven shrugged. "They won't learn much from me." He yawned. "I'm going back to sleep."

Tinker grinned. "I'll let myself out." He passed through the bedroom door and closed it behind him carefully.

French windows, which opened outwards, gave access to the little courtyard. Tinker looked through the panes. Once again, an unmarked carpet of white met his gaze.

Snow had piled up against the glass panes at his feet, on the sills of the windows flanking the French doors, and on the tops of the walls bounding the courtyard to the left and right.

Tinker shrugged, turned away, and let himself out of Raven's apartment. He sauntered upstairs again.

Detective Inspector Stevens was prowling round Garvary's studio. He looked tired and dispirited.

He scowled when he saw Tinker. "Where have you been?"

"Here and there," said the young man evasively. "How are you getting on?"

Stevens gestured expressively. "This case gets madder every minute." He swung and indicated the door to the sculptor's living quarters. "That bolt is so stiff it takes two hands to draw it. And even if the killer could have managed to reach those inner rooms, he would still have been trapped. The windows through there are barred."

"What about these studio windows?"

"You told me yourself they were safely secured on the inside. I examined 'em, though." The Inspector scowled. "My only reward was a handful of dust from the edges. They aren't trick windows that slide into the wall, if that's what you're thinking." Stevens smacked his hands together. "Dammit, Tinker, there was no possible way of escape."

The young man had a momentarily disturbing impression of a faceless assassin melting like a ghost through solid walls. He said lightly: "Perhaps Garvary committed suicide."

"First shooting himself in the leg for practice?" enquired the Inspector caustically.

Tinker grinned. "Don't be sarcastic. What was the medical evidence?"

"He was shot four times. We found bullets in his shoulder, side, and leg. The fourth shot went through his heart. That was the one that killed him."

"Powder burns?"

"Around the heart wound."

"There was a gun by the body." Tinker inflected the words as a question.

Stevens jerked his head. "Four shots fired. The cartridge cases were still in the chamber. No finger prints."

"Can you trace the revolver?"

"I doubt it. The number has been filed off."

Something crashed by the window into the courtyard. Tinker jumped. "What's that?"

"I expect it's Wyatt."

"Wyatt?"

"Yes. We got him on to the roof through one of the top floor windows."

"Why, for heaven's sake?"

"I had some crazy idea," said Stevens frankly, "about the bedroom chimney. It's the only other exit from the flat."

"The inner door," Tinker reminded him gently, "was bolted."

"I know, burn it. But I have to consider every possibility. Including the one," finished the Inspector malevolently, "that you're lying your head off."

Tinker grinned. "You don't believe that."

"No, dammit. I wish I did." Stevens walked across to the open windows and leaned out, resting his hands on the wide sill. The clear polished stone struck cold against his palms.

"Wyatt! Are you all right?"

"Yes, sir." The Sergeant's voice floated down hollowly. "One of the tiles came loose, that's all."

"Anything to report?"

"No. There aren't any marks in the snow. I'd say," finished Wyatt mournfully, "nobody's been up here for years."

Stevens snapped:

"Don't break your neck on the way down." He turned to Tinker, who had moved up behind him. "Now, young fellow. Let's examine *your* evidence."

Tinker squatted on the box seat. "Go ahead."

The Inspector said quietly: "Obviously, there was somebody in this studio with Garvary. There's no sort of booby trap capable of putting four bullets in a man and then dragging him into a cupboard. Two of the exits from this room were locked on the inside, and the third was under your own continuous guard."

He paused. Tinker said firmly:

"No one came out through that door. I'll swear to it."

"The killer must have been hiding somewhere in the studio."

"Impossible." Tinker was positive. "I suspected foul play from the first. I caught the scent of gun smoke as I came in. I searched the room at once. And I was much too wary to let anybody slip out behind my back. Take my word for it, Steve. There was no one in the studio except the victim."

Stevens muttered something under his breath. "I shall go over every inch of the walls, floor, and ceiling. If there's so much as a mouse hole, I'll investigate." His voice sank. "I've even examined that statue."

"You didn't think it was hollow, did you?"

"I don't know what to think," replied the Inspector gloomily.

Tinker stood up. "I think I'll go back to Baker Street."

"I shall require a formal statement of your evidence," warned Stevens. "Perhaps you'd better come back to the Yard with me. The others, too. I'd like to clap all of you in jail!"


"That's that," said Bob Tenison briskly. He looked round and shivered. "What a day!"

"I'm cold," said Linda Martin.

"And hungry," added Tinker gloomily. He had a healthy appetite, and had eaten nothing since breakfast.

They were standing outside the Embankment entrance to New Scotland Yard, waiting for the police car the Inspector had promised them. All three had signed long statements of their evidence. All three were glad to be leaving the grim old buildings.

Tenison's breath misted frostily in the cold air. "Here's the car." They clambered in. The black vehicle moved off.

Tinker had been thinking. He asked suddenly:

"Mr. Tenison, you told me this chap Raven wasn't a very sociable fellow. Was he friendly with Garvary?"

"It's hard to say." Bob's eyes were puzzled. "He knew him, I'm sure. As a matter of fact—." He hesitated. "It's a trivial incident, but—."

"Go on," encouraged Tinker.

"Well, if those two *were* friends, they were distinctly secretive about it. I remember I came down to Garvary"s once—uh—to see Linda,"— Bob looked a trifle embarrassed—"and I thought I glimpsed Raven coming out. Only he stepped back when he saw me, and then nobody answered my ring."

"When was this?"

"Some time back. I don't remember exactly."

Tinker could make very little of Bob's rather muddled story, and they sat in silence till they reached the artist's home.

Linda waved goodbye to Tenison, then sat back with a little sigh as the car rolled towards her own apartment in Chelsea.

Tinker smiled at her sympathetically.

"Tired?"

"A little."

Linda ran her tongue over her lips nervously, then said abruptly:

"You were speaking of Raven. I—I—."

"Yes?"

"I don't like him. He frightens me, somehow. But he did know Mr. Garvary. They were talking in Leo's studio a few weeks ago. He had left the door ajar, and I walked in unexpectedly." She hesitated. "I caught four words before they saw me and grew quiet."

"Four words?"

"Yes. The phrase was so odd, it stuck in my mind. It didn't make sense." Her lovely eyes were puzzled. "It's silly, but I'm positive that Leo said—."

She paused, then finished apologetically: "A stick of tea."

# CHAPTER FIVE

"A stick of tea." The young detective was still considering the enigmatic phrase as he climbed the steps of the old house in Baker Street.

Mrs. Bardell came into the hall to meet him as he opened the front door. "Your dinner's cold," she announced severely.

Tinker greeted her absently. "Never mind, old dear." The young man looked worried.

Mrs. Bardell studied his youthful, abstracted face and said kindly: "I'll bring you some sandwiches."

She watched him climb the stairs with affection in her shrewd old eyes.

Tinker went into the consulting room with strange thoughts stirring in his mind. It was as if the key to the mystery was already in his hand..

Pedro the bloodhound was sitting in the saddlebag chair by the fire. He lifted his great head and barked throatily.

Tinker smiled. "That," he said with mock severity, "is the master's chair. You have a kennel," he went on, stroking the animal's ears, "out at the back."

Pedro looked disdainful. He was a luxury loving hound, and so far as he was concerned, the kennel was To Let.

Tinker tapped his faithful old friend on the nose, then crossed to the window and slumped in the chair behind his desk.

He was staring through the glass with unseeing eyes when Mrs. Bardell returned with a well laden tray. An appetising smell of coffee brought him back to earth. He glanced round cheerily.

"Mmm. That smells good."

Mrs. Bardell put down the tray on his desk, then stood back and folded her hands comfortably. "Eat up, now. You mustn't neglect the inner man."

"No fear of that," said Tinker appreciatively. "Martha, you're an angel. Will you marry me?"

"Get away with you!" said the housekeeper. She bustled out in high good humour.

Tinker finished his meal slowly. His thoughts were busy. He drained a last cup of coffee and clapped it back in its saucer with an air of decision.

He said aloud:

"That's it! That will help me straighten out the tangle."

When Mrs. Bardell returned to collect the tray, she found the young man sitting by Sexton Blake's latest acquisition—a wire recording machine. Tinker was speaking into a small hand microphone.

The old lady eyed it suspiciously. She sniffed. "I don't trust these new-fangled devices."

Tinker laughed. He switched off the machine. "It's only a recording device. It picks up my voice on this wire,"—he flicked a switch—"then plays it back whenever I wish." He finished the speech with his own familiar tones.

Mrs. Bardell listened for a moment in silence, then said firmly: "Unnatural, I calls it. Turn it off, do." She asked curiously: "What's that you was talking about, now?"

"Uh? Oh, that. I'm just telling the story of our latest case."

"You mean," said Mrs. Bardell, who was fond of listening to the American Forces Network, "like they do on the radio?"

"Not exactly," replied Tinker with a grin. "I'm no Sam Spade." His brow wrinkled thoughtfully. "I'm just trying to get things clear in my own mind. I feel that if I can only but record every incident—however trivial—and then play it back to myself repeatedly, I shall find the solution to the puzzle."

"Oh," said the old lady doubtfully. "Well, maybe you're right. At least it might stop you making such an awful mess on those nice clean blotters."

She went out. Pedro jumped down from the saddlebag chair and padded across to his young master.

Tinker fondled the bloodhound's massive head absently. His low, murmuring voice went on. The spools of wire revolved smoothly.

Somewhere beyond the peaceful room, a gun changed hands—and waited.


It was dark in the consulting room. Tinker sat on the floor by the glowing fire, his arm round Pedro's body.

The bloodhound looked up with mournful eyes. The firelight played over the young detective's worried face.

The recording machine played its soft-voiced, insistent commentary. And a theory was taking shape in the young man's mind.

The door opened and the lights came on suddenly. Mrs. Bardell looked in. The good lady was anxious.

"Mr. Tinker! You've been sitting here for hours. Aren't you done yet?"

"Hmmm? Oh, just about, old dear. What's the time?"

"It's past seven. Don't you want some supper?"

"Yes, please." Tinker stood up and switched off the machine. He yawned. He felt a sudden yearning for company. "I'll join you below stairs, if I may."

"Why, of course." Mrs. Bardell was flattered.

The telephone bell rang suddenly. Tinker picked up the receiver and angled it to his ear. "Hallo."

"Hallo, Tinker. Stevens here."

"Hi, Steve. Have you found any way of escape from Garvary's flat yet?"

"No, burn it." The Inspector sounded gloomy. "I had an expert examine every inch of the studio. Walls, floor, ceiling, doors—the lot."

"And?"

"And he didn't find a thing. No secret passages, no sliding panels, no hidden trapdoors. I tell you, Tinker, the killer couldn't possibly have got out of that room. Unless he walked through solid walls."

"Or burst like a bubble as I opened the door," returned Blake's assistant lightly. "Have you set a man to guard the flat?"

"Of course. Why?"

"I think," said Tinker slowly, "I'll pay the place another visit."

"Have you got an idea?" asked Stevens. He was eager, but not very hopeful. "I'd be grateful for any suggestion. I'm due for an interview with the A.C. tomorrow. And he doesn't believe in ghosts."

"Or killers that vanish into thin air," grinned Tinker. "Don't build your hopes too high, Steve. I have an idea, but I shall have to test it before I tell anybody."

"All right." Stevens had a healthy respect for his young friend's capabilities. "I shall have to trust you, I suppose. I'll give orders for you to be admitted."

"Thanks. Uh, Steve—."

"Yes?"

"Whitfield is conducting the post mortem, I suppose?"

"Yes, of course. I expect his report tomorrow. Why?"

"Part of it might surprise you."

"What?" It was partly a question, partly an exclamation. "Hell's blazes! You're not going to tell me that Garvary wasn't shot, or—or—." The Inspector was becoming excited. "Or poisoned first, or something damn silly like that, are you?"

"No, no." Tinker chuckled.

"Then what do you mean, burn it?"

Tinker hesitated. His instinctive response trembled on the verge of speech. Then he thought again. Stevens couldn't act on a mere suspicion. And the report of the autopsy might help to convince him.

His mind made up, the young detective said firmly: "I'll tell you tomorrow. But I'll call in the studio tonight."

Stevens sighed. "All right. Goodbye, Tinker."

"'Bye, Steve."

Tinker hung up. Mrs. Bardell said, with concern in her voice:

"You're going out again, on a night like this?"

He smiled at her. "Later on, old dear. Now where's my supper?" He went down the stairs with his arm round her shoulders.

He didn't know what that moment's hesitation on the telephone was to cost him.


It was nearly midnight before the young man from Baker Street presented himself at the door of Garvary's flat. As he stabbed the bell push with his thumb, an odd feeling of apprehension swept through him. He wondered, queerly, what he would do if the door came open in the dead hand of a bullet riddled sculptor who couldn't possibly have been murdered.

His ring was answered by a reassuring figure in uniform.

"Come in, sir," said the constable. "The Inspector told me to expect you." Tinker glanced round the studio. It was much as he had left it.

The constable said hospitably: "It's a cold night, sir. But I have a fire in the next room." He indicated the door in the corner.

Tinker nodded. "You're—?" He paused invitingly.

"P.C. Craig, sir." He named his division.

Tinker said pleasantly: "Do me a favour, old chap. Go and sit by the fire, and leave me alone for a while."

The constable looked dubious. "Inspector Stevens—," he began doubtfully. "Said he would co-operate," Tinker reminded him gently.

"Come now. Nobody can get into the flat while we're here. You won't be neglecting your duties."

"Very well." The constable did not seem happy. But the police were rarely unwise enough to refuse help from Sexton Blake and his assistant.

Tinker smiled his thanks. He asked casually:

"The other tenants in this part of the building. Are they about?"

"The young fellow upstairs—what's his name? Tenison, that's it— he's in bed, so far as I know. The other chap, Raven—he's out."

"Out? Oh, yes. He works at night."

"If you can call it work." P.C. Craig was slightly scornful. "He has some connection with a night club, so I hear. Won't be back till the small hours." He chuckled. "Proper temper that chap has, too."

"Oh?"

"Yes. When the Inspector went down to interview him this afternoon—purely as a matter of routine, I understand—he got the rough side of Raven's tongue."

"Why?"

"Seems the fellow doesn't like his sleep to be disturbed. Said he'd already been interrupted once that day—."

Tinker coughed.

"—and was fed up with listening to tiles crash past his window. That was the Sergeant," explained Craig in an aside, "examining the roof. Anyway, he stamped out of the building in a fury, and we didn't see him again till evening. Then he went out again."

Tinker nodded. "Now, if you don't mind," he murmured, "I'll get to work."

"Yes, sir." There was a gleam of curiosity in the constable's eye, but he went through the inner door obediently. Tinker thoughtfully bolted it behind him. He glanced through the windows. It was snowing again. He looked round the studio. He said aloud:

"Here's where I know—if it's This Way Out."

# CHAPTER SIX

P.C. Craig shifted uneasily. His glance strayed towards the door in the corner. It was a quarter of an hour since he had left Tinker in the studio, and the constable was feeling a trifle restive.

A sudden burst of wind rattled the window panes. The whirling snow flakes drove at the glass in fury. Despite the fire, the policeman shivered.

He stood up at last and went to the inner door. He paused for a moment with his fingers on the handle, then twisted it hard and opened the door.

The studio was empty.

Craig paced across to the windows. They were securely fastened on the inside. The constable stared round, repressing a vague sense of disquiet.

"Funny," he mumbled. "Where's the young fellow gone? I— Oh, of course." His gaze had fallen on the outer door. Tinker must have let himself on to the landing. The Yale lock would have sprung to behind him.

Feeling relieved, Craig walked with a heavy tread towards the door and grasped the handle.

It would not turn.

The constable stared unbelievingly. The small round stud which was the inner catch had been pushed up and was holding the lock fast.

The door had been secured from the inside. Yet, Tinker was no longer in the studio. Craig swung round. "All right," he called grimly. "No monkey tricks young fellow. I know you're hiding somewhere."

There was no reply. The constable's mouth set sternly. He ran to the cupboards and jerked open the doors one by one.

"Empty!"

Craig was alarmed. A thin beading of sweat showed along his hair line. He scanned the room with fear-tinged eyes.

He continued to search desperately, looking in the most unlikely places, and knowing instinctively it was all in vain.

He stopped at last and wiped the perspiration from his forehead.

He whispered: "It's impossible! A man can't vanish—like a ghost."

A bell shrilled suddenly, shattering the silence.

The constable gasped. Then, feeling ashamed, he went to the door to answer the call. His fingers trembling, he pulled down the catch and released the lock. He opened the door.

"Surprise, surprise," said Tinker cheerily and walked past him into the studio.

The constable swallowed. He shut the door with great care, then said indignantly: "Now, see here, young fellow— ."

"I'm sorry," said Tinker contritely. "I couldn't resist the temptation to startle you."

"Never mind that," returned Craig impatiently. "How the devil did you manage to disappear like that?"

"Ah," said Tinker. "That would be telling."

The constable's temper was fraying. "Now, see here," he snapped again.

Tinker soothed him. "I was just testing a theory. Rather successfully, as it turned out."

The constable grinned suddenly. "You gave me the fright of my life." His voice dropped. "The matter can't rest here, sir. A murder was committed in this room, and Inspector Stevens nearly tore this place apart looking for a way out. You seem to have found it. It's your duty to explain."

Tinker said seriously: "The guv'nor and I have never obstructed the police. I'll explain what I've been doing—but," he warned, "in my own good time. I want to talk this case over with Mr. Blake first."

"But——."

"I'll tell you this," said the young detective amiably. "There's no kind of secret exit anywhere in the flat."

The constable's mouth opened. "That's impossible."

Tinker shrugged. "Seeing," he murmured gently, "is believing."

He turned back to the door. Craig, for one incredible instant, half expected to see the young man dissolve like a phantom through the panels. Instead, Tinker put up his hand and twisted open the lock.

The constable found his voice: "You're going?"

"Why not?" asked Tinker mildly, and closed the door behind him.

Outside in the corridor, he grinned wickedly, then went silently down the stairway to the floor below.

He glanced about him cautiously, then pushed at the door to Raven's apartment. It swung open at his touch.

Tinker stepped inside the flat, closing the door behind him. He left the catch up.

It was dark. "Better not put the lights on," Tinker told himself silently. He fumbled in the pocket of his raincoat and drew out a flashlight. He depressed the button and—.

"Blow!" said Tinker ruefully. The bulb was broken.

He thought for a moment. There had been a small table beside Raven's bed that afternoon. He had noticed an electric torch lying on the top.

He went to the inner door. One of the windows in the main room was open a few inches at the top. A cold blast of air made him shiver.

He opened the door and groped his way towards the bed, guided by a fugitive gleam of light from the barred window. He ran his hands over the surface of the little table.

"Ah!" he breathed with satisfaction.

He picked up the torch and clicked it on. Then—.

"Oh, dear," he muttered inadequately. A dying gleam flickered dully and went out. The batteries were spent.

Tinker glanced around. He strode across to the fireplace, picked up the poker, and stirred the glowing coals vigorously. A thin tongue of flame leaped out of the embers. The meagre, fitful light was enough to guide the young detective's actions.

He replaced Raven's torch on the table top and drew his own from his pocket. He unscrewed the base and let the batteries fall into his hand. Then he emptied Raven's torch and prepared to transpose the batteries.

"Exchange is no robbery," he murmured. "Hallo! What's this?"

Something was uncoiling against his fingers. He thought at first it was the cardboard backing of the exhausted batteries, then a lively interest began to stir in his mind as he realised what he was holding.

He went and knelt by the grate, examining his find by the light of the fire.

It was a thin strip of microfilm, which had been coiled tightly round one of the batteries in Raven's torch. The pictures were evidently photographs of documents, or the pages of a book.

Tinker strained his eyes to make out the tiny characters. Momentarily off guard, he did not notice the almost imperceptible sound from the doorway behind him.

A bright beam of light cut with the suddenness of a knife slash across the darkened room.

Tinker's head jerked round abruptly. His pupils contracted—almost Painfully—in the glare.

He gasped. "What—."

The question died on his lips. A gloved hand came into the orbit of light. It was holding a gun.

"Don't bother to get up," said a soft voice, evilly.

Tinker shut his eyes and opened them again. He was beginning to distinguish a shadowy form behind the powerful flashlight. Still on one knee, he said pleasantly:

"I didn't hear you come in."

The man with the gun laughed shortly. "You left the catch up. That was a mistake."

"Not my first," commented Tinker ruefully.

"But possibly," said the other quietly, "your last."

Tinker felt the sweat break out on his forehead. He said nothing.

The soft voice continued gently: "We'll talk. No, don't move." A chuckle sounded from behind the light. "I'm a cautious man. I prefer to keep you at a disadvantage."

Tinker's right shoulder was turned towards the man with the gun. The young detective's left hand had dropped to the ground beside him. Shielded by his body, his fingers closed around the poker.

The shadowy figure indicated the strip of film in Tinker's right hand. "Since you know of the microfilm,"—the soft voice showed over tones of menace— "you must also know of the little black book."

Tinker stared into the barrel of the automatic pistol.

He said carefully:

"I don't know anything about a little black book. As to the microfilm," he swallowed, "I found it by accident."

There was a silence. Then the other said harshly:

"You don't expect me to believe that, do you?"

"No, I don't," replied Tinker regretfully. "Though it happens to be true." The metal struck cold against his palm.

The man with the gun said abruptly:

"You called on Garvary this morning. Why?"

"He sent for me." Tinker answered absently. He was weighing his chances coolly. The pistol jerked impatiently.

"I know that. What did he have to tell you?"

"I don't know. He was dead."

The other man growled angrily. "Don't trifle with me. He sent you a message of some sort. What was it?"

"He was receiving anonymous letters. The threats alarmed him. He asked for my help."

"Yours or Sexton Blake's?"

"For once," said Tinker unthinkingly, "I'm on my own."

It was a blunder which he recognised at once. A hiss of indrawn breath, as of satisfaction, came from behind the circle of light. "Today — or yesterday, rather— was the first time you heard from Garvary?"

"Yes." Tinker thought quickly. He couldn't see how to retrieve his error. "He sent Lind Martin to Baker Street."

"Linda Martin!" The man with the gun seemed queerly excited. He spoke the name with a rising inflection. "The girl, yes. I wonder— would he trust her?" He broke off. "Listen. Did she bring you a packet from Garvary?"

"She didn't bring me anything, except one of the letters."

"Never mind that. It's the book that interests me."

Tinker"s throat was dry. "I told you. I don't know anything about this little black book."

"You still know far too much." The other"s voice was level. "I'm sorry for you, Tinker. You're a danger to my safety."

The gun steadied in his hand.

Tinker's mouth set desperately. He thought: "It's now or never," and swept up the poker shoulder high and hurled it towards the evil eye of light.

"Ahhh!"

The man in the shadows let out a shuddering gasp of pain as the poker crashed against his forearm. He staggered back. The light danced wildly in his hand and the rays streamed back, showing his contorted features in a brief, revealing flash.

He recovered instantly.

Tinker had thrown himself sideways the moment the poker had left his grasp. He had time enough to scramble up and take the first step towards the man with the gun.

Then two livid flames stabbed from the darkness and the room resounded with the crash of gunfire. Tinker felt a dull thud which was followed by a searing pain and he lurched stupidly, fumbling at his chest.

A voice which he didn't recognise as his own said incredulously: "Why, you—," and bubbled and choked.

He staggered forward. Another tongue of fire leaped to meet him He felt the lash of the bullet and the warm blood streaming across his temple, then the pain went away and he knew no more.

# CHAPTER SEVEN

Sexton Blake climbed the steps of his home in Baker Street with a scarcely audible sigh of relief. The case which the famous detective had just brought to a close had called upon both his finesse as a diplomat and his skill as a fighter. Now an unwonted weariness was flooding his spare, athletic frame, and he was looking forward to rest in the saddleback chair and— despite the lateness of the hour— a chat with his young assistant.

Scarcely had the door closed behind him when his old housekeeper appeared from her quarters below stairs and bustled towards him smiling broadly.

"It's good to see you again, sir."

"It's good to see you, Mrs. Bardell," replied Blake, as she helped him out of his heavy snow-spattered coat. "But you shouldn't have waited up for me. I might not have returned till daybreak."

"Bless you, sir," said the old lady comfortably. "I regards it as a pleasure and an extinction to work for Mr. Sexton Blake."

The detective's mouth quivered humorously. Not for worlds would he have hurt her feelings by correcting her.

Mrs. Bardell went on:

"Besides, Mr. Tinker is likewise out."

"At this hour?" Blake raised his eyebrows. "And in this weather?"

"Yes, sir." Mrs. Bardell folded her hands. "We also 'ave a visitor."

"Detective Inspector Stevens, perhaps?"

The old lady looked at him with admiring eyes. "How did you know, sir?"

Blake laughed. "I detect a pleasing aroma wafting down from the consulting room. And of all my visitors, the good Inspector is the one most likely to help himself to my best cigars."

He walked briskly up the stairs to the floor above. The door of the consulting room was already ajar. He twisted his long, sinewy fingers round the handle and pushed it fully open.

Detective Inspector Stevens was seated by the fire, still wearing his battered raincoat and nursing his bowler in his lap.

He removed the glowing cigar from between his lips and stood up, greeting the detective with a trace of surprise on his heavy features. "Hallo, Mr. Blake, I hardly expected to see you. I understood you were

493

working on that business in—."

Sexton Blake held up his hand. He spoke in friendly reproof. "Better not discuss it, Inspector. It's sufficient to say that the affair has been concluded." His lean, somewhat ascetic face broke into a quick smile. "In England's favour, I'm glad to say."

Stevens nodded briefly. He said irrelevantly: "This is a fine cigar."

"For myself," said Blake, "I prefer a pipe." He dropped into the saddlebag chair and thumbed tobacco from a pouch. He scratched a match over the bowl and murmured, between puffs: "You're a late caller, Stevens. I suppose you know it's after midnight?"

The Inspector inclined his head. He drew deeply on his cigar.

Blake was a man of acute intelligence allied to a fund of human kindliness. He could see his old friend was badly worried. He said abruptly: "Obviously, you came to see Tinker. Why?"

Stevens flung the cigar into the heart of the fire and smacked his hands together heavily. "It's about this blasted case," he confessed. "The murder of Leo Garvary."

"Garvary, Garvary," muttered Blake. "The sculptor?"

"Yes. You knew him, then?"

"I know his work," corrected Blake. "He had, at one time, a very considerable talent. Though he seems of late to have lapsed into a certain obscurity."

"He's obscure no longer," said Stevens grimly. "He's dead, in incredible circumstances."

A spark of interest showed in Blake's steady grey eyes.

Stevens pursued: "To put it briefly, the man died in a room from which there was no possible exit. Since the A.C. doesn't believe in miracles, I have the unenviable task of clipping handcuffs on a killer who has, presumably, no physical existence."

Blake smiled. "You intrigue me, Inspector. What has Tinker to do with all this?"

"Garvary sent his model—a girl named Linda Martin— to see you. Since you weren't here, Tinker took charge of things himself —."

"I remember," interrupted Blake. "I gave him permission. Go on, Stevens." He gestured in apology.

"Young Tinker asked me to let him into the dead man's apartment tonight. Said he had a theory he wanted to test."

"Good for him. I'll back his judgment against the best of New Scotland Yard." Blake waved his hand gracefully. "Saving your presence, Inspector."

"Believe me," said Stevens frankly, "I don't care who solves the case, so long as somebody does. It's driving me insane. Tinker was hinting at all sorts of things on the telephone. I came here to find out what he knows. If he proves obstinate,"—the Inspector sighed—perhaps you can persuade him to co-operate."

"It's true," smiled Blake, "I have a strong affluence over Tinker, as Mrs. Bardell might say. But I'm not sure I should interfere. This affair is the young'un's solo."

Stevens scowled ruefully. "I wish I knew what he's playing at. Mrs. Bardell tells me I just missed him. Why he should want to poke around Garvary's flat so late as this— ." He broke off and sighed. "It's beyond me."

The wind battered at the panes, hurling snow against the glass. Something stirred in the famous detective's consciousness. It was almost a presentiment.

He said slowly: "I gather Tinker implied he had discovered how the crime was committed."

"Yes." The Inspector seemed irritated. "Perhaps he can see farther into a brick wall than I can."

Blake took the pipe from his mouth and cradled the bowl in his palm. "If he knows that," he mused, "obviously he's a threat to the murderer's safety."

There was an uneasy silence. Into both men's minds came the thought, unbidden: if a man kills once, he won't hesitate to kill again.

Sexton Blake knocked out his pipe into the fire. He stood up, his face impassive. "I've changed my mind, Inspector. I shall investigate this crime without delay."

Stevens nodded. He said simply: "I'm glad."

Blake continued crisply: "I suggest we follow Tinker to the dead man's apartment. You"ll have to direct me, of course."

"Gladly." The Inspector hesitated. "It's late, and I have no car waiting—."

"We'll take the Grey Panther. You can give me all the details of L'Affaire Garvary on the way."

They went out together.

The snowflakes stung their faces as they hurried from the car towards the doorway of the old building.

Stevens blinked as the light from the hall caught his eyes. His heavy face was worried. He nodded absently to the man behind the reception desk, and asked a question.

"Yes, Inspector. The young gentleman arrived a while ago. He's still here."

"Thanks. This way, Mr. Blake."

Sexton Blake followed the Inspector up the stairs at the rear of the hall. He walked lightly, on the balls of his feet.

Stevens grunted, as they reached the landing:

"Garvary's flat is here, at the end of the passage. I— Hallo! What's this?"

A burly man was standing outside the door of the dead man's apartment, his finger on the bell push.

"It's Raven," muttered Stevens, and led the way along the corridor.

As the two men approached, Raven glanced around sharply. An odd expression of wariness flickered briefly in his deep set eyes. He greeted them softly:

"Good evening, gentlemen. Or, rather—good morning."

Stevens responded gruffly. "You're home early," he commented, pointedly.

"Yes. As you can see, I"m dressed for work," said Raven, indicating his evening clothes with pleasant self mockery. "But I found my heart wasn't in it. I soon returned."

Sexton Blake spoke for the first time. He said politely:

"You've soiled your cuff, Mr. Raven. Allow me."

Without haste, he took hold of the burly man's wrist and rubbed a clean handkerchief over a long smudge of dirt. Raven's arm jerked instinctively, but then he relaxed and said smoothly:

"It escaped my notice. You have keen eyes, Mr. Blake."

The detective released the other's wrist. He murmured:

"You know me, then?"

Raven said politely:

"All the world knows Sexton Blake."

Stevens interposed impatiently:

"What exactly do you want, Mr. Raven?"

The man"s eyes hooded. "I was about to ring. Excuse me." He prodded the bell push, then plunged his hands in the pockets of his overcoat and against the wall. He explained:

"I'm going to make some coffee before I go to bed. It occurred to me that the constable here might care to join me."

Stevens began to speak and at the same moment P.C. Craig appeared at the opening door of the flat, but before either could complete a sentence they were interrupted sharply.

From somewhere below them came the sound of a report which was followed almost immediately by another.

Raven jerked clenched fists out of his pockets. "Good grief, that sounds like—."

He ran to the back stairway, followed by Blake and the others. The Inspector's face was vivid with alarm. He gasped a question into the detective's ear.

Blake shook his head. "Tinker wasn't armed," he replied grimly. "I'm almost sure of that."

Raven clattered to a halt at the bottom of the narrow stairs. He pointed wordlessly. The door to his flat was open.

Stevens asked: "You didn't leave it like that?"

"No. And I've only just arrived. I called on the constable first—."

"You didn't come down here?"

"No, I—."

Stevens didn't wait to hear the rest of Raven's explanation. He led the way into the darkened apartment. As he clicked on the lights, a gust of cold air played over his face.

He grunted:

"One of those windows is open at the top. Is that how you left it?"

Raven nodded. "I like fresh air."

Stevens stared round the room and pursed thick lips. "What do you think, Mr. Blake?"

"I think," replied Blake evenly, "that I smell gun smoke."

The Inspector's chin lifted. Without a word he went to the inner door which was already ajar and pushed it fully open.

Raven began to say: "That's my bedroom," when his words were cut off by the click of a switch and a cry from the Scotland Yard detective.

Stevens' expression was both angry and fearful. Blake shouldered past him into the bedroom. The he, too, was frozen for a long second in immobility.

Tinker lay sprawled on the floor with an ugly red stain spreading over the tweed jacket beneath his open raincoat. Blood swelled over his forehead, running into his eyes.

A tiny flame danced over the ashy embers of a dying fire. It was the only sign of life in the silent room.

# CHAPTER EIGHT

That moment of paralysis was for Sexton Blake an odyssey of pain. And he knew, almost for the first time, the acrid taste of fear.

Then he strode forward and knelt beside the body of his young assistant. His long fingers felt, without trembling, for the throbbing of Tinker's pulse.

Stevens asked hoarsely: "Is he dead?"

Blake looked up. His face was a frozen mask, but relief, and then anger, showed in the depths of his piercing grey eyes.

He said:

"No. But he's badly wounded. He needs immediate care."

The Inspector breathed something which was probably a prayer. Then he snapped: "Craig!"

"Yes, sir." The constable saluted mechanically.

"Telephone for an ambulance. At once, man!"

The constable ran out. Stevens bawled after him: "And see that no one leaves the building." He jerked round with glinting eyes. "And now we'll search this flat. Raven, come with me."

Sexton Blake pulled the cap from his assistant's curly hair. His fingers probed delicately at the young man's forehead.

He drew in his breath with relief. The ugly wound across Tinker's temple was only superficial.

"Hold on, old son," he said aloud. "Help is coming."

He didn't attempt to move the unconscious young man's body. He stood up and went into the bathroom and damped a towel with water. He came back and wiped the blood from Tinker's eyes. His touch was firm and gentle.

Stevens was hurrying about the apartment with heavy feet. Raven followed him like a shadow. He seemed entirely subdued.

The Inspector came to a halt by the outer door. He looked angry and puzzled. "Mr. Raven!"

"Yes, Inspector?"

"Is there no way of reaching the floor above except by those stairs?"

"There's no other way, no." The burly man's tone was neutral. "To leave the building at all,"—he hesitated—"I have to go up to get out, if you understand me."

"Only too well," replied Stevens tersely. He stepped outside the flat and glared round. "There's nowhere to hide out here. And four of us heard the shots. We can all swear nobody passed us on the stairs."

"That's right, Inspector."

Stevens stepped back and slammed the door. "Right," he repeated. "And there's no one hiding in your apartment. So that leaves— what?"

Raven said doubtfully: "The courtyard?"

Stevens nodded briefly. He took a powerful torch from his pocket and strode towards the French windows. His hands hovered over the fastenings, then dropped to his sides. "Mr. Raven," he said quietly. "You're wearing gloves. Please open these windows—carefully," he added, a note of warning in his voice. "Try not to obscure any possible fingerprints."

Raven pushed open the glass doors, scraping away the piled up snow. A flurry of white flakes swept in to meet him.

The Inspector shouldered past him into the courtyard. It was snowing hard. Stevens clicked on the torch, and let the powerful beam probe round like a questing finger.

He grunted: "There's no way out, no place to hide, and—." His voice dropped thoughtfully. "And no foot marks."

"You couldn't expect to find any traces," murmured Raven. "Even recent ones. The snow's settling fast."

Stevens indicated the walls. He said grimly: "There's your answer. Our man might have escaped from this yard by scaling the walls. But look closely. There's no break in the snow piled on the tops."

Raven made no reply

Stevens clicked off the torch, leaving his bulky figure a silhouette against the light streaming out from the windows behind him.

He whispered:

"It's hard to believe that a flesh and blood killer can fade into air."


"It's hard to believe, said Sexton Blake calmly, "because it's obviously impossible." It was later. The ambulance had come and gone, and Tinker was on his way to a famous London clinic.

Blake had refused to accompany him. "He will have all he needs medically. I can do no more." His jaw had set grimly. "But I can track down the man who shot him."

Stevens had stared at the detective's calm face and shivered.

Now they were discussing the case in low tones while the Inspector's men busied themselves about the apartment.

Blake continued: "Tinker wasn't attacked by a phantom. If the evidence proves he was, then the evidence itself is wrong. Or, at least, misleading."

Stevens looked at him anxiously. "Have you formed a theory?"

"Not yet. Stevens, I'd like to examine the bedroom again."

The Inspector went to the inner door and signed to his men. They filed out of the bedroom, glancing at the Baker Street sleuth curiously.

Stevens gave them a few curt instructions, then followed Blake through the inner door and closed it behind him.

The famous detective glanced briefly at the spot where his assistant had fallen, then let his keen gaze sweep round the room.

Stevens stared at Blake's profile. It was hawk-like and aquiline. Blake asked: "You found the empty shells?"

"Yes." The Inspector produced a small box from his waistcoat pocket. Inside were two cartridge cases, nestling in a bed of cotton wool. Stevens commented tersely: "Ejected from an automatic pistol." He named a probable make and calibre. "We picked 'em up just inside the door."

"Which suggests that the gunman was standing on the threshold." Blake took long strides across the room and indicated a fresh-looking hole in the wall. "And there," he commented grimly, "is the bullet which scorched over Tinker's temples."

"Thank Heaven the angle was what it was," said the Inspector fervently. "Else the shot might have lodged in his skull."

"The damage was bad enough," said Blake, with a rasp of anger. "The young 'un has a chance of survival. But it's only a chance."

Stevens said nothing. Blake's keen gaze focussed on the bedside table. "What do you make of that?"

The Inspector followed his friend to the table. Sexton Blake pointed to two empty torches and a number of batteries beside them.

Stevens looked puzzled. "What about them?"

"One of those flashlights belongs to Tinker." Blake drew a pair of thin gloves over his hands and picked up the torch. He noted that the bulb was broken.

"What was he doing, then?" asked Stevens.

"The answer is simple enough," replied Blake absently. "Tinker discovered the bulb in his torch was shattered, and was about to transfer the batteries to another lamp. Which was, presumably, Raven's."

He glanced up. "Apparently it was at this point Tinker was interrupted."

"And shot," added the Inspector. "But why, exactly?"

"We don't yet know." Blake shrugged. "Be patient, Inspector. We're progressing." He put down the torch and moved away. "When Tinker is attacked," he murmured, "he usually defends himself. So— ah!"

He stooped over and picked up a poker from the floor. He said, over his shoulder: "You saw this, of course?"

"I'm not blind," returned the Inspector, dourly.

"The tip," continued Blake thoughtfully, "is black from the fire. Though part of the dirt appears to have been smeared off."

Stevens merely grunted.

"No matter," said Blake briskly, and replaced the poker in the grate.

The Inspector expected the great detective to move away from the fireplace. Instead, he stayed with his hand on the mantle, staring at the embers.

"Stevens." There was an odd note, almost of excitement, in Blake's quietly spoken summons. "Come here."

"What is it?"

Blake gestured, almost absently. He squatted on his heels and indicated something in the grate. "Look at that. No, don't touch it. Here." He took a pair of tweezers from his pocket and picked up a fragment of thick paper or cardboard from the tiled grate.

Stevens stooped over and stared with puzzled eyes. The scrap had apparently fallen from the fire, since its gaudy colouring was smoked and scorched.

"It's the remains of some sort of packet, I suppose," the Yard man mumbled. "A toothpaste container, perhaps."

"Smell it," said Blake shortly.

Stevens sniffed. "Why, it smells of—."

"Exactly," said Blake curtly. He dropped the fragment into a small, transparent envelope. "Now look at the fire itself."

Stevens arched his eyebrows. "It's out."

"It's smouldering," corrected Blake. "But, if you remember, the coals were still burning when we entered the room." He picked up a pair of tongs and stirred the embers gently.

His face was intent. As the black ashes fell away, his grey eyes gleamed with satisfaction. "Look there, Stevens! Do you see them?"

Similar gaudy coloured scraps showed clearly among the embers. Blake collected them carefully, commenting as he worked: "Somebody has been burning a considerable amount of paper. So much so, in fact, that the ashes have all but killed the remains of the fire."

Stevens muttered: "I'm beginning to understand."

Sexton Blake dropped the scraps into another envelope and handed it to the Inspector. He stood up. "Laboratory analysis will confirm my theory."

"For my money," grunted Stevens, "it's proved already. Those fragments are the remains of cardboard casings of ordinary—." He broke off, then finished disgustedly:

"Fireworks."

"Quite," agreed Sexton Blake. His mobile lips curved in a smile. "At least, Inspector," he murmured, "this discovery dispels the bogey of the vanishing man."

Stevens smacked his hands together angrily. "Fooled!" he growled. "I should have known those reports weren't gunshots."

"To the trained ear, "said Blake didactically, "the difference between the crack of firearms and the explosion of squibs should be immediately apparent. But think for a moment, and you will recall that our attention was cleverly misdirected."

"Hell's blazes! You mean— ."

"Don't jump to conclusions. Let's analyse the situation." Blake dropped into a chair and began to fill his pipe with a leisurely air. "First, we may assume Tinker was shot before we arrived in this building. Why then was his assailant at pains to make us believe he was attacked later?"

"To prove an alibi," answered the Inspector.

"That seems likely, yes." Blake lit his pipe and puffed reflectively. "I don't suppose our mysterious gunman intended to confront us with the enigma of," he chuckled, "a flesh and blood killer fading into air."

"Don't rub it in," grunted Stevens. "I expect he thought we'd conclude he had escaped through the courtyard."

"Yes." Smoke wreathed around Blake's head like a misty halo. "Now. We know those two 'shots' were fakes. Let's consider the mechanics of the device."

Stevens stirred impatiently. Blake went on smoothly:

"An examination of the ashes in the fire leads us to believe that the gunman, after shooting Tinker, wrapped two squibs in a sizable package of thick paper which he thrust into the heart of the fire, banking the glowing coals round it. The embers would, of course, burn through the packing, eventually igniting the fireworks. What's the obvious comment?"

The Inspector pondered. "It would be like a slow fuse."

"Exactly. A slow fuse. And," said Blake slowly, "a short one."

Stevens nodded. He clenched a heavy fist. "So?"

"So our gunman needed a witness. Name a candidate, please, Inspector."

Stevens growled:

"P.C. Craig."

"Who had not heard the shots that wounded Tinker because he was waiting behind a soundproof door. How then could our man make sure that the constable heard the second brace of reports?" Blake took the pipe out of his mouth. "No, don't answer yet. Instead consider this.

"It would be difficult, if not impossible, for any unauthorised person to enter this building at night without attracting the attention of the desk clerk. So the man who shot Tinker was either an official visitor like ourselves, or one of the tenants. And since the fireworks were exploded to prove an alibi, it seems likely the culprit had taken the precaution of placing himself in such a position that at least one independent witness could swear he was not in Raven's flat."

Blake smiled grimly. "I can give you the names of four people who answer to those requirements." He pointed the pipe stem at his friend from Scotland Yard. He said slowly:

"Detective Inspector Stevens. Sexton Blake. P.C. Craig." His lips tightened. He finished dryly:

"And a man named Alan Raven."

# CHAPTER NINE

Bob Tenison was restless and uneasy. He puffed quickly at the cigarette between his lips, then stubbed it out and threw it away half-smoked. Plunging his hands into the pockets of his dressing gown, he considered an unfinished sketch on the easel. He made a motion towards it, then jerked away irritably.

"Oh, what's the use?" He ran his sensitive artist's fingers through thick, tousled hair. A bell rang. Tenison looked surprised, and a little apprehensive. He went to the front    door and opened it. "Raven!"

The burly man said smoothly:

"Do you mind if I come in?"

Tenison shut the door behind him. He burst out:

"What the devil's happening below?"

"Ah." Raven chuckled mirthlessly. "I've got the police in. I need a place to rest.

He was still wearing his overcoat, though now he was hatless. He sprawled in a chair and looked round the studio without interest. He murmured: "I'm afraid I haven't been very sociable to date. Forgive me for intruding now."

"Make yourself at home." Tenison followed one banality with another. "Would you like a drink?"

"Please." Raven regarded the artist thoughtfully. "I didn't disturb you?"

"I couldn't sleep." Bob gave a short laugh. "Having a murder in the house—soda? Right—doesn't make for a tranquil mind."

"Maybe not." Raven took the glass the artist handed him and swallowed greedily. "You knew Garvary well?"

"I? No. What makes you think that?"

Raven's eyelids drooped. "I thought he might have—." He seemed to choose the next word carefully. "—confided in you."

"Heavens, no." Bob flushed slightly. "I called on him sometimes," he admitted, "usually as an excuse to see his model, Linda Martin." He regretted the confidence at once.

Raven nodded. He seemed oddly disappointed. He finished his drink. Slamming down the glass, he asked abruptly:

"What were Garvary's relations with this girl Linda Martin?"

Tenison replied, as politely as he could. "I told you. She was his model."

The burly man said insolently:

"That's all?"

Bob reddened again, this time with anger. "What the blazes are you insinuating?"

"Nothing, nothing." Raven seemed to lose interest. He changed the subject at once. "There's been another killing. Somebody shot Blake's assistant."

"Tinker?" The shock spilled over into Tenison's voice.

"That's right. Somebody caught him prying round my flat." Raven was relaxed and casual. "And that somebody had a gun."

"Tinker's—." Bob broke off and swallowed. "Tinker's dead?"

Raven shrugged. He said coolly:

"He's as near to death as makes no difference. I wouldn't give a penny for his chances."

"This is terrible," muttered Bob sincerely.

Raven lit a cigarette. He said indifferently:

"I can't get into my apartment for policemen. Can you give me a bed for the night?"

"Yes, yes." Tenison agreed absently. "You say Tinker was shot. Do you know—." He hesitated. "I think I can tell the police something about that."

Raven was holding the cigarette lightly between his lips. The glowing end bobbed violently, then was still.

Raven asked softly:

"You? What do you know of the shooting?"

"That's what I ask myself." Bob Tenison hesitated. Raven wasn't a friend of his, but he wanted to confide in somebody. Making up his mind, he dragged round a chair and straddled it. "Listen, then tell me what you think."

Raven nodded. The set of his mouth was ugly.

Bob was too intent on his story to notice. Without preamble, he said: "I was asleep in the bedroom adjoining. It was an uneasy slumber at best, and when I woke up some time after midnight, I gave up the struggle and came into the studio for a book.

"One of those windows was open." Bob smiled. "It's an odd taste, perhaps, but I like fresh air."

"I share that weakness," said Raven. "Go on."

"It was snowing heavily, and there was an infernal draft, so I went across to close the window. Just as I reached it, I heard a noise from below."

"What sort of a noise?"

"Well——." Bob faltered. "Like a shot."

Raven smiled sardonically. "Did you think that," he murmured, "before I told you about young Tinker?

"Frankly," said Tenison, "I don't know. I wouldn't have heard the noise at all if the window hadn't been open. It was a muffled report. It might have come from your flat."

Raven blew out a cloud of smoke. "So you heard,"—he mimicked the words—"a muffled report. Is that all?"

"No. It was followed almost immediately by another report like the first."

Raven was subtly tense. "What time did this happen?"

"I can't say exactly."

The burly man relaxed. "We heard the shots, too. Your evidence won't help much."

Tenison said dryly: "I haven't finished yet. "The noise puzzled me, and I didn't go back to bed. I wondered if maybe I should go down to your flat and investigate. Eventually I remembered there was a policeman on duty in Garvary's studio and I decided to tell him what I'd heard. Just as I started down the stairs I heard voices—and two more reports."

Raven crushed out his cigarette on his thumbnail. He flicked the stub away angrily.

Tenison rubbed his chin. "These sounds were—different, somehow. I couldn't identify them accurately. They might have been shots. They might have been something else."

Raven's right hand slid into the inside pocket of his coat. His face was dead.

Tenison continued:

"There was a cry—I recognized your voice—then a scurrying on the stairs. I went down to the landing outside Garvary's flat and hung about, uneasy and undecided. After a few minutes, the constable came rushing back. I tried to speak to him, but he brushed me aside. He told me to keep out of the way till sent for." Bob lifted his shoulder. "I came back to my studio."

Raven asked: "You've told this story to no one?"

"Not yet."

"Ah." Raven smiled unpleasantly.

Bob stood up. His fingers drummed on the back of the chair. "Well, what do you think?"

"I think," replied Raven carefully, "the police would be interested to hear your story."

"I"d better tell them, then." Bob started towards the door. He stopped as Raven called his name. "Well?"

"Don't hurry," said the burly man, oddly.

"Why not?" asked Tenison impatiently.

"Stevens is a busy man. He won't like being disturbed while he's working. You're forgetting, he virtually turned me out of my flat. He hasn't even taken a statement from me yet. And I am a principal witness."

"Well," said Bob, "he knows where to find you."

There was a brief silence. Something flared in Raven"s eyes, then flickered and was gone. He said without inflection:

"He knows where to find me."

His fingers relaxed. His hand came away from his pocket. It held nothing.


Sexton Blake took a handkerchief from his coat and showed it to the Inspector. "Look at these black smears, Stevens. I rubbed that dirt off the sleeve of Raven's coat."

"I remember." The Inspector pursed his lips. "What about it?"

Blake answered the question with another. "Have you forgotten the poker we found on the carpet?"

"Heavens, yes. You mean—."

"I mean I would like to examine Raven's forearm for a bruise. I'll wager he found the weight of that poker before young Tinker went down."

There was a steely glint in Blake's grey eyes.

Stevens was muttering:

"We can examine the poker for Tinker's prints. And we can compare the sediment on the tip with the smears on your handkerchief. But— Yes, what is it?"

Sergeant Wyatt had glanced around the door.

"Excuse me, sir. The young fellow who lives on the top floor—."

"Tenison? What about him?"

"He's asking to see you, Inspector. Says he has some information which might be important."

"All right." Stevens glanced at his watch. "Give me—oh, a couple of minutes. Then show him in."

He turned back to his friend from Baker Street. "Raven's our man," he grunted. "I've half a mind to arrest him at once."

Blake held up a warning hand. "Be careful, Inspector. As yet, we have no proof."

"But the smears on his sleeve, and the squibs in the fire—."

"Interesting, yes. But, in themselves, not conclusive evidence of the man's guilt."

"But dammit, the thing's obvious. He came back unexpectedly, caught Tinker and shot him, planted the fireworks, ran upstairs to call out the constable and fix his alibi—."

"And was considerably startled to find Inspector Stevens and Sexton Blake included in his audience. Yes, old man. The thing's obvious. But we need more evidence."

They were interrupted by Tenison's arrival. Bob entered diffidently. He was still wearing his pyjamas and dressing gown.

"Now, sir," said Stevens gruffly. "I understand you have something to tell us.

"Yes, Inspector." With an awed glance at Sexton Blake, whom he recognised at once, Bob Tenison repeated his story.

Though he still had no knowledge of the exact significance of his own evidence, the artist could not fail to be aware of the growing excitement on the Inspector's rugged face.

When Bob had finished, Stevens thumped a heavy fist into his palm. "Blake," he cried exultantly, "we've got him!"

Sexton Blake inclined his head.

Tenison looked bewildered. "What do you mean?" he asked. "Is my story so very important? Raven didn't seem to think so."

"Raven?" The triumphant grin froze on the Inspector's lips. "You told Raven about this?"

"Why, yes." Tenison was shocked at the change in the Yard mans tone. "He came up to my flat—."

Stevens said grimly: "You're lucky you're still alive."

Bob stuttered helplessly:

"I—I—."

The Inspector paid no heed. He growled to Blake: "Raven's no fool. He knows now that his alibi's broken. And—." He broke off with an oath.

Sexton Blake snapped a question.

Stevens' voice was hard. "The gun, Mr. Blake. The gun. We didn't find it. It wasn't hidden in this flat. Raven wouldn't be fool enough to hide it anywhere else in the building if he suspects the pistol can be traced to him. He's still carrying it!"

Blake said softly: "I believe you're right."

A knock at the door made them turn. A uniformed policeman appeared. He saluted smartly. "You sent for me, Inspector?"

Stevens stared at him. "No, I didn't. What put that idea into your head?"

The constable stared in his turn. "Why, the gentleman gave me your message, sir. The burly gentleman with the deep set eyes——."

"Raven!" Stevens choked. "Quick, man. What did he tell you?" "Only that you wanted to see me at once."

Bob Tenison muttered:

"I don't understand. I left Raven in my flat. He said he'd wait while I talked to you, Inspector."

"I don't understand either," grumbled Stevens. "I——."

"Inspector." Blake cut in calmly. "Where was this man stationed?"

"Why, in the hall, of course." Stevens groaned. "Burn it! That means the front door is unguarded."

Blake said levelly:

"He has made a bid for escape."

He strode across the room and picked up the telephone. His calm voice cut through the angry babble behind him.

"Hello. Is that the desk clerk? Good. Is Mr. Raven…."

Thomas Heath said softly:

"Yes, this is the desk clerk." He glanced up. He could see Alan Raven standing by the door to the street, looking out at the driving snow.

"Yes, Mr. Raven's here. Do you want to speak to him?"

The "phone crackled. Heath's eyes widened. "I don't quite understand. Keep him here, you say?" His voice dropped instinctively. "I'll do my best, Mr. Blake. Yes. Yes. Goodbye."

He hung up. His mouth was dry. He called:

"Mr. Raven!"

"Yes, Tom?" The burly man's response was pleasant.

"I—I—." Heath's mind was barren of ideas. "I wonder if you could give me a light?" he finished lamely.

"Certainly." Raven strolled back to the reception desk. He produced a lighter and flicked it into flame. "Where's your cigarette, Tom?"

Heath smiled weakly. "I'd forgotten. I've run out of smokes."

Raven glanced at him sharply. He snuffed out the flame and dropped the lighter into his pocket.

He said abruptly: "Goodnight, Tom." He turned away.

Heath jumped up and snatched the burly man's sleeve. "Don't go, sir."

Raven"s eyes hooded. His free hand slipped inside his coat. Heath sat down, still clutching the other's sleeve. He was beginning to lose his nerve.

Raven's voice was soft. "Are you trying to detain me, Tom?"

Neither man moved. Then Raven's keen ears caught the sound of hurrying footsteps. The desk clerk heard them, too. His nerve cracked.

510

"Here! Come quickly!"

Raven said kindly:

"That was a mistake, Tom. I'm sorry for you." He withdrew his hand from the inner pocket.

Dull metal crashed into the desk clerk's face. Heath's shrill scream rose higher than another sound which was like that of breaking wood. He sprawled over the desk.

Raven raised the gun and clubbed it down on the other man's head. Then he ran lightly out into the darkness and disappeared amid the swirling, feathery flakes.

# CHAPTER TEN

Linda Martin struggled with the door of an enormous cupboard. Suspended in a vacuum, the panels melted and blurred and vanished beneath her anguished gaze.

A bullet riddled corpse sat up and smiled at her.

Linda screamed, and woke up. Her frightened gaze went round the darkened room, then she sobbed and buried her face in the pillows.

A bell rang suddenly. Linda fumbled for the telephone and cried into the receiver:

"Hallo. Hallo!"

"Linda! Is that you, Linda?" The voice in her ear was anxious. "This is Bob."

"Bob!" The girl laughed hysterically. "Bob. Oh, Bob."

"Linda, my dear. What is it? You sound upset."

Linda sat up and pushed her hair away from her eyes.

"It's nothing." She clicked on the light. Her voice grew calmer. "A nightmare, that's all."

"That's understandable." Tenison hesitated. "You found Garvary's body. It must have been a shock."

"Yes." Linda was herself again. "Where are you, Bob? In your flat?"

"No. I"m speaking from the switchboard in the hall." He hesitated once more. "There's been some trouble here."

"Trouble?" Linda was wide awake. "What sort of trouble?"

"I hardly know how to tell you this, but—but there's been another shooting."

Linda gasped.

Answering her unspoken question, Tenison went on: "It's Tinker. He's been shot."

"You don't mean—."

"No, no," Bob cut in swiftly. "He isn't dead, thank God. That is—not yet."

"Who shot him?"

Tenison said:

"They—that is, the police—they think it was Raven."

"Raven!" Linda's eyes widened. "But why should he harm Tinker?"

"I don't know." Bob's voice dropped. "The Inspector's here and so is Sexton Blake. From what they've told me, and from the hints I've

513

picked up from the others, I think young Tinker came here tonight to test a theory about Leo Garvary's death. In some way, the trail led to Raven's flat."

"But how?"

"We don"t know the details," said Bob quickly. "And I'll have to be discreet. Strictly speaking, I shouldn't be discussing the case at all. I suppose it's slander, even now, to call Raven Suspect Number One."

"Even now?" Linda's temples were throbbing. "Why should the police think Raven killed Leo?"

Tenison said eagerly:

"I haven't told you everything. You know the desk clerk here, don't you."

"Yes, of course."

"The poor devil's in hospital with a concussion and a broken jaw. Raven clubbed him twice with a gun."

Linda was beyond surprise. She said weakly:

"I'm sorry, Bob. I can't seem to take in anything you say."

"I'm sorry, too." Tenison was remorseful. "I shouldn't have bothered you. I don't know why I blundered so. Heavens above, it's the middle of the night."

"No, no, Bob," the girl protested. "Don't apologise. I'm glad you rang." Her breath caught. "Oh, Bob. When will this nightmare be over?"

Tenison soothed her. "Don't worry, Linda." He laughed encouragingly. "I know it was a shock for you. But after all, your part in the affair is almost finished. You'll have to appear at the inquest, but that's only a formality. Then you can forget all about it." His colourless voice took on a new authority. "I'll look after you. And we can safely leave Sexton Blake to track down the man who shot his assistant."

Linda said dreadfully: "Tinker mustn't die."

Tenison spoke with a confidence he was far from feeling. "He'll pull through." He coughed. "Listen, dear. I shall have to ring off now. The police are here, of course, and they'll be wanting the "phone for their own use. Yes, officer, I'll clear the line. Thanks."

He spoke to the girl again. "I'll see you tomorrow. "Bye, Linda." He hung up.

The girl sat motionless. Then her hand tightened on the silent receiver and she whispered again: "Tinker mustn't die."

Detective Inspector Stevens snarled into the phone:

"What do you mean, there's no trace of the fellow? A man can't walk into the snow and vanish. Yes, I know you're doing your best. That's the trouble, burn it."

His face was red. At his side, like a silent ghost, Detective Sergeant Wyatt gave a warning cough.

Stevens cooled. "Sorry," he grunted. "I spoke hastily. No, I haven't got Raven's photograph. You've got his description, haven't you? Yes, I know it could fit a thousand men. But I don't want a thousand men. I want Raven!"

He slammed down the receiver. He looked rather sheepish. He mumbled: "I lost my temper. But Raven's a dangerous man." He smacked his fist on the desk top. "Where is he, dammit?"

Wyatt said stolidly: "He's gone to ground."

Raven said: "Where else could I go at this time of night?"

The other repeated:

"You should not have come here"

Raven snapped his fingers irritably. "I tell you, I was forced to. I was lucky to escape at all, once that fool Tenison had exposed my alibi."

"Your precious alibi," said his companion, with a thin rasp of contempt. "Was that the best you could do?"

"I had to act quickly. I couldn't smuggle Tinker's body out of my flat without being noticed. And Heath had seen me come in. I nearly lost my head. Fortunately I had those fireworks left over from some foolery in November—."

"You panicked," said the other thinly. "Just as you did after Garvary's murder when you came here snivelling because—."

Raven said evilly:

"Watch your tongue."

The words dropped like pebbles into a pool of silence. Then the burly man went on quietly:

"I shot Tinker because he found the microfilm. I clubbed Heath because he got in my way. That's what I did tonight." His eyes hooded. "I'm ready to kill when I must." He grinned crookedly. "Remember that."

"You showed your hand. Why didn't you bluff it out?"

"I tried but the luck was against me. Did you expect me to wait to be searched when I had the gun on me?"

"Why didn't you leave it by Tinker's body?"

Raven swore impatiently. "Suppose the police had traced it to you. Is that what you wanted?"

"The pistol wasn't registered."

"I didn't know that."

"I wish I'd never given it to you."

"It's a little late to say so now."

"Give me the gun."

Raven said coolly:

"No. I may need it again."

"Haven't you done enough violence?"

Raven said softly: "Understand this. We're not safe till we recover the little black book."

He stood up. His voice was gentle. "If necessary, I'll kill again to get it."

The young man in the hospital bed shifted and groaned unconsciously.

The nurse in charge of the private room got up from her seat and went across to him. She shifted his pillows and moved him into a more comfortable position.

Tinker's head was swathed in bandages. What was visible of his face was almost as white as the sheets. He groaned again.

The nurse stared own on him, pity piercing her professional armour of kindly indifference.

She though: Poor boy. And so young.

She realised, with a start, that she was thinking of him as a man rather than a patient. Tinker's eyes flickered open sightlessly. He seemed to be trying to speak.

The nurse soothed him. "Hush now. Don't try to talk." Her voice was softly Irish. Tinker's lips parted. Sounds bubbled out.

The nurse remembered her instructions. She bent her ear to his mouth. Tinker said clearly:

"Raven... film... black book." His eyes closed.

Sexton Blake sat in the saddlebag chair, his head sunk on his chest. The firelight threw his lean, ascetic face into sharp relief.

The door opened. Blake looked up with a quick, spontaneous smile which momentarily belied the grave cast of his features.

"Mrs. Bardell! Why aren't you in bed?"

The housekeeper stood on the threshold of the consulting room, a slightly comical figure with her hair in curlers.

She clutched the voluminous dressing gown more closely about her buxom figure and said anxiously:

"I couldn't sleep, sir. Not with poor Mr. Tinker lying there in 'ospital and fighting for his life—."

She broke off and sniffed.

The detective said quietly:

"He's in good hands, Mrs. Bardell." He stood up and patted the old lady on the shoulder. "Go back to your room," he said kindly. "I'll call you if there's any news."

"Yes, sir." She blinked away a tear. "But when I think of him as he was yesterday, cheerful like he always was, and spending all that time 'unched over that thingummy in the corner—."

"Mrs. Bardell!" A spark of excitement showed in Blake's eyes. "Do you mean the wire recorder?"

"Yessir." The old lady's speech was beginning to slur. "I think that"s what you calls it. He said as 'ow he was recording every incident in the case—."

She broke off as the detective turned away precipitately. He bent over the machine and adjusted the controls.

Tinker's voice, young and alive, spoke out of the inanimate mechanism.

Daylight peeped through the wide windows of the consulting room.

Sexton Blake stretched out his arms and yawned. He took a pouch from the pocket of his dressing gown and filled his pipe with tobacco. He lit up and drew in the smoke luxuriously.

His eyes were tired, yet strangely triumphant. He had not slept.

He stood up and walked across to the window. Resting his hand on the curtain, he stared down at the deserted street.

He began to think about his assistant. Then, exerting all the iron force of his will, he locked away the searing worry into a closed compartment of his mind. He knew well enough that work was his only refuge. He strode back to the machine and clicked it on.

Tinker's voice started to recite the whole history of the case again. He had recorded even the most trivial of incidents, from the time Linda Martin had called at their house in Baker Street till the time he had left her in the police car.

Sexton Blake listened attentively as the wire unspooled yet again.. Tinker's voice said, in conclusion:

"Miss Martin caught only four words. She didn't understand them, but she was certain Garvary said to Raven: 'A stick of tea'"

There was a short silence. Then Tinker's voice burst out irrepressibly: "We know what that means, guv 'nor, don't we?"

Sexton Blake switched off the machine. He said grimly:

"Yes, old son. We do."

# CHAPTER ELEVEN

Detective Inspector Stevens said gloomily:

"I don't like it. We can't find Raven anywhere."

Detective Sergeant Wyatt coughed discreetly. "After all," he pointed out, "it's only a matter of hours since he ran away from us. Obviously, he's hiding somewhere. We shall find him soon enough."

"Somehow," grunted Stevens, "I don't think that answer will satisfy the Assistant Commissioner. Oh, well. At least we're chasing a man, not a phantom."

The two detectives were sitting in their office at New Scotland Yard, a tiny room high over the Embankment.

"We still haven't solved the problem of the sealed room," Wyatt reminded his chief respectfully.

Stevens groaned. "I know, burn it. If only Tinker had confided in us before he was shot—."

He broke off and sighed. The Sergeant nodded sympathetically. He had already heard P.C. Craig's story of Tinker's odd disappearance from Garvary's studio the night before.

He asked:

"How is the young man, by the way?"

Stevens hunched his shoulders. "He's still unconscious. They operated, but—." He pursed his lips. "We can only wait." He hesitated. "And pray, perhaps." Then, as if slightly embarrassed by his own words, he went on briskly:

"As soon as he's strong enough to talk, we'll take a statement. That should provide the answers to a lot of questions. Where's that nurse's report?" he asked abruptly.

Wyatt handed it to him. He repeated curiously:

"Raven. Film. Black book. What does that mean, I wonder?"

Stevens rubbed his jowl. "Heaven only knows. Tinker was delirious, I suppose. Still, the words must mean something. I—."

He was interrupted by a shrill ring from the telephone.

"Hallo. Yes. Right! Send him up." He slammed down the receiver. "Blake's here," he said briefly.

When the famous detective entered his office, the Inspector shook his hand cordially. "You're up early, Mr. Blake. But I'm very glad to see you."

"Thank you, Inspector." Sexton Blake took a seat. "Is there any news of Raven?" Stevens' eyes clouded. "I'm afraid not. But his description has been circulated, and all our men alerted. He can't escape," he finished hopefully.

Blake said grimly:

"I trust not."

Stevens cleared his throat. "I needn't say," he jerked awkwardly, "that all our resources are at your disposal."

"My dear Inspector," responded Blake, "I have complete confidence in your ability to handle the case. Nevertheless, since it concerns me rather intimately,"—his jaw set—"I would appreciate your complete co-operation."

"Of course, of course," said Stevens hurriedly. "We'll keep you informed of every development. You've heard that Tinker's nurse heard him speak—."

"Four words. Yes. At present, I prefer to express no opinion as to their meaning." Blake reflected. "You've received the surgeon's report on Tinker's condition, of course?"

"Yes. It's fairly encouraging, I'm glad to see."

"I didn't mean that," said Blake quickly, though a responsive and friendly warmth touched his keen grey eyes. "The hospital mentioned there were certain bruises on his feet and legs."

Stevens looked puzzled. "A curious point, perhaps. But I don't quite see—."

"No matter." Blake stood up. "Now, Inspector. If you agree, I'd like to inspect Garvary's and Raven's apartments by daylight."

"Certainly." Stevens rose with alacrity. "We'll leave at once. Wyatt, stay here and keep an eye on things. You know where to find us."

As the two men went down the stairs to the main entrance, Sexton Blake said thoughtfully:

"By the by, Inspector, have you heard the result of the autopsy yet?"

Stevens stopped. "Great Scott! Garvary was shot, wasn't he? We don't need a post mortem to tell us that." He lowered his heavy brows. "Just what are you two getting at? Young Tinker asked me the same question yesterday. He said that part of Whitfield's report may surprise me."

"Did he now? That's interesting." Blake chuckled. He said smoothly:

"Incidentally, Inspector, you haven't yet answered."

"Eh? Oh. No, I haven't heard the result yet. Wyatt will 'phone when the report arrives."

"Good. Meanwhile, have patience, Inspector. The pattern grows clearer."

Stevens stared round Raven's apartment gloomily. He growled:

"Burn it, I had high hopes of a search. But the experts swear there's no possible means of reaching Garvary's studio from this flat."

Sexton Blake said calmly:

"I gather you expected to find a cleverly concealed trapdoor in the ceiling. I could have told you, however, that this particular problem would not be solved so easily."

Stevens muttered rebelliously. "Dammit, the problem must be solved before we can take the case to court."

"Exactly." Blake laughed without humour. "It's an awkward dilemma. And a pretty alibi. However certain you may be of the killer's identity, and whatever other evidence you have against him, he's quite safe until you discover how he escaped from Garvary's studio."

The Inspector swore. "I'll take the place apart."

"I doubt that will help us. No, Inspector. We must match brain with brain." Sexton Blake looked at a desk in the corner. He mused:

"Your men have searched Raven's possessions, of course?"

"Yes. The Inspector looked worried. "It's incredible, but we only have the haziest idea of the man's activities. He's a mystery in himself."

He took off his hat and punched it absently. "He told us he worked in a night club. That wasn't true for a start. We contacted the secretary, and he told us that Raven had worked as his assistant for a short spell, then threw in the job without explanation and stayed on as a member."

Blake was studying a typewriter on the desk. He said, over his shoulder:

"Was Raven a member of other clubs?

Stevens replied:

"Of several. He was a regular night owl."

"I suspected as much," said Blake. He picked a small object out of a drawer in the desk and showed it to the Inspector. "What do you make of this?"

Stevens stared. "It looks like a child's toy to me. My young daughter has one. A cine-viewer, it's called."

"Quite. Its construction is simple, as you can see. An eyepiece, which is an elementary lens in a Bakelite container, at the front—and what may be described as an open screen at the back. Thread a short strip of film through the back, hold it up to the light, and squint through the lens—and Hopalong Cassidy or Mickey Mouse springs up before your eye."

Steve said slowly:

"I'm not stupid, You're thinking of Tinker's message— if you can call it that."

"Yes. In particular, the word 'film'. It may only be a coincidence. But Tinker must have made some vital discovery in this flat, or Raven would not have shot him." He shrugged. "However, we mustn't waste time with idle speculation."

He picked up a sheet of paper and fitted into the typewriter. As he twisted the roller, he said crisply:

"Before we left your office, I asked you to bring along the anonymous letter which was sent to Garvary. Would you please dictate the text?"

Stevens fumbled in the pockets of his battered old raincoat and drew out the note Linda Martin had handed to Tinker. He cleared his throat and read:

"'You'd better be careful, damn you. I won't wait much longer.'"

"Thank you, Inspector." The roller whirred loudly as Blake ripped out the paper. "Now, if I can compare the two—."

Stevens handed his friend the letter. Blake scanned both letters quickly.

Handing the original back to the Inspector, he said incisively:

"The characters are entirely different."

Stevens grunted. "I'd be surprised if they weren't. Raven's no fool. He wouldn't have used his own machine."

Blake smiled, but made no comment.

He turned away from the desk. "Let's go upstairs."

The Inspector shivered. "This place is uncanny. Burn it, I know Tinker's no ghost. So how the blazes did he get out of the studio?"

Blake was examining the unfinished statue which dominated Garvary's flat. He murmured:

"A work of striking merit. It's a pity its creator will never complete it. What's that, Inspector? Ah, Tinker's disappearance. Yes," he chuckled. "I'm afraid the young 'un was rather mischievous. I suppose we can regard the constable's account as completely accurate?

Stevens grunted a monosyllable: "Yes."

"Then," said Blake smoothly, "let me give you a hint."

He strolled around the studio as he spoke, his keen eyes missing nothing. Stevens growled: "Well?"

"Think of this room as a box with three apertures: the windows, the outer door, and an inner door."

The Inspector scowled thoughtfully. He repeated: "Well?"

"When Garvary died, the windows and the outer door were secured on the inside."

Stevens nodded. "Tinker himself knew that nobody left through the front door."

"Exactly. But when the young'un disappeared last night, the windows and the outer door were locked on the inside, while P.C. Craig was, in effect, mounting guard on the bedroom door. So in each case—."

Stevens interrupted:

"We get two exits locked and the third guarded by an unimpeachable witness. So?"

"So," replied Blake mildly, "we arrive at a feasible solution to the mystery."

Stevens looked blank. Then he said eagerly:

"Do you mean you know how the trick was worked?"

Blake said evasively:

"First things first, Inspector. Our primary concern is the arrest of Alan Raven."

"But—."

Sexton Blake walked into the dead man's bedroom. Stevens followed him with a choked off query hovering on his lips.

"Ah." Blake indicated a portable typewriter standing against the wall. He lifted it on to a nearby table and removed the cover.

The Inspector watched him curiously. He began to ask a question, then grew quiet and waited.

Blake inserted a sheet of paper and typed quickly. Stevens handed him the anonymous letter without comment.

Blake studied both notes. Then he gave them to the Inspector.

"Hell's blazes! They're exactly the same."

"Quite. Even to the naked eye, the characters clearly coincide. The threatening letter was typed on Garvary's own machine."

Stevens sat down on the bed. He said frankly:

"It's beyond me. Did Garvary send the letter to himself?"

"I doubt it," responded Blake. "Though it's possible certainly. Failing that, we state what's self evident. Namely, the letter was written by somebody who had access to the typewriter."

"That's a lot of help," grunted Stevens. "I wonder if Raven was ever seen in this flat."

"I can answer that, Inspector. Miss Martin will tell you she encountered him in this apartment."

Stevens eyed him. "How do you know?"

Blake explained:

"Tinker recorded verbal notes of the case on our wire recorder—." He was interrupted by the telephone.

Stevens growled. "That's probably the Sergeant. Excuse me." He stumped into the studio and grabbed the receiver. "Stevens here. Hallo, Wyatt. You wanted me?"

Blake could hear the 'phone squawk plaintively.

Stevens clapped a big paw over the mouthpiece and grunted absently:

"Whitfield's sent in his report of the autopsy. Wyatt's got it now." He removed his hand. "Yes, Sergeant. Go ahead."

Wyatt started to read.

The Inspector's eyes widened. He punctuated his assistant's discourse with little expressions of surprise.

Sexton Blake watched him with amusement.

Stevens finished. "Yes. Yes. Thank you Sergeant. Goodbye."

He slammed down the receiver and stared at the man from Baker Street. "Well! I didn't expect that."

Blake squatted on the box seat beneath the windows and folded his arms. "What was the result of the post mortem, then?"

"Garvary died with a bullet through his heart. We knew that, of course. And there were other wounds in his shoulder, side, and leg. But Whitfield discovered something else." He paused, savouring the news.

"Leo Garvary was—."

"A dope addict," supplied Sexton Blake.

# CHAPTER TWELVE

Detective Inspector Stevens blinked.

He asked weakly:

"How in blazes did you know that?"

Sexton Blake smiled. "It was an elementary deduction, my dear Inspector. And I had you at a disadvantage. Miss Martin told Tinker she had overheard Garvary speak of "a stick of tea"—which is American slang for a *marihuana* cigarette."

"Of course." Stevens was disgusted. "Though they're usually known as reefers."

"Exactly." Blake inclined his head. He said gravely:

"The drug trade is a perennial menace."

"You're telling me," grunted the Inspector. "I was attached to the narcotics squad for a while... To get back to Garvary," he said abruptly, "*Marihuana* wasn't his only drug. The report says he was also addicted to cocaine."

"Really?" Blake raised an eyebrow. "Have you found any in the flat?"

"No. Of course," explained Stevens gruffly, "we weren't looking for drugs."

"No. In any event, Garvary's store might have been temporarily exhausted before he was murdered."

"Or the man who killed him might have taken the dope away." Stevens pulled down his heavy brows. "Just where does Raven fit into this?"

"I imagine," said Blake carefully, "that Raven kept Garvary supplied with his illicit drugs.

Stevens swore. "So the scoundrel was a dope peddler!" His eyes blazed. "Wait a minute! Did Tinker know—was that why Raven shot him?"

"Possibly. The young'un knew from what Miss Martin told him that Garvary and Raven discussed *marihuana* in addicts' slang. He was probably searching the flat below for evidence."

"I wonder if he found any," grunted the inspector. "I'll take my oath there's no dope in Raven's apartment now."

"Once Garvary was dead," Blake reminded his friend drily, "the police were certain to come prowling around this side of the building.

Raven would be careful to dispose of such damning goods as soon as he could."

"But when, burn it? He came in at four o'clock in the morning— and we know he didn't go out again until…."

Sexton Blake smiled sympathetically. "Yes, Inspector?"

Stevens scowled disgustedly. "The fellow picked a quarrel with us yesterday afternoon—complained about the noise, blast him—and stalked out of the building in a fury."

"Smuggling out whatever remained of his store of dope at the same time. Well, don't blame yourself too much, Inspector. You couldn't know then he was a dealer in drugs."

"I might have guessed," growled Stevens illogically. "I told you Raven was a night owl. I suppose he peddled the dope from one club to the other."

"Yes. You might be able to pick up a line from one of the members. Though frankly, I doubt it. That's the tragedy of the drug habit—the victims will rarely betray the man who has enslaved them for fear their supplies will be cut off."

The Inspector clenched his fists. "So help me, once I lay hands on that fellow—." He broke off. "Where did he take the stuff yesterday afternoon, I wonder?"

"If we knew that," commented Sexton Blake, "we should probably know where the man is now."

Raven was cleaning the gun. Laying down the oil-soaked swab, he squinted along the barrel of the pistol and clicked his tongue approvingly.

"A lovely weapon," he murmured. He grinned at his companion crookedly. "I may have more work for this beauty."

The other asked tonelessly: "Haven't you done enough killing?" He slapped a newspaper in front of the burly man. "Look at that. 'Famous Detective's Assistant on Point of Death.' Pah! You were crazy to shoot. Blake won't rest till he catches up with you."

Raven said coolly:

"Have you finished?" He picked up the paper and frowned. "I don't care tuppence for Sexton Blake. But one thing bothers me." His mouth thinned. He said slowly. "Tinker is still alive."

Alarm showed in his companion's eyes. He whispered:

"You're not thinking of—."

"Of finishing the job off? Perhaps."

The other said positively:

"It would be suicide."

Raven shrugged. "Tinker saw my face. And he saw the microfilm."

"The film—where is it?"

"Here. I took it from Tinker's hand when I shot him."

"Give it to me."

"Why?"

The reply sounded impatient. "So I can destroy it, of course. It's evidence against us."

Raven chuckled. "You're right there. It incriminates both of us. My records were complete."

The other said venomously: "You have never learnt caution. Give me the film." He took the film from Raven and dropped it into the fire.

The burly man said regretfully:

"There goes the remains of a very profitable business."

"It has served its purpose." A new authority showed in the dry voice. "Listen to me, Raven. You're a wanted man. We may have to smuggle you out of the country. In any event, you're no longer a dealer in drugs."

"Agreed." Raven picked up the gun once more and slipped it into his pocket.

"And," said the other sharply, "keep your finger off that trigger. We have trouble enough."

Raven grinned slowly, like a wolf. "You'll know what trouble means," he said softly, "if the police get hold of the little black book."

Detective Inspector Stevens said with disgust: "Right under my nose and I didn't spot it."

"Come now," said Blake smoothly, "as you have already pointed out, you weren't looking for drugs."

"But a false bottom in a drawer!" said Stevens, and broke off with a snort of contempt.

The two detectives were in the dead sculptor's bedroom, standing over an emptied drawer from the dressing table. They had lifted out the thin sheet of matchwood which was its ostensible base, and were examining their find beneath.

"The simplest tricks are usually the most effective," commented Sexton Blake. To salve his friend's injured pride, he added:

"After all, you found this hiding place as soon as you suspected its existence."

"Well, it was clear he must have stored the dope somewhere. I—." The sound of a footfall made him stop. He swung round and glared at the man in the doorway.

"Really, sir. You"re intruding."

Bob Tenison flushed slightly. "I'm sorry, Inspector. I came down to ask about young Tinker."

Stevens caught the sincerity of the reply and relaxed appreciably. "He's still unconscious," he said gruffly, "but the doctor's reports are favourable."

"I'm glad." Bob hesitated. "The papers—."

"Aren't always reliable."

Sexton Blake glanced at the artist curiously. "I appreciate your concern for my assistant's welfare, Mr. Tenison. Tell me,"—he put the question suddenly—"did you know that Leo Garvary was a drug addict?"

Bob was genuinely shocked.

Disbelief showed clearly in his voice. "Garvary?" he repeated. "Surely not."

Sexton Blake indicated the contents of the drawer. "Do you know what those are, Mr. Tenison?"

The artist said doubtfully: "Cigarettes. I don't recognize the brand."

"I should hope not," said Blake, with a humourless chuckle. "They are 'reefers'." His tone accentuated the quotation marks.

Bob repeated: "'Reefers'? I don't think— Oh, yes. That's the name for *marihuana* cigarettes, isn't it?"

Sexton Blake nodded. "The slang term."

Tenison stared at the pudgy cylinders with interest. "Well, well. We live and learn." He followed the platitude with an awkward comment: "So Garvary smoked these... Well, I suppose things might have been more serious."

Stevens' eyebrows went up. He asked sarcastically: "Weren't they serious enough?"

Bob flushed again. "I mean,"—he floundered— "smoking doped cigarettes isn't that bad, is it?"

The Inspector was ironic. "Do you smoke 'em?"

"No, of course not," snapped Bob, indignantly.

"Neither does any other decent man or woman," said Stevens caustically. *"Marihuana* is a very dangerous drug. Mr. Blake will tell you that."

"True, Inspector." Sexton Blake went on for Tenison's benefit:

*"Marihuana* is home grown Indian hemp. It causes—" he paused "—erotic fantasies in the mind of the addict. However," he continued smoothly, "that's not its most dangerous property. Hashish also derives from Indian hemp, and was originally used by a religious sect to whip its members into a state of frenzy—and murder. That's how we get the

word 'assassin'. Addicts were capable of extreme violence and cruelty."

"Good heavens!" exclaimed Tenison weakly. "Was Raven an addict, too?" Stevens grunted irritably.

Sexton Blake said quietly:

"Possibly. Though, frankly, I doubt it. Drug addiction implies a certain weakness of character. Raven is a coldly calculating—and very dangerous—man."

"I can believe that." Tenison remembered his interview with the burly man in the small hours and shivered. He had had a narrow escape.

Sexton Blake said:

"We suspect Raven supplied Leo Garvary with his illicit drugs. You knew both men, I understand. Can you throw any light on their relationship?"

The latest development in the case had taken the artist by surprise. He was out of his depth. "No, not really. I think they were friendly— if you can use friendly in that sense—but they were pretty secretive about it." He repeated the incident he had already described to Tinker.

Blake nodded. "Perhaps Miss Martin can clear up the point."

"Linda?" Tenison said positively:

"I'm sure she doesn't know anything about it. She wouldn't have stayed on as Garvary's model if she'd suspected—."

"He was in the habit of taking drugs. No, I imagine not." Blake strolled over to the window. He said, over his shoulder:

"Still, I'd like to meet Miss Martin. I haven't yet had that pleasure."

Bob asked uncertainly: "Shall I arrange it? She's a good friend of mine, you know."

Stevens cut in sardonically: "This isn't a social engagement. If Miss Martin's required, we'll call on her." He added sarcastically: "I think we can dispense with a formal introduction."

Tenison coloured painfully. He mumbled:

"If you don't want me any more...." He fumbled and stopped in mid-sentence.

Stevens said heavily: "No, thank you, Mr. Tenison. And, by the way—."

"Yes, Inspector?"

Stevens was benign. "Don't leave London."

When the young man had gone, Blake asked, with a twinkle: "Weren't you rather severe with him?"

Stevens grunted. He countered:

"Weren't you a little too communicative?"

"Come, come, Inspector. He must have heard us talking. So it did no harm to take him into our confidence." Sexton Blake smiled. "Would it surprise you if I mentioned I was considering requesting that young man's assistance?"

"Eh?" said Stevens inelegantly.

"Tinker is temporarily out of action. And Tenison seems an intelligent fellow."

"You're not serious."

"Perhaps not." Blake looked thoughtful. "Yet I think young Tenison might be useful. He knew both Garvary and Raven, remember. He might recall something of importance."

"True." Stevens mused. He said, at random: "I wish I knew what Tinker meant by 'film' and 'black book'."

"Ah. That's what I'm anxious to clear up. I'm convinced the answer lies somewhere in the tangle of Raven's association with the dead man."

Stevens said:

"We've learnt too little about Garvary's activities. As a matter of fact, I hope to fill in some of the background this morning. I've arranged an interview with the dead man's solicitor. He may be able to tell us something."

"His solicitor?"

"Yes. We found his card among Garvary's papers. I 'phoned him yesterday. He's expecting us."

Sexton Blake took the card and held it up by the edges. His eyebrows went up. "My dear Inspector, this name is almost too Dickensian to be true. However," he chuckled, "let's go and see this aptly styled lawyer Mr. Smyrk."

# CHAPTER THIRTEEN

Oswald Smyrk lived and worked in a luxurious block of offices and flats not far from his ex-client's own residence.

As Blake and Stevens climbed the stairs to the first floor, the Inspector grunted:

"I hope this lawyer fellow can tell us something useful."

"The operative word," Blake said gently, "is 'tell'."

"Huh?"

"Solicitors are traditionally discreet."

"If he starts the mustn't-break-a-client's-confidence stuff," promised Stevens grimly, "I'll strangle him with his own red tape."

He stopped outside a glass panelled door, rapped on it smartly, and led the way into the room beyond.

A dusty little man in spectacles came forward to meet them. "Yes, gentlemen?"

"We want to see Mr. Smyrk. He's expecting us."

"Ah—you have an appointment? I am Mr. Smyrk's clerk," he explained in apologetic parenthesis. "May I have your names, please?"

"I'm Detective Inspector Stevens, of New Scotland Yard. This is Mr. Sexton Blake."

The little man's eyes popped behind the thick lenses. "Will you follow me, please." He ushered them into a comfortably appointed room at the rear. Its floor was covered with a deep rose carpet which cushioned their feet like a caress. Velvet curtained windows looked own on the street.

A man was sitting behind a large mahogany desk. He had a long, intelligent face, faded blue eyes, and a long upper lip below a Punch nose. As he rose to greet his visitors, he seemed to rustle like the leaves of an old manuscript.

Stevens clasped the solicitor's hand and grimaced involuntarily as the dry skin rasped against his palm. He introduced Sexton Blake with his usual gruffness.

"Mr. Blake!" Smyrk's voice was as dry as his handshake. "This is indeed an honour. H'mm! Indeed, yes."

Sexton Blake was six feet tall, yet even with his scholarly stoop, the lawyer more than matched him in height. Dressed in black, he seemed to brood like an elegantly clad vulture.

"An honour, indeed," repeated Smyrk, waving the detectives to seats. "I have followed the reports of your work with great interest, Mr. Blake." He settled himself in the deep chair behind his desk with a flip of his coat tails and put his bony fingers together judicially. "You are, without doubt, the greatest warrior in the eternal crusade against crime. I salute you, sir. In my own humble way," he simpered, "I too am active in the eternal crusade against vice. You may have heard—h'mm—of my little organization?" He named a particularly obnoxious body of self-appointed custodians of public morals.

Sexton Blake replied, with restraint: "I've heard of it."

"I," stated Mr. Smyrk with pride, "am the general secretary."

The Inspector shot his friend an eloquent glance from under his heavy brows. "If you don't mind, sir," he began.

Mr. Smyrk, however, was obviously intoxicated with the heady wine of his own eloquence. He swept on:

"We may be reviled as busybodies, but that is a burden which I, for one, am ready to bear. A stand must be made against the immorality of the age. I am horrified, gentlemen—aye, horrified—by the disgustingly carnal displays every summer at our great national resorts. And nudity is not confined to the beaches! In our London theatre, at this very time —."

"Mr. Smyrk," Blake's voice was not loud, but it killed the words on the solicitor's dry lips. "Man was made in the image of his Creator. Therefore I consider it arrogant at best, and blasphemous at worst, to dub the human body obscene."

Smyrk's eyelids drooped like shutters. He did not reply.

Stevens seized his opportunity. "Well, sir," he said with relief, "as I told you on the telephone, Leo Garvary was found dead in his apartment yesterday morning. He had been murdered. Well, now!" The Inspector was brisk. "You were his legal adviser. Can you throw any light on his— er —circumstances?"

"I"m not sure I know what you mean, Inspector." Smyrk rasped his palms together. "I can hardly help you to elucidate the mystery of Mr. Garvary's death. And, in point of fact, he had virtually severed all connection with this office some time ago."

Stevens looked dissatisfied. "Surely, as his solicitor, you must have an intimate knowledge of his affairs?"

Mr. Smyrk picked up a silver pencil and began to play with it. "You put me in a difficult position, Inspector." He coughed. *"De mortuis nil nisi bonum."*

Stevens bristled. *"Veritas prevalebit,"* he retorted. "To know why Garvary died, we need to know how he lived. If you're aware of anything to his discredit, it's still your duty to tell us."

The solicitor sighed. "So be it, then. Leo Garvary, I'm afraid, was a very reckless and improvident man. He—h'mm— spurned the advice I continued to give him in the face of all rebuffs."

Stevens fiddled with the bowler hat he was balancing on one knee. "In what way?"

"In every way, Inspector. He was, of course, an artist," — Mr. Smyrk spoke the word with distaste— "and we must make due allowance for the artistic temperament. Yet—." He broke off and shook his head mournfully. "You will hardly believe this, Inspector, but poor Leo managed to dissipate the bulk of a substantial fortune in less than two years."

A spark of interest showed in Blake's keen gray eyes. "Please continue, Mr. Smyrk."

"The subject is distasteful," said the lawyer graciously, "but I shall not shrink from the performance of my duty. H'mm! Where was I? Ah, yes. Mr. Garvary's late father left his money in trust with our firm. Three years ago—with the exception of a small annuity which we continued to pay to Mr. Leo—the control of the capital passed into Mr. Garvary's hands. He at once, I regret to say, embarked on a course of reckless spending."

Mr. Smyrk gestured expressively. "Such restraint as he thought to show fit at first was soon cast aside. He realised asset after asset. The end was inevitable.

"Three months ago, he was almost penniless."

Mr. Smyrk replaced the pencil in his pocket with an air of conscious virtue. Stevens asked: "Do you know where the money went?"

The lawyer began to shake his head. Sexton Blake interjected:

"Inspector, I think we should take Mr. Smyrk into our confidence."

Stevens glanced at him in surprise, but made no objection. Blake turned back to the solicitor and said quietly:

"Your client was a drug addict."

The faded blue eyes flickered. The long upper lip quivered. "Surely you're mistaken."

"No. It was discovered by the surgeon conducting the post mortem. And we also found *marihuana* cigarettes concealed in the dead man's bedroom." He described their find briefly.

Smyrk listened attentively. He sighed. "Poor Leo! Yet, after all, what could one expect? The artist is notoriously contemptuous of the conventions. And when he rejects morality, he opens the door to vice." He began to speak with fervour. "Vice takes many forms. My society is ever vigilant. Look around you, gentlemen. Look at literature. In the name of art, appalling novels have found a place in hitherto reputable bookshops. Ah, for a return to the sturdy morality of the Victorians! They knew how to deal with such books." He quoted, with relish:

"Feed the budding rose of boyhood with the drainage of your sewer; Send the drain into the fountain, lest the strain should issue pure."

Sexton Blake heard a muffled squawk from the Inspector, and repressed a smile. He said gently: "Those lines were penned as a reproach to Emile Zola." He paused. "Zola was a genius."

Mr. Smyrk blinked, "Surely you're not defending indecent novels?"

Blake said simply: "There aren't any indecent novels. There are only indecent readers."

The lawyer began to protest. Stevens almost shouted: "For heaven's sake! Let"s get back to the point, Mr. Smyrk! Do you know a man named Alan Raven?"

Smyrk said briefly: "No."

"Garvary knew him."

"He never mentioned the name to me. Why do you ask?"

The Inspector muttered something evasively.

The solicitor had apparently recovered his good humour. He said briskly:

"Well, gentlemen, I'm sorry I was not able to help you more. If you wish, I'm prepared to send you a full statement of the firm's dealings with Leo Garvary. Possibly a minute examination of the details will give you the clue you're seeking. I suggest you also contact the unfortunate man's bankers."

"Thank you, sir," grunted the Inspector.

Mr. Smyrk touched the bell on his desk. The dusty little man reappeared. His employer gave him a few curt instructions, then turned back to the two detectives. "A complete dossier will be at your disposal very shortly."

Stevens nodded his thanks. "Perhaps you'll send it to the Yard, sir."

"Willingly, Inspector. And pray call on me for any help you require. I live on the floor above, so— h'mm—I am always available."

"That's very good of you," returned Stevens, rather sourly. He stood up. "Now, sir, we won't bother you any further."

Mr. Smyrk insisted on accompanying then both to the door. His long face was mournful. "Alas, poor Leo! Caught in the toils of dreadful vice. Cocaine addiction is indeed a dreadful thing." He shook his head. He said briskly: "I am confident, at least, that the police will quickly apprehend the man responsible for this—h'mm—tragic demise."

"You can depend on that, sir." Stevens clapped on his bowler with an air of determination. As they went down the stairs, the Inspector asked his friend:

"Well, what do you think?"

"I think," replied Sexton Blake, "that Mr. Smyrk is full of cant. But he gave us some useful information."

Stevens grunted agreement. "It isn't hard to guess where Garvary's money went. Illicit drugs are expensive."

Blake nodded. He murmured, apparently at random:

"How long had Raven been living in the flat below Garvary's?"

"Oh, about three years." The Inspector's eyes widened.

"Hell's blazes! Three years!"

"Since his victim assumed control of his fortune, in fact. A curious coincidence, Inspector."

"Great grief!" Stevens turned, as if to go back.

Sexton Blake laid a restraining hand on his arm. "No more questions, Inspector. I don't want to renew Mr. Smyrk's acquaintance so quickly."

Stevens laughed. "You're rather hard on him."

Sexton Blake said briefly. "I don't like censors or book burners."

Stevens glanced at him slyly. He asked softly:

"Is that the only reason?"

The two friends stared at each other. Then they both smiled.

## CHAPTER FOURTEEN

From a café across the street, Alan Raven watched Sexton Blake and Detective Inspector Stevens come out of the building and set off round the corner.

He crushed out the cigarette and signalled for his bill. He smiled at the waitress, and left her a generous tip. He handed the cashier a ten-shilling note, received his change and thanked her.

Then he walked unhurriedly to a telephone booth in the corner and closed the folding door behind him carefully. He picked up the receiver, dropped three pennies in the slot, and dialled a number.

He waited patiently. He was relaxed and contented.

A voice squawked in his ear. The burly man put his thumb on Button A and pushed. He said:

"Raven speaking. Yes, they've just left. No, of course they didn't see me. Stop worrying. I can walk the streets as freely as you. Yes, I know they've got my description. What about it? It could fit a thousand men. And there's no photograph of me in existence. That's what counts. All right. I'll be careful."

His gloved hand began to play with the edges of the directories. His voice was soothing.

"I tell you, you've got nothing to worry about. I shan't come back to you now. You've got rid of my evening clothes, haven't you?

"Right, then. Now there's nothing to connect you to me." He laughed, not very pleasantly. "Your skirts are clean. You're still respectable."

His hand slipped into the pocket of his overcoat. His gloved fingers moved over the shape of the gun which had nearly hurled Tinker into eternity. He went on:

"We have to move quickly. To preserve my safety and—," he expelled his breath in a silent chuckle—"your respectability."

He said briskly:

"I've been thinking. We know why Garvary took the little black book, but we don't know what he did with it. He didn't hide it in his studio," — he grinned wryly—"and he didn't hand it over to his solicitor."

The receiver squawked loudly. Raven jerked it away from his ear and said irritably:

"All right, all right. I'm just thinking aloud. Garvary told me the book wouldn't fall into the wrong hands unless something happened to him. Perhaps he was bluffing. Anyway, the police can't have got hold of it yet, or the lid would have blown off everything—and you wouldn't be sitting in that comfortable chair listening to me now.

"So what happened?"

Raven cradled the receiver between the side of his face and his shoulder. He slid the cigarette into his mouth and flicked up a flame from his lighter. He inhaled deeply.

Blowing out a cloud of smoke, he said thoughtfully:

"Here's my guess. Garvary gave that book to somebody with instructions to dispose of it— most probably to the police— if he dies a violent death. For some reason, those instructions haven't been obeyed.

"That's a piece of luck for us, but we can't just sit on our tails waiting for something to happen. We've got to find the person who has the book."

Raven took the cigarette from his mouth and scratched his cheek. "Garvary didn't have many friends. He didn't even know the fellow on the top floor very well, and I doubt he'd trust him with the book. Anyway, I talked to young Tenison, and sounded him out. He didn't know anything."

He jammed the cigarette between his lips again. He said, between puffs:

"There's only one person friend Leo might have trusted. The girl he sent to Baker Street. Yes, the model. Linda Martin. No, she didn't take the book to Sexton Blake. Tinker didn't know anything about it. He told me so. Yes, I know I didn't believe it then. But I believe it now. I don't know why she has kept the book. We can find out later.

"What am I going to do about it?" Raven grinned crookedly. "That's a silly question." He hung up.

He went out of the booth and through the restaurant. Out on the street, he paused for a moment to consider. It wasn't really safe to move till darkness fell. In the meantime, the comfortable anonymity of a seat in a cinema seemed his best refuge.

He flung away the cigarette and strolled along the pavement.

A news bill caught his eye. He walked across to the vendor and dropped two coins into his hand.

Regardless of the passers-by, he flipped open the newspaper and scanned the heavy black headlines.

TRAGIC DEATH OF SEXTON BLAKE'S ASSISTANT, he read. TINKER VICTIM OF UNKNOWN GUNMAN. Then, in smaller type:

Dies in Hospital after Operation.

The newsvendor said hoarsely:

"Gawd, I'd like to get my hands on the dirty tyke what did that to young Tinker."

Raven started. An odd expression flickered in his deep set eyes. He murmured a platitude and strolled on.

When he came to a litter bin, he folded the paper and dropped it inside. Then he walked on, his step jaunty.

He was humming a tune, and smiling.

# CHAPTER FIFTEEN

Sexton Blake was at work in his laboratory.

It was small, but compactly equipped. Every modern appliance was there, from a comparison microscope for ballistic study to X-ray apparatus and violet light. Nothing delighted the detective more than to occupy his leisure secluded in the laboratory lost in some abstruse problem of forensic chemistry or physics. At such times, he was the despair of his housekeeper. It was a struggle for her to induce her employer to leave his work for a meal.

It was late in the afternoon. Outside in Baker Street, it was already dusk. Soon, the muddy slush which had shortly before been a white carpet of snow would be masked by darkness.

A knock sounded on the laboratory door. Sexton Blake said sharply: "Come in! Ah, Mrs. Bardell. What is it?"

The old lady looked unhappy. "Inspector Stevens is 'ere again, sir."

"Show him into the consulting room, please," said Sexton Blake, wearily. "I'll join him in a moment."

His lean, ascetic face was fine-drawn with fatigue. He gathered up the papers he had been examining, then put out the lights and left the laboratory. He crossed the landing and entered the consulting room.

Stevens swung round as his friend entered. He asked abruptly: "You've seen the papers?"

Blake replied briefly:

"I have."

Stevens nodded. By mutual consent, the matter was dropped. Instead, the Inspector said:

"We're investigating—the other. Of course, we have to be discreet."

Blake interrupted without discourtesy. He said:

"There's something you should know. You will recall I asked you for these?" He passed the papers to the man from Scotland Yard.

Stevens took them and frowned. "Yes, I remember. You wanted the threatening letter which was sent to Leo Garvary, and the envelope it came in. What about 'em?"

Sexton Blake selected his favourite pipe and lit up before replying. Plunging his hand into the pockets of his dressing gown, he said:

"You will also remember we established that the anonymous letter had been typed on the dead man's typewriter."

541

Stevens growled an affirmative. "But the address on the envelope was impressed by a different machine. So far, we haven't identified it."

"Quite so." Blake sat down in the saddlebag chair. "We may disregard that aspect of the matter for the moment." He said thoughtfully:

"Type is as easily identifiable as handwriting. Each machine has identifiable idiosyncrasies. It was easy to prove Garvary's had been used for the letter. That was elementary. But now I am in a position to go further. I can tell you something about the man who wrote the note."

"What's that?" Interest showed in the Inspector's question.

Blake explained:

"Just as the machines themselves vary, so do the people who use them. Laboratory analysis of the typed characters show up subtle differences of pressure on the keys, which—as well as obvious errors of back spacing and over-printing—clearly identify both the trained typist and the amateur."

Sexton Blake broke off and chuckled. "A graphologist can look at a specimen of a man's handwriting and then describe his character. Upon my soul, I think I could do much the same thing with an anonymous piece of typing. I have sometimes contemplated a monograph on the subject. However!" He drew deeply on his pipe. "I can tell you this, Inspector. Whoever addressed this envelope was a skilled typist who used the touch system.

"On the other hand, the person who wrote the letter itself was an amateur—a two finger man at best. His system, such as it was, might best be described as 'hunt and peck'."

Stevens pursed his lips. "You're sure of this?"

"I would swear to it."

"Then there are two people involved in the case! Raven—." He finished cautiously. "And another."


Bob Tenison puffed uneasily at a cigarette, then wrenched it out of his mouth and flung it away. The lighted end described a glowing arc in the darkness, then fizzled out in the churned up snow.

Tenison stabbed a finger at the bell push. As he waited on the porch, his thoughts took a sombre turn. The news of Tinker's death had left him badly shaken.

The door opened. A buxom old lady greeted him with a sniffle. Tenison said uncertainly:

"Mr. Blake? He's expecting me."

"Yessir. Come this way, please."

Mrs. Bardell took him up to the consulting room. Sexton Blake rose to greet him. "Ah, Mr. Tenison. I'm glad you came. You know Detective Inspector Stevens, of course."

The artist acknowledged the Yard man awkwardly. He hadn't forgotten the circumstances of their last meeting.

He said:

"I can't tell you... how sorry I am... about Tinker."

A shadow passed over Blake's face. He replied, almost roughly: "Please don't speak of it." He took the pipe from his lips as if the tobacco had lost its savour.

Bob pursued uncertainly:

"I suppose it will mean—legal complications—."

"Because he was chief witness to the outrageous circumstances of Garvary's death?

No, I think not. All his evidence is on file at the Yard. His statement is in order."

"Good." Bob hesitated. "At least you can use it at Raven's trial."

Blake said obliquely:

"Raven will be tried. I can promise you that."

He bent over the fire and knocked out his pipe over the glowing coals. Straightening up, he said briskly:

"I asked you to come here, Mr. Tenison, because you are the only available tenant of that part of the house which you shared with Raven and Garvary. There are many points in their relationship we have yet to clear up. You may be able to help us."

"I'll do my best. But I don't see— ." His voice faded.

Blake was offering him a gun. Tenison took it gingerly.

The detective murmured:

"Don't be afraid of handling it. It has already been subjected to an exhaustive examination."

Tenison said with real revulsion: "It's horrible."

Blake said:

"It"s only a gun." He asked abruptly:

"Have you seen it before?"

"No. Why do you ask?"

"That is the weapon which snuffed out Garvary's life." Stevens interrupted gruffly. "Did you ever see Raven with it?"

Tenison said positively:

"No."

Stevens swore mildly. "He's got another, anyway. The blasted man's a travelling arsenal."

Bob put down the revolver hurriedly. "Can't you trace it?"

The Inspector shook his head. "It's obviously an unregistered weapon. Anyway, the number has been filed off. And," he finished gloomily, "it's of foreign make."

Bob asked:

"How do the infernal things get into the country, anyway?"

"I'll tell you," said the Inspector, grimly. "The bulk of them were smuggled into the most respectable homes as war souvenirs. Quite illegally, of course, but the Customs couldn't look into the bottom of every unthinking chump's kit bag."

Bob protested:

"As souvenirs, they're harmless."

"As souvenirs, yes. But a burglar doesn't treat 'em as souvenirs if he breaks into a house and finds a gun amongst the loot. He sells it." The Inspector finished grimly:

"And there's only one sort of person who will buy an unlicensed gun."

Bob smiled wryly. "You've convinced me."

Sexton Blake resumed control of the conversation. "Mr. Tenison, before Tinker... died...." His tongue seemed to trip over the word. "Before Tinker died, he spoke Raven's name, and then three words: Film. black. book." He paused. "Can you help us explain them?"

Bob was puzzled. "It's a mystery to me," he responded frankly.

Blake mused:

"Tinker was obviously referring to some discovery he had made in Raven's apartment. We believe the man was a dealer in illicit drugs, so it's possible the book in question was a record of his clients. Garvary was an addict. We're wondering if he knew anything about the book."

Tenison said eagerly: "Linda—Miss Martin—might know. Have you asked her?"

"Not yet."

"Shall I, then?" Bob hesitated. "I was going to 'phone her today. She's my" —he flushed engagingly—"my good friend."

Blake smiled. "Perhaps you'd like to use the telephone here. Come, Stevens," he went on tactfully, "I'll show you the laboratory."

"Huh? Oh—oh, yes. Excuse us, Mr. Tenison." Stevens followed his friend out of the room.

Bob sat down at Tinker's desk. He picked up the telephone and dialled a number. He pressed the receiver to his ear. The soft purr-purr of the dialling tone was followed by the tired voice of a girl. "Hallo, Linda. Bob."

The artist's tones were warm with affection.

"Hallo, Bob." There was a note of relief in the girl's response. "I was hoping you'd call."

Tenison felt his throat constrict with pleasure. He said:
"You can always depend on me." He hesitated. "Have you seen the papers?"

"No, I haven't been out. Why do you ask?"

Tenison thought quickly. He knew the news of Tinker's death would shake the girl badly. It would be better to break the news later, when he could be there to comfort her. He said, as casually as he could:

"No reason. Linda, my dear. I'm speaking from Mr. Blake's house in Baker Street." He went on swiftly:

"He thinks we may be able to help him. It's about Raven— and Garvary."

"What—what about them?"

"Linda, this will shock you. Leo Garvary was a drug addict."

"Leo? I—I don't know what to say."

Bob continued. "Tinker made some sort of a discovery in Raven's flat. Before he—before he became unconscious, he spoke four words: Raven, film, black book. You knew Leo well. Mr. Blake thinks the words refer to Garvary in some vague way. Can you suggest anything?"

Linda was doubtful. "N—no," she said slowly. "Though— wait! Leo had a micro camera once. He was very proud of it, and sometimes showed me the films."

Tenison felt a thin prickle of excitement. It was almost as if he had caught the detective fever. "When was this, Linda?"

"About three months ago. He got rid of it shortly afterwards. I thought he might have sold it. I remember he was very short of money at the time— he had hardly enough to pay me to pose for him."

"Microfilm—I wonder." Tenison continued:
"Did he say anything about Raven, or a black book?"

"No. I'm almost sure he didn't."

Bob continued hopefully. "You're sure there wasn't any such thing around the apartment? It might not have looked like a book. It might have been a package, or—."

It was a long shot, but it succeeded. Linda caught her breath. A cell unsealed in her memory. "Bob, wait! I'd almost forgotten—."

That was true: the pressure of events had driven it from her mind. "About the same time—that is, two or three months ago—Leo gave me a sealed package. He said it was,"—her voice faltered—"an insurance policy. I—."

Something was wrong. Her voice died suddenly. Bob Tenison felt a chill of premonition. "Linda! What's the matter?"

A sob sounded in his ear.

The Linda said, fearfully:

"Raven."

The word choked in her throat. There was the sound of a fall.

"Linda! Linda!"

Bob Tenison was frantic.

He heard the sound of a chuckle, then an audible click as someone replaced the receiver in the girl's apartment.

# CHAPTER SIXTEEN

Alan Raven looked down at the crumpled figure with an expression of mild annoyance in his deep-set eyes.

It was a pity the girl had caught sight of him in the mirror before she had finished speaking of the sealed package. It was a pity, too, she had blurted out his name before his pistol clubbed down on her head. But at least he knew now what Garvary had done with the little black book.

He glanced at the telephone and frowned. He would have to move fast. Tenison would already have given the alarm.

Raven slipped the gun into his pocket. He bent down, slipped his hands under the girl's shoulders, and dragged her along the floor to the window.

He peered through the curtains. This was the back of the block, and the window overlooked a mews or short alley. Opposite were some garages, all locked up.

The way was clear.

Raven extinguished the lights. Then he pushed up the window and dragged the unconscious girl across the sill so the upper part of her body hung down over the deserted laneway.

The bottom of the window was not more than five or six feet from the ground. Lithe as a cat, the burly man swung himself over the sill and dropped softly on the cobbles.

His own car was parked at the entrance to the lane. Raven slid behind the wheel and backed the car till it was directly beneath the window.

Then he slithered out and reached up for the unconscious girl. Gripping her firmly, he dragged hard on Linda's arms. The girl's limp body half-slid, half-fell towards him.

His steely grasp did not weaken. He eased her gently to the ground.

He bundled her into the back of the car, shrouding her crumpled form with a travelling rug. A bruise was already swelling beneath her raven black hair—it would be a long time before she recovered consciousness.

Raven returned to the driving seat. His movements were cool and unhurried. He drove out of the lane and into the main road. He turned a corner and cruised smoothly by the front of the block of flats.

A police car roared past and drew up with a screech outside the main entrance. Raven glanced into the rear view mirror and smiled gently at his own reflection.

The car drove off into the night.

Sexton Blake said grimly:

"It's easy to reconstruct what happened. Raven must have broken into the apartment—the catch on this window has been forced."

Stevens asked:

"Why didn't Miss Martin give the alarm?"

"She was probably outside the flat."

Bob Tenison interjected hollowly:

"She sometimes went upstairs to look after a little girl while her mother was out."

Blake nodded. "You might check that, Inspector. Not that it matters particularly. Raven concealed himself and waited for Miss Martin to return. He overheard her talk on the telephone—."

Bob groaned involuntarily. Stevens glanced at him with a momentary expression of sympathy showing in his steely, policeman's eyes.

Blake finished:

"Raven interrupted too soon. Miss Martin saw him —in this mirror, I imagine—and he silenced her."

Seeing the pain in Tenison's eyes, the detective said quietly:

"He didn't kill her. He abducted her."

Bob's mouth trembled. "Why—why, in God's name?"

Sexton Blake said slowly:

"He wants the sealed package."

Tenison ran his hands through his thick, tousled hair. "But—" he began helplessly. Reading the thought in his mind, Blake answered gently:

"It isn't here in the apartment. Raven would have made sure of that."

Bob faltered. "You mean—he's taken Linda—to make her tell where—." He stopped.

Blake nodded. "I fear so."

The blood rushed out of Tenison's face. He cried:

"Good God! That swine might do anything—anything!"

There was a dangerous note of hysteria in his voice. The Inspector said sharply:

"Control yourself, man! There's no need to panic. We've sent out a general call."

He spoke with more confidence than he felt. It wouldn't be easy to track down Raven, even with the girl. If he had taken her away in a car—which was probable, thought Stevens sombrely—they had no description of the vehicle. And they couldn't stop and search every car in London.

Shaking off his depression, the Inspector said briskly:

"We'll soon have him in a cell. In the meantime, you can help us best by keeping calm."

Bob gestured wordlessly, then dropped into a chair and hid his face in his hands. An extravagant gesture, thought Stevens without approval. But in keeping with an artist's temperament. He turned to Blake. "You believe that's Raven's game?" he muttered. "To force the girl to tell him what she's done with this—this sealed package?"

"I believe so, Inspector." Sexton Blake reflected. "Look at it this way, Inspector. Put these facts together. An addict pays heavily for his drugs."

"That's for certain," interrupted Stevens grimly. "Go on, Mr. Blake." The detective continued:

"Two odd things happened at the disappearance of his fortune. First, he obtained a micro camera—which was later sold. Second, he gave Miss Martin a sealed package—his 'insurance policy.'"

"What was in the package? Was it the little black book? And why does Raven want it?"

Sexton Blake clenched his strong white teeth on the stem of his empty pipe. "There you are, Inspector. Three questions and a number of unrelated facts. Or," he asked quietly, "can we fit them together and discover a pattern of events?"

Stevens cursed suddenly, and with certain satisfaction. "Mr. Blake," he breathed, "I begin to see daylight."

"You can hazard a shrewd guess," corrected Blake. "Don't mistake that for proof."

Stevens scowled agreement. "In any case, working out what happened three months ago doesn't help us much. We want Raven."

"And the girl," added Sexton Blake.

"She's safe enough," jerked Stevens. "At least," he mumbled thoughtlessly, "until she tells Raven what he wants to know."

Bob Tenison felt the blood surge back to his cheeks angrily. He jumped up. "What the devil do you mean by that?" He paled again. "You mean that—afterwards—he'll have no further use for her?"

He stuttered helplessly.

Stevens replied uncomfortably:

"Calm yourself, sir. There's nothing we can do for the moment. We can only watch— and wait."

"Watch!" choked Tenison. "And wait—while that swine Raven has

Linda at his mercy?" He was almost crazed with worry. He shouted:

"All right, Inspector! If you won't find Linda Martin—then I will!"

He wrenched open the door and rushed out of the flat. Stevens made to follow him, but Blake intervened.

"Let him go, Inspector. You can't reason with a man in love."

"Poor devil," rumbled Stevens. He stared round the missing girl's apartment. "I suppose we'd better search the place. Not that there's much hope of finding Garvary's mysterious sealed package."

Blake permitted himself the luxury of a smile. "If you were Miss Martin, Inspector," he asked, "what would you do with a package entrusted to your care?"

"Put it in a safe place," replied the Inspector with a tinge of sarcasm.

"Exactly," said Blake. He held out his hand. "What do you make of this?"

Stevens stared at the object in his friend's outstretched palm. "It looks like a key. Where d'you find it?"

"In Miss Martin's jewel case." Blake tossed the key in the air and caught it again expertly. "I make no apology for that, Inspector. I am cursed—or blessed—with an insatiable curiosity."

Stevens grunted. "Well?"

Sexton Blake smiled again. "It's a key, as you said, old fellow. But a special kind of key."

Alan Raven drove through the open doors into the garage. He switched off the motor with a glimmer of relief showing through the impassivity of his face.

He murmured aloud:

"'Journeys end'." He glanced into the rear view mirror and grinned without humour as he completed the tag. "'In lovers' meetings'."

He pushed open the door and slid out of the car into the darkness of the garage.

He pulled open the door at the back of the car. "Good evening, Miss Martin. How do you feel?"

Linda looked up with frightened, tear-dimmed eyes. Her voice slurred badly. "I  f—feel ill."

"You'll feel better soon." Raven's voice was pleasant, almost kind. "I'll take you to your room."

Linda had put up her hand to the bruise beneath her hair. She asked fearfully:

"Where have you brought me?"

"To a house on the river," replied the burly man. "That's all you need to know." Linda dropped her hand. Terror seeped into her blue-grey, slanting eyes.

Raven smiled gently. He took the gun from his pocket and showed it to her. "No tricks," he warned.

He slipped the pistol into his coat again. "Now," he said sharply, "let's go."

Linda pushed the travelling bag aside. She winced with pain. "You'll have to help me," she gasped.

"Right." Raven was patient. He helped the girl to her feet.

No sooner was she out of the car than she slumped against him heavily. Raven was nearly thrown off balance. He cursed inaudibly, grabbed the girl's shoulders, and hauled her upright. She staggered a few paces away from him.

"That's better," he grunted. "I—why, what—." His voice faded. His hands opened.

The girl was standing erect, a new authority in her manner. She was still frightened, but her chin was tilted and determined.

The light from the car showed the gun in her hand. Raven clutched convulsively at his pocket. It was empty.

Linda Martin shook her head. "It's no good, Raven. I took your pistol when I pretended to fall against you."

The burly man said softly:

"You're clever, my dear. But don't think you're going to escape me."

The girl's lips trembled. "Keep back! I warn you—I shall shoot!"

Raven laughed. "I'm calling your bluff, Linda. Fire, if you dare." He kept his eyes steadily on her.

Linda took a deep breath and squeezed the trigger. Nothing happened.

Raven said gently:

"You see. It isn't loaded."

The girl's mouth squared in a silent scream. Then she sobbed aloud and flung the gun with all her strength.

Raven's arm went up to protect his face. The pistol thudded painfully but harmlessly against his coat sleeve, then dropped to the ground.

Linda didn't wait to see the result of her desperate throw. She turned and ran through the open doors behind her.

Outside the garage, she hurled herself recklessly along the drive towards the gates. Her strength was nearly gone. Every step was an agony. Her breath came painfully, squeezed desperately from her heaving breasts. A most of terror obscured her vision. Behind her, Raven followed with giant's strides.

The end came suddenly. The girl's ankle wrenched and she went down heavily. Raven fell over her.

Bruised and sobbing, Linda felt him crush her wrists together with one hand, then pull her cruelly towards him.

He smiled at her.

"Next time you try to shoot me," he murmured, "make sure the catch is off." He nodded. "Oh, yes, my dear—the gun was loaded. But you hadn't released the safety catch."

Linda sobbed hysterically.

"Well," said Raven. "We'll speak no more of that. But, Linda—you threw the pistol at me. That wasn't friendly."

He hit her twice, very deliberately, across the face.

# CHAPTER SEVENTEEN

Bob Tenison was no fool. He knew the magnitude of his self-imposed task. On the face of it, it seemed impossible he could succeed where Scotland Yard had failed.

He refused to give up hope. "I must find Linda," he told himself grimly. "I must!" He had thrown out his challenge to Blake and Stevens in a moment of hysteria, crazed as he was with fear for the girl's safety. By now he was cool, but he was still determined to rescue her. She was the girl he loved.

He prowled restlessly around his studio, puffing nervously at one cigarette after another.

He groaned involuntarily. It was no good. There wasn't a useful thought in his head. Somewhere out in the darkness, Raven was hiding with the girl. But where? Tenison pressed his hands against his temples. The cigarette dropped out of his mouth and smouldered on the carpet.

Raven's home was the flat below. He had been driven out almost without warning. He must have found sanctuary somewhere, or he would never have been able to evade the police. Yet he was a man without roots, without associates. A lone wolf....

Raven wasn't a man. He was a maniac with a gun. Tenison stopped short.

The gun!

The blood pounded in the artist's throat. Excitement blazed in his eyes. Raven's gun was an unlicensed weapon. Somebody must have supplied it. Tenison breathed:

"Who?"

No reputable dealer, obviously. A fellow crook. A criminal associate — perhaps the very man to whom he had gone for sanctuary.

If I can find this man, thought Bob hopefully, I might find Raven himself—and Linda.

His head was spinning. He felt hot and feverish. He groaned aloud: "I have to think!" Tenison went into the bathroom and doused his face under the running taps. The cold water refreshed him. Towelling his face absently, he began to ponder.

What had Detective Inspector Stevens told him about unlicensed guns? That the bulk of them were smuggled into the country as war souvenirs.

Tenison perched himself on the edge of the bath. A man with war service, then. Bob started. He had told Tinker—ages ago, it seemed—that Raven hadn't been a sociable fellow. But that, as he suddenly realised, hadn't been strictly true.

Besides Garvary, with whom he had had secret dealings, the burly man had been on friendly terms with one other person in the building. A man with war service.

Impulsively, Bob Tenison ran out of his flat and down the stairs to Garvary's. He was lucky. Stevens still had a man on duty inside the dead man's apartment.

The uniformed policeman scratched his head when he heard the artist's excited query. "Thomas Heath, sir—the desk clerk? Still in hospital, so far as I know. He was badly beaten."

"Which hospital?" Bob asked impatiently.

The constable told him. "If you were thinking of visiting him," he added dubiously, "I doubt if they'd let you in. I—."

But he was too late. Bob had already left.


Tom Heath said sourly:

"I"m no masochist. I don't enjoy being beaten up."

Tenison said: "I couldn't help noticing how often Raven stopped to chat with you. I thought you must be friends."

Heath indicated the mass of plaster on his face. "Raven smashed my nose," he replied sardonically. "He didn't seem friendly then."

"I know," pursued Tenison. "But—."

Heath interrupted petulantly. He looked white and strained beneath the bandages. "I don't have to be bothered by you. How did you get in here, anyway?"

Bob answered evasively: "I had permission." In actual fact, he had bluffed his way into the ward by showing the card Sexton Blake had sent him with his invitation that afternoon, and by implying he was one of the famous detective's assistants.

Tenison went on: "Never mind that. I didn't say you and Raven were fellow criminals. I just said I thought you were" —he accented the verb heavily "— his friend. You might know some of his associates."

Heath shifted restlessly in the hospital bed. "Look, Mr. Tenison. A lot of tenants stop and chat with me on their way through the lobby. That doesn't mean they're my intimate pals, and it doesn't mean I know every detail of their private lives!"

He sank back against the pillow with a gasp.

Tenison was worried. He didn't want the ward sister to send him away. He soothed Heath as well as he could. "All right, Tom. Perhaps I was mistaken." He appeared to be changing the subject. "You did your war service in the army, didn't you?"

Heath eyed him distrustfully. "That's right," he grunted. "I fought in Italy."

Bob said softly: "You brought back a gun, as a souvenir. Why did you sell it, Tom?" The sudden question jolted Heath like a blow in the face. His voice cracked. "I never—I didn't—."

Tenison smiled. "Don't be silly, Tom. You told us about it once. And though I never saw it myself, you said you'd shown it to other tenants in the building. It's not in your possession now, is it? Suppose I ask the police to look for it—."

Heath croaked:

"No, no, for heaven's sake! Haven't I suffered enough? Don't say anything to the police. If they knew about the gun, and what had been done with it—."

Bob tasted triumph. "All right, Tom. I won't tell the police. But you'll have to tell me everything."

Heath nodded feverishly. Tenison said smoothly:

"To begin with, you admit you sold your pistol to Raven—."

The injured man stared. He interrupted:

"No, no, Mr. Tenison. It wasn't a pistol— it was a revolver. And I didn't sell it to Raven. I sold it to Leo Garvary."

There was a long silence.

Then Bob said hoarsely:

"To    Garvary?"

Heath nodded again. He seemed eager to explain. "Yes. It was three or four months ago. Mr. Garvary had heard I owned a gun, and he persuaded me to sell it. Said he needed it for protection, in case of burglars, and—and it was too difficult to get a pistol from the regular dealers. So I let him have the revolver. Then when I heard he'd been shot—."

Tenison held up his hand. "Wait." His brow furrowed. He thought quickly. After a minute, he looked up. "Tom, I have a theory. How does this sound to you?" He paused, then went on. "Garvary had this gun. Raven got into the studio and shot him. Naturally enough, he left the gun— which was Leo's own— beside the body.

"But then he needed another to do his dirty work. So he went to a fellow criminal and got hold of an automatic pistol. Which he used on Tinker — and later, on you."

Heath said eagerly:

"That sounds like an accurate reconstruction." He hesitated, "Mr.

555

Tenison, please don't talk to the police. I would get into awful trouble for selling the revolver." His lips trembled. "They might even call me an accessory."

"I don"t think there's much fear of that, Tom." Bob spoke absently. "You've disappointed me. I was hoping to get a line on Raven's whereabouts. Still, I'll respect your confidence. If I tell anybody at all, it will be Sexton Blake. He will see the police don't trouble you." He grinned crookedly. "You shouldn't have sold the gun. But I suppose a broken nose and a clout on the head is punishment enough."

"Thanks." Heath was genuinely grateful. "I wish I could help you— about finding Raven, I mean."

Bob said helplessly:

"If only I could find one of his associates."

Heath's eyes narrowed. "Just a jiffy. Maybe I can help you after all."

Bob was eager. "Well?"

"You know that most of the mail for the tenants goes through my hands first. The postman drops it on my desk, and I sort it out—."

"Yes?"

"Raven didn't have many letters, so I noticed the few he did get specially, if you get my meaning. There were one or two letters with the address of the sender stamped on the back of the envelope. I couldn't help noticing, and it made me wonder a bit."

Heath broke off. "Of course, I didn't know he was a crook, then, which makes it even funnier—." He seemed to be confused. Tenison did his best to distil the meaning from the badly constructed, broken sentences. "Even so, Mr. Raven didn't seem to be the sort to be interested in a thing like that. So I wondered why he was getting letters from this—."

He went on talking.

Tenison listened in silence, a desperate hope once more growing in his heart.

# CHAPTER EIGHTEEN

Linda Martin was sitting on a trestle bed in the corner of a bare and dusty room. There were no windows. A naked electric bulb hung down from the blackened ceiling at the end of a cobwebbed flex. An oil stove fused heat from the centre of the floor.

Linda glanced up as the floor creaked open.

Raven entered. He spoke to somebody beyond the range of the girl's vision. "You can bolt the door behind me. Don't disturb us till I call."

The door closed. He leaned back against the panels, studying the girl with vague amusement.

"Well, Linda?"

The girl did not reply. Raven jerked his thumb backwards. "That was my partner. You don't know him."

The silence crawled endlessly. Then Linda asked hopelessly:

"Why have you brought me here?"

"I want to talk to you."

Linda touched her bruised face. She said bitterly:

"Is this what you mean by— talk?"

"You were naughty," said Raven, as if to a child. He walked towards her slowly. He slewed round a chair and straddled it.

Linda watched with fright in her lovely eyes. He stretched out a hand towards her. "Don't touch me!" she cried suddenly, and huddled against the wall.

Raven was reproving. "Don't be silly, Linda. I'm not going to touch you." His hand went past her, and hovered over a bowl of fruit on a small table by the bed. He selected an apple.

He went on:

"In any case, how could you stop me? You might scream. But who would hear you, down in this cellar?"

He sank his strong, animal teeth in the apple.

A tear trickled down the girl's cheek. She burst out:

"Why do you torture me?"

"Torture?" repeated Raven. "That's a nasty word, Linda. You should wash out your mouth with soap."

She sobbed, and dabbed the corners of her eyes with a handkerchief.

"That's right," said Raven cheerfully. He took another bite from the apple. "What do you know about me, Linda?"

"N-nothing."

"Well—scrunch, scrunch—that's tactful. But not strictly true. To begin with, you know I supplied Garvary with drugs?"

Linda shook her head.

"No?" Raven shrugged. "Oh, well. It doesn't matter. I'll explain." He paused to reflect. "Garvary paid me well. He had to, dope addicts can't afford to argue." He arched an eyebrow. "You knew friend Leo was a rich man?"

"Yes."

Raven grinned. "When I had finished with him, he was practically a pauper. A few months ago, he couldn't pay me for the dope. So I cut off his supplies."

Raven dug his thumb into the apple. The thin skin burst and the juice from the fruit oozed over his thumbnail. "I made a mistake," he admitted. "I underestimated Garvary's resourcefulness. He broke into my rooms and stole the little black book."

Linda repeated painfully:

"The little black book?"

"Yes. Garvary was clever. He knew what went into the book—it was a complete record of all my business dealings." The formal words sounded odd. "Where I got the dope, where I sold it, my connection with my partner—everything."

"Why did Leo want the book?" Linda hardly knew why she asked.

"He didn't." Raven showed his teeth. "He wanted me—under his thumb. He knew I dare not let the book fall into the wrong hands."

Linda breathed:

"Blackmail."

"Yes. But Garvary wasn't an ordinary blackmailer. He didn't want money. He just wanted all the dope he could lay his hands on."

"I see."

"I thought you might. There's not much more to tell. Garvary didn't bother to decipher my records. He just photographed 'em with a micro camera and gave me the film strip later. Every time I wanted to refer to something I had to squint at it through a child's toy." He gestured. "But never mind that. I kept Garvary supplied with drugs, and he didn't make much trouble. He was still afraid of me—and he bought a gun for protection." He added softly:

"That, as it happened, was a sad mistake."

Linda was frightened. She tried to speak, but couldn't.

Raven smiled at her. He continued. "I went on looking for the notebook. I didn't find it. Now I know why."

He said quietly:

"He gave the book to you."

"No—."

"Don't lie to me, Linda. I heard what you said on the telephone. Garvary gave you a sealed package. For safe keeping."

Linda's fingers plucked nervously at the blanket beneath her.

Raven mused:

"I can see why Leo entrusted it to you. But why did you keep it? Surely he told you to send it to the police,"—he chuckled grimly—"if and when he died."

"He didn't tell me—." The girl's voice died.

"Ah. He didn't tell you anything? Well, that fits. He was always a secretive devil. He knew you wouldn't break a confidence—the package was safe with you. And he thought he could handle me."

Linda stared at him hopelessly. She ran the tip of her tongue over dry lips.

Raven said pleasantly:

"You can see why I have to recover the book. Without it, the police have no real evidence against me. They could take me for assault, perhaps, but nothing more serious than that."

Linda breathed a name. "Tinker—."

"Tinker"s dead," said Raven shortly.

"No!"

"Yes." Raven studied her curiously. "I didn't think you'd be so upset. Well, I'm sorry, Linda. But he died in hospital. Which means there's one person less to give evidence against me."

Linda stared in misery.

Raven asked  softly:

"What did  you do with the little black book?"

"I—I hid it in my room."

Raven shook his head. "That was another fib, Linda. I searched your flat while you were out. There was no book there. So I waited for you to return."

"I—I—."

Raven sighed. "Let's be friendly, Linda. Tell me what you did with the package."

The girl's lips trembled. Then she shook her head, mutely.

Raven sighed again. He threw away what remained of the apple. It landed with a dull spatter in the corner. Then he stood up, pushing the chair aside.

"Stand up, Linda."

"W-what for?"

Raven smiled at her, "Just stand up." He added politely:

"Please."

Linda wondered why the word sounded like a jeer. Slowly, fearfully, she got to her feet.

Raven hit her in the face with the back of his hand. Linda screamed. She reeled backwards across the bed.

The sound of the slap seemed to linger in the room. Linda looked up, sobbing. Her cheek throbbed numbly, then blazed with pain. The mark of Raven's hand showed red against the whitened flesh.

The burly man stood over her. His fists clenched slowly. He grinned like a wolf. He whispered:

"That's only the beginning."

# CHAPTER NINETEEN

Bob Tenison slipped from the cover of the bushes and ran across the gravel path towards the house.

A fitful moon reflected glassily in the tall French windows. Tenison glanced round cautiously. Then he lifted his gloved hand and smashed his fist against the pane above the latch.

The glass shattered. Tenison reached through and unlocked the window.

Closing them behind him once more, he stepped through the heavy curtains into the room beyond. He stopped to listen. He heard nothing.

He switched on the lights and glanced round. He found himself in a downstairs bedroom.

Tenison's face was hard. Slowly, he pulled the scarf from around his neck and tied a knot at each end.

Footsteps sounded outside the room. Tenison stepped quickly behind the door. It opened slowly. A man walked in.

Tenison put one hand on the panels and pushed the door shut. The man wheeled. Tenison said:

"Good evening." He held the scarf loosely in one hand.

The other responded dryly:

"I thought I heard you. Who are you, sir?"

"My name's Tenison. You don't know me."

"That is correct. What do you want?"

Bob's mouth was hard and ugly. "I want Linda Martin."

The other man's eyelids drooped. He coughed nervously. "I don't know the young lady."

Bob smiled thinly. "Who told you she was young?"

There was a silence. Then—"You had better leave."

"Not unless Linda goes with me." Bob kept his face stiff.

He was bluffing desperately. "I know Raven brought her here."

"There's no one of that name in this house."

The quick reply lacked conviction. Excitement quickened the artist's reactions. He felt sure he was on the right track.

"Don't lie, man! What have you done with her, you swine?"

The other's eyes flickered. He said smoothly:

"You've made a mistake—." He broke off suddenly and made a grab for a heavy ebony hairbrush on the dressing table.

561

Tenison reached him with one stride. His gloved fist swung up and crashed against the other man's jaw. The crisp smack of leather against bone sounded clearly in the room.

The man's knees buckled. He tumbled to the floor. A trickle of blood showed at the corner of his mouth.

Tenison wiped the sweat from his forehead. He picked up the scarf which he had dropped by the door, then went out of the room and along the corridor.

He felt physically ill. He kept on moving. He came to a door under the stairs.

Footsteps sounded beyond the cracked wooden panels. The tread of a stair creaked in protest. Somebody was coming up from the cellars.

Tenison gripped the knotted scarf at both ends. He stepped back in the shadows. The cellar door opened.

Raven appeared. He was breathing heavily, like a man who had been exerting himself. His face was savage and disappointed.

Bob Tenison moved behind him like a ghost. Then, with a hiss of indrawn breath, he dropped the scarf over Raven's head and drew the heavy folds tightly about his throat.

"Ahhh!"

With a strangled gasp, Raven dropped to his knees and clawed madly at the cloth which was choking him.

With the face of a madman, Bob Tenison twisted hard on the scarf. He knew he was no match for Raven physically. He had to subdue him once and for all.

Raven gurgled horribly. His hands dropped. His face had turned black.

Tenison took both ends of the scarf in one fist and held on desperately. His free hand slipped into Raven's pocket.

He sobbed triumphantly. He had found the burly man's gun.

He let go of the scarf. Raven lurched forward till his forehead touched the floor. With his last reserves of strength, he pulled the scarf from his bruised throat. Then he retched.

After a while, the colour came back to his face. He levered his body up painfully, one hand against the wall.

He turned round and looked into the muzzle of his own gun.

Tenison thumbed off the safety catch. "One false move," he said grimly, "and I shoot."

Raven lost his temper. "You—!"

"Swear if you like," snapped Bob. "But keep your hands where I can see them."

"You"ve got my gun," sneered Raven. "What are you worried

about?"

Bob smiled mirthlessly. "I'm an amateur," he said. "I can't afford to make mistakes."

Raven felt his throat. He was beginning to recover his poise. "You'd make a good professional," he replied. "That move was fast—and dirty."

"I'd do more than that," said Bob sincerely, "for Linda."

Raven's fingers spread. "Ah, yes. For Linda."

Bob"s jaw set. "What have you done with her?"

Raven said tonelessly: "I don't know what you mean!"

Bob's eyes darkened. Love had made him, for the moment, a very dangerous man. He jerked the muzzle of the gun. "Go that way, Raven. And remember, no tricks." He followed the burly man along the corridor till they came to a large, curtained recess. Tenison pushed Raven roughly on to a long sofa facing the entrance.

The burly man looked angry, then relaxed and stared at the artist insolently. "You're getting bold, my friend."

Tenison said icily:

"Let's not waste time. You brought Linda Martin to this house. Where is she?"

Raven smiled.

Tenison snarled:

"Tell me, damn you! Or I'll rake open your face with this pistol."

Raven folded his arms. He said softly:

"Don't get above yourself, Tenison. You've got a little nerve, and you've had a lot of luck. Don't press it too hard."

Tenison gave him a tremendous buffet with his gloved fist. Raven's head jerked, otherwise he made no movement.

He showed his teeth in a grin. He said pleasantly:

"I'll kill you for that, Tenison. I promise you."

Bob hit him again. Then he stepped back, his chest heaving. His brow glistened with sweat. He clutched the gun hard.

Raven said conversationally:

"You weren't made for violence. You've been lucky. Now your luck's run out."

Tenison chilled suddenly. He started to turn, then something crashed own on his head with sickening force. His eyes glazed. He tried to level the gun, but it dropped out of his nerveless land and landed with a dull plop on the carpet. He sprawled face downwards on the floor.

Almost casually, Raven stood up, drew back his foot, and kicked the unconscious man heavily in the ribs.

Then he offered two words of commendation. "Good work."

The tall man in the black suit rubbed his punch nose nervously. The ebony hairbrush ell out of his hand to lie beside the fallen man.

"Is he dead?"

"Not yet," replied Raven coolly. He glanced at his partner and smiled slightly. "I congratulate you. How did you find us?"

"I heard you talking," the tall man replied absently. He seemed upset. He stared at Tenison and licked his lips.

"I didn't want to hit him," said the respectable Mr. Smyrk.

# CHAPTER TWENTY

"You had no choice," returned Raven indifferently. He stooped down, dragged up the unconscious man, and threw him across the sofa. Then he picked up the gun and slipped it into his pocket.

Oswald Smyrk looked unhappy. "What shall we do now?"

Raven replied casually:

"We have to get rid of... this."

The solicitor was frightened. "What do you mean?"

Raven grinned crookedly. "This is the turning point," he said. "You'll have to dirty your hands."

He reversed the pistol he had just withdrawn from his pocket and proffered the butt to his partner.

Smyrk struck it away with revulsion. "No!"

Raven said coldly:

"This isn't a pretty business. We can't handle it with pretty methods. Don't you understand what's happened?"

"Tenison tracked you here. How did he manage it?"

"I don't know and I don't care. That's not the point."

A beading of sweat showed above Smyrk's long upper lip. "You mean— he has told the police?"

"Perhaps. Though somehow I doubt it." He added contemptuously:

"A man in love is always a fool."

"Then—?"

Raven explained patiently. "One of us has blundered. Tenison discovered I brought the girl here. How, I don't know. That doesn't matter. The point is, if he could trail us—so can Sexton Blake."

Smyrk repeated:

"What shall we do?"

"I'm leaving with the girl."

The lawyer asked:

"Has she spoken?"

"No." Raven smiled evilly. "But she will. I must get her away from here. Your house is no longer safe!"

Smyrk said fretfully:

"I can hardly believe it."

"Grow up, man! And don't snivel. The game's not up yet."

Smyrk mumbled:

"But the disgrace."

"There won't be any disgrace, if you keep your head."

The lawyer clutched Raven's sleeve. "Tell me what to do."

"Once I've taken the girl away, nobody can prove she was here." Raven pointed. "Except Bob Tenison."

Smyrk squeezed dry palms together. He nodded unhappily.

Raven said calmly:

"There's a motor launch in the boat house. I'll help you get Tenison aboard. Take the launch up the river, find a lonely spot, and then—."

He gestured significantly.

Smyrk whispered:

"That would be murder."

Raven laughed. "You're forgetting that other little matter. You gave me this gun, remember. You're already an accessory to murder. They can hang you for that."

Something rattled in the lawyer's long throat.

Raven laughed again. "Have you another gun?"

Smyrk replied, with an effort:

"There's a revolver in the side pocket of my car."

"The one I brought here tonight? Good." Raven chuckled. "For a man who hates violence, you're remarkably well armed."

Smyrk muttered something about protection.

Raven said:

"Take this gun. No, don't argue. Remember? You asked me to return it."

Smyrk put out his hand with an effort. The butt struck chill against his dry palm.

Raven said:

"That's better." He stepped back to the couch, and slid his hands under Tenison's armpits. "Take his feet. We've no time to waste."

Smyrk hesitated. "What about the girl?"

"I'll attend to her in a moment. We'll dispose of her boyfriend first."

The lawyer caressed his chain. A bruise was beginning to show along the line of his jaw.

"Suppose the girl makes trouble?"

Raven said mildly:

"She'll make no trouble for a while." He explained:

"She fainted."

They tumbled Tenison's limp body on the smooth boards of the deck.

Smyrk straightened up, breathing hard. He seemed more like an elegantly clad vulture than ever. He mopped his brow with a handkerchief. "What now?"

Raven grunted: "He's still unconscious. But we'd better make sure of him."

He disappeared into the tiny cabin, and came out with a heavy strap. Twisting Bob's arms behind his back, he buckled the leather cruelly about the young man's wrists and waist. "There, he won't get out of that in a hurry."

Smyrk whispered:

"He may—float."

Raven snarled:

"Tie weights to his legs. Here, I'll help you." He turned back to the cabin, then stiffened suddenly.

Smyrk croaked: "What is it?"

Raven gestured savagely. He was staring towards the open doors of the boat house. He breathed:

"I thought I heard something. Out there."

His voice tailed off. His hand slipped into his pocket. Then he swore silently—he had given the pistol to Smyrk. He turned to the lawyer, then changed his mind.

"Get going Smyrk. Start the engine."

"But—."

Raven smacked him on the shoulder. "Don't argue, man! There may be danger." He vaulted lightly on to the landing stage.

The motor roared as the lawyer started up. He was an enthusiastic amateur sailor. Raven called a warning. "You know what to do?"

Smyrk replied hopelessly:

"I know what to do." The motor launch slid away into the darkness.

Raven ran out of the boat house and across the gardens. He re-entered the solicitor's house and went at once to the cellars.

Linda Martin looked up fearfully as the door of her prison crashed open.

Her eyes were swollen and red with tears. Her face was bruised and puffy. When she saw Raven, she cowered back. "No—no, please."

The burly man said briefly:

"Come here." He seized the girl by the arm and hustled her through the door, into another cellar, and then up some rickety stairs.

Linda stumbled and almost fell. Raven growled impatiently:

"Come on, come on." He half-carried her out of the house and into the garage. He opened the car door and pushed her into the front seat. Then he ran round to the other side, wrenched open the far door, and slid behind the wheel.

The car rolled out of the garage and along the drive towards the gates.

Raven drove fast. Linda crouched away from him, tears streaking her cheeks. She sobbed:

"W—where are you taking me?"

Raven said evenly:

"Be quiet."

They roared out of the gates and into the road.

From beside the road, a torch beam stabbed at the darkness. It flicked on and off three times.

Linda saw the signal. So did Raven. The car thundered on.

The headlights blazed. Ahead of them was a hastily erected barrier. A uniformed man stood just behind it, swinging a red lantern.

Linda cried:

"Stop!"

The man beside her trod hard on the accelerator. She caught a revealing glimpse of his face as he smiled, horribly. Then the car crashed through the flimsy barrier. The mudguard caught the policeman a savage blow.

The lantern flew from his hand, curved in a blood-red streak, and smashed against the ground.

Inside the car, Linda screamed.

"You beast!" She beat at Raven with ineffective fists.

Raven kept one hand on the wheel. He drove his elbow viciously into the girl's body. She collapsed with a gasp.

The car roared on.

# CHAPTER TWENTY ONE

The launch drifted silently on the dark waters.

Mr. Smyrk huddled over the controls for several minutes after he had cut the motor. His bloodless lips quivered, and his faded blue eyes flickered from side to side.

He forced himself to move at last. He went towards the man lying bound and helpless on the deck.

Bob Tenison was still unconscious. Mr. Smyrk leaned over him and pulled up one eyelid. Bob's eyes had rolled up, showing blood-streaked white.

The lawyer straightened his bony frame. The bruise on his jaw throbbed painfully. His skin was like dirty parchment.

He whispered:

"I can't do it." Then, with decision: "I must!"

He hauled the stunned man into a kneeling position, so that his chest rested on the edge of the boat and his head lolled down towards the surface of the river.

Smyrk stepped back, his forehead glistening. He fumbled in his pocket for the gun Raven had returned to him. He thumbed aimlessly at the safety catch for a long second before he realised, with a shock, it was already off.

Slowly, he levelled the pistol at Tenison's head. His finger tightened against the trigger..

Something stirred in his sluggish brain. Raven had told him—told him what? He lowered the gun. Weights! That was it. He should tie weights to Tenison's legs. Quite suddenly, Mr. Smyrk felt he wanted to be sick. The nausea turned into a brief but furious hatred. Tenison! This was the young fool who had threatened to tear the mask of probity from the lawyer's face.

Smyrk shouted:

"I won't let you do it!"

Almost insane with rage and fear, he jammed the gun barrel against the hair at the back of the artist's head.

Tenison groaned unconsciously. It was as if a dead man had spoken.

Petulant tears glimmered in Smyrk's faded eyes. He muttered foolishly:

"I won't let you stop me now."

His bony finger crooked on the trigger. He shuddered convulsively. His lips drew back over his gums. His features set in a distorted cast of fear. He sobbed aloud. "Die, damn you! Die!"

His hands grew slippery with sweat. His whole body shook uncontrollably. And still his finger refused to obey the shrieking call of his brain.

"Uhhh." It was no good. He couldn't fire the gun.

Frenzied and almost ashamed, the lawyer surrendered to obsession. His only desire was to be rid of Tenison's body. Still clutching the pistol in his fist, Smyrk scrabbled at the artist's inanimate form.

Sobbing hysterically, he hauled his victim across the gunwale.

Tenison balanced crazily. One push would be enough to send him into the river.

A swelling roar sounded in the lawyer's ears. He thought it was the blood pounding in his veins, till a blinding light blazed through the darkness and caught him in its pitiless glare.

Smyrk moaned an obscenity.

A voice barked a warning from behind the eye of light.

Smyrk crouched. The gun in his hand seemed welded to the flesh. The muzzle crashed fire like a discharge of pus and blood.

A point of flame stabbed its reply from the darkness. Smyrk felt a jarring shock which flung the pistol from his grasp. He stared incredulously at the hole punched through his hand. Then the pain ran like fire with the blood and he staggered madly. He crashed backwards against the man he had hauled across the gunwale.

Slowly, lazily, Tenison's limp body slid head foremost down into the dark waters. Bob vanished without a cry, almost without a splash.

He sank like a stone.

Sexton Blake jammed the smoking pistol into the hand of his friend, the Inspector. Then he wrenched off his coat and balanced for a moment of the edge of the police launch. He dived cleanly.

The icy waters closed around him. The shock of the cold was paralysing.

Blake was grimly aware he had only one chance. Expert swimmer as he was, he couldn't stay under water indefinitely. If he didn't find Tenison's bound and helpless body at once, the young artist wouldn't have a chance of survival.

As he plunged downwards, the detective's hands groped and explored tirelessly, in a blind and desperate search.

Chill despair struck through his heart. A heavy iron band seemed to be tightening around his chest.

A few seconds more at the most. Then—.

His steely fingers grasped cloth, and brushed against cold flesh. Sexton Blake took a firm grip with both hands.

Then, threshing the black water with his long, powerful legs, the detective started on the long journey back to the surface.

It taxed his strength severely. Tenison's inanimate weight was a crippling burden. Blake clenched his teeth. His lungs were bursting. He fought on with relentless determination.

He broke surface at last. The first shuddering gulp of air was as intoxicating as champagne.

Sexton Blake turned on his back and floated. His iron grip kept Tenison's head above water. He felt his strength returning. He began to swim, using his body and legs.

The powerful light from the police launch swept over the river like a questing finger. The beam found the two heads bobbing above the surface of the water.

A hail sounded from the launch. "Ahoy there, Blake! Are you all right?"

The detective disengaged one hand briefly and waved it in reply. Then he swam on with determination.

Stevens helped him aboard with his burden. The Inspector was concerned. "Are you sure you're all right?"

"Yes, yes," said Blake impatiently. Now that he was free of the river's icy clutch, he was more than ever conscious of the chill in his bones. "Look after young Tenison."

Stevens turned his attention to the bedraggled figure on the deck. He looked at the heavy strap which pinioned the artist's arms and commented grimly:

"They weren't taking any chances."

He unbuckled the strap and examined the young man carefully. He muttered:

"He's had a bad crack on the head, and he"s swallowed a lot of water. We'll have to get him to a doctor. But he'll be all right."

He called over his shoulder. "Take over here, will you?" He added a few quick orders.

He straightened up. "And now," he muttered, "for Mr. Smyrk."

The men in the police boat had manoeuvred it alongside the motor launch. Stevens jumped clumsily from one craft to the other.

Oswald Smyrk was huddled up against the side of the tiny cabin. He was staring at his injured hand and crying.

Stevens glared at him with silent contempt. His gaze went to the pistol lying on the deck. He picked it up by the trigger guard and wrapped it in a handkerchief.

He grunted absently:

"The make and the calibre—they fit, by Glory! This could be the gun that shot young Tinker."

Smyrk's bloodless lips moved tremulously. He croaked:

"I'm hurt. Get me a doctor. Please."

Stevens said dryly:

"I'll get you to a doctor. Believe me, from now on, we'll be taking good care of you."

He chuckled grimly.

"I hope you enjoy reading about this in the Sunday newspapers."

# CHAPTER TWENTY TWO

Bob Tenison huddled close to a cheery fire in a private room in the local police station. A curious assortment of garments had replaced his own wet clothes, but at least they were warm and dry. A blanket was draped around his shoulders.

Detective Inspector Stevens asked gruffly:

"How are you feeling?"

Bob was drinking cocoa. He pressed his hands against the warm cup. "I'm okay." He strove to keep the panic out of his voice. "How's Linda?"

The teacup dropped and shattered in the grate. Bob shouted:

"What do you mean—you didn't find her? She was there in the house—I know she was there!"

Sexton Blake said firmly:

"Control yourself."

Something in the detective's level tones drove the hysteria from Tenison's flushed face. "I'm sorry," he mumbled. "But I was certain I had found her again."

Blake glanced at his friend, the Inspector. Stevens hesitated, then said:

"We think Smyrk had Miss Martin locked in the cellars."

"Then she was there." Bob sounded dazed. He dared not ask the question which formed in his mind.

Stevens answered it anyway. "Raven took her away," he said flatly. Bob looked at him in mute misery.

Sexton Blake interposed with deliberate banality. "Mr. Tenison, you owe us an explanation."

"I don't quite—."

"How did you know that Miss Martin was being held a prisoner in Smyrk's home?"

"Oh." Bob smiled weakly. "I didn't. I was gambling wildly. That's why I broke into the house without consulting you." He rubbed his chin. "I had fool's luck."

Stevens commented grimly:

"That kind of luck runs out quickly."

Bob nodded. "Raven told me that, too." His voice dropped. "He also told me he'd kill me."

"He left that job to his partner." Stevens scowled at the floor. "If it hadn't been for Mr. Blake—."

Sexton Blake interrupted once more. "Please, Inspector. Mr. Tenison has not finished explaining."

Stevens snorted. "Go on, young man."

Bob grinned wryly. "I'm no detective. I bungled things dreadfully. But I used each blunder as a stepping stone."

Sexton Blake smiled. "That's as good a motto as any. Continue, please."

"Well...." Bob looked uncomfortable. He explained the shrewd guesswork which had led him to Tom Heath, and repeated what the desk clerk had told him about Leo Garvary's gun. "That was a shocking disappointment, of course. I thought Tom might have sold his gun to Raven. I also thought he might know some of Raven's associates—."

"We understand." Stevens was impatient. "Go on,"

"Well, luck was with me after all. Heath is fairly inquisitive—."

"Who isn't?" growled Stevens.

Bob rubbed his cheek. "Tom sorts all the tenants' mail. He noticed Raven received letters from Smyrk—."

"Wait a minute. How the devil could he know that?"

"The old villain was the general secretary of a morality league, wasn't he? Well, Raven got letters with the name of this precious society stamped on the flaps of the envelopes.

"Raven wasn't the man to be interested in cranks like that, so Heath wondered why he was getting the letters.

"Tom told me about Raven's apparent connection with the league, and I jumped to the conclusion Smyrk was corresponding with the man privately."

Stevens muttered a heartfelt oath. "Why, for heaven's sake?"

"It's hard to explain it," admitted Bob. "I was proceeding more by luck than logic. I knew, you see, that Smyrck had been Leo's solicitor, as well as the society's secretary. Garvary used to joke about it. He always laughed at censors."

Tenison gestured. "You had told me that Raven was Leo's evil genius. Smyrck had been his lawyer. The letters pointed to a connection between the two. I decided Smyrck was worth investigating."

Stevens stared eloquently at the ceiling. "Go on."

Bob shuffled. "I went straight to his office."

"So late in the evening?"

"I was too worried to wait. Besides, I'd looked him up in the 'phone book. He had a flat in the same building." Bob stared into the fire. "Smyrck wasn't there but my luck still held. I found a dusty little chap in spectacles. Perhaps he was annoyed with Smyrck for making him work so late—he was the clerk, you see—."

Stevens interjected:

"We've seen the man."

Bob nodded. "I needn't go into detail, but I bluffed him and bribed him till he told me about Smyrck's house on the river."

"Did he tell you anything else?"

Bob smiled slightly. "A man answering to Raven's description called at the office on the afternoon of the day Garvary was murdered."

Sexton Blake lit his pipe. "Another little problem solved, Inspector. You remember our talk yesterday morning?"

"When we agreed Raven had disposed of his drugs in a hurry? Yes, I remember." Stevens scowled horribly. "I'll tear Smyrck's rooms apart with my bare hands."

"I don't think such drastic measures will be strictly necessary. You should find the cache easily enough." Blake puffed comfortably. "But a search of Smyrck's quarters might prove rewarding."

Bob Tenison waited till the two detectives fell silent again, then went on quietly:

"I guessed Raven might have taken Linda to the house on the river. So I broke into one of the downstairs bedrooms. Smyrck heard me. He came in to investigate so,"—Bob gestured—"I knocked him out."

Stevens seemed on the point of exploding. "Hell's blazes! Do you know how many laws you've broken tonight?"

Bob looked him innocently. "I suppose I was technically at fault. Still, I thought I was justified."

"Heaven protect me," said Stevens fervently, "from all amateur detectives." Tenison defended himself. "I got results."

"You got results all right," snapped Stevens irascibly. "You lost us the girl."

Bob stammered. "W-what do you mean?"

"Did you think the police were complete fools? You young idiot, we've been watching Oswald Smyrck since yesterday afternoon."

"W-what?"

Steven said heavily:

"I sent Sergeant Wyatt and another man to watch the house by the river. We wanted the girl—we couldn't show our hand to Smyrck. The Sergeant prowled round the house, wondering what was happening. Eventually, he saw Raven and Smyrck carry you out to the boathouse. He couldn't challenge 'em— they were armed, and he wasn't.

"Fortunately, we were keeping radio contact. Wyatt had a walkie-talkie. He sent an urgent message to the police launch, warning us to look out for the lawyer.

"Unfortunately, Raven must have heard him. Anyway, he took alarm and ran for it. Wyatt managed to get back to the road just as Raven came roaring out in the car. The girl was with him.

"The Sergeant flashed a signal to our man further up the road." The Inspector grimaced. "This one had rigged up a barrier when you busted the window—he and Wyatt guessed you would stir up a hornet's nest. Much good the barrier did him, though. Raven drove straight through it." Stevens looked angry. "The policeman is in hospital," he finished abruptly.

Sexton Blake blew out a cloud of smoke. "Fortunately, he wasn't badly hurt."

"Thank heavens for that," said Bob sincerely.

Stevens was still angry. "No thanks to you," he snapped. "You young fool, you've lost us Raven and the girl, landed one of my men in hospital, and nearly succeeded in getting yourself murdered."

Tenison flushed scarlet. He hit back furiously. "You're not so clever yourself. You knew Linda was a prisoner in that house! Why the devil didn't you raid it?"

"You're being rather unjust," said Sexton Blake quietly. "We didn't *know* Miss Martin was there. We merely recognised the possibility." He took the pipe out of his mouth. "Let me explain.

"One small incident directed our attention towards Mr. Smyrck. We wondered if he was really as respectable as he seemed. The Inspector has described how we set a watch on his house. Similar measures were taken regarding his quarters in the city, though we knew Miss Martin could not be taken there.

"Wyatt saw nothing. Raven, you see, had already hidden himself with the girl before the Sergeant arrived."

Bob interrupted:

"The Inspector said the police had been watching Smyrck since yesterday afternoon."

"Watching Smyrck, yes. But not his house on the river."

Stevens put in gruffly:

"We didn't do that till Miss Martin had been kidnapped. Raven had to take her somewhere. Smyrck's house was one of the possible places."

Tenison asked: "Couldn't you apply for a search warrant?"

Stevens exploded. "Burn it, this isn't a police state! I can't get a warrant just like that. I have to produce strong evidence first."

He unbent slightly. "Between you and me, the Director of Public Prosecutions wasn't any too keen to tackle Smyrck on the flimsy evidence we had then. He knows him of old, you see. Smyrck was always nagging him to ban this, that, and the other. These holier-than-thou boys pull a lot of weight. And they always will, till we clear archaic laws off the statute book."

"You mean you were helpless?"

"No! Wyatt was watching. As soon as he saw any indication at all that Raven or the girl was there, he was to report to me. Then—and not till then—I'd have the evidence I needed.

"So what happened? You crashed in. We had to divert most of our forces to rescue you—and during the confusion, Raven escaped with the girl."

Bob choked suddenly. He hid his face in his hands.

Sexton Blake said briskly:

"Come now. You mustn't blame yourself too much. And you musn't be too hard on this young man, Inspector. Mr. Smyrck, at least, is in your hands."

Stevens brightened. "Yes," he agreed with relish. "We've charged him with attempted murder, assault, shooting at the police, possession of an illegal firearm—."

"Spare us the full catalogue," chuckled Blake. "You'll be able to prove Mr. Smyrck has committed most of the crimes on the calendar."

"Yes." Stevens smacked his lips. "There's no limit to the possibilities. We haven't even investigated the dope angle yet."

Bob Tenison looked up. He asked wearily:

"How did you know Smyrck was a crook?"

Sexton Blake smiled. "He gave himself away. Most criminals do, sooner or later." He drew on his pipe. "We told Smyrck his client Garvary had been a drug addict. As we were leaving his office, he commented:

"Cocaine addiction is indeed a dreadful thing."

Bob looked puzzled. "What's wrong with that?"

"Nothing," replied Sexton Blake softly. "Except for one thing. Garvary doped himself with cocaine, yes. But the only specific drug we had mentioned to Mr. Smyrck had been—*marihuana*."

Tenison's lips formed in a soundless ejaculation. Then he whispered:

"Does nothing escape you?"

Sexton Blake smiled without arrogance. "Nothing," he replied gravely.

# CHAPTER TWENTY THREE

Alan Raven said cheerfully: "Here we are, Linda. Make yourself at home."

Linda's voice was dull. "Where are we?"

"In one of the more desolate quarters of London," replied Raven vaguely, though with the air of one making a great confidence. He held a revolver in one hand, and a flashlight in the other. "Let me see … there should be some candles somewhere. Ah! There they are."

He put down the torch, pocketed the gun, and picked up a box of matches. He touched flame to the wicks of the candles.

Linda Martin watched listlessly. She made no attempt to escape. Fear had numbed all her perceptions.

Raven extinguished the torch. He planted candles at strategic points around the room. He said briskly:

"That's better. Sit down, Linda. You're not going anywhere."

Linda stared round in despair. She sat down on an old divan, against some shabby blankets.

She asked again:

"Where are we?"

The burly man's face was in shadow. He said softly:

"You're very curious." Linda cringed.

Her arm went up, as if to ward off a blow.

Raven laughed. "Don't be scared, Linda. It was a reasonable question. I'll tell you where we are."

He spoke gently, as if he was humouring a mad woman, or soothing a nervous child. "This is a basement room in an old bombed house in the middle of a wasteland. Nobody ever comes here. Since the buildings all around are dangerous, not even the children come to play. The council seems to have forgotten the whole area. They make grandiose plans to clear it, but nothing is ever done. Nobody will find us here."

Linda's shoulders slumped. "Why have you brought me here?"

Raven smiled. "Don't be silly, Linda. We haven't finished our… talk." A whimper escaped her.

Raven said kindly:

"Cry if you wish. No one will hear you."

Linda's fear-struck gaze went round the room, as if she was seeking a miraculous deliverance. Only bare stone walls—stained and damp as though the house itself was sweating—and a heavy door met her eyes. There were no windows.

Raven indicated a door-less aperture in the wall behind the divan. "There's the bathroom, Linda. Through there. You see,"—he showed all his teeth—"I've provided all the amenities."

Linda sobbed.

Raven sprawled his burly frame in an old wicker chair. He leaned back against the cushions and sighed gratefully. "There's food, too. Nowadays you can find anything you need in a tin. I hope you can cook, Linda."

He took a packet from his pocket and flipped a cigarette into his mouth. He left the cylinder unlighted.

"Yes," he went on in the same friendly manner, "I prepared this hide-out some time ago. You never know your luck," he grinned, "in my line of business. Mind you, it isn't an ideal spot for a winter holiday. But there's an oil lamp here, if it gets too cold. All things considered, we can make ourselves comfortable,"—his voice dropped oddly—"you and me."

The last three words had a brittle sound.

A spark of defiance showed in the girl's slanting eyes. "The police will find us."

Raven shook his head. "I don't think so, Linda."

The girl said desperately:

"They'll trace the car."

"Oh, no. I hid it in a deserted, tumbledown garage. Which," Raven added kindly, "is also close at hand."

Linda cried suddenly:

"Please—please let me go home."

"Be patient, my dear. I'm in an awkward position." Raven seemed slightly amused. "I don't know what's happened to my partner. The police may have arrested him, for all I know."

"Your partner." Linda was too tired to inflect the words as a question.

"Yes." Raven appeared to come to a decision. "I think I'll tell you about him, Linda. It can't do much harm now."

The girl made no reply.

Raven made a long arm and picked up the box of matches he had used to light the candle. "Have you heard of Oswald Smyrck?"

"No," returned Linda dully. Then she looked up, interest struggling past the lassitude in her lovely eyes. "At least—wasn't he Leo's lawyer?"

"That's right." Raven threw up the box and caught it again. The matches inside rattled and rustled a sibilant accompaniment. "He was also my partner." He used the past tense instinctively.

"I—I don't understand,"

"No? Well, I'll explain. Mr. Smyrck was—is—a very cautious man. Garvary's father had left his money in trust with Smyrck's firm. Friend Oswald had his eye on that particular nest egg, but he was much too clever to embezzle the funds outright. He handed over the capital to friend Leo three years ago.

"That, in fact, was that. Mr. Smyrck was beyond reproach." Raven grinned. "That was when I took over. We had been partners in the dope racket for some time past. Smyrck had built up some good connections, and we operated discreetly. Smyrck's launch came in useful, too. Where was I? Oh, yes.

"I moved into the flat below Garvary's. It wasn't hard to introduce him to the drug habit—Leo had indulged before, I fancy. Anyway, I made him pay through the nose. One way or another, Smyrck and I fleeced Garvary of his fortune." Raven clicked his fingers. "You know what happened next."

Linda said sombrely:

"You told me."

Fear clutched her by the throat. "Why have you told me all this?"

Raven took a match from the box and rasped the head into flame. The focus of fire threw odd shadows across his face as he lighted his cigarette. "Why not?"

Linda didn't want to reply, yet she whispered:

"I might—tell."

Raven dribbled smoke through his nostrils. He mocked her. "You wouldn't be so unkind."

Linda's lips trembled. "I won't tell."

"Of course you won't." Raven was sardonic.

He thought of the revolver in his pocket.

He drew hard on the cigarette. The tip flared red.

"Now, Linda. We've chatted long enough. Tell me what you did with the little black book."

"Why is it so important?" Linda was struggling for time.

Raven sighed. "It's still the most important evidence against us."

"But if the police have captured your partner, the game's up anyway."

"No, it isn't." Raven and the girl seemed to be playing another, more deadly game. "Smyrck won't incriminate me. He knows me too well. He knows what I might do."

Linda's pupils dilated. She strove to find another objection. Her

581

mind was barren of ideas.

Raven said:

"I can guess what you're thinking. You're telling yourself to keep the secret. Why? Because you're afraid I'll have no further use for you once I've learnt it. You're afraid I'll kill you, Linda." He smiled indulgently. "That's a fear you'll have to overcome. I'll help you."

He stood up. He walked towards the divan. He said pleasantly:

"Undo the buttons of your blouse, Linda."

A tear stained the girl's cheek. "No."

"Undo your blouse," said Raven evenly, "or I'll tear it off myself."

Linda's mouth distorted. With clumsy fingers, she unfastened the top of her dress.

"That's a good girl," murmured Raven kindly.

He drew hard on his cigarette.

Then he took it out of his mouth and ground the fiery, glowing tip into the flesh at the base of Linda"s throat.

# CHAPTER TWENTY FOUR

Alan Raven picked his way through the ruins in the cold, grey light of early morning. Light but persistent rain was falling, washing away the snow.

Raven descended to the basement of an old bombed house. He came to a heavy door, bolted on the outside.

He slid back the bolts, and pushed open the door. He closed it behind him.

Linda Martin looked up dully. She made a motion to hide her hands. They were sore and bleeding.

The burly man clicked his tongue. "Linda!" He reproved her gently. "You've been hammering on the door. Didn't I tell you no one would hear you?"

She made no reply.

Raven dropped the suitcase he had been carrying. "I've brought your things," he said pleasantly. "You can make yourself look pretty."

A bitter sound throbbed out of Linda's throat. It was only the travesty of a laugh. Raven twisted a key in the lock, then replaced it in his pocket. "Don't be bitter, Linda. You're bruised and bedraggled. But you have only yourself to blame. You shouldn't have been so,"— he formed the word delicately—"obstinate."

The girl said huskily:

"You got what you wanted. Now leave me alone."

Raven smiled at her. He took another key from his pocket and showed her the metal glinting in his palm. "Oh, yes. I got what I wanted. Here it is."

Linda's fingernails hooked in the blankets covering the divan.

Raven said:

"Don't be frightened, Linda. I won't hurt you any more." He grinned. "I still need you." He seated himself in the old wicker chair. "Tell me, Linda," he murmured with the air of a man making conversation, "why did you choose to put the book in a safe deposit?"

Linda replied in the lifeless tones of an automaton. "Leo gave me the sealed package. I didn't want to take it, but he said it was valuable, and he wanted to place it with someone he could trust. He made me promise to say nothing about it. He said he'd ask for it when needed. He gave me some money. I didn't want to keep the money in my flat, so I put it in a depository. I had almost forgotten about it, till—till—."

She broke off and sobbed, caressing her bruised cheeks.

Raven spoke with exaggerated concern. "You're exhausted, my dear." He snapped his fingers. "You need a bath."

"W—what?"

"A hot bath. It will do you all the good in the world. You'll feel the fatigue soak out of your bones."

Linda squeezed her eyes shut. The lashes were damp.

Raven stood up and lit the gas ring he had fixed up in one corner. Then he went into the bathroom and filled an old kettle with water. Placing it on the fiery ring, he said cheerfully:

"There, it won't take long to boil enough water to fill the bath. Then you'll be fresh and clean again."

Linda sprawled face downwards on the divan. She lay motionless while Raven heated kettlefuls of water on the gas ring, talking casually all the time.

"I didn't have any trouble breaking into your flat. The police had gone." His voice faded as he went into the bathroom. She heard the splash of water as he poured it into the bath, then the gurgle of the taps as he refilled the kettle with cold.

He came back. "I went through the window, just as I did before. They hadn't even repaired the catch. The key was in the jewel case, as you had said. I had no trouble finding it." He nodded towards the suitcase. "Why don't you unpack? I've brought you some fresh clothes, and make-up—everything a girl needs."

Linda raised her head. She said bitterly:

"You're very kind."

Raven glanced at her thoughtfully. "You're regaining your spirit. Well, that's nice. But don't get too venturesome."

Linda hid her face again.

Raven went on with his work in silence. It took time, but the burly man was patient. Finally, he opened the suitcase and took out a kimono. He handed the flimsy garment to the girl.

He murmured:

"Take your clothes off, Linda."

She shook her head. A tendril of hair came down across her forehead. Raven dug cruel fingers into her wrist and twisted slowly.

Linda moaned. The burly man released her. He said tersely:

"Undress."

He picked up the suitcase and the kettle and took them both into the bathroom.

He put the case on the floor beside the door-less aperture, then emptied the kettle into the bath. The water steamed.

Raven tested it. It had cooled, inevitably, but it was still warm and pleasant. He went to an old chest in the corner and took some fresh towels from a tightly-lidded tin. He put the towels with some soap on a rickety chair by the bath.

Then he opened the suitcase and took out the clothes he had chosen from Linda's apartment. He spread them neatly on a rail screwed into the wall.

He glanced round. A small oil lamp burned in a niche above the bath. It was the room's only illumination.

Raven went back to the other chamber.

Linda stood up. She clutched the kimono about her tightly. Raven said:

"Take your bath, my dear."

Linda's pupils dilated. She whispered indistinctly.

Raven laughed. "Don't worry. We'll observe the proprieties."

He dragged one of the blankets from the divan and draped it across the door-less aperture, catching the cloth on two rusty nails above the lintel.

He held the blanket aside. "There. I think that's all I need to do." He laughed. "Unless you would like me to wash your back."

Linda's chin tilted. She went into the bathroom without replying.

In the shadowy chamber, she looked back doubtfully at the hanging folds of the blanket. Then she heard the unmistakable creak of the wicker chair as Raven flung himself into it. She let our her breath in a delicate sigh of relief.

She slipped out of the kimono. Her body was exquisite.

She stepped into the bath. The water washed about her softly, warming her flesh and soaking the hurt and the exhaustion away.

When the water chilled, she stepped out of the bath and dried herself with the rough towels. The coarse material chafed the delicate texture of her skin, but the smart—and the tingle—was not unpleasant. She felt her body glow. She dressed quickly.

She went back to the adjoining room. Raven was still sitting in the wicker chair. He had stripped to the waist.

He said:

"You look like a different girl. Now you're fit to be seen in public."

"In public?"

"Yes, we're going together, you and I." He stood up. "Makeup your face, Linda. I want you to look your loveliest."

She whispered:

"Where are we going?"

"We are going," replied Raven slowly, "to get the little black book."

Linda understood.

"And now," said Raven, "I'll have a wash myself." He smiled. "Don't be troublesome, Linda. I still have the key of that door in my pocket. And I still have Smyrk's revolver."

# CHAPTER TWENTY FIVE

The depository, besides being one of the strongest places in London, was almost a show-piece. Its security precautions were famous.

Raven and the girl went through the single entrance. The burly man had linked his arm through hers. He kept his right hand in his pocket. The cold butt of the revolver pressed against his palm.

He whispered without moving his lips:

"Remember, Linda. I have nothing to lose. If the police get me, I'll get you first."

Linda said dully:

"I understand."

The strong-rooms and the safes were all in the basement. Linda made her way towards the lift. Raven stopped her as she put a finger on the buzzer.

"No. We'll use the stairs."

They went down the flight of steps which curved round the lift shaft. They did not speak.

They came to a massive grille.

Linda stepped up to the bars and spoke to the man on duty. "My name is Linda Martin. I have a safe rented here." She showed him the key Raven had taken from her flat.

The commissionaire nodded. He manipulated his keys and swung open a portion of the grille.

Raven pressed the girl's arm gently. Responding to the silent instruction, Linda said as naturally as possible:

"This gentleman is a friend of mine. Do you mind if he waits inside?"

"That's all right, Miss," was the cheerful response. "The gentleman can wait in the centre 'all."

Raven and the girl stepped through the grille. They walked along a short corridor and found themselves in the circular hall. From this part of the basement, other passages radiated like the spokes of a wheel. They were all protected by steel bars. Raven asked:

"What now?"

"I have to see the manager—to sign my name and give the password. They won't let you into his office."

Raven covered his anger with a smile. "Make sure you don't tell him

587

anything but the password."

Linda shivered. "I won't."

"Good girl." He released her arm. "Don't forget, angel. There are six bullets in this gun. And I'll save them all for you."

A pulse throbbed in Linda's throat. She walked across to the manager's office and knocked on the door.

Raven saw the door open and heard the manager's voice. "Oh, Miss Martin, isn't it? Come in, please."

The door closed. Raven stared at the blank panels. His body was tense.

A few minutes later, Linda came out of the office accompanied by a plump man in a pin-stripe suit. It was the manager's duty to release the first lock on the safe the firm had rented to the girl.

Raven watched them with the wariness of a cat.

They went through one of the steel grilles, admitted by another uniformed attendant. After a while, they returned. Linda was carrying a deed-box. The manager indicated the door of a private room, then left her with a bow.

As soon as the portly man had disappeared into his office, Raven shouldered his way into the room after the girl.

Linda turned. "You shouldn't—."

"Don't argue," said Raven evenly. A thin glitter of amusement showed in his deep set eyes. "Open the box."

Linda's hands trembled. She lifted the lid.

"Hurry, girl!"

Linda lifted a sealed package from the bottom of the deed-box. She murmured:

"This is the packet Leo gave me—."

Raven didn't let her finish. He grabbed the package eagerly, and tore away the stout paper securing it.

Linda began to tremble. She looked on hopelessly.

A long sigh of satisfaction broke from the burly man's lips. He gazed at the girl in triumph.

"This is it, Linda. This is it!"

She whispered:

"Have you finished with me now?"

Raven's head jerked. A slow, cruel smile touched menace to his face. He said softly:

"Oh, yes. I've finished with you now."

The pulse in her throat pounded madly. She backed against the wall.

Raven laughed. He slipped the little black book into his pocket. Then he stuffed the discarded wrappings into the deed-box and re-closed the lid.

"Take this back to the safe, angel. We're leaving this expensive rat-trap."

Linda picked up the deed-box. She stumbled through the door like a girl in a nightmare. Raven followed her into the central hall. He kept his hand on the gun in his pocket.

He waited with apparent patience while Linda returned the tin box to the safe. She rejoined him again after a short interval, and they retraced their steps to the exit.

The commissionaire swung open the grille once more.

As it clanged shut behind them, Raven's cold heart sang with relief. He murmured:

"We're out of the cage, Linda. Let's go."

He turned to the flight of steps. Linda said clearly:

"Let's use the lift."

Something in the girl's voice warned Raven that to deny her would provoke a scene. He clutched the gun hard.

The lift doors slid open. A uniformed attendant poked out his head. "Going up, sir?"

"Yes," replied the girl quickly. She hurried into the lift. Raven looked ugly, but he had to follow.

The attendant repeated cheerily: "Going up!" He gave a fatuous chuckle. "One way only."

Raven said evenly: "Let's not waste time."

"Yessir. Time's money, as they say. And we don't have much of either nowadays." Raven glanced at him irritably. The attendant was a tall old man with grey hair and a moustache. He stooped over the controls and sent the lift upwards.

He brought it to a stop on the ground floor. He slid back the inner metal guard, then pushed open the outer doors. "Here we are."

He stood back to let the girl pass. Raven made to follow her.

At that moment, the grey haired attendant stepped quickly between them. With one hand, he gave Linda a vigorous shove in the small of her back. She staggered out of the lift and reeled into the lobby. Strong hands grasped her.

The attendant's shoulder caught Raven in the chest. The burly man lurched back. He was taken by surprise.

The lift man was—magically—no longer old and stooping. His features changed subtly. Level grey eyes looked into Raven's own.

"Blake!"

Raven spat out the name with venom. He clawed the revolver from his pocket.

589

Before he could level the gun, Sexton Blake was upon him. Steely fingers fastened round Raven's wrist, forcing the gun away.

The burly man fought desperately. The struggle raged in the confined space of the cubicle.

Raven's breath came in great sobbing gasps. He felt the sweat soak through his clothes.

He gritted:

"Damn you, Blake."

Fury lent him extra strength. The muzzle of his gun moved inch by inch towards the detective's body. Raven's teeth bared in a ghastly grin. He was conscious only of an overwhelming lust to kill.

Blake's fingernails pressed into the burly man's wrist. Blood oozed from the torn skin.

Raven laughed aloud. He screamed:

"Now, Blake! *Now!*"

His finger crooked hard on the trigger.

In that same instant, Sexton Blake made a superhuman effort. He forced the gun muzzle away from his body. The incline altered. The revolver blasted. The sound of the shot was deafening.

Into Raven's eyes, which had been lit with cruel triumph, came a ludicrous expression of surprise.

Something bubbled thickly in his throat. Sexton Blake stepped back.

The burly man swayed. A red stain seeped round the powder-blackened hole in his chest.

He was still holding the gun. He seemed to be trying to raise it, then his fingers opened and the revolver dropped to the floor of the lift.

Alan Raven lurched forward. He put out his hands blindly, as though finding his way in the dark.

He walked with the uncertain, tottering steps of a very young child. His eyes glazed. He coughed blood.

An overwrought voice sounded from the rear of the lobby. "For heaven's sake! Stop him somebody."

Raven's sightless eyes flickered. His head moved slowly from side to side, like a dying reptile's.

A tortured smile plucked at the corners of his mouth. Then he crashed forwards on his face. Nobody moved.

Sexton Blake moved forward out of the lift and knelt beside the fallen man. Detective Inspector Stevens moved forward.

He cleared his throat. He asked gruffly:

"Is he—?" Sexton Blake straightened up.

He answered quietly:

"Yes, he's dead."

# CHAPTER TWENTY SIX

Linda was crying helplessly.

Detective Sergeant Wyatt patted her shoulder.

"There, there," he sympathised. "It's over now. You're safe."

She sobbed brokenly:

"I thought—I'd never escape his—."

Wyatt said grimly:

"You have nothing to fear from Raven now."

Linda looked up with frightened eyes. "Is it true he's dead?"

Wyatt replied sombrely:

"It's true."

They were waiting in a small room on the ground floor of the depository. Wyatt's special charge had been Linda's safety. As soon as Blake had thrust her out of the lift, the Sergeant had hurried her out of harm's way.

The door opened and Sexton Blake entered. He was still wearing his attendant's uniform, but he had peeled off the moustache and his hair was no longer grey.

Linda said weakly:

"Mr. Blake— I—."

Sexton Blake smiled gravely. "We meet at last, Miss Martin."

The girl was at a loss for words. Eventually she said tremulously: "You saved my life."

Blake smiled. "I apprehended a dangerous criminal." He took out his pipe and filled it. "That's all,"

Linda said softly:

"You could have apprehended him at any time after he first appeared in this building. You held your hand for one reason only. You thought he would injure me,"

Sexton Blake squeezed her fingers. "I thought you had suffered enough."

The girl trembled. She nodded dumbly.

The famous detective had heard most of the girl's story from the Inspector, who had already questioned her. He said gently:

"We knew Raven would force you to tell him what you had done with the black book."

"I tried—I tried not to tell him."

"I wish," commented Blake soberly, "you hadn't tried to resist him. You would have saved yourself,"—-he hesitated—"much pain."

Linda sobbed. Her fingers went up to her throat.

Blake went on:

"You see, Stevens and I were waiting for Raven to bring you here. It was our best chance to catch him and save you at the same time."

Linda nodded. "I'm beginning to understand." She ventured a nervous laugh. "I didn't know what to think when the manager told me to be sure to take the lift up to the ground floor."

"Ah, yes. He co-operated handsomely. We took him into our confidence, of course. The company's security rules couldn't permit the Inspector to plant his men in the vault itself, but the manager gladly consented to,"—Blake chuckled— "my little impersonation.

"My make-up was simple, but effective." Blake cradled the bowl of his pipe. "Disguise is as much an attitude of the mind as a matter of false hair and greasepaint. I learnt that from one of the greatest criminals of the age—a man named Leon Kestrel."

Linda nodded again. She asked:

"But how did you know—how could you have known—Raven would come here?"

Blake explained:

"Obviously, he had kidnapped you to make you tell him where you had hidden the sealed package Garvary had entrusted to your care. I found the key to a safe deposit in your jewel case. It wasn't hard to discover which depository had issued it.

"It was reasonable to assume you had put the package in your safe deposit. It was equally reasonable to expect Raven would put in an appearance sooner or later. We had only to wait."

The door behind them opened again. Detective Inspector Stevens came in. "Well, Miss Martin. How are you feeling?"

Linda mumbled a vague reassurance. Now the danger was past, she found herself oscillating between wild elation and black depression.

Stevens studied her shrewdly. He knew the conflicts reaction could bring. He said:

"I've brought some one to see you." He raised his voice. "Mr. Tenison!"

Linda stood up as Bob hurried in. Her face changed colour. The artist cried:

"Linda! My dear."

"Bob. Oh, Bob."

Tears blinded her. She went limp in his arms, pressing her cheek to his breast. Tenison whispered:

"Linda, my darling." His face was blindly happy.

Blake murmured:

"Come, Inspector."

They made a tactful withdrawal, taking the Sergeant with them.

Outside in the corridor, Stevens scowled. "That's that," he said. "Hell's blazes! What a case. I'd better go along to the mortuary, I suppose. It's a pity we didn't catch Raven alive."

Sexton Blake rejoined:

"At least you have the little black book."

The Inspector looked grimly pleased. "Yes. With that in our possession, we'll blast the remnants of Smyrk's organisation from here to Kingdom Come."

His caustic smile faded. He said again:

"It's a pity Raven's dead."

He shrugged his burly shoulders. "Now we shall never know how he escaped from Garvary's studio."

## CHAPTER TWENTY SEVEN

A few days later, Linda Martin knocked rather timidly on the door of Bob Tenison's flat.

The artist appeared immediately. "Linda, dearest!"

He took her in his arms. She submitted to his embrace, but turned her face slightly, so his rather clumsy kiss fell on her cheek.

"Hello, Bob." She disengaged herself gently. They went into the studio.

The girl was her lovely self once more, but there was still something very much like fear lurking in the depths of her blue-grey, slanting eyes.

She touched Tenison's arm. "What does it mean, Bob—this message from Mr. Blake?"

Bob rumpled his already tousled hair. "I don't know, darling. As I understand it, he wants us to join him in Leo's studio,"——he glanced at his watch—"in ten minutes time."

"But why, Bob, why?" Linda's mouth trembled. She asked: "Is this nightmare never going to end?"

"Don't worry, dear. Nobody will harm you now."

Linda took off her hat and coat. She dropped them on the heavy raised couch under the windows, then turned to the artist again.

"But, Bob—nothing is finished. It all drags on." Her voice was tired. "I expected the inquest on Leo to be over by now. But the Coroner adjourned it for seven days."

Tenison soothed her. "It's just a formality, I suppose." He looked puzzled. "Though I had expected the police to tidy up the case and drop it quickly, now Raven is dead."

Linda sat down on the couch. Bob dropped his hand on her shoulder.

She kissed his fingers briefly. "Dear Bob. You're so good to me."

Tenison said: "I would do anything for you."

A rare winter sun streaked through the windows and touched unexpected highlights in the girl's smooth hair. She was very beautiful.

A half smile flickered uncertainly on her innocently inviting lips. She said inconsequentially:

"We'd better go downstairs."

Tenison looked at his watch again. "It's early yet."

"Never mind."

They went down the little back stairway to the floor below. They paused outside Garvary's apartment and gazed at each other. Linda nodded quickly. Bob pressed his thumb on the bell push.

Sexton Blake opened the door. He bowed to the girl.

"Good afternoon, Miss Martin." He nodded to Bob. "Mr. Tenison."

The artist cleared his throat. "You wanted us, Mr. Blake?"

"Ah, yes. Come in, please."

Sexton Blake stepped back. They went past him into the dead man's studio. The room had a curiously lonely air. Linda felt it and shivered.

Sexton Blake closed the door carefully and pushed up the catch. "We don't want to be disturbed."

Tenison said directly:

"What's all this about, Mr. Blake?"

Sexton Blake replied gravely:

"Leo Garvary was a lonely man. You two are the only persons remaining who might fairly be described as having been close to him."

Bob shook his head. "Forgive me. I still don't understand."

"I want you to assist me in a little experiment."

"An experiment?" The words seemed to catch in Linda's throat.

"Yes." Blake smiled at her. "But first I want you to meet an old friend."

He went to the inner door and threw it open. A young man strolled into the studio. The girl gasped. Her hand went up to her throat.

"Hallo, Linda," said Tinker cheerily.

Linda found her voice. She said huskily:

"They told me you were dead."

Tinker grinned. "Don't believe everything you read in the newspapers. I'm still very much alive."

The girl walked over and touched his sleeve unbelievingly. "I still don't understand."

Sexton Blake laughed quietly. "There's no mystery, Miss Martin. We thought it advisable to broadcast the convenient fiction of Tinker's death for one reason only. We were afraid Raven might attempt more violence. He might even have been reckless enough to raid the clinic."

Tinker chuckled. "Yes. He'd done his best to kill me once... The guv 'nor didn't want him to try again."

"Now Raven is dead," said Blake levelly. "Tinker will reappear. In fact, the young 'un will be present when the inquest on Garvary is reopened."

"I'm the reason it was adjourned in the first place," commented Tinker brightly.

Linda said sincerely:

"I"m so glad you're unharmed." A spark of alarm showed in her next question. "You *are* quite well?"

"Uh. A little stiff, perhaps. There's a bandage round my chest, besides this one adorning my forehead." Tinker grinned. "Except for that, I'm fine."

Linda repeated softly:

"I'm so glad."

Tinker smiled at her. His face altered subtly. He was looking at the third finger of her left hand.

Linda followed his gaze and blushed. She covered the bright new ring with her other hand.

Sexton Blake said smoothly:

"It seems that congratulations are in order."

Tenison coughed. He said awkwardly:

"Linda and I—." He broke off and smiled happily. "We're going to be married."

There was a tiny silence. Then Sexton Blake and Tinker murmured the conventional words of congratulation together. Tenison beamed expansively. Linda said very little.

Sexton Blake said at last:

"Well, now. This is all very pleasant. But it's time we dealt with the business at hand." He gestured politely. "Perhaps you would both be seated."

Tinker found Linda a chair. Bob sprawled in another, his amiable face intent. Sexton Blake stood before them. His voice was calm, incisive, and charged with quiet authority.

He said, without preamble:

"I intend to demonstrate the manner in which Garvary's murderer contrived his escape from this studio."

Somebody gasped.

Then Bob Tenison said quietly:

"Shouldn't Inspector Stevens be with us?"

The detective returned an unemphasised contradiction. "No. I'm not yet in a position to offer my theories to the police. As I intimated before, we're here to conduct an experiment."

Nobody spoke. Blake took out his pipe and began to fill it with tobacco.

His quiet voice echoed eerily in the silent room. "The credit for solving the puzzle belongs mostly to my assistant." Warmth and affection touched his keen, grey eyes as he glanced at the young man resting on the box seat under the windows. "Tinker had already worked out an answer to the problem before Raven shot him. Fortunately for me, he had left verbal notes on our wire recording machine. Though he didn't record his theories, he noted all the facts— and more—on which his conclusions were based. I was therefore able to form my own theories which, as I discovered later, tallied with Tinker's."

Blake lit his pipe. "All right, young 'un. Let's hear from you."

Tinker stood up. His cheery young face had grown oddly nervous. He said:

"One thing about this case bothered me badly. It was Garvary's crazy behaviour in the corridor."

He paused as if uncertain—or unwilling—to proceed.

Linda said doubtfully:

"I know it seemed silly. But then Leo was always eccentric."

Tinker replied seriously:

"His behaviour wasn't just eccentric. It was insane. Let's consider it carefully." He ran his fingers through his dark, curly hair. "This studio is soundproof. Therefore Garvary couldn't have heard Linda and me when we arrived at the end of the corridor. Yet he burst open the door just as we reached the landing. There's only one way he could have managed that."

Bob Tenison interrupted eagerly. "He must have had the front door slightly ajar. He was watching for your arrival."

"Right, That sounds reasonable. He wanted to see me urgently. He was nervous, he couldn't wait patiently. He had to keep watch.

"Yet what happened? I arrived with Linda. Garvary rushed out, skipped in the air, and rushed back again, slamming the door behind him.

"For Pete's sake, why? If he was so anxious to see a detective, why did he shut the door in my face? Why didn't he come to meet me? If he wanted me to hurry, why didn't he call out?"

Nobody answered. Tinker went on:

"That was the first puzzle. Then I found another. When I examined Garvary's clothes, I saw his jacket was stiff with blood. In other words, the blood had begun to dry."

Linda whispered:

"That's not possible. It couldn't have dried. There wasn't time."

"Right again. We had both seen him alive and uninjured a few minutes before. There was only one answer. The man we saw wasn't Leo Garvary."

Linda started to protest.

Tinker interrupted her without discourtesy. "Think about it for a minute. It explained his crazy actions in the corridor. He gave us a fleeting glimpse just to establish his identity as the victim—who was already dead inside the cupboard."

Tenison frowned. "This theory explains why the man didn't speak. The voice might have given him away. But it seems fantastic to believe he had made himself up to look like Leo."

Tinker shrugged. "He wouldn't have needed much of a disguise. We saw him for only two or three seconds. All he required was a long white coat, a tam-o'-shanter, and a false beard and moustache.

"Oh, yes. And a pair of gold rimmed spectacles. He probably used Garvary's own. That was another point, incidentally. The dead man's glasses were hooked precariously over one ear. As if they had been replaced in a hurry."

Tinker chuckled with uncharacteristic grimness. "The killer was expecting us to break in at any minute. He didn't have a lot of time to work his vanishing trick."

There was another silence. Sexton Blake puffed reflectively. Through the coiling smoke, he regarded his young assistant with affection and pride.

Tenison's voice was harsh.

"How the devil *did* he work the trick?"

Tinker replied mildly:

"That puzzled me at first. But as this room has only three exits, I considered each of them in turn.

"Obviously, nobody could have left through the front door while Linda and I were waiting outside. That eliminated the first possibility.

"Then I thought of the inner door—that one in the corner. It's sometimes possible to shoot bolts from the wrong side of a door by looping string round 'em—but the bolt on *that* door is much too stiff for trickery of that sort. Besides the killer couldn't have escaped from those inner rooms. There are bars on the windows.

"That eliminated the second possibility. There was only one exit left." He pointed behind him. "These windows here."

Linda said huskily:

"But they were locked, too."

Tinker turned. He stepped up on the long box seat. "Yes, but do you remember? When we came in, I opened the top half of this left hand section,"—he raised the bar and pushed out the transom to disclose the upper metal edge—"and found no dirt on the edges? Yet when Steve examined this one,"—he opened the right hand section—"he got his hands covered with dust. So why had the other window been cleaned while its companion had been neglected?"

Tenison echoed him. "Why?"

"Watch." Tinker felt in his pocket and drew out a bobbin of stout cotton. He broke off a generous length of it and threaded it through the triple notched bar of the left hand section. He passed the cotton through the first hole and out again through the second. Then he took both free ends and passed them over the upper metal edge of the transom, so they dangled down outside the window.

Tinker smiled over his shoulder. "Watch me closely."

He secured the right hand section once more, then opened the middle section and stepped through the open glass panels on to the sill outside.

Then he pushed them shut from the outside and worked his way along cautiously till he reached the left hand section. He thrust his arm through the open transom, seized the handle which secured the centre section, and pushed it home, latching the window securely.

Then he let the transom fall to, and pulled the two ends of the cotton thread. The bar swung upwards. Tinker manoeuvred it gently until the third (and free hole) dropped over the small iron upright set in the ledge at the base.

Tinker released one end of the thread and pulled on the other. It passed easily into the room, through the notches in the bar, and then outside the window again.

The window was securely locked.

Sexton Blake commented:

"Though such a window appears to fit snugly in its frame, there is—inevitably—an infinitesimal gap which permits the passage of slender thread."

He walked forward and opened the centre section once more. Tinker manoeuvred himself cautiously into the room again. He sat down on the box seat and wiped his forehead. "Suffering cats! I'm dizzy."

Bob Tenison had been thinking hard. He said hoarsely:

"I have an objection."

Tinker said politely:

"Yes?"

Bob nodded quickly. "It was snowing the day Leo died. You would have found footmarks on the window sill."

Tinker contradicted him mildly. "No. When Steve leaned out the window that day, I noticed that the stone sill was clear and polished. In other words, somebody had brushed all the snow away—obviously, to destroy footprints.

"That in itself was another pointer to the truth. The snow had only just ceased falling when Linda and I reached this building. So the sill must have been swept after that. Can you imagine Garvary, who was supposed to be awaiting our arrival so eagerly, stopping to tidy up the window sill?"

The intricate pattern of the argument was giving Bob a headache. But he struggled on. "You've worked out your theory very well," he admitted.

Tinker gave him a lop-sided grin. "I've tested it before."

"What?"

"Uh huh. I came back the same night. I persuaded the constable on duty to leave the studio, then worked the window trick—as I've demonstrated. I wanted to test my theory thoroughly."

Blake chuckled. "You were a little *too* thorough."

"Yes. While I was on the sill, I glanced down to the floor below and saw that Raven had left one of his windows open. So I hung down by my hands from the sill here, and dropped the rest of the way into the courtyard. The snow broke my fall, but I didn't come off entirely unscathed." Tinker rubbed himself ruefully. "I bruised myself a bit, and I smashed the bulb of the torch I'd been using. Which had an odd consequence."

He shrugged. "Anyway, I climbed into Raven's apartment through the window. I'd guessed from what you told me, Linda, that Raven was mixed up in the drug racket.

"I thought it was a good opportunity to investigate. But first I had to reassure the constable upstairs. So I unlocked Raven's door and pushed up the catch, so it would open again at a touch.

"Then I went up the stairs and nearly shocked the constable out of his wits. He thought I was Houdini in person." Tinker grinned mischievously. "I went down to Raven's flat again and—well, you know what happened."

Sexton Blake blew out a cloud of smoke. He said:

"Perhaps I should explain from the purely physical evidence what the young 'un had been doing. He inevitably left marks in the snow in the courtyard, and on the window sill. But the storm was still raging, and by the time the Inspector went out to the courtyard,"—he gestured—"every trace had been obscured by a fresh layer of snow."

He chuckled. "I did guess what you'd been up to, young 'un, when the hospital reported bruises on your feet and legs."

Tinker winced reminiscently. "I was too darn enthusiastic. Those bruises were painful." He commented wistfully. "It's at times like that when I wish I were like Waldo the Wonder Man. He can't feel pain at all."

Bob Tenison kept his grip on the essentials. He muttered:

"I can see why the window was wiped clean. The thread would have left tell-tale marks in the dust on the upper edge." He shook his head. "What a pity—artistically speaking—the killer didn't remember to wipe the dirt off the other windows. That was Raven's only mistake."

Sexton Blake took the pipe from his mouth. He said softly:

"Raven didn't kill Leo Garvey." The silence was suffocating.

Tenison seemed to be choking. A dreadful compulsion forced him to ask the obvious question. "Then who—?"

Sexton Blake replied mildly:

"You murdered him, Mr. Tenison."

# CHAPTER TWENTY EIGHT

Tenison laughed. It was a queerly desperate sound. "You're joking."

Tinker took up the tale again. "No. Raven had no reason to kill Garvary. The sculptor wasn't an ordinary blackmailer. He dared not give Raven away because he could have destroyed the source of the drugs he craved. Raven had only to keep him well supplied to preserve his own safety.

"Garvary's death was the last thing he wanted. The black book might so easily fall into the wrong hands."

Sexton Blake said:

"Exactly. When he heard Garvary was dead, Raven panicked. He went straight to his associate, Smyrck, got rid of his store of drugs, and borrowed a gun for protection."

"The pistol," said Tinker drily, "which he later used on me. Oh, well."

Tenison cried frantically:

"I tell you—Raven killed Garvary!"

"No, no." Tinker was patient. "It wasn't possible. When I went down to interview Raven, I looked into the courtyard. The snow was undisturbed. It was even piled up against the French windows, and on the sills of the windows flanking the glass doors. Nobody could have managed the descent from this studio without leaving traces in the snow.

"But an *ascent*— that was a different matter."

Bob asked dreadfully:

"What do you mean?"

Tinker returned:

"You have a lot of gymnastic equipment in your studio upstairs, and your windows are directly in line with Garvary's.

"You let down a rope from your window, tying one end to the leg of that heavy raised couch under the windows. It was strong enough to bear your weight.

"Physically, you resemble your victim. You're tall, as he was. Once you had impersonated Garvary, shut yourself in his flat, and hocused the windows, you climbed up to your own apartment. That left no traces, since you brushed both sills.

"You hauled up the rope, and stowed it away with the white coat and tam-o'-shanter in your studio. You ripped off your false beard and moustache, and burned them in the fire. Then you came downstairs as yourself.

"You had ample time to do it all if you hurried. You'd be a little short of breath, that's all. I noticed your breathing was heavy when I met you.

"Another thing. You said you came down because you heard Linda talking. That wasn't possible. Later that morning, the police surgeon was standing in the same place, calling the Inspector. Steve was in your flat... and he didn't hear a word. You knew Linda and I were there because you saw us."

Tenison said desperately:

"The killer must have climbed up to the roof. He passed my flat."

Tinker looked at him with pity. "The Sergeant examined the roof. Nobody had been up there for months."

Bob's face had crumbled. Only his eyes were stubbornly alive. He clenched his fists hopelessly.

His voice was not his own. "All right. I killed Leo, I admit it."

Tinker sighed. "Thank you. Let's go and talk to the Inspector."

"Just a minute." It was Linda.

Sexton Blake studied her curiously. "Don't protest, please. We haven't made a mistake. Throughout this case, two people have persistently spoken of Raven as your employer's murderer. One was Stevens—he was genuinely mistaken. The other was Tenison, who preserved the fiction desperately, even in his telephone conversations with you. He knew the calls might be overheard."

Linda disregarded the speech completely. She said:

"You can't arrest Bob for Leo's murder."

Tinker replied patiently:

"We must. He's confessed."

Linda's voice swelled in the silence. "You can't take Bob," she said. *"Because I killed Leo Garvary myself."* Nobody moved for three seconds.

Then Tenison said huskily:

"She's lying."

The two detectives kept there gaze on the girl.

Linda's face was tragically intense. She said dully:

"It was an accident." She choked suddenly.

Tinker said gently:

"Tell us about it Linda."

She sank back in her chair and turned her face away. Her voice stumbled.

"It was all so unexpected. When I came here that morning I didn't dream—." She broke off, then went on listlessly: "I felt there was something wrong as soon as Leo opened the door."

She felt there was something wrong as soon as he opened the door. Garvary was trembling. He stood aside with his usual courtesy, but the returned her "Good morning" in a voice which was strangely off-key.

She felt vaguely uneasy.

"Shall I get ready, Mr. Garvary?"

He stared at her. Then he said abruptly:

"Yes. Yes. Of course."

She went into the bedroom and closed the door. She began to think about her employer. He was a brilliant man, but seemed to be subtly off balance. Lately she had noticed a queer, fleeting hunger in his eyes when he looked at her. But, surely, she was imagining things.

She slipped out of her clothes. For the first time, she was aware of an absurd sense of embarrassment.

She struggled impatiently, and pulled the dressing gown over her lovely body. When she came back into the studio she found Garvary staring at the unfinished statue with some thing like pain in his eyes. She murmured uncertainly:

"Shall I.... ?"

She stopped on the platform and fumbled with the cord at her waist, preparing to strike her pose.

Garvary groaned suddenly and threw himself in a chair with his hands pressed against his temples. It was a wildly extravagant gesture which ought to have been funny.

Incredibly, it wasn't.

Linda stepped down and put her hand on his shoulder. She was instinctively sympathetic.

Garvary said tonelessly:

"It's no good. I can't work any more. I can't stand the—the torment of feeling beauty grow under my fingers. A beauty which is mine—yet which I can never possess."

He grabbed her hand and kissed it.

"Linda, don't you understand? It's agony to watch you!"

Linda's pupils dilated. She looked into his eyes and saw naked passion in their depths.

He whispered:

"I want you."

He stood up, gripped her by the shoulders, and pressed his mouth hard against hers. She struggled wildly and threw him off balance.

Garvary staggered back and steadied himself against the wall. He clawed something out of his pocket.

He whispered:

"If I can't have you, no man shall!" There was a revolver in his hand.

Linda thought fearfully:

"He's mad."

Garvary said softly:

"You're so beautiful." He levelled the gun and smiled at her. "This way we can always be together."

Linda stumbled towards the door. Leo crashed his shoulder against it and laughed at her.

She struck at the gun with desperate strength. It jarred out of Garvary's hand and slid across the floor towards the windows. He tried to save it and fell on one knee.

Linda reeled backwards. Her foot stumbled against something hard. Her heart squeezed up inside her. She scrabbled frantically and felt the cold metal against her hot palm.

Across the room, Garvary was rising.

Linda picked up the gun and fired again and again.

When the smoke cleared away she saw he was lying quite still. His clothes were bloody. His face was grey.

She thought incredulously:

"He's dead." And then:

"I killed him!"

Sobbing uncontrollably, she stumbled to the door and wrenched it open. Bob would help her. Bob. Dear Bob.

When he answered her frenzied knocking she was near collapse. "I killed him, Bob. He's dead,"

Minutes, hours, years later, they stood together in Garvary's studio. Tenison drew in his breath sharply.

Linda said dully:

"They won't—hang me, will they?"

Tenison swung round quickly. The pleasant face she could never love was taut with determination.

He said tightly: "Listen to me, Linda. You shot Leo in self defence. But there aren't any witnesses. We can't be sure the police will believe your story. And I won't see you dragged through the dirt of a public trial."

Her head was splitting.

She asked wearily: "What can we do?"

"Plenty." Tenison put his hands under Garvary's shoulders and dragged him into an open cupboard. He closed the door and said gently:

"Go in the bedroom and dress."

She put on her clothes and examined her face in the mirror. Her make-up was smeared badly. She fumbled for the compact in her handbag.

She reddened her mouth with shaking fingers.

She went back to the studio and found Tenison examining the windows. He took her hands and said gently:

"This won't be easy, but you will manage it. Do everything I tell you."

The girl's whispering voice filled the silent room.

"I did everything Bob told me. I couldn't pretend I hadn't been to Leo's studio, because I always came at the same time. Besides, Tom Heath had seen me arrive.

"Bob decided to impersonate Garvary. He remembered the false whiskers, which he had bought for a joke. And he had a white coat like Leo's, and a tam-o'-shanter.

"We needed a witness. A man whose evidence would not be questioned."

Sexton Blake said dryly:

"So you came to Baker Street."

"Yes. But, of course, I needed an excuse for my visit. We decided to invent a story about anonymous letters.

"Bob can't type, but he picked out a threatening message—with two fingers—on Leo's typewriter. We found the envelope amongst Garvary's mail, and destroyed the note inside. It was only an advertisement of some sort.

"All I had to do was to bring you, Mr. Blake—or you, Tinker—and keep you outside Leo's studio with me until Bob came down from his own flat upstairs."

Linda"s voice faltered and died away.

Tenison said brokenly:

"You shouldn't have told them."

Tinker looked at the girl sadly. "I didn't know why you had shot Garvary. But the rest of your story—it was no surprise."

She gazed at him with astonishment. "You mean—you knew?"

"Yes."

"Then why did you accuse Bob?"

"The guv'nor and I... we wanted to see if you'd tell us how it happened."

"I understand." Her mouth was bitter. "I've been rather a fool."

Tinker rammed his hands in his pockets. He didn't look happy. He said:

"Obviously, the only point of the impersonation was to give Linda an alibi.

"Otherwise Tenison would not have needed to make himself up at all. He had only to push up the catch on the front door—as I did—to seal the room at every exit. He could have made his escape at his leisure, and left the police to batter down the door. The impersonation was necessary for his own safety."

Bob put his arm around Linda's shoulders. Tinker gazed at her squarely.

"You gave yourself away so many times. I guessed there was something wrong the minute you walked into the consulting room. An attractive girl like you wouldn't be so careless—unless she was scared.

"Why? Mere concern for her employer didn't explain it.

"Then that anonymous letter was obviously false. It was creased *only* in quarters, but I had to fold it *again* to fit it into the envelope you told me had contained it."

He pointed to the unfinished statue. "When I saw that, you blushed. Why? Models don't get embarrassed about their portraits. Why should they? They give beauty to the world. They have nothing to be ashamed of when they see their likeness in the nude.

"It was a small point. But it suggested your relations with Garvary were maybe a little more personal than you'd admitted. In his life? Or in his death?

"Again, when I asked you to look into those closets, you opened the first and then the third. Why did you avoid the middle cupboard till later? Because, subconsciously, you dreaded the inevitable discovery of the body you knew to be there!"

Linda whispered:

"You devils."

Sexton Blake intervened.

He said quietly:

"Not devils, Miss Martin. Say rather... your guardian angels."
There's something wrong. Go carefully now."

Linda muttered fearfully:

"What do you mean?"

"I mean," replied Sexton Blake, "your story is true in every detail. And it proves you did not kill Leo Garvary!"

# CHAPTER TWENTY NINE

Linda wanted to cry, but she couldn't.

All three stared at Sexton Blake. Even Tinker's youthful face was startled.

Blake addressed his assistant kindly. "Your deductions were accurate, young 'un, but you didn't carry them far enough. You missed the final complication."

He turned to the girl. "How many times did you fire at Garvary?"

Linda struggled for speech. "I thought—three times---."

"Exactly. You wounded him in the shoulder, side, and leg. They were nasty wounds, and he fainted. You thought he was dead. So did Tenison.

"Neither of you examined him properly. You were too scared to do so, and Tenison naturally took your word you had killed him."

Blake's words spilled quickly. "You left the studio. Tenison waited inside. He was nervous and tense. It was nearly time for your witness—Tinker—to arrive.

"Then an impossible thing happened. The man you both thought was dead... recovered consciousness!

"He groaned. Tenison opened the closet and saw the sculptor was still alive. His first call was to call a doctor. And then he thought again." Sexton Blake lifted his hand, then dropped it.

"He had always wanted Linda. Yet he knew he could never have her. He couldn't win her love.

"Yet now she was in desperate trouble. He had stood by her, loyally, without question. Would she refuse him after that? She would surrender herself willingly, with a gratitude that was almost love.

"Their guilty secret would bind them together as though with steel chains. But only if Garvary was dead, and Linda a murderess.

He gestured. "So Bob Tenison, that quiet and colourless young man, picked up the revolver and pressed the muzzle over Garvary's heart."

He smacked his hands together with the suddenness of an explosion.

Linda screamed. "Don't!"

Blake said, with pity:

"You haven't been very lucky. Raven was a ruthless hooligan. Garvary was a drug addict—he probably attacked you under the influence of *marihuana.* As for the third man in your life—." He

609

gestured wordlessly.

Linda looked at Bob with horror in her eyes. Tenison spoke with a cracked and terrifying tone. "Don't listen to him, Linda."

She sprang up from her chair and stumbled away.

Blake turned on Tenison grimly. "She has to listen. Her confession proves she shot him long before the body was discovered. That's why the blood had dried on his clothes. Yet Tinker found him *freshly dead* from a heart wound that must have been instantaneously fatal.

"Miss Martin fired at Garvary from across the room. So why did we find powder marks around the heart wound? Because that was the only shot fired at close range. And who but you could have fired it?"

Tenison's features crumpled.

He muttered a prayer which might have been a blasphemy.

He slumped slowly downwards, and caught at a chair arm to save himself. His face was a death mask.

Tinker watched him with pitying contempt.

Linda clutched Blake's sleeve. "What are you going to do?"

Sexton Blake's face was once more fine-drawn with fatigue. "I'm not going to do anything. Because you're plainly innocent, and yet I can't prove it. You've suffered enough. I can't expose you to the danger of a trial. You would be named as an accessory before, after, and during the fact."

He turned back to Tenison and raised his voice.

"Detective Inspector Stevens is a clever man. We've solved this case. He might, too. I have already given him some broad hints in the course of the investigation.

"Do you realise what you've done? You have woven a rope that might hang you both."

Tenison answered with dreadful sincerity.

"I did all those things. But I did them because I love Linda better than myself. You think you know why I killed Leo Garvary. Well, you're right. But you don't know it all.

"I looked down at Garvary, and saw everything. Leo would be bitter and revengeful. Linda had refused him. Linda would suffer. He would go to the police with a lying story of attempted murder. He would drag her into court. I couldn't let that happen."

Bob bowed his head. "It was agony to do it. But I killed him because I loved her." His voice was indistinct. "I would do anything for Linda."

Sexton Blake said slowly:

"That, you have yet to prove."

He took Linda's hand and led her out of the studio. Tinker followed. The three went along the corridor. Linda Martin did not speak.

Suddenly, she stopped. She looked down at her hand with revulsion. She tore off the engagement ring so madly she broke the skin of her finger.

She flung the ring away.

It landed with a dull plop! on the carpet, rolled over, and was still. It glinted pathetically.

# EPILOGUE

Sexton Blake and Tinker were both in the consulting room.

Blake was seated in the saddlebag chair, reading. Tinker was pasting the reports of the case—including those of his own death— into the Baker Street Index.

The young man stirred restively. He cleared his throat. "Good book, guv 'nor?"

Blake looked up. He said gravely:

"It is *Proverbii in Facetie*, by Cornazano. It's a rare sixteenth century work, complete with the original woodcuts. This is the twentieth edition, which appeared in Italy in 1560. Yes, I think I can describe it as a good book."

He chuckled. "You can't fool me, old son. You're not really interested in my reading. You want to talk about the case."

Tinker grinned. "Do you blame me?"

"No. I—."

The telephone rang. Tinker grabbed it.

He listened with a grave face. The he covered the receiver with his hand. "It's Steve, guv 'nor. You'd better speak to him."

Sexton Blake took the 'phone and spoke his name.

"Hallo, Mr. Blake. Stevens here. I have some new for you."

"Yes?"

The Inspector sounded vaguely upset. "Look, we were all wrong about Raven. He didn't kill Garvary. Do you know who did?"

The question was clearly rhetorical. Blake contented himself with a monosyllable. "Who?"

"That fellow Tenison. He's committed suicide."

"Oh."

"Yes. He gassed himself, and left a full confession by his body. He described how he murdered Garvary and escaped from the studio, but he didn't say why. I suppose it was a grudge killing. Not that it matters, now."

"No. Was there anything else in his confession?"

"No." The Inspector sounded surprised. "Except that he insisted he had no accomplice. I can't think why the point bothered him. We have—and had—no reason to think anybody else was involved."

"No. Goodbye, Stevens."

"Hey, wait a minute! Don't you want to hear the details?"

"Another time, old fellow. Good-bye."

He hung up.

Sexton Blake said thoughtfully:

"That's that. Miss Martin is no longer in any danger." He explained briefly.

Tinker studied his beloved guv 'nor shrewdly. "The police might still arrest her for conspiracy."

Sexton Blake had studied the complex problems of crime and punishment for too long not to know there was a larger justice beyond the letter of the law.

He said:

"No. They know nothing of Miss Martin's complicity. And I do not intend to tell them."

Tinker smiled with satisfaction. He said with apparent inconsequence:

"Linda was really upset when she heard I was dead."

Blake's mobile lips quivered. "I don't want to disillusion you, old son. But I'm afraid it's possible she was more disturbed to think you would not be available to testify on her behalf. Her alibi depended on your evidence."

Tinker looked rebellious. "She's a very lovely girl."

"I agree."

Tinker pursued:

"Some girls only find fulfilment in marriage."

"Some men," said Blake, "are wedded to their work."

Tinker laughed. "All right, guv 'nor," he returned obscurely. "You win." A twinkle in his eye suggested he had opinions of his own about the subject. He asked, more seriously:

"Do you think that Tenison really loved her —unselfishly, I mean?"

"It's possible. His suicide, though a grave sin, was in itself a sign of grace. He knew it was the only way he could be sure of saving her from the hangman."

"So he destroyed his victim and himself because he loved her." Tinker shivered. "It's rather a terrifying thought."

Sexton Blake said:

"Most of the great love stories are also tragedies."

He went back to his chair and picked up his book, but his thoughts did not return to the printed page. He was thinking of the revulsion with which Tenison had put down the revolver the detective had handed to him in this very room. That, in itself, had been a give-away. Tenison had called the weapon horrible before Blake had officially informed him it was the gun used to kill Garvary.

Sexton Blake lit his pipe. He was thinking of Tenison's final speech in the studio. He was wondering how much of it was truth, and how much instinctive self-justification.

He blew out a cloud of smoke.

He decided he would never know.

The blue smoke wreathed lazily, then drifted away into nothingness.

# EDITOR'S NOTE

There is a question about the correct title for the foregoing novel.

The publisher of *Come to Paddington Fair,* Hidetoshi Mori refers to the work as *Model Murder* and is in possession of a dedication which uses that title.

However, the manuscript copy provided by Bob Adey clearly shows *Model for Murder* on the title page, which also has a dimly perceptible © Derek Howe Smith 1952 showing through in mirror image.

The majority opinion of the several people I have consulted favours *Model for Murder,* which is the title I have used.

# THE IMPERFECT CRIME
## The Story of a Strange Experience

# THE IMPERFECT CRIME                    by Derek Smith

"I have strong views about capital punishment," said the plump man cheerfully. "You see, I happen to be a murderer myself."

"Oh," murmured Hamilton feebly; and wondered if he was supposed to laugh.

The two men were the sole occupants in a carriage of the night train which was writhing its way like a blinded snake through the creeping, choking mist.

Hamilton had disliked the stranger from the first. He had awakened from an uneasy doze to find he was no longer alone; and had found out also that the little plump man was regarding him with his head slightly askew, like a bird peering at a worm with its bright, beady eyes.

Regretting he had allowed himself to be drawn into the extraordinary discussion which had preceded this even more extraordinary confidence, Hamilton turned away and peered irritably out into the darkness, and saw nothing more than his own reflection in the in the fog backed glass of the compartment window.

He settled back in his seat with a muffled sigh, and met, once more, the eye of his fellow passenger. He smiled weakly.

The plump man said smoothly, by way of reply:

"Mine is the story of an imperfect crime. I'll tell you about it—the tale might amuse you." He buried his chin momentarily in the fold of the thick muffler swathed round his neck, and looked down his nose with malicious humour. "I won't tell you my name. You wouldn't recognize it, anyway... That is my tragedy." He spoke the word with high good humour. "I was nearly famous once. And then I was merely—and briefly—notorious."

Hamilton made no comment. His companion went on gaily:

"Of course, I never intended to become a murderer. I had talent, and I wanted to write. I completed my first novel. It was accepted, and published. It was almost a best seller. I was almost famous. And then—.""

The plump man broke off and gestured vaguely.

"Almost. That's the story of my life... Oh, well" He sighed. "Perhaps you don't remember those ridiculous years between the wars. Novel after novel was suppressed and destroyed. And why? Because British hypocrisy was at its worst. 'Ulysses' and 'Lady Chatterley's

619

Lover' were seized and burnt by H.M.Customs. 'Sleeveless Errand' and 'The Well of Loneliness' were pilloried, branded 'indecent,' and taken to court."

Hamilton shifted uncomfortably. His companion went on equably:

"The day after my novel was published; a notorious journalist in an equally notorious Sunday newspaper launched a slashing attack on the book, calling for its immediate suppression."—The plump man chuckled soundlessly—"in the name of public decency. The same paper carried full details of the latest axe murder on its front page... But then, the English public don't consider the mechanics of death indecent— only those of life.

"However... The smut hounds were in full cry. An application was made to the stupidest magistrate on the bench. Counsel for the prosecution made a long speech in which immoderate language, distorted judgment, and prurient sex hatred were nicely blended."

The speaker waved a chubby palm. "I was fined, which wasn't important. The book was banned, which was.

"That was the finish. No other publisher would look at my work. My carer was ruined." There was a cold gleam in his pale, almost lidless, eyes. 'And it was all the fault of one man. A newspaper scribbler whom I had never seen. So—I decided he had to die."

Hamilton swallowed nervously. He wondered, desperately, when the train would reach station. He was acutely conscious of the communication cord, so far out of reach above his head.

The plump man continued:

"I laid my plans carefully. I didn't intend to hang.

"I wrote the wretched man a letter—under an assumed name— complimenting him on his public spirit. The reply came a few days later. His literary style was, I might add, abominable. But I had what I wanted. There, at the bottom of the note, was the signature, bold and florid: Gordon Gardnor.

"I copied that signature until I could write it as easily, swiftly, and exactly as my own.

"I began to follow Gardnor like a shadow. I soon discovered he lived alone with his secretary (a colourless fellow who did all the great man's routine work) and also discovered he worked alone in his study every evening."

A thin smile crept over the speaker's lips.

"One night, Gardnor came into that study, switched on the lights, and found me there, waiting. When he saw the gun in my hand, he locked the door as I ordered him, and sat down quietly.

"I told him, briefly, why he had to die. I showed him a letter typed on his own machine, signed with his own florid signature. It was a suicide note.

"Before he could speak, I jammed the gun into his face and pulled the trigger."

The plump man mused: "The noise deafened me. And some of his blood splashed over my mouth. I licked it... It tasted warm, and salty.

"I left the note on a table, and clasped the gun in Gardnor's dead hand. Then I left the way I came—through the windows—straight into the arms of a patrolling policeman."

The little man sighed. "Even then, I kept my head. I told the bobby I had heard a shot and had climbed through the windows to investigate. He seemed to believe me. All went well....

"But, as they told me at the trial, I had made one bad mistake. The signature I had copied so carefully wasn't Gardnor's at all.

"It was the secretary's, using his employer's name. I told you he did all the routine work. Like answering readers' letters."

He fell silent, still regarding his companion with head comically askew.

"I wonder," said Hamilton painfully, "they didn't execute you."

"Oh," said the stranger mildly, pulling the scarf away from his twisted throat, "but they did. I was hanged by the neck until I was dead."

# ACKNOWLEDGMENTS

I am grateful to Douglas G. Greene, Executor of the Literary Rights of Derek Howe Smith, for permission to publish these stories. I have long been an admirerer of Derek's work and it is a privilege for LRI to be entrusted with their publication. I am also grateful to Robert Adey, whose *Locked Room Murders and Other Impossible Crimes* is the definitive bibliography on the subject, and who probably knew Derek better than anyone else, for the insightful Introduction.

Thanks also go to Hidetoshi Mori, renowned collector, reviewer and publisher of locked room myteries; to Tony Medawar, editor of several John Dickson Carr and Christianna Brand collections; and to Nigel Moss, a highly knowledgeable collector, for providing the additional material used in this book and for permission to publish it.

Thanks, too, to the enterprising Fei Wu and Yangbo Zhou—like me, admirers of Derek's work—for supplying texts in machine-readable form and greatly speeding the transcription process. I wish them luck with their Chinese edition.

Finally thanks to another writer of fiendishly ingenious locked-room mysteries, Monsieur Paul Halter, whose books I am also privileged to publish in English, for designing the cover.

John Pugmire
Locked Room International
New York, June 2014

Made in the USA
Lexington, KY
02 September 2014